VENUS OF SHADOWS

Iris Angharads gave her life to a dream—to turn a harsh and barren world into a new home for humankind. Now, a generation later, her descendants find themselves on opposite sides of political battle lines, torn apart by forces they only dimly understand:

Benzi Liangharad—He left Venus to live among a near-immortal race of space-faring engineers. Now he holds the key to his home world's future.

Risa Liangharad—As strong-willed as her mother, she rose to become a powerful leader. Now she must watch as her own children betray her dreams.

Dyami Liang-Talis—Risa's son, he was driven by his hunger for forbidden love, embittered by the hatred of his people. Now he is caught up in a maelstrom of intrigue, deception, and terror.

Chimene Liang-Haddad—Daughter of Risa and an exiled Earth historian, she became the high priestess of a strange erotic cult. Now she must face a bloody day of reckoning.

Spanning four generations, their story is a masterfully woven tapestry of love and hate, triumph and tragedy, which will change the course of human history.

. . . AND FOR

VENUS OF SHADOWS

"This is the generational saga writ large indeed . . . Sargent writes of a time when we have learned to think in larger categories . . . follows [these personal tales] with a patient, insightful eye."
—Gregory Benford,
Los Angeles Times Book Review

"Beyond its gripping political intrigues and fascinating sociological truths, *Venus of Shadows* is a masterly piece of world-building. I could see Pamela Sargent's Venus, hear it, smell it, taste it, and once—a true story—I dreamed about it."   —James Morrow

"A masterful blend of science fiction and the old-fashioned generation-spanning family saga . . . a grand, sweeping tale."   —*Wilson Library Bulletin*

"Pamela Sargent is one of SF's most literate and thoughtful writers. *Venus of Dreams* was a wonderfully rich story peopled with sensitively drawn characters. *Venus of Shadows* enlarges on the themes of personal responsibility and the pain often inherent in emotional ties. It is a brilliant, evocative work. Pam Sargent is simply a great writer."
—George Alec Effinger

VENUS
OF
SHADOWS

Pamela Sargent

BANTAM BOOKS
NEW YORK · TORONTO · LONDON · SYDNEY · AUCKLAND

This edition contains the complete text
of the original hardcover edition.
NOT ONE WORD HAS BEEN OMITTED.

VENUS OF SHADOWS
A Bantam Spectra Book/published by arrangement with Doubleday

PRINTING HISTORY
Doubleday edition published December 1988
Bantam edition/January 1990

Bantam Books are published by Bantam Books, a division of Bantam Doubleday
Dell Publishing Group, Inc. Its trademark, consisting of the words "Bantam
Books" and the portrayal of a rooster, is Registered in U.S. Patent and Trade-
mark Office and in other countries. Marca Registrada, Bantam Books, 666 Fifth
Avenue, New York, New York 10103.

PRINTED IN THE UNITED STATES OF AMERICA

KRI 0 9 8 7 6 5 4 3 2 1

To George, again

THE DREAM

Malik's visitor was late. "Salaam, Linker Malik," she murmured, bowing her head slightly as she entered his apartment.

"Salaam," Malik replied. He led her to a chair and sat down across from her. He had been wary when the woman first called and asked for a meeting with him. Malik's uncle, in his last message, had warned him to be careful; there were complaints about some of Malik's recent writings. The warning had been vague, as most of Muhammad's messages were lately, with hints that the older man felt threatened and might no longer be able to protect his nephew.

Yet this woman seemed innocuous enough. He glanced at her as he poured coffee. Her name was Wadzia Zayed, and she claimed to be one of his former students. Malik had verified that much through his forehead implant; it was still something of a novelty to be Linked, to have all of the information in Earth's cyberminds open to him.

He had remembered her only after viewing an image in the university's records. Wadzia Zayed had been a shy girl with sad dark eyes, another female student from one of his Nomarchy's outlying villages who wore a scarf over her head and kept her eyes lowered whenever she spoke. The attractive, self-assured woman who sat in front of him now hardly seemed the same person.

"I am honored that you agreed to see me," Wadzia said in formal Arabic with a trace of a rural accent. "I was

3

surprised to learn that you are now Linked, although your accomplishments surely merit that honor."

Malik touched the small jewel on his forehead that marked him as a Linker. "I have tried to be worthy of it." His uncle's influence had helped to win him the Link; Muhammad was grooming him for better things. Grateful as he was, he wasn't sure if he shared his uncle's ambitions.

"Well." Wadźia set down her cup, then shook back her uncovered black hair. "I assume you've already viewed my mind-tour." She was speaking in Anglaic now, the official language of Earth, although any truly educated person knew Arabic as well.

"Indeed I have," he answered in the same tongue.

"And what did you think?"

"Your depiction has an impact," Malik said carefully, "but I'm puzzled by your reasons for asking me to see it. I used to view such things as a boy, and had many happy moments experiencing them through my band, but I'm hardly an expert on mind-tours and sensory entertainments." Such visual images and simulated experiences, some of which depicted historical incidents, could impart a bit of knowledge to the many illiterate and unschooled people of Earth's Nomarchies, but to Malik, they seemed much like the more trivial mind-tours with which such people amused themselves.

"I value your opinion," Wadzia replied. "I wouldn't ask for a recommendation, even though one from a historian of your standing might help in promoting it, but I would appreciate any suggestions you'd care to make." She lifted her head and gazed directly at him.

Malik's lingering suspicions vanished; apparently this meeting was partly an excuse to entice him. Women had begun to seek him out when he was hardly more than a boy, attracted by his handsome face and well-formed body. It had become easy to enjoy the novelty of each new love while knowing that he was certain to find another before that love died. Wadzia might have nursed an infatuation since her student days, although any intimate encounter with her then would have been dishonorable on his part. He sighed; anticipation of a new love was now often tinged with weariness.

"Your subject is fascinating, of course," he said. "That by itself makes your mind-tour quite dramatic. You simplified events somewhat, but I didn't note blatant inaccuracies. I know these events have been used in other depictions, but your treatment seemed fresh. I especially enjoyed the way you thrust the observer into various scenes before contrasting them with more distant perspectives."

Wadzia smiled a little. He was being honest; the story of the Venus Project could still move him. The efforts of people to create a livable world from such a hellish planet, a world none of them would survive to see, was surely testimony to the human spirit.

Terraforming Venus had been the dream of Karim al-Anwar, one of the earliest of Earth's Mukhtars. The Earth that Karim and his fellow Mukhtars had ruled more than five hundred years ago was a world ravaged by wars over resources. Many people had abandoned the home world for habitats in space, hollowed-out asteroids and vast globes built from the resources space offered. Karim's Earth was a wounded world, deserted by those who had become the Habitat-dwellers, with the people left behind clinging to the little that remained.

The Nomarchies of Earth had finally won peace. A Mukhtar had ruled each region ever since, and the armed force known as the Guardians of the Nomarchies preserved that peace. But Karim al-Anwar had seen that Earth needed a new dream, one that might rival the accomplishments of the Associated Habitats; without such an achievement, human history might pass into the hands of the Habitat-dwellers. Karim had looked toward Venus, that planet of intense heat held in by a thick atmosphere of carbon dioxide with a barometric pressure ninety times that of Earth, and had seen a place human beings might transform. The Habitat-dwellers might believe that humanity's future lay in space; Earth's people would show that they were wrong.

Karim had lived only long enough to see a feasibility study begun, but his dream had won out. Anwara, the space station named for him, circled Earth's sister-world in a high orbit. The shield called the Parasol, an umbrella of giant panels with a diameter as large as the planet's, hid Venus from the sun, enabling that world to cool. Frozen hydrogen had been siphoned off from distant Saturn and hurled toward Venus in tanks, where the hydrogen combined with free oxygen to form water. The atmosphere had been seeded with new strains of algae that fed on sulfuric acid and then expelled it as iron and copper sulfides.

Venus's first settlements had been the Islands, constructed to float in the planet's upper atmosphere slightly to the north of the equator. Platforms built on rows of large metal cells filled with helium were covered with dirt and then enclosed in impermeable domes. On the surface, construction equipment guided by engineers on these Islands had erected three metallic pyramids housing gravitational pulse engines; rods anchoring those engines had penetrated the basaltic mantle to the edge of Venus's nickel and iron core. The planet, after being assaulted by the release of their powerful antigravitational pulse, had begun to turn more rapidly. Its tectonic plates, locked for eons, began to shift; speeding up the world's rotation would also provide Earth-like weather patterns in later centuries, and the spinning iron core had generated a magnetic field that would protect Venus's settlers from solar radiation when the Parasol no longer cast its shadow.

Now at last, Malik thought, so long after Karim al-Anwar had first had his vision, domed settlements were rising in the Maxwell Mountains of the northern landmass known as Ishtar Terra. The people who called themselves Cytherians, after the Mediterranean island of Cythera where the goddess Aphrodite had once been worshipped, were living on the world that bore one of that ancient deity's names.

Wadzia's mind-tour had hurled him into this world. Malik had stood on barren, rocky ground, peering through a misty darkness as lightning flashed above a volcano. He had seen the Parasol, a giant flower reflecting sunlight away from a world that would bloom. He had watched as tanks of frozen hydrogen flared brightly in the planet's hot, black clouds, brief candles doused by the darkness. He had glimpsed two satellites appearing over the poles, their construction compressed into seconds, and seen their winged panels reach past the Parasol's shade to catch the light of the sun. The ground had lurched and heaved under his feet while thunder slapped his ears as a pyramid, with veins of light bulging from its black walls, released its pulse of energy.

The mind-tour had been filled with great spectacles interspersed with images of individuals who seemed to have no life apart from their obsession with the Venus Project. Wadzia had not mentioned the drain placed on Earth's limited resources by more than four centuries of support for the Project. She had barely hinted at the agreement the Mukhtars and their Project Council had reluctantly made with the Habitat-dwellers, who had decided to aid the Project for their own obscure reasons. Without Habber aid and technology, Malik knew, the Project could not have advanced this far.

Wadzia had also passed over more recent events. The pyramids had finally released their mighty pulse of energy in 555, nearly forty years ago; Wadzia had quickly moved to scenes of settlers inside the surface domes. She had avoided darker events, incidents that might have marred her tale of noble souls and grand feats of terraforming, the years when it seemed that Earth might lose the Venus Project.

The possibility of that loss was not yet past, even with Guardians stationed on Venus's Islands and with settlers moving to the surface. Malik thought again of his uncle's messages and the dilemmas that now faced Muhammad's allies among the Mukhtars.

"Do you have any other comments?" Wadzia asked.

He forced his attention back to her. "It's incomplete, isn't it? Those experiencing this mind-tour will have at least a hazy knowledge of more recent events, and wonder why they were omitted."

"I thought you might say that," she said.

"I don't see how you can avoid mentioning Pavel Gvishiani's ambitions."

"That's exactly what I think." The woman leaned forward. "The rest of my team disagrees. That's why I wanted you to see this. The opinion of a scholar who has a family so close to the Council of Mukhtars might carry some weight with my colleagues."

"The part of the story you left out has its pitfalls. You'd have to be careful in what you show, but since the tale ends with Pavel's defeat—" He reached for the pot and poured more coffee.

"Dealing with Pavel would also add some drama," Wadzia said. "After all those scenes of grandeur and self-sacrifice, we'd see the most influential of the Island Administrators trying to seize control of the Project for himself, even if it means an alliance with Habbers."

"One can feel a bit of sympathy for the man," Malik said. "The Project's progress had slowed, the Mukhtars weren't doing anything about it, and Pavel Gvishiani was faced with people who were impatient for surface settlements and resentful of the Guardian force on the Islands. He knew there wouldn't be much progress without more aid from the Habitat-dwellers."

Pavel had taken a chance, believing that Earth might not risk a confrontation, and had lost that gamble. But Wadzia could not acknowledge that without admitting how crucial the help of Habbers had become, an admission that would tarnish the glory Earth claimed for itself through the Venus Project.

How ironic, Malik thought, that Earth had to lean on Habbers for assistance in a venture meant to rival the Habber vision of humanity's future. The Mukhtars did not appreciate the irony, which only deepened their resentment of the Associated Habitats. Some believed that the Habbers had agreed to work with the Project in order to spy on the people there. Malik, however, suspected that the Habbers meant what they claimed—that working with the Project enabled them to test their own technology in various ways. Perhaps they were also moved by feelings of responsibility to those the ancestors of the Habbers had abandoned. It was hard to know what Habbers thought, given the limited contact Earth had with them.

"I certainly can't portray Pavel sympathetically," Wadzia was saying. "Assuming authority to make all decisions about the Project himself, and issuing what amounted to ultimatums to the Mukhtars, was close to treason."

"Indeed." She also could not discuss the fact that a threat from the Habbers to withdraw all their resources and sever any contact with Earth had persuaded the Mukhtars to resolve the matter peacefully. Pavel had been deprived of his Link; a few of those closest to him, including the Guardian Commander who had supported him, had also been punished. Mercy had been shown to most of the Islanders, since Pavel had misled them; Earth had achieved the semblance of a victory.

"There are also some heroes in this part of the story," Wadzia continued, "who would be inspiring. I'm thinking of Iris Angharads and Amir Azad in particular."

Malik nodded; he had refreshed his memory of recent Project history before his guest's arrival. Iris Angharads had been a climatologist working on the Islands, Amir Azad a Linker and Administrator. Both had died attempting to resolve the situation Pavel had created. Their deaths, according to one sentimental interpretation, had led to Pavel's remorse and his surrendering of himself to Earth for punishment.

"There's a memorial to Iris and Amir in one of the surface settlements." Wadzia sipped some coffee. "Maybe I could show that monument. Earth reclaims its dream, and we end with settlers building a new world for Earth's greater glory."

"A lot of settlers don't quite see it that way," he murmured. "Some still dream of being free of us. A few Mukhtars wonder if they're looking at a world that might try to escape from their grasp again."

"I don't have to dwell on *that.* We'll see a future Nomarchy, and people who are mindful of their loyalty to Earth."

"I almost think you wouldn't mind going there yourself."

She laughed softly. "I'm happier being a spectator, seeing history's grand sweep and dramatic moments, without being drawn into all the smaller struggles and personal disappointments that also play their role in events." She tilted her head. "I imagine you feel much the same way."

"I suppose I do." She was reminding him of his current worries. His uncle might be too involved in the Mukhtars' political disputes for Malik's family to remain spectators for long.

Wadzia's legs were crossed; the body covered by her blue tunic and pants was slightly arched, as though she was subtly trying to display herself. "You also never touched on one important reason for the Project," he said, "namely, that we might need what we learn from terraforming Venus here on Earth." Karim al-Anwar might have been a dreamer, but he, along with others, had noted the rise in Earth's temperatures, the slow melting of its polar ice caps, the gradual flooding of coastal cities, and the increase of carbon dioxide in the atmosphere. He had seen Earth's possible future under Venus's clouds.

"I don't want to alarm people," she responded. "The ones who are likely to experience this tour may not stop to think that Earth will hardly become a desert any time soon. Besides, we've postponed the day of reckoning by moving so much of our industry into near-space, so it's not anything to worry about now." Wadzia's hand tightened around her cup. "May I tell my team that you're in agreement with me, that we should include what this version omits?"

"If you think it'll do any good."

Her face brightened a little. "Oh, it will. Maybe I can show you an early version. It'd be a mock-up, just the images without the sensory effects, and you could point out anything the authorities might find objectionable."

"Be sure that I will." What a mind-tour designed for ignorant people showed could not matter; advising Wadzia to shade the truth could not really count as intellectual dishonesty. Refusing to state certain conclusions in his writings, or keeping his lectures safely ambiguous so that they did not contradict the accepted historical theories, would be more serious failings. I may come to that, Malik thought, wondering exactly how much he might restrict his own thoughts in order to keep what he had.

His cowardice disgusted him. "The Venus Project is problematic," he said. "Here we are, hoping for a new world and a new culture that might revitalize our own, and yet for Venus to have a chance at doing that, it should be left to grow in its own way. By placing too heavy a hand on those Cytherian settlers, we risk losing what we hope to gain."

"The Mukhtars wouldn't like to hear that."

"A few of them think it," he said. "It'd be more sensible to grant the Cytherians autonomy and allow the Habbers to contribute even more to the Project. Some resent what it's cost us already."

"Impossible." Her eyes widened in shock. "The Mukhtars can't take a Project they've touted as our greatest effort and turn it over to Habbers who affront us at every opportunity. Even people who don't care about Venus would see that as a betrayal. It's bad enough that we needed Habber help in the first place."

"Does it really matter in the long run?" He suddenly felt a need to display some courage and recklessness, even if only with words. "Habbers are one branch of humanity, we're another, and the Cytherians will undoubtedly be a third. We'll diverge for a time, but we may draw together eventually and find a common destiny, as the different regions of Earth did so long ago. Venus could be a bridge between Earth and the Habitats, and there's much we could gain from more contact with Habbers." Malik fell silent; this was the kind of talk Muhammad had warned him against.

"Dangerous words, Linker Malik."

He rose, knowing that it was time to end his brief show of bravery. "Much as I would enjoy prolonging this visit, my duties require my attention." He was speaking in Arabic now, anxious to find refuge in its formalities; Wadzia seemed a bit disappointed as she got to her feet. "I shall look forward, God willing, to your presentation at another time." Her eyes were lowered, her lips turned down; Malik took her arm and guided her toward the door. "I would like to hear more about what you've been doing these past years—perhaps you are free for dinner this evening."

"That would be most pleasurable," she replied. "Since my bondmate's work has taken him to Baghdad, my evenings have often been lonely." There would be a bondmate, of course; young women of Wadzia's age in this Nomarchy were rarely unpledged. The man was probably from her village; she might have been promised to him even before attending the university. The two would have made their pledge, and perhaps gone through the rite of marriage as well, because their families would be shamed if they refused. Now, he supposed, they had an understanding that allowed them other companions as long as they were discreet. It was a common enough arrangement.

Her novelty would divert him for a while; he was already trying to determine which restaurant might provide the most seductive atmosphere. He sighed as he once more felt his familiar weariness.

The University of Amman was near Malik's residence, and he usually walked there instead of taking the private hovercar provided for his use. The towers of the school and the tall, terraced apartment buildings surrounding it rose above a city of small, pastel-colored houses packed tightly together on low mountainsides. Other towers dotted Amman, looming over dwellings that might have been carved from the multicolored stone.

Malik had grown up in Damascus, but this city had claimed his heart when he first came here to study. Its clear, biting air invigorated him, and he had never tired of exploring its rocky hills and twisting streets. He had been happy to win a position in Amman; it was the city in the New Islamic Nomarchy that he loved most.

Olive trees and cedars lined the pale paths of the university complex; they were tall, straight trees unlike the tiny, stunted ones that grew in the crags and small spaces between houses. A small group of students walked toward him, chattering in Hebrew, then nodded respectfully as they drew near.

"Salaam, Linker Malik," one of the young men said in Arabic. "May I ask—we have been told that you will be visiting Jerusalem next term."

"As God wills." Malik touched his forehead. "Isaac Alon has invited me, and I am looking forward to spending more time in the Eastern Mediterranean Nomarchy."

"I must tell my brother, then—he is a student there. He will be hoping to meet with you."

One of the female students was ogling him quite blatantly; her large hazel eyes were much like Luciana Rizzi's. Malik drew his brows together. He had promised Luciana he would see her tonight, before Wadzia's visit; his Link would have reminded him had he bothered to consult it. Even after two years, he was not entirely accustomed to the Link; now he would have to change his plans. Perhaps not; he could find an excuse to give Luciana. It was always a sign that a particular love was fading when he began to make excuses.

"I shall hope to meet your brother, then," Malik said. He could not remember this student's name. He opened his Link to call it up, and heard only a dead silence.

The shock of meeting a block in the Link's channels made him tense; it had to be a malfunction. What could be wrong? He trembled and swayed unsteadily as another young man caught his arm.

"Is something the matter, Professor?" the student asked. Two other men were coming toward him. One wore the khaki garb of the local police; the other was in the black uniform of a Guardian.

"Malik Haddad?" The Guardian spoke gruffly, omitting Malik's title. Malik nodded; the student released his arm and stepped back. "You're to come with us. We have orders to detain you."

"You must be mistaken," Malik said. "I have a seminar to conduct." His Link was still blocked; he was suddenly afraid. "I think you should know—"

"Come with us," the Guardian said. The students were watching him with blank expressions as he was led away.

THE DREAMERS

One

The spires of Tashkent lay far behind him. To the south, above the port outside the city, a shuttle climbed Earth's sky. Malik trudged east along the side of the road, feeling the weight of the pack on his back. The people with him had held their heads high as they left Tashkent's port; now their pace was slower, their heads bowed.

The asphalt of the ancient thoroughfare was broken; hundreds of feet had already worn away a path under the row of bare-limbed trees that lined the road. A young woman near Malik suddenly stumbled on a patch of uneven ground. He reached out and caught her by the elbow.

The weariness left her strong-boned face as she smiled up at him. "The Mukhtars dream of their new world," she said in Russian, "yet they punish some of those who seek it."

"They want the way to be hard," Malik replied in the same language. "If it were otherwise, too many would want to leave, and even the Habbers couldn't find ships for them all."

The woman's smile faded as her tilted black eyes grew hard. "They think we'll forget when we're on Venus, that gratitude will wipe our memories clean and make us honor the Mukhtars again."

A young man near her turned; his eyes narrowed with suspicion as he glanced at Malik. Malik had seen that look from others, back in the port. "Do not speak to him, Katya," the young man muttered.

Malik had done what he could to conceal what he was. His long sheepskin coat was like those many of these people wore, and he had wound a turban around his head. He had·given himself away somehow, perhaps when he had forgotten himself and addressed the Guardian at the port in formal Arabic.

He could imagine what the man and the woman were thinking—either that he was a spy sent to ferret out those who might prove troublesome or that he would not be among these people now unless he had offended someone powerful. In either case, he did not belong, and it would do no good to speak to him.

He would have to live among these people. He had thought they would accept him as a fellow emigrant, one who shared their dream; now he saw how foolish that hope had been.

Malik glanced back at the distant city and recalled other visits to Tashkent. On his last trip there, he had taken an airship from Bukhara. From his window, he had enjoyed the sight of a Central Asian spring—flat green land irrigated by canals, fields white with the cotton that was still grown for the formal robes of Linkers, slender trees with pink and white blossoms. A student from the university had been sent to greet him; Administrators had invited him to their homes and accompanied him to Tashkent's lively markets. He had not been allowed to enter the city this time. A Guardian had greeted him, then scanned the identity bracelet on Malik's wrist before pushing him roughly in the direction of this road.

The plain stretched before him. A touch of winter was still in the air, but spring came early to this region; on the horizon, machines were already tilling the soil. He thought of how far they still had to walk, and of the people who had traveled over this land in past times. Persians and Greeks had carved out their conquests, caravans had brought silk from China, horsemen of the steppes had come in search of loot, and Russians had expanded their empire here. Now the land bore the footprints of those seeking a new world far from Earth.

The small group of fifteen people moved away from the road and settled on the grass to rest. The woman who had spoken to him looked away as he sat down. The young man seated himself next to her, warning Malik away with his eyes.

Silence would not help him now; he had to speak. "I

have heard," Malik said in Russian, "that the barriers separating us on Earth do not exist on the new world, and yet I see those barriers here." He looked around at the others as he spoke but saw only cold stares and averted eyes. "I am to labor on Venus with you. I've given up all I had to join you, yet you shun me."

No one spoke. He repeated his words in Anglaic, then waited.

"You know why we're here," the young man near him said at last. "However hard our lives may be on Venus, we'll have the chance to rise and to see our children rise. The Nomarchies may scorn us now, but we'll win their respect. You have the look of a man who held a higher place than ours. Why would you choose to travel with us? Why do you try to hide what you are?"

Malik forced himself to gaze directly at the man. "To show that, whatever I was before, I am one of you now."

The young man shook his blond head. "Perhaps you're a spy." He smiled mirthlessly. "But you'd make a poor one, since we so easily see what you are. Why would you wait with the likes of us, hoping for passage on a ship?"

"Because I lost everything." Malik shrugged out of his pack. "My family was dishonored by my fall from favor, and told me that their shame might be lessened if I left Earth. There's no chance that, disgraced as I am, I could be chosen for the Project, so if I want to get to Venus, my only choice is to wait with you."

"You think your chances will be better than ours," a bearded man said.

"I have less of a chance. They need willing workers there more than they need my kind."

"I'm still puzzled," the black-eyed young woman said. "It seems—"

The young man gestured angrily. "Don't speak to him."

"I'll speak if I wish, Alexei." The woman turned back to Malik. "I am Yekaterina Osipova, and this man who thinks he can speak for me is my younger brother, Alexei Osipov." The blond man scowled but was silent. "I would hear more of your story, should you wish to tell it."

"Our pasts don't matter now," another woman muttered.

"Unless we find out more about this man," Yekaterina

replied, "we won't be able to trust him. Do you think we can build a new world on suspicion?"

Her words were sincere, but Malik supposed that the Guardians had planted a few spies among the hopeful settlers in the camp that was this group's destination. That was one of the reasons for allowing such camps.

"My name is Malik Haddad," he said. "I was a professor at the University of Amman, but I also had an uncle who was close to the Council of Mukhtars. He had hopes of rising to a place on the Council and of one day giving me a position on his staff."

Alexei's green eyes narrowed. "Then you had even more than I thought."

"My uncle's ambitions weren't mine," Malik responded. "I was happy teaching history and doing my writing. It's true that my uncle's position smoothed my path, but it was my own work that won me my place. Some had questions about what I said and wrote. That didn't matter until my uncle lost favor with those who now have more power among the Mukhtars. My uncle, you see, was close to those who forced Abdullah Heikal from the Council twenty-six years ago."

His companions stared at him blankly. Most of them, he realized, were probably illiterates who had only the sketchiest knowledge of past events.

"In 568," Malik continued, "you may recall that Earth had to punish an Administrator on Venus's Islands who had allied himself with Habbers in order to seize power over the Project for himself."

"My parents told me the story," one man said. "I hadn't yet been born. They said nobody here really knew much about what happened until it was over."

"I'm not sure I understand it all now," a woman added. "I know Earth sent Guardian ships to blockade the Islands until that Linker gave himself up, and that some Islanders died in a surface explosion when they—"

"Perhaps I may tell you about it," Malik said. "I have some knowledge of those events, and those who hope to be settlers should be familiar with them."

The group gazed at him passively, apparently willing to listen if only to pass the time. He had seen a similar look on the faces of a few of his students. "I should begin by reminding you of an earlier incident in 555, since it's con-

nected to what followed. A small group of pilots, dissatis-
fied with their lot on the Islands, managed to board a
shuttlecraft and fled to the nearest Habitat. Naturally, the
Project could not ignore such an act of betrayal—those
pilots, dreaming of an easier life among Habbers, had betrayed Earth's greatest effort. The Habbers refused to return them, arguing that they had always accepted any who
wished to join them, so most of the Habbers remaining on
the Islands were forced to leave, and a Guardian force was
stationed there to reassert Earth's rightful authority."

"I think I heard about them," a man muttered. "But
what does that have to do with the blockade?"

"Pavel Gvishiani, the most powerful of the Island Administrators, had ambitions of his own. He believed that,
with the Habbers as allies, he could wrest control of the
Project for himself and become its sole ruler. Naturally, his
ambitions suffered a setback when most of the Habbers
working with the Project left and Guardians arrived." Better, Malik thought, to give the official version of events.
"But Linker Pavel plotted with the Guardian Commander
there, won her support, and brought more Habbers back
to the Islands. It was a blatantly rebellious act. He'd totally
ignored the Project Council's authority by taking such action on his own."

"So Earth blockaded the Islands," a woman said.

Malik nodded. "The people there were cut off from
the outside and warned to surrender. With Earth's ships in
orbit, any shuttle leaving or arriving at the Island port
called the Platform could be disabled or destroyed. The
Islanders had the use of only their airships after that,
which, as you all know, are useless for travel through space.
Earth might have attacked, but the Mukhtars, in their
wisdom, knew that damaging or destroying the Islands
would set the Project back for decades, maybe longer.
They were also compassionate enough not to want a battle
that would take many lives."

"And the Mukhtars are so kind," one young man said
with a sneer.

"The Islanders knew they couldn't resist a blockade
indefinitely," Malik went on, "and the Habbers were making no move against Earth's ships, even though some of
their own people were still on the Islands."

"That's because Habbers are cowards," someone whispered.

Malik ignored the remark. "Then a small group of Islanders decided to take matters into their own hands. They made plans to board an airship, seize part of the Platform, plant explosive devices, and threaten the entire port with destruction if Earth didn't back down. You can understand how serious a threat that would have been. Earth would have lost everything the Mukhtars were trying to regain."

The plan, considered objectively, had not been so foolish, however insane it appeared. The Islands drifted slowly around the planet in the thin upper atmosphere of Venus, nearly one hundred and forty kilometers above the surface. The location offered certain advantages. The Islands were held by Venus's gravity and were at a safe distance from the fierce winds that still raged below; the atmosphere also provided some protection against meteor strikes. But the protective domes enclosing the ten Islands made it impossible for shuttlecraft to land there. Helium-filled dirigibles were the only vehicles that could land in the Island bays; the Platform, an eleventh Island without a dome, was the port for the shuttles carrying supplies from Anwara and the dirigibles that conveyed cargo and passengers to the other Islands.

Had the port been seized, all of the Islands would have been hostage; Earth would have had either to retreat or to see the Platform destroyed. The Islands, with their thousands of trained specialists and workers, would have been completely isolated from the outside until a new port could be built, and that wouldn't have happened in time to save those Islanders. The Project would have been set back indefinitely. The Mukhtars, after investing so much in Venus, might never have made up for that loss.

"But those people never got to the Platform," Yekaterina said.

"No, they didn't. A worker named—named—" Malik had to think for a moment before coming up with the name. "It was Liang Chen, I believe," he said at last. "This man found out about the plan, and the personnel on the Platform were warned not to allow a landing there. Unfortunately, Liang Chen himself was taken prisoner by the plotters, who immediately headed for the surface when they learned they wouldn't be able to land their airship, with its cargo of explosive devices, on the Platform. They managed to get to one of the three domes the Project had built in the Maxwell Mountains. The dome wasn't yet habitable, but several specialists were working there, housed in a shelter inside. The plotters took them prisoner and said they would blow up the dome and everyone inside if Earth didn't call off its ships. They wanted what amounted to a declaration of independence from Earth. By this time, Linker Pavel must have seen that he had lost control over his Islanders and that others might also risk such suicidal gestures."

"Did anyone ever use all this in a mind-tour?" a man asked. "Seems to me you could."

"One was being planned," Malik replied. "It's why I became more familiar with the story recently."

"You worked on mind-tours?"

"Not exactly. Few professors bother with such things."

The questioner looked a little disappointed. "At any rate," Malik continued, "two Islanders, a woman named Iris Angharads and a man named Amir Azad, went to Pavel and offered to travel to the surface, hoping that they could persuade the plotters to give up peacefully. Pavel let them go, and the plotters agreed to see them. They did succeed in winning freedom for the specialists being held, but only by taking their place as hostages. Their gesture had a tragic result. When the people holding the dome realized that the Mukhtars would never grant their demands, they set off the explosives. Iris Angharads and Amir Azad died with the plotters."

"How sad," Yekaterina murmured; most of the others looked solemn. Malik had not bothered to mention that some Habbers had been among the hostages in that dome, people who had been working there with the Project specialists. Their deaths might have caused the Habbers, who made a show of avoiding violence, to retreat from the Project for good. Earth had needed an apparent victory over the brief Islander rebellion, after which it could surreptitiously turn to Habbers for aid once again.

There was the true dilemma that had faced the Mukhtars then—not the possible loss of a dome and a few lives but the loss of Habber help. The Project could not have continued without straining Earth's resources to the

limit. Discontent would have spread among those on the
home world who already resented the Project, thus threatening the power of the Mukhtars and the peace they had
maintained. If the Mukhtars gave in to the plotters, they
would lose; if they did not, they might lose anyway.

But the Habber hostages had been saved, through the
efforts of the unfortunate Iris and Amir; that small act,
Malik supposed, had helped to preserve the Project. It had
apparently moved the Habbers—who had seen two Islanders sacrifice themselves to save a few of their people—to
promise Earth that they would continue to work with the
Project if Earth showed mercy to most of the Islanders.

"What about that worker?" a woman asked.

"A pilot who was one of the plotters was holding him
aboard the airship in the dome bay," Malik replied. "When
she realized that her friends had set their charges, and that
the dome was going to be destroyed after all, she decided
to save herself instead of joining her companions in death.
The airship, with Liang Chen aboard, managed to reach an
Island."

"I guess he was a hero, too."

"I don't imagine it gave him much joy," Malik responded. "Iris, the woman who died, was his bondmate."

A woman sighed. Malik wondered if Wadzia Zayed
was still working on her mind-tour. No wonder she had
wanted to include this part of the Project story; it had so
many of the suspenseful and touching elements that would
appeal to her prospective audience.

"I think you're all aware of what happened after that,"
Malik said. "Pavel Gvishiani's Link was taken from him,
and he lost his position, but he was allowed to go on labor-
ing for the Project as a humble worker; so Earth showed
some mercy." He closed his eyes for a moment; the fate of
that man, he knew now, had not been so merciful after all.
"His allies among the Habbers were content to let him
suffer that fate. Earth allowed the Habbers to come back to
work on the Project. We'd learned they were powerless
against our might, so there was no need to reject their aid
then." Earth had won at least the appearance of a victory.

Alexei's lip curled. "That's not what I've heard," the
blond man said. "Some say that, without the Habbers,
there wouldn't be more domes on the surface for settlement."

Malik gazed back at Alexei, who had come close to the truth. "We could have gone on without them, but it was thought wiser to let the Habbers make up for the delay that they helped cause. Better to use them in whatever way we could and save more of our resources for Earth itself. The Project is still ours, and the Habbers only tools for us to use."

"Is that why Earth calls on the Habbers and their ships to take us to Venus?" a blue-eyed woman asked.

"Of course," Malik replied. "And it gives Earth a chance to observe the Habbers more closely, learn more about what they might be hiding. We on Earth don't get too many chances to observe them at close range." That was also easier to say than the truth—that Earth needed those ships to transport some of the settlers and that the Habbers could always be blamed if a prospective emigrant was refused passage.

"You're one with many words," Alexei said. "What does all this have to do with you?"

"Some on the Council of Mukhtars thought that Abdullah Heikal had inflamed the situation by sending Guardian ships to blockade the Cytherian Islands instead of trying to reach a resolution more quietly. He and those closest to him were removed from the Council of Mukhtars, and my uncle was among those who forced him to give up his position." Malik had been only four years old at the time, but he could still recall how Muhammad had raged at Abdullah's carelessness. Abdullah's show of force, and the necessity to back down later, had only revealed Earth's weakness to the Habbers.

"I still don't see—" Yekaterina waved a hand. "Why would you be punished for what happened then?"

"Because some close to Abdullah feel he was treated unfairly. His people have more influence now. Abdullah Heikal may never be a Mukhtar again, but he has eyes and ears on the Council, and those who will act for him there. They singled me out, knowing that my disgrace would weaken my uncle even more and shame my family as well. They took what I had written and said, ideas I meant only as speculations, and accused me of harboring dangerous notions. I could no longer teach or write. A Counselor came to speak to me. I saw that it might be better to remove myself entirely from the scene of my disgrace."

"Counselors," a woman said. "They can seem so kind when they're giving their advice, but it's the Nomarchies' interests they think of, not ours."

Malik did not deny the statement. The regional Counselors who advised those in their Nomarchies were there to promote stability and defuse tensions within a community. They consulted with people on every aspect of life, and their advice had nearly the force of law. They granted permission to families who wanted more children, steered people to various jobs, and noticed when a few discontented souls might be better off in a different Nomarchy. In return, Earth's citizens could feel that the Administrative Councils, and the Mukhtars those Councils served, were intimately concerned with their welfare.

The people with him now might believe that they had chosen to be here, but he suspected that Counselors had manipulated a few of them to make that decision. Some of them might be troublemakers, and their communities better off without them. Anyone expressing a willingness to start over on Venus, even with no hope of being chosen officially by the Project Council, would be one a Counselor might steer here.

"The Mukhtars!" Alexei spat. "Venus won't be theirs. It'll belong to the people who build it, whatever the Mukhtars say. If anyone tells me what to do, he'll soon see what he's up against."

Malik leaned forward. "I've learned that it does no good either to get close to the powerful or to work against them. Better to live out your life in the hope that they won't notice you at all."

"Those are a coward's words."

"Silence, Alexei Sergeievich," a black-haired man with the flat cheekbones of a Mongolian said. "Words don't make a man brave."

Yekaterina put a hand on her brother's shoulder; Alexei pulled away. "I'm still confused," she said. "Couldn't a time come when your uncle might rise again? You would only have to wait."

Malik was silent. There was no point in explaining the true situation to these people. Guardian Commanders were among Abdullah Heikal's allies now, Guardians impatient with being only the arms of the Mukhtars. Muhammad was powerless against them as long as so many of the

Mukhtars did not resist their growing influence. Abdullah had been ready for a battle with Habbers, while Muhammad had counseled against that fight. The Commanders had felt themselves shamed and would always regard Malik's uncle as one of the causes of that shame.

"Whatever they took from you," Yekaterina continued, "the Nomarchies must have spent much to train you —surely they could have found other work for you here. However humble your position, it would have been higher than ours, and your work easier. Do you really need to run to Venus?"

"They took more from me than you know," Malik said. "The shock of that loss was too great. Everything here only reminds me of that loss, and I need to forget."

"So our choice," Alexei said, "the chance we've given up everything for, is only a punishment for you."

Malik shook his head. "Being here isn't my punishment. I suffered my punishment earlier."

He reached up and pushed his turban back a little, revealing the tiny scar on his forehead. "That was my punishment. I was a Linker, and my Link was taken from me. I could have borne the rest if they'd left me my Link, but I was to be a useful example to others. Other scholars will now be more cautious in their speculations, while Abdullah and his friends have shown my uncle that their power is growing."

Yekaterina raised a hand to her mouth; he thought he saw sympathy in her dark eyes. Alexei frowned, looking even more suspicious than before, while the rest of the group was silent.

Malik listened to the silence inside his head. A simple procedure, the physician had said. Malik would suffer a headache for only a day or two after the implant and its microscopic components were removed and the slight damage to his nerve endings repaired. A simple procedure, to remove the Link connecting him to Earth's cyberminds; the simple procedure had seemed more like an amputation. He had felt like a man suddenly blinded and deafened and made mute as well, cut off from certain senses and forced to communicate through other means. Even the band he could put on his head was not able to replace his lost Link. The band opened channels to the artificial intelligences only to block his path when he probed too far and reached a road open only to Linkers.

"Now you know about me," Malik said. He wondered if he had dispelled some of their suspicions or had intensified them. "Losing my Link nearly destroyed me—I feel the loss still. I can't imagine what such a punishment would be like for one who had lived with a Link longer than I had." He drew his turban back over his scar.

Alexei's mouth twisted. "You lost only what most never have."

"It was as though I'd lost part of my soul. A world had suddenly been taken from me."

"That isn't what you regret," Alexei said. "It's the jewel you once wore on your head, the jewel that marked what you were and made even strangers bow to you."

Yekaterina touched Malik's sleeve. "Don't listen to my brother."

Alexei stood up and walked on; the others began to follow him. Malik rose and helped the young woman to her feet. "Thank you for what you said."

"I didn't say it just for your sake," she replied. "What good will it do to leave this world if we carry our resentments to the next?"

"I wonder if we can avoid that," he said, feeling the burden of history.

The group trudged on in silence. Toward noon, a floater passed overhead, casting its elongated shadow on the broken road. The helium-filled dirigible was long and sausage-shaped, with a windowed cabin for its passengers; Malik thought of those carefree travelers and lowered his eyes. High-speed trains and tubeways connected most major cities, but travel on a floater was often the only way to get to smaller towns. Malik wondered where this one was bound, and what its passengers were thinking as they gazed at the group below.

The sun had quickly burned away the chill in the air, and a sharp wind was dying down. Yekaterina pulled off her fur hat and let her hair fall over her shoulders. Malik, having noted her black eyes and olive-skinned face, had expected her to have dark hair, but she was nearly as blond as her brother. The wind had heightened the color on her broad cheeks while the blond curls softened her features.

She glanced at him from the sides of her eyes and smiled a little; he had seen such glances many times. His beauty was a curse. Without it, he might have found a bondmate by now, a companion who could have eased his pain and loneliness. Instead, he had gone from one love to the next only to find, during his disgrace, that none of them loved him enough to share his shame. He thought of Wadzia, who had been quick to let others know her connection with him was a casual one, and of Luciana, who had found only excuses to give him.

Malik rubbed at the stubble on his face; he might not seem so attractive now, disheveled as he was. Maybe Yekaterina Osipova only pitied him.

He and the woman had fallen behind the others. Malik halted for a moment, took out his canteen, drank, then offered his water to Yekaterina. She took a sip, then handed the canteen back.

"You spoke of yourself, Malik Haddad," she said as they walked on. "Perhaps I should tell you a little about myself."

"If you wish."

"I applied to be a worker with the Venus Project. My Counselor tried to talk me out of it and said I had no chance, but I insisted."

"Then you were rejected," Malik said, "or you wouldn't be here."

"Perhaps I should have listened to the Counselor. Those I went to said they had no need of a woman whose only work was growing vegetables. I told them people had to eat wherever they were. They said I had no skills, and I said that I had learned to read, could speak Anglaic, and that I could learn anything else they felt I needed to know. They said a settler's life wasn't easy, and I said that I came from people who took pride in how much suffering they could bear. They turned me down. I went home to think of ways to make them change their minds."

"What happened then?" Malik asked.

"I had a lover, Yuri. That was enough—I wanted no more from him. But I was nearly twenty, and he kept after me for a pledge. Soon, my parents were taking his side— they were going to renew their bond and wanted a ceremony for me at the same time. My mother told me I was a fool, that Yuri wanted me enough to pledge two decades or

even three. It's the way she thinks, that you should have a
bond with a man for as many years as possible, so that
when it's time to renew the bond or let it lapse, it's harder
for him to leave."

Malik nodded. Yekaterina clearly came from a community where such bonds were valued, and her Counselor
would have insisted that she follow custom.

"I know a little of other lands," Yekaterina continued.
"I told my parents there were places where people
scorned bonds or wore them lightly, but they wouldn't
listen—their ways are the law of the world in their eyes. I
had some love for Yuri. He was strong, and a hard worker,
and his smile made my heart dance, but I knew that he
would demand too much from me. Yuri was content in our
village—he didn't want me to think of trying to leave it
again. He mocked my learning and said it was useless."

Malik arched his brows. "Your learning?"

She smiled. "It isn't learning like yours, only what I
could find out with my screen and band. I can read. I've
had some lessons, but not enough to be chosen for a
school." She lifted her head. "On Venus, all children can go
to a school. They don't have to hope that a Counselor will
choose them or find a way to pay for the lessons if they
aren't chosen."

The rest of the group was getting farther ahead of
them; the two picked up their pace. "Why did you come
here?" Malik asked. "Did you decide there was no point in
applying to the Project Council again?"

She shook her head. "Alexei wanted to come. Even
our parents saw that it might be better for him to be away
from our village. I couldn't let him come here alone. My
mother wept, but she knew that I'd try to look out for
him."

"He seems old enough to look after himself."

"He's seventeen." She paused. "I don't like to say this
about my brother, but he thinks freedom is only the
chance to do what he likes, with no one to hold him back.
Whatever freedom is on Venus, it cannot be that kind,
but—"

Yekaterina put on her hat, then thrust her hands into
her coat pockets. "Alexei has often been troublesome," she
murmured, "and he'd fallen in with a few like himself. The
Counselor would have done something about that eventu-

ally, but happily my brother chose to come here. I had to
come with him, and it's also a chance to have what I want.
Maybe when we reach Venus, his anger at the world will
cool."

Light danced on the horizon, reflected by facets of
glass; Malik lifted a hand to shade his eyes. A town lay
ahead, with rows of wooden dwellings and glassy greenhouses for the fruit grown in this region. He had been
taken to a town much like it once, to sit under the trees
eating shashlik and drinking tea while dark-eyed Uzbek
and Russian children gathered to gape at the unfamiliar
sight of a Linker. Much as he longed to rest, this village was
not likely to welcome them. Already, the people ahead
were following a dirt path that led away from the town.

They walked rapidly, refusing to rest, pushing themselves on until a few of them were panting. The prospect of
sleeping out in the open sent fear through the group. The
night might be cold; there was talk of wolves. Malik found
himself worrying more about what lay ahead in the camp.

Most of the specialists working with the Venus Project
were selected from among students at the Cytherian Institute, a university in Caracas, one of the cities of Nueva
Hispania. Some of them came there from various regions
of Earth, while others were chosen from among young
people who had grown up on Venus's Islands. Skilled workers who wanted a place with the Project could apply to the
Project Council, but most of them were turned down.

The camp that was Malik's destination held ones who
were more impatient or more desperate.

Ten years earlier, people had begun to make their way
to various shuttle ports, to camp there until they were
granted passage to Venus. Those who could pay might
have been allowed to go, but this would only encourage
others to make the same demand. Domes were being built
on Venus, but there was room for only a certain number of
people. Some of the hopeful emigrants lacked needed
skills, while others were likely to be a disruptive influence.

The crowds might have been dispersed, but the Council of Mukhtars had been wiser than that. Better to let
some of the discontented gather where Guardians could
keep an eye on them, and where their restlessness could
cause trouble only to themselves.

Near three of Earth's cities, including Tashkent, isolated land at a distance from each city's port had been set aside for those who wanted passage to Venus. There, they were allowed to wait until passage could be found for them, but a price was extracted for this. Those traveling there had to pay for their journey and surrender the rest of their credit when they reached a camp. They had to wait, with no guarantee that they would ever leave Earth. If they then chose to give up waiting, they had to take whatever labor was found for them elsewhere, and Malik knew that only the most burdensome work and conditions were offered to such people.

Malik had heard of riots in the camps, outbursts born of despair; some had died in the violence. The Mukhtars, although they prided themselves on their restraint, did not trouble to hide measures taken to quell the disturbances; there was no point in encouraging too many people to join those in the camps. Given the uncertainty of life there, and the capriciousness involved in choosing those who would be allowed to leave, it was a wonder that thousands still dreamed of finding a new life on Venus.

"Look there," the Mongolian man said as he pointed toward the horizon. A few lights were shining in the distance; a beam from a tower swept across the ground. The group strode more rapidly. A large, egg-shaped cradle was to the east of the tower; a floater rested inside it.

As the travelers came nearer, two Guardians left the tower and waited outside. The camp was now visible; prefabricated shacks, tents, and yurts, rounded structures made of felt and wood, were surrounded by posts with scanners. Three other towers loomed over the dwellings below.

"Halt right there," one of the Guardians, a short, stocky man with dark eyes, called out in Anglaic. "I trust you understand me. You can speak whatever you like here, but you'll need Anglaic on Venus."

"Don't you think we know that?" a woman asked.

"We've seen a few who thought they could fool us. They had to be turned away." The Guardian motioned toward the tower door. "Line up there—we'll take you one at a time. We have to do a med-scan before you go in."

"We're tired," Alexei said in accented Anglaic. "Can't we rest and get something to eat before—"

"Quiet!" the taller Guardian shouted. "The sooner we get through this, the sooner you can rest."

People began to line up behind Malik. Tired as they were, they seemed willing to let him go first and find out what was in store for the rest of them; maybe they thought they'd be treated better when the Guardians learned Malik's identity. He walked toward the door, then glanced back at Yekaterina; the dark-eyed Guardian shoved him inside.

He was in a small room. A man with an officer's pin on his collar sat behind the desk; three other Guardians, all in black uniforms, were sitting at a table. Two were women; one lifted a brow as she stared at him.

"Let's see your bracelet," the officer said. Malik moved toward the desk and thrust his arm toward the ID console; the officer gazed at the screen. "Well, well—never thought I'd see one of you here." The officer glanced at the other Guardians. "We've got a scholar and a Linker here, comrades—a former Linker, I should say." He narrowed his eyes. "Fair amount of credit, too. Maybe this place will break even this month." The officer motioned with one hand. "Drop the pack and strip."

Malik tensed.

"Come on, man—you heard me. Take off your clothes for a med-scan. We can't have medical problems here."

"I need not undress," Malik replied. "The med-scan will pick up anything I might have anyway, and you'll see from my record that I'm—"

"Strip!" The officer rose a little from his seat. "Get those clothes off now, or you and your friends can sleep outside the camp tonight. They might not like that, and I'll tell them who's to blame. Better drop your Linker airs if you want to get along here."

Malik shrugged out of his pack, then took off his clothes. One of the women giggled as the stocky Guardian circled him with a portable scanner; Malik lowered his eyes, shamed. "There's one for you, Lana," a man said.

"Too bad they aren't all like that," a woman's voice replied.

The room was silent as the Guardians studied the results. "Guess we can pass him through," the officer muttered. "Get dressed and wait outside until we're done with the others."

Malik pulled on his clothes, grabbed his pack, and hurried outside as Yekaterina entered. He sat down a few paces from the others, refusing to look at them. He wondered when they would be fed. There was a little food in his pack, but if he took it out, the others might expect him to share it.

He looked up as Yekaterina left the tower; her face was red as she settled next to him. "That officer," she whispered, cursing in Russian. "I wanted to spit in his face. He didn't have to—"

"I know."

"Alexei won't stand for it."

"He'd better, or they won't let him in."

Alexei came outside. He had a bruise near one eye. His hands were clenched fists as he sat down next to his sister.

The sky was almost completely dark by the time the rest of the group had been scanned. The stocky Guardian left the tower, then beckoned to them. "Follow me."

As they drew nearer to the camp, Malik saw tents with torn flaps, shacks with painted walls, and worn-down paths winding among the yurts. Several people were standing near one long, low building; the Guardian waved an arm in their direction. "Showers and toilets," he said. "You go to the one closest to your part of the camp—someone'll show you which one. You get two showers a week, and the scanner keeps a record, so don't try for more unless you want to lose the privilege for a month." He chuckled. "That wouldn't make you too popular."

He stopped near one of the posts. "Don't leave the camp without permission. The scanners will alert us to that, too." He pointed at another large building not far from the nearest yurts. "That's one of the dining halls. You get fed twice a day, and you can eat there or anywhere else, but take your trays back when you're done and don't throw garbage around."

"Where do we stay?" Yekaterina asked.

The Guardian stared at her for a long time before replying. "I trust you knew enough to bring a tent. You can pitch it here, on the open ground. If you didn't, you'll just have to sleep in the dining hall when people are through eating. Start making friends, and you'll get another place to live. Don't get sick, or you'll have to leave—we can't have disease going around. Don't break any rules, or out you go."

"What are the rules?" a man asked.

"You'll find out when you've been around long enough." The Guardian paused. "Too bad this little talk took so long. We can't give you any supper now, so you'll have to wait until breakfast." He leaned against the post.

Several people had come out of the yurts to look at the new arrivals. Behind them, light wands stood in the ground along the paths or hung over doorways. Malik glanced at these people, noting that most of them seemed very young, as he had expected. Children under a certain age would not be accepted here, and the old would be turned away.

No one spoke or offered any sign of welcome. Malik supposed that he and the rest of his group were being judged. Every additional person meant another competitor for a place aboard a ship; in the meantime, they all had to get along. After a few moments, people disappeared inside the yurts, but one young man remained outside, staring past Malik at the Guardian.

Some of the new arrivals were already drifting away, seeking out places to pitch their tents. Malik turned toward Yekaterina. "I brought a small tent," he said, "but it's hardly large enough for me."

"We have our own," Alexei said stiffly.

"We'll set it up next to yours," Yekaterina murmured. Alexei glared at her; she stared back at her brother until the blond man took off his pack.

Malik had carried stakes with him, but the ground was hard. As he pitched his tent, the same one he had used when backpacking in the desert outside Amman, he wondered what Karim al-Anwar would have thought of those now pursuing his dream.

Yekaterina was driving a stake into the ground as the Guardian walked over to her. "If you're hungry," he said, "I can get you something to eat."

"That's very kind," she said, standing up.

The stocky man shrugged. "It depends on how kind you are to me." He motioned with his head. "I can take you to the tower, or we can use your tent." He reached out and caught her arm; she shook him off. "Don't be a fool," he said.

"I'm not that hungry."

"I'll tell you what it's like here. You might need a little extra food or a warmer place to sleep."

Alexei stepped toward the Guardian. "You heard my sister."

"What's the problem?" the Guardian asked. "You want some food for yourself? I can take care of that, as long as she—"

Alexei raised a fist; the Guardian's hand moved toward the wand at his belt. Malik leaped up and grabbed Alexei's arm. "Steady," he murmured; Alexei twisted away. "Don't strike him—it'll just mean trouble for you."

The Guardian turned toward Malik. "This isn't your business."

"The woman doesn't want your attentions."

"You probably think she'd prefer yours." The Guardian smiled. "You're not a Linker anymore, Citizen. You can't do a thing to me."

"I'll complain to your officer," Malik said. "I'm sure he wants an orderly camp, one where his people don't stir up trouble."

"Let the woman speak for herself." The uniformed man reached for Yekaterina; she recoiled.

"I've already spoken," she said. "I'm not hungry."

The Guardian spun around, then strode toward the distant tower. The young man standing outside the nearest yurt grinned. "He would have fed you," he called out.

Yekaterina lifted her chin. "I'm not a whore."

The man walked toward her. "Just as well that you refused him," he said. "We don't care for people who get too friendly with Guardians." He brushed back his unruly brown hair, then bowed slightly from the waist. "I'm Nikolai Andreievich Burian."

Yekaterina introduced herself and her brother, then motioned at Malik. "His name is Malik Haddad. We met him in the port."

Nikolai Burian studied Malik for a moment. "That Guardian said something about your being a Linker."

"I was. I'm not now, as you can see." Malik lifted his turban a little.

Nikolai frowned. "Let me give you some advice," he said as he glanced at Yekaterina. "Keep near the camp, and around other people—don't go wandering around in the open alone. The Guardians won't bother you if you're near others, but you might not be safe by yourself."

"I can look out for Katya," Alexei said.

"Maybe you can and maybe you can't. That Guardian might still try something when he thinks he can get away with it."

"His officer—" Malik began.

"It'd be this woman's word against his." Nikolai folded his arms. "An officer wants discipline, but some are more sympathetic than others. Best thing to do is to just keep away from them."

"If he comes near Katya again," Alexei said, "I'll—"

Nikolai waved an arm. "You won't do a thing. The Guardians don't choose people for transport, but if you make trouble, they'll force you out, and you can forget Venus. If you have any questions, come to me. I sort of manage things at this end of the camp, mostly because I've been here longer than anyone else—almost three years."

Yekaterina let out her breath. "That long?"

"Knew some who waited even longer before they left. Blame the Project Council—blame the Habbers, too. They must have something to say about who gets on their ships."

"Actually, the Habbers have nothing to say about it," Malik said. "Their agreement with Earth only allows them to provide pilots and ships."

"That's what they'd like us to think," Nikolai answered. "I don't know why you'd want to speak up for Habbers anyway, but you Linkers probably think you know it all." Nikolai gazed at him steadily until Malik looked away. "They feed us about an hour after dawn, so make sure you get to the hall over there on time. It's breakfast at dawn and supper before sunset until summer comes—then it changes and you get breakfast at sunset."

"Why is that?" Yekaterina asked.

"The only way we can stand the heat is to sleep during the day then. They don't do a lot to keep us cool and comfortable. You'll see—you'll start feeling as if you're on Venus already when summer's here."

As Nikolai walked back to his yurt, Alexei knelt to drive in another stake. "Thank you for speaking up for me," Yekaterina said softly. "You also kept Alexei from doing something foolish."

"It's nothing. I have a little extra food, and I won't ask any favors for it."

"I wouldn't mind if you did." She smiled. "Keep your food, Malik. You may have need of it yourself."

Alexei motioned to his sister. Yekaterina entered their tent; the young man followed and let the flap fall.

Malik went inside his own tent and rolled out a blanket, grateful that he had come here in early spring but wondering how he would endure the summer. He stretched out, trying to get comfortable. His loneliness deepened as he listened to the voices in the camp. The thought of sex was far from his mind, but he would have welcomed physical closeness with someone who might ease his fears.

He didn't belong here. He could never live among these people. All along, he had assumed an unlikely turn of events, a message from his uncle Muhammad that would call him back to Amman and restore his old life. That could never happen now; by entering this camp, he had cut his ties.

The others in the camp hoped to escape Earth's bonds. Malik only wanted a refuge and a second chance for a quiet, largely uneventful life. There were Habbers living among the Cytherians. Islanders had fled to a Habitat before. Perhaps he could even find a place among them, away from the toil of a new world and safely distant from the pain of the old.

The emigrants around him would despise such dreams, Malik realized as he closed his eyes and tried to sleep.

Two

"I don't know why you called," Angharad Julias said. "I don't know why I'm speaking to you at all. I thought you'd forgotten us long ago."

Benzi gazed at the screen. His grandmother's image stared back at him with tired brown eyes. Angharad had to be close to ninety by now, but he was still shocked at how much she had aged. Her once-brown hair was completely white; her skin had been lined and roughened by the prairie winds of North America's Plains. Earth's primitive rejuvenation techniques could postpone aging only for a time; he had been among Habbers for too long and had lost sight of that fact.

"I haven't forgotten you," Benzi said.

"I see you're calling on a private channel. Do they allow you to send messages from that camp?"

"My room's monitored," Benzi said, "but I found it easy to block those devices. The Guardians here will think I'm sleeping now, and I won't leave any record of this call. Even if I did, I doubt that anyone would hold the call against you."

"You can be sure they won't. Erase it if you like, but I'll keep a record. I won't have my Counselor scolding me for talking to a Habber, and he'll see I didn't say anything I shouldn't." Her flat Plains voice had changed very little. "Mother of God—you must be sixty, and you're still a young man."

"Fifty-six," Benzi corrected. "We live long lives in the Habs." He did not mention the tiny implants that allowed his cells to repair themselves, one of the gifts he had received when he joined the Habbers.

Angharad shook her head. "I never expected to hear from you again. When you went to the Habbers, you broke your ties with us, with everyone. I can't believe they let you come back to Earth."

"They had no choice," Benzi said patiently. "It's part of our agreement. The Nomarchies have to allow pilots to wait in these camps until—"

"So you can spy on us, I suppose. The Mukhtars must have their reasons, but I never understood how such people think."

"We're only here to take settlers to Venus."

"Venus!" Angharad's brown eyes were fierce. "Venus took my daughter's life! I have a granddaughter there I'll never know, who sends me a message once a year. That's what Venus and that fine Project did for me."

There was some justice to her words. Her daughter, Iris Angharads, had left the North American Plains for the Cytherian Institute. Benzi knew that Iris had never expected to be chosen for advanced training at the school; she was sixteen and already pregnant with him when the news came. Iris couldn't have refused the honor; even Angharad had seen that.

Iris had left her home town of Lincoln soon after Benzi's birth. She had become little more to Benzi than a screen image after that; Angharad and her household had cared for him. The mother who returned shortly before his fifth birthday was a stranger, one who had come there only to take her son to the Cytherian Islands.

Iris had claimed that more opportunity awaited them both with the Project. The Plains Communes were households of women who tended their farms and often had children in their teens, choosing fathers for their young from among the workers who passed through their towns. Plainswomen scorned bonds; each might welcome many men to her bed, but none would tie herself to one man. Many Plainswomen were illiterate and had little desire for learning; they preferred to dwell on their people's glorious past. Had Benzi remained with Angharad's household, he would, he supposed, have become yet another wandering Plains mechanic, a man who moved from town to town and shared his bed with any woman who was willing. He would have had no real home in the communities Plainswomen controlled.

It was a wonder his mother had escaped. Iris, he knew, had suffered the mockery of her household while pursuing her lessons; she had even flouted custom by secretly pledging herself as a bondmate to Liang Chen, Benzi's father. At most, she had hoped to leave Lincoln with Chen to join the Project as a worker; she had not thought the Institute would choose her.

Benzi had been afraid to leave his grandmother, but anticipating his journey to Venus had dulled those fears. Now he recalled the warmth and affection Angharad had always shown him, and how she had wept when Iris took him away. His bond with Iris, despite his mother's efforts, had always been more tenuous.

"Your line will continue on Venus," he said. "Your descendants will be part of a great enterprise." Angharad had always given in easily to what she called the sin of pride; such dreams might console her a little.

"If your sister Risa ever finds a man," Angharad muttered. "She's in her twenties, and no sign of a child." She shook her head. "I don't understand you, Benzi. You abandoned the Project, and now you're back on Earth, helping those fools in that camp to get to the place you left."

"Pilots are needed, and it's a chance to try to overcome Earth's distrust of us. I've lived on Earth and the Islands, so I was a logical choice to come here."

"Everything's changing now," she said, "and I wonder what will come of it. Your cousin Sylvie is head of this household now, and she's thinking of having us merge with another household. There are fewer households now—we don't need to farm as much land. Our ancestors found a wilderness here long ago and made it their home, and now much of it may become a wilderness again."

"Angharad—"

"But I've said enough about that." She went on to speak of her housemates, LaDonna and Constance, both old women now, and of the new generations living under her roof; Benzi nodded absently as she gossiped about the town's mayor. "She's a good enough woman, I suppose," Angharad said, "but I don't mind admitting that she sometimes benefits from my advice. Frankly, I think I was a better mayor—you wouldn't have seen me walking

around with such airs. I remember when you used to come
to the town hall while I was meeting with people—you
were so solemn, even then—the mayor's assistant, they
used to call you." She paused. "And has the life you chose
made you happy?"

"I suppose so." He mentioned a few of his friends and
told her of some of the difficulties he once had in adjusting
to his Link. There was much about Habber life she would
not comprehend, much he didn't quite understand himself.

"I shouldn't be speaking to you," Angharad said when
he was finished, "but I'm old now, and the chance might
not come again. I don't like what you've done, but you'll
have to live with that, and God and His Holy Mother will
judge me for my sins soon enough."

"I'm happy we had the chance to speak, Grandmother."

"God be with you, Benzi, and Mary's blessings upon
you." Her mouth twisted. "Unless you Habbers have no
God."

"Farewell."

The screen went blank. Benzi leaned back in his chair.
Angharad might think of him as a Habber, but even now,
he often wondered if he would ever truly be one.

He had been in his teens when he fled the Islands of
Venus with a few other pilots who had dreamed of shedding their bonds with Earth and its Project. He had kept
his plans secret from his mother and father; he had even
hurt them by severing his familial bond with them for-
mally, in the hope they would thus be spared any blame for
his actions. He had been sure of his decision then; he had
viewed Earth as a dying civilization refusing to let go of its
children.

His actions, and those of his accomplices, had forced
the Island Administrators to expel most of the Habbers
from the Islands in response to their deed. That had set the
Venus Project back, which in turn had eventually led to
the Islanders' confrontation with Earth. His mother had
died trying to prevent one mad group from destroying one
of the surface domes, but she had saved the lives of several
Habbers there; that, as much as anything, had convinced
the Habbers to push Earth into a face-saving settlement.

Had it not been for his and his fellow pilots' deed, Iris

might still be alive, living on the world she had given her life to build.

Few Earthfolk grasped the Habbers' motivations for assisting the Project. Even the Islanders, many of whom had grown closer to the Habbers there in recent years, did not fully understand their purpose. The Project provided the Habbers with their only direct contact between themselves and the people of Earth; it was their last link with the rest of humanity.

Benzi thought of the Habitats near Mars and just beyond that planet's orbital path. Habbers had made homes for themselves inside the two Martian satellites and had built others using the resources of the asteroid belt; the location of their worldlets had established their claim to Mars. Terraforming Mars would have presented fewer problems than transforming Venus, but the Habitat-dwellers regarded planets in much the same way as some ancient Earthfolk had seen their Earthly environment. To make use of some planetary resources was acceptable; to alter a world completely was unnecessary and undesirable. Habbers lived in space; they had no need to make other planets into replicas of the Earth they had abandoned.

Long ago, Earth had been gently but firmly warned that the Habbers would not welcome efforts at terraforming Mars. The Nomarchies might have looked to the satellites of the gas giants then, but any settlements there would be farther from Earth and its influence. That left Venus, Earth's sister-planet. The obstacles to terraforming there were great, but that would only make Earth's eventual triumph more glorious. The Habbers had established no claim to Venus; there was only one Habitat orbiting the sun between Venus and Earth, built before an agreement with the Nomarchies limited the Habbers to the space near Mars and outside the red planet's orbit. As long as Earth allowed them that small outpost in the part of the solar system the Mukhtars claimed for themselves, the Habbers were content to let Earth proceed with its Project. Later, when Earth turned to them for help, the Habbers had readily agreed. They had not been able to stop Venus's transformation, but could learn much from assisting the Venus Project, whatever their own doubts about the wisdom of that effort.

The Habbers feared cutting themselves loose from the

rest of their kind, yet already many of them had begun to diverge. Benzi had never visited the Habitats near Mars and beyond, but those who came to his Habitat from there seemed as distant and alien to him as they would have been to a citizen of Earth. They wore human shapes, but their minds, Linked to the artificial intelligences of their own worlds, were as engineered, molded, and shaped as their Habitats. These Habbers had shed their earlier passions and surges of irrationality, erased their cluttered memories of decades or centuries after storing them in the cyberminds, had made themselves what they once aspired to be—a society of mind, links in a vast intelligence. He often wondered how much of themselves they had given up; some of them seemed hardly more than the eyes and ears of cyberminds.

He had joined the Habbers to be free of Earth, but he was still bound to Earth's people. His home was the one Habitat between the orbits of Venus and Earth. Those who lived there saw themselves as a bridge between Earthfolk and the rest of their own kind. He had dreamed of someday exploring the stars beyond this solar system, but the people of his Habitat feared such a break with all that they knew, while the Habbers near Mars thought only of probes, of exploring space only through cybernetic intermediaries.

He and his fellow pilots had planned their escape flight carefully. They had chosen the perfect moment, the hours when the gravitational engines on Venus's equator would release their pulse of energy. The nearest Hab, with an orbit nine million kilometers beyond Venus's orbital path, was within reach of a shuttle at that time. Benzi and his comrades had volunteered for Platform duty, knowing that nearly everyone on the Islands would be gathering by their screens to witness the awesome events below.

Probes transmitting from the planet's surface had given the Islanders images of crumbling mountains, hills swaying on molten lava, pyramids crowned by lightning as Venus was assaulted. Few had paid attention to the shuttle as it left the port and began to orbit Venus, ostensibly to view the world from above. Benzi remembered the bright fan of colored bands that had suddenly appeared above the northern pole as the dark world below began to turn more rapidly. That had been his last glimpse of Venus before the shuttle thrust out of orbit.

He had arrived at an asteroid enclosed by a vast metallic shell. The Hab was a world of wide corridors, simple rooms, and a garden of forests, lakeshores, hills and plains at its center that seemed meant to be a monument to Earth. Its people were individuals whose strongest passions were apparently directed toward knowledge and speculation. He saw them not as inhuman, but rather as people whose true humanity had triumphed over qualities that were usually linked to his species' baser instincts.

Benzi avoided thinking of Iris and Chen during his earliest years in the Hab. They had their dream and he had his; their lives could no longer touch him. News of the Project's setbacks had left him unconcerned, since he was beginning to think as Habbers did, to see most events as little more than transitory stages in a long life. The Project would need more Habber assistance again; eventually Earth would allow more Habbers to return. He had forgotten that Islanders, with briefer lives, could not be so patient. Iris's death had reminded him of that.

He had given up his life on the Islands. He could never have remained happily in those gardened environs or lived on the surface, where the dark clouds would always have hidden the heavens from him. Iris could live in her dream, seeing Venus as it would be; he had seen only a prison. He was free now, but could still not think of himself as a Habber. By his own choice, the Link inside his head that connected him with his Habitat's cyberminds was often silent.

The guilt he felt over his mother's death separated him from many of his fellow Habbers. Iris had once represented everything he was trying to escape, so driven by her own dream that she was unable to see his. He had escaped from her, but now she held him once more; he was aiding others who shared her dream. He had sought to shed a little of his remorse by agreeing to ferry settlers from this camp outside Tashkent; he wondered if he would ever be free of that guilt.

Four Guardians sat in the small room at the base of the tower; they were hunched over the table, playing a game on a portable screen. They fell silent as Benzi stepped out of the lift. The uniformed people spoke to him only when it was necessary and muttered about him when they thought he was out of earshot.

The Guardians had various assumptions about Habbers, many of them contradictory. The Habbers were here to spy on Earth; they were here because they secretly longed to return; they had altered their bodies somatically to the point where they were hardly human, or else their rational, distant manner was only the pose of people pretending they were different. Habbers dreamed of conquering Earth, sabotaging the Venus Project, or of abandoning near-space altogether. Whatever the Guardians believed, they also seemed to think that the Mukhtars now had the upper hand in their dealings with the Associated Habitats and were using the Habbers for their own ends.

None of the Guardians here knew that Benzi had spent his early life on the Plains of North America and had grown up on Venus's Islands, and that was just as well. He preferred being seen as an odd creature in human form rather than as a traitor to the Nomarchies.

The door slid open as he walked outside. Dawn had come; in the camp, lines of people stood outside the dining halls, waiting for their morning meal. The Mukhtars, he admitted to himself grudgingly, were handling this situation in a fairly rational way. The camp's primitive conditions and the impossibility of knowing when one might be allowed to leave discouraged most of those who might otherwise have come. Earth could rid itself of a few potential troublemakers while ensuring that those who got to Venus would be strong, determined, and willing to work for that world. Fear of losing a chance to emigrate kept the camp relatively quiet; the confiscation of nearly everything the hopeful emigrants owned made it possible to run the camp more economically. It might have been wiser in the long run to treat these people more kindly, thus gaining their loyalty and gratitude, but that would only have encouraged too many others to join them.

Benzi sometimes pitied the people in the camp, but at least they were aware of the price they would pay to reach their goal, something he had not known when he joined his life to the Habs. The would-be emigrants did not harbor kindly feelings toward him; they assumed that any delays were partly the work of the Habbers, and the Project Council let them believe that.

He shivered a little in his long coat. The air was warming rapidly, but he was still unused to the extremes of temperature here. He thought of the Plains on the other side of Earth. His grandmother's town of Lincoln, like this camp, had been a lonely outpost set against a wide and beckoning horizon, its only connection with the outside world one floater cradle where an airship arrived from time to time.

Te-yu was circling the tower. She thrust her hands into the pockets of her blue jacket as she walked toward him. "You're up early," she said.

"I couldn't sleep."

"Your Link is there to calm you, among other things."

Benzi smiled. "I don't imagine you open yours any more often than I open mine."

"You're wrong. Sometimes I need it more here. I feel very far away from our Hab when it's open but entirely cut off when it's closed."

Their Links, unlike those embedded in the foreheads of Earth's Linkers, were hidden. They wore no tiny jewels on their brows to indicate the presence of a Link, but Earth's authorities had insisted on outward signs that they were Habbers. As a result, he and Te-yu wore pins made of silver circles on their collars. They never left their rooms without pinning the circles to their coats or shirts; it was a way to be certain that others knew exactly what they were.

The people here, like those he had known on the Islands, were uncomfortable and anxious without such outward signs of status—jewels for Linkers, pins for various specialists, uniforms and insignia for Guardians, and the lack of pins for workers and ordinary citizens. One could see immediately what another was and consequently know how to behave.

Habbers needed no such signs. Before Benzi had joined them, he had believed, as did so many others, that this was because Habbers disdained such distinctions. They were all given the Links that on Earth were the privilege of an elite, and were all equals inside their own worlds. He had learned instead that other signs marked the difference between one Habitat-dweller and another —a stance, a gesture, a distant, contemplative gaze, a mind that could almost pierce his own through a channel in his Link.

"I spoke to my grandmother last night," he said. "She's aged so much. It wasn't until she spoke that I knew she hadn't really changed. I told myself she might be happy to hear from me, but maybe I only awakened memories she'd rather forget."

"I suppose I must have some relatives on Earth," she said, "but there's no point in trying to contact them. I can just imagine it. 'Greetings, I'm Hong Te-yu. You don't know me, but I'm a relative, even though I've become a Habber.' That's just what they'd need to hear. Well, I never knew them, so I'm under no feeling of obligation. It must be worse for you, being here."

"I chose to come."

"Do you ever regret it—what we did?" Te-yu asked.

She had not asked that question in a long time. "No," Benzi replied, "I don't regret it. I'm sorry I didn't know what it might cost, and sometimes I think I might have made another choice if I had known, but that's probably just a way of dealing with some of my guilt."

Te-yu was one of the pilots who had fled from Venus with him almost forty years ago. Her parents had left the Islands shortly after she became an apprentice, and her few close friends had been among other pilots. There had been nothing to keep her on the Islands, no family who might think of her act as a betrayal.

Two Guardians had left the tower; Benzi could sense them watching him. He slipped his arm around Te-yu's small waist as she glanced at the Guardians for a moment. "I wonder which bothers them more," she said, "when we seem inhuman or when they see we can be human after all."

They walked toward the camp. "A group arrived last night," she continued. "I got into the lift before they started bringing them inside." Her mouth twitched. "I don't know what they gain by humiliating the new arrivals, but it's probably the only entertainment they have. I did hear an odd piece of news later, something about one man in the group being a former Linker."

"Strange that any Linker would come here."

They halted several paces from the nearest post. He and Te-yu had been warned not to enter the camp alone.

They would be either shunned or besieged with pleas from desperate people whom they were powerless to help; the Guardians wanted no incidents. "I wish the Council would make its selections," he said, "so that we could be on our way."

"Maybe they think the officer here will find out more about us if we're kept here for a while." She leaned against him. "At least we've had a chance to see a little of Earth."

"This isn't the Earth I knew." He looked down at the still-youthful face under her cap of short black hair. Te-yu had come here with him only so that he would not have to face Earth alone. Even after decades with the Habbers, his closest bonds were still with those who had fled from the Islands with him.

They could not keep him here too much longer. His ship was waiting for him up in the Wheel, one of the space stations where freighters, torchships, and other craft were docked. The two Habber pilots who had accompanied him and Te-yu that far would be getting impatient while trying to prevent the Wheel's personnel from examining the ship too extensively. Benzi's ship, with its passengers, would later dock at Anwara, and perhaps there he would be able to get a message to his father and the sister he had never seen.

He had sent a message before, just after Iris's death, through a Habber on the Islands who had known her. "Tell him," his father Chen had replied, "that his mother will always be alive in me." He had said nothing more, and Benzi had wondered if Chen was blaming him in part for her death or trying to console him.

Tents had been pitched near the yurts at this end of the camp. A dark-haired man was standing outside one tent, gazing in Benzi's direction. Benzi turned and led Te-yu back to the tower.

Three

The camp's mosque was a rambling structure of wood, where Muslims could gather for their prayers. Malik was kneeling, his hands on his knees; he raised his head. It had been much easier to recall an appropriate *sura* from the Koran with his Link to prompt him.

"God hears those who praise Him," Malik recited as he glanced at his fellow worshippers. Several of them seemed as unpracticed in such observances as he was. The men rose, knelt once more, then went into a prostration, pressing their foreheads and noses to their prayer rugs. "God is most great!"

The call to prayer issued forth from a speaker in the roof of the mosque five times a day. Except for the dawn prayer, which he performed quickly outside his tent before lining up for the morning meal, and the night prayer, which he raced through before going to sleep, Malik came to the mosque for the others. It was a way to pass the time, which was probably why most of the Muslim emigrants came here to pray even on days other than Friday; he had seen few signs of true devotion. Perhaps that was just as well. On Venus, these people would have to be tolerant of others who held various beliefs, people they might otherwise have rarely encountered; diverse groups from many different Nomarchies had to live together there.

The men near him were speaking now. "Peace be upon thee, O Prophet," Malik murmured with them, "and the mercy of God and His blessings! Peace be upon us all, and all righteous servants of God. I witness that there is no

God but God, I witness that Muhammad is His servant and messenger. God is great!"

When they were finished, they rose, rolled up their rugs, and filed out from the mosque. The camp also held a church, a ramshackle building used at different times by both Old Catholics and Marian Catholics. Sharing a church would hardly have been possible for those two groups anywhere else. Old Catholics regarded the Marians, who had elevated Mary to a status equal to Jesus, as trapped in theological error; in the camp, however, their status as fellow emigrants clearly overrode such differences. Malik supposed many of the Catholics were as casual in their practices as he was in his.

Those who followed other beliefs usually gathered in small groups for prayers and other rites in the dining halls between meals. As Malik walked toward his tent, he saw that Nikolai Burian was sitting outside, waiting for him. Nikolai, along with many of the Russians, did not bother with religious observances, since he came from a community that held to older atheistic beliefs.

The young man had attached himself to Malik. He usually showed up at Malik's side when it was time to line up for food or to use the showers; he was often squatting outside Malik's tent, alone or with other young men, when Malik came out to pray at dawn. They had already dispensed with such formal terms of address as "Nikolai Andreievich" and "Linker Malik"; Malik's old title was inappropriate now anyway. Lately, Nikolai had insisted that Malik address him by the nickname of "Kolya."

Nikolai and the men living in his yurt apparently controlled this end of the camp. They roamed along the paths, asked questions, offered advice, and settled a few disputes best kept from the attention of Guardians.

Nikolai had given Malik advice on which people to avoid, the times when toilets were usually free, and the few amusements the camp offered. Occasionally, he listened while Malik told him a little about his former life. Rumors that Malik was once a Linker had spread through the camp, and at last he guessed why Nikolai sought his company. People were still suspicious of Malik, but he had once held a place among the powerful. Nikolai was undoubtedly curious but also might want to see if some advantage could be gained from getting closer to the scholar.

The young man smirked a little as Malik sat down. "I hope your prayers were a comfort," he said. "The Mukhtars probably just use all that talk of God to impress the likes of us, keep us in line, make us think God tells them what to do."

"That's an oversimplification," Malik replied. "They all have a respect for the *ulemas* and the law. There are many devout ones among the Mukhtars, even though they realize, in their position, that some tolerance of others is required." It was useless to explain too many subtleties to Nikolai. What the man probably enjoyed most was the reversal in their stations.

Two of Nikolai's friends were wrestling on the open ground beyond the tents. Several in the camp filled the long hours with such pursuits—footraces, wrestling, acrobatic feats, or violent games with tattered balls and sticks. The efforts kept them fit, and a serious injury, which could always be passed off as an accident, might eliminate at least one competitor for a place aboard a ship. Malik was careful to avoid such contests, as well as the betting of food or personal possessions that often accompanied them.

A female Guardian stood near the post, watching the wrestlers. Nikolai gestured at her. "I'll tell you what I heard about that bitch. She got tired of waiting for passage, so she joined the Guardians instead."

Malik frowned. "Was she in this camp?"

"Of course not. They wouldn't keep somebody like that in the same camp—there'd be more chance of trouble. A couple of people joined from here, and they got sent somewhere else afterward. They'll take ones they can use, and she'll probably be more grateful to them than most. Just as well we won't have that sort on Venus—someone who'd join the Guardians instead of patiently waiting."

Malik rubbed at his chin; the skin of his face felt slightly raw. He had removed his stubble, but the harsh depilatory cream the lavatory provided irritated him.

One of the wrestlers pinned the other, then released him. The two men rose and began to wander toward the yurts. "The officer in charge now, Keir Renin, got here a few months ago," Nikolai continued. "The one before him was harder in some ways. She'd use any reason to throw someone out, and always kept to the rules, but at least the women were a little safer. It's better for them if the of-

ficer's a woman and keeps the male Guardians in line. Keir
Renin will just look the other way. It's why I told Yekaterina Osipova to be careful—there wouldn't be much she
could do if a Guardian or two caught her alone."

Malik felt his own helplessness. "Her brother would go
after anybody who hurt her."

"He'd be a fool if he did. They're armed and we're not.
He'd just ruin things for himself, and he wouldn't help
her."

The Guardian was gazing at Malik now. She seemed
vaguely familiar; she might have been in the room where
he had been scanned.

"You'd better look out for her," Nikolai muttered.
"You're probably used to women eying you like that, but if
you let her get you alone and don't give her what she
wants—" He shrugged. "She could make it look bad for
you. There are some here who don't mind trading themselves for food or favors, but they usually learn better and
they aren't well liked. We'll remember who they are when
we're on Venus."

Malik thought of all the times he had dismissed Guardians with no more than a gesture. Nikolai was grinning; he
wondered what the young man was thinking. He remembered how easily he had once called up the records of any
person who interested him and how rarely he had concerned himself with how vulnerable that person might
feel. He knew nothing of what had brought Nikolai to this
camp; he was a stranger, his record now inaccessible.

"Yekaterina likes you, too," Nikolai went on, "and
she's a pretty enough woman. You probably wouldn't mind
getting her inside your tent when Alexei's off somewhere.
But you were a Linker—maybe it won't be the same for
you now. I heard a Linker can look through someone else's
eyes and see what they're seeing or hear what they hear."

"You've been misinformed," Malik said. "We can't
read minds, you know. We can communicate, of course,
and the cyberminds can show us images of what another
Linker's seeing if his Link is open and he's willing to—"

"Must come in handy during sex," Nikolai interrupted. "You could let others look on or watch them yourself if they let you."

"No. You've got some odd ideas about Linkers." In
spite of his denial, Malik had heard of Linkers who occa-

sionally shared images of their sexual encounters with others through their Links. The practice was not all that common and had never held much appeal for Malik, who preferred privacy.

"Maybe that wasn't your way. You probably liked to look at yourself through your partner's eyes. You're good-looking enough to have preferred that."

Malik flushed with anger. Nikolai had guessed correctly; Malik had often chided himself for his vanity. "Linkers aren't as interested in such pursuits as you think," he responded. "Those who have been Linked for many years become more indifferent to such things." Was Nikolai mocking him? Was he clumsily expressing an interest in Malik himself? That was unlikely; any potential settlers whose inclinations ran to their own sex would have to be discreet here. Venus was peopled by many who came from more backward areas of Earth and bonds between couples were greatly honored there. The new world was less tolerant of certain practices than many Nomarchies.

Malik lifted his head and was surprised to see a gentle, sympathetic look in the other man's blue eyes; he could almost imagine that Nikolai was feeling sorry for him. The young man glanced toward the tower, where a small woman in a blue coat was taking a stroll. "One of the Habber pilots," Nikolai said. "Whatever they are, at least they leave us alone. That one must be getting impatient by now." He stood up. "If you want some company later, come over after supper."

Malik nodded. The brown-haired man strode away. Malik looked toward the Habber woman again; she was walking toward the tower. He suddenly envied the pilot's Link; for a moment, he could understand why the Habbers held themselves aloof from Earth and its troubled souls.

Malik sat inside Nikolai's yurt, listening to the men as they gossiped and occasionally offering a brief remark. A few of the men seemed to be studying him; perhaps they had expected more talk of his fine friends in Amman. Malik had already learned that comments about his old life were best accompanied by gentle mockery and a tone of indifference; he did not want his companions to think he believed himself better than they.

He got up and said his farewells as the others began to

gamble with sticks and dice; Nikolai followed him outside. "I'll walk back with you, Malik," the young man said. "There's something I want to ask. We talked it over, all of us. Ahmad's been seeing a woman in another yurt, and they're hoping to make a pledge when they both reach Venus. She told Ahmad there's enough space for him to move in with her, and the others don't mind if you take his place with us."

"I'll think about it," Malik replied, knowing he should be grateful for the offer.

"I guess we're not the kind of company you're used to."

"It isn't that," Malik said quickly. "Actually, I'm surprised you want me to live with you."

Nikolai shrugged. "A couple of them wondered a little, but I convinced them. Frankly, it'd make things a little easier for you here. If we take you in, others won't be as suspicious of you, and you can use a few friends."

"I'll decide as soon as I can."

"You can't think about it too long. There're others we could ask, men who wouldn't mind moving in."

They were near Malik's tent. The flap of Yekaterina's tent was open; she was sitting there, barely visible in the dusky light. Alexei was nowhere in sight; he had been spending more evenings and nights in the camp lately.

"Don't think I haven't welcomed your kind offer," Malik said, "but maybe you should ask Alexei to live with you. His sister says he can be moody. It might do him good to live with a group."

Nikolai shook his head as he drew Malik aside. "Listen, I wouldn't mind having him on my side in any fight, but you can't tell what he'll do a lot of times. I've seen him with a few who don't mind stealing when they can get away with it, and he looks willing to go along with them. Either he'll quiet down and learn to be patient or he'll make trouble, and I don't want him close to me until I know which. He's probably just waiting to strike out at somebody—I see it in his eyes." Nikolai paused. "Let me know tomorrow what you want to do."

The evening call to prayer was sounding as Nikolai walked away. Malik thought of beginning his ablutions, then decided to ignore the call this time. He was about to enter his tent when Yekaterina called out to him. "Malik?"

"Yes?"

"Alexei won't be back tonight. I thought you might like to talk."

She sounded lonely. He sat down in front of her tent. "He doesn't like to see me talking to you."

"It isn't for him to decide, is it?" She smoothed down her coat collar. "He may have this tent to himself soon, unless he finds a place somewhere else. A few women asked me to move in with them. They think they haven't gotten passage yet because they don't speak Anglaic all that well, so they'd like to practice it with someone who's more fluent. I'd also be safer with a group."

"Kolya offered me a place in his yurt just now."

"Then you should accept it."

"I know," Malik said. "He seemed a little insulted that I didn't take him up on the offer immediately. I couldn't explain. I've had my own quarters for years—I don't know how well I'd get along."

She laughed softly. "Hadn't you better find out before you get to Venus?"

"I suppose so. Where's Alexei been spending his evenings lately?"

"He's seeing a woman named Anya," she replied. "When he talks to her, he's full of words about how much he cares, and when he talks to me about her, he calls her a whore."

Malik raised his brows. "That's hardly gracious of him."

"It's how most of the people in my village think. They see any woman who lies with a man as a fool if she's not trying to bring him around to becoming her bondmate later. But how can Anya hope for that now? It's useless to make a pledge here, when we don't know how long we'll be waiting or where on Venus we'll end up. I told Alexei there was nothing wrong with Anya wanting companionship while she waits and that he should think more kindly of someone who shows him love, but he won't listen. He thought I was foolish for taking Yuri as a lover and not accepting his offer of a pledge."

There was little he could say; some of his own people held beliefs as unreasonable. Even in the easygoing atmosphere of Amman, he had always avoided inexperienced women, in case any of them came from an old-fashioned family that might view the young woman's actions as a stain on the family's honor.

"That's why Alexei doesn't like to see me with you," Yekaterina continued. "He thinks you would only amuse yourself with me and would never seek a bond with someone so far beneath you."

"You're not beneath me now," he said. "I'm just another inmate of this camp. I don't understand why Alexei's so worried about me. I haven't given him any reason to think—"

"You haven't, it's true. But he knows how I feel. He thinks I wouldn't turn you away, and he's right."

Malik lowered his eyes. Her admission came as no surprise; he had sensed it from the beginning.

"I wouldn't expect anything more of you," she said. "We don't know when we'll leave this camp, or even if we'll leave it together, but we could forget our worries for a while."

He wanted to hold her, but restrained himself.

"What is it?" she whispered as she leaned closer to him. "Are you afraid of Alexei? He'll only make trouble for himself if he does anything to you, especially now that Kolya's looking out for you. He'll say his harsh words to me, not to you."

It seemed cowardly to admit that he was wary of her brother, but Alexei wasn't his only concern. He felt trapped, imprisoned by what he had always been, and realized now that he had dimly hoped he might escape part of his nature in the new life into which he had been forced.

"It's my choice, isn't it?" she said. "Alexei has to learn that eventually." She drew back suddenly. "But maybe it isn't my brother." Her voice was pained. "Maybe I was wrong to think you wanted—"

"No, Katya." He reached for her hand almost automatically. "You aren't wrong about that." I'll only hurt her if I turn away now, he told himself; it was easier to give in. Anticipation of a new love was already arousing him, as it always did.

His lips brushed against hers lightly; her fair hair smelled of soap. He stood up, helped her to her feet, and led her inside his tent.

* * *

Malik's first day in Nikolai's yurt was much like the days that followed. He had been given a space by the wall near the door; one of the men helped him hang a shabby blanket between two poles to mark off the space. His sleep the night before had been disturbed by the sounds of men leaving the yurt. The Guardians had forbidden them to relieve themselves anywhere except in the camp's toilets, and their own fears of spreading illness made them content to obey that order.

His day began with his morning prayer, said outside the yurt, after which he lined up with the others to wait in a line for their morning meal. This time they ate at one of the long tables instead of taking the food back to the yurt. Breakfast, as always, was a bowl of lumpy cereal served with a slice of melon and milk-laced tea, while their evening meal was usually fish with wilted vegetables or a piece of textured soy protein with a potato. Malik had learned not to ask too many questions about the food, which was often so tasteless that it was impossible to tell what it was.

The men lingered over their meal as long as possible before going to the lavatories; a few took showers while the others groomed themselves by the sinks. By then, a line had already formed by the camp's laundries, where people could clean and mend their clothes. Malik had brought only three changes of clothing with him; the Guardians would issue new clothing on request, but only if one's old garments were practically in rags.

After noonday prayers, Malik returned to the yurt to find that the others were planning to exercise outside. He retreated to his space, pulled his blanket shut, and took out his pocket reading screen.

The blanket was abruptly pulled open; Nikolai and a Chinese man named Howin peered inside. "What do you have there?" the Russian asked.

Malik tensed a little. Only Yekaterina knew about his screen, but he could hardly keep it a secret now. "It's just a reading screen," he replied. "I brought a small library on microdot. I enjoy reading in the afternoon." He gazed at the two apprehensively; they would probably spread the news about his screen. He tried to reassure himself; his possessions would be safer in this yurt than in his tent. Few in the camp would risk angering Nikolai and his friends, who had no compunctions about confronting any suspected thieves when the Guardians weren't around.

But Nikolai and Howin seemed amused and indifferent. "Reading," Howin muttered under his breath before letting the blanket fall. "Be better for him to strengthen himself instead of ruining his eyes."

"You're forgetting," Nikolai answered. "Malik's a scholar. They must get used to reading, or they couldn't keep doing it."

"I don't know why they bother," another man said in the distance. "Screens and mind-tours can tell you all anybody needs to know."

Malik read for most of the afternoon, having no desire to join the others in their athletic pursuits and strolls around the camp. In the evening, he went with them to the dining hall; they collected their food and carried it back to the yurt. After eating, they threw dice to determine who would carry the trays and bowls back to the hall; Malik lost.

Yekaterina approached him as he left the hall. A few Guardians passed, beginning their nightly patrol; they would wander the paths for a bit and then retreat beyond the posts. He took Yekaterina's arm. "I moved in with those women I told you about," she said. "It's crowded, but I'll get along."

He was disappointed; he had been expecting to join her in her tent for part of the night. "That's good," he said. "But I was hoping for your company tonight, and now—"

"I've seen Kolya's yurt," she said. "They keep it clean enough, and they've marked off their spaces with curtains and blankets, haven't they? It's not as if they'll see anything, and we can always wait until they're asleep."

He could not argue with such practicality. He led her to his new residence, where the others were already pulling their blankets shut in preparation for sleep. Two of the men also had female visitors; they grinned at Malik before he closed his own blanket.

Yekaterina seemed content to look through part of his library as he lay at her side; he had almost forgotten that she knew how to read. From time to time, she held out the screen and whispered a question about an unfamiliar word or phrase. He waited until he could hear the sounds of even breathing and soft snores, then drew her to him.

She responded to him readily, as she had before. The simplest touches and most straightforward thrustings seemed to satisfy her, and he felt no need for more, perhaps because she was still new to him. The darkness hid her firm body, and his hands lingered around her small waist before caressing her rounded hips.

In spite of her words about wanting only a temporary bed-partner, he was sure she could grow to love him. She had shown some courage in coming here, in her willingness to reach out for more than her old life had offered. She was a steady, caring woman who would make someone a good partner on the new world. For a moment, he could imagine himself asking her for a bond and promising a pledge when they were both safely on Venus; with her, he might know some peace. His previous loves had never lasted; perhaps this was as much as he would ever find.

He held her afterward as he let his mind drift into a reverie, and when he came to himself, she was gone. Could he be so certain she would eventually welcome a bond with him? During his old life, he had never felt such doubts, but he had been a man from a prominent family and had held a respected position; all that had been stripped from him now. How would Katya view him when the novelty of his lovemaking and physical beauty wore off? Perhaps she would see him only as a strange, unfortunate creature, made weaker by the privileges he had lost and unsuited for what lay ahead. However infatuated she was, she might be too sensible to join her life to such a man.

He should never have come here. He imagined a world filled with other sturdy people who might view him with pity or contempt, of women who might treat him only as a passing amusement. He had little else to offer them. His past life now seemed buttressed with shields that had kept him from facing what he was.

Malik left the dining hall. As usual, he had lost that evening's throw of the dice and had won the task of returning the men's bowls and trays to the hall. Almost everyone in the camp was sitting outside along the paths; now that the weather was warmer and the days a little longer, people had taken to spending more time outdoors.

Lately, most of their conversation involved speculations about when the next group of emigrants would be chosen. Five new arrivals had set up tents, and the Habber pilots had been living in one of the towers for more than a month; surely a group would have to be picked soon.

Malik counted the days in his mind. He had been in the camp for a month, but he had learned that the Project Council kept to no particular schedule in selecting emigrants. Two groups might be chosen in less than a month, and then several months might pass before others were picked. But the camp also knew that Habber pilots usually did not remain here for longer than two or three weeks, and the two here now had to be growing impatient.

Yekaterina was sitting in front of her yurt with five other women. She smiled as he passed, then turned back to the young woman beside her, who was speaking haltingly in Anglaic. He could read Yekaterina's expressions readily by now; her slightly apologetic smile told him she would not be sharing his bed that night. He smiled back and nodded to show that he understood.

He strolled to the edge of the camp; the recent arrivals, sitting outside their tents, averted their eyes as he passed. They had greeted him easily enough before but had probably been told that Malik was a former Linker; now they held back. He felt his loss once more and longed for the Link that had always kept any loneliness at bay.

A man dressed in gray was walking just beyond the posts. Malik recognized the short, stocky form and dark hair of one of the Habber pilots; the man often took walks, alone or with the Habber woman who, like this man, had an Asian's features. Perhaps the pilot did not mind the delay; his Link would keep him connected to his world.

Malik suddenly wanted to go to the man, ask him if there was a way to join his people. Among Habbers, he could be Linked again, and such people wouldn't mock him for his learning. His uncle's enemies had accused him of too many sympathies with Habber views; perhaps he should prove to them that they were right.

Such hopes were useless. He turned to walk back to his yurt, wondering how Nikolai had endured the years of waiting.

The men were sitting outside, listening as Bogdan analyzed their chances for winning passage soon. "Kolya's been here the longest," the stolid young man was saying, "and the Council must know how patient he's been and how he's kept some order here. On the other hand, maybe they think he's useful here because of that." He went on to assess Howin's chances while the Chinese man nodded solemnly. Bogdan spoke in his slow, deliberate way, as if struggling with the Anglaic, but he sounded the same way in Russian, his native tongue.

Malik leaned against the doorframe of the yurt. He longed to go inside to read, but even Nikolai was complaining lately that he kept too much to himself.

Nikolai cleared his throat as Bogdan lapsed into silence. "The trouble is," Nikolai said, "that every reason you give for letting us go seems to be a reason for keeping us here, too." Bogdan scratched at his dark hair, as if this were a new thought to him. "Maybe they just pick names by chance."

"They have reasons," Malik said. "The problem is that you can't ever know what they are. They might need people with certain specific skills, or the demographers might say more women are needed. Bogdan's right, in a way— anything that's to your advantage one time could work against you at another. There's also the chance of the Council being capricious in the choice if several people here can do the same kind of work, because it wouldn't much matter which one they select."

Howin gestured at Malik. "What do you think his chances are?"

Bogdan scratched his head again. "He's here because he has enemies, isn't he? They might want to keep him here forever." He slapped his palm. "On the other hand, Venus might need a man with some learning now."

Malik could no longer endure this useless discussion. "I think I'll get some rest," he said.

"Yekaterina's been tiring him," Hisoka muttered; a few of the men chuckled. "Better keep yourself strong," the Japanese man continued, "or she might look somewhere else."

Malik went inside; he could read a little before sleeping. He ducked under his blanket, knelt, and searched for his screen, certain he had left it next to his sleeping mat. At last he pulled out his small light wand and looked carefully through his belongings. The flat panel that held his microdot library was still there, but the screen was gone.

He sat back on his heels and knew immediately that none of the men outside would have touched it. Except for Hisoka, none of them could read. At any rate, they would never touch another man's possessions without asking first; that was one reason they got along in such close quarters. Yekaterina often enjoyed glancing through some of the more accessible books written in Russian, but she wouldn't have borrowed the screen without telling him.

Most of the camp knew he had a screen; Nikolai had jested about Malik's solitary pursuit often enough. But without the library, the screen was useless, and the library was still here; he knew of no one in the camp who had another. His more useful possessions—the light wand, his other clothes, his grooming aids—were untouched. Why would the thief take something he could not use?

The answer came to him at once. The thief held a grudge, and Malik could think of only one person who disliked him enough to do this. Alexei knew that he and Yekaterina were often together; she and her brother had exchanged harsh words about that. The young man had not confronted Malik openly, probably because he feared Nikolai's reaction; Nikolai would not hesitate to stand up for any of his friends.

Malik could go to Nikolai, who would settle the problem one way or another. Alexei's life here would not be easy after that, and Yekaterina might blame Malik for her brother's troubles. Even knowing what her brother was like, she still persisted in believing he could change; she would wonder why Malik had not gone to Alexei to deal with this quietly.

He would have to handle this alone.

Alexei had recently moved to a cabin near the dining hall; a hard-looking man seated outside the door told Malik that Alexei was taking a walk on the open ground to the south. Malik hurried there and found the blond man loitering by one of the posts with three companions.

"Look who's here," Alexei said in Anglaic. "We don't usually have such fine company." He did not seem surprised to see Malik.

"I have to speak to you," Malik muttered.

"What about?"

"It'd be better if we speak alone."

Alexei glanced at the other men, then nodded. The three wandered off and sat down several paces from the post. The Habber pilot was still outside walking; two Guardians trailed him at a distance.

Malik said, "I've lost my screen."

"Careless of you."

"It was stolen. It's an old screen, one that can only be used with a library. I thought you might know where it is."

Alexei's green eyes widened. "Now, how would I know that? I can't use that kind of screen. I didn't have your advantages, I don't know how to read. Are you saying I'm a thief?"

Malik swallowed. "The screen's gone. Few people in this camp can read, and if one of them were to risk taking the screen, the library would have been taken as well. Anyway, I don't see how anyone could use it without others finding out, so the thief must have had another motive."

"And you're accusing me? I don't take kindly to that." Alexei did not sound terribly indignant. "Anyway, how could I possibly take it without being seen?"

"I don't care how you did it. If you give it back, I won't say anything."

"But I don't have it," Alexei said, "and you can't prove that I do."

"Use your sense," Malik said angrily. "Do you want Kolya and his friends to know something was taken from their place? They'd make things very hard for you."

"And I'll deny it. Go ahead, see what people think when you can't offer any proof. See what Kolya thinks when you drag him into your personal grudges." Alexei's eyes narrowed. "You think you're better than the rest of us, with all your learning and your airs. You think you can use Katya as you like just because you were once a Linker. I came here to be rid of people like you—you don't deserve to have more than anyone else. You'll just have to get along without your precious screen."

"I want that screen back," Malik said evenly. "It had better be with my belongings by tomorrow, or I'll go to Kolya with this story."

Alexei laughed. "You can't tell me what to do now."

He motioned to his three friends; the men stood up and came toward them. The Habber pilot and the two Guardians were closer but not near enough to hear Alexei's words. Malik knew he could not go to the Guardians with his problem; everyone in the camp would despise him for bringing such a matter to their attention, and the uniformed men were unlikely to take his side anyway.

"The Linker's saying some evil things to me," Alexei said to his companions. "He just accused me of something I didn't do, and you know how he's treated my sister. I don't think I should stand for that, do you?"

The three took up places around them as Alexei raised his fists. Malik stepped back; he was taller than the blond man, but Alexei was more muscular and probably used to fighting. Alexei came at him; Malik ducked and managed to block the blow with one arm. If Alexei hurt him badly enough, he'd be taken away for treatment and probably not allowed to return; maybe that was what the younger man wanted.

Alexei jolted him with another blow. Malik kept his arms up, trying to protect his head and chest. A foot kicked him in the thigh, narrowly missing his groin. Alexei swung and caught him in the belly; Malik doubled over, nearly retching as he was knocked to the ground.

Hands grabbed the collar of his coat, then suddenly released him. "What's going on here?" a voice shouted. Malik struggled to his feet; Alexei drew back as the two Guardians and the Habber approached.

"What's going on?" one of the Guardians asked. "We can't have this."

Malik knew what he would have to say. He took a breath, trying to ignore the pain in his abdomen. "It's nothing," he rasped. "My friend here was only showing me how to defend myself. Just a little exercise, that's all."

The Guardian peered at him. "You're the Linker, aren't you?" The Habber seemed surprised as he glanced in Malik's direction. "Maybe you do need some practice at such things. Well, we can't have fighting in this camp— pretty soon, others start taking sides and then we have a riot on our hands."

"It wasn't a fight." Malik hoped he sounded sincere. "You can see I wasn't hurt."

"I won't ask who started it, but if I see you two fighting

again, out you go. I wouldn't want our Habber friend here
to think you're the kind of folks he'll be taking to Venus.
Just be grateful I'm in a good mood at the moment."

Alexei led his friends away; the Guardians turned toward the tower. The Habber was still watching Malik; as
he was about to follow the Guardians, Malik saw his chance
and motioned with his hand.

"I'd like to speak to you alone," Malik whispered.
"Find a way if you can." He hurried away before the Habber could reply.

Nikolai took Malik aside after breakfast the next morning. "I heard you and Alexei Osipov had a disagreement,"
he said.

"It's nothing," Malik replied. His body still felt
bruised.

"Guardians saw you—that's what I heard. If you've got
a gripe, settle it where they can't see you."

"I told the Guardians he was just helping me learn
how to defend myself."

Nikolai nodded. "You've learned something then."

Malik left the other men at the lavatory and went back
to the yurt alone; Yekaterina was waiting by the entrance,
her face grim. She went inside without speaking and
looked around as he entered, then thrust one arm inside
her coat.

"I brought this back," she said as she pulled out his
screen.

"You took it?" he asked, surprised.

She shook her head. "I heard about your argument
with my brother. I kept after him until he admitted what
he'd done. I told him I'd bring it back and make sure no
one else finds out. You didn't say anything to Kolya, did
you?"

"No."

"See that you don't. If you do, I'll deny it, say that I
only borrowed the screen and that you're blaming Alexei
unfairly. I don't want any more trouble for him." Her
expression softened a bit. "One of his friends said you
spoke up for Alexei when two Guardians saw you fighting.
That hasn't warmed my brother's heart, but I'm grateful."

He examined the screen; it was scratched in one corner and stained by dirt, but otherwise undamaged. "You'll

lie for him," Malik said, suddenly irritated by her dogged devotion to her brother. "You refuse to see what he's really like. How do you expect him to change if you're always there to save him from the consequences of his mistakes?"

"He's my brother."

"You may not be doing him any favor, Katya. What's he going to do when you're not around to clean up after him? You may not even be sent to Venus together—how is he going to get along there?"

"It'll be different there," she replied.

"Do you think so? He may just find something else to resent. Perhaps I should have said something to Kolya, so Alexei could learn that he can't just do as he likes, but I wasn't really thinking of him then. I was thinking of how upset you'd be if he got in serious trouble."

"I spoke to him," she said softly. "He won't do anything like that again. It's time we saw no more of each other, I think. I don't want to part from you now, but seeing you only makes him angry, and we always knew that our time together wouldn't last."

"Do you think that's the only reason he struck out at me?" Malik clutched his screen tightly. "He hates what I am—he would have hated me even if I'd never welcomed you to my bed. I represent all the privileged people he hates—he doesn't see what I am now. He can work out his resentments on someone who's lost the power to do much about it."

"He may be willful," she said, "and he's done reckless things, but is it wrong for him to want more than he was given? Venus will give him a chance to change, and I should do what I can to see that he gets there safely. I shouldn't give him any more reasons to be angry with you —I can put my own wants aside for a time. Maybe later—"

"Then you're a bigger fool than I took you for." He clenched his teeth. He had not meant to say that; she was glaring at him now. He had wanted to speak of his need for her, of his feeling that there might be more for both of them in time. Could he grow to love her that much? Could he ask her to consider a bond with him later? Or did he want to cling to her desperately only because he feared being alone and was trying to convince himself he was capable of love? He probably did not love her at all but only wanted her to love him, as he had with all the other women he had known.

"I must go," she said quietly. "You aren't losing so much, Malik. There will always be other women for you."

"Katya—"

She left the yurt before he could say more. Perhaps it was just as well. If that Habber pilot did find a way to speak to him, he now knew what he would ask the man.

Four

Benzi waited by the tower. The man from the camp was walking toward him, two Guardians at his sides. The inmate's whispered request to speak to him had roused Benzi's curiosity; the officer in command here had told him there was one former Linker in the camp and that his name was Malik Haddad. He wondered if he should be speaking to this man at all, and then remembered the desperate look in his dark eyes.

Malik Haddad bowed his head a little as he halted; the Guardians lingered near him. "Your officer told me," Benzi said, "that I might speak to this man in private."

The female Guardian shrugged. "Think you can worm some secrets out of him?" she muttered. "He probably won't tell you anything you don't already know—I mean, if he knew anything important, he wouldn't be here now, would he?"

Benzi tried to look indifferent. "As interesting as I find your company, and that of your commander, one does occasionally long to see a new face, and I ought to know a little more about the people who may soon be aboard my ship."

The male Guardian glanced at Malik. "Maybe it isn't just talk he's looking for," he said. The other Guardian laughed as the pair entered the tower.

Benzi motioned to Malik Haddad. "Do you mind taking a walk?"

"Not at all. They said I was wanted here, but not why."

"I hope I won't cause you any difficulty," Benzi said as

they ambled away from the tower. "Your friends may see us and wonder why I wanted to talk to you."

"They find me odd enough already," Malik replied. "I can always tell them that even Habbers want to hear gossip about the Mukhtars and their foibles—that might make you seem a bit more human."

"Keir Renin is humoring me lately," Benzi said, "although I don't know why. When I told him I was bored and wanted to talk to the Linker in this camp, he seemed amenable."

"I'm not a Linker now."

"You were, and a scholar as well—so I was told."

Malik's mouth twisted. "That'll be of little use to me on Venus."

The man was taller than Benzi and quite striking; even life in this camp had not noticeably marred his appearance. His thick black hair curled a bit around his chiseled, pale-brown face, and he wore his plain gray clothes and sheepskin coat with an easy grace.

"Even Venus may need scholars," Benzi said.

"Disgraced historians? I doubt that very much." Malik's Anglaic was clear and unaccented, but his voice had a musical lilt. "How strange it is to be talking to one of you, and yet I suppose it's exactly what those who disgraced me might expect me to do."

"How so?" Benzi asked.

"I was criticized for, among other things, implying that Earth would be better off with closer ties to your people. It was a convenient excuse for those who wanted to shame my family to use, since it meant I was questioning the assumptions behind the Mukhtars' power. I might have been ignored if my family had been less prominent and my uncle hadn't had enemies close to the Council. The Mukhtars might have settled for suggesting that I make my comments more ambiguous."

"I'm mystified," Benzi said, "as to why your Mukhtars remain so distrustful of us. Oh, I can understand why Habbers would be resented for abandoning Earth centuries ago, but can't the Mukhtars see that our intentions aren't hostile? We aid you in whatever way we can, and our confrontations with you were provoked by Earth. We have all of space to live in—surely the Mukhtars can see that we have no designs on Earth."

"It doesn't matter whether you do or not," Malik replied. "Even your existence is a kind of affront, and the Mukhtars are bound by a certain historical perspective."

"I was never much of a student of history."

"Perhaps Habbers see themselves as free of it." Malik paused. "Centuries ago the Mukhtars united Earth under their rule. They were wise enough to see that allowing some autonomy and diversity in various regions would be beneficial, but, even so, part of our destiny as Muslims had been achieved. The world had become what we call the *Dar al-Islam*—the Abode of Islam. Long before the era of the Nomarchies, we had believed that the reign of those we called infidels was only temporary, and then Earth was ours. It didn't matter that many still held to other faiths; the Mukhtars could afford to be tolerant. Islam ruled. Most of the Mukhtars, whatever their origins, have submitted to Islam, however lightly some of them wear their faith. Islamic law, with appropriate modifications and a great deal of leniency in certain areas, prevails. Much of the land in our New Islamic Nomarchy—the first of Earth's Nomarchies—had once been ruled by a socialistic empire, and those people had once believed that their way would prevail. It wasn't too hard for the earliest Mukhtars to adopt a few of their ideas and reshape them in accordance with Islam."

The historian was silent for a bit as they walked on. "This world was ours," Malik continued, "but other worlds remained. The time for holy wars to expand the Abode of Islam was past, or so my people thought. There was Venus to conquer and make our own, and perhaps other worlds in times to come. But there were also the Habitats and a people who believed the future might be theirs. As long as you exist as you are, we're still far from the destiny Islam has ordained for us."

"And if your Abode of Islam doesn't eventually include us," Benzi murmured, "the Mukhtars have lost, and their faith becomes more dubious."

"Even the most skeptical Mukhtar knows where the justification for his power lies. Those who oppose the Mukhtars aren't just *their* enemies, but God's. Earth will make its agreements with you and hold to them. The Mukhtars always honor their formal agreements, but they also see any they make with Habbers as temporary ones.

Surely your people still know that Islam means surrender and submission to the truth. I would have done well to remember that myself, but my faith was always weak and my practical sense almost nonexistent." Malik glanced at Benzi. "Well, I've lectured enough—old habits are strong. I don't believe I've heard your name."

"Benzi. I was named for a friend of my father's."

"Your father? I was under the impression your people don't have family ties."

"That isn't quite true. Some are raised by their genetic parents, while others have close ties to the adults who brought them up and to those children among whom they were raised. Habbers are encouraged not to assign those connections the importance they have here, where a family can often put its own interests above those of their community." He was speaking of Habbers as though he weren't really part of them, but then that was how he often felt. "Benzi Liangharad is my full name." The words sounded strange to him; he had not said his full name aloud in years. Habitat-dwellers did not customarily use family or ancestral surnames.

"Then you weren't always a Habber," Malik said. Benzi tensed a little. "I think I've heard your name before or seen it somewhere, but I can't place it now. It's one of the few drawbacks to a Link. Your memory gets weaker, since you don't have to rely on it, but you must know about that."

Benzi hesitated, wondering how much he should reveal. The Guardians here knew nothing of his past. They could have done nothing to him even if they had known, but it was simpler to keep his history to himself. The secret now seemed like a burden, and a man in Malik's position would hardly be anxious to admit to others that he had spoken to one whom Earth would see as a traitor.

Maybe, Benzi thought, I still feel the need to justify my actions.

"You may recall," he said, "that a group of pilots fled from Venus's Islands to the nearest Hab almost forty years ago. You might remember that incident, since it was partly responsible for various problems afterward. I was one of those pilots."

Malik slowed his pace. "Of course. Iris Angharads, the

specialist who—part of your name is like hers. Can you be—"

"Yes, I'm the martyr's son." His throat tightened a little. "Your memory's better than you think."

The Earthman shook his head. "Not really. As it happens, a mind-tour producer spoke to me about Iris Angharads not long before my subsequent difficulties, although it seems your mother is more widely known on Venus than here. That was something this particular producer hoped to remedy. Your own name is fairly obscure. When Iris Angharads lost her life, I suppose it was better to forget what her son had done."

"So that her memory wouldn't be tarnished," Benzi whispered.

"So that her act could be seen as a sacrifice for the Nomarchies and the future of the Project rather than, perhaps, as an attempt to make up for her son's deed." Malik did not appear terribly shocked by Benzi's admission or disgusted by his action. "How fascinating that you should come here."

Benzi felt the familiar twinge of guilt. "Iris is something of a minor heroine to Habbers, too, since she managed to save Habber lives. That was one of the reasons some of us decided that the Habs owed her a debt and continued to aid the Project she so loved."

"It must have been hard for you when you learned of her death."

"It was. It still is. But Iris acted as she did for her own reasons. I doubt that she was thinking of me, or had any fondness for those Habbers she saved—she would have been concerned with the Project's future and the fact that it still needed our help. I'm sure she had no intention of dying. She'd simply lived so long for the Project that she couldn't imagine her life without it." Even after all this time, he could not keep the bitterness out of his voice.

"I'm sorry," Malik said.

Benzi knew that he had said too much already; being on Earth again had awakened too many memories. "No need to be sorry," he said tonelessly. "My mother would have been gratified to know that some remember her and that a daughter of hers now lives with my father on Venus." He paused. "You seemed anxious to speak to me, but I'm sure that history is not what you had in mind."

Malik halted, then turned to face him. Benzi had to lift his head to gaze into the taller man's brown eyes. The Earthman's face was tense; he seemed to be trying to come to a decision. "I can ask you," Malik said. "Now that I know who you are, I can see you'd understand. You can tell me how to reach your Hab—there must be a way. Maybe you could take me there yourself, but there isn't much chance I'd be chosen to go on your ship."

Benzi was too startled to speak.

"Habbers don't turn away those who reach a Habitat." Malik twisted his hands together. "You have a Link—you could easily let any other pilots who'd come here later know of my wishes. It wouldn't be difficult—a Habber ship could head for your Hab instead of Anwara, and by the time anyone knew, it would be too late to stop it. The other passengers could always be sent to Venus from there, and I could stay behind. Your pilots could always claim that something went wrong with the ship—they could think of a likely story."

The man had apparently been dwelling on this notion. Benzi took a step back, suddenly suspicious; could the Mukhtars have sent this scholar here to lay a trap for unwary Habber pilots? He could not think of why Earth would want to jeopardize its agreement with the Habbers now.

It did not matter whether Malik was being devious or sincere. Benzi would have to give him the same answer in either case.

"It isn't possible," he replied. "There's nothing any of us can do to help you. If you wanted to flee to a Hab, you came to the wrong place."

"It doesn't matter why I came here. Every day I'm here convinces me I made a mistake. I don't belong on Venus, and I can hardly go to the Guardians and say that— I'd be even worse off than I am now. I'm not one of those people who thinks of yours with suspicion and distrust— I've always thought that both our societies could find a common purpose."

"We have one now," Benzi responded. "The Venus Project has drawn some of us together in a common effort. I'm sorry, Malik. If you found a way to reach a Hab by yourself, which is hardly likely, you'd be welcomed, but none of us will risk the agreement we have with Earth to help one man. I can't do anything for you, and I won't try. Too many other lives would be affected. Some on Venus have grown closer to us, and maybe even Earth will learn to trust us in time."

Malik moved closer to him. "Were you thinking of that when you made your escape? You, of all people, should understand how I feel."

"I do, but I also learned what my actions cost others, and I haven't found what I'd hoped to find. Maybe you're thinking that you'd have a Link again and your life would be much as it was, but it wouldn't. A Link gave you power here. It won't in a place where everyone has a Link from late childhood on and there's no power to be had. You'd be an exile. You want to escape Earth, but you'd end up among people who find a purpose in trying to reach out to Earth. I doubt that you'd ever be ready to give up enough of yourself to become one of the others."

"The others?" Malik asked.

"One might call them the true Habitat-dwellers. Earth thinks all Habbers are much like the ones they see, but they're not. We're only a bridge they choose to maintain."

"You sound as if you have regrets."

"It's done," Benzi said. "Regrets are pointless now."

"I had to ask. I had to see if there was a chance. Maybe you're just trying to make it easier for me by making me think I'd regret such a choice."

That was partly true; Benzi would do the Earthman no favor by encouraging his dream. "You'd be better off accepting your lot and making your peace with whatever you find on Venus." He kept his voice as firm as possible. "You don't really want to escape to a Hab—you want to recapture what you've lost—your easy life, your quiet pursuits. If you were offered your old life now, you'd take it without a qualm, I suspect. You're probably used to having others ease your way, but no Habber's going to do that for you. Accept what you have now, or you'll never make a life for yourself."

"Did you?"

Benzi smiled ruefully. "I was young then and not overly reflective, and now I'm here, helping others reach the world I abandoned. A new world needs such people— those who take a risk to get there and who will value what they find. Maybe you should try to become more like them."

Malik was silent. Benzi turned away from him and walked back to the tower; there was nothing more to say.

Keir Renin, the officer in charge of the camp, was a broad-faced man, who seemed to regard his assignment as some sort of punishment. He skulked in the tower for much of the day, complaining about supplies, glancing at records, and questioning his subordinates about matters in the camp, which he rarely entered. He seemed as much a prisoner as the people he guarded.

The officer had unexpectedly invited Benzi to share a meal with him, and Benzi had accepted, unsure of how to refuse without offending the man. The invitation included Te-yu, who had come along so that Benzi would not have to endure Keir's company alone.

The small table in Keir's room was laden with fresh vegetables and melons appropriated from supplies sent to the camp, whose people could survive on minimal allotments. Many of the Guardians were not above trading the food to inmates for favors. The would-be emigrants were in no position to complain, and records would show that the provisions had reached the camp safely.

Benzi was expecting Keir to ask him about his conversation with Malik Haddad; he had prepared an innocuous story about their talk. Instead, the officer was droning on about his home near Odessa and his hopes for his next assignment. Te-yu's face was calm, her eyes blank, her lips curved in a half-smile; Benzi saw that she was profoundly bored.

Keir got up, rummaged among some belongings on a shelf, and pulled out a bottle. He waved it at Te-yu's cup as he sat down again. "We aren't supposed to drink here," Keir said, "but I've got a little trade going with a village nearby, and I don't see the harm in a bit of refreshment." He motioned at the cup once more.

"No, thank you," Te-yu said.

"Habbers don't drink?"

"Some do and some don't," Benzi replied. "We generally prefer to keep our minds clear." Keir Renin would be expecting such haughty remarks from a Habber, and

Benzi could not resist making them. "I'll try some, though."

Keir poured some of the liquor into Benzi's cup. "I had some schooling, you know," the officer said, "but I wasn't chosen for advanced education." His Anglaic was fluent enough, but he lingered a bit over longer words, drawing out each syllable. "My Counselor sort of suggested that I try the Guardians, and after I thought about it, it seemed like a good idea. They sent me to Baghdad for officers' training. I've been a Guardian for twenty years, and this is the first time I've had my own command." He gulped down some liquor, then folded his arms across his broad chest. "I keep hoping they'll send me for Linker training, make a Commander out of me."

"Well, maybe they will," Benzi said politely, although that seemed a goal beyond Keir's reach.

"I doubt it. You can't show what you're made of here. They give two kinds this post—young ones who look promising and older ones they can't find anything else for. The young ones get a little experience, and the older ones just mark time. A lot of people don't like Guardians, you know. They think of the few times we've had to be harsh and forget about what we do most of the time, when we just keep order and repair the old weapons systems in orbit. Maybe they ought to think about what it used to be like a long time ago, when you had one army here and another there and everyone could get dragged into the fight. They're a lot better off now."

"Indeed," Benzi replied. "The Mukhtars could hardly maintain their control without your services."

Keir's broad, ruddy face brightened, as though Benzi had complimented him. "True enough," he said, "and some of the Commanders think it might be time for the Mukhtars to pay more attention to their views. Sometimes the Mukhtars wait just a little too long before doing what has to be done. The people here—they think things'll be different on Venus. They'll see what it's like when we—" He leaned back and took another drink.

Benzi was silent. Any political struggle among Mukhtars and Guardians would distract Earth's attention from the Project, and that might be to the Cytherians' benefit—unless, of course, the Guardians won. That was a troubling thought.

"Did you have a nice chat with that man from the camp?" the officer asked suddenly.

"I'm afraid it wasn't very informative. As you might guess, he wasn't anxious to say much to me. In fact, he seemed to resent the imposition. I was foolish to think he wouldn't."

"You two aren't so bad," Keir said expansively. "But you're not like a lot of Habbers, are you? Maybe you're a little homesick, and that's why you're here. Anybody can make a mistake, but sometimes there's a chance to make up for it. You two might like to see your old homes and the people you left behind."

He knew about them, then. Benzi kept his composure. Angharad had told him she would mention their conversation to her Counselor; that information might have been passed on and found its way to Keir. His fears faded; the agreement would still protect him.

"Maybe you're not so ready to leave," Keir went on. "I could help you out, or you could deliver your passengers first and then come back. You could keep your Links and tie up with the cyberminds here—you'd do all right for yourselves."

Keir, in the aftermath of such a defection, would certainly do all right for himself; a promotion might be won. Benzi's own fate would be more uncertain. After a flurry of praise for the Habber who had returned, there would probably be interrogations, which would become less gentle when the questioners found out that Benzi could not tell them the sorts of things they would wish to know.

"There's nothing in the agreement that says you can't stay if you choose," the officer said. "In your case, even the Habbers would understand if you did. I'll tell you something, Benzi. You'd be smart to come back to us while you can. Things are changing here, and Guardians will have more to say about what happens later on."

"You'll still need Habber help on Venus," Te-yu said softly.

"Maybe the people there won't always welcome you," Keir replied. "A lot of them don't particularly like you as it is. I'd rather see that Project rot than stand by and let Habbers treat it as if it's theirs, but we've put too much into it to abandon it now. It'll continue, but on our terms. If progress slows a little, the settlers will live with that—they'll learn their world still belongs to Earth."

Benzi was repelled by the man's pride and resentments. Keir reminded him of everything he had wanted to escape.

"We're only too aware that the Project is Earth's accomplishment," Benzi said carefully. "It's not a venture that the Associated Habitats would have chosen, believing as we do that our future doesn't lie on the surface of planets, but we can learn a little by contributing in our own small way to its efforts." If, he thought, Earth did not strangle the development of a new culture that might revitalize the two older ones, and if the Habbers did not decide to retreat from the Project.

Venus should have been a world free from the evils of the old. Unlike Earth, its people did not have to build a civilization on the ruins of ancient wars; unlike the Habbers, its settlers would not have to feel guilt about the Earth left behind. Venus could mend the breach between Earth and the Habitats. Benzi had not appreciated that possibility when he had been younger. He had seen only Earth's dead hand clutching the new world, and had dreamed of escaping to the stars. He had convinced himself in time that he might instead find a purpose among the worlds he knew. Now, in Keir Renin's presence, with the memory of Malik's words still fresh, he felt a new quickening of his old dream.

"You'd contribute more by giving up your ties to the Habs," Keir said. "I don't think you'd be here if you didn't miss what you once had. Maybe you left the Islands because you didn't think you'd get a chance to rise, but we could do something about that. We might find a place for you even there."

"I have missed my childhood homes, both here and on the Islands," Benzi said. Keir had become unpredictable; there was no point in provoking him. "Being here has brought back many memories."

"I'll be getting a list of passengers in a day or so." The Guardian toyed with his empty cup. "I guess it would delay things if you didn't make this run, but you'll be coming back, and maybe then—" He lifted his brows.

"I'll definitely give it some thought," Benzi said. The man could fix on that false hope and perhaps leave him

alone until he and Te-yu were safely away. He stood up.
"Thank you for the dinner. We'll look forward to getting
the list."

"You almost made me think you were considering that
ridiculous suggestion," Te-yu said when they were outside.
"What a clumsy, obvious man he is."

"Maybe you're underestimating him," Benzi replied.
"From his point of view, it's reasonable for him to think I
might want to come back. If I don't, he's still given me a
warning to pass along to our people. The Guardians must
think of Habbers as cowards who will easily retreat if they
feel threatened, and they do have evidence for believing
that, along with reasons to resent the Mukhtars for making
an agreement with us."

"Oh, I understand him. We can still think the way
Earthfolk do, can't we? How unlike true Habbers we are."

"Do you know what that man from the camp said
today?" Benzi asked. "He wanted to know if there was a
way he could get to a Hab, if I could help him. And I had to
tell him there wasn't. He said he didn't belong on Venus,
and I gave him a lot of stern words about accepting his fate
and making the best of it."

"You couldn't have done anything for him," she said,
"without violating the agreement."

"Maybe the agreement isn't worth what may happen
to that man, and the others with him, if Earth tightens its
grip on Venus again. Are they going to labor there just so
that Earth can impose its will and take away their dream?"

"It isn't up to us," she said quietly. "It's up to the
Cytherians."

"I shouldn't have come here, Te-yu. When I get to
Anwara, I'm going back to our Hab. Someone else can
ferry all these lost souls."

"I came here only because you did," she murmured,
"and yet I'm sorry to hear you say that. It makes me think
the ones like Keir Renin will win out in the end."

The warm wind was picking up. It would be fierce
before long and howl as the colder winds had howled outside his boyhood home on the North American Plains. He
gazed through the darkness at the camp and the small, dim
lights that shone against the night.

Five

The announcement came at dawn, before the morning call to prayer. Malik was barely awake when the amplified voice sounded through the camp.

"Line up in front of the south tower," a man's voice droned in Anglaic. "Pack up everything you wish to bring with you in case you do not return to the camp. Say your name clearly as you enter the room. If you are on the list, go directly to the floater cradle. If you are not on the list, return to the camp with your belongings."

Malik sat up quickly, pulled on his clothes, then began to pack his things. The announcement was being repeated; by the time he opened his blanket-curtain, the other men were already leaving the yurt.

Nikolai caught Malik's arm as he emerged. "Better take a piss first," he said. "We'll be standing on that line for a while."

Malik followed the other men toward the lavatory. "Why do they want us to bring our packs? Surely everyone can't be on the list."

Nikolai sighed. "Because if you're picked, they don't want you coming back here to collect your things. Some who aren't picked could get a little nasty with the ones who are, and they want to make sure there's no trouble."

"I shouldn't think there'd be any point in having me wait on the line," Malik said. "I haven't been here very long, so it isn't likely I'd be selected."

"It doesn't matter—everyone's got to line up. I waited on a line like that a week after I got here."

The men's section of the lavatory was crowded. The

81

sky was lighter when Malik came back outside; a large
shadow moved toward him over the ground. He looked
up. A floater was overhead, moving slowly above the
camp; he could see the airship's cabin clearly. As he came
to open ground, he saw that the Guardians were already
taking up positions by the posts.

The line was long; at least three hundred of the two
thousand inmates were already waiting. A few were couples who held hands or clung to each other; most had their
heads down, refusing to look at those nearest them. In the
distance, a small figure left the tower and began to walk in
the direction of the floater cradle.

"Someone got lucky," Nikolai muttered.

Malik lowered his eyes and stared at his feet. Nikolai
had been here longer than anyone; that had to mean his
chance of being chosen was greater than Malik's. Perhaps
some of the young Russian's friends would be picked as
well. Malik was beginning to dread returning to the yurt.
Nikolai had mocked him but more gently than the others
had; he had spoken up for Malik when his friends began to
press for more details of the conversation with the Habber
pilot. He wondered what his days would be like if Nikolai
were no longer there to ease life a little for him.

"Malik!"

He raised his head, recognizing Yekaterina's voice.
She was farther up the line, waiting with a group of
women; Alexei was nowhere in sight. He waved tentatively; she left the women and made her way back to him.

"I'll wait with you," she said. Nikolai, standing just
behind Malik, averted his eyes from the pair.

"You'll just be waiting a while longer," he responded.

"I won't be chosen so soon, I think. This will give me
more time to pretend I might be." She lowered her dark
eyes. "I have been sorry for what I said to you," she whispered.

"I've also regretted my words."

She touched his arm lightly. The day was already
growing warm. Behind him, Bogdan was once more labori-
ously assessing his friends' chances; others were already
returning from the tower. Malik glanced at the people as
they passed; their faces were grim, their eyes hard and
resentful.

Malik thought of the Habber who had refused to help

him. He knew that the man could do little for him, but his hopes had risen when he realized who Benzi Liangharad was. He had been foolish; even the bit of compassion he had glimpsed in Benzi's eyes was probably feigned. Malik was nothing to the Habber, useless in whatever game Benzi's people were playing with Earth, only someone to be ignored and dismissed; Benzi had lectured to him in the end as though Malik were a child instead of a man of thirty.

The pilot, of course, could easily view him that way. His boyish appearance was deceptive; Benzi had to be somewhat older than he looked. His life among Habbers enabled him to observe life from afar, as a series of events that might affect him only in passing; he could remain indifferent to the individual lives he momentarily touched. Malik had once seen his own life in that way.

The line was moving more quickly now. More people filed past, their heads lowered as they strode back to the camp. A woman left the tower and ran to the arms of a man waiting for her; they remained locked in their embrace until one of the Guardians stationed outside shouted at the pair. The woman freed herself and began to walk toward the cradle; the man covered his eyes for a moment. Yekaterina's friends walked by, their eyes fixed on the ground.

When Yekaterina's turn finally came, the people near Malik had grown silent. The Guardians paced, hands on their wands. The door opened; Yekaterina came outside, shook her head as she glanced at Malik, then shrugged.

He entered the tower. The officer in charge was behind the small table; two Guardians stood behind him. The two Habbers were nowhere in sight.

"Malik Haddad," Malik said.

The officer stared at his small screen, then raised his head. "You're on the list." Malik tensed in surprise. "Give him his med-scan and send him on his way."

Another Guardian approached Malik with a scanner; apparently he would not have to disrobe this time. Had someone interceded for him with the Project Council? Somehow, he doubted that, having no practical skills that would be of immediate use to the settlers. His name might have been picked at random, or perhaps someone on the Council had felt a bit of pity for a former Linker. He was not likely ever to know the true reason.

"Go to the cradle," the officer was saying. "The floater will take you to the port in Tashkent." Malik did not move. "Don't you hear me? Get going."

Malik stumbled outside; his head was swimming. Yekaterina was waiting; she hurried toward him as Nikolai went inside. "What is it?" she asked. "You look so pale."

He said, "I'm on the list."

She drew in her breath sharply. "I'm happy for you, Malik. It'll be better for you away from this place, but I'll miss you."

"When you get to Venus—"

She shook her head. "Make a life for yourself—find a home. You don't know when I'll be on the list."

She was right. Better to allow her to find someone who could commit himself wholeheartedly to her instead of making promises he was not likely to keep. "I wish I had something to give you," he said.

"You must keep what you have—you may need it there."

He had one small gift. He shifted his coat to his left arm, then fumbled at the pin on his collar. "Take this, Katya." He held out the tiny gold pin of a scroll with Arabic lettering, the symbol marking him as a historian. "It's my specialist's pin. I won't need it among the settlers. They say that the dome-dwellers and even many of the Islanders don't bother with signs of rank." He put it into her hand and closed her fingers around it.

"On your way, man," a Guardian shouted. Yekaterina touched his face lightly, then hurried away. Malik had gone only a few steps before he felt a hand on his arm.

"I'm on the list, too," Nikolai said.

"Maybe we should say farewell to the others."

The Russian shook his head. "They wouldn't want that. No sense in rubbing it in. I can't believe it—I got so used to the bad news."

They had not moved far from the tower before Howin joined them, followed by Bogdan. The men congratulated one another in Russian; Howin narrowed his eyes as he turned toward Malik. "Your Habber friend must have put in a good word for you," he said. "Maybe you didn't tell us everything he said."

"He had nothing to do with this," Malik replied. "You

don't seriously think the Council would listen to a Habber's recommendation. It's luck, that's all."

"Don't question our good fortune, Howin," Nikolai said. "If the Habber helped Malik, then maybe he decided to put in a word for us. There's no use thinking about it now—just be grateful."

Evening had come before the last of the fortunate ones joined those aboard the floater. The mood on the airship had grown more subdued; Malik had taken his turn in the floater's lavatory and was wondering if they would be fed before the journey began. Nikolai slouched in the seat next to his; perhaps he was now brooding about whether the long wait would be worth it.

Two Guardians walked down the aisle and passed out packages of dark bread and cups of tepid tea. The two Habber pilots came inside; the woman raised her arms for a moment.

"We'll board a shuttlecraft in Tashkent," she said. "My companion and I will be the pilots on the shuttle, but a few Guardians will accompany us. When we get to the Wheel, you'll follow us to the bay where our own ship is waiting."

The two Habbers disappeared behind the door up in front with the airship pilot. Malik gazed out the window as the floater slowly lifted from its cradle.

At the port, Malik and his fifty companions were herded aboard the magnetic train that was to take them to the shuttle field. The people they passed in the wide, lighted halls of the port looked away when they saw the uniformed Guardians among the group; even the children who hung around the port trying to sell their services as guides to unwary travelers avoided them.

The shuttlecraft turned out to be a small, ancient vehicle with few comforts, and it lacked a lift to carry them to their seats. Malik and the others were forced to climb up worn ladders through the center before easing themselves into their seats.

Malik lay back and fumbled at the tubes in the armrest as Nikolai climbed in next to him. "Ever been off Earth before?" the Russian asked.

Malik shook his head. "I imagine this is the first time for most of us." He opened a panel in the armrest, took out two tablets, and handed one to Nikolai. "Here's what I was looking for. Better take one, Kolya—you may get sick otherwise." He put the tablet into his mouth and sucked some water from the tube.

"We've got a trip ahead of us," Nikolai muttered as he swallowed his tablet. "I hope I'm not one of those people who can't adapt."

"It's too late to worry about that now." Malik strapped himself into his seat. This ship had no screens through which the passengers could view images of their journey; he only knew that they were on their way when an invisible weight pressed him against his seat and the loud humming of the ship's engines drowned out even the sound of Nikolai's moan.

The shuttle journey was an ordeal of discomfort, relieved only by two periods of restless sleep. From time to time, a Guardian drifted by weightlessly, showed the passengers how to pull themselves along the handholds on the seats, led them to the zero-g toilets, and explained how to use them to those who could not read the instructions.

Most of the travelers seemed weak by the time they docked at the Wheel. They followed the Guardians passively through lighted halls and up elevators until they arrived at another bay, where a small vessel carried them to the waiting Habber ship.

This ship was unlike the smaller, sluglike freighters and sturdy torchships housed in the other docks of the tubular space station's hub. The Habber vessel was a long, silvery cylinder connected to a giant globe that housed its engines; inside, a soft light permeated the ship.

The Guardians had remained behind in the bay. The passengers waited restlessly in a corridor while Benzi Liangharad and his companion greeted the two Habbers already aboard; the Anglaic they spoke among themselves seemed filled with unfamiliar or shortened words.

"That shuttle trip was bad enough," a woman near Malik said. "I don't know how I'll get through this."

"How long do you think it'll take?" Nikolai asked Malik. "I don't know much about this sort of craft."

"I can't take weightlessness again," Howin said.

"If this ship is anything like Earth's spacecraft, you won't have to," Malik responded. "Our torchships use laser-induced pulse fusion." He shifted the pack on his back, which felt heavy even in the one-half g of the Wheel. "What that means is that you'll experience some weightlessness at the beginning of the trip, but as the ship continuously accelerates, you'll feel the illusion of gravity. A torchship keeps accelerating until the midpoint of its trip, and then it begins to decelerate, so—" His voice trailed off; he was hardly an expert on such vessels, and it was possible the Habbers had something more sophisticated.

"They're Habbers," Howin said. "Maybe they like weightlessness."

"Come with me," Benzi said.

The group followed the pilot down the corridor. "How long do you think we'll be on this tub?" Bogdan asked.

"That depends on where Venus is now in relation to us," Malik replied. "It might be a week, it might be three."

A door slid open; Benzi led them into a large room filled with platforms covered by transparent carapaces. "This is where you'll pass the journey," the pilot said when they were all inside. "Pick out a sleeper and stow your pack next to it. A red button on the side of the sleeper will open it, and it closes automatically when you're inside. Remove your clothing if you think you'll be more comfortable that way. You'll be awakened when we reach Anwara."

Nikolai gaped at the Habber. "What is this?"

"You'll be in suspension during the trip. Our own people often avail themselves of the sleepers during a long journey. You won't have to be fed, and you'll avoid the boredom of the trip. Believe me, it's for your comfort."

"Sure," one man said. "You really care how we feel."

"You wouldn't be very comfortable at two g's or more," Benzi said, "since we'll be accelerating to make faster time."

"They want us out of the way," a woman whispered. "They just don't want us roaming around their precious ship."

The same thought had occurred to Malik; the Habbers might not want the Earthfolk examining their ship too closely. "Coffins," Bogdan said suddenly. "They look like coffins. How do we know he'll wake us up at all?"

Benzi frowned. "Don't be ridiculous. Don't you think

word would have reached Earth by now if previous settlers hadn't arrived safely?"

Bogdan did not seem reassured. "Coffins," he said again. "You won't get me into one of those things."

"Then you'll have to leave the ship," Benzi said. "I don't imagine the Guardians in the bay will be happy about having to take you back."

Malik walked toward one of the sleepers, set down his pack, and pressed the button; the carapace yawned open. He put his coat on top of the pack and climbed inside as a few other people went to the sleepers. He had thought there might be a chance to speak with Benzi again, or to see if one of the other Habbers might be more sympathetic.

The sleeper closed over him. He caught a glimpse of Nikolai in the sleeper next to his own before a cool mist bathed his face and a darkness as thick as Venus's clouds enveloped his thoughts.

THE MONUMENT

Six

Risa opened her eyes, adjusted the harness holding her in her seat, and gazed absently at the large screen in front of the shuttle's passenger section. The vessel was just beginning its descent to Venus's upper atmosphere. Weight pressed her against her seat as the shuttle's retros fired to slow its speed. The Platform was visible on the screen; circles of light marking its docks shone against the Island port's dark metal surface.

Risa was on her way home to Oberg. She looked away from the screen, still weary after the party a few of her friends had given for her on the northern Bat.

She had finished her last shift on the winged satellite above the north pole of Venus. The northern Bat, and its twin over Venus's south pole, had large wings that extended beyond the Parasol's shadow to provide the satellites with solar power. Below the workers' living quarters, each Bat had a latticework of docks for the scooper ships that traveled to the surface.

The process of terraforming was releasing much of the planet's oxygen. Some of the oxygen would remain locked in rock; some would combine with the hydrogen brought from Saturn to form water. The rest of the excess oxygen, however, had to be removed if the atmosphere was ever to support life. Two installations near each of Venus's poles drew in the atmosphere, separated the oxygen from other elements, and then compressed it. Robots ferried the oxygen containers to the scooper ships, which carried it up to the Bats. Much of the oxygen was dumped into space; the rest was used on the two satellites or was ferried away for other purposes.

This process was automatic, but people were needed on the two winged satellites to maintain the docks and service the ships, and all the workers there lived with the fear that the volatile oxygen might explode. Risa had never experienced such a disaster, but she knew a few older people who had lost friends in an explosion.

Along with other able-bodied young people who were not needed for other tasks, Risa had volunteered for duty on one of the Bats. She had worked two-month-long shifts ever since her sixteenth birthday. Her father had not been happy with her decision; he knew that some young people saw Bat duty partly as a rite of passage and also as a chance to be away from their families for a while. Such motives did not concern her. The Project needed workers on the Bats, and she wanted to be useful.

Risa had gone back to Oberg between shifts to train for the work she would be doing when she returned to her settlement for good. She would now become a permanent member of the team that had trained her and would work at maintaining dome installations. She would also be free to spend more time on her household's business and at work that would earn more credit for herself. Once she had looked forward to this time; now she felt a pang of regret. Decisions she had been free to postpone might soon have to be made; her adult life as one of Oberg's settlers would truly begin.

The weight holding her down dissipated. Risa waited until a light overhead signaled that the ship was safely lowered into its dock and the entrance sealed off above, then released herself from the harness. The floor under her feet was now a wall. She reached for her duffel and began to climb down the center of the ship, clinging to the handholds and securing her feet in the small indentations along the wall while trying to keep out of the way of other passengers.

She was inside the large, cylindrical dock that held the shuttle. Most of the others were already pushing through the dock's door. The pilot climbed down the shuttle's ladder, followed by a Guardian in a black uniform. Risa's nose wrinkled in distaste; she disliked the Guardians. A Guardian pilot always accompanied each shuttle, as though the travelers were simply waiting for a chance to flee to the nearest Hab; she viewed such suppositions as an insult. Seeing the Guardians who were stationed on the Platform made her grateful she lived in a domed settlement, where they had no need of such people.

She walked into a long, lighted corridor. Most of the passengers had already climbed into one of the carts that would take them to the airship bays. A couple of women in the cart beckoned to her; she was about to walk toward them when she spotted Evar IngersLens striding in her direction. The young man waved at her; she stepped back from the cart as it rolled away.

"Risa," Evar said as he took her hands. "I thought I'd catch you. It just so happens that I'll be piloting the next airship to Oberg, so you'll be traveling with me. They're still loading cargo, so it won't be leaving for a couple of hours." He smiled, obviously glad to see her; his blue eyes shone with anticipation.

Two hours, she thought, enough time to find a free cubicle in the pilots' quarters for some hasty lovemaking before departure. Then, after they arrived in Oberg, Evar would expect her to invite him to her house. In her last message, she had told him that she needed time to consider their relationship. Evar had clearly taken her words literally. He had given her the time; presumably she was now prepared to plan their future.

"I'm not quite myself today," she said as she slipped her hands from his. "I just want to stretch my legs a bit and then rest until it's time to go."

"I'll walk with you, then." He took her duffel before she could refuse and slung it over his shoulder. Her eyes fell to the black and red sash he wore with his blue pilot's coverall. More people, especially among the pilots, were wearing it lately. As they walked down the corridor, the sash reminded her again of the true reason she was unwilling to make any commitment to Evar.

The sash marked him as a member of the Ishtar cult. Risa had always prided herself on her tolerance of any system of beliefs, as long as the believers left others free to reject them. Ishtar's followers were not so tolerant; they imagined a world where everyone believed as they did. To her, this was utter folly; how could people from so many different Nomarchies and traditions get along if concessions weren't made to the beliefs of others?

Two pilots passed them, both wearing the sash of Ishtar. The cult had originated among the more ignorant Project workers. Those simple people had believed that the effort of terraforming would rouse the Spirit that now lay dormant on Venus, and that this Spirit had to be placated. The believers, dimly aware of theories that Venus might have developed into an Earth-like planet if its planetary evolution had not taken a different turn, saw terraforming as a way to restore Venus to what it should have been. But Venus, and the Spirit now called Ishtar after an ancient goddess, would resist humankind's efforts. Risa did not care to think of the rumored rituals by which Ishtar was appeased.

She hoped that Evar was sensible enough not to believe in the actual existence of such a Spirit; he could hardly see every quake as a sign of Ishtar struggling against Her transformation. Along with many others, he probably saw Ishtar only as a symbol of what the cult's followers longed to create—a future world free of barriers among the settlers, when the technology that now separated them from their world would no longer be needed.

She understood why Evar and so many of the pilots might be attracted to such a group. The pilots were the most mobile of all the groups here and were often away from their primary residences for long periods. Knowing that others sometimes did not view them as true settlers, they tended to be more fervent in their professions of loyalty to their world. They also had to endure the presence of Guardians aboard shuttle flights, a reminder to them of the pilots who had deserted Venus long ago; wearing the sash was a way of showing how the pilots felt about the Guardians and their suspicions.

Being in Ishtar, according to Evar, marked him as a true Cytherian, one yearning for a world free of both Earth and the Habbers. The problem with Ishtar's adherents was that they seemed to regard other people as less loyal to Venus.

"This was your last shift on the Bat, wasn't it?" Evar asked.

She nodded; he knew perfectly well that it was.

"You'll be back in Oberg then, tending to your household's affairs," he continued. "Time to think of a bondmate and the next generation, wouldn't you say? You're twenty-four now—you shouldn't put it off much longer."

"I couldn't think of it while I was working on the Bat."

"Well, plenty of others do. I mean, accidents don't happen all that often, but if they do, it's a consolation to a family to know that the ones they lost left children or stored seed behind. But you don't have to think of that now. There's nothing to stop you from settling down."

His conventionality suddenly irritated her. "Maybe I'll have a child without a bondmate," she said. "I might find a man who'd be willing to donate sperm and renounce any formal ties with the child. It'd certainly make things simpler."

He halted. She had expected to shock him a little; instead, he laughed. "Oh, Risa. You don't mean that. People would wonder."

"My father and his companion never had a bond."

"That's different." Evar shook back his sandy hair. "Bettina's older—she grew up on Earth, and her people didn't have bonds, and I suppose she's a bit old-fashioned. Anyway, she and Chen live together as if they're bondmates, so it comes to the same thing. And everyone says you have a chance to be on the Oberg Council someday, so you ought to think of your reputation. You don't want people to say you act like a Habber, without any ties."

She glared at him, wondering exactly what he meant. Was he telling her that, because her brother had abandoned the Project for a Habber's life, she had to be careful? She had never known her brother Benzi; his actions had nothing to do with her. Benzi had broken with his family; as far as she was concerned, he did not exist.

Evar's eyes widened a little; he smiled blandly. He was only giving her commonplace advice. Among diverse groups of settlers, it was wise not to be unnecessarily offensive; that usually meant conservative public conduct and keeping more questionable pursuits to oneself.

"It's funny, hearing you tell me how I should act," Risa said. "You should save your advice for some of the people in Ishtar's inner circles. They don't bother with bonds, and I've heard plenty about their rite. If anyone else acted the way your precious Guide does, people would have some choice names for her."

He peered at her earnestly, almost pityingly. She had hoped that, just this once, she could rouse him from his placidity.

"You don't understand," he responded calmly. "Their bonds are with Ishtar and among themselves, and there's no need for them to be formal. They're breaking down the barriers that divide people, living the way all Cytherians will someday, sharing themselves and all they have with each other. Yet they're wise enough to know that most of us aren't ready for that. They're examples of what we might become, and it's the obligation of our Guide to allow the Spirit of Ishtar to fill her."

Risa sniffed. "That isn't the only thing that fills her. What does she do at those rites—take on every man there?"

"Certainly not. You should come to our meetings sometime. We do allow people to find the truth in their own way, you know—belief is harder for some than for others. What's important is fellowship and knowing that we're part of something larger than ourselves."

"We're part of the Project, and we're settlers. That should be enough."

She walked on; Evar paced at her side. "I thought you were more open-minded," he said. "You usually go out of your way to be fair, but you aren't very fair to us."

"I'm fairer than you. I don't care how many people join Ishtar or rut with your Guide, as long as they don't keep harping at the rest of us about their wonderful truth."

She pressed her lips together. Evar had been her lover for two years; it had been easy to let him assume they would become bondmates. He eased her loneliness, and she did not expect to meet anyone who might fire her passion among the relatively limited number of available men. Evar was steady and reliable; because his pilot's duties would take him away for extended periods, she would be freer to run her household as she saw fit. But she could not abide the thought of suffering endless lectures on Ishtar or the likelihood that any children they had would grow up wearing the sash.

Like Evar, she dreamed of building a new world, but she had hoped that the new society would be rooted in more rational ways of thought.

"You should join us," he said. "It isn't as if you have to

accept everything right away—it's making the effort that's important, and showing the willingness to become a true Cytherian. You ought to be more sensitive to that than most, after what your brother did so long ago—you'd only be showing where your true loyalties lie if you join."

She stopped and faced him. "How dare you bring that up." She lowered her voice as another cart rolled past. "You know what I think of him and what he did. Everyone knows I'm loyal." Rage brought her an odd feeling of relief. He had finally given her an opening for the arguments she had avoided. His patience and even temper always made her feel vaguely guilty for saying anything in anger, but reproaching her with her brother's deed was unforgiveable. "If you feel that way about me, maybe you'd better find someone else. I don't want a pledge from you, and I'm not even sure I want you as a lover any more."

Evar blinked; his smile did not waver. She reached for her duffel; he slid it from his shoulder and handed it to her. "I guess you are tired," he said. "Why don't you go to the mess and have a cup of tea? I'll see you in the bay when you've had time to collect yourself." He kissed her lightly on the forehead before she could pull back, then stepped out to the center of the corridor to wave down a cart. He turned to grin at her as the cart rolled away.

She bit her lip in frustration. She could never make a dent in his placid insistence. To him, her outbursts were no more than the occasional quakes that rocked Venus's surface as its tectonic plates shifted after being locked for millennia, a distraction that was often predictable and disturbed him only momentarily. He would wear away at her gently but persistently, as the acid rains falling steadily through the Cytherian mists ate away at the rock below. He would wait, secure in his assumption that she would eventually see things his way and that her loneliness and physical need would bring her back to him. Like many who dreamed of a world they would never see, he was used to waiting.

Even her resistance to his beliefs was, she supposed, a challenge. For people so convinced they possessed the truth, there would be more virtue in winning a new adherent than in seeking out those who already believed.

It would not work, she told herself, hoisting her duffel to her shoulder.

* * *

The airship, like most dirigibles here, had a cabin that could hold fifty people. Only ten passengers were aboard; the aisle was filled with crates of cargo that had been secured to the floor. In front of Risa, Evar sat with a female pilot. The bands around their heads linked them to the ship, and they were now concentrating on the panels before them as the airship glided out of the bay. Risa had pointedly ignored Evar's glances while finding her seat.

The screen above the pilots revealed the darkness of a world in the Parasol's eclipse. Risa had greeted the passengers she recognized; she closed her eyes now and listened to the drone of their conversation. Two young men were, it appeared, seismologists who had recently returned from the Cytherian Institute. Only a small number of the dome-dwellers won admission to the Island schools, where they were trained as specialists; an even smaller number were chosen for the Institute. Risa often found the new graduates a little hard to take, since they seemed to feel they should be grateful to Earth for their opportunity to study there.

"It was crowded," one young man said in response to a question about Earth. "I didn't think I'd ever get used to all the people, and being outside—well, you can imagine."

Risa tried to imagine it. She had lived on Island Two until she was eight, and then in Oberg; she had traveled to the Islands and the northern Bat aboard airships and shuttlecraft. She had spent all her life in enclosed spaces. What would it feel like to stand under an open sky?

"I didn't go into Caracas," the other graduate said, "until I'd been at the Institute for almost a year. Even the students from Earth were cautious about trips to the city. We heard all kinds of lurid stories about thieves who'd get someone into an alley, torture him into giving up his codes, and then steal his identity bracelet and clean out his credit before anyone knew the difference. Sometimes the victim was even killed."

"Well!" one woman muttered. She sounded quite appalled at Earth, as she had every right to be.

"I notice," the first young man said softly, "that one of our pilots is sashed. Has Ishtar become more popular since we left?"

"Not really," a woman's voice replied. "A few here, a few there—it's still a fairly small group, thank God."

"That's reassuring," the graduate said. "I could never stand their proselytizing or those ridiculous meetings. I went to one once, out of curiosity. We were given what they call a lecture—I never heard such distortions of history." Risa found herself liking the young man.

She settled back in her seat. Chen had hoped that Risa might be chosen for advanced training, and even for the Institute, which her mother had attended. Instead, she had left school at fourteen to apprentice herself to a maintenance worker, dashing her father's hopes. Chen had a lot of faith in the value of education, perhaps because he had been given so little. He had railed at her for not trying for more, especially since her schoolwork had been good.

She had learned what she needed to know; her work had included lessons in soil science, botany, geology, and some elementary chemistry and physics; she knew how to read and could pursue other lessons from time to time. She could not see that becoming a specialist would make her any more valuable to the Project; learning practical skills made more sense. Chen had accused her of being like her grandmother on Earth, and that was a failing in his eyes; he had often told her how proud Angharad was of her ignorance of what she called useless learning.

The airship shook a little; riding out the fierce winds that still raged below the Islands took some skill. She relaxed a little; the bay workers had been very careful with maintenance since the latest accident a few years ago, which had involved an airship on a routine trip to the Platform from Island Two. A pump had locked, the ship's helium cells had filled with atmosphere, and the dirigible had descended precipitously and crashed. Most Cytherians remembered that accident well, since several Administrators had died.

She shifted in her seat, anxious to be home.

On the screen, the four domes of Oberg shone through the misty blackness, blisters on the planet's hot surface. The roof to the bay adjoining the main dome was open as the airship slowly dropped toward one of the egg-shaped cradles below. When the ship was securely clamped to its cradle, the roof began to slide shut. The passengers waited in their seats as air cycled into the bay.

"Welcome to Oberg," a woman's recorded voice said over the airship's comm; Evar took off his band. "Please wait until the wall separating the cradles from the rest of the bay has been lifted, then go directly into the main dome so that the unloading of cargo can be expedited. I trust your journey was a pleasant one."

The passengers ignored the voice as they rummaged for their belongings. Risa moved toward the door ahead of the others, hoping to avoid Evar. She hurried down the ramp at the side of the cradle and walked swiftly through the cavernous bay. Gantries, cranes, and consoles lined the walls; to her right, a wide closed door sealed off the area where some of the diggers and crawlers used in surface operations were stored.

An entrance twenty meters wide and thirty meters high was ahead, at the far end of the bay. Its door, a vast sheet of metal, was only partly open; she nodded at the members of the bay crew as she passed.

Near the entrance, she saw that it was still light inside the dome; a large disk of light embedded in the dome's center gave the settlement twelve hours of daylight, followed by a dim, silvery glow that passed for night. She left the bay and entered the main dome.

On the grassy land near the bay, twenty tents were pitched to house arrivals who had not yet found permanent residences. In the distance, under the center of the kilometer-high dome, stood the broad, three-story windowed building that housed the External Operations Center. Laboratories, along with the Refining and Recycling Center, were closer to the western side of the dome, not far from the community greenhouses.

She drew in her breath, welcoming the familiar scent of grass and trees. The land inside the main dome was flat, with only a few hills, and dotted with trees; carts carrying workers and crates rolled by along the flat main road that circled the land under the dome.

Her arm was jostled; she looked up into Evar's blue eyes. "Glad I caught up with you," he said. "Feeling rested enough to have me over for supper later?"

"I'm not going to my house right away, and I may get home late," she replied.

"Then maybe I can come by after supper. Now that Noella's moved out, you have plenty of extra space, so I can always stay in her old room when you need time to yourself."

She had space for him in her house, and of course that space had to be made available. It made more sense than having Evar stay in the more cramped quarters of the pilots' dormitory between trips, and she would have been the first to comment disparagingly on people who built houses with more rooms than they needed. She sighed as she thought of the days ahead. Evar could continue to ingratiate himself with the rest of her household, and soon they would grow accustomed to his presence. It would seem only natural for him to come there again between trips, and even more natural for Risa to agree to some sort of pledge at last.

"My father told me in his last message that he wants to bring in someone who might take on some of our household work. He's thinking of one of the new immigrants. He feels a little guilty that we haven't taken one on, even temporarily, and he'd probably like to hear some talk of Earth."

"Well, he hasn't taken one in yet, has he?" The young pilot smiled. "I'll see you later, after dark." He marched away toward the pilots' dormitory before she could say anything else.

Risa raged silently against Evar's obstinacy as she walked toward the main dome's eastern wall. She would have to be firmer with him. A few days of barring her bedroom door ought to do the trick, and then—

She would be alone again. Not many men had ever had the patience to break through her wall. In fact, there had only been Evar and, before him, a young mechanic named Rafael Tejada. Bettina, her father's companion, had often wondered about Risa, but Bettina came from the North American Plains and thought any woman without a strong interest in bed-partners was abnormal. Plenty of men came to Risa for advice on their problems and disputes, but she knew most thought her cold. Her problem was quite otherwise; her needs were strong, but she feared surrendering that much of herself to any man.

Evar could satisfy her and leave her mind unclouded

by thoughts of him the rest of the time. She might have settled for that if it weren't for his insistent, almost interminable talk of his cursed cult.

She moved under a grove of trees, still and silent in the windless dome. The low wall that circled the dome was visible; the transparent dome, made of a ceramic developed by Habber technology, revealed the blackness outside. Rods sunk deep into the crust of the planet anchored the wall and drew on geothermal power to maintain the structure.

She was near the monument to her mother; Chen would expect her to stop before going home. He would ask if it had been polished lately or if any visitors had left a tribute, and she would have to have something to tell him.

Five women stood around a small metal column. A worn-looking wreath had been left at its base, and she could safely tell her father that there was no need for him to come and polish the monument himself. As she was about to leave, one of the women motioned to her.

"Excuse me," the woman said, "but do you know how to read?" Risa nodded reluctantly. Most of the people who had grown up with the Project knew how to read; these women had the rather disoriented look of recent arrivals.

"Could you read this inscription to us?" the woman continued. "We were told about it when we got here, but we'd like to hear the words."

Risa wanted to refuse. She had read the inscription often enough; she hardly had to glance at the Anglaic lettering. "In honor of Iris Angharads and Amir Azad, the first true Cytherians, who gave their lives to save our new world." She swallowed. "They shall not be forgotten. May their spirit live on in all those who follow them. They rest forever on the world they helped to build."

The woman sighed. "They were very brave. We heard their story, of course."

Risa stepped back. As a child, she had often come to this spot whenever she saw people viewing the monument. Someone would be reading the inscription, or she would be asked if she could read it to the group. She had enjoyed following her recitation with a statement sure to elicit attention.

"I'm her daughter," she would announce dramatically. "Iris Angharads was my mother." This usually brought gentle sighs, pats on the head, an occasional treat, and sometimes a few questions about Iris, which Risa answered as well as she could.

More sympathy always followed whenever she admitted that she had never known Iris. She had been brought to term in one of Island Two's ectogenetic chambers and born in 570, two years after her mother's death. Chen and Iris had stored their sperm and eggs against the day when Iris was ready to bear another child. The Islanders, knowing that Chen had averted a grave threat to the Island Platform, had been willing to honor his request for a child —all that would remain to him of his lost bondmate.

Risa had not minded such attention when she was younger, but that was before Iris's memory had become burdensome. Whatever she did, there were those who would compare her with her mother. The comparisons were never made to what Iris had actually been but to the symbol she had become. Risa found the monument and everything connected with it morbid now. It might have been more sensible and meaningful to honor those who had lived out full lives working to transform Venus, rather than dwelling on two people who had, in the end, done less than others.

She gazed at the two sculpted faces on the pillar. Chen had made the carving used as a model for this monument. Amir Azad's eyes were partly closed, as if death had brought him peace; Iris's large eyes were open. Her strong-featured face was that of a very young woman, although she had been in her forties when she died. Chen had told Risa often of how he had failed to carve his dead bondmate's face, until he finally captured a vision of the girl he had first loved, who had dreamed of coming to Venus.

Chen often dwelled on his memories of Iris even now. Her records, messages, and even her school papers were preserved on a microdot panel he had brought with him to Oberg sixteen years ago. Risa had viewed her mother's image while Chen told her stories of their life together. He might have done better to forget her. He did not even seem to mind that Iris's monument also honored Amir Azad and that the two had once been lovers; Iris had been a Plainswoman, and her bond with Chen had not kept her from the beds of other men.

But Chen had also forgotten the real Iris and seemed to remember only what he chose to recall. Even his companion Bettina had not vanquished Iris's ghost.

Whenever Risa had stood here and told people that she was Iris's daughter, at least one would comment on the resemblance. She had not minded such comparisons then; later, she had found them absurd. She had her father's black hair and his almond-shaped brown eyes; she might have been any woman's daughter. Lately, however, she had noticed how her prominent cheekbones, full lips, and strong chin were like the features Chen had molded for the monument.

She hurried away from the column. The resemblance was not so marked that these women would notice it, but she had lingered there long enough.

Several paces away from the column, two other memorial pillars with holo portraits of Oberg's dead stood near a glade. There had not been many such deaths yet; it would be some time before the space on these pillars was filled. She passed them and entered the glade.

Birds twittered above her. The small birds fed on both the worms used to enrich the soil and the insects that pollinated the flowers that lent some color to the landscape; cats that some of the settlers kept as pets preyed upon the birds in turn. Cat births were even more closely regulated than those of the settlers, lest the settlement be overrun by them.

The peace of the wood soothed her. New arrivals often complained about devoting space to trees and shrubs rather than building more dwellings for settlers. Later, most of them learned to appreciate such spots and preferred to complain about the still newer immigrants.

She left the wood. Ahead of her stretched a plain of houses; many of the residences had small, glassy greenhouses adjacent to them. The houses were one-story, flat-roofed structures made of light prefabricated plastic or ceramic walls. In the regulated environment of the dome, the settlers needed no more protection from the elements. Small streams flowed in narrow channels, fed by liquid collected from the steady rain outside the dome; that liquid was collected in receptacles and channeled under the dome's wall to be cleansed and chemically altered. These streams had recently been restocked with a few small fish;

a group of children were loitering on one of the walkways bridging the stream, trying to glimpse the fish below.

Her destination was a house overlooking the main dome's small infirmary and biological laboratory. Risa hesitated for a moment, then approached the front door. Chen disapproved of her visits to this house; she shrugged the thought aside. Pavel would want to know she was back.

She pressed her hand against the door.

The door opened; a dark-haired man in gray workers' clothes ushered her inside. Two other men sat on the floor at a low table in the center of the room; they looked up from their game of cards.

"When did you get back?" the dark-haired man asked.

"Just a little while ago," Risa replied.

"Your last shift, wasn't it?" one of the men sitting by the table said. "Lucky you."

"I thought I'd stop by and see Pavel on my way home. Is he around?"

The man standing next to her frowned. "He's resting in his room. Been weaker lately, but then, he's an old man." He lowered his voice. "I tried to talk him into going over to the infirmary, but he wouldn't hear of it, kept saying it'd be a waste of medical resources. I guess he's right, but—" He shrugged. "Go on—he won't mind a visit from you."

She turned right, entered a small hallway, and pressed her hand against the first door to her left. It slid open; she entered the tiny room and saw the empty bed. A white-haired man sat on a cushion in one corner with a reading screen on his folded legs.

"Dawud said you were resting," Risa said. "I hope I'm not disturbing you."

Pavel's heavy white brows rose slightly as he peered up at her. "Not at all. You know I always enjoy seeing you."

She studied the old man for a moment. His dark eyes no longer seemed as alert, and he had lost weight. Rejuvenation could do little for him now; she knew the signs. But Pavel Gvishiani had been an old man when he first came to Oberg. When his disgrace had faded in people's minds, merciful Administrators had decided to let him spend his last years on the world he had helped to build, and which he had once hoped to rule.

"Sit down, child." She sat on the bed. "I trust you stopped by the monument."

"Chen expects it of me." Memorials to the dead were not a topic she would have chosen for a talk with Pavel. "He worries about that monument too much—always thinking about whether it's properly tended and that people remember what it was for."

"That's understandable. Even my thoughts have turned to it lately. It's one of my regrets—that your mother died as she did."

Risa shook her head. "Pavel, don't be sentimental with me. You're only sorry that you miscalculated."

"How harsh you are sometimes."

"I'm realistic." They rarely discussed her mother. Iris's death, and that of Amir Azad, might have been avoided if Pavel had not played for time in the hope of keeping his position. That was how Chen viewed the matter.

Risa saw the past differently. Pavel had seen what the Project required and had acted. He had seen himself as a Cytherian rather than as a minion of the Mukhtars and had acted in the interests of his world.

"My mother was somewhat brave," she went on. "But the people who seized that dome might also have been brave in their own way. They knew Earth would win if they didn't take action—the Islands would have had to surrender completely if the siege had gone on long enough. The plotters who died with my mother also gave their lives for the Project."

"How odd to hear such words from you, Risa."

"I may not approve of their methods, but I understand their motives."

"They foolishly threatened some Habber lives. They'd hardly have kept helping us if they no longer felt safe among us."

Habbers, she thought. Tolerable because they were useful, but they were not people to depend on. Habbers retreated from difficulties, or were the descendants of those who had. The Islanders who saw them as new friends were deceiving themselves.

"But what lies ahead for you, now that you're back?" Pavel tilted his head. "A run for the Council, perhaps?

Enough people rely on your advice—you ought to put
yourself in a position where it'll carry more weight."

She shrugged. People sought her advice, in the hope
of avoiding public hearings over their disputes or the need
to call in a Counselor from the Islands to settle those that
could not be resolved. She had gained a reputation for
fairness, but a good amount of the advice she gave was
Pavel's. His Administrator's experience was valuable.

"And you might make plans with your young man,"
Pavel continued. "You're at an age when many have a
bondmate and children."

She smiled; Pavel had never had either. "If I take a
bondmate, it won't be Evar. I'm not going to spend the
next ten or twenty years listening to his tedious talk about
Ishtar."

"Ah, yes. You told me that he had grown quite devout.
It's dismaying to see people involved in such foolishness,
but we can be grateful their numbers are still small. One
might almost think that Earth was surreptitiously encouraging that cult."

Risa folded her arms. "Earth? Members of Ishtar dislike Earth—they dream of being free of the Mukhtars."

"They dislike Habbers more, and without them, we'd
be even more dependent on Earth's help. Well, I won't live
long enough to see what role, if any, they'll play here."

Again, she worried about what might happen when
Pavel was gone, when all the older Cytherians were gone.
They had lived to see surface settlements and had ex-
pected little more.

Many of the younger settlers were not quite so patient. They resented the Project Council, distrusted Habbers, and dreamed of a world where the distinctions they
wanted to escape would be erased. At times, the desires of
the younger settlers seemed contradictory; each wanted to
rise as high as possible while hoping for a world where no
one would be higher than anyone else.

"Sometimes I'm sorry that I never had children," Pavel murmured. "I wouldn't have minded having a daughter like you—someone who understood me, who'd listen
and be frank with me."

"You have that now," she replied. "Plenty of people
seek you out." Pavel was being more maudlin than usual,
wistful about the past and sentimental about the present.

"Anyway, if I'd actually been your daughter, I might not have understood you as well, and you probably wouldn't have been honest with me."

He set down his screen, tried to rise, then settled back on his cushion. "Could you help me to the bed?" he asked. She stood and helped him up; he leaned against her and hobbled toward the bed. He stretched out; she propped a small pillow under his head, then handed him his screen. "I'll fetch you some food, Pavel."

"I won't be awake long enough to eat it."

She embraced him, pressing her cheek against his. "You flatter me, Risa," he said weakly. "I was past this when you were still a child."

"Rest and get stronger, and maybe you'll surprise yourself."

When Risa left Pavel's house, the overhead disk of light was fading. The growing darkness gave an illusion of space; she could almost forget that the dome was there. She walked past the houses, nodding at the people she knew as they hurried home. Beyond Pavel's dwelling, the evening call to prayer was sounding from the mosque's small minaret.

She still had a walk ahead of her; the main dome was five kilometers in diameter. Oberg's able-bodied citizens moved through their settlement on foot whenever possible; the walking exercised their bodies and kept the domes free of too many roadways and vehicles. She moved away from the houses and followed a small creek to the west.

At the western end of this dome, just beyond the Buddhist temple, she met the flat main road again; a cart was rolling toward the tunnel that led to Oberg's west dome. She followed the cart down the gently sloping ramp that slipped under the wall.

Overhead panels lighted the underground passageway; two empty carts stood against the walls. Part of one wall had been painted in an abstract pattern, while other sections were marred by lettering in Anglaic, Arabic, and a few other languages. Someone had added an inscription she hadn't seen before, in black Anglaic letters: HELP! I'M A PRISONER OF FREEDOM! She smiled and walked on.

She came to another sloping ramp and went up into the west dome; ahead of her, a curved path led away from the main road toward a group of dwellings and small greenhouses. Trees hid some of the houses from view, and much of the flat land surrounding them was covered by shrubs and high grass.

Engineers, aided by Habbers, had begun to build this dome, and another one like it to the southeast, soon after Risa and her father had come to Venus's surface. They had lived in a dormitory in the main dome for four years while this one was completed; she remembered peering over the main dome's wall as airships lowered the second dome over the cleared and leveled land.

Their home now was a one-story building with two small rectangular wings; it sat among slender trees about thirty meters from the entrance to the tunnel. Chen had built most of the house himself, from materials given to him. She and her father had been among the earliest settlers, those who had come to Oberg sixteen years ago when only its main dome was ready, Tsou Yen was uninhabited, and two other settlements, Galileo and al-Khwarizmi, were not yet habitable. Now, ten domed settlements sat on plateaus among the Maxwell Mountains, and thousands of settlers had followed Risa and Chen to the surface.

She turned onto a tree-lined stone path, glanced at her household's small greenhouse, and pressed her palm against the front door's lock.

The door opened. Her father was sitting alone in the common room. Bettina, who was a physician, was probably off tending to a patient elsewhere, while her son, Paul, would be with the young woman he loved.

Chen sat on the floor at the corner table where he kept his carving tools and supplies; a lump of clay, partly molded into a face, was in front of him. He looked up as she approached; his smile was quick. "Welcome home, Risa."

She leaned over and kissed him on his brow. "I stopped by the memorial. Someone left a wreath, and the monument's been polished. A few people asked me to read the inscription to them." Maybe he would assume that she had lingered there, although he could probably guess that she had visited Pavel. "Starting something else? Have you finished the carving for Paul and Grazie?"

Chen shook his head. "It'll get done."

"You don't have much time. They'll be making their pledge in a few days." Chen had once hoped that she and

Paul might someday make a pledge, but Paul had always seemed more like a brother. He was two years older than Risa and had lived with his father before joining Bettina in Oberg three years after her arrival. Risa had often thought that Bettina and Chen wanted their children to be bondmates because they had never made a pledge themselves.

Iris still held him, she thought. He had a life with Bettina, but Iris would be his only bondmate. Perhaps his affection for Bettina rested largely on the fact that the physician was a Plainswoman, as Iris had been.

Chen's once-dark hair was gray; tiny lines marked the pale brown skin around his eyes. His small, stocky body was still sturdy. He had always been strong and would have at least three decades of life still ahead of him, even here. Bettina scanned him regularly and found no cause for concern, but Chen was eighty, older than most of the settlers.

Risa gestured at the clay. "Who's the subject?"

"I thought I might try to capture your brother."

She frowned. "I can't imagine why." The mention of Benzi dismayed her; Chen rarely spoke of the son he had lost.

He gazed at her steadily. "I had a message from Benzi yesterday," he said. "He was on Anwara, preparing to return to his Hab. The people there didn't trouble him over the message, in spite of who he is, and I said I was willing to accept it." He waved a hand at the large wall screen behind him. "He looks much the same, your brother, even after all these years."

She hardly knew what to say. "But why did he want to talk to you?"

"He wanted to see how we were. He said he wanted me to know he hadn't forgotten me."

"After all this time? Does he really think we'd care? Why didn't he ask a Habber here to pass along a message to you earlier if he was so concerned?"

"You mustn't be too hard on him, Risa. He might have thought his new life would be easier if he left this one completely behind."

"And exactly what was he doing on Anwara?" she asked.

"He was one of the pilots bringing new settlers from Earth."

"Really!" Her jaw tightened. Benzi was a part of Chen's life best forgotten, a son who had wounded both his parents and the Project. Iris was the mother she could not emulate, and Benzi was the brother for whose actions she was supposed to atone. "Is he feeling remorseful now? It's a little late for that, isn't it?"

"He still feels a bond with us."

"I don't feel one with him! You shouldn't have spoken to him at all. He doesn't deserve your love—he didn't care about you when he abandoned the Project."

"He's my son, and Iris's."

"He cut his ties to you long ago."

"I can't forget that he's still our son."

She said, "I'd never forgive a child who treated me the way he treated you."

He lifted his chin. "You won't feel that way when you have a child of your own."

Benzi had cast Chen aside. Risa had tried to fill the void in her father's heart. She had not fulfilled some of his hopes for her, but she had done her best to be a good daughter. The love Chen still held for his son seemed a betrayal of his love for her.

"Benzi told me something else," Chen continued. "When he was on Earth, he talked a little with a man there —this man was a passenger on his ship. He was a Linker once, but his Link was removed. Benzi gave me the man's name—I think he felt a bit sorry for him."

"How kind," Risa said acidly. "And just why did he feel compelled to tell you about this unfortunate man?"

"He seemed concerned about what might happen to him here, how he would adjust. The man was a historian, and once taught in a university. He isn't the kind of settler we usually get. As it turns out, Benzi may have done us a favor."

"How so?"

"After I spoke to Benzi," Chen said, "I asked the screen to tell me what it could of the man's public record. His name is Malik Haddad, and from what I could tell, he lost his Link only because of things he'd said or written that the Mukhtars didn't like. I went to see Theron last night and told him what I'd found out, since he'd said our school here could use a new teacher. Theron's already put in a request for the man by name, and it's been granted."

"So the children will have another teacher. Theron might have found someone who knows something more practical."

"We need all kinds of knowledge," he replied. "If he was a Linker, he'd know more than any of the teachers we've had here—we wouldn't find anyone else with his training so easily."

"A historian," she said mockingly. "What use is that?"

"We'll have our own history. We'll need people to remember it. The children here should have a chance to learn everything they can, even if they don't use much of it." He paused. "There's something else. It'll be simpler for him to live in this dome if he's going to teach at our school, and we have the space now that Noella's moved out. She and Theron would take him in if they had the room, but—I spoke to Tina and Paul. They've agreed to let him stay here, in Noella's old room."

"Here?" She shook her head. "What use can he be to us? We need someone to help with the household work."

"When he's been here a while, he can find somewhere else to live. I'll have to add a room anyway, now that Grazie's pregnant, and this Malik might be able to help with some of that work."

"I doubt that very much," Risa said. "If he was a Linker, he probably didn't dirty his hands too often." Chen had not even asked about the immigrant's more useful skills; he was simply enthralled with the notion of having a scholar in his household, a man with the learning Chen so prized.

"Malik Haddad will be here tomorrow," her father said. "I hope you'll agree with my decision and bring him here."

"He was a Linker. He might find our home a bit beneath him."

"He'll find it more comfortable than living in a tent near the bay and having to walk all that distance to our school."

She would have to agree; she had no real reason to refuse. It occurred to her that she would now have an excuse to turn Evar away when he arrived, one that even he would have to accept. "Very well," she said.

"I kept a record of Benzi's talk with me. He was sorry he couldn't talk to you, but you can view it if you like. He spoke to your grandmother when he was on Earth. You might like to hear about their talk."

"No." Her grandmother was only a distant image, and Benzi was even less than that; she preferred to keep it that way. Her own life was here, among her people, where the past did not matter.

Seven

Nikolai was saying farewell to Bogdan. Malik stood to one side as the two men embraced, then wished each other well in Russian. Nikolai stepped back; Malik clasped Bogdan's hands.

"Good luck," Malik said.

Bogdan smiled weakly. "They say you make your own luck here," the young man replied. "Mtshana. I wonder what that settlement is like." He embraced Nikolai again, then walked toward the group waiting with a Guardian by the door.

Malik and Nikolai sat down again. After arriving at the Platform, they and the others from the camp had been led to a small room adjoining one of the airship bays. Every hour or so, a Guardian had appeared to read off a list of names and then the settlement that was their destination; groups had already left for Hasseen, Kepler, Curie, and ibn-Qurrah.

The ten settlements on the surface had been named for scientists of the past, but Malik doubted that his fellow immigrants were aware of their contributions. They would not know or care about al-Khwarizmi's contributions to astronomy and algebra during the first flowering of Islamic civilization. That Tsou Yen's elemental theories, developed nearly three thousand years ago, had laid the foundations of Chinese scientific thought would be a matter of indifference to the people around him. Malik had not bothered to tell Bogdan that his new home bore the name of a man whose biological work was partly responsible for the algae used in seeding the Venusian atmosphere. The

114

names would evoke no historical musings on the part of these settlers; they were only places where a new life would be made apart from the past.

Now, except for three women who had pointedly ignored Nikolai's efforts at conversation, the two men were alone. Nikolai leaned back and folded his arms. "Guess it doesn't much matter where we end up," he murmured. "One place must be a lot like another." He closed his eyes.

They had been revived when the Habber ship docked at Anwara. Malik, like most of the others, woke with stiff muscles and a headache knifing through his skull. Anwara was three circular tubes that turned slowly around the hub where the ship had docked. When the passengers were able to move, they were conveyed by smaller vessels to Anwara's inner circle. There, a man had raced through a short speech of welcome before a few Guardians herded them to the shuttle that would carry them to the Platform. On the shuttle's screens, Malik had looked toward the planet thirty thousand kilometers away, but had seen only darkness under the bright curving crescent of the Parasol.

He glanced at the clock on the wall; he had been in this room for six hours now. The room's foodmat had given him some bread and dried fruit, and he had relieved himself in a nearby lavatory, but had not yet had a chance to remove the stubble from his face.

The door to the room opened; a female Guardian entered with a pocket screen. Malik nudged Nikolai awake as the Guardian read off three unfamiliar names and finally their own. "You'll be going to Oberg," the Guardian said. "That's not a bad place to get started."

"Why is that?" one of the women asked.

"Oberg was the first place to get settlers," the Guardian replied. "It's got more people than most of the other domed settlements, and it's kind of a center—the other nine settlements almost see it as a kind of capital."

"Lucky us," Nikolai whispered. Malik was relieved that he and Nikolai would not be separated.

The Guardian frowned at the screen. "You—Malik Haddad." She looked from Nikolai to Malik. "Do you have family or friends here?" Malik shook his head. "Well, somebody's requested you by name. That doesn't usually happen. Normally, people just get sent to where their particular skills are needed."

The women's eyes narrowed; even Nikolai seemed a bit suspicious. "I can't imagine why anyone would ask specifically for me," Malik said. "I have no connections here."

"Let's hope you can all adapt nicely." The Guardian smiled a little. "It gets to some people, being under a dome all the time—they get to feeling trapped. I've heard of a few people going to pilots and begging to be taken away."

Nikolai stood up. "That won't happen to me," he said. "I'll just remember that I finally got away from Earth."

The remark wasn't one to make to a Guardian, but she seemed indifferent to it. "Your airship leaves in half an hour," she said at last. "I'll take you to the bay."

Malik, overcome by fatigue, dozed during the airship's descent to Oberg. He awoke when Nikolai poked his arm. "We're here." The other man sounded a bit apprehensive.

Their fellow passengers were already leaving the cabin. The two men shouldered their packs and followed the others down the ramp into the large bay. Mechanics and workers ignored the new arrivals. When they reached the wide door that led into the dome, Nikolai beckoned to a gray-clad man. "Where are we supposed to go?" he called out.

"Inside and sit down near the door. Somebody'll meet you and tell you what to do."

The group left the bay. A disk of light floated far above them; a wide halo of paler light surrounded the disk before fading into blackness.

"God be praised," one of the women muttered as she gazed at the grassy land beyond the door. "We could almost be on Earth."

Malik wasn't sure he agreed. Oberg, with its cluster of buildings under the disk and small houses that dotted the landscape, might look like a town on Earth, but it did not feel like one. The warm air was thick with the odors of plant life and so still that he found himself longing for a breeze. He felt as though he were enclosed in a terrarium. He glanced toward the low wall that circled the settlement and could see only darkness through the transparent dome above the wall.

A tall blond woman approached them. "You three," she said to the women, "come with me. We'll find a place to pitch your tents, and then I'll show you where you'll be working." She led them toward the small plain of tents ahead.

Nikolai took off his pack and sat down. "I hope we won't be living here too long."

Malik seated himself next to him. A cart carrying cargo and two men rolled by along a roadway; a few workers leaving the bay ignored the seated men. He was beginning to wonder how welcome they would be. A man in a red and black sash standing near the tents caught sight of them, then hurried over.

"Welcome to Oberg," the man said as he approached; his round, dark face bore a broad smile. "When you've rested from your journey, I hope we'll have a chance to meet again. I'm a member of Ishtar, and we'll do our best to make you feel at home." Nikolai was about to rise; the man motioned to him to stay seated. "We'll be having another meeting in two days, just after last light, and I know you'll be interested in what our Guide, Kichi Timsen, has to say. Anyone can tell you how to get to her house, and I hope I'll see you there. By the way, my name's Ilom Baraka."

"What's Ishtar?" Nikolai asked, not bothering to introduce himself.

"A fellowship of those who reach out to the Spirit of this world, and who strive to be true Cytherians," Ilom replied. "We welcome all who wish to be our brothers and sisters."

Nikolai rolled his eyes. A pale young man was coming toward them now; Ilom's smile faded. "Any questions you have will be answered at the meeting," Ilom said quickly. "Farewell." He hurried away.

"Which one of you is Nikolai Burian?" the pale young man asked.

"I am," Nikolai replied.

"That fellow must have been telling you about Ishtar. Don't pay any attention."

"I didn't plan to," Nikolai responded.

"I'm Jed Severson." The man shook back his blond hair. "Your record says you worked in a greenhouse and that you're also trained in airship repairs and maintenance."

Nikolai nodded. This was a revelation to Malik; the young Russian had never mentioned his past.

"That's good," Jed Severson said. "The more skills you have, the better. You'll be working with my team in the bay, and you can earn extra credit if they need someone in the community greenhouses. After you've been here a while, you can find a household to give you a room, but for now, you'll be over here." He waved at the tents behind him. "That building back there is the pilots' dormitory—you can use their foodmats and lavatory."

Jed thrust his hands into his pockets. "I hope you're not troublemakers." He turned toward Nikolai. "I didn't see anything on your record that says you are, but I'll give you some advice. We don't have Guardians here on the surface, and we've never needed police. We don't much care to consult Counselors. The Oberg Council can handle disputes, but most people would rather settle them by themselves instead of asking for a public hearing, because the Council can be pretty quick with fines and reprimands."

"Fines and reprimands?" Nikolai shrugged. "Doesn't sound like too bad a punishment."

"Get enough reprimands, and people start treating you differently. That may not sound like much, but it can get to you in a community this size, with only about ten thousand people so far. We have to trust each other. When you lose that trust, it's hard to get it back. A reputation means something here."

"I lived in a small village," Nikolai said. "I know what that can be like."

"Make friends," Jed said, "and keep out of trouble. I wouldn't have to tell you this if you'd been picked by the Project Council or were one of those dreamy Institute graduates, but you came here from a camp."

"I thought," Nikolai muttered, "that we were all the same here."

"Oh, we are." Jed's mouth twisted. "But some think the Nomarchies are a little too free with dumping your sort here. You weren't born here, and you weren't chosen. You're here because Earth doesn't mind getting rid of you, we can use you, and you don't have anyplace else to go."

Nikolai got to his feet. "Where do I go now?"

"You can pitch your tent any time. You're free to wander around and get the feel of the place. Come to the bay tomorrow at eight, about an hour after first light—I'll meet you there."

A young woman was crossing the roadway; Jed turned to greet her. "Risa! What brings you here?"

"I'm supposed to meet an immigrant." She halted in front of Nikolai. "Malik Haddad?"

Malik stood up and touched his forehead. "I'm Malik Haddad."

"I'm Risa Liangharad."

Malik raised a brow, surprised. Benzi had briefly mentioned a sister, but it seemed an unlikely coincidence that this woman, of all people, should have come here for him. She was short, with wavy shoulder-length dark hair and a sturdy, compact body clothed in a brown shirt and pants. She resembled her Habber brother, but her brown eyes were larger than Benzi's and her cheekbones attractively broad; she was, in fact, quite pretty.

"You're not what I expected," she said in a flat voice. Her gaze was direct but cold, as if she was sure of her own position and accustomed to the respect of others.

"What did you expect?" he asked lightly, assessing her, looking for a glance or gesture that might betray some interest in him.

She continued to stare, and he could not discern even a faint gleam of interest. "Someone a little more scholarly looking, I suppose. We need a teacher in the west dome's school. That's why we requested you. You'll be living with my household."

She was assessing him, Malik realized, and she didn't look terribly pleased. He thought of how he must appear, with his unkempt hair, worn clothes, and stubbled face.

"Fortunate for you," Jed murmured, "getting a room to live in right away, and with a future Council member, too."

Risa's eyes shifted toward the blond man. "I'm not on the Council yet."

"You will be. Everyone says so."

"We'll see." She waved a hand at Malik. "You look as though you could use a bath and a meal. I hope you're not too tired to walk."

"I slept on the airship."

"I've got to get back to work," Jed said to Nikolai. "I'll see you tomorrow."

As Jed wandered toward the bay, Nikolai hoisted his pack. "He told me I have the rest of the day to myself," he said. "Do you mind if I come along with my friend here? I'd like to spend the time finding out more about Oberg."

"Are you going to be working with Jed?" she asked.

The Russian nodded. "But I was a greenhouse gardener before—that was the work I did in my village, along with homeostat repairs. I spent some of my credit learning airship repair because I wanted to get work in a port, but that was before I decided to go to a camp instead. I'm Nikolai Andreievich Burian." He smiled; Risa smiled back. Nikolai was wasting no time in telling the woman about himself.

"I don't suppose *you* know much about greenhouses." Risa glanced at Malik; he shook his head. "Too bad. Most of us have household greenhouses. It gives the Project a chance to try out new kinds of plants, and us an opportunity to earn some extra credit by selling or trading part of what we raise."

Malik looked down; apparently she had found something else to hold against him.

"Your friend Jed didn't seem all that happy with us," Nikolai said. "He doesn't seem to like people from the camps."

"It's a common feeling, but don't let it worry you. After you've been here a while, you can sit around and complain about the next arrivals. Come along with us if you like."

Nikolai smoothed back his brown hair. They followed Risa along the side of the main road; a couple of blue-clad female pilots sitting outside their dormitory waved at Risa as they passed. "One man seemed happy to see us," Nikolai said. "He told us he was in something called Ishtar and asked us to a meeting."

"Don't bother with them," she responded. "They're always trying to get their hooks into new settlers. Ishtar's a cult. They think all Cytherians should believe what they do, and they have irrational beliefs about some sort of spirit on this world that they worship."

"I believe in what I can see, nothing more."

Risa smiled a little more, obviously approving of Nikolai's answer. They were now near three large, glassy buildings set back from the main road. "Those are the main

dome's community greenhouses," Risa said. "That's where
our basic allotment comes from, and we supplement it
with what we grow in our household greenhouses. You've
got to wear a face mask when you work in there. The
plants do better with a higher percentage of carbon dioxide, and it gives us a chance to test the strains that may
thrive outside someday." She stopped to point at two long,
low buildings in back of the greenhouses. "We've got laboratories there, and the building to the right refines and
recycles. That's where we'll all end up, so useful elements
can be extracted from our bodies. Of course, you'll get
your space on one of the memorial pillars."

They walked on. "What's this Council Jed mentioned?" Nikolai asked.

"The Oberg Council. It has five members, who are
elected by the settlers in these domes. The Council listens
to complaints, settles any disputes people can't work out
privately, or appeals to the Island Administrators if necessary. Occasionally, it meets with the Councils of the other
settlements."

"And everyone here picks the members? They aren't
chosen by the Administrators?"

"No," Risa said. "This is our home. If we have a problem specialists should handle, we go to them, but we make
our own decisions about a lot of things. When you've been
here for two years, you'll get to vote as well."

"We heard everyone has a say here," Nikolai said. "I'm
glad to know it's true."

She glanced at him. "I'm always surprised at how
many of you come here knowing so little about us."

"What do we have to know, except that we'll be freer
here and able to build something for ourselves?"

"Come with me." The three crossed the road and
moved toward the low wall at the base of the dome. "Look
out there."

Malik peered through the dome. Lightning flashed for
a second, revealing black, barren mountains so high he
could see no valleys below. Droplets of acid rain glistened
on the impermeable dome surface; in the distance, on
another rocky shelf, he glimpsed the faint glow of another
settlement. He had assumed that one reason for using a
transparent material for these domes was to keep the settlers from feeling too closed in, but this sight made him

uneasy and aware of how precarious humanity's hold on this world was.

"We have our limits, Nikolai," Risa continued. "The Mukhtars may often be far from our thoughts, but we aren't exactly free to do as we please. Out there, the atmospheric pressure would crush you, the heat would boil your blood, and the rain would eat away at your bones. Every time there's a quake, the dome's able to withstand it, but we have to send out our diggers and crawlers to make sure rocks are cleared away, and then see that none of our installations have been damaged."

She turned around and leaned against the wall. "Oberg has three domes with settlers and a fourth being made ready for more, but everything we build has to be maintained. Every Cytherian, including the children, learns at least one skill that can aid the community as a whole. Every action has to be measured against certain limits. You may, like many immigrants, be wondering why we don't clear more land for houses here so that you don't have to live in a tent, but those trees and plants help to maintain our oxygen level inside. We have a small lake in the center of the west dome, but it isn't there just for our pleasure—it and the streams you'll see keep the air from becoming too arid." She paused. "Much of the work we do involves simply trying to hang on to what we have."

"You almost make it sound like Earth," Nikolai said.

She shook her head. "Not quite. You'll have a chance to learn more than you would have there because that may make you a wiser and more valuable citizen. You'll be rewarded for good work, not just with credit, but with the respect others will give you if you earn it. You can make your life what you want it to be, instead of letting the Mukhtars and their representatives decide that for you. You can know that your children have a dream and a purpose. That's our real freedom—to know that our children will have more."

"I guess that's enough for me," Nikolai responded. "I don't mind work, as long as there's some reason for it. I couldn't see living and dying and making no difference to anybody, and that's what it was like where I was."

Risa was clearly devoted to her world. She seemed, Malik thought, totally without guile, unlike most of the people he had known. "You must be an inspiration to your own children," he said.

Her eyes grew colder. "I have no children."

"Surely some young man has made a pledge to you by now."

"No."

"In your case," Malik said, "with your attributes, certainly a temporary state of affairs."

She gazed at him indifferently. "My home's in the west dome," she said in a toneless voice. "I share it with my father, his companion Bettina Christies, and her son, Paul. The woman Paul loves is pregnant now, so she'll be joining us when she becomes his bondmate." She moved away from the wall and led them toward the main road again.

"When did you come here?" Nikolai asked.

"I was born on Island Two. I came here with my father when I was eight, with the first settlers. My mother died some time earlier." She fell silent, apparently determined to say nothing about her mother's deeds or the brother who had become a Habber.

They neared a slope that led from the road toward an opening under the wall. Risa nodded and smiled at a group of women as they walked by, then went ahead into the tunnel.

Risa's house was smaller than Malik had expected. He glanced around at the common room and the narrow hallways on either side of it, wondering where she would find space for him.

"That's Bettina's wing." Risa pointed to her left. "She has a small examining room where she can see people with complaints—she's a physician. We added a small lavatory for her recently. That's a bit of a luxury, but sometimes her patients need to use it. Our bathroom's over there, second door to the right." She turned toward the other hallway. "Which one of you wants to wash first?"

Nikolai chuckled. "Do we reek that much?"

"I've smelled worse."

"Go ahead, Malik," Nikolai said expansively. "I could use a meal, if you don't mind."

Malik walked to the hallway, noting the space as he moved toward the bathroom; these rooms had to be small. In the bathroom, there was barely enough space to set down his pack. The water in the tiny stall was tepid, and probably recycled. When he had finished bathing, he slapped depilatory cream to his face, wiped off his beard, and changed into clean clothes.

As he left the bathroom, he heard laughter in the common room. Risa and Nikolai were seated on the floor in front of a low table, eating from a tray filled with vegetables and pieces of bread. The Russian seemed to be making himself at home; Malik was surprised at how much that irritated him.

"Not bad," Nikolai said as he munched on some bread.

"Our food used to be pretty dull," Risa said, "but we've learned more ways of storing and preparing it. The community greenhouses grow a lot of beans and peanuts, along with enriched dwarf strains of wheat and rice. We've got beets, cabbage, parsley, onions, tomatoes, and some households keep rabbits and goats. We don't really need the protein from their meat and milk, since we can get enough from some of the other foods, but the animals can eat things we can't, and they do add some variety to our diet. It's also simpler than building vats to manufacture animal protein, the way the Islands do."

"What about your own greenhouse?" Nikolai asked.

"I've been doing pretty well with berries and spices, but I raise some basic foods, too. I trade some of the surplus or exchange it for credit."

"I wouldn't mind seeing your greenhouse." Nikolai got to his feet. "But I'd better wash up while I have the chance."

He left the room; Malik seated himself. Risa pushed the food toward him. "The experiment seems to be going well," he murmured as he helped himself to some bread.

"Experiment?"

"I meant these domes. They are a kind of experiment, since the terraforming of Venus could have gone on without them. The Islands were here, and people could have waited out the centuries for Venus to cool before building surface settlements. In a way, they're here partly for political reasons—a lot of people working for the Project, especially common workers who saw a chance for a different kind of life, became impatient and didn't want to wait."

"Why should they have waited?" Risa pushed back a

loose curl of dark hair. "They had the means to build these domes, and people willing to live in them."

"I was only saying—"

"We're the ones who are really committed to this Project. The Islanders—well—it doesn't mean the same thing to them."

"Surely they're equally devoted to this Project."

"In their own way, but most of them are specialists. Sometimes you get the feeling that their scientific work means more to them than the Project as a whole, and I don't know if it's wise for some of them to be as close to the Habbers as they are."

"If you work with someone, it's natural to form friendships."

"I doubt that Habbers really know what friendship is." She poured him a cup of herb tea. "Your record says you were a teacher," she continued. "We need a teacher in our west dome school, and since my friend Noella Sanger's moved out, we have room for you here. She's living with Theron Hyland, the teacher who put in the request for you. I'll introduce you to both of them tomorrow."

"I was a historian," Malik said. "I'm not sure why you need me here. Don't your young people go to the Islands for more specialized training?"

"Yes, but we don't need you for that. You're here to teach the small children. We have screens, of course, and a lot of recorded materials, but teachers can guide and motivate the students. They gain so much more in a group than if they only pursued their lessons alone, and here every child has a chance to attend a school. It's important work, Malik. Earth only gives such an opportunity to the most promising children."

He felt disappointed; he had imagined older students already past their early training. "I don't know if I'm suited for that, Risa. I taught in a university. I—"

"You can read, and you must have studied other things before you specialized. There's not much chance that we'll get someone with your kind of training too often. You should do well enough."

"I've never taught children."

She frowned. "Maybe you think that because you were a Linker, you're entitled to something else. I didn't see that you have many other useful skills. You're lucky to get work that'll win you some respect. What did you expect, anyway?"

"I suppose," he said slowly, "that I must be grateful."

"There isn't much else you can do here—even the Islands don't have much use for historians, as far as I know. And isn't history just a bunch of stories the Mukhtars would like people to believe?"

He was stung. "Not in my case. The Mukhtars didn't much care for some of my writings. That's why I lost my Link—one of the reasons, anyway."

"Well, you can write what you like here. Most won't be interested enough to pay it much mind."

Her bluntness and frigid stare were annoying; he was beginning to see why, attractive as she was physically, no man had warmed enough to her to make a pledge. "That's very reassuring," he snapped. "It's always good to know that no one cares about what one does."

She flushed a little and lowered her eyes. "I shouldn't have put it quite that way. I only meant that you wouldn't be bothered about it." She paused. "My father has some records. He brought them along when we came here— they're mostly records of my mother, messages, what she did and thought. He probably wouldn't mind showing some of them to you. My mother is something of a historical patron saint to people here."

"Iris Angharads," he said. Risa looked up; her eyes widened a little. "I know a little about her. A mind-tour producer on Earth was hoping to use her story in a historical mind-tour about Venus—your father's, too."

"With appropriate distortions, no doubt." She sighed, apparently unimpressed. "Actually, you're here now because my father learned about you from a Habber pilot. I might as well tell you—you'll learn soon enough. My father had a son who abandoned the Project to join the Habbers. He sent a message here and told Chen about you, and my father went to Theron with the news."

He stiffened in surprise. "Benzi did that? I spoke to your brother on Earth, but I didn't think—"

"I don't need to hear anything about him." Her voice was once more cold and toneless. "He broke his bond with us, and there's no reason I should care about him—I never knew him anyway. He's just another Habber now."

"You have Habbers working with you here. The Project couldn't have come this far without their help."

"They're useful. That doesn't mean I have to like them. Maybe they think they can use us against Earth someday, but I don't care about that as long as we get whatever aid we need from them."

He was not off to a good start with this woman. His learning was of little interest to her, and his brief acquaintance with her brother was another mark against him.

"I'm sorry," she said suddenly. "I am being a bit rude, aren't I? No one's ever accused me of being excessively friendly, but I don't usually act this way. It's just that—"

"I'm not what you expected."

She poked at a vegetable. "No, you're not."

"I'll do my best to be useful," he said. "People here must think something of you if they're planning to put you on the Council."

"People come to me for advice, and I try to be honest and fair with them—I suppose that's why. Some see me as a little bit like a Counselor. Actually, I get advice from an old man who was once an Administrator—he's almost like another father to me. His name's Pavel Gvishiani. He's made his own mistakes, but I guess he's learned from them."

Malik tensed. He had not known that Pavel Gvishiani was still alive. He was going to ask about him when Nikolai entered the room.

"I feel better already," the younger man said. "Mind if I look at the greenhouse now?"

Risa stood up, obviously relieved to see him. "I'll show it to you." The two hurried to the door. "Would you like to come along?"

"No, thank you." The door closed behind them; Nikolai would appreciate some time alone with her. Malik nibbled at a sweet pepper. Nikolai was ingratiating himself as quickly as possible; Risa probably preferred his company to Malik's. A sturdy man with practical talents was more valuable here than a learned former Linker. He smiled at his wounded vanity. He had felt some desire for Risa when she spoke to him more warmly, but that was only a response born of old habits. He would have to live here for a while, and it would be easier without entanglements.

He surveyed the room. A small table in one corner

held small blocks of wood, chisels, and a knife; a lump of clay was being molded into a face. A cloth was draped over another object.

"It's a hobby," a voice said as the door whispered open. A small Chinese man was walking toward him; his hair was gray, and he carried a small tool chest. "I saw a young man going into the greenhouse with my daughter, but I assume you're the teacher. I saw your image while listening to your record."

"I am," Malik replied. "You saw Nikolai Burian—he lived with me in the camp." He was about to stand; the old man held out a hand, motioning him to stay seated. "I'm Malik Haddad."

"Liang Chen." The old man set down his tool chest. "Maybe you'd like to see a little of my carving. I don't have any training, but it's something I always enjoyed. Risa's mother used to say it's because I'm not good with words and have to let my hands speak for me, and she was right."

Chen removed the cloth and held up a carving of two long-necked birds with webbed feet; the head of one bird rested against the neck of the other.

"That's beautiful work," Malik said, marveling at the detail of the feathers on one outstretched wing.

Chen covered the carving again. "It's a gift," he said. "I don't want Paul to see it yet—he's the son of my friend Bettina, and I'll give it to him and his new bondmate when they've made their pledge. When I was a boy on Earth, the people in my village sometimes gave a pair of geese to a young couple. Geese mate for life, so it was a way to wish the couple well. We don't have those birds here, so this bit of wood will have to do."

Chen sat down on a cushion near Malik. "Has Risa told you about your work?"

Malik nodded. "It seems I'm here to teach the children. She didn't tell me much more than that."

"We were lucky to get you."

"Maybe not. I haven't taught young children before."

"You'll find ways, as long as they want to learn. I never had much learning myself. Screen lessons taught me a little reading after we got settled here, but my mind's too old for much new learning." The wrinkles around Chen's eyes deepened as he frowned. "Risa had the chance, but she left school early—she said learning more wouldn't be useful."

Malik could not tell if the man was disappointed with his daughter or simply stating a fact. "Risa doesn't sound like an unschooled person to me."

"She was always quick, and her teachers praised her, but she said she could learn whatever else she wanted to know by herself. I wanted more for her, but—" Chen shrugged. "She has what she wants, and she's respected by people. She may be on our Council soon, and that will make her an important person here."

"I know a little about your life," Malik said, "what you and your bondmate Iris did. That must make you a person of some importance yourself."

The old man smiled. "I saw a danger and did what I could. It's no more than anyone else would have done. I never wanted power over others, or to be near those who had it—it fills them up until there's no room for anything else, and makes them see others as only pieces in a game. From where they stand, that must seem what life's all about."

Chen was better with words than he had admitted, and his sentiments reflected Malik's. He thought of what Risa had told him about Pavel Gvishiani. Clearly, she did not share her father's views and probably saw Pavel's deeds in a different light.

Was the disgraced Administrator once again trying for some power or influence through Risa or others? Malik felt apprehensive at the thought. He did not want to be near power of any kind again, where someone with influence might strike at an enemy through him, and yet its attraction was still there. He could be tempted by his desire to be respected and honored once again.

By the time Nikolai and Risa returned from the greenhouse, she was calling him Kolya. When the Russian left, just before dark, he was promising to visit again soon.

Risa then led Malik to his room, where he managed to conceal his dismay; the enclosure was not much larger than one of his closets in Amman. Drawers were set into one wall; a bed with a large drawer under its mattress sat under a small, curtained window. A cushion was in one

corner; he saw no other furnishings except for a clothes rod
and a few hangers.

"I hope this will do," Risa said. "We're still working on
designs that might give more of an illusion of space, and
the houses we have are relatively easy to build and to
expand if we need more rooms. You're probably used to
more."

"I'm sure I'll be comfortable," he said, wondering
what other illusions he would have to accept. "All this
room might need is a large wall screen with a mirrored
surface. The mirror would give you a feeling of space, and
you could call up landscapes for—"

"It would cost," she said flatly. "Some might also find it
a bit ostentatious."

She left him alone to get settled. After hanging his
clothes on the rod and storing his other belongings in the
drawers, he went back to the common room.

The other residents of the house had returned and
were already gathering around the low table for supper.
Risa introduced Malik to the others. Bettina Christies was a
plain, narrow-faced, middle-aged woman with reddish-
blond hair; her son, Paul Bettinas, had hair like hers, but he
was stockier in build. Paul had brought along a young
woman named Grazie Lauro who was to become his
bondmate; she was slender, dark-haired, and took every
opportunity to hold Paul's hand or to gaze into his eyes as
they ate.

"We don't stand on formality," Bettina said as she
handed Malik a plate of bread. "We're usually all here for
the evening meal, but if you're late or have to eat earlier,
just go to the kitchen and fetch a meal for yourself. You do
know how to cook."

"A little."

"Well, there's always bread, and you can help yourself
to the stored fruits and vegetables. We don't have a foodmat in the house, but the school and some of the larger
buildings do." She peered across the table at Malik with
her pale blue eyes. "You look healthy enough, but then,
you wouldn't be here if the Platform Guardians found
anything on your scan."

"The Platform Guardians? I was scanned before I left
Earth, but no one at the Platform gave us even a basic
med-scan."

Risa let out her breath. "They're getting careless again," she said angrily. "We've told them over and over—"

Bettina raised a hand. "It's unlikely that he picked up anything during the journey, but I'll do a scan now, just to be safe. Come with me." Malik rose and followed the physician from the room. "It's probably best to be careful," she continued. "Anything contagious could spread quite rapidly in a settlement."

The examining room, with its desk, stool, cushion, and padded table, was not much larger than Malik's room. He sat on the table while Bettina passed her med-scanner over him. "What kinds of medical problems do you treat here?" Malik asked.

"Accidents, usually—chemical burns, broken bones, pulled muscles, that kind of thing. Everyone's scheduled for a routine scan with a physician once a year, and the older folks who need it get their rejuv shots to clear out their protein cross-linkages. I can treat a lot of things here or in the patient's home, but anything more serious gets sent over to the main dome's infirmary. More serious than that, and you get bumped up to one of the Islands, to the real medical specialists. Had one patient who lost an arm when something fell on him during a quake, so he went to Island Three for a prosthetic replacement. And I deliver babies, of course. My son's able to handle that, too—he's a paramedic—but some expectant mothers don't want a man with them when they're giving birth. It was like that on the North American Plains, where I came from. We always thought it was bad luck if a man was in the room during childbirth."

"And if it's something the Island physicians can't treat?" Malik said.

"Then you live with it, or die with it, and we do what we can to make you comfortable. It costs the Project too much to do anything else—we can't ship every disabled or dying person back to Earth. Frankly, we don't have a lot of the equipment you'd find in the average city hospital on Earth, even though some of the Habbers have helped with a few difficult cases, and that's why we stress prevention. I can't tell you how many times I've told people to be more careful doing their work or to take some basic precautions when the seismologists have predicted a quake."

She sat down at the desk and stared at her small screen. "Just what I expected—there's nothing the matter with you. You look just as good inside as you do on the outside." She lifted her head and batted her eyes a little; he remembered that she was a Plainswoman and probably used to flirting.

They returned to the common room; Malik noticed that Risa had left the table. "Where's Risa?" Bettina asked.

"Leilani came by," Grazie answered. "She wanted to talk with Risa alone, outside."

"About that bondmate of hers, I expect." Bettina sat down and gazed affectionately at Chen. "Turkan Belis told me today he'd like to have you do a carving of his daughter."

Chen looked up. "If she'll sit still long enough, which she won't."

"Do her from memory, then."

Chen shook his head. "I'll have to ask for a holo image to look at."

"Chen does very well with his carvings," Grazie murmured as she slipped her hand into Paul's. "He'd do even better if he demanded more credit for them. He still gets requests from some of the Islanders."

"I'd do them for no credit at all," Chen said.

"Hush," Paul said. "You don't want people to know that."

The group was soon pursuing the topic of Paul and Grazie's upcoming ceremony to mark their pledge. It appeared that the ceremony would be small, with only the household and Grazie's family in attendance, since Paul seemed anxious to avoid any showy displays. Malik listened as he sipped tea, wondering at the young couple's certainty about their life together; they were to pledge a bond for twenty years.

"You're invited, too," Paul said to Malik, "since you'll be part of this household, at least temporarily."

"I'm honored."

"A lot of the unattached young women will probably drop by when they get a glimpse of him." Bettina smiled at Malik. "Maybe even some of the attached. Better look out, Malik—you don't want somebody's bondmate to bear you a grudge. And if Kichi Timsen spots you, she'll have all those fools in Ishtar trying to get you to their rites."

The comments about his appearance depressed him. He knew little of these people's customs and no longer held a position that could protect him from the consequences of an unwise dalliance. He thought of Yekaterina and how he had felt fleetingly that a bond with one woman might give him some peace.

He stood up. "If you'll excuse me—I haven't seen your dome after dark. I'd like to take a look." He went to the door and stepped outside.

The air felt cooler; he might almost have been enjoying a moonlit night on Earth. Birds twittered in the trees beyond the door; three children raced by along the main path. Above the trees, the pale disk seemed to float on the darkness. Risa stood under a tree, speaking to a taller woman; the shadows were too dark for him to see their faces.

A desire for Risa came into him. He supposed that he only wanted the comfort of another body near his; it was a longing mixed up with loneliness and the memories of other women who had once shared his bed and who seemed so distant now.

The other woman was leaving. He waited, then walked toward Risa; she folded her arms and leaned against the tree, hidden in its shadow.

"Just a talk?" he asked. "Or did she need your advice?"

"Advice, and some help."

"What's her problem?"

"I don't talk about what people say to me—that's one reason I'm trusted. I try to be fair, and I don't take bribes."

"I wouldn't think there'd be much to bribe with here."

"Oh, you'd be surprised," she said. "Nobody'd use credits, of course—that would show up on the records. But people can offer a service of some kind or try to give you something they own. I never accept any of those offers. I listen and I give advice, and if there's a dispute, I make a decision."

"But how can you enforce your decisions?" he asked. "You don't have any real authority."

"If they disagree with me, they can always take the matter to the Council and ask for a hearing. Usually, people will go along with what I advise, because it's simpler and keeps the matter off the public record—no one wants a blot on their record. My advice often works well. People know that."

"They could go to Counselors," he said. "That's what they're there for, to handle certain problems."

"We consult them as little as possible. We take pride in settling our own affairs, but it isn't just that. We don't much trust Counselors, and we haven't got any on the surface— they're all on the Islands, the few of them that are needed there now. We prefer not to give the Islanders any excuse to decide we can't govern ourselves."

"You're all part of the Project. Surely the Administrators concern themselves with what happens down here."

"They're Islanders. They can seem quite distant from our concerns. Anyway, they have to worry about what Earth wants, rather than what might be best for us."

"And why do people come to you?" he asked.

"It started when I was younger," she replied. "A couple of people asked me for advice. I guess they thought I had some special wisdom—they told others, and people began coming to me."

"Perhaps your mother's reputation—"

"That has nothing to do with it." Her voice was harder. "Well, maybe in the beginning—Pavel told me that Iris used to intercede with him for some of the Islanders she knew, and others trusted her judgment, but I've earned the respect I get."

"What kinds of problems do they have?"

"Oh, someone on a team is slacking off at work, or a household has a disagreement about who's supposed to do a chore, or a couple of people have an agreement over how to divide the proceeds from a private greenhouse garden and never bothered to make a record of that agreement, so I have to come up with something that's fair. Those are the easy ones."

"What are the hard ones like?" he asked.

"Someone may want to sever a bond. Usually, people will settle for separating, to avoid the trouble of a hearing and looking as though they used bad judgment in selecting a bondmate in the first place. Often, they just need some time apart to sort things out, but if not, I try to work out a fair arrangement. That isn't easy when you have children and other members of the household involved, along with the problem of where one of the bondmates is going to live afterward. We take our bonds very seriously here."

"Anything else?"

"Sometimes something's stolen," Risa said. "You wouldn't think anybody would steal when it's pretty certain it'll be discovered, but it happens. Usually the victim has a good idea of who the thief is, and I can just go to the suspect and point out how hard life can get when a person isn't trusted. That's usually enough to get the object back, because nobody wants a charge like that on a public record."

"And what if you don't know who the thief might be?"

"I let it be known that if the thief's found out, the matter will be settled in a public hearing. You'd be surprised at how many stolen objects suddenly turn up after that. Besides, having a stolen object is useless if you can't use it openly, and everyone knows it's been stolen—you'd always worry about who might see it."

"But what kinds of punishment do you have?"

"Reparations," Risa said, "payments in credit or goods, or a service of some kind to repair any damage that's been done. If there's a public hearing, a note about the offense in the offender's record. That may not sound like much to you, but we have to trust one another, and when that's lost, you don't get it back so easily. We tend to look the other way if some wrongdoers suffer at the hands of people they've wronged badly enough."

She thrust her hands into her pockets. "It works well enough. The proof is that most of us get along most of the time. We've had only a few cases of violence without cause, and if it looks as though the offender might repeat such acts, we call in a Counselor."

Risa stepped out from the tree's shadow. "We've done all right so far," she continued, "but sometimes I worry about what may come. We don't want Guardians here, and we have no police. We certainly can't spare people to guard prisoners or spare the resources to build a prison. All we have to restrain anyone is a sense of obligation to others or fear for their records and reputations. That's been enough, but it might not always be. It's why some of us aren't too happy about accepting people from those camps. They weren't born here, and they haven't been through the same selection process as those picked for the

Project or those who come here from the Cytherian Institute."

"Troublemakers in the camps aren't likely to get here." Malik hoped that was true; he had not been in a camp long enough to know. "People from the camps gave up everything to get to Venus—they'd hardly throw their chance at a new life away."

"And you?" she said. "You wouldn't have gone to a camp, judging by your record, unless everything was taken from you. I don't suppose your choice was entirely voluntary."

"I lost much, but no one forced me to go to that camp."

"Do you want to walk?" she said suddenly. "I can show you a little of the settlement."

"I'd enjoy that." He was about to take her arm, but she moved toward the small path in front of the house before he could reach for her. They walked toward the main path, then turned left. The other houses, like Risa's, sat several paces back from this walkway, with trees shielding them from their neighbors. Four children were playing a game in front of one house; near a greenhouse, a young couple was sharing a meal outside.

"There aren't many people about," he murmured.

"They're doing household chores or having supper or getting ready to sleep. A few will be taking their turn on the darktime shift."

"You seemed to be getting along with Kolya," he said, "and he apparently likes you." She did not reply. "But perhaps another man has a claim on your affections."

"There's a pilot I've been seeing, but I find his talk of Ishtar insufferable. I'd never be able to stand years of listening to it. He's been persistent, but I didn't hear from him at all today, so maybe he's finally getting the message."

"Surely others have paid court."

She smiled at his turn of phrase. "Not really. You sound a bit like a settler already. People do find it strange when you don't make a pledge as soon as possible with a likely prospect. Some women wait until they decide to become pregnant, like Grazie, and others become bondmates first and wait a while for children, but it comes to the same thing. All of us want to leave descendants to live on the world we make—there wouldn't be much point in being here otherwise, unless you're a specialist who can find similar satisfactions in your work."

"Then you'll assuredly find a bondmate in time."

"And what about you?" She glanced sideways at him. "Your record didn't note any bondmate, but then, with your looks, you probably had too many opportunities. There would always have been another woman for you." She had hit close to the truth. "Maybe men, too, for all I know."

He shook his head. "Men never interested me in that way."

"That's just as well. Not that it matters to me, you understand, but many people here brought the prejudices of their old homes with them."

"I suppose it's easier to fit in here if one tries not to offend others too openly, even if there's no real reason for anyone to take offense."

"True enough. As I told your friend Kolya, there are freedoms we don't yet have. It can be a hard life for those who have trouble conforming."

He could now see a lake in the distance, shimmering under the silver light of the dome. "We've just begun to stock the lake with fish," Risa said. "If it's successful, we'll have another source of protein." She pointed to her right. "The school's over there—you can't see it, but it's just past the trees on that side of the lake. We'd better head back—I have to be up early tomorrow, and Theron will want to meet with you."

They began to retrace their steps. "Maybe I should give you some advice, Malik, because you look like a man who's used to the attentions of women. We value our bonds, as I've said. It'd be wiser for you to avoid any entanglements with women who have bondmates—most of them, anyway. There are a few who have different arrangements or provisions in their pledges that allow them other companions occasionally, but they're usually discreet about that. You might meet a pilot who's in Oberg between trips and doesn't mind a bed-partner for a couple of days, or someone like Tina who scorns bonds, although there aren't so many like her here. And there are the Habbers who work with us here—they don't seem to care about formal ties at all. But you probably shouldn't seek them out unless you have to work with them. Maybe Islanders don't mind being close to Habbers they work with, but they're not like us."

"And are Islanders so close to the Habbers?" he asked.

"Some are. I imagine the only reason the Project Council looks the other way is that they think the Islanders may learn more about Habbers if the Council ignores it."

"Since people here value your advice," he said, "I'll take it. There will be enough other things to keep me occupied, and perhaps I'll find companionship among the unattached."

"Anyone who's unattached will be regarding you as a potential bondmate. Don't mislead anybody about your intentions."

"I'm not a child," he said. "I don't lack experience in these matters."

"You were a Linker. You probably did as you liked."

"I didn't delude my companions. They knew what I was like from the start. Sometimes I wished for something more, but God has not yet ordained such an attachment for me." He moved closer to her and took her arm gently. "There might be a few pleasant moments for you and me while we wait to see what is written for us."

She halted, then withdrew her arm from his. "You'll be living in my house for a while. Things'll be simpler if we keep our distance."

"Very well. I'll respect your wishes." He felt a little disappointed, but the young woman might change her mind when she knew him better. There were pleasures to be had in anticipating a future encounter; when their time together palled, Nikolai might be waiting to claim her.

She gazed at him pensively, almost pityingly. Maybe she was feeling sorry for a man who had come here more as an exile than a settler; perhaps his attributes held no attraction for her. She was one who might win a place on the Council of these people, while he had no credits, few skills, and no position except as a teacher of children; he was hardly what she would call a likely prospect. A dalliance with him would lead nowhere, and she was clearly a practical woman; she might even regret that her household had not requested the sturdy Nikolai instead.

He felt a twinge of jealousy and was surprised that he could feel it.

Eight

The eighth day of Risa's shift at the west dome's External Operations Center began with a minor quake, which the seismologists had predicted for sometime that day. She waited outside the building with her team as the ground trembled slightly, then entered. No alarms had sounded; the damage to their installations, if any, was probably minor. The Maxwell Mountains rarely endured a severe quake; that had been one of the reasons for building settlements here, even though the domes could easily withstand great shocks.

In the consistent, temperate climate of the domes, houses did not have to protect them from weather. Most of the structures were made of light materials, and the houses were only one story in height. Often it was not possible to wait out an expected quake outside, in an open area away from trees. A wall of one house near Risa's had collapsed a couple of years earlier; the residents trapped inside had suffered only a few bruises.

Alasid ibn-Faraki, the head of her team, was reassuring Sarah Shirer, a young woman who had come to Oberg only a few months ago. "That one was nothing," he said as they walked through the hall. "The Center's built to take much stronger shocks than that."

"What if the dome goes?" Sarah asked.

Alasid shrugged as he pressed a door open. "Then it's God's will."

"Or a mistake in engineering," Risa muttered; she did not find Alasid's Islamic fatalism very comforting. "But the Habbers contributed a lot to the dome design, and they

139

don't make mistakes—not about that sort of thing, anyway. Besides, there's no point in worrying about it."

The room where she worked here was filled with screens, consoles, and small platforms that served as desks. Risa sat down on the chair in front of her station, checked to make sure that everything was secured against the inevitable aftershock, then picked up her band and put it around her head.

She was viewing the mountain plateau outside through a robot's eyes and seemed to feel its squat body around her as it rolled forward. Lights swept through the thick, dark mist as diggers and crawlers, ghostly tractors and tanks on treads, moved over the flat, rocky land. The domes of Oberg stood near the center of this wide plateau, which had been carved out near the peak of one vast mountain. The machines moved west, toward a high cliff where Oberg had a small-scale mining operation; the mined materials would be conveyed to the west dome's small digger and crawler bay before being taken to the main dome for refining. The robot was following the crawlers and diggers; if one of the larger machines developed a problem outside, the robot would be there to replace any failing components.

Tiny lines as thin as hairs danced before her eyes. The plate through which the robot viewed the world was already slightly scarred by the hot, acidic droplets of rain that fell through the mist; it would have to be replaced before long. To the southwest, just beyond that edge of the rocky plain, she could barely see a distant, eerie glow on another plateau where the domes of al-Khwarizmi stood. On a shelf of rock near that settlement, one awesome installation was hidden in the darkness, one Risa had seen only on the screen: the vast, square structure where the domes themselves were made. That building dwarfed the settlements and seemed almost like another mountain itself. Habber machines had erected the structure and maintained it. When another dome was ready, the roof would open and a fleet of airships equipped with cables would carry the dome to a prepared site.

The atmospheric pressure, even after centuries of terraforming, was still forty times as great as Earth's. She would view this landscape only from inside a dome, in images on a screen, or through the eyes of a machine.

Risa closed the channel to the robot; a signal would alert her when it needed to make its repairs and her intervention might be required. She was now gazing at a room of panels and thick pipes, looking out through the eyes of a robot inside one of the life-support installations. In this bunker, which abutted the dome wall, nitrogen needed to feed the dome's atmosphere was extracted from traces of ammonia in the misty rain collected by the installation. Nitrogen had once been a scarce element on Venus, but ammonia from Saturn was present in the compressed hydrogen sent here from that planet.

A few panels were likely to fail soon. The robot's claws, guided by Risa, carefully lifted one panel from the wall and quickly replaced it with another. She frowned. Cyberminds could have handled much of this work, but the cost to the Project would have been greater. Cheaper to use human beings wherever possible and to let the settlers return more to the Project with their labor. They had chosen to settle this world and could feel that they had a greater role in making it.

Malik Haddad had called these settlements an experiment; perhaps the work, however necessary, was also a way to test the Cytherians. She pushed that notion away. Thinking about the new immigrant was distracting; thoughts of Malik made her feel uneasy and uncertain. She forced her attention back to her work.

By the end of her eight-hour shift, with two short breaks and a longer one for a meal, Risa had finished replacing the panels inside the bunker and had made a minor repair on one of the diggers outside. She lifted her band from her head and set it down. Her muscles ached from the hours in her chair; the walk home and a quiet dinner with her household would refresh her. She had one day off ahead, and then eight days working in the west dome's community greenhouses, where the work would be soothing in comparison.

Alasid nodded at her. "Enjoy your day off," the young man said.

"You're sure you don't need me back tomorrow?" she asked.

He seemed surprised. "There's nothing the next team

can't handle. What is it, Risa—trying to prove yourself, now that you're off-duty on the Bats?"

"I just wanted to be certain," she murmured before leaving the room. She had planned to spend the next day doing household tasks; it was likely she and Malik would be alone in the house part of the time, after he came back from the school. That prospect made her uncomfortable; she did not want to examine the reasons for her unease too closely.

The west dome's External Operations Center was much smaller than the one in the main dome, hardly larger than a good-sized house. It sat about twenty meters from a small bridge over a stream that fed the lake. Risa had crossed the bridge and was moving toward the wooded area used as a park before she recalled that she had promised to visit Andrew Dinel on her way home.

Andrew's house was just past the park, on a small hill overlooking the lake. The house seemed larger than when she had last visited; more space had been added to one wing. Andrew Dinel's household was looking a bit too prosperous lately; his house had to be one of the largest ones here.

She frowned as she came closer to the front door and saw its tiny lens; Andrew had installed a scanner. Most of the settlers had contented themselves with simple metal locks until recently; a palm-print lock was only another device to be tended and repaired. But thefts, almost unknown a few years ago, were slightly more common, and even she had given in to Chen's insistence on a palm-print lock. Yet, having a scanner, and a record of everyone who came to call, seemed too much.

She supposed this was progress of a kind—having a few more items someone might be tempted to steal and therefore a few more thefts.

She waited until the door opened. Usually someone came to the door to greet her, but perhaps Andrew's household was growing too grand for that small courtesy. This common room was somewhat larger than her own but so cluttered that it seemed smaller. Andrew's two sons and their three cousins sat on cushions around one low table, reading lessons on their screens. His bondmate, Grete Soong, sat at her sewing machine, working on a shirt. A shelf near the large screen contained two small boxes holding a microdot library—an obvious affectation, since Andrew himself could not read much more than his name and the numbers that helped him keep track of his accounts. A carving of Chen's sat next to the library; her father had captured Andrew's fine-featured face well but had given his eyes a slightly predatory look.

"Risa!" Grete looked up from her sewing. "Andy said you'd be by today." Andrew's bondmate was a pretty, dark-haired woman with a slightly glazed expression in her brown eyes. "Say hello to Risa," she shouted to the children.

"Hello," one of the boys said tonelessly. The other boy and the three girls looked up, mumbled a greeting, then resumed staring at their screens.

"I won't be staying long," Risa said. "I want to get home for supper."

"Sorry you can't eat with us, but I can see why you'd want to dine with that new teacher instead. My nieces are so taken with him. Marta says he looks just like a hero in one of those adventures she likes to watch on the screen."

"Grete!" one of the girls wailed as the other children snickered.

"Now, you know it's true, Marta. You couldn't stop talking about him."

"Let's hope his looks give them an incentive to do well at their lessons," Risa murmured. "Where's Andrew?"

"Oh." Grete waved a hand languidly to her right. "Just go down this hall, second door to your left. Now that we've added more space, Andy has his own little room for seeing his friends or going over the accounts. So much nicer than using our bedroom or having everyone clear out of the common room."

"How convenient," Risa said, wondering how many more affectations Andrew would acquire. "I'm glad to see you're doing so well."

"No better than you, I'm sure," Grete replied politely.

Risa walked into the narrow hallway and paused in front of the door before knocking. "Andy? It's Risa."

The door slid open. Andrew Dinel sat on a cushion, staring at the small screen on his lap. A voice was reciting numbers; Risa caught a glimpse of a graph and the blue and red lines that marked the household's credit and debits before Andrew turned off the screen. He looked up.

"Come on in, Risa. Hope Paul and Grazie got my message of congratulations."

"Of course." Risa seated herself on another cushion. A second carving of Chen's, this one of Grete, sat on a small table in one corner of the tiny room. She had never known whether Andrew actually appreciated her father's carvings or had bought them only because others considered them valuable.

"I would have come over myself to wish Paul well, but this is the first free moment I've had in days, and it'll be like this until we finish that tunnel." Andrew ran a digger, and his team was now working on a tunnel that would connect the still-uninhabited south dome of Oberg with the one to the southeast. "What with that and my household work—well, you know how it is."

She studied him for a moment; he was wearing his usual affable expression. He was a tall, lanky man with thinning brown hair, but his stomach was showing signs of a paunch and his fine-boned face was developing jowls—perhaps less-welcome signs of prosperity.

"There's a problem we have to discuss," Risa said. "I spoke to Leilani a few evenings ago and promised her I'd speak to you."

"About what?" Andrew was still smiling, but his blue eyes had narrowed.

"Kosti's been drinking quite a lot."

Andrew raised a brow. "That isn't news. What he does in his own house is his business, don't you think?"

"As long as he can control himself, it is," she replied. "But now his team is complaining about his work, and Leilani says he's been threatening her when he's drunk."

"So she can't control her bondmate. If it's reached that point, it's a matter for the Council—maybe even an Island Counselor."

"We can avoid that. I'd rather not see Kosti shamed. He's all right when he's sober—it's only the drinking that affects him."

"Then tell him to stop," Andrew said. "If he can't, it's his problem."

"It's everyone's problem. Do you want him on your team, where you'd have to look out for his errors as well as doing your own work?" She took a breath. "You've been selling him the liquor."

"I sell it to anybody who has the goods or credit to pay for it. As long as I do my work for the Project, I have the right to profit from anything I do in my own time. It's Kosti's problem, not mine."

There was some justice to his objection. Andrew, with the small distillery he had designed, had found a way to make a palatable whiskey using the rapidly maturing dwarf strains of grain he grew in his private greenhouse. The liquor, which he had pretentiously labeled Dinel's Cytherian Whiskey, was the source of much of his good fortune; there were some who claimed that it rivaled the whiskeys of Earth.

"Leilani told Kosti she'd spoken to me," Risa said. "That startled him enough for him to promise her he'd try to stop. He's not a bad man, Andy—he'll be all right if others help him out now."

Andrew shrugged, apparently unmoved. "He needs a hearing—that might shake him up. If not, there's a Counselor, and, at worst, a physician could give him an implant that'd make him sick if he ever touches alcohol. It isn't my responsibility."

"Do you want Earth and the Project Council to have even more excuses to interfere with our lives? You know what Counselors are. They can be useful in certain cases, but in the end, they represent Earth's interests. If we call on them too much, the Administrators might decide they should send a few to live in the domes permanently. That means an extra expense for the Project, which we'll ultimately pay, and our own elected Councils won't have as much authority. We've always prided ourselves on handling most of our own problems. Do you want that changed?"

"I don't know what you expect me to do," he said.

"I was hoping you'd have the sense to see it for yourself, and make the offer." Risa leaned forward. "I want you to stop selling liquor to Kosti. For that matter, you ought to consider putting limits on how much you sell to any one person. Your computer can easily keep track of the records for you, and Kosti will be grateful when he's past this. He won't relapse if he knows others are giving him support."

Andrew shook his head. "He could always get his liquor from somebody else."

"I doubt it. You're the only one selling it here so far,

and he doesn't have enough credit to import any. You've got a chance to help him and to set an example for others. Kosti won't be the only one with this problem—there could be others, if there aren't already. I'd like to see something done about it now."

Andrew fidgeted. "You always were smart, but there are some things you don't understand. You think anyone here can make something of himself, but I know better. We'll get some who fail and maybe a few more who'll steal, and the more some of us have, the more others'll want it and won't care how they get it. You may not want Counselors here, but they'll come, even if we have to train our own. We get along without Guardians on the surface, but we'll have to use our own people to keep order in time. We worked hard to get what we have, and we're not going to lose it because of some idea about making a different kind of world."

Risa steadied herself. There were a few more like Andrew Dinel lately, people who displayed what they had earned in various ways; she was not immune to such urges herself. But there was a difference in acquiring a few small luxuries that weren't beyond the means of anyone willing to work and the ostentatious display of goods that only emphasized a growing distance between some people's means and those of others. Such displays created resentments, and the fools in Ishtar were ready to feed on such resentments with their talk of sharing all.

She had assumed that the Project's ideals might restrain people's greed; maybe Andrew was right in thinking that she was naïve. His attitude seemed a betrayal of everything the Cytherian settlements were meant to be.

"My household worked to grow that extra grain," Andrew went on. "I spent credit to get parts for my distillery and put it together with my own hands. It took a couple of years to come up with something that tasted right, and a couple more to make a profit. You can't tell me I don't have a right to earn what I can. Are you going to tell Chen not to carve anything? Will you tell your friend Noella to stop selling that jewelry she makes?" He peered at the polished Cytherian stone that hung around Risa's neck. "People wouldn't like hearing that kind of advice."

She suppressed her irritation. "I have no wish," she replied calmly, "to take away anything from you. If you sell less whiskey to each person, you'll be making it more valuable. Seems to me that you could ask more for it then."

Andrew straightened, obviously surprised by this elementary economic point. "You'd be earning just as much," she continued, "without having to sell as much. That should appeal to you."

Andrew shook his head slowly. "It won't work. Some people may decide not to buy or trade with me after that, and a couple of households in al-Khwarizmi and Galileo are building distilleries of their own." He drew his brows together. "Look, all I did was find a way to make something people wanted and earn some credit and goods for myself. It isn't right to make me pay because a few people are weak."

Appealing to his sense of responsibility was ineffective, and there was no threat she could make. She could hardly make a complaint against Andrew that might bring about a hearing without dragging Kosti into the dispute, and a lot of Cytherians would take Andrew's side. She would have to try something else.

"Very well," Risa said. "I know you've been sending some of the whiskey to the other settlements occasionally."

"Nothing wrong with that. When pilots have room for a little extra cargo, there's no reason they can't put it aboard. I guess Evar told you."

"It isn't exactly a secret, Andy. Have you ever thought of trading with the Islanders, too?"

He frowned. "I never thought they'd be interested. They've got better stuff when they want it, and a lot of the Administrators are Muslims. They might disapprove."

"They've got better stuff if they import it, at great cost, and you know perfectly well a lot of Muslims aren't above taking a discreet nip once in a while. I don't see what you have to lose. You'll be doing just as well in the end, and if you send more to the Islands, you'll have a reason for restricting what you trade away here. No one's going to blame you for trying to expand your market, so to speak."

"I still don't know—"

"Surely you take some pride in your product," she interrupted. "You were the one who told me some immigrants found it as fine as any they'd tasted in their Nomarchies. Just think of how nice it would be to have some visiting Project Council member sample your genuine Cytherian whiskey at Administrator Sigurd Kristens-Vitos's table."

Andrew's smile had returned. "It's an idea, Risa—I have to admit that."

"I'm willing to discuss this with Administrator Sigurd. He'll be amenable when he understands the reasons, and I'm sure he'll find someone reliable who can handle your shipments there and draw up a contract with you. I'll let you know as soon as I've talked to him. Do we have an agreement?"

"I guess so."

"And you'll limit how much you give each individual here, and you won't sell any to Kosti for now?"

Andrew nodded. "It might not matter in the long run, though. If I don't sell it, people can always trade with those who have it or even try to steal it."

Risa gestured at his screen. "Let's put the agreement into our records. We can keep it private as long as you live up to it."

"My word's good."

"Indeed it is," she said acidly, "but I've seen too many disputes caused by vague memories of agreements. It never hurts to be clear and have it recorded."

The west dome's light was just beginning to dim as Risa left Andrew's house. She nodded at his brother, John, who was carrying a crate of returned bottles up the path.

She had found a solution. Both Leilani and Andrew would be satisfied, and she could tell Kosti that Andrew was acting as a friend should, a statement he would understand in his present, although potentially precarious, sobriety. But she knew that this was only a temporary solution. Andrew would prosper as much as before, and other settlers would note that and think of providing similar products. She had to hope their greed did not overtake their sense of responsibility.

Couldn't people like Andrew see that their settlements, their very lives, depended on acting responsibly? Too often, she worried about how many others shared her feelings for this world. Sometimes she longed to rage at the ones who came to her with their petty disputes and problems; she was tired of having to tell them things they should have seen for themselves.

Perhaps she had done them no service by offering her advice in the first place. They might have been forced to settle their difficulties themselves and become the self-reliant people they aspired to be. Paradoxically, she could even wish for the authority to force them to be what they should have been.

That was not a wish to indulge in for long. Pavel had begun with wanting to serve the Project and had ended by assuming that Venus's future depended on his maintaining his own authority. She would not make his mistake.

Her neighbors greeted her as they walked toward their own houses. A cat was sharpening its claws on a tree near her house; it scurried away as she passed. Malik would be home by now. She suddenly wished that she had worn something more flattering than her plain gray shirt and pants. Maybe she should have offered to trade with Grete Soong for some new garments. Most of the settlers contented themselves with the coveralls and work clothes the Project provided, along with shifts, tunics, and pants that were easy to make from imported fabrics, but lately a few were wearing slightly dressier clothes. Grete had a talent for sewing; clothes made by Andrew's bondmate always had extra touches—embroidery on the edges of sleeves, or tailoring that flattered the owner. Risa thought of how she might look to Malik in one of Grete's silken shirts; she had never concerned herself with clothing before.

The man was a disgraced Linker; apart from his education, he had no useful skills. She suspected he was vain; his clothes, plain as they were, always seemed neat, and she had seen no stubble on his face since their first meeting. After preparing his lessons, he preferred to spend his evenings with his reading screen and library instead of offering to help around the house or trying to learn more practical skills. He did not even know how to prepare his own food, and the formal manner he adopted with visitors seemed affected.

She could find enough flaws in him. None of them, however, had any effect on her feelings. She thought of him when she was alone in her room and knew that only a narrow hallway separated them.

He was the most beautiful man she had ever seen. His

features were so perfect that they were unnerving; she had been relieved to notice the slight hook of his slender nose, a minor defect that made him seem more human. She had glimpsed a sad, pensive look in his eyes that drew her sympathy, as well as a darker, more passionate glance that hinted at strong emotions.

She had persuaded herself that living as she did might make her better able to advise those who came to her with their problems, which she could then view with a detached objectivity unmarred by sentiment and too great an attachment to another human being. She had imagined finding a bondmate who would be a friend and companion and ask for little more.

Malik's presence had upset those plans. She wanted him to care about her even when she acted in ways that would discourage him. She sensed his need; even worse, she suspected that he knew what she felt.

She could guess at how he saw her. She was pretty enough in her own way, but he was probably used to beauties. She had some learning, but Malik was no doubt accustomed to wit and brilliance. She was a woman who had never lived anywhere except on Island Two and then in Oberg; he was familiar with several of Earth's cities. She knew none of the classical, formal Arabic Malik favored; his talk of the poetry and literature he loved made her feel even more ignorant. She could never be anything to him except a provincial settler and a passing amusement.

What kind of advice could she give herself? To take him as a lover if he were willing or else to put him out of her mind. She could find another household that might give Malik a room.

"Risa!" a voice called out as she turned toward the path leading to her door. Nikolai Burian came toward her from the tunnel; she remembered then that Malik had mentioned inviting the young man to dinner.

She smiled as he came to her side. "It's good to see you again. How are things going?"

"Better. Jed's starting to treat me like everyone else. I'm learning how to repair diggers in my spare time—can't hurt to learn another skill."

"Has anyone offered you a place to live?"

"Not yet." Nikolai tilted his head. "I wouldn't ask for

much—just a place to unroll a mat, and maybe a chance to get to know a woman as pretty as you."

She flushed a little. It was too bad that she was not more attracted to Nikolai. He wouldn't scorn her lack of learning; he might be grateful she wasn't overly educated. His interest in her was evident. Part of her attraction for him might lie in the fact that she was a person of some importance here, but she could not object to that. He was the kind of man who would make a good companion, even a bondmate. Encouraging him might help her put thoughts of Malik from her mind. But such dishonesty was repellent—a pretense of caring for one man so that she would not have to confront her growing feelings for another.

"You'll find a home before too long," she said.

He took a step along the path, then halted. "I wanted to ask you—how's Malik getting along?"

"He seems fine. I don't see that much of him except in the evenings, and he's usually preparing lessons or reading then. He brought quite a nice microdot library with him, with books we don't have here. Most of what we have was recorded from Island libraries and whatever Earth can send when the channels aren't taken up with essential communications. Some of his students seem quite taken with him already—especially the girls."

Nikolai chuckled. "I'd expect that. Is there any other work he can do?"

"I suggested that he offer his services as a tutor," she replied.

"Screen lessons can teach."

"True, but some people happily pay teachers to go over the lessons with them or just to discuss what they've learned—debate, ask questions, suggest other readings, and so forth. It's a little more interesting sometimes to have a real teacher to talk to instead of a screen image with programmed responses, and a few who didn't have a chance at more advanced learning can enjoy a lecture or a seminar."

Nikolai shrugged. "People have fun in different ways, I guess."

"Why were you curious about Malik?" she asked.

"I worry about him a little. That probably sounds strange." He walked toward a tree and leaned against it.

"It's a good thing he came here when he did. He might not have lasted that long in the camp. A lot of people avoided him. One man tried to start a fight with him once, and I don't think it was just because Malik was sleeping with his sister."

So there had been a woman in the camp. That did not surprise her.

"It's funny," the young man continued, "but I felt kind of sorry for him, knowing he was a Linker once. That camp was hard for him, even if he tried not to show it. The rest of us could look forward to having something more, but he's never going to have what he had."

"I know," she said softly.

"He doesn't belong here, really. He'll be thinking of what he lost."

"He has more than most new settlers get right away," she said, "interesting work and a place to live."

Nikolai moved away from the tree. "I wanted to ask you something else, Risa. You don't know much about me, so you don't have to give me an answer—you can just think it over, maybe. I wouldn't mind staying here and helping in your greenhouse. I can get up earlier to go to the bay, and I'll sleep in the hallway or the kitchen if there's no other space."

Risa did not know what to say. With Nikolai's assistance, the greenhouse might earn more credit for the household; if she was elected to the Oberg Council, which seemed likely, she might need extra help here.

"It's something to consider," she responded at last. "I'll have to look at your record, of course. For that matter, you may want to examine ours."

"I've seen a little of what your people are like. Listening to a public record probably won't tell me anything new. You won't find much to hold against me. I didn't leave any kids on Earth. There was a girl I wanted for a bondmate, but she wouldn't follow me to the camp. I missed her for a while, but that's past."

"I'll think about this," she said. "It isn't just up to me—the others will have something to say about it. If they're agreeable, you could probably use Tina's examining room at night. I'll let you know as soon as possible."

"Thanks." He took her arm. "I think I'd like it here."

They walked toward the door. Perhaps if Nikolai were living here, she could ignore Malik.

Risa felt restless. She sat down on her bed and stared at the small screen in one corner of her room. She would call Sigurd Kristens-Vitos tomorrow; the Administrator did not need to be bothered with Andrew Dinel's petty affairs at this hour. It was too late to visit Leilani; she could speak to her after talking to Sigurd.

Nikolai had done his best to be friendly during dinner. He had congratulated Grazie and Paul on their pledge, asked Chen about his carvings, and entertained Bettina with a few bawdy jokes. Her household probably wouldn't mind having him live here for a while. Chen would still be awake; she could see what he thought of the idea.

She crossed the room and opened her door. Malik, with a towel draped over his bare shoulders, was about to enter his own room; he turned his head.

"I was just going to talk to my father," she said as she gestured at the door to Chen's room.

"Nothing important, I hope. I think he's with Tina—I saw him enter her room just a little while ago."

"Oh." She looked down, feeling awkward. "Well, it can wait until breakfast, then. Kolya asked me before if there might be room for him here, and I said I'd speak to everyone about it."

"That's your decision," he said.

"Yours, too, now that you're living with us."

"I'm more of a guest," Malik responded. "Anyway, I don't have any objection. Kolya looked out for me before, and he'd be of use to you, I think. How long would he stay?"

"That depends. We'd offer him an informal, private agreement stating our obligations to each other—how much credit he'd contribute to the household, things like that. Eventually, he can decide if he wants to stay on as part of the household or build his own house somewhere else. There's still plenty of room here and in the southeast dome, but if he waits until the south dome is ready to be occupied, he'd have his choice of sites."

Malik pressed his door open. "Would you like to come in?" he asked. "We haven't had much time to talk since I arrived."

She wanted to refuse. This is my house, she told herself; I ought to listen to what he has to say if he's going to be living here.

He stepped aside, allowing her to enter; the door slid shut behind him. She sat down quickly on the floor, leaving him the cushion in the corner. He smoothed down his pants before seating himself. His torso was broader than it had seemed under his shirts; his chest was covered with swirls of hair that fanned out over his upper body before narrowing into a thin dark line.

"Actually, I thought you might be able to advise me," he said, "since you say you're sometimes helpful to others. I can't help feeling I'm already a disappointment."

"Have Theron and the other teachers found fault with you?"

He shook his head. "It isn't that—as far as I know, they think I'm doing reasonably well up to now. I think you're sorry I'm here."

She lifted her head. "What makes you think that?"

"We're sharing a house, yet even in these close quarters, you try to avoid me. Maybe you can tell me what I'm doing wrong so that I can remedy my faults."

"I've been busy," Risa replied. "As it is, I'm going to have to spend my day off settling another problem. I don't really have any complaints about you—we're just getting used to you, that's all. In fact, I think you've behaved quite well, under the circumstances."

"What circumstances are those?"

"You know." She should not be bringing this up. "You don't think we always have so many neighbors stopping by before and after dinner, do you?" Almost every young woman in the vicinity, or so it seemed, had found an excuse to visit lately. Even her friend Noella, with a pledge to Theron pending, had not been above flirting a little with Malik while hinting heavily that Theron would overlook any trysts before the ceremony. "About the only thing they haven't done is to throw themselves at your feet. You're very strong-willed to resist such temptations."

"You warned me the first night I was here. I have to live with these people." He sighed. "I'm not strong, Risa. Maybe I'm just tired of all that. Every time, I'd think maybe this one would be different, and I'd feel I was in love for a while, and then another woman would come along." He sounded bitter. "It gets to be a habit. There was always someone else—they'd make it so easy that I couldn't refuse. It's like being at a banquet where there's always some new delicacy to tempt you even when you've eaten enough, and then it's more like an addiction. The longer it goes on, the less satisfying it is, and in the end, I went to Tashkent alone."

She recalled what Nikolai had told her. "I doubt you were alone for long."

"There was someone. I didn't love her, but I needed her. She wasn't a beautiful woman, and what learning she had was limited to some screen lessons, but she had an inner strength I admired. I see something of that in you. I didn't see it in most of the women I knew. Maybe it was there and they simply had no need to develop it."

Risa pressed her back against the wall. He was sitting too close to her; she wanted to retreat from the tiny room.

"I still can't believe I'm here," he continued. "I keep thinking that I'll suddenly get a call telling me I've been forgiven, that I can be a Linker again and return to Earth —not that such unlikely good fortune could really befall me. Even if it did, I'd remember how precarious my position would always be."

"You have to forget your former life," she said. "People who get too nostalgic about Earth make others wonder how committed they are to this life. It's not as if you can't earn respect here."

"Have you more advice to give me?"

"You might see if some parents want additional tutoring for their children—you could earn extra credit that way. You may even find adults who'd like some tutoring or a few seminars and lectures—when people get a little more prosperous, they often like to take on a few airs."

"Anything else?"

"Try to learn a worker's skill. Your teaching counts as work for the Project as a whole, but we can always use mechanics and greenhouse gardeners. Or you could learn how to operate the robots, diggers, and crawlers. The more you can do, the more valuable you'll be."

"And what other advice can you offer?"

Was she supposed to tell him how to lead his life? Risa sighed impatiently, then noticed the earnest, almost desperate look in his brown eyes. She had known men who had the usual weaknesses of a quick temper, obstinacy, impatience, insensitivity, or pride, but she had never encountered one who seemed so unable to help himself.

"Why did you go to a camp, anyway?" she asked. "You could have stayed on Earth. Even in disgrace, someone with your training and connections shouldn't have had that hard a life."

"My family would have been embarrassed further if I'd remained, but that wasn't the only reason. I couldn't see any purpose in staying and hoping others would help me eventually. I had to do something for myself, however incapable of that I prove to be."

He wanted to be stronger than he was; there was something to admire in that. "Don't dwell on your doubts," she said. "You won't feel the same way when you've been here a while, after you begin to see yourself as a Cytherian. You'll have your work and your new friends, and when you find a bondmate and have your own children, you'll understand why you're here, and know you're working for those who'll follow you."

She was about to rise when he took her hand. "Stay with me, Risa."

"I can't," she whispered.

"Why not?" He pressed her hand against his cheek, then released her. "But perhaps I'm not the sort of man you want. Someone like Kolya would undoubtedly be a better choice."

"For someone else, maybe. I don't think he could be more to me than a friend."

"Then why?"

"Maybe I'm simply too proud to be just another in what must be a long list by now."

"You wouldn't be saying that," he said, "if you didn't feel something for me. My past would hardly matter otherwise." He reached for her hand again. "I wanted you when I first saw you. That's natural enough—you're attractive and I was lonely, but oddly enough, I feel more for you now. I can't promise that anything will come of it, but it might if you give it a chance." His mouth twisted a little. "What trite words I can utter. I'm usually a bit more eloquent, but I want to be honest with you. Stay with me. At the very least, we could share—"

"You'd hurt me sooner or later."

"How can you be so sure?"

She lowered her eyes; his hand gripped hers more tightly. "I have a sense for things like that," she said. "It's useful when I give advice—I have to know what might be too much for someone. I wouldn't help people by giving them advice they can't follow."

"And what if you're wrong about me? You're willing to risk living here, where any number of mistakes could bring trouble, and yet you won't reach out to a man who wants you when there's no reason to hold back."

People had come to her with all sorts of problems, but never with troubles of the heart. Perhaps they sensed that she had no expertise in that area, that she was either incapable of love or afraid of it, that she was unwilling to take any risk that might bring her love.

I wouldn't be chancing that much, she thought; I'm free, and at worst I'd have a pleasant interlude to remember later. Malik would be kind as long as he was living in her house, and when he left, as he surely would one day, his absence would make it easier to forget him. She could even tell herself that she was helping him by keeping him from being tempted by more troublesome entanglements.

He stood up and drew her to him. As he embraced her, she forgot all of her rationalizations and thought only of him.

Nine

Sigurd Kristens-Vitos had made time to speak directly with Risa Liangharad, as he usually did, even though the matter she had raised hardly merited much discussion. Too many of his fellow Islanders, especially the other Administrators, did not take the trouble to maintain contacts with individual dome-dwellers. It was important to have the settlers feel that the Islanders were Cytherians, too, and not just people indifferently watching over the domes from above.

There were, he mused, still some Islanders who considered the domed communities a premature development. The work of terraforming might have gone on without them; settling the world below could have waited until the surface had cooled and a few of the Parasol's shades could be removed. A few Islanders might not even mind if the settlements were abandoned; the specialists here would still have their scientific work to occupy them, while knowing that their own descendants would be the ones to inherit Venus.

Sigurd, however, felt an obligation to the settlers. Whatever Earth's reasons were for wanting surface settlements, the people in them had committed their lives to this world.

Sigurd nodded at the image of Risa on his wall screen. "You handled the problem well enough," he said. "I'll have one of my aides deal with the matter of Andrew Dinel's whiskey, and we'll make it clear that anyone else producing such products will be expected to show some restraint in how they're distributed. Forbidding them altogether would only create more problems later—even the early Mukhtars, despite their devotion to the holy Koran, learned that."

"I'm sorry I had to bother you with this," Risa replied. "Sometimes I think Andy's getting a bit above himself. He'll probably be flattered that one of your aides will be paying such attention to him."

Sigurd tapped his fingers on the small table in front of his screen. Andrew Dinel deserved a reprimand for not being more responsible instead of additional credit from his enterprise. He smiled at that thought. He was an Administrator and had to use such people or work around them rather than forcing them to adhere to the Project's ideals.

He studied Risa's image. Often her face was taut with tension. Now she was almost glowing; her cheeks were rosier and her dark eyes sparkled.

He had met Risa Liangharad a few years earlier, when the Administrator whom Sigurd was assisting had sent him to the northern Bat; a workers' dispute had seemed to require a personal visit. Sigurd had been in his early twenties. Although he had grown up on the Islands, he had only recently returned from Earth's Cytherian Institute. He supposed that his visit to the Bat was a test of his ability to negotiate.

Risa was seventeen at the time, yet even then her fellow workers had been willing to have her present their complaints to Sigurd. Some respected her simply for being the daughter of Iris Angharads, but she had earned his respect with her reasonableness and her concern for those with whom she worked. He had spoken with her intermittently over the screen since then, and she had proven to be useful both in handling some problems the settlers faced and in giving him a closer glimpse at their day-to-day lives through her impressions.

"You ought to visit Island Two sometime soon, God willing," Sigurd said. "This was your home once."

"I've thought of it, but—" She shrugged. "I'd have to make the time."

"I've spoken to my colleagues," he continued. "We so rarely meet with your dome Councils, and we should do something about that. Maybe when you're elected to the

Oberg Council, we can invite the Councils here, and you and I can meet again."

"If I'm elected."

"I'm sure you will be." Part of Risa's charm was that she did not seem interested in power for its own sake and saw whatever influence she had as a burden. Such modesty made her seem trustworthy, but he occasionally wondered if it was a pose. He knew that she visited Pavel Gvishiani fairly often and that their involvement was clearly not romantic. Pavel might still be dreaming of what he had lost and might see the young woman as a way to regain some influence.

"I made exactly one recorded message for people here to view if they like," Risa said, "and all I did was point to my record and say I'd serve with integrity. I haven't made any promises, and I've got better things to do than go in person from house to house asking for votes."

"That may strike many as refreshing," Sigurd said.

"Anyway, I don't know if I really want to be on the Council. It'll just demand more time, and I doubt that I'll be of much more use than I am now. Besides, I may want children before too long, and I should allow time for them."

This was something new from Risa. "The Council will give you more authority," Sigurd said. "Better you should have it than others who are not so wise. Your household and the nursery will help you care for any children, so they'd hardly be neglected."

"I suppose." She sounded more tentative than usual; her mind seemed to be elsewhere. She smiled suddenly. "Anyway, don't we all know that a Council member is only another Cytherian and really no better than anyone else?"

"Indeed," he replied. "By the way, how is the new settler in your household getting along?" He did not have to ask; he could have called up recent data about Malik Haddad through his Link, but he was curious about her impressions.

Risa reddened, then looked down for a moment. "He's fine. I haven't heard any complaints about his teaching, and he's settling in here." She seemed embarrassed; her eyelids fluttered. Could she be infatuated with the man? "I've taken up enough of your time, Administrator Sigurd." She was clearly anxious to cut the conversation short; he wondered why. "I'll let Andy know I've talked to you."

"Of course. Farewell."

The screen went blank. Sigurd considered the man who was now living in Risa's house. He had pitied Malik Haddad a little when he first heard about him; now he began to worry about the effect he might be having on Risa. She hardly needed the distraction of a man whose record implied that he was a skilled seducer, and Malik Haddad had to be a man with divided loyalties even now. Unlike the other settlers, he had not joined the Project willingly or gone to a camp in the hope of finding a better life; he was here as an exile.

Sigurd was certain that the Council of Mukhtars had various ways of watching the settlers, ways that were not shared with the Islands' Administrative Committees or even with the Project Council. A few among the dome-dwellers had to be their eyes and ears. Through his Link, Sigurd had studied the records of many settlers, looking for anything that seemed not to fit. It would be easy for the Mukhtars to plant spies in one of the camps where people waited for passage; if some obscure person vanished on his way to a camp and another took his place, that fact could be hidden. Identity bracelets could be altered and records changed.

Could Malik Haddad be such a spy? He was atypical enough to make that a possibility. His family apparently had enemies on the Council of Mukhtars, but Malik's disgrace could be part of a ruse.

Sigurd chided himself. In his position, he could see deviousness even in the most commonplace events. Many of the settlers would be curious about the former Linker; that was hardly the best position for an operative. Perhaps he was only what he seemed, a disgraced exile from Earth. Even so, he did not want the man to interfere with Risa's usefulness to him. If necessary, he might have to find an excuse to bring Malik to the Islands.

He got up from his screen and paced in his room; his Link was silent. He had been given this room five years ago; the records had told him then that Pavel Gvishiani had once lived here. That had amused Sigurd at first; now, as he pondered his own ambitions, the fact disturbed him.

Only an accident had given Sigurd the place he held,

an airship accident that had taken the life of Walid Amani
and fifteen Administrators; the Islands had lost some of
their most experienced people in that crash. There was no
doubt that the tragedy was accidental, although other possibilities had been checked before being dismissed.

Sigurd had been Walid Amani's closest aide. In the
normal course of events, he would have remained a minor
member of the Island Two Administrative Committee for
many years. But Sigurd's mentor had held the post of Liaison to the Project Council, which had made Walid the most
important of the Island Administrators. Sigurd had worked
closely with him; it seemed appropriate for the Council to
allow him to assume the dead man's duties temporarily.

The temporary appointment had soon become permanent, much to Sigurd's surprise. He did not flatter
himself by believing that only his work had won him the
position. The Project Council, he was sure, saw him as a
young, easily malleable man, indoctrinated by the Cytherian Institute with loyalty primarily to Earth. His fellow
Administrators, despite their own ambitions, showed little
resentment at Sigurd's apparent good fortune. Sigurd
would presumably make a grave error before too long, as
he struggled to balance the interests of the various people
he served; such a mistake was probably inevitable. Earth
remained unsure of its hold on Venus, the dome-dwellers
pushed for more control of their lives, and the Habbers
clung to their role in the Project. If anything went wrong
during this precarious time, Sigurd would be a convenient
scapegoat, and a successor could take over when the problem had been resolved. He might fall as far as Pavel had.

Sigurd would not let that happen. His five years as a
student at the Cytherian Institute had only convinced him
that Venus would be better off free from Earth's grasp.
Pavel had provoked a confrontation, but the old man had
done the right thing, whatever his mistakes. Even Earth
would benefit more in the future if Venus were allowed to
diverge. The new culture would revitalize the old and
perhaps even heal the breach between Earth and the Habitats. The denizens of this solar system might finally see
themselves as one human community instead of as opposing societies with irreconcilable visions. Sigurd could
reconcile such a possibility with the Islamic faith he had
tentatively adopted during his sojourn on Earth. Earth

wanted to bend the future to its will; surely there was more virtue in allowing people to draw together freely and in reaching for a universe instead of clinging to the past.

Pavel, as it happened, had even made his punishment a kind of victory. After his Link had been taken from him, he was sent to the northern Bat to labor as a worker; by the time he had requested a chance to go to the surface as a settler, several people were willing to speak for him. The settlers might honor Iris Angharads and Amir Azad, who had died trying to resolve a dilemma Pavel had helped to bring about, but many of them also knew that the old man had dreamed their dream.

Sigurd could admire Pavel, but he was not about to make the other man's errors. He would find another way to loosen Earth's bonds.

As Sigurd came through the curving hallway, a man called out to him. He slowed reluctantly, recognizing the voice.

"How pleasant to run into you," Rafi ibn-Ali said cheerfully as he caught up with Sigurd. "I stopped by your room, only to find that you were absent."

Sigurd gazed at the jewel on Rafi's forehead. The man could have summoned him through his Link. The Guardian Commander often acted as if he had no Link; that was one of his little conceits, pretending that his position was unimportant. "Was there something you wished to discuss?" Sigurd asked.

"Oh, not at all. I thought perhaps we might share some tea and some gossip. We haven't had a chance to visit lately." The two passed more doors adorned with Arabic calligraphy; the Commander thrust his hands into the pockets of his rumpled black uniform as they approached the door leading out of the Administrators' residence.

Sigurd lingered at the top of the steps leading down from the ziggurat where he lived. The dome above him glowed with a soft yellow light; the Islands followed the same twenty-four-hour cycle as did the surface settlements. A white stone path was below the steps; a few people were sitting on benches under the trees that lined the path. He might have been in a park rather than on a domed platform floating in a deadly world's upper atmosphere.

Three Guardians stood at the foot of the steps, ready to question anyone who approached the ziggurat. Sigurd found their presence both annoying and useless. Anyone coming to the Administrators' quarters would either have an appointment or be visiting a friend. He did not care to have the Guardians interrogating his visitors, but the Commander insisted on posting a few there.

He descended the steps, Rafi at his side. The three Guardians saluted their Commander, then nodded at Sigurd as they touched their foreheads. "Salaam, Commander," the female Guardian said. "Do you and the Administrator require an escort?"

"That isn't necessary," Rafi replied.

He and the Commander had in common a dislike of escorts, at least. Sigurd did not care for escorts even on ceremonial occasions, and he also avoided wearing his formal white robe and headdress most of the time. Too much concern with outward signs of position seemed a mark of insecurity. Such signs were important on Earth, of course, where the Mukhtars were probably a good deal more insecure than they would admit.

The woman and her two male companions stepped back, allowing Sigurd and Rafi to pass. These three were tolerable, Sigurd thought; they did not go out of their way to be unpleasant to visitors. That meant, he supposed, that the three would soon be sent back to Earth. Guardians were always removed from their Island posts before they could grow too friendly with Islanders.

He had learned a little about these Guardians. They were three more young people who had come from towns where there was no real future for them. They had probably been seduced by talk of Guardian traditions and the opportunity to become one of those who kept the peace, served the Mukhtars, maintained Earth's weapons, and were prepared to move against anyone who might raise an opposing force. That was their mission—to be ready for a battle while hoping that their readiness made any battle unthinkable.

"And where are you bound?" Rafi asked as they strolled along the path.

"To visit a friend."

"I'll walk with you for a bit." The stocky Commander's suggestion had the sound of a command. "It's been one of the pleasures of being stationed here—walking about this peaceful place."

They passed a few people seated at a table in a grove; a small apelike creature was serving them tea and fruit. The genetically modified monkeys could handle simple tasks once performed by robots or workers; they had been most useful in tending the Island plants and gardens and in doing uncomplicated repairs under human supervision. There were more of the monkeys now and fewer workers. Among the few workers who did live on the Islands, most would eventually choose to join the surface settlers, who had steadfastly refused to allow the tailored apes there, even though the creatures could have freed them from a few tasks. More monkeys, so they reasoned, meant fewer places for people; the Islands were proof of that. Each Island had once been home to some five thousand people, the largest number each could support; now the average was barely more than three thousand.

Rafi sighed. "Much as I've enjoyed being here, I do miss Earth. I'll feel some regrets when I leave, but I'm looking forward to my return."

"You sound as though your departure is near," Sigurd said.

"Perhaps it is. I had a message from the people on Anwara today. There's talk of bringing more of us back, but I'm not sure who will replace us. It's beginning to seem unnecessary to go to the trouble and expense of maintaining a force here, when it's so clear that your people are unlikely to be troublesome."

Sigurd tried not to look startled. Could it be that the Islanders might finally be free of the Guardian presence? He had hoped for that; now, he was not so certain that such a decision would be welcome news. He knew that a few Guardian Commanders had more influence with the Mukhtars. Withdrawing the Island force might only mean that the Guardians hoped to consolidate their power on Earth. It could be a tactical retreat designed to lull the Cytherians before Earth tightened its grip once more.

On the other hand, this could also mean that the Guardians were weaker and that more reasonable and less suspicious Mukhtars were thinking of recalling those here.

"I'd be sorry to lose your company," Sigurd murmured.

"How kind of you to say that. You wouldn't be terribly pained to see us go, I expect, and your Habber friends would be delighted." They had come to a curve in the path; beyond the trees ahead lay a round stone building. "That's where you're headed, isn't it?" Rafi went on. "To visit the Habbers."

"Yes," Sigurd admitted.

"There isn't anyone who doubts you, Sigurd, but maybe you should keep more of a distance from them. Some of your Islanders are a little too cozy with them, and you could set more of an example."

He halted. His dealings with Habbers were hardly a secret, and the Commander had never rebuked him for them before. "We have to work together," he said in a steady voice. "It's natural that some friendships would form, but we don't deceive ourselves that they're anything more than passing relationships. Better to let the Habbers believe they're entirely welcome here, and such contacts give us a way both to learn more about them and to control them."

Rafi folded his arms. "I'm hardly condemning you, my friend. A man has his needs, and yours haven't affected your performance of your duties, but it might be wiser to satisfy them elsewhere."

"The Project Council hasn't found fault with my actions. If they did, I'd follow their directives, but they quite rightly regard such matters as unimportant."

"I'm giving you good advice," Rafi responded. "Earth can tolerate some of your Islander foibles at the moment—after all, there's always a chance your people might bring a few of them around to seeing things our way, and that could spread a little discord among them. But Earth might not always be so tolerant. Well, I'll leave you to your friends."

The Commander turned back; Sigurd walked on toward the stone building where the Habbers who came to Island Two lived. Two Guardians were stationed outside; the uniformed men smirked a little as they glanced at him. These two had come to the Island only recently, and they had admitted their surprise upon learning that Sigurd was an Administrator. His mop of disorderly blond hair and his boyish face often startled those who expected a more imposing figure; he had always looked even younger than he was. These two grizzled Guardians obviously found his youthfulness amusing.

"Salaam, Administrator," one Guardian said. He stepped aside as the door slid open. The common room, as usual, was empty. Sigurd turned to his left and walked through a dimly lit curving hall until he came to the fifth door on his right. He pressed his palm against it; the door opened.

Tesia was sitting on a futon. She wore only a white loincloth and a thin silver chain on one wrist. A few clothes hung on a rod behind her, and her wall screen held the image of a distant constellation. She did not open her eyes until he had seated himself next to her.

"Sigurd," she said softly. Her lips curved in a smile, but her hazel eyes stared past him. She always accepted his presence passively, without revealing whether she was happy to see him or not.

Her fine-boned, angular face was partly covered by her long reddish hair; he smoothed a lock back as she rested her head against his arm. He thought of their first time together nearly a year ago. They had been meeting in his room to discuss the study she was conducting with some of the Island's geologists. Tesia had stood up to leave; he had found his arms around her. She had responded to him almost as though lovemaking were a normal conclusion to such a meeting. For all he knew, perhaps it was for her people.

He had not troubled to hide their encounters; he had even brought them up himself in conversations with others before dismissing them slightingly. This had convinced the Project Council that his deeds were not a sign of potential disloyalty; if they had been, Sigurd would hardly have been so open about them. They could ignore what he did with Tesia for now and use it against him if he ever fell from favor.

Sigurd knew he had been reckless. That was part of Tesia's attraction in the beginning. He had always tried to live up to the expectations of the teachers and Counselors who cared for him in place of the parents who had died when he was a boy. After years of being only what others wanted him to be, he had acted impulsively for the first time. Perhaps the act had been a sign of rebellion, a way of testing the limits that had always pressed in around him.

A few other Islanders had bed-partners among Habbers; the Habbers treated such entanglements with the same lack of concern as Tesia apparently viewed theirs. Perhaps the Habbers also joked about such encounters in secret or else saw them as a way to reach out to the people they were helping. He could not know; there was so little that he knew about Tesia even now. Their talk was of the Project; their lovemaking was a search for purely physical pleasures. He knew nothing about her past before she had come to Island Two three years ago, not even how old she was. Her slender body was hardly more developed than a young girl's, but her eyes never revealed a young person's uncertainty. Her mind was locked away from his, and her Link was closed to him, although he sometimes wondered if it remained open to other Habbers even during their most intimate moments.

She knew as little about his thoughts, he supposed. She was unaware of how much it pained him now to speak slightingly of her; he longed for her too often lately. He wanted to tell her how he really felt, but loyalty to his own people held back the words he wanted to speak.

He stroked Tesia's hair; his hands were soon moving over her body. She helped him out of his clothes, caressing him as she did so, then drew him down next to her. She had never refused him, had always responded to him, had never shown any sign of hurt or disappointment on the few occasions when he had gently refused her overtures because of sudden doubts and fears. He explored her with his fingers and tongue until she was ready for him and listened to her soft sighs and gasps as he entered. She shuddered and sighed; her cheeks flushed as she moaned. For a moment, the barriers between them were gone.

The moment passed; he withdrew and lay silently at her side. "Sigurd," she whispered. Her hand touched his face; he could almost imagine that she too was holding back words that she wanted to speak.

She kissed him, then sat up slowly; he ran his hand along the ridges of her ribs as she stretched. She turned her head; the distant look in her hazel eyes had returned.

"You seem troubled," she said. Her expression did not change, but her voice was a little warmer.

"I had a conversation with Rafi ibn-Ali before coming here. He thinks he may be leaving us soon—in fact, he hinted that the Guardians might be removed from the Islands altogether." He paused. "Your people would probably find that a welcome development."

"Earth will hardly take our feelings into account. But removing the Guardians would show that your people are now considered trustworthy, as well as saving Earth the expense of keeping them here. Frankly, I think it would improve morale on the Islands, and that can only be to the Project's benefit. There's no point in my people raising the issue—that might only convince the Project Council that the Guardians should stay on. Actually, I'm not so sure that some of my people would welcome their absence."

"And why not?" he asked.

"They provide a kind of balance. Having them here quells some of the Mukhtars' suspicions and makes them feel that they're still in control of the Project. They know that many of my people are reluctant to come here as long as Guardians are present, but there are enough of us here to give you what aid you need. Without them, matters could become more uncertain. Maybe the Mukhtars only want to see if you and your fellow Administrators can keep control of this Project without them, or if you'll move closer to us and give them an excuse to expel us once and for all."

"I've had similar thoughts," he said.

"The Guardians also provide a focus for any resentments your people may feel. If they were to leave, that would remove one source of discontent and perhaps convince your surface settlers that Earth has no intention of interfering too much in their lives. But they'd also be freer to direct their resentment toward us."

Sigurd frowned. "You've always claimed that Habbers only want to help, with no aim other than observing us and learning what you can. It doesn't matter how the dome-dwellers feel about you as long as you can work together, and I'm sure—"

"Earth may want to see if their resentment of us will flower," she said. "That could work to the Mukhtars' advantage." Tesia lifted her head. "You'll inform your colleagues of my thoughts, of course. They'd enjoy thinking that we're worried over what might happen."

"You don't sound like a Habber now, Tesia."

"Maybe I'm becoming more like one of you. Those of

us who come here are often those who feel more distant from other Habitat-dwellers, and perhaps that makes us more vulnerable to certain mental afflictions. I was young when I came here, young even by your standards. My Link is often closed now, and I wonder if I could be fully a part of my world again even if I went back." Tesia bowed her head; she seemed very young then, hardly more than a child. "You can tell your friends that, too—it ought to provide them with some amusement."

Was Tesia being honest with him? Was she trying to say that her feelings for him were as troubled as his for her? "Your people say they're helping us," he said at last. "But you're also contending with Earth for the future, whether you admit it or not. You want to drive a wedge between Cytherians and Earth, and you'd enjoy seeing Habbers in control of what comes to pass. That would be a victory for you, seeing the Mukhtars lose their hold on their greatest accomplishment, and turning it into your achievement." His words were harsher than he had intended. She had spoken more openly of her feelings than she ever had before, but he could think only of how little he still knew her.

"I thought you knew me better than that," she said.

"I don't know you at all. Maybe you think you can manipulate me, but my only loyalty is to this Project. I may complain about the hold Earth has on us, but only because it's an unnecessary distraction. I may seem sympathetic to your people, but only because you can help us. I won't see Earth's domination replaced by yours, whatever your designs."

Her hand rested on his arm for a moment. "Your argument isn't with my people, Sigurd—it's with me. I don't want to manipulate you. I don't want anything from you except—"

"Except what?"

Her face paled; he had never seen her look so distressed. "I should open my Link and steady myself," she whispered. "I care too much about you. I thought you saw that, that it didn't need to be said. But even love is a struggle for power with your people, isn't it? We can't be just two people sharing part of ourselves. I know you run some risk in being with me at all, whatever you've done to minimize the danger. Maybe I should show my concern by sending you away and telling you there can be no more between us."

"That isn't what I want," he admitted. He lay down and pulled her to his side, wanting only to hold her for a while. His feelings would not prevent him from telling others what she had said to him. He might want to love her openly and freely, and he felt some joy in knowing that she cared for him more deeply, but he would not forget his duty. If Tesia interfered with his obligations, he would have to give her up or find a way to use her.

He supposed that she harbored similar notions. She might want only love from him now, but she would not give up what she was for that love; she would choose her people over him. They were never likely to see a time when they could share any more than what they already had.

He kissed her gently, as though in apology for his thoughts.

Ten

The explosion happened two hours before Risa was to go off duty. It ripped through one of the installations adjoining the west dome, shattering panels, circuitry, part of a computer, and several of the conduits that held oxygen extracted from the atmosphere of carbon dioxide.

The heavy walls of the installation contained the explosion, and the dome was unaffected, but the damaged interior of the bunker would have to be repaired.

Alasid immediately took charge of his team. Three other installations would continue to extract oxygen for the west dome; unless something went wrong in one of them, there was no need to issue a general alert. Finding the cause of the accident, and whether a worker's earlier carelessness had brought it about, would have to wait.

Risa and two other workers quickly guided robots into the bunker and began to clear away debris while the damage to the system was assessed. Two small carts on treads entered the bunker's lock; Risa's job now was to sort out relatively undamaged parts from those damaged beyond repair. The carts would carry the material to the digger and crawler bay; there, other workers would salvage what they could.

She worked, unaware of how much time was passing, then felt a hand on her shoulder. "Risa," a voice said. For a moment, she felt disoriented, her mind still with the robot, her body stiff with tension in her chair.

She took off her band and looked up at Alasid's broad face. "Go home and get some rest," he said. "An engineering team's here, along with the next shift. They'll work through the night on that installation."

"I can finish—"

He shook his head. "You've been at this long enough—I don't want you making mistakes. It's the engineers' job now."

She blinked and rubbed at her eyes. A few engineers were already in the room; Noella Sanger was among them. Risa's head throbbed. "I'll need you back here by twelve," Alasid was saying to the rest of his team. "No point in coming here just after first light. By then, we should be ready to make that bunker operational again." Risa noticed then that the engineers were staring at her pointedly.

"Congratulations, Risa," Willem Van Eyck called out from across the room.

"For what?" she asked as she stood up.

Noella came to her side. "The last votes were registered just before I left my house. You're now officially a member of the Oberg Council."

Risa managed a smile, too tired to feel gratified. Her thoughts were still on the accident, less serious than it might have been but still a reminder of how precarious their lives here were. "I didn't think—"

"I suppose it just slipped your mind after you cast your own vote," Noella said more softly. "You don't have to be modest with me." The tall blond woman walked with Risa toward the door. "Go home and celebrate a little with Malik—it'll be something new for him, having a Council member sharing his bed. I've got to get to work."

Risa hastened from the room before anyone else could congratulate her. She was beginning to regret that she had confided in Noella, although her friend would have found out about Malik sooner or later from another member of Risa's household. Noella seemed convinced that her attachment to Malik would eventually become more formal, while Grazie Lauro, whose child would be born in less than six months, kept asking when Risa and Malik intended to have their contraceptive implants removed. Even Chen was assuming that Malik would become a more permanent member of his household before long. Risa had not told any of them that Malik seemed content to leave matters as they were.

The dome was nearly dark as Risa emerged from the External Operations Center. She walked until she came to a small bridge leading over a stream near the lake, crossed it, and strode past Andrew Dinel's house and the dwellings near his until she reached the path that led to her home. She glanced past the trees lining the path; most of the windows of the houses she passed were unlit, their inhabitants now asleep. At least she would not have to endure more congratulations.

Her mouth twisted. She had expected the victory, in spite of her comment to Noella; it was not only her fatigue that robbed her of the joy she should have felt. Malik was the source of her discontent. She had learned that she could feel love after all, but instead of filling a void in her life, that love had revealed other needs in her without satisfying them. She was afraid that she wanted more from Malik than he could give; her love was making her doubt herself. She had deceived herself by thinking that she could control her feelings for the man.

Malik was now earning extra credit with tutoring, but he showed no interest in learning any practical skills. He was like a few other people in Oberg, who seemed content to work at tasks they chose while trying to avoid any they found uncongenial, and Malik was doing well enough with his small students now that he had learned more patience. His looks and his courteous manner had helped him to make friends; people easily found excuses for his lack of more enterprise. Malik was a learned man and a former Linker who had held a high place; better to value him for what he was and to be grateful that one of such unusual accomplishments lived among them. It was as if seeing Malik labor at more humble tasks might tarnish him somehow.

Risa understood such attitudes because Malik could evoke similar feelings in her. She was always mindful of what he had lost and dreaded doing anything that might bring an unhappy look into his eyes. Pressing him to attempt more work usually evoked such unhappy glances; gentle questions about his feelings for her brought only poetic words about love that did not address their possible future together. She had learned not to discuss the problems that others brought to her after he had criticized her for being too hard in her judgments; he was willing to let her shoulder those burdens alone.

She could become aroused whenever she recalled the touch of his hands or his practiced, demanding kisses; she could still marvel at his slender, muscled body and perfect face. He had not sought out other women; gossip would have reached her by now if he had. She should be content; wasn't love the willingness to accept someone for what he was?

How could she ever imagine that he might pledge himself to her? He was the kind of man to take as a lover, not as a bondmate. She had put off having children for too long, but to have his child would be folly; he would fill the child's head with fancies and impractical dreams or dwell on his own disappointments. She no longer knew why she wanted a child. Was it to continue her line, to have a young one to nurture and teach, to reach out through her descendants to Venus's future? Or did she only seek to bind Malik to her more closely?

Nikolai was coming out of the greenhouse as she neared her door. "You're working late," she said.

"No later than you. I got back late from the airship bay. We heard another rumor about the Guardians from one of the pilots—she says Earth might be removing them from the Islands and stationing some of them on Anwara with the Guardians there."

"Maybe they've finally realized they're not needed on the Islands." Sigurd Kristens-Vitos had not mentioned the Guardians, but that was not a matter he was likely to discuss with her.

"By the way, congratulations," Nikolai said. "Your father said he was going to wait up and share a drink with you, but I wanted to tell you myself."

She thought, not for the first time, of how sensible it would be to have someone like Nikolai as a bondmate; it was too bad her feelings refused to follow her reason. Perhaps Malik, with his skill in bed and his poetic professions of love, had made it impossible for her ever to be content with another man.

"I've been thinking," he continued. "Now that you're going to be busy with the Council, you'll need even more help around here, and somebody you can count on. I spoke about this to Chen and Paul before, and they didn't mind the idea. Maybe I could become a real member of this household."

"I can't think of any argument against it," she replied, "but you've only been with us a month and a half. Are you sure that's what you want? You'd have a chance to build your own quarters after you've been here a while."

"We'd be better off as partners, and I can do well enough working here. It makes more sense than starting my own household—I mean, if it's all right with you."

"Well, I'm grateful that we won't be losing you."

"I can add a couple of rooms to Tina's wing—there'd be almost as much space for me there as I'd have in my own house, and it wouldn't cost so much credit to build."

She smiled. "A couple of rooms?"

"Grazie and Paul'll need some extra space for their child." Nikolai gazed at his feet as he thrust his hands into his pockets. "And there's Emilia. We get along, and she kind of hinted that she'd rather live here if we ever decide to make a pledge—with her brothers and her cousins, there wouldn't be much room for us in her house."

Emilia Knef was an apprentice of Chen's. Risa had noticed that the young woman and Nikolai often spent evenings talking under the trees outside, but she had not realized the pair had grown so close. She would have seen that, she supposed, if Malik were not distracting her so often. "Emilia's hardly more than a girl."

"She's old enough to know what she wants, and she's a good worker. I thought you ought to know—I'm kind of serious about her, so I wanted to be sure she'd be welcome later on."

"Of course she is. Chen would be pleased—he says she's one of the quickest apprentices he's had." That would simplify matters; she would no longer have to reproach herself for being unable to feel more for Nikolai. The young Russian was eminently practical; having seen that Risa's affections had already been claimed by Malik, he had turned his attention elsewhere. She felt a twinge of regret.

"Malik ought to think about making a pledge to you," Nikolai muttered.

"Maybe he doesn't feel he knows me well enough for such a commitment."

"Why wait? I don't know what more he could want. He reads too much of that history in his library—he talks about things that happened a hundred years ago as if they happened yesterday. Maybe he thinks he'll be alive forever and have time to decide everything later. I could talk some sense into him."

"Don't," she said firmly. "I won't have him feel that he has to—"

"You won't be around forever, either. You ought to think of yourself."

She did not want to discuss Malik any more. She pressed her hand against the door. As it opened, she saw her father at his table, staring at a carving. She had thought that Malik might have waited up with him to congratulate her; she should have known better.

Chen lifted his head, then stood up quickly. His face was troubled; he did not look as though he was about to offer any congratulations. "You didn't have to wait up for me," she said as she walked toward him. "What's wrong? Don't tell me that you decided to cast your vote for someone else."

He did not smile. "Dawud al-Askar called just a little while ago," Chen said quietly. "I'm only giving you his message because I promised him I would. He thought you'd want to know. Pavel Gvishiani's dying. Dawud doesn't think he'll last longer than a day or two more."

Risa tensed, suddenly alert, her tiredness gone. "Did he say—" She swallowed. "Is Pavel still conscious? Is a physician looking after him?"

"I didn't ask." Her father scowled; she had never seen such a dark look on his face. "Your mother died because of him. He had to play for time instead of preventing that— do you think I can ever forget? She could have been here now, alive, with me. I'll be glad to see him dead."

"That's past," Risa replied.

"It'll never be past for me. He thought he could use her—that's why she died."

"Pavel did what he felt he had to do, and Iris did the same. She knew the risk she was taking—don't demean her memory by calling her a tool of Pavel's." Her voice had risen; she choked back more words.

Chen took a step toward her. "I can understand why others would forget," he said, "but not my own daughter. I should have tried to stop you from seeing him at all, but I thought you'd come to see things my way. Well, he'll be dead soon enough."

"Whatever he did," she burst out, "we're here because of it. Whatever mistakes he made, he was thinking of this world. He's paid for what he did."

"He didn't pay enough."

"And he's been my friend," she shouted, "almost like another father."

Chen raised his arm; for a moment, she thought he might strike her. "You shame your mother's memory by saying that!"

"I have to go to him. I should be there to say farewell to him."

Chen lowered his arm as he looked away. Malik had entered the common room; Risa glanced at him briefly. "Stay with my father," she whispered to Nikolai before she hurried from the house.

By the time she reached Pavel's house in the main dome, her strength was nearly gone. The old man was dying; she had expected it but not so soon. She had visited him only a few days earlier; he had listened attentively and patiently while she discussed her feelings about Malik and her doubts about herself—matters she could not discuss with Chen, who would only find them another failing.

Jeannine Loris, another Council member, greeted Risa at the door. Other visitors had gathered with Pavel's household in the common room. Risa beckoned to Dawud; he walked toward her. "How is he now?" she asked.

"A physician's with him." Dawud's eyes were resigned rather than sorrowful. "He was awake before, but he might be sleeping now."

"May I see him?"

"The others have. He'd want to see you. Go ahead."

She went to Pavel's room. The old man lay in his bed, eyes closed; Gupta Benares was leaning over him. A small scanner sat on the table next to the bed; she saw no other medical equipment.

Gupta's dark eyes met hers. "It's his heart," he said; the physician's brown face was composed. "He had an attack a few hours ago. I estimate that he may have a day or two more without intervention."

She clasped her hands together. "Why aren't you doing anything, then? He should be in the infirmary. Can't you—"

"Intervening now will only prolong his passing, and the strain of moving him might kill him. He's refused treatment. I told him he should have had a heart replacement before, but he didn't want it and our facilities are limited in any case."

"There must be something you can do."

"He's made his choice."

She moved closer to the bed. Pavel opened his eyes. "Risa." His voice was faint. She knelt and bent her head toward him. "I trust you aren't going to cry. I heard the news about you. I'm a little sorry that I won't see you on the Council myself."

"But you can. Tell Gupta to take you to the infirmary."

"And have limited medical resources prolong an old man's life? That doesn't sound like a new Council member speaking or the daughter of Iris Angharads." He was silent for a moment. "What Venus could get out of me now wouldn't be worth the effort."

"He can help you," she insisted.

"Stop it, Risa. This isn't like you, and it's a strain on me to scold you." Pavel cleared his throat. "You look tired— you ought to be sleeping. Have you had a talk yet with that young teacher in your house?"

Risa shook her head.

"I thought you valued my advice. You know what I said—tell the man what you want from him and give him the choice of deciding if he can grant it. Don't be so indecisive. You want a child and you ought to have one soon."

She clutched at his hand; his fingers were icy. "How conventional you sound."

"It isn't that. With some, it wouldn't matter, but I know what you're like. You'd be happier with a bondmate and a child, and that'd make you more useful to Oberg." His voice was weaker. "I'm happy you came," he continued, "but say your farewell now. I lived most of my life alone, and I don't need companions to face death. You've done your duty. Don't linger outside with the others—say your farewell, go home, and turn your thoughts to life."

She pressed a hand to her mouth.

"Do you hear me?" Some of Pavel's old strength had returned to his voice. "Go home."

"You won't be forgotten, Administrator Pavel."

"No—I'll be remembered for the wrong reasons, no doubt."

"Farewell." She touched his forehead. His dark eyes closed.

Risa went to the airship bay. Three workers on the darktime shift were loading cargo into a cart. She rode with them as far as the tunnel, then walked the rest of the way on foot.

The common room was empty. She went to her room, too tired to get a meal in the kitchen. Malik was lying on her bed; a covered tray sat on the floor.

He opened his eyes and sat up. "Have you eaten yet?"

"No."

"There's food for you on the tray." He helped her off with her clothes, then handed her bread, goats' cheese, and a cup of fruit juice. She chewed the food listlessly.

"Did you see Pavel?" Malik said at last.

"Yes. He's awfully weak. It's probably a wonder he's still alive." She swallowed the juice and put the cup back on the tray. "He refused to have any treatment. At least he didn't see me cry—he would have despised that." She fell silent until the lump in her throat eased. "I could always count on Pavel. All those people who turn to me for advice never think I might need advice, too. I think Pavel might have taken an interest in me because he was a little sorry about what happened to my mother, but I could never explain that to Chen."

"Your father calmed down after you left. His anger's past. I told him I'd wait here for you. This should have been a happier day for you, Risa." His hand rested lightly on her shoulder.

Pavel had told her to think of life. All she could see was death making its inevitable demands. "I'm not just mourning for Pavel," she said. "I'm thinking of my father, too. I don't imagine most of us will live quite as long as people on Earth. I might lose Chen sooner than I think, and I haven't even given him a grandchild. He probably thinks I never will. He gave so much to this Project and I—" She stared at the spot on the inside of her left arm where her contraceptive implant had been embedded when she reached puberty. She had thought then that there would be a bondmate and children for her by now.

Malik's grip tightened. "Is that what you want? A child?"

"Yes." She had to say it now but was afraid to turn her head and see his reaction. "I love you, Malik. It's your child I want."

His hand fell away.

"Please don't say anything until I've finished," she said. If she did not speak now, she might never find the courage to broach the subject again. "I want your child, but I won't ask anything more of you. We can draw up an agreement so that you have your rights as a father, but you needn't make a pledge."

"Some in Oberg may find that odd," he said tonelessly.

"Tina's a Plainswoman and so was my mother. Their people didn't care for bonds, and those who disapprove are free to gossip if they like. You can live here as you have, without ties, and if you leave to live somewhere else, I'll see that the child has time with you." She wondered if Malik could sense the urgency in her request, if he could see that this was her way of pushing death from her for a while.

"That's what you want?"

"Tina can do the genetic scan and remove our implants. I don't expect she'll find any problems. I'd rather not wait." I can't wait, she thought; too many years might pass before she loved another man, if she ever found one to love at all. "If you'd prefer not to have ties to the child, we can arrange for that, too. I can always say that I was the one who didn't want a bond so no blame will be attached to you."

"Why are you telling me this?" His hand lifted her chin, forcing her to gaze into his face; she was surprised to see the pain in his dark eyes. "Is it because you don't want me for a bondmate or because you believe I couldn't be a good one? You think I'll fail you. That's what it is, isn't it? You love me enough to have my child, but you're too sensible to tie yourself to someone so useless. Our first night together, you told me I should find a bondmate, but I suppose you had someone else in mind."

"I just don't want you to feel obligated or pressured."

"I understand," he said softly. "I couldn't possibly

change. It never occurs to you that I might need you or want you for a bondmate. I'll make a pledge to you, Risa. I don't know what kind of father I'll be—I never felt the need to become a parent—but I'm willing to try."

This was what she wanted. Why couldn't she feel happier about it? Even now, she wondered if Malik was speaking out of love or from pride and a desire to prove that she was wrong about him.

"Will you be my bondmate, Risa?" he asked. "Even if it's only for a little while, I'll try to make you happy. You may even find that you want to renew our pledge later. I'll try to be more than I've been—I can—"

She touched his lips, silencing him; she did not want to hear too many promises he might not be able to keep. "I'll make a promise to you. When I'm pregnant, when we know there'll be a child—we can make our pledge then."

"If you wish it that way." His hands moved over her as she lay down next to him.

Eleven

Chen stood near the main road, at the edge of the crowd that had gathered outside the mosque in Oberg's main dome. He had not expected to see so many people here; of Oberg's nearly eleven thousand inhabitants, he guessed that nearly three thousand had made their way to this spot, and there might have been more if others had been able to leave their work for this occasion.

He did not see anyone weeping. Pavel Gvishiani had been an old man, and his death was expected. Most of those here were not mourning Pavel; instead, they were marking the passing of an era in their world's history. A few, like him, had probably come to the mosque with a hidden, dimly felt desire to make sure that Pavel was dead.

The mosque was no more than a minaret and four walls surrounding an open courtyard. The entrance to the mosque opened; Pavel's body, wrapped in a white shroud and laid out on a flat bier, was being carried out. Sigurd Kristens-Vitos, dressed in his formal white robe and headdress, walked next to the bier, leading the procession in the direction of the recycler that would receive Pavel's remains.

The people in front of Chen pressed forward. "God is great," Sigurd called out. Others took up the chant. "God is great!" It was one of the few Arabic phrases that Chen understood. He had never heard that Pavel was particularly devout or regular in his observances, but it was rumored that he had made his peace with his God at the end. Chen almost wished that he could believe in such a God, one that might make Pavel suffer for his sins.

"God is great!" several people near Chen cried. Several in the crowd, those wearing the black and red sash of Ishtar, were silent. Chen caught a glimpse of Malik, who was standing near Paul and Nikolai. Like Pavel, but for much less reason, Malik had been disgraced and had lost his Link; he wondered what the scholar was thinking about the honor being paid to Pavel now.

It wasn't right, Chen thought. Didn't these people remember that the dead man had risked the future of the Islands to defy Earth? Didn't they know that Pavel had wanted more power for himself as well as success for the Project? Had they forgotten that Iris had paid for Pavel's miscalculations with her life? To see Pavel honored and mourned in the way Iris had been after her death seemed an obscenity.

Sigurd Kristens-Vitos should not have come to Oberg to pay his respects; it was as though the Administrator approved of Pavel's past actions. Did Sigurd think he could finish what Pavel had attempted, that he could free Venus entirely from Earth? That freedom would have to come slowly, in its own time. Much as Chen wanted such freedom himself, it would have to wait for his descendants. He had seen the price some had to pay when others reached for freedom too soon.

Women were following the men away from the mosque; his daughter was among them. He had hoped Risa would be satisfied with standing among those outside; instead, she had left the house early to be sure of a prominent place with the female mourners. She had always done as she liked, regardless of what he felt; she was like her mother in that.

He had always looked for part of Iris in Risa and had been disappointed when he could not find it. Perhaps that had driven her to confide in Pavel and to see him as another father.

Chen walked among the trees until he came to his bondmate's monument. His fingers fluttered as he remembered how he had molded Iris's face. He had wanted to capture the girl he had met in Lincoln, the one who had dreamed, but those who came here did not see that girl; they saw a self-sacrificing woman whose legend made her seem not quite human. Chen knew how human she had been and how flawed; she had never aspired to be a martyr, yet she was one now, and even he often viewed her in that way.

It was easier to believe that she had been thinking of the Project, even that she had been used by Pavel. Chen did not want to think that she had gone to the threatened dome only to save him.

He was in the airship again. His captor, the pilot called Teofila, had freed him from his bonds. Iris and Amir were still inside the dome, trying to convince the plotters to disarm the charges they had set around the dome's perimeter. The strain of the long wait showed on the pilot's face; her eyes were glassy as she stared at the panels in front of her. She clearly knew that he would not try to attack her now, not while his bondmate was inside. He could only wait and hope that Iris would make the conspirators see reason.

He strained to listen to the voices over the ship's comm. Pavel Gvishiani was saying that Earth was prepared to come to an agreement if the people in the dome dismantled their charges. Did that mean that the Administrator was giving in to their demands? Somehow Chen did not believe it.

The comm was now picking up voices from inside the dome's shelter; the conspirators seemed ready to grant Pavel the concession he wanted. They don't want to die, Chen thought. Perhaps they were too worn down by the endless hours of negotiation to care if Administrator Pavel kept his promise. Maybe they preferred risking punishment rather than accepting certain death if they carried out their threat.

He knew then that Pavel would not give them what they wanted; the man was only playing for time. Once the charges were disassembled, and the box inside the shelter that controlled the charges was taken apart, there would be nothing to prevent an attack on the dome. The Guardians probably had a way to override the controls in this bay from outside and to bring an airship in here. The conspirators would not have time to reassemble their charges; in their present state, they would hardly be able to mount much of a defense against a trained force.

Chen, along with Iris and Amir, might die during such an assault, but that would not matter to Pavel. The hostage

specialists and Habbers were already free, thanks to Iris
and Amir. The Administrator could sacrifice three small
lives to crush the plotters and show Earth that he was still
in control here.

Teofila leaned toward the comm. "They're suiting up
to leave the shelter," she said. "They're going to remove
the charges and take them apart. We've won, I guess."
Chen wished that the pilot would be quiet so that he could
hear what was going on inside. "It didn't take much, did it
—just a threat. I knew they'd give in when they saw we
meant what we said." Her face was sallow. He wondered if
the woman had really been that ready to die.

More voices murmured over the comm; he realized
then that Iris and Amir were still inside the shelter with
two of the plotters. A woman was speaking; he recognized
the voice of Eleanor Surrey. She had not yet surrendered
her control box; the charges could still be armed. Chen was
suddenly afraid.

"You two came here to wear us down," Eleanor was
saying. "Pavel Gvishiani will find a way to hang on now,
and you two will be showered in glory for helping him."
She paused. "No."

Chen heard a thud, then a crash as something hit the
floor. "Can you do anything?" Amir shouted.

"She's already armed them," the other conspirator
replied. "They'll go off in five minutes."

"Listen, all of you!" That was Iris's voice; Chen caught
his breath. "You've got to get to those charges fast. They're
armed now. You've got to take them apart out there." The
people outside the shelter would hear her voice through
their suit comms. He wondered if they would listen, or
would panic and try to get to the bay. "Teofila. You've got
to get your ship out of the bay now. We can't reach you in
time. Get away as fast as you can. If we disarm the charges,
another ship can come for us. I'm closing this channel now.
Farewell, Chen." She had been thinking of him all along,
not just the Project's future; her voice told him that.

Teofila had decided to save herself and Chen, as Iris
had clearly hoped she would. The pilot had ignored his
plea that they wait. The dome had blazed with the bright
white light of an explosion only a few moments after the
airship lifted from the bay. Even then, he could not believe
that his bondmate was gone.

He looked up at the face of Amir Azad, the Linker who had died with her. There had been other lovers for Iris while she and Chen were bondmates; Amir had loved her once. Chen's resentment and jealousy had long since faded. Iris had demonstrated her love for her bondmate in the most final way possible, and he found some solace in knowing that she had not had to face death alone. The two were now a monument to the Project, ennobled by death; love and guilt had no place in their legend.

Chen sighed. Had Iris been here now, she might have gone to the mosque with Risa and said a prayer to her own gods, Mary and Jesus, for Pavel's soul. She would have been happy that Risa was trying to have a child; Bettina had removed Risa's and Malik's implants only yesterday, just before the news of Pavel's death. Iris would have been pleased that the couple, after consulting Oberg's demographic statistics, had decided to have a daughter; female children were more valued on the Plains, and Iris, in spite of choosing to have a son earlier, had retained a few Plains prejudices. She would have sympathized with Malik; Iris had known what it was like to live in a household where intellectual pursuits were mocked or considered impractical.

He closed his eyes for a moment as he ached once again for the woman he had lost.

"Greetings, Liang Chen."

He opened his eyes. Kichi Timsen, the Guide of Ishtar, stood near him; she was dressed in a plain black robe with a sash around her waist. Two young men, also wearing the sash of Ishtar, were behind her.

Chen nodded to the woman. The Guide had to be in her middle years, perhaps as old as sixty, but her light brown face was unlined and her black hair unmarked by gray strands. "Pavel is gone," Kichi said.

"I didn't think you would mourn that," Chen responded.

She lifted a brow. "You don't either, I would guess." She glanced at the image of Iris. "No, I'm marking this moment, not mourning Pavel. He saw that we would have to be free of Earth, and yet he was willing to deliver us to the Habbers. He was far from knowing the truth. Others are far from the truth as well—they don't see that the

Habbers may be greater enemies of our aspirations even than Earth."

"They help us and we need them. They don't want any power over us."

"They separate themselves from planets and the Spirit that dwells within the people who live on them. They wed themselves to their technology instead of seeing it as a tool we won't need in time. Habbers would have us become no more than isolates communing with cyberminds and imagining that our world can be encompassed and bound by conscious thought, but we can't be free by closing ourselves off from part of our nature. When we're able to leave these domes, such barriers will fall away and we'll embrace the Spirit."

The Guide repelled him. Kichi had come to him years ago with her babble about Ishtar, clearly hoping to ensnare the bondmate of Iris Angharads. Her words made little sense to him, and not because he lacked the learning to understand them. He could not see any use in believing in unseen spirits, and he did not know why people would want to give up the technology that had made their visions a reality; that would be like resenting his chisels because he could not shape his pieces of wood with his bare hands.

"I've heard," he said, "that it's more than spirits you embrace." He glanced at the two men with her.

Kichi smiled. "Come to our meetings, Chen. That would ease your pain at the losses you've sustained. You can forget the son who betrayed you to join the Habbers, and the old man who let your bondmate risk her life. You can see Iris in the Spirit of this world and in the women you encounter during our rite."

She must have guessed at how troubled his thoughts would be today and imagined that he would be susceptible to her words. "If Iris were here," he said slowly, "she would have scorned your foolish talk. I won't listen to it in front of her monument."

"More will come to our way," Kichi said as she turned to leave. "Your descendants will see our truth. You'll—"

He hurried away, refusing to hear more.

The crowd had gathered on the plain just beyond the main dome's External Operations Center. Sigurd Kristens-Vitos stood on a low hill with arms outstretched, as if he were about to speak. Chen had intended to return to his home but had little desire either to push his way through the crowd or to detour around it. Risa and the other members of his household were near the foot of the hill, looking up at the Administrator.

"People of Oberg!" Sigurd called out. The crowd's murmurings grew softer and then faded. "It was God's will that Pavel Gvishiani suffer for the errors that he made. Yet even after his disgrace, he continued to labor for this world and won some mercy for himself when he was allowed to spend his last years among you. We can honor him for that and for his devotion to Venus before his head was turned by dreams of power. We can take consolation in knowing that God, the Compassionate and Merciful, allowed Pavel to repent, and that God ordained that Pavel should live to see the beginnings of what he wanted to build. He has won his right to a place on one of your memorial pillars."

Chen could dimly see the fair-skinned man's pleasant features. That face probably served the Administrator well, Chen thought; it was so boyish, so open and ingenuous, with wide-set eyes and a gentle mouth, that Sigurd hardly seemed capable of deception.

"I came here to say a farewell to one who once bore the burden of my responsibilities," Sigurd continued. "Even the Project Council saw no reason not to honor Pavel this day, since he atoned for his deeds. The Mukhtars will always be swift to act against treachery, but they will also forgive those who repent."

Chen's mouth twisted. He doubted that Pavel had ever regretted anything except his failure to become this world's ruler.

"I did not, however, come here only to mourn. Pavel is gone—our Project continues." Sigurd paused for a moment. "It has long pained me that Earth still distrusts us, that the Mukhtars are still mindful of the few Project pilots who fled to a Habitat decades ago and also of the man who wanted to seize the Project for himself. But that man is at peace with God, and now that we can see our world beginning to bloom inside these domes, could anyone wish to betray us by following the example of those pilots? The Habbers who labor here with us only serve our ends and those of Earth, and there is nothing to fear from them. They know that their way is not ours. They know that those who are strong enough to become Cytherians will never surrender power to Habbers, and Earth is coming to see that as well."

Chen recognized most of the people in the crowd by sight; there seemed to be no Habbers among the mourners. He looked toward the round windowless building where some of the Habbers working in Oberg lived, and saw no one standing outside. Some claimed that Habbers could extend their lives past any normal span. The story could not be proved because no Habber had remained with the Project for more than two or three decades, but seeing Benzi's youthful face on his screen had lent some credence to such tales. A funeral might seem meaningless to Habbers.

Perhaps the Habbers were not so wise as they sometimes seemed. Malik had once spoken to Chen of past times, before the rise of the Nomarchies, when well-meaning people with an abundance of resources had tried to help those who had little. Sometimes, such efforts had been successful, but often they had created other problems—people who tried to emulate the more powerful culture only to become alienated from their own people, dependence on the gifts of the wealthier culture, even the destruction of the weaker one.

"The Linker may say that," someone near Chen muttered, "but it's said he's grown closer to Habbers." Chen turned his head slightly; Kichi Timsen and her two companions were near him.

"To one Habber in particular," the second man replied to his friend.

The Guide shrugged. "Too many Islanders think that they can be close to Habbers and remain uncontaminated by their ways. Sigurd can be forgiven by some as long as he's useful. When he no longer is—" Kichi's voice trailed off; her eyes were cold as she stared toward the Administrator.

"Guardians have remained on the Islands," Sigurd was saying, "and yet we have long felt that any reason for their presence is past. Earth must preserve the peace, but we have peace here. We are Earth's children, but children can honor a parent freely without being compelled to obedience. We have pointed this out to Earth on several occasions, and the Mukhtars have listened."

Everyone was very quiet now; even the small children a few paces in front of Chen had stopped fidgeting. "You will be pleased to know," Sigurd said, "that within a week's time the Guardian force will leave the Islands. A few will remain on Anwara, and the others will return with their Commander to Earth. This is a sign of Earth's trust and faith in us. God grant that this trust is never abused."

The crowd began to cheer. Chen was silent, wondering what this announcement meant. Did Sigurd have enough influence over the Project Council and its colleagues on Earth to bring this about? Chen doubted that, even though the Administrator had implied that he did. Earth would not be removing the Guardians only because Sigurd thought it wise; the Mukhtars surely had other reasons for this withdrawal. Chen disliked the Guardian presence as much as anyone, but knowing that the force was on the Islands had kept the settlers subdued. They might now grow more impatient with Sigurd and with those Islanders who had to balance the Cytherians' interests against Earth's. Risa would be on Oberg's Council; he suddenly feared for his daughter.

Kichi Timsen was smiling as the crowd continued to cheer. The pilots had resented the presence of Guardians on the Platform most of all, and many pilots were members of Ishtar. The Guide seemed pleased by the news.

Sigurd lifted his arms, silencing the crowd. "Fellow Cytherians!" he called out. "It is fitting that on this day, when we gather to remember Pavel Gvishiani, we look forward to a future in which we can demonstrate our loyalty to Earth freely as we pursue our destiny here. God be praised!"

"God be praised!" the crowd echoed.

Sigurd moved down the hill and stopped in front of Risa. He spoke with her for a few moments before he greeted another Council member. Chen shook off his darker thoughts. Iris would have greeted this news with joy, been proud of her daughter's new prominence, and chided him for his worries.

He waited until the crowd began to disperse, then made his way home alone.

"I wonder what it means," Bettina was saying. "I used to think Sigurd was too young to hold his position, but he's raised himself in my estimation. If he could make the Project Council see reason on this point—"

"He probably didn't convince them of anything," Paul interrupted. "Earth will save an expense, and there'll still be some Guardians on Anwara. Sigurd was only trying to make himself look good with that little speech."

"It doesn't matter," Grazie murmured. "It means we'll be a little freer than we were, without those wretched Guardians and having to worry that they'd be sent to our settlements. It's too bad the Administrator couldn't have said so outright instead of speaking of how loyal we'll be to Earth."

Malik picked at his food. Most of the talk at supper had been of Sigurd and the Guardians; Pavel had hardly been mentioned. He looked across the table at Risa. Her eyelids were lowered, and her food remained untouched; she alone seemed to be sorrowing for the dead man.

Chen rose and excused himself. The events of the day had clearly tired him, and Malik knew Risa's father had few reasons to mourn Pavel.

"That was something," Nikolai said, "having the Administrator come over to us afterward to greet us—well, to greet Risa anyway."

"Risa's consulted with Sigurd before," Grazie said, "over the screen. He does think something of her."

"Maybe something of Malik, too." Nikolai lifted his brows.

The Administrator had made Malik uneasy. Sigurd's gray eyes had been studying him during the brief encounter; he had seen the man glance from him to Risa speculatively. The Linker had murmured a few words about a paper of Malik's he had recently read while hinting that he might enjoy future discussions with him. He had succeeded only in reminding Malik that the two men were no longer equals.

"You haven't said anything about Sigurd's speech," Bettina said as she gazed at Malik. "You know more about what goes on among the Mukhtars than we do—maybe you have some ideas."

"I can't shed very much light on this topic. When I went to the camp, I knew that various Guardian Commanders were trying to gain more influence over the deliberations of the Council of Mukhtars. I have no way of knowing which faction in that struggle was responsible for recalling the Guardian force here, and no way of finding out. The one message I've had from my family was confined to family news, and it wouldn't be prudent of me to ask if they know more about the current situation."

"Then I might be right," Paul said. "Sigurd probably didn't have much to do with the decision."

"What about you?" Nikolai leaned toward Malik. "It might mean better things for you if your family gets stronger again."

"Little would change for me even if that were the case. My life is here now—that choice was made when I came here. At most, my family might erase the record of my disgrace, but that would be only in the interests of their own reputation. You should hope that whatever struggle's taking place now goes on for a long time, Kolya. That would keep Earth distracted from Venus's affairs."

Malik stood up. "Excuse me," he went on. "I should prepare a discussion for my pupils. With today's events fresh in their minds, it might be appropriate for them to spend some of their free time tomorrow learning more about the Project's history."

Paul set down his cup. "That's something we all know."

"Then my young students must be the exception," Malik replied, "since they seem to know only family stories or exaggerated and misleading tales of individual exploits, along with a few vaguely defined and poorly thought-out ideals." He was revealing too much of his sour mood. "Good night."

He went to Risa's room. He had moved his belongings there the day after her last visit to Pavel. She had explained that they did not need separate rooms now that they were planning to have a child, and since Nikolai was to remain in the household, it was time the Russian moved out of Bettina's examination room. Her request had been reasonable; he could find no objections.

The door closed behind him; he felt trapped. Why had he ever agreed to this? He knew that Risa's feelings for him had deepened, but he had been unprepared for the desperation in her voice. She had given him a way to avoid any real ties; only wounded pride and a half-formed hope that he could grow to love her more had led him to promise a pledge. He was still drawn to her, but the novelty of making love to her and the challenge of surprising her comparatively inexperienced body with his caresses would soon pall.

He had convinced himself that he could find contentment in what he had and know some peace; Administrator Sigurd's speech had changed everything. Guardians would be leaving the Islands, and a few Islanders had fled to the Habbers before. There was a chance, a small one, that he could escape; all it would take was one or two disaffected pilots whom he could trust and the time to make some plans. He could forget the Earth that had disgraced him and the new world that imprisoned him inside a domed settlement. He could free himself from being only a pawn in the game played by the more powerful. How could he happily bind himself to Risa now, with such a possibility, however improbable, tantalizing him?

Bitterness welled up inside him. He thought of the children he taught. Basic skills would be enough for most of them; he was little more than someone who guided them through their lessons. His talk of literature and history was only a momentary diversion for them, his assigned readings only exercises. Even if he found a student who had the makings of a scholar, the demands of life here would eventually force the child to put aside such an ambition. The specialists here and the settlers who arrived from the Cytherian Institute were learned in their way, but they could never replace the community of scholars he had left behind.

He sat down on a cushion in the corner and leaned against the wall. He heard voices outside; Risa was saying good night to Nikolai. The door opened and she walked toward him. Her head drooped; her face was drawn. She sank to the floor and reached for his hand. Knowing that he did not truly love her, and that he would hurt her deeply if he ever admitted it aloud, made him feel a sudden tenderness for her.

He said, "I'm sorry about Pavel."

"He didn't want me to mourn." She lifted her head. "At least you had a chance to meet Sigurd. I didn't know he'd read something of yours."

"It surprised me, too. The piece was a somewhat specialized one on how a scholar during the New Islamic

Nomarchy's earliest days reconciled certain points in Islamic law with the socialist ideology that was prevalent in Central Asia even after those lands were no longer under Russian control." Risa's eyes widened as he spoke; she was trying to seem interested, although he suspected much of his talk mystified or bored her. "On the other hand, the essay might have been of interest to the Administrator, since he's trying to reconcile Cytherian hopes with Earth's desires."

"I've been meaning to speak to him about you," she said, "and now I have a bit of an excuse. If he's curious about your work, then others might be also. Maybe he could arrange some lectures or seminars for you on the Islands when your students have time off from school to learn other skills. Some of the Islanders would probably enjoy that sort of meeting, and you could earn some extra credit."

"Provided, of course, that I avoid problematic or ambiguous speculations."

"You'd have a chance to meet a few of the other Administrators. You probably miss that kind of thing."

He was moved by her concern. Even now, with her other worries and sorrows, she was thinking of him. But the gesture irritated him as well, making him feel even more obligated to her.

"Sigurd's close to a Habber woman," Risa murmured. "I'm sure I don't know what he sees in her, but maybe she'll want to meet you, too."

"We can think of this another time." He suddenly wanted to change the subject, afraid she might glimpse his hidden hopes. He smoothed her dark hair back from her face. "You're getting too thin, Risa." Her small, round body was leaner, her face more angular; the more sharply defined bones made her seem both more beautiful and more fragile.

"I'll get fatter when I'm pregnant. I'll have Tina scan me again in a couple of weeks. I might be pregnant already." She lowered her eyes. "Maybe you've had second thoughts. Some people do after their implants are removed."

"Well, I haven't." His throat felt tight.

"We haven't even talked of how long we'll be bondmates. A lot of people ask for twenty years because they think their children are better off with a longer commitment between parents, but I wouldn't ask for more than ten—we can always renew it after that. I'd rather have our child seeing us choose whether or not to continue a bond instead of being bound by a pledge made years ago."

His lungs felt constricted as he took a breath. He had been hoping she might want only a few years. "Ten years, then, if that's your desire."

"I love you, Malik," she said, "but there's a part of you I can't touch, that I don't know how to reach. I wish I could feel—"

He pressed his lips against hers, silencing her, then pulled her toward the cushion, wanting to lose his doubts in her embrace.

THE COUNCILOR

Twelve

The celebrations marking the beginning of the year 600 had passed two weeks earlier. As Sigurd strolled in the direction of the Administrators' ziggurat, he wondered what this new century of the Nomarchies would bring. More demands from the dome-dwellers, he supposed, and more uncertainty about the resolve of the Mukhtars. During the five years since the Guardians had left his Islands, there had been no changes on the Council of Mukhtars, no news of any shift in alliances or of any Mukhtars losing their posts to be replaced by those more sympathetic—or more hostile—to the Guardian Commanders. The representatives of the Project Council who were stationed on Anwara were content to leave most decisions to Sigurd. That, of course, was to be expected. The Project Council would wait to see which faction grew stronger before acting more directly in Venus's affairs; they had to consider their own positions.

And I, Sigurd thought, have to retain the loyalty of those here while giving no one on Earth cause to doubt my intentions. He did not intend to be pushed aside by whichever faction triumphed.

Alim ibn-Sharif hurried around a bend in the path. The chubby Administrator nodded at Sigurd, muttered a greeting, and then hastened away as if intent on urgent business. Sigurd frowned a little; his colleague Alim might pose a more immediate problem than any Mukhtars. He had taken to chiding Sigurd in a fatherly way about his attachment to Tesia, pointing out that, in the absence of any clear directives from Earth, it would scarcely do for

199

Sigurd to seem friendlier to Habbers in the interim. At the same time, Alim was also cultivating Kichi Timsen and occasionally spoke to Ishtar's Guide over the screen, even though her cult was as hostile to Earth's overt influence as to Habbers. Alim surely harbored ambitions of his own. The man might have given more thought to what was in the Project's interest rather than to what might further his own hopes.

Sigurd had spent part of the past two days in meetings with the Oberg Council. In a month, it would be the turn of the Curie Council to visit, and he supposed he would hear from them what he had heard from the Oberg settlers and from the Tsou Yen Council a few weeks ago—requests for more aid, speedier work on dome construction, and, most of all, complaints about troublemakers among the new arrivals.

Often, he regretted his decision to invite the dome Councils to Island Two for meetings. He had thought such visits would be largely a formality and a way for the settlers to feel more united with Islanders. Instead, they had turned into sessions of complaints and demands for various actions on his part; the Councils didn't seem to realize his limits. Perhaps he had only himself to blame for that. By inviting them here, he had led them to believe that he had the power to handle what they could not solve for themselves.

As he came to the open space in front of the ziggurat, he noticed that Risa Liangharad was at a nearby table under the trees; she was speaking to a white-haired woman. The other woman stood up and clasped Risa's hand; he recognized Alexandra Lenas, one of the Island's embryologists.

Alexandra strolled away; Risa looked toward Sigurd, then beckoned to him. He went to the table and sat down across from her as a small ape cleared away a teapot and cups. "I thought you'd be on your way to the Platform with the others," he said.

"Alexandra caught up with me after the meeting and asked me if I'd stay in her room tonight. Frankly, I didn't know how to refuse, and Oberg can get along without me for one more day. Alexandra's an old friend of my mother's."

Sigurd nodded; he was familiar with the embryologist's record. "She supervised your gestation after your mother's death, didn't she? I suppose she wants to reminisce."

"I imagine so," Risa replied. "She sends us a message once in a while, but usually she's too preoccupied to talk for long. She's like a lot of your people—unless we dome-dwellers are actually here or have some problem that requires your attention, what we do isn't of much concern."

"That is a situation," he said, "that I've been doing my best to remedy."

"Oh, I can understand their feelings when I'm here. Oberg seems almost as far away as Earth."

"I trust your daughter won't miss you too much," Sigurd said.

Risa's expression softened. "Oh, she'll be fine. Chimene gets prettier every day, but that's to be expected —she does take after her father. We both sent a message to her great-grandmother on Earth just before the New Year celebration, and Angharad's reply came the day before I left. I do wish she hadn't gone on about how pretty Chimene is and how many lovers she's bound to have— she'll get quite vain."

"And how is she doing with her lessons?" he asked politely, although his Link could have informed him of the child's progress in school.

"Very well, especially for a four-year-old—she can already read a few words. Actually, I have to tear her away from her screen to get her to do her chores."

"With a father who can tutor her at home," Sigurd said, "I suppose she'll be a good student." A more troubled look came into Risa's brown eyes; he had seen that look before when Malik was mentioned. "Some of the students studying here with our specialists are hoping that Malik will give another set of lectures soon. It is a diversion from their normal courses, yet I'm told he's made no arrangements to come here, and it's been nearly a year since his last visit." His eyes narrowed a little as he peered at her. "Perhaps it's only that he wants more time with you and your child."

"He spends quite enough time with Chimene as it is," she murmured before falling silent.

"As he should," Sigurd said. "Of course, when she's older and more able to look after herself—"

"I've told him you'd like to have him here. I'd rather have him earning more credit and doing what he likes— it'd be one less thing for me to worry about. He seemed a little anxious after his last time with your people." Her mouth twisted. "Maybe he expects a formal invitation from the Islands now."

He wondered if Risa was aware of her bondmate's visits to the Habber residence during his last sojourn on Island Two. Malik had been discreet, and few knew of his visits there, but Tesia had told Sigurd of the Habber woman the scholar had seen. He guessed that Risa was ignorant of those encounters; she would hardly be urging her bondmate to return here otherwise.

"Perhaps he needs a different audience," he said, "one that might offer him more of a challenge and would expect more than merely an intellectual entertainment. Several of the Administrators here have studied more deeply in his field, and a few people on Island Eight have expressed an interest in having such a diversion there. I'll see what I can do."

"It's kind of you to bother about this," she said.

He leaned back in his seat. Risa was a useful ally, and he did not want other concerns interfering with that usefulness. He had sensed for some time that she and Malik were having some difficulties, and he was a little sorry she had taken the man as a bondmate. Separating the pair for a short time would ease one of her worries, and perhaps he could find out from Malik how matters stood between them.

Risa folded her arms. "I should tell you," she continued, "that the others on the Council were disappointed with what you told us today. They were hoping for something a bit more definite."

He sighed. "I should think they'd be somewhat reassured. They complained about some troublemakers among those arriving from the camps. I pointed out that fewer of them have been coming here and that there's every sign Earth will be sending even fewer in the future." He had spoken the truth; the fact that Earth was sending fewer immigrants here, and discouraging others from coming to the camps, was another sign that the Mukhtars were more uncertain. "There's every indication that you won't have so many troublemakers to worry about before long."

"That isn't enough. The others wouldn't say it, but I will. We ought to have more to say about the people who are sent to our settlements from the camps."

"You have that now," he replied. "Your needs are taken into account. You can ask for certain types of workers or even a particular individual who comes to your attention, and it's not in anyone's interest to burden any community with too many settlers at once." He knew that this statement was unlikely to satisfy her, and waited for her response.

"We should have the right to refuse those whose records show they might be a problem. Even some people who came from the camps themselves are saying that. You should hear Kolya on the subject—he thinks a few people are putting them all in a bad light."

Sigurd said, "That's impossible."

"Well, it isn't all we'd like. If anyone persists in creating trouble, we ought to have the right to expel him and send him back to Earth."

"That's even less possible."

Risa struck the tabletop lightly with a fist. "There's more stealing, and not just in Oberg—you must have heard complaints from the other Councils. It used to be enough to threaten thieves with public hearings and marks on their records and restitution, but now we have a few who just shrug that off. They know we're reluctant to call in an Island Counselor, and that they can't be sent back to Earth. They don't care about the disgrace, and there's a small group that almost admires them for being able to get away with something. It's always people from the camps, too—after all, everyone else has been approved by the Project Council or has grown up here."

"It seems," Sigurd said, "that one Cytherian is no longer as good as another."

"Thievery isn't even the worst problem," she said. "I hear rumors about incidents the victims are afraid to report, because they think it'll just bring them more trouble in the end. If we had more to say about the people we admit in the first place—"

"Some of your upstanding citizens are people whose previous records are dubious at best. Will you deny others a chance for something better?" He did not wait for her reply. "And having the power to expel others—" He tapped his fingers against the table. "Aside from the trouble and expense to the Project, it sets a somewhat dangerous precedent, don't you think?"

"That would be a last resort, Sigurd."

"You say that now. Anyway, that's not my primary worry. If the Administrators here grant you that power, we'll be giving you authority Earth doesn't yet want you to have. It can't be done."

"Earth withdrew its Guardians from the Islands, didn't it?" she said. "Seems to me that's giving you more authority to decide things here."

"That's exactly why I refuse to use it," he answered. "The situation remains uncertain, and I'm not about to give the Mukhtars an excuse to tighten their grip once more."

She said, "You're thinking of your own position."

"Consider whether or not you'd be better off with someone like Alim ibn-Sharif in my post as Liaison to the Project Council. My interests and yours coincide—surely you don't want the Mukhtars to have cause to doubt my loyalty."

She gazed at him steadily for a few moments. "If you're so concerned about that, maybe you should put more distance between yourself and the Habbers here— one Habber in particular. That's something else the Oberg Council was reluctant to bring up. We can accept their presence, but we're not foolish enough to view them as friends. It isn't just Earth's opinion you should worry about either—your actions give those fools in Ishtar a way to sow doubt about your loyalties."

"I've considered that," he admitted reluctantly. He thought of Tesia and quickly suppressed his feelings.

"That wretched cult's also complaining about our problems," Risa said. "Kichi Timsen keeps threatening to bring up the subject at a hearing—she says several members of Ishtar are willing to volunteer their services as a patrol, to protect people and ferret out any wrongdoers. She'd just love to have that power—it'd be like having Guardians in our settlements."

"You needn't resort to anything so drastic," Sigurd responded. "There are other alternatives. You can stop

thefts by simply making sure every house has a palm-print
lock and a scanner as well. Tell your people that they must
wear their identification bracelets at all times instead of
only when they're leaving their settlement, and make certain a record is kept of their movements. Make it clear that
anyone who doesn't report an offense he knows about risks
a reprimand or any other punishment you deem suitable.
Call in a Counselor more often for the recalcitrant."

She slumped in her chair. "All of that seems contrary
to our ideals—to everything we've worked for."

"No more than expelling those you can't handle and
depriving them of the chance to atone for their deeds. You
may have to temper your idealism with some realism.
Work this out, or admit that you aren't able to govern
yourselves after all." A few specialists were seating themselves at a nearby table; Sigurd lowered his voice. "You
may tell your colleagues in Oberg that I'll report your
discontents to the Project Council, and tell them that serious problems might be avoided if they exercise more control over the immigrants they send here. It'll be better if
they think of this as my suggestion rather than yours.
That's all I can do."

"They won't act—they'll just dither about it and do
nothing, and if something comes up that we can't handle,
it'll be on the record that you warned the Project Council.
That'll be to your advantage, I suppose, but perhaps not to
ours."

He said, "You sound as if such a situation is inevitable."

"Probable. Let's hope it's not inevitable." Risa rose.
"I've taken enough of your time, Administrator."

Sigurd stood up as Tesia entered his room. Bewilderment flickered in her hazel eyes momentarily; he was
wearing his white robe, and he had set out some tea on a
low table. She was clearly puzzled by such formalities; he
had not told her why he had invited her here.

"Salaam, Tesia." He bowed a little and touched his
forehead. "My Link is open, since it was my wish that other
Administrators here witness our meeting. I've discussed
with them what I'm about to say to you. You may open
your own Link if you like. My colleagues are aware that
I've often communicated to your people through you, but
perhaps you'd prefer to have other Habbers view this

meeting directly. You've often spoken of the lack of a hier-
archy among your people, and this discussion concerns all
of you. I don't want to offend any Habitat-dwellers here by
acting as if I assign you more importance than you have."

She stared past him, her face now composed. She
was wearing a pale green coverall that clung to her slight
body, as if she had anticipated a more intimate encounter.
"I shall open my own Link then," she said, "although
they're hardly offended by having you treat me as an inter-
mediary."

She walked toward the table and sat down; he seated
himself across from her. "In the Name of God, the Compassionate, the Merciful," he muttered quickly. "May His
hand guide us all." Tesia did not respond to the ceremonial
phrase.

Sigurd gestured at the wall screen on his left, where
an image of the Ishtar Terra landmass was visible. He sent
a directive through his Link; the image expanded until the
Lakshmi Plateau and the mountains bordering it filled the
screen. To the west, the narrow range of the Akna Mountains met the Freyja mountain range in the north. Among
the Maxwell Mountains in the east, tiny blisters representing the ten domed settlements glowed.

"Oberg's fourth dome is ready to be settled," Sigurd
continued. "Kepler's and Galileo's new domes can be occupied in three or four more years, and construction on
additional domes for Lyata and Mtshana will soon be completed. As you know, we intended to keep these settlements small, with some twenty to twenty-five thousand
people in each cluster of domes."

"We're aware of that," Tesia said. She was probably
wondering why he was stating the obvious; she would not
guess that he was trying to postpone what he planned to
say. "There will soon be less to occupy my people in the
Maxwell Mountains." She was, he noticed, gently mimicking his stiff, formal tone. "At the current rate of settlement
and reproduction among the dome-dwellers, what you
have there now should suffice for another two decades at
least, according to the statistical projections you have allowed us to see."

"The settlers will no longer require so much aid from
your people, and it was never our wish that we grow too
dependent on your help. Our agreement with you allows

us the right to decide the course of the Project without consultation with you, while you are free to withdraw from here when you wish."

"We promised we would stay," she said, "as long as we were needed and our help was welcomed by your people."

"Then you are prepared, I trust, to begin withdrawing more of your people from the surface settlements. You may leave behind those who are still training some of the settlers in various operations, but within five years your numbers there should be reduced by half. It may ease some of the more distrustful settlers to see this demonstration of the fact that you have no designs on this world."

Her eyes widened. "You know that we don't. We came here—"

"—to help and observe," he finished, "and you have. We remain grateful and now grant many of your people the chance to return to their own home soon. Those of you working on the Islands are free to stay, although I know some of those who have been with us for a decade or two are planning to return to your Habitat. For the time being, you needn't replace them with others. With the pace of the Project slowing, at least temporarily, we won't need as many of your people here either."

Her right hand fluttered for a moment, and then her body was still. "I'm puzzled." She turned toward the screen. "I thought that you were to begin moving more industrial operations to the surface so that the settlers would no longer be so dependent on what's shipped to them from the outside. It's been part of your plan all along —setting up factories in new domes and training those needed to operate them. We've just about finished surveying the Freyja Mountains, and once we clear a site, we could—"

"I think it's best that we not proceed with that phase of the Project for now."

"Has Earth told you this?" she asked. "Have the Mukhtars decided not to proceed?"

"The Mukhtars haven't decided anything yet," he replied. "In the absence of any clear directive from Earth or from the Project Council that represents the Mukhtars on Anwara, we think it best to wait."

Tesia was silent. The moment he dreaded was approaching; he could not delay it any longer.

"Let me be honest with you," Sigurd went on, "as your people claim to be with us. Earth, at the moment, appears uncertain about the Project's future course, although I don't doubt that we shall continue with this glorious venture, God willing. You are not going to use this interim to try to further your own influence."

"I fail to see how helping your settlers to be more self-sufficient would further our influence. Once they have more industrial capacity, they'd have less need of us. Earth would also benefit in the end—they would no longer have the expense of supplying the settlers with things they can make for themselves." Her eyes narrowed slightly. "One might almost think that you fear making them too independent, that Earth is too uncertain of their loyalty to allow that for now."

"The settlers have some distrust of the Mukhtars. That will change. But many of them are also skeptical of your ultimate motives, and this doesn't seem to be the time to make them more dependent on you, as they would be during this phase of the Project."

"That dependence would be temporary," she said.

"But it would also present your people with another chance to drive a wedge between the settlers and Earth—that's how some will see it. Matters are too uncertain now for us to risk that. It would be best for your people and mine to keep more of a distance. This should present no problem for you—after all, you say you have no designs."

"I see." Her voice was very calm, her face composed.

"The geologists here have benefited from your contributions. I was told that your recent study and computer modeling of erosion patterns on Ishtar Terra proved most fruitful. But you've been with us for a few years now, and you must miss your home. You'd probably like to go back."

"I intended to stay, to see my study used to determine sites for domes in the Freyja range." Her voice was strained. "I would also miss my friends here."

"Acquaintances, Tesia, not friends." His chest was beginning to ache; he took a breath. "Surely you don't believe that your people and mine are anything more than two groups whose purposes happen to coincide at the moment. We may mimic its form for a while, but true friendship can never exist between us."

She smoothed back her reddish hair as she gazed

steadily at him. "We can still observe," she said. "We can maintain at least some contact with your people, a connection we value so much. It remains our hope that friendship will eventually be possible." He wondered if these were her thoughts or only what her people now expected her to say. He had spoken as an Administrator; she would have to speak to him as a Habber.

He stood up. "God go with you," he murmured, signaling the end of the meeting. "Do let me know if and when you plan to leave us. There's much to occupy me now, and I doubt I'll have a chance to speak with you again, but you can always leave a message on my screen."

She rose and moved slowly toward the door. The other Administrators would be viewing her through his eyes. He wondered if any of them noticed the slight slump of her shoulders or the hesitancy of her steps in the images they saw. For an instant, he was afraid she might turn to gaze at him and break his resolve.

The door opened, then shut behind her. He closed his Link before any of his colleagues could comment on the meeting. He felt a sudden rage at the circumstances that would always separate him from Tesia, then pushed the feeling aside.

Thirteen

Malik found his daughter loitering outside the pilots' dormitory. A woman in the blue garb of a pilot was talking to Chimene; as Malik approached, the little girl looked down.

"Chimene," he muttered, trying to sound stern. "I thought you and your schoolmates were supposed to be visiting the airship bay today."

"I'm afraid I'm to blame," the pilot said. "I was showing the children one of the airships when we had to clear out suddenly—a ship had to land unexpectedly. We brought the children back inside, and their teacher said he'd take them home, but this one insisted on asking me more questions. I promised the teacher I'd walk her to the west tunnel later. Is she your daughter?"

"Yes, she is."

"Charming child." The pilot hooked her fingers around her red and black sash. "She told the teacher her parents wouldn't mind if she stayed behind for a bit, and I think he had his hands full with some of the crankier kids, so he made her promise that she'd give her schoolmates a report tomorrow on whatever else she learned from me. I hope you don't mind."

Chimene peered up at Malik guiltily, then lowered her long thick lashes. The child knew perfectly well that she should have stayed with the others, but he didn't want to scold her in front of the woman. "It's all right," he said. "I appreciate your taking the trouble to look after her."

"No trouble at all. I told her all about the ships, and

I'm sure she'll give a fine report. She's certainly inquisitive."

"Yes, she is." Malik took Chimene's hand. "Are you ready to go home now?" She nodded. "Thanks again."

The pilot entered the dormitory as Malik led the girl toward the greenhouse complex. "She told me all about the helium cells," Chimene said, "and how the valves work. That's why the other ship had to land all of a sudden —one of its valves was stuck, and Oberg was closer than where it was going."

"You know that you should have gone home with the others, Chimene. Risa's told you not to go wandering off without letting the household know where you are. Did you even think to go to a screen and send a message before you went off with that pilot?"

"No."

"I'm glad you're being honest about that. You were stretching the truth somewhat when you told Yoshi we wouldn't mind if he left you here. I thought you were old enough now to be trusted without a bracelet and tracer, but maybe I was wrong."

She squeezed his hand. "You can't make me wear one now! Everybody'd call me a baby." He slowed down so that she could keep up with him. "You won't tell Risa, will you?"

"I may have to tell her if she gets home before we do," Malik replied.

"Please!"

"Very well. I won't tell her if you promise me you'll let us know where you are."

"I promise."

He smiled a little; he could never stay angry at Chimene for very long. "I hope that pilot was just telling you about her work and not Ishtar." The group was capable of trying to interest even young children in the cult.

"No. She just talked about the airships. Why don't you and Risa like Ishtar?"

"It isn't that we don't like it. We simply have different beliefs. We feel that people should be able to practice any faith they choose without one group trying to tell them that their way is the only right one, that's all."

"But when you told me some of your prayers, you said—"

"I told you what my people believe about God and His Prophet and that they see this as the truth. But they also learned that this isn't something to be forced on others and that different beliefs should be respected. It took them a great many conflicts to find that out, and even now, some can forget. Look at our household—we have different beliefs, and we get along."

"Sometimes you don't," she replied.

"Malik?"

He turned his head to see who had called out to him. A woman was standing near the main road outside the nearest greenhouse. "Malik?" she said again. Her blond hair was shorter and her Russian cheekbones sharper, but her dark upturned eyes were the same. "Don't you remember me?"

"Katya!" He released his daughter's hand as Yekaterina hurried toward him, grabbed his shoulders, then kissed him lightly on the cheek.

"You haven't changed," she said. He hugged her; the body under her gray coverall seemed thinner.

A hand tugged at the hem of his brown shirt; he looked down as he let go of Yekaterina. "Chimene," he said, "this is Yekaterina Osipova. We met on Earth before I came here."

"Salaam," Chimene said solemnly.

"My daughter, Chimene Liang-Haddad."

"I could have guessed that," Yekaterina said. "She's as beautiful as I would expect your child to be."

Chimene beamed. She was, Malik knew, used to such compliments; Risa considered her a little too accustomed to them. His daughter brushed back her curly black hair, then smoothed down her dark green tunic, as if preening herself. "I'm five," Chimene announced. "I had a party for my birthday last week."

"Congratulations," Yekaterina said.

The rosy blush on Chimene's golden-skinned face deepened; her lashes fluttered over her large brown eyes. Malik grinned and ruffled her hair. "I teach at the school in our dome," he said. "Chimene's with another group and another teacher, but I tutor her when I can. Her teacher says she's doing very well."

Chimene drew herself up. "Sometimes I help my friends with their lessons."

"Then you must be very smart," Yekaterina responded.

Malik reached for the woman's hand. "When did you arrive?"

"I've been here since 598, in al-Khwarizmi."

"Three years? And you never sent me a message?"

Yekaterina lowered her head. "I thought of sending one. Then I learned of your bondmate and your new home, and I—" She shrugged. "I didn't know how much you wanted to be reminded of the camp."

"Nikolai Burian still refreshes my memory from time to time," he said. "He's a member of our household, he and the bondmate he found here." Her fingers slipped from his. "But what brings you to Oberg?"

"We were coming in from the Platform. The ship had to land here for repairs—Oberg's bay was closest. I was working on the southern Bat, but this was my last shift, and now I can tend more to my home."

"And how long will the airship stay here?" he asked.

"They said a few more hours."

"Come to my house, then," he said. "We'll have a chance to visit, and you can have supper with us."

"I wish I could." Yekaterina's smile faded. "Alexei's here in Oberg. I learned that he arrived about a month ago."

"I didn't know."

"He would have no reason to seek you out," she said. "He waited so long to get here—it was worse after you left. Some gave up hope and went away from the camp, and fewer came there. I have to see how my brother is now. A man near the tents told me he was working in this greenhouse, and he should be coming out soon."

"Well, I'm sorry you can't join us."

The blond woman sighed. "Maybe I don't want to see him as much as I thought. It seemed such luck for our ship to have to land here, but now I don't know. You remember what he was like—trouble often found him. I had to bribe a Guardian one time so that Alexei wouldn't be expelled." She did not say what the bribe had been. "But he's my brother, and being here may change him."

"I'm sure it will," Malik said as sincerely as he could. "Such a long wait would try anyone's patience."

"I hope he didn't have to wait too long."

Chimene began to pull at his sleeve, clearly impatient with a discussion that did not directly involve her. "But those are my worries," Yekaterina continued, "not yours. Your bondmate is on the Council here—I learned that, too. You must be proud of her."

"Indeed. I'm lucky to have her as a bondmate—people often tell me so." His tone was a bit too sharp.

"We have to go home," Chimene said.

"Yes, I know." Malik took the child's hand. "Katya, send me a message after you get back to al-Khwarizmi. Maybe I'll even arrange to call you so that we can really talk."

"I'll send a message. I'm happy I was able to see you and your daughter."

"Farewell," Chimene said, and glanced from Yekaterina to Malik. He led her away from the greenhouse. He had not even had a chance to ask Yekaterina about her household, or if she had found a possible bondmate for herself, but he was not anxious to encounter her brother.

The tunnel lay ahead; Malik followed a cart into the passage. His spirits lifted as he looked down at his daughter. Chimene, the child he had feared to have, was now one of his consolations. He loved her beauty, her quickness, her delight in the stories he told her, even her often willful nature.

Yet Chimene also bound him to this world. He thought of Aryis, the Habber woman who had diverted him for a time on Island Two. When he had finally worked up the courage to admit his secret hopes to her, the thought of Chimene had prevented him from speaking. Even if Aryis had been willing to help him, he could not abandon his child. He would not leave Chimene to live with the disgrace of having a father who had chosen the Habbers, or the pain of losing a parent.

How the Project might handle such a defection did not concern him. Sigurd Kristens-Vitos was putting some distance between himself and the Habbers; he had even given up his Habber woman nearly a year ago. The Administrator's position would certainly be weakened if any settler managed the almost insurmountable task of fleeing to a Habitat, and Earth might again take sterner measures. Both Islanders and dome-dwellers would no longer be trusted.

Malik left the tunnel. The west dome's disk of light gave off the glow of a late afternoon. Behind fences around a few of the houses, goats were grazing; two young women were carrying rabbit cages into one house. Inside a greenhouse, he saw the shadowy forms of two neighbors tending their tiers of peanut plants and beets.

The settlers were content to labor and live their circumscribed lives in the hope that their children would inherit a world. The Mukhtars would allow them the illusion of freedom to give Earth a foothold here. The domes seemed nothing more than a vast laboratory in which to test various subjects, to discover if people would willingly become prisoners of the dream of terraforming, to find out if human beings could transform other worlds without losing their ties to the old or shedding their humanity, as it appeared the Habbers might.

Chimene tugged at him. He knelt down and let her climb onto his back. He would not see his daughter limited by the Project's demands; he would help her to reach for what she wanted. He would not let her become only another link in a chain that stretched toward an indefinite, hoped-for future; she would find her freedom in this life.

By suppertime Risa had still not arrived. The rest of the household began to sit down for the evening meal. They were used to having Risa get home late; someone was probably pestering her about a minor dispute.

Bettina, after ushering a patient to the door, came to the table just as Nikolai was setting down a large bowl of stew. Although Bettina was a simple physician and not a medical specialist, the amount of contact she had with patients had surprised Malik at first. During his former life, he had encountered physicians only rarely. His genes had been mapped before birth, as were everyone else's, and the potential for various genetically linked diseases eliminated. He had expected attention from physicians only if he suffered an injury, when he grew old enough to require rejuvenation treatments, or later, when age began to take its toll and intervening might be able to give him a few more healthy years. His family had disapproved of the techniques some used to postpone puberty in the hope that this might make a child better able to concentrate on his studies without the hormonal distractions of adolescence.

Bettina could have assessed her patients simply by viewing results of med-scans on her screen most of the time, yet she visited them often, and they came to her. Gradually, Malik had come to understand why. Many problems, the sort that a Council member could not handle, were brought to the physicians and paramedics here under the guise of being medical concerns. Bettina and some of her medical colleagues had taken the place of the Counselors the settlers so distrusted.

"Some blight's affecting the potatoes in the community greenhouse," Nikolai said as he helped himself to stew; he now worked in the west dome's greenhouses between his shifts in the airship bay. "We'll have to dig up a lot of the plants."

Emilia poured herself a small glass of whiskey. "That means there'll be more demand for ours. Lucky for us that you and Risa decided not to try those new plants." Nikolai's bondmate was a thin young woman with mousy brown hair and a pale, narrow face. "Our soybeans are doing well enough, but I think we ought to try for more spinach."

Malik tried to pretend he was interested. In the nearly four years since Emilia Knef had joined this household, he had rarely had a real talk with her or, for that matter, with Nikolai. The couple were not people to waste too much time in idle chatter when work was to be done; their conversations revealed two unreflective minds immersed in practicality. Nikolai and Emilia spoke of soybeans, plant blights, faulty door-opening circuitry, clogged plumbing, and ways to increase the household's credit as if these were life's greatest challenges.

He sniffed; a faint odor of fish had permeated the room. Lately, Nikolai and Paul would get up early to go to the lake whenever fishing was allowed from the small docks recently built along the shore. The Russian had quickly discovered that others would trade with him for fresh fillets. He cleaned his catch in the kitchen; now the common room often stank of Kolya's enterprise.

Paul and Grazie, at the other end of the table, were questioning their son Patrick about his lessons. "How do you know you're not interested in geology?" Grazie said.

Patrick glared at his food. "I just do." He had his fa-

ther's reddish-blond hair and his mother's dark eyes; he
wore the pout that was his usual expression. "Anyway,
what do I need it for?"

"That isn't for you to decide," Paul responded. "Don't
you want to learn enough to be able to make certain decisions about what others tell you? That's why you're in
school, you and the other children. Would you rather have
Linkers and specialists decide everything for you?"

Patrick shrugged. "They decide a lot of stuff, anyway."

"But we have something to say about it. You should be
grateful for the chance to have lessons. Your grandmother's people weren't so fortunate—where Tina came from,
only a few could go to school."

"Look at Chimene," Grazie added. "A year younger
than you, and already she has to help you with some of
your work. You could follow her example."

Patrick gazed sullenly at Chimene. She blushed and
hunched over her food, having the grace to look embarrassed. Malik sighed. He had suggested gently to Grazie
and Paul that harping at their son was not likely to produce
the desired results. They were like several of the parents
who interrogated him about their children. The ones without much learning wanted their young ones stuffed with
knowledge; the ones with more education wondered if
their children were learning the right things. Most of them
wanted a rather improbable result—a child who would
master the curriculum thoroughly while never raising difficult or troubling intellectual questions. What they usually
got was a child who limited his ambitions to mastering a
useful skill or a necessary scientific or technical specialty.

Free Cytherians, he thought bitterly. They were free
to imprison themselves.

"Patrick does his tasks around here," Chen said then.
"He deserves some praise for that." Patrick shot a triumphant look at Chimene; this was an area in which the girl
was often negligent. Chimene, Malik thought, took after
her father in that way.

Malik picked at his food. Nikolai and Grazie were the
best cooks in the household, but they had been eating
rabbit stew for three days now, and the food was growing
tiresome. Nikolai, sensibly enough, made a lot of whatever
he cooked so that he wouldn't have to bother with the
same task the next day.

Malik could not find fault with the manner in which this household treated him. They were kind enough; if he still knew little of their inner thoughts and fears, he supposed they knew even less about his. They had to be aware that his feelings for Risa had cooled, but they probably ascribed that to Risa's preoccupation with the Oberg Council and the stresses of rearing a child. The other couples at the table had their own disputes; the difference was that they seemed to settle theirs.

Bettina stood up. "I've got some scans to study," the physician said, "and a couple of people to talk to." She left the common room. Nikolai and Emilia cleared the table, while Paul murmured of a promise to share a drink with a friend.

"I'll be out in the greenhouse," Grazie announced. "Patrick, I want to see you in your room and asleep by the time I get back." The children waited until the door closed behind her, then sprawled on the floor with a small screen to play a game.

Nikolai and his bondmate soon retreated to one of the rooms they had added to Bettina's wing. Malik stared after them, then knelt to wipe off the table. Even after nearly four years of being pledged, the two often found excuses to be alone. He grimaced as he stood up, remembering that he had not told Emilia about the slightly unpleasant smell in his wing's bathroom. He guessed that either the toilet's suction tube or the waste dryer-compressor was to blame, but there was no use in trying to pinpoint the problem himself. Even Risa had learned that it was easier to let someone skilled handle such problems than to nag Malik into making futile efforts at repairs.

Chen could attend to the toilet, but the old man was sitting at his table, carving a piece of wood, and Malik did not feel like disturbing him. Chen had always been tolerant of Malik's failings; he had even reproached Risa for dwelling on them. "I can do things Malik can't," Chen would say, "and he knows things I don't. There's no harm in that." It was a pity Risa could not share her father's more philosophical attitude.

She knew what I was like, he told himself; she knew from the beginning that our bond might be a mistake. He had never failed her as a bed-partner and gave her what affection he could. She had admitted to him that she had once expected little more from any bondmate, but that admission had come during their first months together, when he had found it easier to soothe her with talk of a love he occasionally felt.

Yet she had also given him Chimene. He glanced at his daughter's dark head; his love for her was unclouded by doubts.

The door opened; Risa entered the common room. Malik smiled automatically as he went to her, took her hands, and kissed her on the cheek. "Have you eaten?" he asked.

She nodded. "With Noella and Theron. That reminds me—he wants to talk to you. He was going to invite you over, but—"

"I'll call him up."

"You're stupid," Chimene said suddenly.

Patrick sat up. "I'm not."

"Yes, you are. That maze is simple."

"You're stupid," Patrick replied. "At least I don't go wandering off by myself in the main dome."

Chimene pushed the screen aside. "You said you wouldn't tell!"

"What is this?" Risa asked. "Who's been wandering around in the main dome?"

Patrick bit his lip, then glanced at Chimene. "I didn't mean it," he said, "but you shouldn't call me stupid."

Risa tapped her foot. "I want to know what you're talking about."

Patrick stared at the floor. "Yoshi took us to the airship bay," he muttered, "and then this ship had to land, so we went inside, and Chimene wanted to talk to the pilot some more, so she asked Yoshi, and he said it was all right."

"He did?" Risa frowned.

"Chimene said you wouldn't mind." The boy's voice was now a whisper.

"And I don't suppose you bothered to contradict her." Risa folded her arms as she gazed down at her daughter. "I've told you not to wander around without supervision, especially anywhere near those tents. You know there have been complaints about some of the newer settlers. Did you even bother to send a message here about what you were doing?"

Chimene did not reply.

"Probably not, because you know what I would have said about it. It seems I'm going to have to speak to Yoshi and tell him to disregard any excuses you give him in the future. I'll have to let him know—"

"I was going to leave a message!" Chimene looked up at Malik with a look of desperation. "And I wasn't alone, I was with the pilot, and then Malik came by, and I knew he would, so I didn't do anything wrong."

"Really," Risa said. "Then why did Patrick say you were wandering around?"

"I didn't mean it," Patrick said glumly. "I just said it because I was mad."

Chimene was still gazing at Malik. "It's all right," he said as his bondmate turned toward him. "I left my students at our greenhouses with Leilani, and they'd finished their work for the day, so I thought I'd take the time to go over to the southeast dome and speak to Helder Arneld— he wanted to ask me about a small seminar I'm planning for him and a few of his friends."

Risa's eyes narrowed. "You could have settled that over the screen."

"He invited me, and I thought it would be rude not to go—anyway, I needed the exercise, and Chen said something a few days ago about wanting to check the monument, so I decided to do that as well." So far, he was telling the truth, although his elaborate explanation made it seem like a lie. "Chimene obviously knew I'd be in the main dome when she was there, so I can't see that this matters. The pilot answered a few of her questions about the ships —in fact, she seemed quite taken by Chimene's interest in her work. I hardly think that Chimene should be punished for being curious, especially when she knew I'd be there to look out for her."

Chimene's large dark eyes widened with relief, and obvious admiration of his cleverness. He had shaded the truth a little, but surely his promise to his daughter that he would not tell Risa about the incident outweighed any demand for total honesty.

"I see." Risa pursed her lips. "And I suppose you were both going to tell me about this adventure just before Patrick spoke."

"You have so much on your mind lately," Malik said. "Chimene sometimes gets the feeling that you don't have much time to hear of her doings, and perhaps her reluctance to tell you about her day led Patrick to think she was keeping a secret."

Risa was silent; he had disarmed her, at least for now. Chimene still looked impressed. Chen lifted his head and watched Malik and Risa for a moment before turning toward the children. "Patrick," the old man said, "the next time you make a promise to someone, try to keep it, or else consider if it's a promise you should make. You shouldn't make promises you might have reason to break. And you, child." He focused on Chimene. "You shouldn't demand privileges your friends don't have until you've earned them. Perhaps you should have stayed with the other students even if Malik was nearby, instead of deciding you were free to do what you liked."

"Yoshi let me stay," Chimene objected. "I'm more ahead in my lessons than the others. Why shouldn't I—"

"People don't like it when you demand too many favors," Risa answered. "You'd better start learning that, Chimene."

"It wasn't a favor. Anyway, Yoshi said I have to do a report tomorrow about what the pilot told me, so the others'll hear all about it."

"And have you prepared one?" Risa said.

"Yes."

"Then you can come to your room with me and help me mend the tunic and pants you ripped. If your father insists on wasting credit having Grete make nice clothes for you, the least you can do is learn how to take care of them. Patrick, you should probably be studying instead of playing games."

Chen resumed his carving; Patrick heaved a sigh as he picked up his screen. Malik walked toward the hallway, deciding that he would call Theron from his room.

"So you think the children need more lessons in history and literature," Malik said when Theron had finished speaking.

"Among other things."

"I'm not sure why. Some of the parents will complain that they're pursuing those studies at the expense of more important parts of the curriculum."

Theron frowned as he stroked his short brown beard.

"I thought you'd leap at the chance to design a new program for them," the other teacher said. "It's at least as important as setting up your little lectures and discussions for Islanders and others—maybe more so."

Malik had to agree. He and Theron had often talked of the deficiencies in the curriculum. The children were largely taught skills and knowledge that had a practical end in view. Theron felt that they needed a broader base, a wider perspective from which to consider their own lives, more knowledge of the achievements and failures of the past, and the intellectual tools that would enable them to arrive at their own values and goals. In short, if they were to govern themselves, they needed to know how to think.

Malik had not expected that his colleague was now ready to put his views into practice. Perhaps he had encouraged Theron too much by agreeing with him and pointing out that the power of the Mukhtars lay partly in their control of information and the education offered to the citizens of the Normachies.

"You see what most of our charges will become," Theron continued, "people who will do their work with a vague sense that it's worthwhile and contributes to the Project, and who measure their progress mostly by whatever credit or goods their households manage to attain. Oh, they think they're better off than they would be on Earth, but they couldn't say why. They believe our way has more to offer a human being than that of the Habbers, but they wouldn't be able to explain that either."

Malik leaned toward his small screen. "Most of them may not be capable of much more."

"Now you sound like an Earthman again. I thought you knew better by now. You've complained to me often enough. You've got a daughter, and you'd like to broaden her mental horizons, wouldn't you?"

"Of course." He refused to admit that he rarely discerned the mental spark in other children that he saw in Chimene. His child was better than the others; that was also an Earth-like thought.

"They begin by being curious," Theron said, "and then they learn to close their minds to things that don't appear useful, but they yearn for something we don't provide. They're too vulnerable to a group like Ishtar, which feeds their longings and resentments with its high-flown

talk of a spirit that lives in us all and the perfect world we'll
have. They don't even have the tools to assess the way
Kichi Timsen distorts history in her talks. All they know is
that, if it makes them feel better to believe it, then it must
be true."

"I haven't noticed that Ishtar's made many inroads
lately." Malik looked away from Theron's image for a moment. "Maybe we worry about them too much. I can't say
that I care for their notions, but—"

"What is it, Malik?" Theron tilted his head. "Is it the
extra work? I know you'd earn more credit elsewhere, but
you're the only teacher we have with enough education in
these fields to set up a worthwhile program. I've discussed
this with one of the Island Administrators, and she thinks
it's worth pursuing, even if some object."

"People who think too freely and openly for themselves can be troublesome," Malik replied, "as I've had
ample reason to discover."

"This isn't Earth."

Malik smiled a little. Even if their students willingly
accepted these intellectual offerings, the demands of their
lives would force them to put such pursuits aside. Did
Theron think that the children would learn how to reason
their way to a clear-eyed acceptance of their lot? They
might instead become more conscious of their limits here;
perhaps some would begin to long for what the Habbers
offered, as Malik did.

"Do consider this," Theron said. "It could be a real
contribution."

A contribution I'm not making now, Malik thought.
His lectures and seminars were only a minor intellectual
recreation; his words, like Chen's carvings, were little
more than toys to be amused by and to display to one's
friends. He was no longer bitter about that; since his audience expected so little, he did not have to confront the
issues and doubts that troubled him directly.

But if he were to give his young students a meaningful
experience, he would have to raise such issues and contend
with them openly. He would have to be provocative, and
some were certain to see that as dangerous. His spirit
warmed to the challenge for a brief instant and then faded.
Time spent on this venture would have to be subtracted
from the lectures that both earned him more credit and

removed him, for a little while, from Risa's troubled
glances and petulant complaints. Challenging his students
to think for themselves and ask difficult questions might
raise doubts about his loyalty to this new world—doubts
that would, in a way, be justified.

He had won a kind of peace for himself, even if it was
only the peace of surrender. Better to keep what he had,
win what he could for Chimene, and leave the future of
this world to others.

"I will think about it," Malik said at last. He was committing himself to very little, and wondered if he could
cleverly devise an innocuous program that would also satisfy Theron.

"Good. Do come by when you want to discuss this
further. You've done so well with the students you've
taught."

Theron's image faded. He had failed his students already, whatever the other teacher thought; they mastered
their lessons and little more.

The door opened. "Something's wrong in the bathroom," Risa said as she entered the room.

"I know. I'll speak to Emilia."

"I put Chimene to bed. She claims you promised her a
story, but I told her she'd just have to do without one. You
didn't fool me, you know. You probably just happened to
be in the main dome while Chimene was wandering
around, and then you craftily cover up for her while telling
me that I don't pay enough attention to her."

"She didn't do anything so wrong."

"She knows the rules," Risa said, "and you're not setting a very good example by showing off in front of her."

"You're too hard on her."

Risa sat down on the bed. "You indulge her too much,
Malik. I know she's young, but she has to learn that she
can't always do what she likes. I don't want her to get the
idea that she'll be treated any differently from anyone
else." She paused. "She told me you met someone today—
a woman named Katya."

"Yekaterina Osipova. I knew her in the camp. Kolya
knew her, too."

"And was she—"

"Katya and I were lovers, if that's what you want to
know." He lifted his head. "It was over even before I left

the camp. She was only here waiting for her ship to be repaired before going on to al-Khwarizmi. We didn't talk long. Her brother Alexei Osipov is one of the new settlers here, and she wanted to see him."

Risa's eyes narrowed. "I hope you and he weren't close."

"We weren't."

"Just as well. His name's come up in a couple of complaints lately—fights, that sort of thing. We'd be better off without such people."

"Camps wear people down with waiting," he said. "Maybe he just needs time to adjust."

"You can find excuses for anyone, can't you?"

He did not feel like contradicting her. "Helder Arneld wants me to meet with his little group in a few days, when our youngest students have a couple of weeks off from school. His younger sister's still on the northern Bat, so he told me I could stay there for the three days we'll be meeting—it makes more sense than walking all that distance there from here every day. I thought Chimene might come with me."

"Have you promised her she could?" Risa asked.

"I thought I'd ask you first."

"I'd rather she didn't, then. She might better spend the time doing her chores and helping in the greenhouse instead of traipsing around the southeast dome."

"Don't you think a change might be good for her?" He stood up and moved toward the bed as Risa got to her feet.

"Sometimes," she whispered, "I think you only stay with me because of her."

"That's ridiculous," he said evenly, and covered her mouth with his before she could reply. His hands slipped under her shirt. He still had one way of reaching her and of pretending that everything was right between them. Her lips softened under his as she clutched at his back; he closed his eyes.

Fourteen

"You don't need a consultation," Bettina said as Risa sat down on the examination table. "Your med-scan is perfectly normal, as I expected." Risa said nothing. "Are you looking for a medical excuse not to run for the Council again?"

Risa shook her head.

"You and Malik are thinking of another child, then."

"I'd like one," Risa admitted, "but I don't know if Malik does."

"Why not ask him?"

Risa folded her arms and hunched forward. "Tina, I don't know what to do."

The physician settled back in her chair. Bettina, Risa thought, had probably guessed that her problem was not medical when Risa had asked to speak to her here. Grazie and Emilia would be of no help. Grazie would sympathize but was also likely to gossip; Risa had gained various nuggets of information from her in the past. Emilia assumed that almost everyone shared her even, placid temperament and would be surprised that Risa had a problem.

"I haven't heard that kind of thing from you since you were a girl," Bettina said. "What's wrong?"

"It's Malik," Risa responded. "That can't be much of a surprise."

"It is. You two seem to be more distant, but that's normal enough, and we always knew he was a different sort of man."

"I've tried not to be too obvious about my feelings." Risa sighed. "We certainly can't have a Council member

226

looking as if she's got troubles with her bondmate. I can't even talk to Noella—she'd probably say something to Theron, and then he'd try to give Malik some friendly advice, which wouldn't help."

"Is it that your feelings for him aren't as strong or have his cooled?"

Risa stared at the pale green floor. "I feel the same way I always have. I love him, Tina, but he doesn't love me."

Bettina cleared her throat. "Has he said so? Does he fail you in bed? Is he cruel to you in some way I'm unaware of?"

"No, it's nothing like that. He probably thinks I'm cruel to him. I say things before I can stop myself, words I know won't do any good."

"Why do you say them, then?" Bettina asked.

"Because when I do, at least he looks at me and sees me—he knows I'm there. The rest of the time he closes himself off. It'd almost be better if he hated me, because then he'd be feeling something for me. Even when he makes love to me, he seems to be somewhere else, as if he's imagining another woman." She thought of the night he had returned from the southeast dome. In the middle of their lovemaking, she had suddenly cupped his face in her hands, forcing him to gaze into her eyes; he had looked shocked, almost surprised to find her there.

"Do you think his affections have strayed?"

"I don't know," Risa said. "If there were anyone in Oberg, I would have heard some gossip by now, and whatever happens on the Islands can't matter or he'd find excuses to go there more often. Anyway, he'd hardly risk actions that would make Chimene think less of him, and she's too young and possessive to understand anything like that."

"You sound almost as if you view the child as a rival."

"Maybe she is," Risa muttered. "If he could find an excuse to leave and take her with him, he might. He thinks I'm too hard on her and that I don't love her enough. It isn't true, but if I left her upbringing entirely to him, he'd give her anything she wants so that she'd love him all the more."

"He's not a bad father—better than some."

"I know that," Risa responded, "and I'm grateful, but I

don't want him passing on his own failed hopes to her. He's
tried to adjust, but he lost so much when he came here. I
want him to be content with what he has now and to feel
he has something to offer, but I always end up sounding as
though I'm criticizing him. And Chimene's like him—she's
beginning to think she was made for better things. I don't
want her to be like that. I see the same look in their eyes
sometimes—as if they both see me as somebody who's
imprisoning them."

She had thought that speaking to Bettina might ease
her mind, but the self-pitying words that imperfectly captured how she felt disgusted her. Her chest ached, and if
she wasn't careful, she might cry; she had always loathed
such sodden displays. She had made her choice; what
Malik had given her should be enough.

Bettina said, "What you need is another man."

Risa gaped at her, then laughed softly. "That sounds
like something my grandmother Angharad would say, assuming I could ever explain this to her." She wiped at her
eyes. "You sound just like a Plainswoman now."

"There's some wisdom among Plainsfolk. It's easier
when men and women come together in bed and live
separate lives the rest of the time—it keeps you from mud-
dling your life and confusing sex with your need for love."
Bettina smoothed back a few gray strands in her reddish
hair. "But that isn't possible here, and your father's shown
me that deeper attachments can exist."

"I have a bond," Risa said. "I can't live like a Plainswoman."

"I'm not saying you should. Malik's awakened a need
in you, one that you didn't feel before, one that grows.
Now you believe he's the only man who can satisfy it, but
that isn't so, and you should find that out. Surely you know
of a few men who might make good bed-partners and who
would be discreet. When you learn that one of them can
satisfy you, too, you won't cling to Malik so much. You
wouldn't have to demand what he might not be able to
give. You could then see exactly what you can have from
your bondmate—a deeper love, perhaps, or a lasting
friendship, or a bond as parents of your child. You wouldn't
confuse that with your other needs anymore." Bettina
shifted in her seat. "It's a pity that Malik wasn't younger
when you met."

"I wonder if that would have made any difference."

"Why do you think your parents were able to love for so long?" Bettina said. "They met when they were very young, so they didn't have too many burdensome memories to hold them back from each other. Oh, they had their problems and their times apart—Iris was a Plainswoman— but when they were older, they had the memory of that early love to bring them together again. They knew it was possible to reach out to each other and share themselves without restraint. That's why an early love is so important. It's why the most lasting bonds are often among those who come together when they're young, before they're hurt and scarred. Age doesn't bring wisdom in love, in spite of what some will tell you—only caution and a desire to protect yourself."

Bettina rested her narrow face against her hand. "Malik has too much of a past—his old life, his disappointments, his intellectual pride. Find what you need somewhere else. When you're not clutching at your bondmate so much, he may feel freer to offer you more. If he doesn't, you'll have something for yourself. Malik isn't the only one holding back, you know. You do the same—you always have."

"It's the way we have to live here, Tina. We can't just forget—"

The door opened suddenly; Paul stepped into the room. "Sorry to interrupt," he said, "but Istu Marnes is on the screen, and he wants to talk to Risa. He says it's important, but he won't say what it's about."

"Talk to him here." Bettina rose and left the room with her son. Risa slid off the table, went to the small screen on the desk, and opened a channel.

Istu Marnes's dark brown face appeared. "We have a problem," he said quickly. "A woman's been killed."

"What?"

"Murdered—or so it seems."

Risa sagged against the narrow desk. "It can't be. There must be some mistake."

"No mistake. The victim was Nora Toland. One of her housemates found her body at first light in the house's common room. Three men were seen leaving the house earlier. They're confined in the Administrative Center at the moment."

Risa leaned toward the screen. "But why—"

"Nora's household called me after a physician told them nothing could be done for her. I took what steps I could and then called Jeannine. She'll be at your house soon. To save time, she'll fill you in on what I told her when you're both on your way to the main dome. We'll have to have a Council meeting now, with all of us present, and make it appear we're in control of this until we figure out what to do. Tell your team you won't be working today, but don't say exactly why—they'll find out soon enough."

Risa nodded, unable to speak.

"I'll get hold of the other Council members. Get here as soon as you can."

Jeannine Loris had been one of the first settlers to move into Oberg's recently completed southwest dome. She and her daughter's family had disassembled their house in the main dome, left the stone foundation for another household to build upon, and moved to the newer dome, where, Jeannine claimed, there would be more space, at least for a while. That she would also be farther away from the new arrivals was an additional benefit.

"I knew we'd have more trouble," Jeannine muttered to Risa as they left Risa's house, "but I never expected this."

"Tell me what Istu told you."

The middle-aged woman lacked Istu's conciseness, but Risa had heard most of the story by the time they were inside the main dome. Nora Toland's body had been found, and her household had summoned Gupta Benares. The physician had determined that the cause of death was a severe blow to the head, an injury he might have been able to treat had the victim been taken to the infirmary immediately. One of Nora's housemates had called Istu, the Council member nearest to the house; by the time he arrived, neighbors were already gathering at the scene. One neighbor, an engineer named Yakov Serba, had described the three he had seen leaving the house when he was returning home late from work.

"You couldn't ask for a more reliable witness than Yakov Serba," Jeannine said as they moved past the slender trees surrounding the Buddhist temple. "Everyone knows he'll be on the Council himself someday."

"Was he sure?" Risa asked. "The light would have been very dim."

"He was sure. The door opened while two of them were still inside, and there was plenty of light there. He saw enough of the third to see that he had blond hair. Anyway, he'd seen them all before because they'd come to Nora's house a couple of times. When he described them, the others in her household said they knew who the men were. No signs of any forced entry were found, so it seems Nora let the three inside."

To hear of a murder was bad enough; to think someone could die at the hands of those invited into her house made Risa shudder. She had been assuming that the men were intruders who had entered while everyone was asleep in order to steal, and that Nora might have surprised them in the act. Someone clever enough, with the right tools, could find a way to circumvent a palm-print lock or enter through a window, but the chance of being caught was great.

Her security had rested in the knowledge that she could trust most of the people around her and that the few who engaged in misdeeds were almost always called to account. When they were not, it was only because their victims, for whatever reasons, refused to complain. A new evil had entered her world.

"Istu finally convinced everyone to go about their business," Jeannine continued, "which must have taken some doing, given the circumstances. He and Yakov, along with a few others, went with the household to the tents near the bay and found the three men."

"They were new settlers, then," Risa murmured.

"Did you expect anything else? Yakov identified them, and Nora's housemates confirmed that they'd come to the house before. They didn't deny that, but they insisted Nora was alive when they left. They're in the Administrative Center now, under guard. A few people in Ishtar volunteered for that job."

"Ishtar?"

"Nora Toland's a member—was a member. One of her housemates said she'd been trying to interest the three men in the group. Maybe that's why she invited them in—probably thought she'd snag some new members. Why they killed her, I can't begin to guess."

"Maybe they didn't," Risa said. "If they deny it, what proof do we have?"

Jeannine halted in front of the white rectangular building that was used as a church. "Who else could have done it?"

"I don't know, but—"

Jeannine took her arm as they walked on. "We've got trouble enough, Risa—don't borrow more. It doesn't look as if anyone else came to that house, so you'd have to accuse the people who live there. You can't seriously believe—"

"It isn't impossible. I've heard enough complaints about troubled households, and so have you. Unless we can prove—"

The Administrative Center lay ahead, directly under the main dome's wide disk of light. The building's two wings were set at right angles to a central one-story structure that had served as a shelter after the dome had been erected. Risa recalled the day more than twenty years ago, when she and her father had first come to Oberg. They had been full of hope as they looked out over the empty grassy plain and low hills; Chen had told her this world would be safe from the evils of the old.

Only a few people had gathered outside the Center, most of them in the blue garb of pilots and the red and black sash of Ishtar. They stared at her in silence as she and Jeannine approached the building. Evar was among them; his blue eyes gazed at her steadily.

The two women went inside. Others were sitting on the floor of a large, empty room. Outside a door on Risa's left stood four young men in Ishtar's sash.

The door directly opposite that one opened; Istu Marnes beckoned to Risa. This room was where the Oberg Council usually met on those occasions when they felt the need to discuss matters in person or to hold hearings. Istu did not speak until the door closed behind them. Alain al-Kadar and Curcio de la Cruz were seated behind a low table near one wall, a large screen to their right.

"We're all here now," Istu said as he ushered the two women to cushions, "and I've got some more information. Yakov and a few others searched the tent of the three we're holding, and found a spot where something had been buried. They dug it up. A large stone carving of a bear was there, along with a shirt. The carving had been wiped, but traces of blood were found on both the stone and the shirt. Two housemates of Nora's identified the carving as one the dead woman owned, and then Yakov took it and the shirt to the infirmary. I just had a message from one of the physicians—the blood is Nora's. And there's something else." Istu heaved a sigh. "Three bracelets were found in one man's pack. Seems those were Nora's, too."

Jeannine sat down and brushed back a lock of graying hair. "I guess we have proof," she said. "What do we do now?"

Curcio de la Cruz looked up. "There'll have to be a hearing. And then what? Do we give them a reprimand, or sessions with a Counselor? Do they make reparations? What kind of reparations would be enough for something like this? We never expected to hold a hearing for murderers."

Alain al-Kadar frowned at the pocket screen on the table in front of him. "Maybe they don't deserve a hearing."

Risa seated herself. "We'd better review everything Istu's discovered and look at the records of these three men. Then I think we should talk to them." She still felt numb from the shock of hearing about this murder. "We have to find out exactly what kind of men they are."

The Council members were silent as the three men were led into the room, their hands behind their backs. Risa saw then that their wrists were bound. The four who had volunteered to guard them lingered at their sides.

"No telling what they might do," one of the guards said as he adjusted his red and black sash. "We thought it'd be wise to restrain them a little. Do you want us to stay?"

"You might as well," Risa replied, "although I doubt they'll make matters worse for themselves by threatening us."

The guards stepped back. Two of the accused were staring at the floor; the third gazed directly at Risa. She had expected to see fear and perhaps repentance, but his dark eyes gleamed with defiance. He was tall; she had to strain a bit to look up at his face. He had to be the one named Ciceron Davan, and his record was mixed at best. He had worked as a mechanic in one of Earth's ports before going to the camp outside Tashkent; he had also hired himself out as a guide to travelers. Chen, who had seen several of Earth's ports, had told her that such guides were often thieves who preyed on the unwary.

She studied the other two men briefly. The small Chinese man had to be Chang Ho, who had been given work as a chemical laboratory assistant here. The blond man was Alexei Osipov; apparently stern words from the others on his greenhouse team about his bad temper had produced little result.

Everything in her recoiled from these men. Her hands trembled a little; she kept them under the table, where the three could not see them.

"We're going to ask you some questions," Risa said. "This meeting will be recorded, so think carefully about how you reply. As you know, we don't have any of the devices Earth's police sometimes use in questioning, but don't assume you can deceive us. Our recording can be analyzed later if necessary, and vocal stresses and facial expressions can reveal a few things."

"We've said what we have to say," Ciceron replied. "We were invited to the woman's house. We'd been there before—she met me a couple of weeks ago and started telling me about this group she's in—Ishtar."

"Seems rather late for a visit," Risa said.

"She'd been working later shifts in refining. I told her she could just stop by our tent before going home, but she said it'd be better if we came by. That's all that happened. Everyone else was asleep when we got there, and we talked, and then we left. I don't know what happened after that."

Chang Ho lifted his head; his eyes shifted uneasily before he looked down once more. The three did not yet know what had been found inside their tent; Istu had mentioned that to the Council during their review. He had also said something else—that an analysis of perspiration stains on the blood-stained shirt showed that it had been worn by the tall man.

"Your answer puzzles me a little," Risa said quietly. "You see, your belongings were searched after you were brought here. A couple of bracelets were found, ones that belonged to the dead woman. I'd like to know how they got there."

Chang Ho stiffened; Alexei Osipov, she noticed, seemed a bit paler. Ciceron's lip curled. "She gave them to me," he replied. "She knew it'd be a while before I earned enough credit to buy anything like that, and said she didn't need them. That group she's in always talks about how everything's going to be shared someday."

Alain al-Kadar cleared his throat; Risa motioned to him to be silent. The other Councilors were still; they were in the habit of allowing Risa and Alain to ask most of the questions during hearings. She had learned how to seize on contradictions, assess someone's veracity, and ferret out the truth.

"You say the bracelets were a gift. We can verify that statement with her household."

Ciceron shifted on his feet. "They might not know. She probably didn't tell them everything she did."

"Do you have anything to add to the statement you've made?"

The tall man shook his head. "We went there and we left."

"We'll have to have a hearing. Things won't go well for you if you're lying now. You'd better consider that. We don't have to be as harsh with those who admit they've done wrong and are sorry for it."

His dark eyes were contemptuous; she had to struggle not to look away. She could guess at what he was thinking; this Council could do nothing to him if there was room for doubt, especially about such a serious offense. He did not yet know that their other evidence had erased those doubts. Very well, she thought, I know what kind of man he is. Even if his deed had been impulsive and not planned, he was showing no sorrow over it.

"You're only accusing us," Ciceron said, "because you don't want to deal with her household. You don't want to admit that one of them could have done it. It's easier to accuse somebody who doesn't have as many friends. Go ahead and have your hearing—there will be some who'll speak for us."

"Since that's all you have to say, you can leave." Risa gestured at one of the men near the door. "Take him to the

room where you were holding him. I'll let you know what
to do with him after we've spoken to his friends."

Ciceron's eyes narrowed as he turned toward the
door; the guard grabbed him by the arm as they left. Jeannine's broad face wore a look of puzzlement; she was obviously wondering why Risa had not confronted the man
with the rest of their evidence.

"You two haven't said anything yet," Risa said. "Was
Ciceron telling the truth?"

"You heard him," Alexei said; his green eyes stared
past her. "We went there and we talked, and then we went
back to our tent."

"You're sure of that."

"I'm sure."

"You're not showing a lot of grief over the death of
someone who tried to befriend you."

Alexei's mouth tightened. "I'm sorry about that, but
it's nothing to do with me."

"And you?" Risa turned to Chang Ho. "I'd better say
this again. Things will be easier for you at any hearing if
you tell the truth now."

"You heard it," Chang Ho mumbled. "They said it."

She had given the men their chance. Had they admitted the deed and shown some repentance, she could have
believed they might be reformed. "I'm sorry to hear you
say that," she said softly, "because we already know it's a
lie. A carving belonging to Nora Toland was found in a hole
dug under your tent, along with a blood-stained shirt. The
blood on both has been analyzed—it was Nora's."

Chang Ho's head shot up; his face was constricted with
fear. "It wasn't our doing," he shouted. "Ciceron—he's the
one who killed her. We didn't do anything. He struck her
before we could stop him."

"Be quiet," Alexei said.

"You can't blame us for this. Ciceron did it—we didn't
expect anything like that to happen."

Risa sighed. "I think you'd better tell us the whole
story."

"She asked us to come to her house," the Chinese man
replied. "That's the truth—we thought it'd be more talk
about Ishtar. Then she told us that she knew we'd stolen a
couple of her things when we'd been there before." His
voice caught.

"And had you?" Risa asked.

"Just bracelets. It wasn't hard—just slipping into her room on the way to the bathroom and taking them. We didn't think she'd miss them. You have to understand—in the camps, the way it is, you sometimes need something for a bribe. We thought it might be the same here, and besides—"

"She always talked about how everything would be shared," Alexei muttered.

"She said if we gave them back, she wouldn't say anything about it—that's why she wanted to talk to us alone. I was ready to say we should give them back then, but Ciceron told her we wouldn't and that she'd better not say anything about it either. She said she was trying to help us, let us make up for it, and then Ciceron started saying that she was just like everyone else—she'd talk about people sharing things, but she'd rather keep more for herself. She got up all of a sudden and said she was going to make a complaint right then, even if she had to wake up the whole Council to do it. He hit her before she got to the screen."

The sordid story had the sound of truth. Risa glanced at the other Councilors; their eyes were hard.

"You have to understand," Chang Ho went on. "He just wanted to keep her away from the screen, maybe scare her into leaving us alone and not talking. He didn't mean to hit her so hard. I don't know how long we stood there, and then we were outside the house, and when we got back to our tent, Ciceron said we'd have to keep quiet, that we couldn't do her any good anyway. I didn't know what else to do. But Alexei and I didn't kill her."

"You've admitted you stole," Risa said slowly. "Then, when you saw your friend strike Nora Toland, you didn't even bother to call for medical help immediately. You let her lie there dying, her brain swelling from that injury until it was too late to repair the damage. She might be alive if she'd been tended to immediately. I might believe there was some hope for you if you'd called a physician. Instead, all you thought about was hiding what you'd done. You're as responsible for her death as your friend."

"We didn't mean—" Alexei started to say.

"We all have enough chances to die here," Risa burst out, unable to restrain her anger and disgust. "We're surrounded by air we can't breathe, barren mountains and plains, and sterile oceans. We came here to bring life to this world, and the only life it has so far is what lies under these domes. And you've brought death inside." She looked toward one of the volunteer guards. "Take them away. Make sure they and their friend don't leave that room."

"What are you going to do?" Alexei cried.

"Get them out of here."

The other Council members had been silent for some time. Alain pulled nervously at his thick mustache as he stared at Risa; Jeannine's fingers drummed against the tabletop.

"Well," Curcio said, "what do we do now?"

"Let the Administrators handle it," Istu replied; his dark face sagged with weariness. "They could demand that Earth take the men back and decide what to do with them."

"I wonder," Alain said. "That'd be like admitting that when we're faced with a difficult problem, we're unable to deal with it. The Islanders might feel compelled to take charge here more directly and do away with elected Councils. Earth may decide that if we have to turn to them now, it's time for them to take more control. We could even end up with Guardians in the settlements. We've got to act ourselves and in a way that ensures this kind of deed won't be repeated."

"How?" Curcio asked.

"There will have to be a hearing," Risa said, "and as soon as possible." Her mouth twisted. "We wouldn't want our Habber friends to think they aren't safe here, and they're probably not used to anything like this. They've been withdrawing some of their people lately, and letting murderers run around loose is hardly likely to make them feel secure."

"There's another way," Jeannine said. "My grandmother used to tell me stories about her town on Earth. Sometimes they didn't have hearings or trials. If they knew someone was guilty of anything like this, they'd do away with the murderer and present their area Counselor with an accomplished fact. It spared the Nomarchy some trouble, and it's hard to act against an entire community. Generally, people looked the other way, and a town could get off with a warning." She rested an elbow against the table.

"If we delay, some people might take matters into their own hands. We'd have to hold a hearing for them afterward, of course, but many would accept a black mark on their records and punishment in the form of extra labor for a chance to be rid of those three."

"No," Risa said quickly. "That's just another way of admitting we can't control events, and it would be a poor precedent—the next time people might not wait for proof."

"You sound," Curcio said, "as if you expect this to happen again."

"I want to make sure it doesn't, and it won't if we make an example of these three. They'll have their hearing. Anyone who thinks there might be hope for them can speak up, and they can cite any circumstances that might have contributed to their deed—not that any of that is likely to make a difference. Then we'll make our judgment."

"What kind of judgment?" Alain asked.

They were waiting for her to say it. "When a thief's caught, we make him return what he stole or make restitution. When somebody inflicts bodily harm on another, he usually pays both in credit and in helping to care for the sick in our infirmary. Nora Toland isn't here to receive restitution for her death. Those men have to pay for her life with their own."

"The Administrators will never allow our hearing," Istu muttered.

"They'll allow it," Risa responded. "They'll wait to see what we do, and they won't have time to stop us after the judgment is made. When Earth learns what happened to these three, people like them may think twice before they decide to go to those camps. They'll see what happens to people who prey upon their community." She gazed steadily at each Councilor in turn. "Are we in agreement?"

"We usually decide what to do," Jeannine said, "after the hearing's been held."

"We've had what amounts to a hearing already. The rest is just a formality—presenting the evidence and making sure that everyone's aware of how serious this is. We also want them to back our judgment." Risa folded her hands; her fingers felt cold. "Let's decide when and where to hold this hearing. It'll have to be soon—we should get this over with. Then I suggest that we all go to Nora's house to pay our respects to her household."

Nearly two hundred people had gathered at Nora's house. Risa and the other Council members made their way through the throng and murmured a few words to the mourners inside. The body had already been taken to recycling by the household, who had held a simple ceremony in keeping with Ishtar's ideals. Risa was relieved to hear that; turning the funeral into a large public occasion might have roused too many passions. She consoled one sobbing woman while promising to come to the memorial pillars when Nora's image was put there.

"She is Ishtar's now," Kichi Timsen was saying to another woman. "Her spirit is with the One we have roused and with Whom we will all converge."

Risa left the house. The light was beginning to fade; almost all of Oberg knew of the murder by now. She longed to be home, to look into her household's familiar faces and banish the memory of the evil she had seen.

She walked quickly until she came to a wooded spot overlooking a small bridge and a creek. She had often seen children playing in such places at this hour; now, she supposed, their parents had pulled them inside to safety. She thought of all the times Chimene had wandered off; she had scolded her for wasting time and bothering other people, but she had rarely worried about her daughter's being safe in the company of others.

Chimene suddenly seemed even more precious to her now. She would not allow her daughter's world to be inhabited by those three men.

"Risa?"

She turned around at the bridge. Kichi Timsen was coming toward her, dressed in a plain gray coverall and her red and black sash. "I've been trying to catch up with you. I think we should talk. Istu told me you'd be holding a hearing in three days."

Risa leaned against the bridge and gazed at the water below. "Yes, we are. We can't wait too long. As it is, there's probably time enough for anyone in the other settlements who can find an excuse and a ship with space to come here for the hearing. Most of them haven't seen anything like this."

"They can view it over the screen, and you can hardly fit them all into the Administrative Center."

"We're not having the hearing there," Risa said. The Council had always allowed anyone who wished to attend a hearing in person to do so. Few hearings elicited much interest, but that would hardly be the case with this one.

"The mosque then?"

"The mosque couldn't hold them all either. We'll have to hold it on the open ground between the External Operations Center and the airship bay."

Kichi drew in her breath sharply. "I don't think that's wise, Risa. You may find it difficult to control such a crowd during this hearing. My advice is to make an exception this time and allow only those who have testimony to offer to be present at the hearing. Anyone else who wishes to speak can do so over the screen."

"We've already decided," Risa replied, "and the announcement will go out after dark. I'm not going to bother trying to convince the others to change our plans now."

"They'd listen to you." Kichi rested her back against the railing. "The other Councilors often defer to your judgment. And what kind of decision will you make concerning those three men?"

"Come now, Kichi—you know we have to hold the hearing before we can make a decision."

"You're being disingenuous. You would have discussed a probable sentence, and I have some interest in what it might be. Nora was my sister in Ishtar, and she died at the hands of three she had hoped to lead to the truth."

Risa studied the woman in silence. Kichi Timsen had always been a mystery to her. The Guide's fine-boned handsome face wore its usual serene expression, as if Kichi could no longer be troubled by the emotions others felt.

Could the Guide really believe all that nonsense she professed? Risa had always doubted it. Kichi was a geologist, educated at one of Tokyo's universities before joining the Project. Surely she had too much learning to accept what she claimed to believe, and yet during her youth, she had become a member of the cult. Ishtar's adherents then had come from among the more ignorant workers on the Project; Kichi and those closest to her had soon attracted others to the cult by giving its tenets a more sophisticated philosophical veneer.

Kichi's slender fingers toyed with her silver necklace. The woman was always wearing at least one costly looking ornament, and her house, by Oberg's standards, was spacious. Ishtar might talk of sharing while encouraging its members to share some of what they owned with less prosperous adherents, but the Guide's household apparently got a generous portion of goods and services. Such gifts, along with the respect paid to her, were enough to account for Kichi's look of serenity. Her position in the cult had given her a relatively pleasant life, and she often traveled to other settlements, since much of her work as a geologist could be done elsewhere.

It was easy to understand Kichi's motives for professing her faith, and yet Risa had heard no rumors indicating that the Guide's beliefs were less than sincere. Could the woman have worn a mask for so long without ever letting it slip? Had the pretense finally become real to her?

"You do have a right to be concerned," Risa said at last. "Some will probably see Nora as a martyr to Ishtar. She should have complained about those men instead of asking them to her home, but then she wouldn't have had much chance of getting them into your group. You'll get your chance to speak at the hearing if there's anything you want to say."

"It'd be better if I say it to you now. I've been telling you and the Council that we were willing to organize patrols, keep an eye on things, offer people some protection, but you wouldn't listen to me. If we had, maybe those men wouldn't have risked doing what they did."

"That would be like having Guardians here," Risa said. "I suppose you want to bring that up and make it seem we were negligent."

"I'd rather not," Kichi murmured, "but you could make the suggestion. You'd have support for it—people will need to feel safer after this incident. Ishtar will be happy to organize the patrols, but the Council has to give them some authority to act. It would also solve the problem of what to do with those three men."

Risa frowned. "I don't see how."

"They can't be freed, and you have no place to send them. You'll have to strip them of everything and have them confined, it seems to me. We could build a small place for them, program the scanner in the doorway so they can't leave, have their identification bracelets permanently attached to their arms or embedded so we'd know immediately if they found a way out, and take the additional precaution of posting a guard. We could find work they'd be able to do in confinement or under guard, and the credits they earn would go to Nora's household. They'd never be free again. That would be punishment enough for their deed."

Kichi wanted a prison here, and her proposed punishment seemed worse than death. Their world would be poisoned if such places were allowed to exist. They would be tempted to lock away others in time; it would be such a simple solution but one with risks Kichi had not considered. Such confinements would need to be foolproof in a place where everyone's life depended on the maintenance of the domes that surrounded this community. Those condemned to a perpetual imprisonment might have little to lose by threatening an entire settlement, and prisoners clever enough could probably find ways around scanners, tracers, and guards. Oberg was vulnerable in so many ways. The airship bay could be seized, the water that was chemically treated and channeled into the domes poisoned, the installations sustaining their air supply destroyed.

The settlers would be creating a class who would have every reason to hate them and who might pose a danger in the future. Guards and prisons would only make a mockery of what they had tried to achieve. Yet condemning the men to death was also an admission of failure.

Risa shook her head; no, that wasn't the same. They would expel the evil from their community and, with that example, make it less likely that it would ever return.

"You talk of how we should all be brothers and sisters in Ishtar," Risa said. "Somehow, what you propose doesn't seem in keeping with that."

"But it is. They would have the chance to reflect on their deed, repent, and come to the truth. Their fate needn't keep them from becoming our brothers in time. They may not have freedom in this world, but they could win it in the next, when their bonds fall away and they're one with Ishtar."

Risa shuddered. Kichi was not thinking of their souls. What a triumph it would be for the Guide to win such people for her cult; what pleasure in having captives who would have few ways to resist.

"And you intend to propose this at the hearing?" Risa asked.

"I think not. Even if suggestions for how to resolve a problem aren't out of place there, I've always felt that it makes more sense to offer them to a Councilor ahead of time, so you have a chance to take them under advisement."

Risa pressed her lips together. Of course Kichi wouldn't speak at the hearing, when even Ishtar's followers were likely to demand death for the accused. She wanted Risa to make this suggestion to the crowd and take full responsibility for anything it brought.

Her resolve stiffened. She would not allow the Guide to use her. "Thank you for taking the trouble to speak to me, Kichi. If you have any other suggestions, please feel free to enter a message for me. I must get home."

She hurried from the bridge. The recording of her interview with the three men would have to be reviewed, the evidence assembled, and the hearing organized, while her team would expect her to make up the work she had missed today. She and her colleagues might be sentencing three men to death; she felt the weight of that possibility. Kichi's alternative could spare her from such a choice but might lead to something even worse.

She came to the main road and followed it toward the tunnel. She suddenly wanted to flee this time, to vanish from this world altogether, to return when the clouds had parted and sunlight touched Venus. She imagined herself in space, hurtling toward the speed of light where time slowed, letting the lives of generations slip past her. She saw herself returning to those Cytherians who would live in the garden created by their ancestors. She yearned for the future that she would never live to see, and knew then what she would have to do.

Risa stirred under the coverlet. A cylinder of light glowed in the corner; Malik had not yet come to bed. She closed her eyes and waited until she heard the door slide open.

She sat up. "I thought you'd be asleep," Malik said as he began to undress.

"I've got too much to think about to sleep."

Malik's skin was golden in the dim light. His back arched as he pulled on the light tunic he usually wore to bed. Noella claimed that sex with a bondmate palled after a while unless one worked at it, but Risa had not found that to be true. Malik could always arouse her, even after the bitterest exchange of words, even when she sensed that his mind was elsewhere as he held her.

"Katya left a message for me," he said. "Katya Osipova."

Her desire cooled a little. "I know the woman you mean."

"I called her after everyone went to bed. She wanted to give me a statement. It's recorded, and she'd like—" He sat down on the bed and turned to face her. "It's about her brother. She wants you to read it at the hearing."

"I don't see why. We'll certainly show anything she wants to record, or she can deliver it over the screen then. She can even come to the hearing in person—under the circumstances, she could probably get space aboard an airship."

"She's afraid to come, Risa. Your Council's making such a spectacle of this thing that she might not be safe herself, and she's worried about how Alexei might react to her presence—it'll be hard enough for him to know she's watching elsewhere. Composing the message was difficult for her, and she's afraid she'll break down if she tries to read it herself. She pleaded with me. I promised I'd speak to you."

"I have to decide this matter," she said. "I can't read statements made by those wanting to speak for the accused—why, it would look as though I'm pleading for mercy. If she can't read it herself, let her find someone else to do it." Here was still another person who wanted to use her, Risa thought.

"Not many would be willing. You could make an exception for this."

"Her brother will have his hearing. We'll listen to everything that's said and then make our decision. It's more than that wretched man gave to Nora Toland. If you really want to help your friend Katya, tell her she ought to forget her brother instead of staining her own reputation with some sentimental plea in his defense. She's going to have to live among people who will despise him."

"How merciless you are." A muscle near his jaw twitched. "I heard quite a bit of talk today. People were saying you'd already decided what you'll do—all they were wondering about was the means of execution. I said they were mistaken, that you'd keep an open mind and decide only after you'd heard everything, that you'd be just. But I see now that I was wrong. You've already made your judgment, and what Katya says will make no difference."

Risa clutched at the coverlet. "You show a lot of concern for a man who let a woman die and thought he could get away with it."

"Do you think I care about Alexei?" he said hoarsely. "I saw what he was long ago, and I pitied Katya for caring about him. I'm worried about what this decision will do to you. You're so lost in your vision of what this world is supposed to be that you no longer care about the means you use to bring it about. You've grown harder, Risa, and after this—well, it'll get easier for you to sentence people. There won't be anything to hold you back."

"Maybe I am hard," she responded. "Maybe I have to be. You've never tried to ease my burden—you just endure me and feel sorry that you're stuck with me. I can't count on you, and you've never really loved me."

He stared steadily at her; he was not denying her accusation this time, as he always had before. A lump rose in her throat; she swallowed. "The point of this hearing isn't just to punish those men," she went on. "It's to make sure this never happens again, that an example's set—"

"Do you think you can frighten people into being what they should be? Perhaps you should have made time for more historical study, and you might have learned better." He turned his head away from her. "And now your Council's turning this hearing into some sort of festival. What a diversion this will be for your citizens. You should have heard my pupils—they're all looking forward to it and praying that their parents will take them along so they can say they were there."

"It may do them some good to see it," she said. "They should know how evil deeds are rewarded."

"Their parents will have to decide that, but I won't

have Chimene watch that hearing. She's staying home, and I'll put a lock on the screen if I must."

Risa drew in her breath. "She's going," she muttered. "I won't have people say that I couldn't make this decision in front of my own child. She's not going to think that I have any reason to be ashamed of what I do or to keep her from seeing it. She'll see the kind of men they are, and she'll learn a lesson from it. You've always protected her too much, but you're not going to do it this time."

"Risa—"

"She's going, and you're not going to stop it. If you try, I'll see you out of this household before I let you shame me in front of my daughter and make it seem I'm in the wrong, and I won't let her leave with you. You'll see what she thinks of you then, when you're gone—"

Her voice caught in her throat. She had expected to see rage; instead, his face was weary and resigned. She had said too much, had pushed him past anger into disgust and indifference. His dark eyes seemed to bore through her, as though she had suddenly become invisible to him.

"I didn't mean it," she said hastily.

"Why, how can you say that?" His voice was light and tinged with mockery. "You almost always mean exactly what you say. It's one of the things we all admire in you— your honesty."

She twisted the edge of the coverlet in her hands. "Anyway, she'll want to go, especially if most of her friends are going. She'll wonder why you wanted to keep her away from something so important. It isn't good to shield children from too much. You can see that, can't you? You want her to be able to make up her own mind, don't you?"

"Oh, yes." He was still speaking in that same high-pitched tone, as if he were only bantering with her. "Perhaps you're right. I certainly don't want to keep her from drawing her own conclusions."

"If you don't want to come yourself—well, I'll understand." She had to grant him some sort of concession now. "If anyone wonders why my own bondmate isn't there, I can think of some excuse."

"Oh, no. I never intended to stay away myself. I'm willing to see you and the Council deliver your verdict. You should have your bondmate there. I know you won't shrink from having me view the decision in person, and it can scarcely alter my feelings toward you." He got up, pulled back the coverlet, and got into bed with his back to her.

"Malik, I'm sorry," she said. "You understand, don't you? Please forgive me." I need you now, she wanted to say. I know you don't want me to face this, but I can't turn away from it now. You'll see I was right, you'll see that nothing else could have been done. Why can't you give me some support now?

She touched his arm, then reached around and gently caressed his chest; he recoiled. He had never rejected her advances before. She withdrew to her side of the bed; he did not move. She sensed him lying there, awake, indifferent and walling himself away from her.

Fifteen

Chimene clung to her mother's hand. She had never seen so many people in the tunnel at once, but almost everyone seemed to be going to the main dome. Some people weren't going, of course—the ones who were needed on darktime shifts or who had to look after babies, but they would see it on the screen. Todd Hansen-Barini wasn't going because his household didn't like crowds; he had complained at school about that.

At first, it had been hard to keep up with her mother, but now, in the press of bodies, they could hardly move. "Let Risa Liangharad through," someone shouted up ahead. "Let the Councilor through." A space began to open up in front of them, allowing Risa's household to pass.

Her grandfather had decided not to come. Chen was old and had said he was too weary for the walk, but he hadn't seemed anxious to come anyway; he had looked worried when he hugged Risa before she left. Malik seemed upset by the hearing, too; he had been very quiet while the household was preparing to leave. Her teacher Yoshi Shigeta had told the children how serious a matter this was, and maybe that accounted for her father's mood, but Malik had also known the sister of one of the accused on Earth.

Chimene remembered the dark-eyed blond woman she had met. She hadn't really liked the warm and familiar way the woman had greeted Malik, and was somewhat pleased to have another reason to dislike her.

Lately, her friends were talking of little except this hearing; Lena Kerein had told them all that Chimene had actually met the sister of the accused Russian. They had gaped at Chimene when she admitted that both Kolya and her father had also known the man on Earth, but she hadn't been able to tell them much more than that. She had tried to ask Kolya about the man, and Malik had told him not to answer her questions; she had never seen her father so angry before.

They left the tunnel and followed a stream of people along the main road. The dome's light was dim, but the greenhouses near the road were lighted, and many in the crowd were carrying light-wands or small, glowing globes. The spots of light made her think of the stars she had seen only on the screen, the distant suns hidden by Venus's thick dark clouds.

We won't get good seats, she thought impatiently. Malik was bringing a pocket screen along, on which they could see and hear everything that took place, but if she had to look at a screen, she might as well have stayed home. She sighed. At least she could say she had been here, and that was the important thing. She felt a little sorry for Todd Hansen-Barini, who wouldn't be here, and for Maryam Nishimoto, whose parents had said she might have to stay home with her little brother.

People were already seated on the ground just beyond the airship bay. Some sat on blankets; others settled on the grass. Near the tents, a platform had been set up; two gray-garbed men were adjusting the lights on the poles around it. A wide screen sat against the poles, and the other four Council members were waiting on the platform.

The people near them stood up as Risa's household was ushered toward the platform. They would get good seats after all. That had to be because Risa was on the Council. Her mother was an important person, even if she did always tell Chimene that one Cytherian was as good as another and it was wrong to think you were better than anyone else.

Kolya and Emilia seated themselves; Grazie helped Tina to the ground before sitting down herself. Risa released Chimene's hand and walked toward the steps that led up to the platform. Chimene looked up at her father, but his eyes were on Risa.

Patrick nudged her. "I see Maryam." Chimene looked around for her friend. "Over there—she's with her aunt and uncle." Chimene waved in that direction but still couldn't see the other girl. Her friends were probably envying her for getting to sit up here.

"Sit down," Paul said to Patrick, "and behave yourself. You're not likely to see another hearing as important."

The two children settled on the ground; Malik sat down next to Chimene. Three men were being led to the platform by others wearing Ishtar's sash. The first man looked like one of Chen's people; the second was tall and dark-haired, and the third was blond.

A woman had died because of them; that hardly seemed real. Such things had never happened here before, and some of her friends had been told by their parents not to wander around after dark and to be careful about those they let inside their houses. She squinted as the three men climbed onto the platform, surprised to see how much they looked like other people. She noticed then that their hands were tied behind their backs.

Risa stood up and raised her arms; the murmurs of the crowd faded. Alain al-Kadar pinned a tiny microphone to Risa's collar. "Fellow Cytherians!" her amplified voice rang out. "You'll have a few more minutes to get settled, and then this hearing will begin." The men standing with the accused began to pin microphones to the collars of the three.

Patrick leaned toward Chimene. "Gur told me they'll probably die."

"A lot of the kids say that," Chimene replied. "I don't know why they're so sure. They haven't had the hearing yet." She recalled what she had learned about hearings. "They get to defend themselves."

"What good'll that do?" Patrick scratched at his reddish-blond hair. "Everyone knows what they did. You want them to come after you?" Patrick lowered his voice. "Gur said they—you know—did things to that woman before she died. He said nobody'll talk about it, but—"

"Be quiet," Malik muttered angrily. "Those men are in enough trouble without having lies told about their deeds." Chimene shivered a little and wondered why her father was here if the hearing disturbed him so much. Risa might have told him to come, but there had been plenty of times when he hadn't done what she wanted.

"I hope this doesn't take too long," Kolya whispered behind her. "Won't help to drag it out."

Malik turned his head. "Don't be so impatient to see the end. It isn't likely to lead to anything good."

"Even the Administrators haven't tried to stop it," Kolya answered.

"Of course not," Malik said. "They'll wait until it's over before they act—that way, they won't have to deal with those three themselves or worry about how to control this mob."

Risa was standing up again. "Silence," she called out. "This hearing will now begin. The other Councilors have asked me to present the facts in this case." Risa accepted a pocket screen from Jeannine Loris and studied it for a moment.

Chimene sat up a little straighter. All of these people would be listening to her mother, and the other settlements would watch on screens. Chimene had attended a couple of hearings before to learn how they were conducted, and she had noticed then that Risa did most of the talking for the Council. But those hearings had been held in the room where the Council usually met and had involved only minor disputes. This was different.

Chimene wondered what it would be like to have all these people listening to her words. It would be frightening but also thrilling, perhaps a little like those times Malik asked her to recite some of the Arabic poetry he had taught her to a few of his friends. She always enjoyed the attention, and the smiles and words of praise when she finished.

"Here are the facts," Risa continued. "Nora Toland's body was found in the common room of her house just before first light. The physician Gupta Benares was called to examine the body, and he determined that Nora's death was caused by a severe blow to the head. A neighbor, the engineer Yakov Serba, saw three men leave Nora's house some hours before, after dark."

Chimene watched the three men as her mother told how they had been identified and what had been found in their tent. The tall dark one seemed angry, while the Chinese man sat with his head bowed. The blond one was studying Risa intently. What were they thinking? They had to be afraid. She was often a little frightened of Risa herself when her mother knew she had misbehaved, and she had never done anything this bad.

Chimene tried to pay attention to what her mother was saying. "That concludes our preliminary summary," Risa said. "If you look at the screen behind me, you will now see the two interviews the Council had with Ciceron Davan, Alexei Osipov, and Chang Ho. The first took place four hours after the men had been identified by Yakov Serba and the members of Nora Toland's household. We conducted the second yesterday." Risa crossed the platform and sat down with the other Councilors.

Chimene had already seen the first interview, although she'd had to sneak over to Lena Kerein's house to call it up. Malik had pulled her away from the screen in their common room when she tried to look at it there. "Your mother's smart," Lena told Chimene after they had watched it. "She fooled them into admitting it." Chimene, after thinking of the times Risa had tricked her into saying she had done something she shouldn't, had felt a bit sorry for the men before reminding herself that they had killed a woman. One of them had anyway; the others had apparently only tried to help their friend hide it. Did that mean they wouldn't be punished as much?

She looked around at all the people sitting in the clearing. The ones farthest from the platform were peering at pocket screens; others were whispering to the people near them. A few had climbed up into the trees at the edge of the open area for a better view. Most of them had probably seen the interviews before, since they were in the public record. She turned back to the large screen as the second interview began. The Chinese man was telling the same story he had in the first; when he finished, the blond man said only that the story was true and that he had nothing to add except that he was sorry. The dark-haired man refused to say anything at all, even though he had been the one to kill the woman.

The screen went blank. "I'll call the first witness," Risa said. "Gupta Benares." Chimene sighed as the physician climbed up to the platform and accepted a microphone from Istu Marnes. This was the part of the hearing when witnesses would testify in detail about what they knew, and it was likely to go on for a while. She began to wish that she had brought her own pocket screen so that she could have played a game in the meantime.

Gupta Benares droned on as the screen showed images of the scan he had conducted. Patrick was fidgeting; Chimene poked him in the arm. "The tall man didn't say anything," she whispered.

"It doesn't matter," Patrick whispered back. "We already know what happened. I don't know why we have to listen to all this stuff."

"It's their hearing." Patrick often didn't seem to know the simplest things. "They have to—"

"Hush," her father muttered. She noticed then that the blond Russian man was staring directly at Malik; the cold look in his eyes made her shiver.

The physician left the platform; Yakov Serba was called. Chimene tried to concentrate. The last time she and her friends had gone to a hearing, Yoshi had questioned them in school about the Council's decision and whether or not any of them would have decided differently. Yoshi might ask about this hearing, and Chimene, who was usually quick to respond, did not want to look as though she had not paid attention.

Three women and two men followed Yakov to the platform, but their voices were faint and subdued, difficult to hear even with microphones attached to their collars. They were members of the dead woman's household. Chimene nearly choked at the idea of finding a body in her own common room. She glanced at Malik. Maybe he and Risa would let her sleep with them tonight, even though she hadn't for a long time.

Her mother was walking across the platform. "You've all heard the testimony," Risa said. She turned toward the three men. "Do you have anything to say in your own defense?"

The tall man got up awkwardly, then wobbled a little on his feet as his companions stood. "You've made up your minds," he said. "I've got nothing to say to you."

"You can't blame me," the Chinese man shouted. "I didn't kill her."

"You could have gone for help," Risa replied; she lifted an arm, then let it fall. "Something might have been done for her if you had, but all you thought about was hiding what you did." Chimene was startled by her mother's en-

raged tone; a Council member was supposed to be calm
during hearings.

"Ciceron was a friend," the blond man said. "I told
myself I couldn't betray a friend. Maybe that was a mistake, but we didn't know what to do, and he didn't mean to
kill her. She got him angry, pretending she was our friend,
and saying she was going to complain we'd been stealing.
If she hadn't said that—"

"You're not helping yourself," Risa said. "Nora Toland
admitted you to her home, offered to forgive you if you
gave back what you took, and was trying to befriend you."

"I'm sorry for what happened," Alexei Osipov said
quietly. "I was trying to protect my friend. He'd never do
anything like this again—none of us would."

Risa stepped toward the front of the platform. "The
records of the accused have been studied," she said. "We
found no medical or psychological disorder that might
have contributed to their deed, a brutal act one of them
committed so that he would not be revealed publicly as a
thief, and which his companions sought to conceal. If they
had called a physician immediately, they might have been
judged as others are who injure another person in rage. If
they had confessed to the deed willingly, we might have
believed repentance was possible."

"We've heard all we have to," a man behind Chimene
shouted. "What are you going to do about it?"

"Silence!" Risa called out. "Some facts about people
aren't always part of their records, and they have the right
to have others speak in their defense. Perhaps someone
here, or in one of our sister settlements, can tell us of their
more worthy deeds or of circumstances that would show
them to be deserving of more mercy. If anyone wishes to
speak, step forward now or give your message over the
screen."

Chimene craned her neck. The crowd was murmuring, but she did not see anyone stand up. Maybe their
friends were afraid to speak. Perhaps they had no friends.

"Those three are trouble," a bald man near the platform called out. "I had to work with that one in the greenhouses." He pointed at Alexei. "He'd start a fight over
nothing at all!"

"Sit down," Risa commanded. "Previous complaints
don't concern us now, and any judgments about them

have already been made. We're asking for those who will speak in their defense."

Malik suddenly rose. Risa tensed as he walked to the platform and climbed the steps. "What's he doing?" Patrick whispered. Risa seemed stunned; she moved back a little as Alain gave Malik a microphone. Chimene wanted to shrink away; what would her friends think of her father now?

Malik was holding his screen in his hands. "I promised to read this statement from one who can't be here to speak. Her name is Yekaterina Osipova, and she's the sister of Alexei Osipov. She came here from one of Earth's camps, and she's lived in al-Khwarizmi for the past three years. She volunteered to work on the Bats, a task which, as a new arrival, she could easily have avoided. You won't find any black marks on her record."

Malik looked down at his screen. "I'll read her words now. She would have offered them herself, but her grief has made that impossible." He cleared his throat. "My brother Alexei has made mistakes, but please see him for what he is. He knew that Earth could offer him little, and so he chose to go to a camp. I went with him—I was happy for him then because I believed there would be something better for him here. I didn't like some of the companions he found in that camp, and maybe they led him astray, but life there is hard, and waiting can seem endless. There's little reward for goodness in a camp, especially among Guardians who look for weakness and prey upon the people there. Alexei had to survive and stay strong enough to reach Venus, and sometimes that meant doing things he wouldn't have done at other times. Whatever our disagreements, he always tried to protect me, and one Guardian nearly expelled him from the camp for that. I pleaded with the Guardian for my brother, and I say that without shame. I wanted Alexei to have his chance."

Kolya whispered something in Russian; it sounded like a curse. Chimene thought of how her father and Kolya never spoke of their time in the camp, and how grim they both looked the few times she had tried to ask them about it.

"Alexei can make a life here," Malik continued, "if he's allowed to make amends for his mistake, and maybe his friends can, too. Give him a chance to overcome what the camp and the Guardians and the waiting did to him. He'll suffer the shame of his deed all his life, even if he's too proud to say that. Give him a chance to make up for what he did. Let him become what I know he can be."

"Fine words," a man near Chimene murmured. "Wonder what the Guide and Nora's household think of them. If the Council's too gentle with them now, nobody's safe. We have to scare anyone else who'd try the same thing."

"I wonder how they'll do it," a woman replied. "We have no weapons—it could be messy."

"Is that the end of the statement?" Risa asked. Chimene had heard that scornful tone in her mother's voice before, usually just before her parents retired to their room to argue. She hated it when their door closed and she knew they were fighting; it made her want to run into the room and beg them to stop.

"This concludes Yekaterina's statement." Malik lowered his screen. "But I have a statement of my own to make. For those of you watching who don't know who I am, my name is Malik Haddad. I teach the children in Oberg's west dome. I knew Alexei Osipov in the camp outside Tashkent when I was waiting for passage. We wouldn't call ourselves friends by any means, but he's a young man who spent years in a place that might have broken some of you. I was fortunate. I waited for only a couple of months, and even that was enough to make me despair at times."

"You were a Linker once," someone shouted from the crowd. "Anything would have seemed hard to you."

"I came here after three years in a camp," a woman called out. "I was grateful for the chance to start again. I didn't go around stealing or trying to hide a murder."

"Your virtue is praiseworthy," Malik said, "but not everyone can be so strong. This is a place where you claim people can start afresh. These men have committed a terrible crime, but don't commit one against them that will poison what you have. You might consider Earth's history —it's a subject I know something about. Acts of violence and revenge only lead to other such acts. I'm not asking that these men be set free, only that any judgment allow them the chance to repent and change."

"Nora Toland didn't get a chance!" a voice shouted.

"You've made your plea," Risa said, "but you've offered few facts in their defense."

"I'm not just pleading for them," Malik said more
softly. "I'm pleading for you and this settlement not to—"

"We have very few choices," Risa interrupted. "If we
expel them, Earth might take them back, but they'd also
exact a price. Do you want to see Guardians in these
domes?"

"No!" several people answered.

"We could turn them over to the Administrators,
which would be admitting that we're incapable of making
our own decisions. Shall we disband the Councils we ourselves elect and turn over all authority to others?"

"No!"

"Shall we allow them to stay among us and affront all
who loved Nora Toland with their presence? Will our children be forced to look at every new arrival with suspicion
and fear?"

"No!"

"I told you," Patrick whispered to Chimene. "They're
going to die."

"Let me speak!" Chimene looked up at the sound of
that familiar voice; Kolya was getting to his feet. "My
friend Malik means well, but he insults every one of us who
came here from the camps. Those men aren't like us, and I
won't have it said that any of us might have done what they
did in rage and fear. They deserve—" More shouting from
the crowd drowned out the rest of his words.

Risa lifted her arms. "Be silent!" She waited, then
moved toward Malik. "Have you finished?"

"This isn't a hearing," Malik said. "It's a spectacle for a
mob." He pulled off his microphone, threw it at Risa, and
descended the steps to the sound of jeers.

Chimene felt torn. Malik was always kind; his students
said that he would often give them a second chance before
issuing reprimands about their work. She could go to him
whenever Risa was being unfair. He had probably only
agreed to read that woman's statement out of kindness,
because he felt sorry for her. Chimene could understand
that, but her friends were sure to wonder why he had
defended these three men.

Anyway, the men wouldn't die, whatever Patrick said.
Her mother couldn't do anything like that; she'd make

another judgment, and the Council would go along with it. People always talked about how clever Risa was, how she could settle disputes when no one else could figure out what to do.

Malik sat down, shaking. Chimene was afraid to touch him. Risa would settle this, and then she and Malik would make up with each other, as they always did, at least for a while. Maybe someday, their making up would last and they wouldn't fight at all anymore.

"Does anyone else wish to speak?" Risa was staring at the part of the crowd to her left. Chimene looked in that direction; her mother was gazing almost directly at Kichi Timsen, Ishtar's Guide, and the people sitting with her.

A dark-skinned man was climbing the steps to the platform. He wore a gray coverall; as he came to Risa, she started a little, then picked up the microphone Malik had dropped. "This isn't a matter that concerns your people," she said.

The man pinned the microphone to his collar. "Even so, I request an opportunity to speak. What happens among you, especially a matter this grave, concerns us." He turned toward the crowd; Chimene now saw the pin of silver circles on his shirt. Habbers never attended hearings; she had never heard of one making any kind of statement or recording any complaint that might lead to a hearing.

"My name is Lluthu," the Habber said. "I have worked with the people of Oberg for nearly five years. I have discussed this incident with my own people. I do not wish to make a statement, only to offer a suggestion."

Chimene leaned forward. She had seen Habbers only at a distance and had kept away from the small residence in the west dome where a few of them lived. Risa always said that there was no point in associating with Habbers unless one had to work with them. In this case, Chimene was content to obey her mother; she had heard about how Risa's brother had betrayed the Project by joining them. Chimene did not want anyone to think that she was like her uncle.

"You must decide the fate of these men," Lluthu continued. "I am free to tell you that, if you wish, you may give them to us and we will convey them to our nearest Habitat. You would no longer have them in your midst, and we would have a chance to make observations that may prove interesting."

The accused men gaped at the Habber; the Chinese man was shaking his head. They seemed more frightened of this Habber than of any sentence the Council might give.

"And how will they be punished there?" Risa asked.

"Punishment? I'm not speaking of punishment, exactly, but of exile, a time for reflection, a way for them to know what they've done, face it, know what they are and then to transcend what they are. They would come to learn exactly what they are, and if they are unable to deal with that part of their nature, that may be punishment enough."

"Some punishment!" a man cried out. "Giving them a Habber's long life and letting them get away. What kind of sentence would that be?"

"Nora was a sister in Ishtar!" A woman near the Guide was speaking now. "The Habbers affront the Spirit by imagining that they can dwell apart from planets and the living spirits with whom planet-dwellers will converge. Will you give these men to such people? Will you deny Nora any justice at all?"

"That's your suggestion?" Risa said. The Habber nodded. "Surely you see the impossibility of such a judgment. Some might say that living among Habbers is a punishment in itself, but you would probably also exact a price for accepting these men. Maybe you think your people should participate in the deliberations of our Councils. We'll make our decision without your advice."

"Poor Risa," Tina murmured to Grazie. "This crowd won't accept any sentence but one. I hope the Council can pronounce it—if they don't, people will try to take those men anyway, and then where will we be?"

"This hearing showed what they are," Kolya muttered. "They don't deserve much mercy."

"The Council," Risa announced, "will begin its deliberations now."

The Council members retreated to the back of the platform. Chimene felt her father's hand on her shoulder; his fingers were gripping her so tightly that it hurt. "Malik," she whispered.

"Be quiet, Chimene." His voice frightened her. "Your

mother has a very important decision to make—pay attention."

The Councilors spoke for only a few moments before they stood up. Chimene was surprised; they usually took longer to make their decisions at the hearings she had seen.

Risa stepped to the front of the platform. "The others have asked me to pronounce the sentence, with which we are all in agreement. Allow me to say a few words first. We live here without police and without all those functionaries of Earth—the Counselors who think only of controlling under the guise of helping, the Guardians allowed to keep order in whatever way they see fit. Consider how precious that freedom is and how fragile. What we have rests on trust, but it must also rest on our willingness to mete out the most severe penalties to those who abuse that trust. If we show that willingness now, our trust is not likely to be abused in the future."

The Habber who had spoken was standing at the bottom of the steps, looking up at Risa with a curious smile. Chimene almost thought he was amused, but he couldn't be; this hearing was too serious for that.

"These men believed they could abuse our trust," Risa continued. "They saw that we do not use officially sanctioned violence, that we have no police, that we attempt to settle our problems through private negotiations or hearings in which all sides are heard, and that we try to be fair to all concerned. They saw we had a freedom here, and they took that as license to do whatever they wished. They saw us as weak people they could prey upon, who had no power against them. If we allow such people among us, we'll destroy what we have. If we act now, we'll preserve it."

The crowd was silent.

"All of these men are guilty of Nora Toland's death and of concealing evidence of their deed. I pronounce their judgment now."

Chimene held her breath; Patrick stopped fidgeting. Risa turned to face the accused; Chimene noticed that her mother's hands were trembling a little.

"Ciceron Davan, Alexei Osipov, and Chang Ho, you will be taken to the airship bay." Risa's voice sounded uncertain. "There, you will be left by the airship cradles while the roof above you is opened. You will have no memorial on our pillars. Venus will have your lives in place of the one you took."

"No!" Chang Ho shouted. "You don't have the right—we don't deserve—"

Part of the crowd was already moving forward. Risa hurried down the steps and stopped in front of Chimene, then held out her hand. "Come with me."

Malik stood up as Risa pulled Chimene to her feet. "Where are you taking her?" he asked.

"The judgment must be carried out. I want my daughter with me."

Malik grabbed at Chimene; Risa began to drag her away. "No!" Malik shouted. Chimene looked back; her father was caught in a knot of people, unable to reach her. The three condemned men were already being led down the steps; the Chinese man was sobbing.

Risa held Chimene's hand tightly as they followed the stream of people toward the bay. Kolya and Emilia were at Risa's side; Chimene caught a glimpse of Patrick and Paul.

The men were going to die. Chimene recalled what she had learned about the bay. The thick wall that separated the cradles from the rest of the bay would have to be lowered before the roof above the cradles was opened. The air pressure would increase to match the atmospheric pressure outside, so the men would already be dead from that by the time the roof was being opened. She tried to imagine what that would feel like and felt an invisible weight against her own chest; the thought terrified her.

"I wonder if the Administrators will allow this," someone near her said.

"They can't stop it now—it's gone too far."

Chimene thought of the Administrator named Sigurd, the one who sometimes spoke to Risa. Maybe he would try to stop it somehow. Suddenly, she was sure he would; maybe Risa was waiting for that. Chimene thought of the times when her friend Lena tried to dare her into doing something foolish, and how relieved she always was when another friend intervened and told Lena how silly she was. Maybe Risa only wanted to scare the men so that they would never do anything like this again, in the way that she sometimes threatened Chimene with dire punishments that were not carried out.

The bay door was opening wider; the Council members walked through the entrance, trailed by part of the crowd. They passed the gantries and machines that lined the bay on both sides. Chang Ho stumbled as he walked, sagging against one of the men who held him.

Chimene soon saw the cradles. The crowd came to a halt. Alain moved toward the three men, who were being held tightly by others. The tall man and the Russian seemed pale and oddly calm; the Chinese man was still weeping.

"Do you have any last words?" Alain asked.

"Only this," the tall man said. "I didn't plan what I did. Call it what you like, but it wasn't murder. This is murder —what you're doing to us."

Was it? Chimene asked herself. She was suddenly confused. Were her mother and the Council being just as bad as the men? But Risa was on the Council; that meant this wasn't the same, didn't it? Some people could decide such things, and others could not.

The two other men said nothing. "Do you want any rites," Alain asked, "or time to say prayers?"

"Prayers won't help us," the blond Russian said.

"You'll be given an injection," Alain said. "It will make things easier for you." Another man approached with a silver wand and pressed it against the tall man's arm.

Risa's hand was icy. Chimene closed her eyes, unable to bear the sight. When she opened them once more, the men were lying next to the nearest cradle. The Russian's green eyes were staring directly at her; she looked away.

The wall was being lowered from the ceiling now. It was all happening too fast; there wouldn't be time to stop it. Risa pulled Chimene toward the wall to their right, where a technician was standing near a console.

"Have you overridden the safety controls?" Risa asked. The technician nodded.

Chimene pulled her arm loose. If I'm bad, she thought, they'll bring me here, too, they'll put me in there. She wanted to run to her father and hear him tell her that everything would be all right, that he would always protect her.

She spun around, clawed at a pair of trousered legs,

and fell. Her stomach lurched; she was afraid she might be sick. She lay on the floor, looking up at Paul as he held her head.

Voices were speaking; her ears throbbed, making it hard to hear their words.

"—dead by now."

"We'll open the roof anyway." That was Risa's voice. "Show me which panel to push."

"—deserved it—"

"—got off easy, if you ask me."

"—maybe we shouldn't have—"

"—the Council may pay for this."

"—nobody tried to stop them—"

The wall was rising. Kolya picked Chimene up; she buried her face against his chest, refusing to look. "I'll take her home," Kolya said.

"Very well." Risa's voice sounded muffled. "I have to go to the recycler, see this through."

"You did the right thing."

"Oh, yes."

Kolya carried her all the way home. When Patrick complained about not getting to follow the crowd back to the recycler, Grazie told him to hush. The rest of the household did not say anything, not even when they were in the tunnel and other people called out greetings. The greetings seemed strangely cheerful; one man commented that the settlers would sleep more easily that night, knowing they were safe.

Tina insisted on scanning her when they were home, to make certain the fall and loss of consciousness hadn't injured her. "Your mother had a difficult decision to make," Tina said as she lifted Chimene off her table, "she and the rest of the Council. Maybe she shouldn't have taken you there, but—" She carried Chimene into the common room. "The Council did what they thought was right. You'll understand someday. It might seem harsh, but they had to think of the settlement and how to protect it from people like that."

The rest of the household was sitting around the table; Patrick lay on a cushion, asleep. Chimene noticed that Malik was not with the others. "Can you sleep," Tina asked, "or do you want to wait up for Risa?"

Chimene shook her head violently. Tina moved toward Chimene's room; the door opened.

Malik was sitting on her bed. Tina lowered her to his side. "I'll stay with her," he said.

"She fainted in the bay. The excitement must have been a little too much for her—maybe she should stay home from school tomorrow."

"My bondmate might object to that. After all, it's likely to be the primary topic of discussion, and Risa will want her daughter to participate. We mustn't have anyone think that Chimene lacks her mother's fortitude."

"I understand your feelings," Tina said, "but Risa will need you even more now. It's done, and there's no point in dwelling on it."

"How practical of you."

"And it couldn't have helped her to have her bondmate reading a statement from a woman who could have offered it herself, or speaking up for those men."

"She'll get over that." Malik's voice was nearly a whisper. "People will undoubtedly praise her for not listening to a weak-willed bondmate."

Tina was silent for a bit, then said, "I'd better put Patrick to bed."

As she left the room, Malik got up, helped Chimene off with her clothes, then dressed her in her white shift. Her arms and legs felt as though they didn't belong to her; she leaned against Malik as he tucked her into bed.

He sat down and began to stroke her hair. "I didn't think they'd die," she said. "I thought they'd only scare them."

Her father did not reply. She curled up next to him, resting her head against his thigh. Everything would be all right now; Malik was with her.

She dozed, dimly aware of her father's presence. She was sitting with the crowd again, waiting for her mother to speak.

"They didn't suffer," Risa said. Chimene, waking, realized that her mother was in the room. She kept her eyes closed, feigning sleep. "They were probably unconscious before they could even feel an increase in pressure." Risa's voice was low. "I doubt they felt anything at all."

"And of course that makes it all right," Malik replied. "Are you going to sit here all night?"

"Maybe."

"You won't be very alert for your students tomorrow."

"It doesn't matter," he said softly. "They'll be too busy talking about this spectacle to pay much attention to their lessons. Maybe I'll send them home, give them a free day so they have a chance to analyze it in detail with their households. It's a fine lesson for them. Gather a mob, hold a hearing that's no more than a charade, and you can commit a crime and call it justice."

"What else could we have done?" Chimene heard the soft sound of footsteps as her mother paced the room. "I didn't want to make this decision. You don't know how hard it was for me. We had no choice. Others would have settled this themselves if we hadn't, and that would have led to worse things."

Malik was silent.

"You saw all those people," Risa said, "and how they felt. How long do you think those men would have stayed alive if we'd spared them? We could have had more violence on our hands and no way to control it, and another excuse for the Project Council to think we can't govern ourselves." She paused for breath. "They died for our settlements—that's how I view it. They died so that others won't repeat their deeds and so that we can keep what we have now."

"You think you're strong," Malik muttered. "You think your decision was so hard, but it was easy. The hard thing would have been to try to convince that mob to live up to the ideals you claim to have."

"You would say that, wouldn't you? You're more used to fine words and fine feelings than doing anything practical. You leave everything that's hard to me, and then feel disappointed because I can't be as sensitive as you."

"What you did wasn't hard, Risa. All that talk about how you're just another Cytherian serving Oberg—you don't want to lose the praise of the crowd, that's all. Maybe you were thinking of the next election or the power you might lose if you surrendered those men to someone else. You can't admit that now you're ruled by the mob, that you couldn't bear to lose what you have."

Chimene wanted to plead with them to stop. Their soft, bitter voices were more frightening than the shouts she had sometimes heard from behind their door.

"You think I'm weak," Malik said. "Speaking to that mob was the hardest thing I ever did, but I knew I couldn't live with myself if I didn't. I thought you, at least, might listen."

"What sentimentality," she said. "A plea from a sister and fine words from my bondmate. We had to be objective."

"And I can't forgive what you did to Chimene. You had no business taking her to that bay just to show others that you weren't afraid to have your own daughter see—"

"I won't hide what I do from her." Risa's voice sounded closer. "But you—you didn't make your little speech because you wanted mercy. You just wanted me to look cruel in front of Chimene, that's all. You couldn't try to give me any support. You've always wanted her to hate me and love you."

"That isn't true."

Chimene had dreaded this. There were too many times when she had overheard one of their disputes and heard her own name mentioned. Was it her fault that they weren't getting along? Was Risa right when she said that Malik spoiled her? Was Malik right when he claimed that Risa simply didn't understand her?

Please, Chimene said to herself silently, please don't fight over me.

"You want to look so noble in her eyes," Risa said. "You'd like her to think you're better than the rest of us, with all your learning and your sensitive feelings. You'd like to turn her against me."

"I was thinking of you," Malik said softly, "of what this decision would do to you."

"If it weren't for people like me, there wouldn't be much of a world for people like you."

"Why, a Mukhtar might have uttered those words—or a Guardian Commander, or any one of a number of people in the past who could find reasons for allowing the deaths of thousands."

"Stop it!" Chimene cried, unable to listen anymore. "Stop it!" She sat up. Risa stepped back from the bed, her eyes wide; Malik threw his arm around Chimene's shoulder.

She began to cry. Risa was always telling her that if she cried too much, she'd use up all her tears and wouldn't have them when she needed them, but she couldn't stop crying.

At last her cries faded to a whimper. Risa stretched out her arm; Chimene shrank back.

"Are you coming to bed?" Risa's voice was lower now. Malik was silent. "You'll see—nothing like this will ever happen again. You see that, don't you? You can't really think—" She bit her lip. "Are you coming to bed?"

"I'll stay here. Chimene might need me."

"I need you, too."

"No, you don't. You never did. I needed you once, and it was your misfortune that you thought you loved me—otherwise, you might have seen that you didn't need me. When you do see that, you'll get along well enough."

Risa spun around and ran from the room. "Malik?" Chimene said. "Malik?"

"Go to sleep."

"Was it wrong, what Risa did? Does it make her like those men who—" She swallowed.

"No, Chimene. Those men knew they'd done something wrong. Your mother believed that she was doing the right thing. She didn't intend to do a bad thing, but sometimes good intentions aren't enough. She isn't able to see that she might have been wrong, and maybe she never will." He drew the coverlet over her. "Go to sleep."

Sixteen

The technicians, pilots, and workers inside Oberg's bay fell silent as Sigurd passed them; they did not look especially pleased to see him there. He had said only that he would be visiting each of the settlements to consult with their Councils, but the settlers had to know the matter was serious since he was here in person.

He paused near the wide door to adjust his headdress; this meeting seemed to call for his formal headgear and white robe. He glanced back at the airship that had carried him here; the ship's cargo was rolling down ramps alongside the cradle. Three men had died in this bay; he clenched his teeth.

He stepped into Oberg's main dome. Risa Liangharad was waiting near the road that circled the dome; next to her, a lanky brown-haired man who looked familiar was speaking to a pilot. Sigurd consulted his Link briefly and came up with a name: Andrew Dinel.

The pilot bowed as Sigurd approached the group, then moved toward the bay. "Greetings, Administrator Sigurd," Andrew Dinel said, smiling. "What a delightful surprise, being able to greet you in person."

Sigurd doubted that the man's presence was a coincidence. "Salaam."

"I hope my whiskey still meets with your approval."

"Some of my guests have praised it. I don't drink myself."

"If it's at all possible," Andrew said, "my household would be pleased to offer you supper this evening."

"I'm afraid it isn't. I must leave for Tsou Yen before dark."

"Well." Andrew touched his forehead. "Have a safe journey then." He bowed, then walked toward the bay.

"I think Andrew was hoping he could ask you about our meeting later," Risa said. "He's always thought he should have been on the Council himself." She gestured at the duffel hanging from his shoulder. "Would you like to have someone carry that?"

"I'm capable of carrying my own bag."

Her mouth tightened; she was clearly worried about why he wanted a meeting with the Council. "We'd better go then. The rest of the Council is waiting."

They began to walk toward the center of the dome in silence As they passed the mosque, the call to prayer sounded, but no one seemed to be heeding it. "Perhaps you want to pray before meeting with us," Risa said.

"I think not, may God forgive me." She knew perfectly well how careless he was in his observances. Perhaps the Oberg Council only wanted a little more time to prepare for the meeting; he hadn't given them much warning.

Risa said no more until they entered the Administrative Center. "We were surprised that you decided to come here," she murmured. "It would be simpler to use the screen—we had no desire to take you away from your other demands."

"My presence was necessary," he replied, "and I haven't visited these settlements in some time. I thought it appropriate to come here now, especially since your recent actions have greatly troubled my thoughts."

Risa stiffened a little as she pressed a door open; surely she must have expected that. But perhaps not. The Council must have thought that since he had not acted before, he would have little to say now.

The rest of the Council was seated on cushions, their pocket screens on the low table in front of them. Risa sat down next to Istu Marnes; the only cushion left was on the side opposite the five people. Sigurd seated himself there and smoothed down his robe, then slipped his duffel off his shoulder.

"In the Name of God, the Beneficent, the Merciful," he recited automatically, "Whose Hand guides us all. May

He guide us now." The five stared at him blankly. He knew that they rarely, if ever, began their meetings with an invocation, but he felt a need for the comfort of tradition.

"May His name be praised," Alain al-Kadar said at last.

"In the name of Our Lord Jesus Christ," Curcio de la Cruz muttered as he bowed his head.

"May the Holy Mother Mary bless us," Jeannine Loris offered.

Sigurd felt irritated. Mentioning other faiths at the start of meetings was not unknown but was certainly not common, since it was often a sign of disagreements to come. Risa and Istu said nothing, apparently having no deities of their own to invoke.

Alain gestured at a teapot and tray of small cakes. "Would you care for some refreshment, Linker Sigurd?"

"No, thank you. I would like this meeting to be a private one. I shall keep a record of my own, of course." He tapped the jewel on his forehead. "Considering what I'm about to say, you may not wish to record this for yourselves."

Alain touched a button on his screen. "Very well."

"Now," Sigurd said. "I'm free to tell you exactly how much you've disappointed me. I thought you were capable of governing yourselves. Instead, you've abused your authority."

"Are you talking about those three men?" Jeannine asked.

"Of course I am."

"They were responsible for a woman's death," Risa said. "There was no doubt about that."

"That fact counts in your favor," Sigurd said, "but it doesn't excuse what you did."

"What could we do?" Risa asked. "Nora's household deserved justice. Some would have killed those men without a hearing, but we gave them one and the chance to speak—"

"Spare me your arguments," Sigurd said. "I already know what they are."

"You didn't try to stop the hearing. You allowed us to—"

"I had a misplaced faith in your judgment, and once you'd sentenced them, I was powerless to intervene. What I should have done was to summon Guardians from

Anwara immediately, but then the people you represent would have said I hadn't given you a chance to show you could handle this yourselves."

"You must have seen the hearing," Istu said, "or looked at a record of it. We did what the people who elected us demanded."

"Does being an elected representative mean following a mob?" Sigurd asked. "It was your duty to lead, to make them aware of the possible consequences of such an act—instead, you pandered to them. Your people are going to have second thoughts about this—it's come to my attention that a few already have. If they suffer for what you did, they'll turn on you. People who have power should think of how quickly those they serve can turn against them. Pavel Gvishiani, may God give his soul peace, learned that lesson."

Alain lifted his head. "They were murderers. Even the Koran tells us that a murderer may be punished by death."

"The Koran also tells us that expiation is received by those who show mercy to such people. I doubt very much that you were pondering the revealed Word of God while you were holding that hearing. You passed a death sentence. There hasn't been a death sentence on Earth in ages. How ironic that you, who pride yourselves on building a new society free from Earth's flaws, should resort to a punishment that even Earth gave up."

Jeannine's lip curled. "We're not that ignorant, Administrator. We know that some on Earth disappear and aren't seen again and that some communities execute wrongdoers without suffering more than a reprimand. At least we made our decision openly, in a hearing. Are you telling us that Earth would have preferred that we send those men back and give them the problem of dealing with them?"

Sigurd did not reply.

"If we'd given them up," Risa said, "Earth would have used that as an excuse to increase its own authority here. They would have wanted that, I suppose, but we—"

"Be silent," Sigurd said firmly. "As a matter of fact, the Project Council hasn't informed me of any displeasure on the part of the Mukhtars. They regret the action, of course. They feel it shows a certain brutality on the part of those who should have been ennobled by participating in this glorious Project. They won't praise you for what you did, but they see that it solves a few small problems for them. They, like you, had been concerned about some of the people waiting in Earth's camps for passage, people like the three you executed. They're perfectly happy to unload a few malcontents on you, people who will do well enough if they feel there's something in it for them, but they hardly want violently antisocial types to impede the Project's progress."

Sigurd paused. The Councilors seemed puzzled by his words, as he had expected. "Some people have decided, in the wake of rumors about what has happened here, to leave the camps and remain on Earth, where you can be sure they are pursuing unpleasant but necessary work. Others will probably be more circumspect. The camps will be easier to control, and the Mukhtars may be relieved that they don't have to settle a few problems for you or have the trouble of transporting troublesome settlers back to Earth. The more cynical may even take a certain pleasure in seeing people who prate about their ideals sink to the level you did."

Risa frowned. He had hoped that she, at least, might show a few regrets. "But if Earth feels that way," she said, "then why are you here?"

"You forget that the Habbers are also concerned with what happens here. I had a talk with two of their people a few days ago. Both men made it quite clear that they're unhappy with what you did."

Risa sniffed. "The Habbers? What business is it of theirs? Surely they didn't expect us to hand those men over to them."

"For all their brilliance in other respects," Sigurd responded, "the Habbers are often naïve."

"They'd like us to think so," Risa said. "They're always so calm and rational, as if darker thoughts never pass their minds. That Habber at the hearing was probably just trying to look—"

Sigurd shot her a glance. "Oh, no. He meant what he said. The Habbers who spoke to me made that quite clear. I had to explain the obvious to them—that Earth would hardly be reassured by their intentions if they knew Habbers were willing to harbor killers. They understood, but they found your action distasteful, to say the least. Their

own ships brought those men here only to be executed—
they find that hard to stomach. They're not happy with the
idea of having their people living among those who could
carry out such an execution."

Risa said, "I suppose they'd be happier if we'd let
them go. Those men might have killed a Habber instead—
how would they have liked that?"

"They wouldn't have demanded other deaths in return. As I said, they're very displeased. They don't like to
feel that their aid may only help yet another brutal society
to exist, or so they claim. Perhaps they're not willing to
admit that they're also concerned about their own safety
here, but I suspect they are. Another mob might turn
against them, you know. For people who have such prolonged lives, death holds even more terror than it does for
us."

Sigurd drummed his fingers on the tabletop. "The
Habbers do not want to see such an incident repeated. If it
is, they'll remove their people and their resources from
this Project altogether. They didn't put it quite that way, of
course. They don't like to make threats so baldly."

"If the Habbers leave—" Risa looked down.

"You're beginning to understand," he murmured.
"You know that I'm one who shares your dream. I have to
balance Earth's interests against those of the Habbers in
order to keep this Project going, while leaving you as free
as possible. Things are uncertain on Earth. If the Habbers
abandon us now, there will be a vacuum here that some
factions among the Mukhtars will rush to fill, and you'll be
even more dependent on Earth. You'll have to accept
more control from them to keep your world. Is that what
you want?"

"An incident like this won't happen again." Risa
sounded a bit more uncertain this time.

"You'll see that it doesn't." Sigurd folded his arms.
"That will require changes." There was no point in telling
the Council that Kichi Timsen had sent him a message a
few days ago, although Risa would guess that when she
heard what he was about to say. "You could have prevented this unfortunate incident by being more vigilant in
the first place. You do so at your other work—taking care of
smaller problems before larger ones develop that aren't so
easy to handle. You ought to secure your homes—you

should have done more about that as soon as you noticed an increase in thefts. You should require that anyone who's found guilty of any action that involves the property or safety of others be required to wear an identity bracelet at all times so that a record of his movements can always be traced. Those who prove they're trustworthy after that can be allowed to remove them after a time."

"Those are your suggestions?" Risa said. "I can't say I care much for them. We've always worn those bracelets only when leaving our settlements."

"When I called them suggestions," he replied, "I was being diplomatic." He paused to let that sink in. "You should also form some sort of patrol, people who will see that order is maintained, who will handle problems and restrain others when necessary, and who can hurry to a person's aid immediately—a kind of police force, if you will. On the Islands, our Counselors handle the few problems we have well enough, but since you don't want Counselors, you'll have to pick your patrol from among your citizens. I've been informed that there are several who will volunteer for such duty and who can organize the patrol. I suggest that you make such an announcement as soon as possible."

"I never thought I'd see that here," Istu muttered.

Risa glared at Sigurd. "I can guess who'll be the first people to volunteer. Ishtar will love the chance to look out for everyone else."

"Such intolerance is unbecoming," Sigurd said. "If, in spite of these measures, you have another sad incident that results in grievous harm or death, you would be well advised to find other punishments. Death is much too final a sentence."

Risa gestured with one arm. "Police—imprisonment. That's what you're talking about. It's contrary to everything—"

"Sentencing people to death hardly bodes well for the future of your communities." Sigurd leaned forward. "You've always trusted your fellow Cytherians, or so you say. Trust them with a little more authority to patrol themselves and prevent more trouble."

"Is that all?" Jeannine asked.

"No. You have an election coming up soon. You've all been on this Council long enough, so you needn't run again. Use the excuse that you're tired and feel that others should take your place."

"That's almost like admitting we were wrong, " Risa said.

"You're lucky I don't ask you to resign right now."

"Did the Habbers demand that, too?"

"Not at all," he said. "But it may reassure them if you leave the Council. Do I have your agreement? I'm sure you'll honor your word, especially since I'll keep a record of our talk. You'll maintain your authority as Councilors if you present my suggestions as your own, and you're hardly in a position to defy me."

"So that's what it comes to," Risa said bitterly. "Oberg can elect us, but the final power rests with you."

"It rests with me when you prove incapable of handling it yourselves."

"And you're trying to save your own position."

"Of course. You should be more concerned about who might replace me if I displease the Project Council now— someone who might not be so patient with you and who might consider Earth's interests more important than yours."

Sigurd got to his feet. "Are you going to act on my suggestions then?" The Councilors nodded passively; only Risa gazed at him directly. "I'll mention your plans during my meetings with the other Councils. They'll have to be persuaded to take similar steps. God be with you."

As he was about to turn toward the door, Risa spoke again. "These settlements are all we have. The Project Council can return to Earth, and the Habbers have their homes elsewhere, but where can we go? I doubt most of us could even function in some other environment. We were only defending what we have—there'll never be anything else for us."

"I want to preserve it, too."

Sigurd had the rest of the day ahead of him before an airship would take him to Tsou Yen. He wandered through the main dome and stopped by the community greenhouses, where a few people greeted him tentatively and began to offer carefully qualified remarks: The Council members had done what they had to do, but— The three men were clearly guilty, but— Severe punishment was necessary as a deterrent, but—

Obviously all of them were trying to figure out exactly what he thought. He uttered a few vague generalities, implying that the Oberg Council now had doubts about their action and had asked for his advice.

He made his way toward the main road. A cart with two men and a few crates passed; Sigurd motioned to it, discovered that the cart was headed for the west dome, then climbed aboard. By the time they came to the tunnel, the men had overcome their shyness enough to talk.

"I wasn't at the hearing," the older man said. "Had some plumbing to do in my house that just wouldn't wait, so I had to look at it later. I thought maybe they did the right thing, but now I don't know."

"You *did* let them hold the hearing, Administrator," the younger man said. "I guess you thought whatever they decided was fine, didn't you?"

"They are your representatives," Sigurd said. "They act in your name. I was not about to deprive them of their rightful authority. They are always free to consult with me, but it's up to them whether or not they follow my advice."

"Maybe I shouldn't ask this," the older man murmured, "but what *do* you think?"

Sigurd glanced at him. "That there are more constructive ways of dealing with such offenses. Fortunately, your Council seems to think so as well and may soon have suggestions to offer."

The cart emerged from the tunnel into the west dome. Sigurd waited until the cart was passing the trees that bordered the school, then raised a hand. "I'll get off here. Thank you for the ride."

"Maybe they should have listened to that teacher," the younger man said.

"Maybe they should have," Sigurd replied.

"I thought he was just being soft-hearted, but—" The man shrugged.

Sigurd strolled toward the trees. Maybe Risa should have listened to Kichi Timsen earlier; the Guide had claimed, in her message to him, that she had offered suggestions to Risa on how to deal with the accused men. Kichi had not bothered to make her suggestions openly at the hearing. She had assessed the mood of the crowd and of some of her own followers, had seen that little could be gained by speaking then.

He did not care for Ishtar and knew that Kichi was trying to use this incident for her own ends, but her group would be useful to him now. Letting them think that he was a bit more sympathetic to their aims would make them useful while giving him more control over them.

The west dome's school was a small one-story rectangle with wide windows. Children raced through the open doorway, then halted to stare at the unfamiliar sight of an Administrator. Risa had spoken of their future welfare at the hearing. He wondered how many of these children had been there and what sort of lesson they had drawn from the fate of the three men.

"What an honor!" a bearded man called out as he came near. "I didn't expect to see you here, Administrator. I'm Theron Hyland, one of the teachers here. Would you care to see the school?"

Sigurd shook his head. "I thought, as long as I was in Oberg, I'd visit with Malik Haddad. Some of my Islander friends are so anxious to know if he plans any more lectures. Please don't let me interfere with your obligations."

"Oh. He should be along any minute. We're letting the children out earlier today. To be honest, they've had trouble concentrating on their work lately."

Several children and a few adolescents were still gaping at Sigurd; Theron shooed them away as Malik came outside. A little girl was with him; Sigurd had seen her image before, during a couple of his talks with Risa. The child, with her long black hair and large dark eyes, was quite beautiful; he wondered if she was aware of that.

"Salaam, Malik," Sigurd said.

"Salaam, Administrator." Malik motioned to the child. "My daughter, Chimene Liang-Haddad. Chimene, this is Sigurd Kristens-Vitos."

"I know that," she said. "I saw him on the screen." She lifted her head. So much beauty in a child made him uneasy; having such attributes so early in life could not be good for one's character. "You came to talk to the Council."

"Yes, I did. I thought I'd speak to your father, too." Sigurd raised his voice a little so that Theron, who was now walking back to the school, could hear his words. "I have a great deal of respect for your father, you know."

Chimene leaned against Malik, clinging to the edge of his shirt. "The Administrator wants to talk to me," her father said. "Do you think you can go home by yourself?" Her eyes widened. "Or maybe you'd like to play with your friends for a bit." The girl shook her head vehemently. "Very well."

Malik looked up. "Her thoughts are often troubled now," he said in Arabic; Sigurd guessed that the child did not know the language well enough to understand them. "She is afraid to be distant from me for too long. I walk with her to the school and guide her home, and her sleep is often broken by evil dreams. I have been sleeping on a mat at the side of her bed—I hear her screams when she awakes."

"I am sorry to hear it," Sigurd replied in the same language.

"Her mother tells me I should leave her alone to cry out by herself, that this will heal her." Sigurd heard the bitterness in the other man's words. "But this is not your concern, Administrator. It is the same with some of the other children, the more sensitive ones. They dream that the Council will come to sentence them. This now leads the other teachers here to remark that they should have defended my words at the hearing, although not one of them rose to do so there."

"It took some courage for you to speak."

"My words swayed no one, and perhaps they only hardened the heart of my bondmate even more."

"Your words have been heard," Sigurd said. "I stand here speaking with you now so that others will know I have heard them and regret that they were not heeded."

Malik's mouth twisted. "Yet you did nothing."

"One must pick a time to act. Had I interfered before, I would only have won more support for the Council's proposed punishment among the people here and in the other settlements. Now others have doubts about what they did. Those doubts can be used to bring about change. This will not happen again, God willing."

"Risa." Chimene looked up as Malik spoke her mother's name; her face was tense. "I might have forgiven what she did if she had shown regrets. I might have understood it if she had done it with reluctance, but she would sweep aside anything in the service of her dream and what she sees as her duty. Now she justifies herself to our daughter, who was forced to witness her deeds. She teaches the child only that those with power can justify any evil act." Malik paused. "But she remains my bondmate. I am tied to her, bound by my pledge and our child."

"Your bondmate has been of value to me in the past," Sigurd said. "Perhaps I am partly at fault for not seeing more deeply into her heart. It may be the will of God that some time must pass before she finds repentance, but she will soon see that her deed is not without unfortunate consequences. I have spoken to the Council, and they have listened."

"How I wish it were written that I could be free of her now!"

"There are Islanders who seek your company," Sigurd responded. "Lectures can be arranged—you could join us soon."

"I could not leave Chimene now. Risa might welcome seeing me go—if I were away from her side, she would have an excuse to account for my absence from her bed. But she would keep our child with her. Chimene is the only weapon she has to use against me."

"Perhaps, when some time has passed—" Sigurd shrugged. "I must go now. My ship will be almost ready to leave by the time I reach the bay." He looked down at Chimene. "Farewell, child," he said in Anglaic.

"Good-bye, Administrator."

Sigurd turned and walked toward the trees. He could easily find a way to bring the historian to the Islands, and perhaps the girl as well. At least two of the teachers on Island Two had made it known that they wanted to settle in the domes, so Malik could be replaced here. The girl might be chosen for an Island school. That was unusual for one so young, but Risa could hardly refuse her the opportunity if her father was on the Island to look after her. She would not be happy to let her daughter go, but she would be in a weaker position when she was no longer on the Council—more doubtful of herself, easier to persuade.

He pitied Malik somewhat, but pity did not motivate him now. Risa had been useful, and she might be useful again. She would lose her present position but would retain some of her influence. She would be better off not living with her bondmate's open resentment, which might affect how she dealt with others. Better to separate her and Malik as soon as possible.

Sigurd had never grown used to Anwara. On Island Two, there was the illusion of space, and the pleasure of seeing grass, flowers, trees, and the few small animals allowed there. He appreciated Anwara most when approaching it in a shuttle, when the space station was only a distant pale circle set against a dark backdrop of pinpricks of light.

Once inside, he felt cramped. The satellite's curved halls were too bright with light, and the spin of Anwara's three circular tubes around its hub made him feel vaguely disoriented and unsteady on his feet. He would almost have preferred remaining in the weightlessness of the hub, where his shuttle had docked.

Anwara made him think of Earth, a thought that was probably responsible for some of his unease. Freighters and passenger ships from Earth docked here, as did Habber ships, but Anwara's personnel did their best to ensure that no Earthfolk or Cytherians fraternized with Habbers temporarily on the satellite. Islander specialists occasionally came here to work, where the presence of Guardians and Project Council members always reminded them that Earth still claimed this Project; the arriving Habber pilots were never allowed to stay for long. Anwara had remained Earth's outpost, a place where Sigurd was always mindful of the limits on his actions.

He had been given a room to himself this time. Sigurd pulled the small bed from the wall and stretched out on it, tired from his journey. The last time he had been forced to share Salim Berkur's quarters, which were not much larger than this tiny room. Salim had not minded, but along with most of the people on Anwara, he had grown used to the lack of space. The men and women stationed here greeted one another or gathered to talk only in the large common rooms, meeting rooms, or gymnasiums; the rest of the time, they avoided even a glance. That would have seemed rude anywhere else; here it left them with a feeling of more privacy and kept them from getting on one another's nerves.

Sigurd's door chimed; he heard a voice through the speaker. "Salim Berkur and Chang Hsin-sheng. We'd like to talk to you when you feel up to it. We'll be in Hsin-sheng's room within the hour, but if that's inconvenient—"

Sigurd was already on his feet. The two might have alerted him through their Links, but Salim was often reluctant to intrude in that way. "Come in," he said as he pressed the door open.

He ushered the two men inside, then pushed his bed into the wall. "We wanted to talk to you before the meeting," Salim said.

"Of course." Salim and Hsin-sheng had always been his allies on the Project Council. "Shall we talk here or go somewhere else?"

"This is good enough," Hsin-sheng said. The three men sat on the floor. The gray-haired Chinese man wore a dour expression on his bony face, but Sigurd had never known him to smile very often. "The Council is pleased with you at the moment. They were afraid that we might be impelled to station Guardians on the surface, but now that the settlers have announced that they will begin to police themselves, that's settled."

Sigurd rested his hands on his knees. "I didn't know anyone was seriously considering stationing Guardians there."

"If the Commanders had more power, that unpleasant incident in Oberg would have given them an excuse to do so. But Ali Akar's faction rules the Council of Mukhtars now. He was planning to recall many of the Guardians by now, but then that unfortunate business occurred in Oberg, so I imagine he thought it best to wait. Now he can proceed."

Sigurd was silent. He had not known that Ali Akar's influence had increased, but there was much that did not reach him over the channels from Earth. This was welcome news. Ali, according to rumor, believed that the Project should have more autonomy, that if the settlers were kept on a looser leash now, they would more willingly give their allegiance to Earth later. There would be fewer restraints on Sigurd's actions and more of a chance for the Project to proceed.

He smiled. "I was expecting more objections from the

Project Council this time, but if Mukhtar Ali is stronger, they'll have to listen to my plans."

Salim was not smiling; Sigurd wondered why. The dark-haired man, unlike his companion, rarely concealed his feelings. "Oh, yes," Salim said. "They'll listen. They know you've been itching to get on with domes and industrial installations in the Freyja mountain range. Now you can tell your Habber friends that you're finally ready to proceed and that the Council can back you with Mukhtar Ali in control. That is what you want, of course."

"God willing," Sigurd replied.

"The Council will support you," Hsin-sheng said, "and so will we, but I fear you may be making a mistake."

"How so? With Ali more powerful—"

"That could change again," the gray-haired Linker continued. "Don't think the Commanders and their allies have given up entirely. The struggle for power over the Council of Mukhtars is far from being concluded. If you push ahead too rapidly now, Mukhtar Ali's enemies may think you harbor dreams of independence for Venus or, worse, they may see you as a tool of the Habbers, working for their ends."

Sigurd shook his head. "I don't see how anyone could draw that conclusion now. I bided my time while Earth's desires were uncertain—I didn't try to take advantage of the situation or allow the Habbers to use it for their purposes. It's true that we must rely more on the Habbers during this next stage of the Project, but I've also taken steps to minimize their influence."

"True," Salim said. "We know about the overtures you've made to Ishtar, and extreme distrust of the Habitats is a tenet of their faith." He did not have to say more; he was clearly aware of Sigurd's strategy. Any influence the Habbers hoped to gain would meet with resistance from the cult, which would now have more power in the settlements. Volunteers for the patrols that would help to police the domes were being drawn largely from Ishtar's ranks, since the cult seemed the only group organized enough to mobilize them.

Ishtar's Guide could mutter what she liked about the evils of Earth, but the Habbers drew most of her scorn. Earth was far away, while the presence of Habbers was a constant affront. Earth's people were planet-dwellers and therefore presumably capable of eventual convergence with their own planetary spirit, while the Habbers had rejected the life of planets altogether. Help from the Habitats might be necessary now, but that would change. As Ishtar saw it, the Habbers could not possibly have altruistic motives; they could not actually want the Cytherians to thrive. Habbers could only be waiting to subvert the Islanders and settlers, make Habbers of them eventually, and strike a blow at Earth by seizing the Project for themselves.

Ishtar's distrust of Habbers had allowed Earth to tolerate the cult. Kichi Timsen would never admit it openly, but Sigurd was sure that if it proved necessary, Ishtar could live under Earth's rule as long as the group was left free to win adherents. Kichi could rationalize such an agreement by imagining that it was temporary, since her perfect society lay far in the future. Earth could believe that the cult posed no danger to its ultimate authority.

The execution in Oberg, however unfortunate, had worked to Sigurd's advantage; it had given him a way to make use of that accursed cult. Earth could hardly believe that anyone who would willingly allow Ishtar a more important role in the settlements was an ally of the Habbers. Everything would be so nicely balanced now, and the cult could be dealt with later.

"You think you can manipulate Ishtar," Hsin-sheng said. "I've often felt that some on Earth may believe the same. It might have been better to put more restraint on them, so that they don't become more powerful."

Sigurd shrugged. "They claim less than fifteen percent of the settlers now. Every projection I've done indicates that they're unlikely to win over many more unless something catastrophic occurs that they could use to their advantage."

Salim's mustache twitched. "Catastrophic events can happen. A community can be weakened enough to become vulnerable to various ideological infections. I've never had much faith in sociological projections—introduce just one new or indeterminate factor and you can get quite a different chain of events."

"I thought you two were on my side. I don't want the settlers becoming demoralized, and they will if we keep stalling. They'll wonder why—"

"Oh, you'll get what you want." Hsin-sheng rubbed his chin. "Let me give you some advice, Sigurd—fatherly advice, if you will. Spend a few months getting this next phase under way, and then resign as Liaison. You can always say that you've been at the job long enough, and you'll still be an Administrator. Let someone else be the Liaison."

Sigurd lifted his brows. "And just why should I resign?"

"Mukhtar Ali isn't only recalling Guardians from Anwara. He's thinking of bringing some of the Project Council back as well. His reasoning is that if the Liaison is loyal, he shouldn't need quite so much direction from the Council."

"But that also helps me."

"Alliances among the Mukhtars are likely to shift again, and if they do, you won't be in a good position. Every year you spend at your current post gives you more power here, and if the Mukhtars decide to reclaim much of that authority, they may not be overly concerned with your fate. Bide your time, Sigurd. You're young—you can wait. Show them that you harbor no dreams of personal power by resigning soon. When the Mukhtars resolve their internal struggle, they may turn to you again."

Sigurd gazed steadily at Hsin-sheng. "I have to see this through. My position means nothing to me except as a way to serve the Project. Too many of my colleagues would be ready to sacrifice the Project's future, given the opportunity, if their own positions were assured. I won't let that happen. I can't allow myself to be replaced by someone who may not be willing to put the Project above all else. I might be needed even more now, if things are as uncertain as you imply."

"Don't think that Venus's future rests entirely with you," Hsin-sheng said fervently. "Don't confuse your own ambitions with the Project's goals to the point where you can no longer distinguish between the two. I'm old enough to remember Pavel Gvishiani's time—don't make his mistake and see yourself as the Project's only savior." The elderly man paused. "But I see you won't listen to me."

"It's in God's hands," Salim muttered as he rose. "We had better prepare for the meeting."

* * *

The airship had landed in its cradle. The cradle moved slowly through the lock and then into the bay of Island Two. Sigurd got up from his seat and absently exchanged a few pleasantries with the other passengers before moving toward the door.

He walked past the row of cradles and dirigibles to the entrance. For a few moments, during his journey aboard the shuttle from Anwara's high orbit, he had found himself toying with Hsin-sheng's suggestion that he resign. Weightlessness often induced such longings for freedom from his responsibilities, as if he could drift away from them as easily as he propelled himself along the aisle of the shuttle. His duty, along with Venus's gravity, captured him again at the Platform. He had looked into the faces of those he passed and convinced himself that they would not welcome his resignation.

I wouldn't welcome it myself, he thought as he followed a white tiled path past the slender trees just beyond the entrance. Freedom would be a void, and he had nothing with which to fill it.

He strode quickly, barely nodding at those who greeted him. He would have to meet with some of the Habbers first. His aides, and perhaps some of his fellow Administrators, would have told the Habbers about the meeting on Anwara by now. They would all be pleased by the results. Everything had turned out better than he had anticipated before leaving Island Two. It was odd that he did not feel more gratified.

He hastened on, then turned toward a path to his right. He might as well speak to a few of the Habbers now; it hardly mattered which people he talked to, since any one of them could speak for the others. It was one of the qualities Kichi Timsen particularly disliked, the ability of the Habbers to seem in complete accord with one another. That was ironic, since Ishtar's adherents dreamed of the time Cytherians would reach such a state themselves. But Ishtar was also convinced that the Habbers' equanimity hid evil intentions. Ishtar, after all, had the truth, while the Habbers seemed to question everything.

A woman was walking toward the Habbers' stone residence; Sigurd slowed to a stop. She turned, and he was gazing into Tesia's hazel eyes.

"Greetings, Administrator," she said in a flat voice.

"Salaam. I hadn't realized you were back. I didn't think you'd return so soon."

"Word of your recent meeting with the Project Council reached my home a short time ago. Those of us who thought we might be needed now decided to return. I was sorry to leave my home—being there brought me into balance again. But I'm also anxious to see the work I did here bear fruit, as your greenhouse gardeners would say." She seemed very stiff; her eyes refused to meet his.

"I'm pleased you did," he said, unsure whether he really meant it.

"I came here with some reluctance, Administrator. My people know you're showing more favor to Ishtar now, people who are so hostile to us."

"Your people were perturbed by that execution in Oberg," he said. "I had to see that it wouldn't happen again, so that you wouldn't be tempted to abandon the Project."

"Oh, I understand your reasoning. Earth mustn't see you making things too easy for us. We can work with you now, and Ishtar's patrols will see that no one becomes too friendly with us. I explained that to many of my friends, that you were a man capable of mimicking friendship and kindness in the service of the Project's goals and that you'd see that the cult did not impede our work."

He took a breath. "I'm sorry I said what I did to you. I know it was cruel to do it that way—you must have seen—"

Tesia seemed amused; her lips curved into a smile. "It accomplished your purpose. You showed your colleagues that we had no hold over you, and now we can get on with the work you postponed. You have no reason to be sorry."

She entered the building; the door closed behind her. He waited only a moment before he followed. The only freedom he had known was with her, before his sense of duty had put an end to it. He wanted to find that freedom again, have something for himself apart from the Project's demands. He wanted to touch one person without thoughts of how that person might become one of his tools.

He reached the door to her room before it could close and stood in the doorway as she stepped back. She would turn him away and taunt him with the words he had spoken to her. She would reproach him for not having the sensitivity to have said his farewells in private or to prepare her for their meeting. She would remind him that she was a Habber and that no true bond could ever exist between them; he had said so himself. Then she would turn away, indifferent to him, or find that she could take a bittersweet pleasure in his pain.

"Tesia," he said hoarsely.

Her arms opened. He stepped forward and embraced her.

THE GUIDE

Seventeen

"You're certain this is what you want," Malik said to Chimene. They were nearing the entrance to Island Two's airship bay; it seemed a little late for her father to be asking her that now.

"Yes," Chimene replied. "Anyway, I can always come back if I change my mind."

"In six months, you can," Malik reminded her, "so I hope you're sure now. You made the request, after all, and Risa will expect you to keep to your commitment."

"I *know* that." She hugged him; he handed Chimene her duffel. "I'll miss you."

"Well, it won't be that long, and Risa will be happy to have more time with you." Malik kissed her on the forehead. "Send me a message as soon as you can."

"I will."

She walked toward the bay, then turned to wave at Malik one last time before the door closed behind her. Cargo was being taken off one airship; passengers were ascending the ramp to another. "Go to the third airship on your right," a voice from the small screen near the door said as her wristband was scanned. "Departure for the Platform in ten minutes."

She hurried to the line of people and followed them into the airship. The two pilots, both in Ishtar's sash, were already seated by the controls under the large screen in front of the ship; the passengers began to settle themselves in the worn and stained seats. Chimene found a seat near the back, rummaged in her duffel for her pocket screen, then stowed the bag under her seat.

She was the only child aboard. She strapped herself in, then looked down at her screen, pretending to read.

"—Malik Haddad's daughter," a voice near her murmured.

"What a beautiful child. Gets her looks from him, I guess."

A blossom of Astarte—that was what her father called her in Arabic. She liked such compliments, even if Risa often told her that Chimene was not responsible for her appearance and could not consider it an accomplishment.

She stared at her screen. Usually, she did not mind talking with the other passengers, but she had a lot to think about during this trip. She had surprised her father by asking to spend all this time in Oberg, but she had convinced him that she wanted more time with her old friends and her mother's household. She had not told Malik that she was equally anxious to be away from him.

"Sigurd's favorite." She had heard one Linker whisper the words to another. "The Administrator's pet" was another term she had overheard. The Islanders who referred to her father that way seemed amused rather than contemptuous, but their words made her wince. Malik either did not know what some people called him or did not care.

She and Malik had come to Island Two five years ago, when Chimene was six. Her father had unexpectedly been offered a chance to trade places with a teacher there, news that came as a relief to her parents and the entire household.

The long months preceding that offer were not times she wanted to recall. Risa had decided not to run for the Council again, which only gave her more time at home to glower at Malik in silence or to snipe at him about some small lapse. Malik had finally moved to Bettina's wing of the house, where Nikolai made room for him.

The estrangement and the household's forced cheerfulness, as they pretended this was only a temporary problem, left Chimene with a gnawing guilt. She knew her father wanted to leave and was staying only because of her. She saw that Risa, once so sure and confident, was now so uncertain of herself that she could not make the simplest decision without consulting the rest of the household.

It was all her fault; Chimene could not escape the feeling. Her father would not leave without her, and Risa would never let her go. Clinging to Malik for comfort made her feel disloyal to her mother, while her efforts to cheer Risa seemed futile. She did not want to give them any reason to hate each other more because of her. She continued to hope that one day she would wake up, go to her mother's room, and find Malik there again, holding Risa's hand, their disputes forgotten.

The offer for Malik to go to Island Two came just in time. Nikolai and Emilia, affected by the household's uneasy mood, had been muttering about voiding their agreement in order to set up their own household elsewhere. Chimene did not even get a chance to worry about how much she would miss her father because she was invited to accompany him.

The Island Administrators, according to the message, were beginning a new program to promote better feeling between the settlements and the Islands. Some of the Islander children would trade places with children selected from each of the settlements. Promising students from among the dome-dwellers had studied at Island schools before, but this program was to involve much younger children; they would begin with a small number and see how things went.

It was, Chimene supposed, an honor to be chosen, and even Risa was unable to come up with any objections. Chimene could live with her father rather than an Islander family and would be gone only for a few months. So Risa had believed then, but in Chimene's case the months had turned into years, with Malik pointing out to her mother that Chimene would benefit from more contact with the Island specialists.

Once, Risa would have given Malik an argument about that, but Chimene soon saw that her parents' separation had, instead of driving them even further apart, brought them closer together. Their messages to each other, at first limited to uneasy talk about various events in their lives, grew warmer, and often they spoke directly over the screen. Whenever Chimene visited Oberg, as she always did during the periods when the children were given time off from school, Risa pestered her for more news about Malik; when she returned, Malik seemed eager to hear about Risa. It was enough to make her think that her parents might renew their bond, but it had lapsed, an occasion they both marked with carefully worded messages saying they would always feel linked through Chimene.

Maybe that was just as well, Chimene thought. Risa might not like to see what Malik was now. It was odd that living alone with her father had given Chimene a little more sympathy for her mother's former complaints—that Malik was impractical, that he wanted an easy life, that he felt no true devotion to the Project.

"We are departing from Island Two now," a voice announced from the front of the airship. "Make sure your harnesses are fastened, and do not move about the ship until we're aloft."

Chimene felt a wave of relief, and then a twinge. In the past she had been reluctant to visit Oberg; now she was looking forward to the journey. Malik would have been surprised if she had told him just how much she wanted to get away and what her reasons were.

Sef, she thought to herself; she loved to think of his name, turning it this way and that in her mind, caressing it with her voice as she whispered it to herself. Sef Talis. She had met him only a few months before, during her last visit to Oberg. She settled back in her seat, remembering, savoring the thought of him.

Risa had put in a request for a new immigrant, and the record of one young man had indicated that he might be useful around the house. Sef Talis had experience as a farmer, which would make him useful in the greenhouse, and he also had some of a mechanic's skills.

Chimene, along with her friend Lena Kerein, had gone to meet the new arrival in Oberg's main dome. They found two men loitering outside the bay. Both were tall; one had thinning brown hair and a short beard. The other seemed hardly more than a boy, in spite of his height; his thick chestnut hair curled slightly around his pleasant face. Each man was carrying a pack, and both had the glazed look of fatigue.

"Is one of you Sef Talis?" Chimene asked.

"I am," the chestnut-haired man replied.

She blinked, a little surprised. Risa had told her the man was young, but not how young. "I'm Chimene Liang-Haddad. This is Lena Kerein. My mother's Risa

Liangharad, but she couldn't come herself because she has to work today, so she sent me to get you."

"Yes," the man said. "I was told someone asked for me. Guess I'm lucky I don't have to live in a tent right off." He smiled then; the smile made his face seem even more attractive. His teeth were white and straight, and she noticed that his warm brown eyes were flecked with gold.

"You're tall," Lena said. Chimene felt irritated with her friend for making such an obvious statement. "We don't have many people that tall."

"People grow tall where I come from—the Pacific Federation, in North America. They grow pretty tall in the Nomarchy of New Deseret, too—some of my mother's people came from there."

"We'd better go," Chimene said. "It'll be getting dark in a couple of hours." Sef hoisted his pack to his broad shoulders, shook hands with the other man, then followed the girls toward the main road. "I thought you'd be older," Chimene added.

"I'm almost eighteen. How old are you two?"

"Eleven," Lena said. "Chimene's ten."

"*Almost* eleven," Chimene said quickly.

"Maybe you can tell me a little about your household."

"Well, there's Chen," Chimene replied. "Liang Chen. He's my grandfather. He's old, but he's still pretty healthy. Then there's Bettina Christies—she's a physician. She and Chen are sort of like bondmates, but they never made a pledge. And there's Kolya—Nikolai Burian—and his bondmate, Emilia Knef, and they had a daughter a few months ago—her name's Irina. Then there's Paul Bettinas and his bondmate, Grazie Lauro, and their son, Patrick Lauro—he's about a year older than I am."

"Sounds like a good-sized household," Sef said. "And there's your mother and you, of course."

"Well, I don't actually live here—I'm just visiting. I've been living on Island Two with my father, Malik Haddad. His bond with my mother lapsed a little while ago."

"Malik's a teacher," Lena said. "He's kind of a scholar, too—he gives lectures and stuff for the Islanders, and even the Administrators sometimes go to them."

Chimene glanced at the brown-haired girl. When Lena made such comments, she was never sure if her friend was praising Malik or mocking him a little. "He's handsome, too," Lena continued. "My mother says she's never seen a better-looking man."

"I guess he must be to have such a pretty daughter."

Chimene blushed a little; now it was Lena's turn to look a bit annoyed. "Anyway," Chimene said, "Kolya and Emilia will put Irina in their room, so you can use hers until I leave." She was beginning to feel even more sorry that she would have to return to the Islands.

A cart rolled by toward the tunnel; one of the women on it was wearing a red and black sash. "I saw that sash on a lot of the pilots at the Platform," Sef murmured. "What's it mean?"

"They're members of Ishtar," Chimene explained.

"And what's Ishtar?"

"The fellowship of true Cytherians," Lena said in her slightly sarcastic tone. "It's sort of like a religion, and every settler's welcome to join. If you go to a meeting, they'll tell you all about it. My parents are thinking of joining soon."

"And are many people here members?" Sef asked.

"Not that many—about two thousand here in Oberg. They'd like everybody to join, but it doesn't look like they will. Still, they are kind of important—most of the pilots are members, and almost all of the patrol volunteers. If my parents join, I guess they'll have me join, too." Lena sounded indifferent to the prospect. "Kichi Timsen's the Guide—Ishtar's Guide. That makes her the most important member."

"Not really," Chimene said. "I mean, she *is* the Guide, but they're all brothers and sisters in Ishtar, so nobody's really more important than somebody else. It's just that the Guide and the people closest to her have broken through the things that divide other people. They kind of set an example, but they're not really more important— they just know not everybody's ready to live the way they do."

"The Guide can say that," Lena objected, "but she's still more important. Kichi—"

Chimene made a sign at her friend; Lena fell silent. For a moment, Chimene had feared that the other girl might tell Sef that they both occasionally went to the Guide's house, and if Sef ever mentioned that to Risa— Chimene shuddered. She had kept those visits a secret so far; Risa would never understand. Risa did not like Kichi

Timsen. She did not know the kindly woman who listened to Chimene's confidences, spoke to her as if she were an adult, and looked forward to their talks.

"My mother doesn't like Ishtar all that much," Chimene muttered.

"Really?" Sef said. "But you seem to know something about it."

"Well, everybody does, but—" She waved at two other children as they came to the tunnel. "Risa just doesn't like them, that's all."

That seemed strange, the more she thought about it. Weren't Kichi and Risa working toward the same goal? Didn't Risa say that they were all Cytherians and therefore equals? Risa probably didn't like Kichi because the Guide had become more influential, and Administrator Sigurd spoke to her more often, while Risa no longer had as much influence.

"My father came here from a camp," Chimene said, wanting to change the subject. "So did Kolya, but he doesn't talk about it very much."

"I can guess why. I was in the camp outside San Antonio. It was hard—not many people try to get to a camp now, and the Guardians don't make it easy for the ones who do." He smiled down at her. "Seems it was worth the trouble now."

She smiled back; his smile made her feel warm inside.

Sef rested in Irina's room before joining the rest of the household for supper. Chimene listened intently as he told them all a little about himself. He was the only son of parents who had him late in life; they had apparently urged him to emigrate. He knew how to read a little, and he was willing to work. Risa seemed satisfied; that was just the kind of statement she liked to hear.

After supper, Risa and Nikolai took the plates to the kitchen, Emilia went to her room to nurse Irina, and Chen took out a few of his carvings to show Sef. Chimene sprawled on the floor near her grandfather, staring at Sef's large hands as they gently handled an image Chen had carved of her. "This is nice work," Sef said, "but Chimene must be a good subject."

"She is." Chen picked up a carving of Malik's head and

shoulders. "This one's of her father. Maybe I can do one of you sometime."

"I'd be honored."

Chen got to his feet slowly. "You can leave them there on the table. I'd sit up with you for a bit, but I need more rest these days."

"Of course. Maybe I'll take a look outside, see what the dome's like after dark."

"Don't wander too far," Chen said. "Some of the patrol might ask what you're doing. Normally, they don't bother people too much, but you're new and they might question you."

"I'll stay close to the house then," Sef responded.

"I suppose we need the patrol. They caught a man just about a month ago trying to take liberties with a woman, and a good thing they did. He's under restraint with a few others that caused some trouble, but still—" Chen paused. "It doesn't seem right to have settlers forced to wear their bracelets every time they go to their work, and having to live in that shack they put up in the main dome for them. I never thought I'd see that here."

"At least they can stay," Sef said as he stood up, "and maybe they'll learn something. We heard in the camp about some men who were executed a while back—that's worse."

"Risa was on our Council then," Bettina said from the corner. "She was one of those who passed that sentence." She looked down at the shirt she was mending. "You might as well know—somebody'd tell you that before long, and I can't see that she had too much choice. Whatever some tell you now, there wasn't anybody who spoke against it then, except Malik."

"Maybe their punishment wasn't worse," Chen said. "They had a hearing, and their sentence was to be a warning to others. No one ever thought they'd have to make a judgment like that again. I didn't know if the Council was doing the right thing, but now I wonder. A settler'd have to do something pretty bad to die like that, but some of the ones who get restrained now—" The old man gazed at the floor. "It's easier for people to do that, demand it from the Council, even when it's somebody who regrets something and probably wouldn't do it again. It's easier than trusting and finding some other way to make reparation, but it also means giving those people a chance to learn how to hate the rest of us."

Chimene bit her lip. Her memory of that hearing was a hazy recollection of crowds, Risa speaking from a platform, a man pleading for mercy, a sudden sharp stab of fear when she understood that the three men were to die after all. Her memory of the aftermath was more vivid—her fear of her mother, Malik's bitter words.

"I see your point." Sef cleared his throat. "I wouldn't want to have to decide anything like that, and it couldn't have been easy for your daughter."

"It wasn't." Chen moved slowly toward his room.

As Sef walked toward the door, Chimene said, "Want some company?"

"I don't see why not."

She followed him outside. "Let's sit there, under the trees," Sef said. "I'm a little too tired to walk around anyway." They went toward the trees and sat down near the path that led to the door.

"Why'd you come here?" she asked.

"I'm young and had nothing to lose. The most I could have hoped for on Earth was some extra credit to buy a little more comfort. I guess I wanted a chance to work for something else." She liked listening to his husky voice. "Your mother seems a fine woman," he continued. "Maybe another man's planning to make a bondmate of her if it's over between her and your father."

"She was seeing a man on her team, but I think they were just friends." Chimene plucked a blade of grass and toyed with it. "A lot of the men she knows have bondmates already, and the others—well, they'd have to decide whether to live with his household or hers, and she wouldn't want to leave this house."

"What about you, Chimene?" Her cheeks flushed as she heard him say her name. "What's it like on the Islands?"

"It's all right. It isn't like Oberg. More scientists live there, and other specialists."

"More Habbers, too, I guess."

She did not like to think of the Habbers. Every time she came back to the room she shared with Malik and found a message from him saying he would be back later, she knew where he had gone, and sometimes he didn't bother to return before first light. Once he had even brought Chimene to the Habber residence and had introduced her to a fair-haired woman, as if that Habber and his daughter could ever be friends. The Habbers seemed friendly enough, but Kichi Timsen had told her that Habbers wanted to lure Cytherians into closer ties with the Habs and seize the Project for themselves. She hated thinking of her father with one of their kind; Kichi would call it a perversion.

Maybe Malik thought he could act the way Sigurd did, but the Administrator was different. Sigurd might have a Habber woman, but some people said that was only his way of keeping an eye on the Habbers and staying in their good graces. Malik could not have such a motive.

"What's it like on the Islands for you?" Sef asked.

She felt flattered by his interest, but the subject was a painful one. "I don't know," she answered. "The students there—they're supposed to get along with us, but they really don't. The ones whose parents are workers aren't so bad, but the rest of them—they like to think they're a little better than we are just because they live on the Islands. They call us grubbers."

"But your father's on the Islands. That makes you just as much of an Islander as a dome-dweller, doesn't it?"

"Not really. My mother's here and Malik was once, and he came here from a camp, so they don't see him as a real Islander." Sigurd's favorite—that was how a lot of them saw him, but she couldn't tell that to Sef. Even worse, she knew that some of the Islander children believed that the only reason she had remained on Island Two for so long was because Sigurd allowed it as a favor to her father. She was quick enough at her lessons but not brilliant enough to be a potential specialist. Her teachers were always saying she could do better, but they didn't know what it was like to have schoolmates who thought one did not belong there.

"Kids can be hard," Sef said. "When they're older, they'll see how silly they acted. I'll bet some of them are jealous of you for being so pretty—maybe that's some of it." He ruffled her hair. Normally, she did not like it when people other than Malik patted her on the head, but she welcomed the touch of his hand. "When do you go back?"

"In two weeks."

"I'll be sorry to see you go."

He would be sorry to see her go! The statement thrilled her. She drew up her legs and rested her chin on her knees. "Oh, I'll visit again pretty soon," she said casually. "I won't be gone that long." She wanted to wish the months away.

"And what do you want to do when you're older?"

"I'm not sure." The door to the house opened for a moment, casting light along the path, then closed again. "Malik wants me to be a specialist, maybe even go to the Cytherian Institute, but I don't think I want to go to Earth, and they might not choose me anyway." She did not want to be chosen if others were going to assume that was another favor of Sigurd's. "I'm pretty good at botany, and that's useful, and Chen shows me how to repair circuits and things when I'm here."

"My daughter hasn't always been so practical." Chimene started at the sound of Risa's voice, then looked up at her mother's shadowy form. "But maybe being on the Islands makes her appreciate what we have here."

Chimene resented the intrusion. "I'll show you the greenhouse, if you like," Risa continued. "Then I suppose Tina will want to scan you—I don't expect they bothered on the Platform."

"They didn't, but you won't find anything wrong with me."

"Chimene, you might help Patrick with his lessons if you can tear him away from his mind-tour, and then you should probably go to sleep."

Chimene got to her feet reluctantly.

"Good night, Chimene," Sef said as he rose. "Maybe you can give me a tour of this dome tomorrow, after I finish whatever work the others find for me."

She grinned in the darkness, happy again.

Chimene was the first passenger off the airship when it was docked in its cradle. She raced through the bay, slowing as she neared the door, then held out her arm.

"Destination?" a voice said.

"Oberg."

"An airship for Oberg will leave in three hours. Go to the waiting room, first door to your left. Don't wander—"

She did not wait to hear the rest; she had been on the

Platform often enough. She walked toward the waiting room, where several people were asleep on the long couches. A glassy booth with a screen in the corner was already occupied by a man; she walked toward the booth and waited.

Two boys were sitting on the floor next to the booth, playing chess on a pocket screen; they were younger than she was, perhaps no more than eight. The red-haired one looked up. "Where are you headed?" he asked.

"Oberg."

"We're going to Lyata. They picked us to live with the grubbers for a while. I hope it isn't too awful."

Chimene glared at him. "You'll get along," she said evenly. "I just hope they don't mind putting up with a couple of gasbags." She stared at the boys in silence until the man ahead of her left the booth.

She went inside, sat down, and spoke into the screen. "I want to talk to Lena Kerein, west dome of Oberg, at her house. If she isn't there, I'll leave a message—I'm Chimene Liang-Haddad."

Lena's rosy-cheeked face appeared. "Chimene! Risa said you were coming back for six months this time."

"Maybe longer. I don't want any of our friends to think I'm turning into a gasbag. My ship leaves in three hours—can you meet me?"

"I'll try, but my father told me I'd have to clean my room and feed the rabbits first, so if I'm not there, I'll meet you at your house. Are you going over to the Guide's?"

"I'd like to."

"When she heard you were coming back, she made a point of telling me you were invited. I'll let her know, all right?"

Chimene nodded, hoping that Risa would not find out. But Lena would be careful not to let her household know where they were going. Lena's parents might be flattered at Kichi's apparent interest in their daughter, but Chimene did not want them bragging about their good fortune in front of Risa.

"See you," Lena said. The screen went blank. Kichi wanted to see her, and that cheered her, even if it meant a little more time would pass before she saw Sef again.

Sef! She would have six months with him, and he'd have to notice how much she'd grown since the last time;

she was almost as tall as Risa now. He wasn't so much older than she was, and surely he would wait until she was old enough for him. He would never dream of approaching her now, but later— She could not tell him how she felt or he might leave the household; he wouldn't want anyone to think he might take liberties with a young girl. But when she was older—

Her grandfather Chen had met his bondmate Iris when she was fifteen. Four years couldn't be so long to wait. It seemed like an eternity.

"Sef," she whispered.

"I need more information to make your call," the screen replied.

She got up abruptly and left the booth, dreaming of Sef.

Eighteen

Lena was able to meet Chimene after all. They walked east, following the main road toward the memorial pillars. The Guide's house was on the southeast side of the main dome, but Lena always chose a roundabout route to get there. The brown-haired girl had a contented smile on her face; Lena enjoyed conspiring with Chimene to make these visits.

Chimene sighed. They had three hours before the light began to fade, and she disliked having to waste any of that time. Lena might like conspiracies, but Chimene resented the need to keep this secret. She wanted to be able to see Kichi openly, to convince her mother that the Guide was her friend. Surely it wasn't wrong to visit a woman who made her feel better about herself and more able to confront her problems. But Risa would never understand; she saw the Guide as a spider, weaving a web in which to trap the unwary. Risa had said so in exactly those words.

"I'm glad the Guide didn't have to work today," Chimene said. "I didn't think I'd be able to see her right away."

"I'd better tell you." Lena looked a bit more solemn. "She hasn't been working as much. Oh, she goes to the lab for a few days every so often, but she has to rest more now. She isn't as strong as she used to be."

"But Kichi isn't that old. She can't be more than seventy or so—my grandfather's older than that."

"She's weaker. She doesn't visit the other settlements as much lately, and I've heard that her rejuv treatments aren't working the way they should."

304

Chimene frowned. She had heard Bettina talk about some of her patients, people who did not seem to adapt to dome life as well as others physically and psychologically, who grew listless too soon, whose immune systems broke down sooner than they should. Eventually, Bettina claimed, the medical researchers would find out if a genetic predisposition was responsible for this tendency, but such a study was unlikely to yield results that would help Kichi in time. The settlements were an experiment; that was Malik's view. The settlers were living in a new environment, and unforeseen problems were bound to surface.

"Don't worry too much," Lena said. "The Guide still has years ahead of her even now, and she won't lack for care. Everyone in Ishtar'll see to that."

The two girls halted in the road. A cart, looking like a box on wheels, was rolling toward them; five passengers sat in its seats. Since Chimene's last visit, the surface settlements had finally arranged for this modest transportation system; now, inside each dome, two carts, traveling in opposite directions, carried passengers along the main roads that circled the land under all of the domes. The cart stopped; she and Lena climbed aboard through one of the openings on the sides. The five older people sitting in the vehicle nodded and smiled at the girls.

Chimene settled in one seat next to Lena. She was home now; Oberg was home, not Island Two. The cart passed the wooded area near the memorials; to the south, rows of houses bordered by trees and shrubs stood on a grassy plain. The panes of their small, private greenhouses glinted with light; tethered goats were grazing near a few of the residences.

Island Two had never seemed this homey. The Islanders did not have houses, but lived in residences that were more like dormitories. The Administrators had their ziggurat, the tallest building on that Island. Its curved hallways were quiet, empty places where she only rarely saw a white-robed figure emerge from one of the rooms. A spiral housed almost two hundred of Island Two's scientists, a few of whom had been friends of her grandmother Iris. She and Malik had a room in the building where most of the teachers and nursery workers lived, but her two favorite places were the pilots' residence and the steel-blue building where workers lived. The pilots' dwelling had

two triangular wings, and she sometimes lingered in the
common room hoping to see someone from Oberg among
the pilots who gathered there between trips. The workers'
residence was a noisy place where people propped open
their doors and sat in the hallways gossiping or playing
games. They reminded her a little of the people in Oberg;
they always welcomed her warmly, although that might be
because her father was one of Administrator Sigurd's
friends.

The Islanders, whatever their pretensions, were
aware of various distinctions. A scientist was more important than a worker, and an Administrator held a higher
place than anyone. They might say that they were all
working for the Project, but each group of people preferred to live among others like themselves. They might
claim that their loyalty was to Venus, but they seemed
more interested in the details of their work. Many of the
Islanders probably wouldn't care what happened to the
Project as a whole as long they were free to go on with
their scientific and intellectual pursuits. No wonder her
father preferred to be there, where he did not have to care
about anything beyond his own interests.

They were approaching the tunnel that led into the
southeast dome. The cart rolled to a stop; Lena and
Chimene disembarked as another passenger boarded the
vehicle. They waited until the cart was out of sight, then
ran toward the trees opposite the tunnel.

Oberg's people kept their wooded areas cleared, yet
there was a wildness here that the tamer Islands lacked.
Amid these trees, away from the road, Chimene could
pretend that she was in a wilderness, that she could roam
without ever seeing anyone else; it was an illusion impossible to maintain on the manicured grounds of Island Two.

A cluster of houses were just beyond the trees; these
dwellings stood near the bank of a small creek. Kichi's
house, like the others, was shielded from its neighbors by
trees on either side. Lena hunched forward and crept toward one wing of the house, glancing from side to side.
This seemed an unnecessary precaution to Chimene; no
one was outside, and most of Kichi's neighbors were also
members of Ishtar. They would hardly go running to Risa
to tell her of her daughter's visits.

They stopped in front of the side door. Lena pressed

her hand against it, then waited. Chimene fidgeted; as Lena touched the door again, it opened.

Eva Danas quickly ushered the two inside. "The Guide's in her room," Eva said; she was a young blond woman who had moved to Kichi's house only three years before. "She's been expecting you." She led them down the hall, pressed a door open, then stepped back as the girls entered the room.

Kichi sat in a chair by her desk, peering intently at a screen; she looked up. "Greetings," she murmured. "Please do sit down." The girls settled themselves on cushions in front of the Guide. "Lena tells me you'll be staying with us longer this time."

"Six months," Chimene said.

"I'm delighted to hear it." The Guide's light brown face was a little paler, and the black hair pulled back on her head was streaked with silver, but she did not look as though she was ailing. Kichi's dark eyes narrowed a little. "Lena, you're not wearing your sash."

"I forgot. But I wear it most of the time."

"It doesn't matter. It's what's in your heart that counts." Kichi lowered her voice. "I'll tell you a secret. Sometimes I forget, too, and one of my housemates has to remind me. Tongues would wag if the Guide wasn't wearing her sash."

Lena giggled. "And what have you been doing, Chimene?" Kichi leaned back in her chair. "Did your parents decide you should spend more time in Oberg, or was this your idea?"

"It was mine," she answered. "I missed it." She had not meant to say much more, but she suddenly found herself talking about the slights of her schoolmates and her feeling that she did not belong. It was always easy to talk to the Guide, who never dismissed her worries as unimportant. She was about to speak of Sef as well but stopped herself; she had not even mentioned that to Lena yet.

"It's a pity some of the Islander children treat you that way," Kichi said when Chimene was finished. "Such attitudes shouldn't exist among fellow Cytherians. Too many Islanders think of their scientific work as an end in itself, instead of as knowledge that must serve all Cytherians, and the Habbers encourage them in that view. Some Islanders grow too close to Habbers, and then they begin to see themselves as different from us. We're wiser here in having as little to do with them as possible."

"Habbers don't seem so bad," Lena said boldly.

Kichi nodded calmly. "You're right, Lena—they don't seem so bad. Often, in fact, they seem quite nice, but that's exactly why we must be cautious in dealing with them. They don't want us to see what they really are or what their true purpose is." Kichi's hands fluttered against the arms of her chair. "This is a particularly problematic time, since one of the domes in the Freyja Mountains will soon be ready for settlement, and more of our people will join the few who are working there with the Habbers. Part of our industrial base will lie there, and the Habbers are quite capable of taking control of it and forcing us to bend to their will. The Islanders grow so lax in their dealings with Habbers that they may not even stand with their own people."

"Administrator Sigurd's still seeing that Habber woman," Chimene said. She had met Tesia a couple of times, and although the woman had addressed Sigurd only in formal language, Chimene had not been fooled. She had seen how Tesia's face softened a little when she looked at Sigurd, as if she were sure of her hold on his affections. "But maybe that isn't the same," she continued. "People keep saying it's just an amusement, that she doesn't really mean anything to him."

"Sigurd has done much for this Project," Kichi said, "but now, I fear, he's beginning to see himself as a ruler. It's a disease, in a way, to see yourself as that. He thinks he can't be touched, that he can do as he likes, and his example leads others to act in the same way."

Chimene thought of her father and how he went to Habbers. They wanted to take him away from her; she could not escape that feeling. He often told her how much could be learned from the Habbers, who were probably only trying to use him; they had to know Malik had not joined the Project as willingly as others.

"Sigurd may be forgetting that he's only another Cytherian," Kichi went on, "and that his loyalty must lie with that. It's the disease of rulers, to consider themselves above the obligations that bind the people they rule. It's why we must all strive to become brothers and sisters and have no more rulers."

Chimene glanced around the room, imagining what Risa would say about these quarters, which were nearly as comfortable as Sigurd's room. Kichi's room was almost three times as large as other bedrooms, and it even had a low table around which several people could sit. "But aren't you kind of like a ruler yourself?" she asked.

Lena rolled her gray eyes. "Oh, Chimene."

The Guide smiled, apparently unperturbed. "I'm only the Guide," she said softly. "I have no privileges, only responsibilities to my brothers and sisters in Ishtar. I have nothing that isn't shared with others. I have no possessions, only objects that I use in service to Ishtar and which belong to all of us. I and those closest to me try to live as all Cytherians will someday, and often that is difficult even now. There is always the fear of affronting the Spirit or the temptation to erect barriers around oneself, instead of reaching out to all Cytherians."

"But if we're all supposed to be brothers and sisters," Chimene persisted, "then why are there some people Ishtar doesn't want?"

Kichi tilted her head. "I don't know what you mean. Ishtar welcomes all who are ready to become true Cytherians."

"You know." Chimene's cheeks felt warm; she lowered her eyes. "Men who like other men too much or women who—"

"Oh, Chimene!" Lena burst out. "What a question!"

Kichi raised a hand. "Lena, being open to others also means sharing one's doubts and questions so that they can be answered. Chimene does no wrong by asking—anyone who truly seeks the truth must ask. Some of those closest to me had grave doubts once, and even I have doubted." She rested her arm in her lap. "Your friend deserves a reply. Lena, tell us what the obligations of a man and a woman are to Ishtar."

Lena scratched her head. "Well, the woman has to be open to the Spirit of our world, which we're transforming, and the man seeks to appease that Spirit and be united with it. The man's like the sun that'll shine on Venus again, and the woman's like the planet that'll receive the light. As children come from a woman's body, life comes from a planet, but the man's seed, like the sun's rays, makes that life possible."

The brown-haired girl let out her breath. "Go on," Kichi said.

"By changing Venus now, we're restoring this world to what it would have been if the heat of the sun hadn't changed it, but we also have to make ourselves what we once were before we were led astray. Women must remember that they carry life, and men that they give it, and if they forget, their world will become like the growing desert in their souls."

"Very good, Lena," the Guide said. "And what about our most important rite, the one in which you'll participate when you're older?"

"The man and the woman have to come together without barriers and be united in Ishtar. They have to reach out to each other and the Spirit in love. The man sees the woman as all women, all of his sisters and the Spirit, and the woman embraces all men through him."

"Some," Kichi said, "many, in fact, can share themselves during this rite only with a bondmate or with others who are close. They haven't yet reached the point where they can share themselves willingly with all their brothers or sisters, as those closest to me strive to do. Yet we accept that. We understand that many aren't ready to share themselves more freely, but at least they've taken a step along the road that will lead us to unity and convergence with our planet's Spirit." Her eyes focused on Chimene. "So why do you say that there are those we don't welcome?"

"But there are," Chimene responded, "the ones I mentioned."

The Guide shook her head. "We welcome all. I know that some in Ishtar's fellowship say that such people can't truly be part of us, but they're wrong—even our brothers and sisters can sometimes not glimpse the truth clearly. There's nothing to prevent anyone from becoming one of us and sharing our rite."

"But then if these people join," she said, "and have meetings and believe in Ishtar and practice the rite when they're supposed to, why should it matter what they do in their beds the rest of the time?"

"Ishtar must be a part of one's life," the Guide replied. "It isn't like going to a mosque or a church and living the way one likes at other times. It's why we always meet in our homes, instead of in some building apart from the place where we conduct our lives. Every good action brings one closer to the Spirit, and every evil deed separates one from Her. One must ask of everything one does whether it will affront the Spirit. Men who cannot share themselves with a woman and women who cannot go to a man are affronts to Ishtar. The men separate themselves from the Spirit that reaches out to them through a woman, and the women refuse to accept the offering a man must make. Such people can become part of Ishtar only if they give up their former practices, but when they do, we welcome them."

"But if you want to get rid of barriers between people—" Chimene bit her lip; perhaps she should not be questioning Kichi about this. She did not want the Guide to become angry with her. But she had never scolded Chimene before. "I mean, isn't that making another barrier, telling a man he can't love another man that way?"

"It's those people who create a barrier," Kichi said, "not us. No life can come from such acts, which only lead those who perform them to think that they can transcend all natural limits. It is an error that Habbers make in other ways."

Chimene pondered this. The settlers already did not accept certain limits; the Guide herself was hardly likely to refuse her rejuvenation therapy. Their children's genes were scanned not long after conception, with genetic transplants made if needed in order to prevent physical disabilities. In certain cases, people could appeal for the use of ectogenetic chambers for the gestation of fetuses; her own mother would never have been born without such tools.

It was not possible for life to result when two people of the same sex joined, but the same could be said of sex between a man and a woman if they did not have their contraceptive implants removed. Biological techniques could also give children to those who loved their own sex, although no settler had yet risked public disapproval by making such a request. Some regions of Earth might accept such practices, but Earth was not an example the settlers cared to emulate. Habbers probably saw nothing wrong with such things either, but that was yet another argument against them.

Anyway, she already knew what Kichi would say if she

raised these issues. Ishtar could accept technologies that furthered natural ends; these included medical techniques and also the technologies needed to terraform Venus, since they were directing the planet along a course it might have taken. But they disapproved of any technique that risked severing people from nature altogether. All technologies, in the end, were only temporary means to be used until the day when they could free themselves altogether and live as the sisters and brothers they were meant to be, in harmony with their planet's Spirit.

Chimene knew all of this, and yet it did not seem fair that some should be scorned because they could show love only in certain ways. She felt some sympathy for them because she knew how it felt to be mocked. Maybe she had simply been on the Islands too long, where people were slightly more tolerant of such foibles.

"I understand how you feel," Kichi said. "We are all the descendants of people who practiced many different customs and who must be tolerant here. Your kind feelings for others are a mark in your favor, Chimene, but kindness shouldn't be misplaced."

Kichi's eyes held her; she could not look away. The Guide, she felt, could see her thoughts and answer all her doubts. The Guide understood.

"The Spirit demands love, and love is often hard." The soft, mellow voice seemed to surround Chimene. "Love makes demands. A parent who truly loves a child must sometimes demonstrate that what the child wants may be wrong. A friend who loves a friend will try to keep that friend from injuring herself. Some people here say that it doesn't matter what one believes or does in certain situations, and call that tolerance, but what it means is that they don't really believe in anything. When one grasps the truth, shouldn't that truth be shared? If you know the truth and tell yourself that others should be free to live in error, aren't you only putting a wall between yourself and them?"

Chimene did not reply.

"Someday you may see the truth for yourself, and then everything will be clear to you. You won't feel uncertain and lost. You'll understand that guiding others to the truth is the highest form of love."

Chimene looked away, breaking the spell. Much as

she loved and admired Kichi, she did not know if she could ever really believe in Ishtar's way. She wanted to live in the kind of world the Guide spoke of, where all would be brothers and sisters, but she did not know if she could ever believe in a Spirit. Maybe she only wanted to be with people who would make her feel that she belonged.

Kichi stood up and helped the girls to their feet. "I'm happy you both came here."

"Thank you for letting us come," Lena said.

"Chimene, you should go to your household now— your mother will be anxious to see you."

Chimene smiled, wishing again that Risa and Kichi could be friends. The Guide never said anything cruel about Risa; it was Risa's fault that she had to sneak here and lie about where she had gone.

"I'll invite you both again soon." Kichi opened the door and led them down the hall to the exit.

Lena was silent until they reached the main road. "The Guide really likes you," she said at last.

"She likes you, too."

"But I think you're the one she really wants to see."

Chimene glanced at her friend. "Does that bother you?"

"No. It's nice that she wants to talk to us, and I respect her, but I don't know if I'd have that much to say by myself. After all, I'm only in Ishtar because my parents and my aunt and uncle decided to join, so it doesn't mean the same thing to me."

"But you must believe in it," Chimene said.

"I guess I do. I try to anyway. There can't be anything wrong with wanting everybody to be happy and share things and get along." Lena had slipped into her usual slightly mocking tone. "Anyway, the Guide says it's all right to wonder and ask questions, so she'd probably say I'm fine as long as I try to walk the road to the truth."

"I don't know how much I could ever believe," Chimene murmured. "Maybe that's because Chen and Risa never had a religion, and Malik—well, he says his prayers sometimes, but they don't mean that much to him." Nothing, she thought, seemed to mean much to her father lately. The Guide would consider him steeped in sin, with his occasional Habber women and the emotional distance he kept between himself and other people. "Anyway, I can't join Ishtar. Risa would never let me."

"You've got your rights, Chimene. It's not like you're a little child."

"If I joined, though, she'd probably ask for a hearing and make it look as if I'm not mature enough yet to make up my mind. I couldn't stand that." It would be hard enough to renew old friendships without that; the other children would already be watching to see how many Islander airs she had picked up.

"Don't worry about it," Lena said. "You can join when you're older if you want, and she can't do a thing then. Anyway, you're home now—bet you're looking forward to seeing Sef again. I mean, you do still like him, don't you?"

Chimene flushed. "What's that supposed to mean?"

"Oh, come on—I've got eyes. I saw how it was the last time you were home—you used almost any excuse to be around him."

Could she have been so obvious? No, she told herself, she couldn't have been; if she had, Patrick wouldn't have missed such a fruitful opportunity to make fun of her. "I suppose I do like him," she said casually, "but that's just because he's sort of like having a brother or an uncle, that's all."

"Well, it's a good thing you like him because it looks like he'll be staying in your household for a while. Grazie told my mother that they were getting ready to draw up an agreement with him so he could be a permanent member of the household."

"Really?" Chimene tried to hide her joy.

"Didn't they tell you?" Lena shrugged. "Maybe they wanted to wait until you were home." She turned around, stepped into the road, then motioned to Chimene. "Cart's coming—let's ride to our tunnel." The passenger cart rolled to a stop; the two girls climbed aboard.

An older woman, a friend of Lena's household, quickly drew the brown-haired girl into conversation. Chimene leaned back in her seat, wanting to indulge in some daydreaming. Sef would be staying with Risa's household, which meant that he hadn't yet been lured by some young woman into joining her household or building a house of his own, a possibility Chimene had feared. Maybe he intended to wait until he was older to find a mate, until he had more credit and had established himself here.

Her daydream was formless and vague. She imagined herself as a woman, sitting with Sef under the trees outside the house as he embraced her and words of love fell from his lips. He would tell her that he had loved her for years and had been waiting for the right moment to speak of his longing for her. He would confess that he had remained with Risa's household hoping for this time. She saw herself standing with him in the common room, making her pledge with the rest of the household as witnesses.

How could she possibly go back to the Islands now? She would have to find a reason to stay without revealing her feelings . On the other hand, Sef might miss her if she went away again and appreciate her more when she returned, when she was older and could drop a few hints about how she felt. She did not want to think of obstacles; she would discover a way to be with him.

She and Lena parted at the end of the path that led to Risa's house. Chimene noticed then that Risa's wing had been expanded; no one had told her about that either. But since Sef would be staying here, he would want to have his own quarters, and now that Chimene had arrived, he could not use her room.

Her footsteps slowed; maybe Sef had already forgotten her. She glanced at the greenhouse; through the misty windows, she saw the tall broad-shouldered shape of a man.

She pressed her hand against the palm-print lock; the door opened. Sef was leaning over a tier of spinach, a basket at his feet. She walked toward him, then said, "Greetings, Sef."

He straightened and dropped his trowel. "Chimene!" He was smiling as he held out his arms. "You're taller."

"A little."

"And even prettier, I see."

He *was* happy to see her! She hurried toward him and hugged him as his strong arms closed around her.

The entire household was in an unusually festive mood; even Patrick seemed glad Chimene was home. Risa arrived a few moments after Chimene had unpacked her duffel in her old room.

"I saw Lena Kerein on my way home," Risa said as Chimene entered the common room. "She said she met you at the bay. I suppose you two were wandering around in the main dome again." Chimene nodded. "I hope she wasn't telling you a lot of foolishness about Ishtar, now that her household are members."

"Don't bother yourself about that," Grazie said as she set a plate of vegetables on the table. "They wear their faith fairly lightly, from what I can tell. Roberto Kerein told me just the other day that it's the ideals that appeal to him—not the mysticism."

Risa seemed content to drop the subject. Chimene studied her mother as they sat down around the table. Risa's cheeks were pink, and her dark eyes glowed; she looked, Chimene admitted to herself, extremely pretty. She also seemed a little distracted. She nearly dropped one of the dumplings Sef had made while serving herself, then giggled as her eyes met Bettina's.

"Sef's decided to stay with us," the physician said.

"I know," Chimene replied. "Lena told me."

"Her family heard it from Grazie, I'll bet." Paul looked at his bondmate affectionately. "I always say that when you want to send a message, Grazie's quicker than using the screen."

Grazie laughed. "I didn't say anything I shouldn't have said."

"I hope you're happy about it," Sef said, "now that you're going to be here longer."

"Of course I am," Chimene said. Her cheeks were growing warm; she looked away from Sef's gold-flecked brown eyes.

"Maybe you won't turn into a gasbag after all," Patrick muttered.

The others were soon filling Chimene in on recent Oberg gossip. She listened, trying to look attentive. Bettina kept casting conspiratorial glances in Risa's direction, as though the two had a secret. Only Emilia, stolid as always as she fed her daughter, Irina, from a small bowl, seemed untouched by the cheery mood around her.

Something was going on. Chimene wondered if Risa was planning to run for the Council again. By now the memory of the men the Council had sentenced to death would have faded, and some might be willing to trust Risa once more. Risa was older now and presumably wiser; she and her former colleagues had as much as admitted they might have been wrong by setting up patrols, and deciding such matters would be handled differently. Yakov Serba, who was on the Council now, sometimes consulted with Risa; Chimene had learned that during her last visit. Ishtar's people weren't likely to vote for her, given her dislike of the group, but there might be enough support from others to make up for that.

When they had finished eating, Chimene was about to help clear the table; Nikolai motioned her back to her seat. "It's your first night home," he said. "You can start on any chores tomorrow." Bettina whispered to Risa as the two women stood up; Risa was nodding.

"I'll get my screen," Chimene said to Patrick. "Maybe we can play a game."

"All right. Take your time—I have to finish a chemistry lesson first."

"I'll meet you in your room then." She wandered toward Risa's wing. Maybe if she got Patrick alone, he would tell her what was going on.

She had left her screen on the small table next to her bed. As she picked it up, she heard a tap on the door. "Come in," she called out.

Risa entered, followed by Sef. "We'd like to talk to you," her mother said, "and I think this is the time." Chimene frowned a little. "Don't look so solemn, dear—it's good news."

Chimene sat on the bed; for a moment, she had worried that Risa might have found out about the visits to Kichi Timsen. Risa and Sef seated themselves in one corner. "What is it?" Chimene asked.

"You're pleased that Sef is remaining in this household, aren't you?"

"Yes—I mean, I really am." She was flushing again; she continued to gaze at Risa, avoiding Sef's eyes.

"Well, he likes you very much, too, and he's glad you're going to be here these coming months." Risa's blush deepened as she glanced at Sef. "What I'm trying to say is that Sef wants to be a member of this household for years to come."

"We wanted to tell you first," Sef said. "Bettina knows, and I think everyone else got the idea when we started adding a couple of rooms to this wing. But this involves you, so I guess they saw that they shouldn't say anything until we'd talked to you. Things will still be the same—you can think of me as your friend."

"You're my friend now," Chimene said, a little bewildered. "Aren't you?"

"I'm glad you think so." Sef ran a hand through his chestnut hair. "I don't want you to think that I want to take Malik's place—he's still your father and I won't get in the way of that."

Chimene swallowed, "But why—" Her voice trailed off.

"I know this is a surprise," Risa said. "It's surprised me, too. I didn't think—" She looked at Sef again. "But we've been lovers for three months now, and Sef is sure, and we don't want to wait. Tina's going to remove our implants in a few days, and we'll make our pledge after that."

"I hope you'll be as happy as we are," Sef said. "I know it must seem sudden, but I always hoped I'd find someone like your mother."

Chimene stiffened with shock. They had deceived her. Sef couldn't be doing this; he couldn't love Risa. Pain welled up inside her chest; she was afraid to speak, afraid she would begin to cry.

Sef reached for Risa's hand. "She's insisting that we have a bond for only ten years," he continued, "in case I want to be free later, but I don't think I will."

She struggled for breath. "But—" Her eyes stung. "But you—she's too old."

Sef chuckled; now he was laughing at her. Chimene could hardly bear it. "Thirty-seven isn't old. Anyway, I always was drawn to someone older and steadier."

He had been in love with her mother all along. How could she hope that he might wait for her now? She wanted to lash out at them both.

"We're going to try for a child," Risa was saying. "I'd always hoped I could give you a brother or sister. Would you like that, Chimene?"

Sef slipped his arm around Risa's waist. "But that won't change how we feel about you. You'll always have a special place in our hearts."

She hated him for saying that. She thought of all the times he must have gone to her mother's bed. A scream was rising in her throat; she swallowed hard and held it back. What could she do? Plead with them not to become bondmates? What could she tell them?

"You'll do what you want," she said at last. "It doesn't matter what I think."

Sef frowned. "But that isn't true. Your feelings matter very much to us. I thought you'd be as happy as we are."

"What is it?" Risa's voice was a little more strained. "You didn't think—were you hoping Malik and I might renew our bond? I know children sometimes imagine such things, but that was over long ago—you must see that."

Chimene grasped at this small thread. "He'd come back if you asked him to. It isn't so great on the Islands for him. I think he wants to come back, but he won't admit it. If you just talked to him and asked—"

"Believe me, that isn't true. I loved your father very much, but—" Risa sighed. "That's past. Even Malik wouldn't object to having me find some happiness with Sef now."

Her mother would not listen to her; she never had, not really. She forced herself to look into Sef's eyes. "You don't know what you're doing," she said softly. "You're too young, you think—" She pressed a hand against her mouth for a moment. "She lured you, she—"

"Lured me!" Sef seemed angry now. "I went to her—she didn't lure me. I wanted her to love me—she didn't know if she could at first. Don't you want your mother to be happy?"

Shock and resentment were muddying Chimene's thoughts. It was Risa's fault that Malik had stopped loving her and had ended up leaving her house; it was her fault that he had become what he was. She wanted to scream accusations at Risa and warn Sef that she would only make him miserable, too. I love you, she thought; why couldn't you wait for me? Why did you have to go to her?

She did not speak. Her old fear of Risa gripped her once more, the fear that if she ever made her mother angry enough, Risa would find a horrible way to punish her. Risa was glaring at her, with the same hard look she had directed at those three accused men during that hearing so long ago.

"It's the shock," Sef murmured to Risa. "We've surprised her—she just needs time to get used to the idea." He turned toward Chimene. "When we're bondmates, you'll understand. You won't feel the same way. When you see how happy that makes us, you'll be happy, too."

He was treating her as a child who had to be soothed. She wanted them out of her room; she longed to be as far from them as possible. "Make your pledge then." She nearly choked on the words. "I'll get used to it. Will you please leave me alone now?"

"Are you sure you're all right?" Sef asked.

"I'm all right." He did not care if she was or not. She continued to stare at the floor until she heard them move toward the door.

"Chimene—" Sef started to say.

"She's tired from her trip," Risa said. "Probably needs to rest." The door whispered open. "I don't know what's gotten into her—"

The door closed. Tears streamed down her face; she shook with rage. Sef would be with Risa tonight. Chimene would have to witness their pledge and pretend to be happy; she would have to live in this house during all the coming months and watch him go to her mother's room. How could she stay here now?

She stumbled toward the door. As she stepped into the hallway, she heard the sound of laughter in the common room as Nikolai congratulated Sef. "—happy for you, but I can't say it's much of a surprise."

"Chimene's upset." That was Risa's voice. "I think she actually thought that Malik and I could be bondmates again, and I'm sure even he wouldn't have led her to believe that."

"Tell Malik to send her a message," Bettina said. "When she hears from him, she'll get over that. Children often have such fantasies."

They all saw her as a child; nothing she felt was important. If they had known about her hopes, they would have laughed at her and told her she would forget. Older people were always saying that her problems weren't real and that her feelings would change in time.

She could not remain in this house. She spun around and ran toward the nearest exit.

* * *

She ran through the darkness toward the tunnel, knowing where she had to go now; only one person could help her. Two men paced near the tunnel, silhouetted against the light; she had forgotten about the patrol. She slowed, wanting to hide herself, but one man was already walking toward her.

"What's wrong?" he asked.

She halted, trying to compose herself. "Nothing. I'm taking a walk, that's all."

"A little late for that, isn't it?" He hooked his fingers around his sash; a wand hung at his side, the kind of weapon volunteers were given when they were on patrol. "Are you sure nothing's the matter? Don't forget—it's a serious offense if you hide what you know about any wrongdoing."

"Nothing's wrong."

"Does your family know you're out here? Maybe we should check with them so they know we're looking out for you."

"No!" The other man was moving toward them. "They won't worry about me," Chimene continued, "really they won't. They'll just get upset with you for waking them up." She took a breath. "I have to see the Guide. That's where I was going, to see her. There can't be anything wrong with that."

"Bring her along," the second man said. "It won't hurt to check on this." He took her by the arm and led her toward the tunnel. "I don't think I've seen you before—what's your name?" Chimene was silent. "Come on, girl—we'll find out from the records in a minute anyway."

"Chimene Liang-Haddad. I just got here from Island Two." Risa would learn that she was trying to see Kichi and would probably elicit a confession about her other visits. She no longer cared. "I'm staying with my mother, Risa Liangharad."

"Funny," the taller man muttered, "Risa Liangharad's daughter wanting to see the Guide." They stopped in front of a small screen at the tunnel's entrance. "Take her over there—I'll call the Guide's household and see about this story."

The shorter man led her to the side of the tunnel; she leaned against an empty cart. Maybe Kichi would not want to see her now; being roused at this hour would annoy her. Chimene rubbed at her eyes, feeling miserable and alone.

The other man spoke into the screen for a few moments, then hurried toward them. "It seems the Guide wants to see you after all," he said; he quickly lifted her into the cart. "I'll take her into the main dome," he murmured to the shorter man. "If anyone comes looking for her or asking about her, you're to say that a volunteer there's watching out for her and will bring her home later."

His companion shrugged. Neither of them would question the Guide. Chimene's spirits lifted a little; Kichi would help her somehow.

A woman on patrol met the cart at the road and led Chimene toward Kichi's house. Eva Danas met them at the door, thanked the woman, then brought Chimene inside.

This common room was larger than Risa's; the Guide often held meetings here, with as many as one hundred people in attendance. Cushions sat against the wall, along with a few of the mats used during Ishtar's most important rite. Under the large wall screen, Kichi lay on one mat, her head resting in the lap of Matthew Innes.

Kichi sat up as Eva and Chimene came near. "My dear girl," the Guide murmured. "You look so unhappy." She brushed the hair back from Chimene's face. "What's wrong?"

"I shouldn't have come," Chimene replied. "I didn't know where else to go. I—"

"You mustn't say that. Haven't I told you that I'm here when you want to see me, or that I'll make the time to see you when I can? I don't ever want you to feel that you can't share anything with me."

Chimene sank to the floor; Eva seated herself next to her. Matthew Innes's gray-green eyes gazed at her kindly. Like Eva, he was young, with pale blond hair that was nearly white. He had joined Ishtar only a few years earlier, as a recent immigrant from the camps; his devotion to the group was so great that he had quickly become one of the Guide's inner circle. Chimene felt a pang of envy. She longed to be like Matthew and Eva, and all of those closest to the Guide—handsome, confident people, secure in their faith and united by the love they had for one another.

"I can't go home," Chimene said. "I have to stay here for six months, and I can't live here now. I couldn't stand it. But if I say I want to go back to Island Two now—I don't know what to do."

"Is that what you want?" Kichi asked. "To go back?"

"I don't have anywhere else to go."

"But why?"

Chimene looked around at Eva, then lowered her eyes. "You may speak freely in the presence of my companions," Kichi continued. "Eva and Matthew are my sister and brother in Ishtar—my concerns are theirs. What has your household done to make you so unhappy? What grieves you so much that you had to come to me? It hurts me to see such sadness in one who deserves only joy."

A lump rose in her throat; she was unable to speak.

"There are barriers enough that separate us from the world that will be ours," the Guide said, "domes that surround us, ships that enclose us whenever we venture outside, screens that show us images of things we cannot touch. There must be no barriers between us."

"It's Sef." She had loved the sound of his name once. "Sef Talis. He's been living in my mother's house—they're going to be bondmates." She could not hold back her tears.

Kichi reached for her; she clung to the Guide as she spoke of her dreams, her love for Sef, her hope that he would somehow see it and be willing to wait for her, her pain at his betrayal of her secret longing. "He'll never love me now," she sobbed. "She took him away—she tries to take away everything I want, and I couldn't tell him, he doesn't know—"

Kichi wiped her tears with the sleeve of her shirt. "He thinks I'm a child," Chimene gasped. "He'd just laugh if he knew."

"Chimene, my dear. I know how you feel. You have so much love in you—I understand what it's like when you want to give it to one who can't receive it. This is the first time you've felt such love, isn't it? How I wish it could have brought you some happiness."

Kichi did understand. Chimene rested her head against the Guide's chest. "I'm so sorry," Kichi went on. "So many men will love you—they will, you know. How

unfortunate it would be if the hurt you feel now scarred
you and kept you from sharing your love with others." The
Guide stroked her hair gently. "You mustn't allow your
love to become bitterness and hatred. Perhaps this Sef also
has love that he needs to share—I must assume that he
does, that he's worthy of what you feel for him—and that's
why he's given it to your mother. I wish he could have
gone to you, but your time for such love will come when
you're a woman."

"It isn't fair—being too young, having to wait."

"Chimene, if this man had known of your feelings and
hadn't been willing to wait to take what you can offer, he
would only have shown himself unworthy of receiving it.
He would have been seeking only his own satisfaction, and
your capacity for love would have been destroyed, more
surely than if he had mocked you or scorned you."

Chimene twisted in her arms. "You always say there
shouldn't be any barriers."

"The Guide speaks the truth," Eva said softly. "You're
like the world we live on, still being formed, not yet ready
to feel the rays of the sun—if they touched you now, your
heart would become as barren as the rocks outside. Venus
will feel the sun again when it's ready to yield life, and it is
the same with you. Barriers must fall when it is time for
them to fall."

"You should rejoice that you can feel love," Kichi said,
"whatever pain it brings you now. Be grateful that this
man has shown that he can love. Love for others often
grows out of love for one. Keep love in your heart and let
Sef share what he can, the love of a father for a child. The
years will pass, and maybe he—"

"But he'll be her bondmate."

"Bonds lapse," the Guide said, "and they are barriers
we can learn to transcend. You needn't give up your hopes.
Sef loves a part of you by loving your mother, and you can
show him love by honoring that pledge for now. More for
you may come later—you may even be the one who guides
Sef to Ishtar."

Her tears were gone. Kichi's words had revived her
dream. A bond meant nothing; the Guide had never re-
stricted her love with bonds. Chimene's sorrow had grown
out of seeing barriers where they did not have to exist. If
she loved Sef enough, all the barriers between them would

disappear; she could still hope that when she was a woman—

She looked up at Kichi as she recalled the rest of her words. "What did you mean," she said, "that I might guide Sef to Ishtar? I'm not even in Ishtar myself."

"You have reached out to us."

"To you, but the rest—I don't know if I can believe in it. I think about it, and then I have all these questions. Even if Risa didn't care, I don't know if I could join, trying to believe and not being able to."

"But many of us began that way," Kichi responded. "I did myself. Do you know how I became the Guide?"

Chimene knew part of the story but waited for Kichi to continue.

"I came to the Islands from Earth in 570, not long after Pavel Gvishiani's disgrace. It was a time of great hope for the Project—a battle had been averted and the surface would soon be settled. But I couldn't share the joy of others. I believed in nothing then. I saw Venus as no more than my planetary laboratory, a place where I could study the movements of tectonic plates that had been locked for millions of years. I never supposed that Venus might create fault lines within my own soul or unlock my heart."

She paused. "I joined Ishtar because a man I wanted brought me to the group, and I supposed that making this small concession might entice him to my bed. Ishtar was a small group then, and most of its people were superstitious workers. Anna Deriss was their first Guide, and even she was only an old woman who babbled about a planetary Spirit and the need to placate Her. She and her followers often went to the platform around Island Two, where they would peer through the dome and offer prayers to the spirits below. I rarely went there with them—when I did, my only prayer was that none of my colleagues would see me in the company of such deluded fools."

Chimene nestled in Kichi's arms. The Guide had never told her this much about her early life before.

"What I didn't know is that my lover had more love for me than I knew. He saw that there was a void in me and that it was growing. Soon, even my work meant nothing to me. Those around me seemed trapped in an illusion—the world they wanted would bring them only a pointless struggle and then death. My work would be used only to create a world that would mirror the emptiness and despair I saw in myself."

"What did you do?" Chimene asked.

"I went to a Counselor, of course. She spoke of fatigue and the need for a short rest, and when that didn't help, she sent me to a psychological specialist, who muttered about depressive tendencies and chemical imbalances and passed me on to a physician. He gave me an implant that altered my moods slightly, but it didn't really change how I felt—it only masked my symptoms. My team began to complain about my work. My position became precarious —after all, if I began to cost the Project more than my work was worth, my Counselor would eventually have to take further steps." Kichi laughed softly. "Advice, they call it, when they're telling you what to do."

Chimene thought of her father, who also seemed unable to feel hope. Often she had awakened, opened the curtain around her bed a little, and peered out to see Malik sitting in front of his screen, his head bowed, his body slumped and weary.

"I didn't want to go back to Earth," Kichi went on. "That would have been admitting that my life was over, that I would never be more than I was. I wanted to give myself wholly to this world, yet something held me back. I wanted to reach out to my lover, but my despair and demands on him were poisoning his love, and I saw I might lose him, too."

The Guide was silent for a long time. "Anna began to visit me in the evenings," Kichi said at last. "She didn't speak to me about Ishtar—in fact, she rarely said much at all. Sometimes she listened and sometimes she only sat with me while I brooded, and then, one day, she told me her thoughts. She had been waiting for the Spirit to reveal who the next Guide would be, and now she knew—she had been led to me."

Chimene knew that part of the story. "And this was enough to change you?"

"Oh, no. I thought she was deluding herself. Only my gratitude for her companionship kept me from mocking her then. She knew I didn't believe, and yet she offered me her love and the opportunity for her guidance. I had nothing to lose by accepting it, and I was sure she'd realize her mistake eventually."

"But you came to believe," Chimene said.

"Yes, I came to believe. The Guide's love, along with the love of those closest to her, healed me, but that healing was a struggle. I had seen Ishtar as a rival for my lover, its women as others who would take him from me—I had to see past that barrier and understand that allowing him to give his love to others left him freer to love me more. Even then I still balked at Anna's talk of the Spirit—that was the last barrier that fell."

Anna's simple, childlike faith had reflected a deeper truth. Time itself was an illusion, a barrier that could also be overcome. The Guide and her followers were able to apprehend the Spirit that the minds of future Cytherians would create, and with Whom they would all converge. During their most important rite, they could capture, for a brief instant, the time when all would be united in Ishtar with no barriers.

"Some can believe in the Spirit easily," Kichi murmured. "They don't need to be told that our concepts of space and time are limits imposed by the way our minds perceive the world, or that a mathematician or physicist might see all time as one instant, or that each of us may be only one aspect of a Mind that is a Unity. They sense the Spirit's presence, and that is all they know—their minds aren't as cluttered with some of the illusions we call knowledge. The Guide was one such person, but as I drew closer to her, I saw why she had been led to me. Worthy as Anna was, she could lead only those much like herself to the truth. She believed I might be able to bring many others to the fold because I understood the intellectual barriers that stood in their way."

"And that was when you believed, when you saw that?" Chimene said.

"No, my dear. Anna died, and I became the Guide while I was still trying to find my faith. My despair then was greater than any I had felt before. I was a fraud, pretending a belief I didn't feel—I had been chosen to guide others and could do nothing for myself. The disciplines that a Guide must practice seemed no more than a sham. I decided to give it up, to tell my brothers and sisters that another would have to take my place, and then, in my darkest moment, as I prepared to reveal the deepest doubts I had always hidden, I glimpsed the Spirit and knew that Anna was with Her. My doubts fell away. I was truly the Guide at last."

"Lock yourself in this moment of time," Matthew said, "and there is no Spirit, for we haven't yet created the Spirit. Open your soul and time falls away, leading you into Her Presence."

"Do you understand, Chimene?" Kichi asked. "The Spirit's potential lies inside all who will become Cytherians. It lies inside you."

Chimene wanted to believe. Whenever she was with Kichi, she almost thought that she could, but she knew that later, she would ponder what she had heard and her doubts would return. "I want to believe," Chimene said, "but I don't know—"

"If you want to believe, then one barrier has been removed." The Guide hugged Chimene, then released her. "I once asked Anna how I would know who was to follow me as the Guide. She said I would know her when I saw her, that I would see the light in her soul, that I would be guided to her. When I found my faith, I accepted that, and yet years passed without such a sign. Once I thought that a child of my own might prove to be the next Guide, but in the end I chose to have a son and not a daughter. I didn't want to be misled by genetic ties or have a particular love overshadow the love I had to give to all."

Kichi reached for Chimene's hands. "I've waited," she said, "and I've prayed, and now I know I've found the one who will follow me. You are that person, Chimene. You will be the next Guide."

Chimene started in shock. She tried to pull her hands away, but the Guide's grip was strong. "You have a Guide's beauty, the beauty that can bring others to love the Spirit. You have the mind that can reach out to those who doubt. You have the soul in which I see my sister. You are my successor, Chimene—I've seen it."

"But I can't be. I'm not even—"

"You will join us, and I promise you that your faith will come. It may come to you at a dark time, as it did for me, or you may surrender yourself to it at a moment of joy, but I know it lies within you. Your love will grow until it encompasses our world, and all of your brothers and sisters will love you."

Could it be true? Could she imagine such a destiny for

herself? Could she ever become like Kichi, serene in her love and certain of the love of others? Her chest swelled; she could not tell if she was feeling joy or pain.

"You will come to us." The Guide's voice was so all-encompassing that it might have been coming from inside Chimene's own mind. "There is so much I have to teach you in the time I have left before my soul is freed by my body. You'll come to us, Chimene—you are one of us already in your heart."

Chimene lowered her eyes. "But I'm not. I want to be, but how can I?"

"You need only pledge yourself to us."

"I can't even do that." Too many obstacles lay in her path. "I still have all these questions, and even if I didn't, I can't even come to your meetings without my mother finding out, and she—" Risa would be appalled enough to think that her daughter was interested in Ishtar or had visited the Guide; she would be enraged if she ever learned of Kichi's hopes.

"Say that you're willing to travel this road with me," Kichi replied. "That's all we require. Together, we'll remove the barriers that lie in your way. Others don't have to know what we're doing now. You may visit me as you always have and begin to learn what you must know."

"Isn't that wrong? You don't want barriers, but you want me to keep secrets. Isn't that like—"

"We see a world where people will walk on the surface unprotected, and yet we do not leave our domes to do so now. We feel the presence of Ishtar, even though we know that the Spirit lies in our future. This secret will be no more than a temporary barrier, one that will fall away in time. Nothing can be wrong if it leads to the truth."

Kichi turned and extended a hand to the wall screen. "Look there, Chimene." Chimene lifted her eyes. An image had appeared of a green, sunlit world. It turned slowly, revealing rippling blue oceans with deeper azure currents and small continents mottled with green. One continent along the equator, a landmass shaped like an open-mouthed lizard with a long, curling tail, reminded her of Aphrodite Terra. To the west, a large island in the midst of a vast sea had to be the Rhea and Theia mountains. In the north, the massifs and high peaks of Ishtar Terra loomed over the deep green of forests and the paler green of mountain valleys.

Kichi said, "Tell me what you see."

"Venus," Chimene answered, "the way it will be someday."

"You see the world you'll help to build. You see the planet whose Spirit resides in you. Reach out and that vision will live inside you and all whom you touch." Kichi cupped Chimene's face in her hands. "Turn away now and the wall you build inside yourself will imprison you as surely as this dome does."

Chimene shivered. She would have to try. This was all the Guide was asking, that she try. She could not bear the thought of disappointing Kichi, of being unable to come to this house and its loving residents, of being alone with parents whose love for each other had finally failed.

"I want to be with you," she said. "I will be—I am."

A member of the patrol conveyed her to the tunnel; Chimene walked the rest of the way. She would be the Guide; she clung to that thought. The future Kichi had evoked for her was still vivid; she could almost imagine that she was already joined to her future self, the Chimene secure in her faith who would love and be loved, who was looking back on this time of uncertainty and doubt with compassion for the girl she had once been. All the barriers would fall away; she knew that now.

But Kichi had also said the way would be hard. Chimene would have to endure months in Risa's house and conceal her visits to the Guide. Later, she would have to return to the Islander schoolmates who would only mock her new dream if they ever learned of it.

How would she ever get through the long months away from the Guide? But Kichi had insisted on that; more Islanders would also have to be brought to Ishtar, and Chimene could learn much by living among them. The Guide had even implied that Chimene could be of use to her; by being observant, Chimene might learn which Islanders were likely to be sympathetic to Ishtar and which might present barriers to the truth. She wanted to be useful to Kichi and show that she had the discipline necessary to be a Guide.

Tests lay ahead of her, and the first such test was approaching. She would have to pretend to be happy that Risa and Sef were to be bondmates, and she wondered if she had the strength for that. She tried to summon up the vision of her future self once more, the woman who had moved past this time, who would find a way to bring Sef to herself.

As she walked toward the house, the door opened. Risa stepped aside as Chimene entered, then grabbed her by the shoulders.

"How could you do this?" Risa muttered. "You sneak out, you call the attention of the patrol to yourself—they must wonder just what kind of a household this is."

"I'm sorry. I didn't want you to—"

"I went out looking for you ages ago with Sef, and a man on the patrol said you were in the main dome. I wanted to go there, but he insisted someone was watching you and he'd make sure you got home safely." She let go of Chimene and stepped back. "Needless to say, I didn't want him thinking I couldn't trust the patrol to look out for you, so I came home. Sef wanted to wait up with me, but I didn't see why anyone else had to lose sleep over you."

"I'm sorry," Chimene said.

"That's all? You're sorry? I thought this would be such a wonderful day for us, and now—"

"I mean, I'm really sorry." Chimene forced herself to look up at her mother. Risa was only another obstacle, one she could overcome. "You were right. I was hoping you and Malik might make another pledge, and that's why I was so upset. I just needed to be alone, to think about it all, but now I'm happy for you—really I am. I'm glad Sef'll be living with us, and Malik will feel the same way—I know that now."

Risa blinked, apparently surprised. "Well. It seems you've come to your senses."

"And I won't wander off like that again. I'm used to the Islands—I forgot about the patrol."

They walked toward Risa's wing. "Good night, Chimene." Risa kissed her on the forehead, then entered her own room. A small light was glowing in the corner; Chimene caught a glimpse of Sef's head against a pillow before the door closed. She squeezed her eyes shut and held her breath until the pain passed.

She pressed her door open. She would be the Guide, and Sef would be among those who would love her. Kichi had said so; it had to be true. She moved toward her bed, already dreaming of the destiny that awaited her.

Nineteen

Risa did not begin to make her way home until a couple of hours after dark. She strolled along the path that led past her neighbors' houses, feeling mildly drained and a little bit drunk. A small group of people in front of one house were playing music on homemade stringed instruments while others danced; one young man took Risa's hands, spun her around, then let her go as she laughingly shook her head.

The year of 614 was ending; 615 would begin just after the twenty-fourth hour. Everyone in the domes and on the Islands would be celebrating, except for small crews of volunteers who would remain on duty at various installations in case they were needed, most of them older people who had seen their share of festivals. The people in Ishtar might complain that it was inappropriate for Cytherians to mark the passing of another year of the Nomarchies, but even they had joined in these festivities. Ishtar held its own more subdued celebrations to mark the passing of the shorter Venusian year, but it was easier for the settlements to keep to Earth's calendar.

She had seen no Habbers among the celebrants. There were fewer Habbers living in the Maxwell Mountains now anyway; most of those who remained on Venus's surface were up in the Freyja range, working with the Cytherians who had joined them there.

That stage of the Project had not gone as smoothly as expected, in spite of the Habbers' efforts. After nearly fourteen years, only two connected domes had risen among the Freyja Mountains, with no more than a small

333

mining and refining operation to show for all the work. Administrator Sigurd was slowing the pace deliberately.

She could guess, however, at Sigurd's motives. He might talk of the need for careful planning, but what he really wanted was a continuing Habber presence. When the settlers had more of an industrial base, they would also be more self-sufficient; Ishtar would increase its demands that the Habbers at last be expelled from the Project or limited to a few observers. It was part of Sigurd's game— balancing Habbers against Ishtar's influence and both groups against those on Earth who feared the settlers might grow too independent. It was a balancing act designed to give the settlers as much freedom as possible for now.

Risa wondered how long the Administrator could go on with his game, treating all sides with sympathy and objectivity, leading them all to think that their various and conflicting desires could be met by keeping him in his position. Perhaps his power was not all he wanted to retain; he might also want to keep his Habber woman near him. She could not know; Sigurd had not shared many of his thoughts with her for some time. He still answered her calls and murmured a few words of praise for Malik's latest lectures before he listened to her talk of Oberg's affairs, but their discussions remained impersonal. She, along with Kichi Timsen, Yakov Serba, and several people in the other settlements, were only pieces in his game, individuals to be cultivated in case they might be useful.

Sigurd probably thought she might run for the Oberg Council again; he had implied that she and her former colleagues had been punished enough. He did not see that once she had overcome the shame she felt earlier, she was happier as she was. She had regretted her actions mostly because they had driven Malik from her, but that was past. She had her work, her household, and her two children with Sef; she found it easy to refuse those who sometimes asked her to run for the Council.

Sef was sitting outside near the greenhouse. Their daughter, Eleta, lay on a blanket fast asleep; Dyami, their son, was playing cat's cradle with Bettina. As Risa approached, he handed the string to Bettina and smiled. Dyami had his father's smile and his flared cheekbones; his thick reddish-brown hair was only slightly darker than

Sef's, and he moved in the same deliberate way. But his brown eyes lacked Sef's open, friendly gaze; Dyami's expression was more guarded.

"Irina's staying with Noella's children tonight," Risa said. "Apparently they're having a party later—I didn't think Kolya and Emilia would mind." She removed the sling from her shoulder and handed Sef a bottle. "A present from Andy Dinel, along with his best wishes for the coming year."

"Damn," Sef muttered. "We didn't give his household anything, did we?"

"Don't worry about it. He hinted that Grete might like some of our strawberries—I'll take her some another time." She looked around at the small group. "Where is everybody?"

"Emilia and Kolya went to her parents' house," Bettina replied. "Paul and Grazie decided to go to that gathering in the main dome with Patrick. They wanted me to come, but I think I prefer to celebrate quietly this year."

"And Chen?"

"He's inside," Sef said. "A message from Earth came—I don't know what it was about. He was getting ready to view it just before we came out here."

"I'll go get him," Risa said. Sef reached for her hand and squeezed it before letting go.

She walked toward the house. Chen sat in the common room at his table, his head bowed. "Don't tell me you're going to sit here carving tonight," Risa murmured.

Her father lifted his head. "I had a message from your cousin Sylvie Lilias before." Chen cleared his throat. "Your grandmother Angharad died a few days ago."

She had expected such news. Angharad was old, and had been failing for some time. She had not expected to feel so moved at the death of the grandmother she had never met.

"You gave her some happiness," Chen continued. "You must know that. It helped make up for Iris's death, knowing she had a granddaughter here, and it kept her from grieving too much over what Benzi did. She lived to see great-grandchildren and know her line would go on here."

She knelt beside him. "You knew her," she said. "This must be harder for you."

"She was so angry when Iris and I told her we wanted a bond. We had to keep it a secret during the years Iris was at the Cytherian Institute—Angharad couldn't have the town think her daughter wasn't leading a proper life as a free woman with many lovers." Risa nodded at the familiar tale. "I remember how she cursed at me in her message after your mother's death," he added. "I didn't think she'd ever contact me again, but you changed that."

Chen was not that much younger than Angharad. She shivered. Perhaps that was the source of her grief, the realization that she might lose Chen before too long. But he was still strong; Bettina was sure he had at least another decade ahead of him and maybe more.

"I should send Sylvie a message," she said.

"Tomorrow's soon enough. Let Sef and the children have their celebration for now." He gripped her hand as she helped him to his feet. "I'll come outside."

She led him to the door; he was leaning against her a bit more than usual. As they stepped outside, he released her and walked toward Bettina with a surer step.

Sef drank some whiskey, then motioned to Risa with the bottle. "Care for some of this?"

She shook her head. "I've had enough to drink already." She sat down on the blanket next to her daughter. Eleta was still sleeping, with one fist nestled next to her broad, chubby face; she had Risa's stocky build. Unlike Chimene, she might never be more than a mildly pretty young woman, but maybe that was for the best; Chimene's perfect beauty was a little intimidating. Perhaps that was why Risa had heard no talk about a potential bondmate for her other daughter, even though Chimene was almost nineteen; many young men thought they stood no chance with her.

She sighed. Much as she hated to admit it, even to herself, her love for Eleta was warmer and stronger than her love for Chimene. Perhaps that was because she was more certain of Sef's love than she had ever been of Malik's or maybe because Chimene had always seemed to be more of a visitor than a part of the household. During the past years, Chimene had continued to spend half the year with Risa before returning to her father, but she had grown more reserved as she grew older. Chimene rarely complained, almost never argued about anything, and did her schoolwork and chores diligently enough, yet Risa could not escape the feeling that her older daughter was only playing a part, mimicking feelings she did not have.

Risa shrugged off her doubts about Chimene. It couldn't have been easy for the girl to migrate between this house and Island Two. Risa had suggested that Chimene remain with her for the entire year and make short visits to Malik, but her daughter had rejected that idea, probably out of loyalty to her father.

At any rate, Chimene had turned out well enough. Malik might complain mildly that she could have done more, but there was nothing wrong with following his profession and becoming a teacher. Chimene was finished with her studies and would be coming back to Oberg in a few days after completing an apprenticeship under an older teacher in ibn-Qurrah. Theron had told Risa earlier that the west dome's school needed no new teachers, but presumably one of the other domes did. She had not asked Chimene where she would be teaching, and she had not bothered to check the records; she would not be the kind of mother who pried into an adult daughter's plans.

Chimene would let her know and was probably preparing to live here for the time being; Risa would have more time with her. She had heard stories about Chimene being seen at meetings of Ishtar in ibn-Qurrah, but Sef had calmed Risa's worries by pointing out that many attended such meetings only out of curiosity. Chimene knew how she felt about Ishtar and would probably abide by her wishes. Maybe living here, and seeing how Risa's bond with Sef still endured, would turn Chimene's thoughts to a bondmate and family of her own; even if they set up a household elsewhere in Oberg, they would still be close by. Risa pondered the future and felt content, her happiness marred only by the fact that Angharad would never receive more messages from the next generation.

She leaned over Eleta and smoothed back the child's dark hair. "Wake up," she murmured. "You don't want to miss the show, do you?" The little girl rubbed her eyes. "Come on, it'll begin very soon."

Eleta sat up. "I'm hungry."

Sef laughed and handed her a piece of dried fruit. Risa leaned against her bondmate; Dyami settled himself in front of them, flexing his already broad shoulders in the

same way his father did. Across the way, in front of Thierry
Lacan-Smith's house, a young man Risa had seen on patrol
earlier lay with his head in the lap of Thierry's daughter,
Valerie, his wand at his side. Farther down the path, she
could hear the music of a flute; the tune died.

She lifted her head. The disk of light at the dome's
center suddenly blazed brightly; directly above her a
green-and-blue globe appeared, Venus as it would be. Dyami sucked in his breath; Eleta giggled with delight. The
globe turned as it began to revolve around the disk that
was now its sun.

Risa's team had let her go early, but Chimene was
already sitting outside the house, watching Eleta crawl
over the grass. As Risa approached, Chimene rose in one
graceful movement and held out her arms. Risa embraced
her, then stepped back. She had not thought that Chimene
could become more beautiful, but her dark eyes glowed
and her long black hair was so thick and lustrous that it
didn't seem quite real.

"Grazie got home a little while ago," Chimene said. "I
told her not to fuss, but she and Kolya are already in the
kitchen, and they insisted that I relax, so I brought Eleta
outside. She's growing, I see."

Risa smiled at her younger daughter. "She'll be three
in a few months. It's hard to believe, but then it often
surprises me when I remember you're a woman now."

Dyami emerged from the greenhouse, carrying a basket of fruit and beans. He moved toward the house; Risa
beckoned to him. "Where are you going?"

"Kolya needs this," the boy replied.

"That can wait for a bit. Your sister's just come home—
you can spend some time with her."

Dyami walked toward them warily; he often had that
veiled expression on his face when he looked at Chimene,
but for a boy of seven, he often seemed solemn or contemplative around others. Maybe now that Chimene was back,
he would grow more used to her and treat her more
warmly; she had always been kind, if a bit distant, to him.

Chimene and Risa sat down; Dyami seated himself
near the path. "I was talking to Dyami before," Chimene
said. "He tells me he's been enjoying his lessons." She

turned toward the boy. "And what do you think you'd like to do when you're older?"

"I don't know," he replied. "I like testing designs on the screen, and math, too. Maybe I'll build something."

"This is a new interest," Risa said, "but Dyami takes it quite seriously. A Habber woman who advises some of the engineers is even taking the trouble to teach him a little about dome design." Chimene frowned. "I can't see the harm. It's just a few lessons and computer simulations and talks over the screen—he knows I don't care to have him over at their residence. Bartai may be a Habber, but she doesn't seem a bad sort."

Chimene arched her brows. "You've certainly grown more tolerant."

"She keeps her distance. Anyway, I'd rather be open about it than having him hide things from me."

"You wouldn't have been so easygoing with me when I was his age."

"I don't suppose I was. Maybe I was too hard on you sometimes, and maybe I've learned more since then."

"Bartai's all right," Dyami said.

"It may seem so." Chimene leaned forward. "But you mustn't be fooled by Habbers, Dyami. They try to find our weaknesses so that they can play on them. They may pretend to be kind, but they're devious and tricky—don't ever make the mistake of thinking that they're people like us. They claim they want to help us, but all they really want is to bend us to their will and force us to serve them."

Risa cleared her throat; Chimene was rather overstating the case. "Habbers may be deluded," she responded, "and I'll confess to feeling uneasy around them, but I don't think—"

"They help us," Dyami said.

"For now," Chimene replied. "They'd like to have us dependent on them, but that will change."

Dyami gazed at her indifferently; he had again retreated behind his customary mask. Eleta crawled over to Chimene and tugged at one of the silver buttons on the young woman's long black vest. The well-tailored red coverall under the vest was becoming; Chimene had always been as vain as Malik about her appearance. She took her little sister's hand and gently removed it from herself.

"Sef!" Eleta suddenly shouted. Chimene's eyes narrowed a little. "Sef!" The little girl stood up and ran down the path toward her father; Sef scooped her up in his arms.

He strode toward Risa, then set Eleta down. "Welcome back, Chimene." He grinned. "Now that you're here, maybe you can help me talk some sense into your mother. I've been asking her to renew her pledge with me, and she keeps saying we can wait."

"You could." Chimene lowered her eyes. "Your bond won't lapse for a while."

"I know, but I'd like to renew it before it lapses—another twenty years, maybe. After all, I'm not going anywhere."

"You seem very sure of yourself," Chimene murmured. "I guess you must be happy still."

"And why shouldn't I be?"

Chimene's lips curved into a smile; her long lashes hid the expression in her eyes. Sef's contentment often seemed to surprise her; Risa wondered why she sometimes felt that Chimene regretted their happiness together. In Chimene's presence, she could still feel a bit insecure, as though her bond with Sef was luck she did not deserve.

"I'm glad you're happy." Chimene looked up at Sef. "You should renew your bond if you feel that strongly about it."

"I'd better see if I'm needed inside." Sef waved a hand. "Stay out here and visit with Risa—she'll want to hear all about your plans. I don't suppose there's some young man—"

"Not at the moment," Chimene said quickly.

"Bound to be one before long, though." Sef ruffled her dark hair, as if Chimene were still a young child, then walked toward the house. Dyami scooped up his basket, took Eleta's hand, and hurried after his father.

"Well," Risa said. "I hope you'll be comfortable enough in your old room."

"I have to tell you—I won't be living here. I didn't say anything about that to Grazie—she noticed that I didn't bring a duffel, but I let her assume my things were being sent on later. I wanted to speak to you first."

Risa felt a twinge of disappointment. It did not matter; Chimene would be in Oberg at any rate. "You see," Chimene went on, "I'm going to be teaching in the southeast dome, so I should be closer to my students in case they or their parents need to visit with me after school."

"Of course. So you'll be living there?"

"No, in the main dome, but I won't be far from the tunnel. It'll be close enough."

"Well, you must come to see us as often as you can. Which household is taking you in?"

Chimene did not reply.

"Is this only until you decide to set up a household of your own," Risa said, "or is there a chance this arrangement might be more permanent? Not that I mind—we would have liked to have you here, but you're certainly free to make your own decisions."

"I'll be living with Kichi Timsen's household." Chimene tilted her head as she gazed into Risa's eyes. "They invited me to stay with them just before I left ibn-Qurrah, when I told them where I'd be teaching. I was grateful for the offer. I left my belongings there, but I thought I should come here to tell you myself."

Risa was stunned. "But you—I don't understand." It could not be true; only those closest to the Guide lived in her house. "Is she so desperate for new members that she's inviting prospects to live with her now?"

"I'm not a prospect—I'm a member." Chimene slowly unbuttoned her vest and showed Ishtar's sash around her small waist. "I joined some time ago. The Guide wants me near her, and it's what I want as well."

"You don't know what you're doing!"

"I know perfectly well what I'm doing," Chimene said softly. "Do you think I decided this yesterday? I've been Ishtar's for years—the Guide saw what was in my heart long ago. It was only out of respect for you that I didn't wear the sash openly before. I knew what you'd say and do, and it would have brought you trouble. I've learned much from Kichi. I didn't want to hide it from you, but I told myself you'd know the truth eventually and see why it had to be this way."

Risa could bear no more. "What has that woman done to you?" How long had this been going on? When had Kichi first started to ensnare her daughter? She thought of all the times Chimene had gone off for a few hours, always with plausible excuses Risa had not bothered to check.

How many people had known about this and concealed it from her?

But it would not have been that difficult to deceive her. Her own complacency had made this deception possible. Once, little in Oberg would have escaped her notice, but she had been willing to leave many matters to others in order to savor her own contentment. It had been easier not to pry into Chimene's doings and risk opening old wounds; if she could not love her as much as she loved her other children, she could at least be a kindly and forbearing parent. She had deceived herself.

"The Guide has given me her strength and her love," Chimene said. "I'd hoped I could share it with you, that when you saw how happy it's made me, you'd see—"

Risa jumped to her feet. "I won't have the sash worn in my house! All that damned nonsense—claiming the truth, turning people against each other—"

"We're not the ones who do that—you do, by refusing to understand our way."

"I won't have it! Not in my house!"

Chimene got to her feet and looked down at Risa. "Then it's just as well I'm not staying. I have no wish to disturb the harmony of your household. Under the circumstances, perhaps I should excuse myself from supper tonight." She stepped toward the path, then turned around. "I can be patient. You can't resist us indefinitely. A time will come when everyone on the Council will wear the sash, when everyone here will be brought to the truth."

Twenty

Chimene sat in Kichi's common room, bowing her head as the Guide offered an invocation. At least fifty people were there, although most members would be holding this weekly meeting in their own homes or be attending one with friends. Her sisters and brothers in Ishtar were free to go to whichever meeting they chose, and often the Guide herself attended meetings elsewhere. Those who weren't yet members were also welcomed; when one room could not hold them all, the meeting was held outside. No one would be turned away; Ishtar raised no barriers to any who sought the truth.

Chimene was trying to summon up a feeling of fellowship with those who were now gathering in Oberg, in the other settlements, and on the Islands, but other thoughts distracted her. She had been back in Oberg for three days now, and Risa had not responded to any of her messages; perhaps she had even refused to view them. Kichi was training her to be patient, but patience was often difficult. Chimene had explained in her messages to Risa that, although she would not hide her beliefs, she would refrain from speaking about them during visits, yet even that concession had brought no response.

She tried to view the matter as Kichi might. Others in Risa's household, whatever their feelings about Ishtar, might think that Risa was being too harsh in shunning her daughter. Risa was caught in a contradiction, practicing the intolerance she condemned in others. Her housemates would see that and might even feel more sympathetic to Chimene.

When she looked at the situation that way, Risa no longer presented a barrier, but rather an opportunity. Chimene could reach out to others in her mother's household and show them that only Risa was responsible for this breach. Her mother might be giving her the means to win the others for Ishtar eventually.

At any rate, Risa's reaction had not been totally unexpected. Chimene had been prepared for anger and her mother's feeling that she had been deceived. Malik presented a more formidable barrier. She could have dealt easily with rage or bewilderment; she had not expected his laughter.

"Ishtar?" he had said. The mocking expression that had distorted his handsome features was still vivid in her mind. "The fellowship of true Cytherians?"

He started to laugh then; she had nearly turned off her screen. "You called to tell me that? Congratulations, Chimene—you've joined one of the most absurd assemblies of human beings that ever existed. I must, however, say this for them—they do provide some of us with a great deal of amusement and free entertainment. I attended a meeting of theirs recently, and I'm afraid I wasn't able to restrain my merriment, so I apologized to one of them afterward for my conduct. Do you know what he said? He told me, in the most solemn and deadly way, that laughter needn't be an obstacle to the truth and that he was happy I had shared some of their joy."

He paused. "Really, I'm surprised at you. But maybe it isn't just the meetings that attract you—maybe it's those rites of theirs. No doubt your brothers in Ishtar will be grateful for a chance at you, but I would have thought you could attract enough men to your bed without that." He chuckled. "My Habber acquaintances will find this a choice topic for discussion—my daughter living in the Guide's household. Needless to say, they'll be too polite to laugh in my presence, but when they're by themselves—" Malik shrugged. "You must keep me informed of your doings, so that I have some choice tidbits to share. When you come to your senses and see how ludicrous it all is, we'll have a little celebration to mark your return to rationality."

"One doesn't leave Ishtar," she said.

"I suppose that's true. They take themselves so seriously, but then that's one of the qualities that makes them so amusing."

"You shouldn't mock the beliefs of others."

"Quite right, but I hardly think the mockery of someone as insignificant as I am will disturb those who have such grandiose visions." Malik had looked more serious then. "I'm disappointed in you, Chimene. I had some hopes for you. Be grateful I can laugh at my own disappointment."

She winced as she remembered her father's words. But Malik believed in nothing and saw the settlers' hopes as delusions. Even his own faith, as he had admitted, was partly habit, a cultural bond with his people's history, and partly a hypothesis he sometimes found comforting. Of course he would laugh at others, and even mock himself, so that he did not have to face the failure he had made of his life.

Risa had probably called him by now to discuss the latest incident in their child's life. Chimene could imagine the discussion—Risa muttering her complaints, Malik assuring her that she needn't take the matter so seriously. Her cheeks flamed with rage as she tried to control her emotions.

Anger was useless. It was only another obstacle. She was angry with her parents only because she still had her own doubts; if she were as secure in her faith as Kichi, their reactions could not have touched her. She had spoken to Risa with more confidence than she felt. But she should not be thinking of this now, during a meeting, when she had to open her soul to love for her brothers and sisters.

Boaz Huerta was speaking now. He had come to Oberg from one of Earth's camps a few years ago; Matthew Innes had brought him to Ishtar. The two young men had experiences in common—a time in the camps and a devotion to Ishtar that had rapidly brought them both to the Guide's attention. Boaz lived with a household in the southeast dome, but Matthew had told her he often came to the meetings here.

Theoretically, anyone was free to stand up and speak at a meeting; in practice, the task was usually left to the most eloquent and to those who lived closest to the truth. Chimene herself had spoken at a few meetings in ibn-Qurrah, and she had won some praise from Kichi's son,

Grigory, but for Boaz to speak with the Guide present was an honor.

She narrowed her eyes as she studied Boaz Huerta. She could not fault his delivery; his voice was clear and resonant, and he had the ability to make each member feel that his words were addressed to him or her alone. That he was a good-looking young man, with large expressive black eyes and a muscular build evident even under his loose gray shirt and trousers, certainly helped. Yet she found herself seeing places where he might have used an expressive metaphor to good effect instead of plainer words.

"We hide behind barriers," he was saying, "as Venus's Parasol shields Her from the sun. Our minds are trapped behind clouds as thick and dark as those outside." His eyes focused on Chimene for a moment; she gazed back steadily, impressed by the warmth and strength his gaze revealed. "But we can sweep away the clouds that surround us and open our minds to the sun."

He spoke well, but the words seemed obvious and trite. Boaz turned toward an older man near him, one whose face was worn with worry; she saw the man brighten a little as Boaz talked of the loneliness Ishtar could ease and of the power that lay inside all souls. She glanced around the room surreptitiously. Several pilots dressed in blue coveralls sat near one wall; two families from the houses near Kichi's were just behind them. A brown-haired man wearing a wrist bracelet was a few paces from Chimene's side. She knew about that man; he had beaten up another man badly in a fight, and Oberg's Council had decided his fate. He had been remorseful, and the other man had recovered from his injuries, so the offender would soon be freed from the house of detention that adjoined the Administrative Center, although he would have to wear his bracelet for another year.

Only those considered dangerous to others spent time in detention; among them were a woman who had beaten her child severely and a man who had assaulted a young girl. The Guide felt it was important to reach out to such people, and the patrol volunteers brought those who were interested in meetings. Kichi had told her that she hoped Chimene would visit the house of detention; Chimene shrank from the prospect. Better to rid the settlements of such people altogether and expel them from their midst.

She shook off the thought, which reflected her mother's sentiments. If such people could be brought to Ishtar and changed, she would have to regard them as her brothers and sisters, too.

If only her faith were stronger. She felt it most when she mused about Ishtar's eventual triumph or imagined herself as the Guide, loved by all. It was weakest when she was apart from other believers, or confronted someone like her mother, or lay alone in her room. But Kichi had doubted, and the Guide had told her that her faith would grow. Chimene had to cling to that promise. Kichi would not have spent the past years summoning Chimene to her side in secret, training her in how to clear her mind of distractions that obscured the truth, teaching her ways to speak and to carry herself, and arguing philosophical points with her, if she had not been sure of her choice.

Lena Kerein leaned toward Chimene, then widened her gray eyes as she ogled Boaz. "I sense the Spirit already," Lena whispered very softly. "I'd feel it even more if he weren't hiding behind the barrier of those clothes. I wouldn't mind having *him* appease the Spirit through me."

Chimene glanced at her friend, annoyed. Lena wasn't above poking some gentle fun at the fellowship, in spite of her faith, although she usually restrained herself in the Guide's presence.

"We welcome all who are true Cytherians," Boaz said, "all who see that much must be swept away before we can become what we must be. We welcome those who sense the Spirit of this world, the one we must appease and embrace with both our strength and our love."

The room darkened suddenly. On the large screen behind Boaz, images appeared in rapid succession—the volcanoes of Beta Regio, with lightning dancing around their peaks; a sterile ocean beating against a black shore; bands of bright light leaping up from the northern pole as Venus turned; the glow of the four domes of Oberg clustered together on a rocky mountain plateau.

The Spirit still eluded her. Lena took her left hand; Chimene slipped her other hand into the palm of the man at her right. She bowed her head as the room filled with sighs. Kichi was saying a prayer; Chimene closed her eyes.

* * *

The meeting ended after the last prayer; no one had come forward to join Ishtar this evening. Chimene walked with Lena toward the creek that ran past Kichi's house.

"I just had to come to this meeting when I heard," Lena said. "Becoming part of the Guide's household—but I always knew Kichi thought a lot of you." She poked Chimene's arm gently. "One of us for all these years, and you didn't even tell me."

"I couldn't. Kichi said keeping that a secret was part of my training." A secret in the service of Ishtar was no sin, only a temporary necessity. "But that's past now. I've learned a lot from Kichi."

"I suppose you have. Most of us have to settle for discussions and guidance from folks who aren't much closer to the truth than we are. You've certainly been favored by the Guide. Everyone's saying you must have proven great devotion to be so favored."

"I'm only another sister."

"You're a sister who lives with the Guide herself."

She wondered if Lena resented that but dismissed the notion. Eva Danas and Matthew Innes had become part of the Guide's household after being in Ishtar only a short time; everyone knew that some could grasp the truth more quickly than others. It did not make them better than anyone else in the fellowship; instead, it imposed burdens most would not want to share. Their lives had to be above reproach; they had to set an example for everyone else.

"You might not want what you call a privilege," Chimene murmured, "preparing to live your life without a bondmate, with every spare moment apart from your work taken up with service to Ishtar, having to strip away every barrier that threatens your faith."

"Still, there must be compensations," Lena said dryly. "I notice that the Guide always sets a good table, with all the contributions she gets. Her household doesn't lack for much."

"We use only what others choose to give us. We own nothing, not even what we've earned with our own labor."

Lena chuckled. "Once the food's in your belly and the clothes are on your back, it's a distinction without a difference."

"We share what we have."

"Well, of course," Lena said, "but the traffic seems heavier in one direction than the other. No matter. People certainly wouldn't be very attracted if they thought being part of the fellowship meant they had to live in tents and wear rags, and spreading goods around equally has more appeal if there are more goods to hand around. I'll concede one point, however—I wouldn't want to be in your position. I can still look forward to my journey down the road toward the truth and have something to hope for. You're probably nearer the end of that path. It's got to be harder to hope you won't slip back into error than to admit that you've got a long way to go."

Lena had touched on one of her fears—that she could not be what Kichi expected her to be. Others had been close to Ishtar's most virtuous adherents only to fail in some way. Such brothers and sisters were still loved, but they were also pitied.

But Kichi could not be wrong about her. The Guide was still convinced that the Spirit had guided her to Chimene. Kichi would never have chosen her if there were any chance she might fall into a more imperfect state. Kichi knew about her remaining doubts and fears, but she was patient. She was sure that in a few years Chimene would be ready when Kichi announced to all what her own household already knew—that Chimene would succeed her as the Guide.

"Still, you must be thrilled," Lena went on, sounding more like the old friend Chimene remembered. "You should have told me as soon as you got back."

"I meant to, but—"

"I can guess. Grazie told us Risa wasn't terribly delighted with your news—furious was the way she put it. I know she doesn't care for Ishtar, but she manages to get along with others who have joined—we do all have to live together."

"I'm her daughter," Chimene said, "and I'm living with the Guide. I had to tell her that this wasn't a sudden decision, that I've been part of Ishtar for some time."

"It'll pass. She thought my family was deluded for joining, but eventually she was coming around again, trading for a couple of rabbits and sitting with my mother over tea. She'll get over it. Sef will wear her down—Grazie said he's telling her that she's being too hard on you."

Chimene smiled in the darkness. Perhaps she should send Sef a private message. He often tried to smooth over disputes among the household; he always said he regarded her as his own daughter. She could tell him how deeply she regretted this estrangement. He would tell Risa about the message; as far as she knew, he and her mother had no secrets from each other. He would intercede for her.

Lena halted near the bridge. "I'd better get home," she said. "Carlos probably came by already, after his meeting. I expect he's sitting in my room, full of religious fervor and waiting to share the rite with me, and by the time I get back, I'll be too tired to accept his offering. Carlos seems to think he'll offend the Spirit if he doesn't try to appease Her after every meeting." She grinned suddenly; despite her words, she seemed to be looking forward to the encounter.

Chimene felt a pang of envy. Lena had someone who loved her, with whom the rite was an act of love as well as worship. Carlos Tokugawa wanted to be her bondmate, and eventually the two would make a pledge. They were free to do so; like most of Ishtar's followers, they weren't expected to lower all barriers, only to make the effort. Chimene's love had to encompass everyone; she had to be ready to reach out to all her brothers. Sometimes it hardly seemed like love at all.

"You're lucky to have him," she said.

"I do love him, I suppose." Lena tilted her head. "I should love all my brothers, of course, but I care for Carlos more. It only shows how steeped in error I still am, but, as the Guide says, love for one can grow to be love for others." She was silent for a moment. "Maybe I shouldn't be saying some of the things I do to you. I mustn't cloud your mind with muddy thinking."

"Oh, Lena—you're my friend. I don't ever want you to think you can't say anything to me. Even the Guide doesn't mind questions or criticisms—she wants everyone to be open with her."

"She may want it, but I wonder how many besides her inner circle really are. She's more isolated from a lot of us than she used to be."

"It's only because she's older," Chimene replied. "She has to save most of her strength for her work and her service to Ishtar, but she relies on all of us here to be honest about what others are thinking." She touched Lena's arm.

"And I expect the same of you." I might need you, she thought to herself, not wanting to admit aloud that Kichi's increasing isolation troubled her, too. If she were ever to be the Guide's successor, she wanted no barriers separating her from others in the fellowship.

"Come and see me soon," Lena said. "We can sit around with Carlos and talk about old times. He used to be a little infatuated with you when we were girls, you know. I hope your love for all your brothers doesn't require you to demonstrate any for him right away. He might be willing to move that much closer to sanctity, but I can still be trapped behind the barrier of jealousy."

Chimene laughed. "Don't worry about that. I'm not past all barriers yet, and the Guide wouldn't approve of anything that might drive you further from us. I hope you'll invite me when you decide to make a pledge."

"I will." Lena clasped her hands, then crossed the small bridge. A patrol volunteer on the other bank greeted the young woman; Chimene could not hear her friend's reply.

She turned and climbed the small slope to Kichi's house. The common room was nearly empty. Eva Danas and Galina Kolek sat in one corner, speaking to Boaz, who had not yet left; Josefa Huong's head rested on Yusef Deniz's shoulder. Lang Eberschild and Matthew Innes were with Kichi, reclining on cushions in the center of the room. Matthew looked up as Chimene approached, then quickly got to his feet.

He led her toward the screen, away from the others; she looked up into his gray-green eyes. His arm encircled her waist; she leaned against his slender body. Matthew had brought her to his room three years ago, when she was sixteen, during one of her visits to this house. He had been her first lover, and Chimene knew he had welcomed the chance to instruct her, but Kichi had chosen him for her. He was gentle with her and spoke of his love for her, but the delight he took in being with her would not keep him from others. That had been one of her most difficult lessons —learning to love Matthew, and then realizing that she would have to share his love with other sisters in Ishtar.

But she had to share herself, too. That had been even harder; the first time she had been with a man other than Matthew, she had imagined that she still held Matthew in her arms. She was past that now; she knew she could love others. She wondered why she sometimes felt that she had lost something rather than gaining more love.

He stroked her hair; she brushed back a pale blond lock from his forehead. Perhaps he wanted to come to her room now and share the rite with her.

"You seem pensive," Matthew said. "I think I know why. You're still new to this household and worrying about whether you'll ever feel you're one of us." It was true; Matthew had the Guide's gift for knowing how she felt. "That's over, Chimene. You won't have to move between one place and another, wondering if you'll ever be at home in either place. You're with us now, and every household of believers will be your home."

She was about to speak; he pressed a finger against her lips lightly. "It's time you shared the rite with us. We've asked Boaz to stay—he's been with us several times before. You should be with us as well."

She was suddenly afraid. "I don't know."

"But you've participated in the rite before."

"Only the way you and I celebrated it—alone, with one man, never with others present." Matthew had to know that already; she had admitted as much to Kichi, who kept no secrets from her household. "I'm not ready for this."

"The Guide believes you are, or I would never have suggested it. We want you with us, Chimene. This is a barrier you have to conquer if you're ever to become the Guide yourself."

He was right, however much she recoiled from such an encounter. To be asked to join those so close to the Guide was an invitation no one in Ishtar could refuse; only the worthiest of believers would be asked. She had known this would come sooner or later. How could she refuse? She recalled what Kichi had told her years ago, on the night when she had first told Chimene she would be the next Guide. *Turn away now, and the wall you build inside yourself will imprison you as surely as this dome does.* That threat had always lain behind Kichi's promises and the faith she claimed to have in Chimene.

"The Guide will watch over us," Matthew continued, "but you must take her place. You must join us. You'll see we were right."

"Very well." Her voice sounded hoarse.

He kissed her lightly on the forehead, then beckoned to the others.

Chimene moved toward her room in a daze, trying to keep her mind as blank as possible. She took a breath as the door closed behind her, then quickly shed her clothes before removing her shroud from a drawer.

I mustn't be afraid, she told herself. She was loved; that was why they wanted her with them. The Guide would watch over her, and Matthew would be there; surely sharing the rite in the presence of the others could not be that different from the times they were alone. But maybe Matthew did not expect her to go to him; perhaps this was another test for her, to see if she could reach out to another while he was present.

She steadied herself. The rite was what mattered; which man shared it with her did not. She had to be willing to love any of her brothers in Ishtar.

Chimene covered herself with her shroud. The dark cloth reached from the top of her head to the floor. She swayed a little on her bare feet, then opened the door.

Four shrouded figures waited for her at the end of the corridor. She caught a glimpse of one golden-skinned foot before its owner drew it under her shroud; that had to be Josefa Huong. Eva Danas was the tallest of the women; her shroud hid her form, but not her height. "The Spirit is with us," another woman whispered; she recognized Kichi's voice.

Chimene felt nothing. Galina Kolek had told her that this was when she felt closest to the Spirit, that the rite always freed her from herself. Faith came so easily to some.

She followed the others into the common room. The ceiling light panels were dim. Through the dark fabric concealing her face, Chimene saw a blurred image on the screen, a vista of high mountain peaks topped by snow and covered with evergreens, overlooking a wide, grassy plain —Ishtar Terra as it would be.

The men were waiting for them. Each man was clothed in a long dark robe and stood by the mats in the center of the room. One shrouded woman seated herself in front of the screen as the men opened their robes, then let them fall.

The three women with Chimene did not move. Were they waiting for her to make her choice? She shivered, wanting to bolt from the room. Matthew was standing next to Boaz Huerta, his pale skin a contrast to the other man's darker hue. Lang Eberschild's head was bowed; his graying hair hid his eyes. Yusef Deniz lifted his bearded face and gazed directly at the shrouded women.

For a moment, Chimene felt a stirring inside her mind, as though something outside herself was trying to touch her thoughts. Could it be that she might feel the Spirit now? She emptied her mind, giving herself up to the dimly felt sensation; she would let it guide her, whatever it was.

She lowered her eyes and moved toward the men; the soft padding of the other women's footsteps followed her. She stopped before one man and touched him lightly on the hand, then looked up at Boaz's dark eyes.

She tensed as he drew her down onto a mat. She caught a glimpse of Matthew, only a few paces away on another mat, as he embraced another shrouded form, and then Boaz stretched out at her side. His hands roamed over her, feeling her body through her shroud. She was the Spirit of Venus to him now, the Spirit of the world still veiled in thick, dark clouds and hidden by the Parasol, as she was by her shroud. He had to appease her, placate the Spirit of the world they were transforming. His touch was gentle at first, as if he feared that she might not accept him. He reached under the cloth and caressed her belly and thighs.

Did he know who she was yet? He had shared the rite with the others before; had the unfamiliarity of her body already revealed who she was? It made no difference; she was all of his sisters now, only another aspect of all those who would be united by the Spirit.

His fingers explored her; she heard herself gasp. Another woman was moaning; a deeper cry answered hers. Boaz lifted Chimene's shroud above her hips, then lowered his head. His lips brushed against her belly; she opened her legs wider as his tongue found her slit.

She was ready for him more quickly than she had expected to be. He lifted her hips as she guided him into her. It was time to remove her shroud, to imagine the day when the clouds of Venus would finally part and the land below lay open to the sun. She drew the shroud up and lifted it from her face.

His arms tightened around her. She saw the delight in his eyes as he gazed into hers, his joy that the Spirit had guided her to him. This was the reason for her beauty—to make men even stronger in their devotion to Ishtar; Kichi had told her that. She embodied the Spirit of this world, demanding their love, reflecting the beauty this world would have when it was transformed. She was Ishtar as she moved under him, accepting his offering to Venus, certain once again of her purpose.

Matthew was groaning; she recognized the sound. Josefa was kneeling astride him; her black hair swayed as she threw her head back. Chimene hoped the others were feeling the joy she felt. Boaz was thrusting more rapidly inside her; she caught a glimpse of the Guide as she glanced past Boaz's brown shoulder.

Kichi's head was bare, her shroud draped around her shoulders. She was looking at Chimene with a cold, distant stare; a strange, almost mocking smile played about her lips. Chimene faltered, and then Boaz lowered his head, hiding Kichi from view. She clawed at his back and surrendered herself to him.

Twenty-one

Dyami sat at the edge of the grassy plain, just beyond the trees. From here, he could see the entrance to the residence where the Habbers working in the west dome lived. Once the windowless circular structure had sat at some distance from the nearest dwellings, but more houses had been built, and the walls of a few more were rising on the plain. Ten Habbers lived in that gray-walled house now; soon most of them would be gone. Some would go to their Habitat; two or three might stay on the Islands or go to work in the Freyja Mountains.

Bartai would be leaving; she had told him so a couple of days ago. She had said she would miss their talks, but she didn't seem unhappy about going home. Habbers were like that; they didn't get too attached to anyone here. Risa told him that was their way, but it seemed to him that it was partly the settlers' fault, too, since they avoided the Habbers whenever possible.

His parents would not want him to be here, but he couldn't see that sitting here was actually disobeying them. He wasn't visiting the house, which they had forbidden; he was only looking at it. If Sef or Risa asked him where he had gone today, Dyami would tell them that he had been in the community greenhouses helping out, and that would be the truth.

Theron had taken his students there earlier, since their classes wouldn't begin again for another week, and had turned them over to the adults in the greenhouses. The children had been put to work checking the water gauges, weeding some of the tiers, and packing produce.

One man had instructed them in how to put on the face masks and rebreathers anyone working in the large greenhouses had to wear. The plants flourished in an atmosphere with a higher percentage of carbon dioxide, and the man had been very stern about telling the children to make sure their masks were on tight. Alicia Hamlyn-Kateri clearly hadn't been listening; after she had fainted and was revived, the children were lectured about safety before being allowed to leave a bit early.

Bartai might come to the Habber house soon, or maybe she was inside and would decide to take a walk. He would not be disobeying his parents if he spoke to the Habber woman outside the residence; he wouldn't have too many more chances to talk to her. He wondered if she was leaving because of all those people in Ishtar who couldn't stop talking about how creepy Habbers were, the ones like his sister Chimene.

He glanced at the timepiece he wore on one finger and decided to wait another hour. If his friend Teo Lingard got here before then, he might wait a bit longer, but then he would have to head home before the light began to dim. The patrol was always out early along the main road that ran behind the Habber residence, and they usually questioned anyone who was loitering nearby.

Dyami did not like the patrol. They were nosy, always asking where you were going. Once, one patrol volunteer had asked him if he had seen one man leaving the Habber residence. Dyami had, but refused to admit it. The volunteer had muttered something about "offenses to Ishtar," whatever that meant, before sending Dyami on his way. He hadn't seen the man doing anything wrong; therefore, he did not have to say anything about him. People on the patrol sometimes seemed much too curious without a good reason.

Almost all of the patrol volunteers were in Ishtar, even though most of the people in Oberg weren't members of the cult. Dyami had once asked Kolya why people put up with the patrol. "They're annoying sometimes," Kolya had replied, "but they've prevented some trouble, and we're all probably safer because of them. You can say what you like about Ishtar, but at least they can get people organized when something needs to be done." It was the way adults thought; they would put up with something they didn't much like, while telling themselves it was for their own good.

In the distance, a passenger cart was rolling along the main road; it stopped and a dark-haired boy jumped out. Dyami lifted a hand and waved as Teo Lingard ran toward him across the open expanse.

Teo was panting by the time he reached Dyami. "Sorry I took so long." He threw himself onto the grass. "I had to get the goat shit cleaned up and into the sterilizer, and then my uncle had to go to a friend's, so he told me to take my cousin over to the nursery before I went anywhere. Seen Bartai yet?"

Dyami shook his head.

"She's really going?"

"Yeah."

"Don't feel too bad about it." Teo stretched out on his back; Dyami lay down next to him and gazed at the dome overhead. The disk of light was beyond the trees behind him, but a paler halo of light surrounded it. The dome was a vast, banded bowl, white at the center, then blending into yellow, gray, and at the edge, where it met the low wall that circled the settlement, black.

Teo said, "I wonder what a real sky is like, with clouds and all, I mean one where it isn't always dark the way it is outside."

"Take a mind-tour and find out."

"Maybe a real sky's very different."

"My grandfather told me a little about it," Dyami said. "He says it looks different, depending on where you are. In some places, you've got all these tall buildings and hills, so you can see only a little bit of the sky, but in others—" He slipped one arm under his head. "He met my grandmother on the North American Plains. He said that there the sky was sometimes like this huge kettle over the Earth."

"That makes it sound like a dome," Teo muttered.

"A lot bigger than a dome, and blue, with all kinds of different clouds. You know what it's like when you're in the middle of this dome and you can't see the edge? It's sort of like that, he says, except that you think you'll never get to the end of it. And it changes—sometimes the clouds seem close to the ground and sometimes there're hardly any clouds at all. And the wind—he says sometimes it would howl for days."

"Sounds scary."

"I guess it is, if you're not used to it."

"It's always the same here," Teo said, "except for the quakes. I wonder when the next one's going to hit."

A quake had been predicted days ago. "They can't always pinpoint it—you know that." Dyami thought of the little he had already learned. Earth's seismologists knew much more about the home world's fault lines and the patterns quakes followed there; here, prediction was somewhat more uncertain, since the planet's tectonic plates had only recently begun to shift. The landmass of Ishtar Terra was on one such plate. The Maxwell Mountains were far enough away from fault lines to make it safe to build settlements here, but they often trembled to the vibrations of powerful distant quakes. Dyami was used to the tremors, which usually did no more than shake the ground a little.

"I heard a good one yesterday," Teo said. "My father told it to my uncle. Why do women in Ishtar wear shrouds during the rite?"

"I don't know."

"Because they want to make sure the men will go through with their offering." Teo chuckled. Dyami smiled tentatively, not sure he understood the joke, although he did know something about what happened during the rite. Maybe Teo didn't really get it either, but he was nine, a year older than Dyami, and seemed to think that extra year made him more knowledgeable.

"I heard another one, too," Teo continued. "Why do men on patrol always carry wands?"

"The women do, too."

"Come on, Dyami—it's a joke. Why do the men carry wands?"

"I don't know."

"Because if the Spirit fails them during the rite, they've got something they can use."

Dyami did not bother to laugh at this one. He sat up and peered toward the Habber house; the door opened as a man stepped outside. He sighed.

"Maybe you don't think they're funny," Teo said, "with your sister and all."

"Come on—you know what I think about that."

"My father says it'd almost be worth joining if he could

get close to her, but he didn't say it in front of my mother. How long are you going to wait for Bartai?"

"Not much longer."

"We could make the rounds."

"You know we haven't got time for that," Dyami replied. Making the rounds was a game some of his friends played. They would go to the tunnel that led to the main dome, race through it, catch a passenger cart there, ride it to the tunnel that joined the main dome to the southeast dome, and keep going in the same manner until they were through the southwest dome and back at the point in the west dome where they had started. The object of the game was to get through all of Oberg's four domes in the shortest amount of time, which required running along the main roads if a cart didn't show up immediately.

Teo folded his arms across his chest, apparently prepared to wait. The slender black-haired boy was like Dyami, curious about things others said they shouldn't be curious about. He sometimes joined Dyami in his room for talks with Bartai over the screen, but not because he was particularly interested in engineering design; he was curious about Habbers.

Teo was unlike him in being more reckless. Dyami thought of their latest adventure, when Teo had dared him into sneaking out of his house after dark. Dyami had waited until the household was asleep before leaving by the side exit in his wing; he still remembered the sharp, almost pleasurable stab of fear he felt when meeting his friend outside.

The object of this venture was to cross the dome and get to the digger and crawler bay without being seen by the patrol. They got only as far as the lake before seeing two sashed volunteers talking to a man. The boys had hunkered down behind a shrub.

Dyami recognized the man then. He was Lucas Ghnassia, one of his neighbors, and even in the dim light, he could see how frightened Lucas was. What could the patrol want with him? Lucas Ghnassia was so respectable that he was often the topic of jokes; he was a chemist who spent most of his spare time doing chores around the house he shared with his sister's family. Dyami had never known him to smile or waste time visiting with his neighbors. Some of his schoolmates often loitered around Lucas's greenhouse, knowing that he would soon come out and, in his odd, rasping voice, lecture them about idling. His bondmate, Sirisa Wallis, was a pale, pretty woman as reclusive as he was; even Grazie had never been able to lure Sirisa into a session of gossip.

"We know where you've been," the female volunteer said.

Lucas drew himself up; his hands trembled as he looped them around his red and black sash. "I was visiting a friend." His voice was even more raspy than usual.

"And we know just what kind of friend. Did you think we wouldn't find out? We know what goes on—where you meet, what you do."

"You must be mistaken," Lucas replied. "Unless you have a reason to detain me, I must be on my way home."

"We have to look out for you," the male volunteer said. "You're our brother in Ishtar now. Don't you want to move closer to the Spirit? What you do affronts Her. Did you think that donning the sash and practicing a deception would protect you from the consequences of your offense?"

Dyami frowned. The patrol was supposed to keep order, not pry into someone's personal business. If Lucas posed no threat to persons or property and was on his way home, why were they bothering with him?

"I've done nothing that concerns the patrol," Lucas said; apparently the same thought had occurred to him.

"We have to love you," the woman said, "but you're making it very difficult to do so. Very well—we'll try to forgive you this time. Even those close to the truth can occasionally fall into error. But the patrol will be looking out for you, and if you persist in your affronts, it may be time for you to confess them at a meeting. The fellowship will still love you if you're truly repentant, but others may not be so kind—many here would despise you for what you do."

Lucas covered his eyes. "Go home," the male volunteer said, "and open your soul to the Spirit. Reflect on your errors and gather the strength to resist them."

Lucas stumbled away toward the path that led to his house. Dyami held his breath as the man passed; he heard a choked sound and wondered if Lucas was weeping. The man and the woman watched him in silence, then walked away along the shore of the lake toward Andrew Dinel's house.

"Shit," Teo whispered when the two were out of sight. "Shit." Dyami saw that his friend was trembling. "I wish I was anywhere except here."

Dyami touched his arm. "Lucas could complain to the Council," he said. "Yakov Serba would be on his side—the patrol isn't supposed to—"

"Don't be stupid, Dyami. Even if he did, those two would just get a reprimand, and then he'd be in even more trouble with them." Teo wiped at his face. "We'd better go home."

"Don't you want to try for—"

"Not now."

Dyami glanced at his friend. Teo was still staring up at the dome, as if hoping that the clouds he was probably imagining might suddenly appear. It was strange that Teo had so rapidly abandoned their adventure the other night, after daring Dyami into being his accomplice. He had seemed almost as frightened of the patrol as Lucas.

Dyami pondered the incident. Lately, he had begun to feel that unseen threats lay all around him and that his only protection was in being guarded with others; seeing Lucas with the patrol had given some substance to his vague fears. He had always been reserved, sensing dimly that he had to be. Sef sometimes kidded him about his solemnity, but somehow Dyami knew that he could never be as open and demonstrative as his father was. Only with Teo did he feel he could let down his guard, in spite of his friend's occasional recklessness. Teo was like him in often wanting to be alone, in being more distant from their schoolmates, in feeling that their class discussions were often a waste of time when they could learn just as much from their screens. "They want us to learn how to get along," Teo had said once, in a tone that implied this was an impossible goal. "That's all those discussions are for."

"That uncle of yours," Teo said then, "the one who's a Habber—maybe he was right."

Dyami smiled a little. Teo liked to say startling things, at least to him; he was more careful around other people. "You wouldn't really do that, would you—try to get to a Hab?"

"I don't know. Maybe I would if I could, but I won't
have the chance."

"Well, I wouldn't," Dyami said. "If I could go there for
a while and come back, maybe, but—my mother never
forgot what her brother did. I think that's the real reason
she doesn't want much to do with Habbers."

He thought of Bartai. With her black hair and almond-
shaped eyes, she looked a little like his mother; her
straightforward manner even reminded him of Risa.
Maybe that was why he liked her, although Risa wouldn't
be happy to have herself compared to a Habber.

"I don't think we're going to see Bartai," Dyami said,
"and if I don't pick up in my room before Risa gets home,
she'll—"

"Yeah, I know." Teo sat up. His dark eyes seemed sad
as he gazed at Dyami, and then his face brightened. He
jumped to his feet. "I'll race you to my house."

Dyami kept up a swift pace with his long legs, but the
smaller, slighter Teo won the race. He waved a farewell to
his friend before heading home. Perhaps Bartai had left a
message on the screen; he could not believe that she would
leave without saying good-bye to him.

He could clean his room and still have time with his
screen before dinner. On his own, in addition to his schoolwork, he had been learning more about the history of the
Project. These lessons were ones Theron would have come
to eventually, but Dyami saw no reason not to master them
now. Dawud Hasseen, the engineer who had designed the
Parasol, was one of his heroes; Dyami had viewed scenes of
the Parasol's construction many times, marveling at the
calculations and effort that had gone into building it.

A teaching image named Simon presented these lessons, commented on the visual images, and answered Dyami's questions. Dyami knew that the fair-haired Simon
was only an image presented by a cybermind, modeled on
a real man who would be leading his life elsewhere, and
yet he sometimes felt that the image was his friend. Often,
he imagined that he could feel Simon's hand on his shoulder whenever the image praised him for a correct answer,
and wondered why he felt more drawn to an image than to
his own teacher. Sometimes he daydreamed and saw himself leaving his house to find the real Simon waiting out-

side. He would imagine Simon's arm around him and the
man's deep voice promising to be his friend, but he had
never mentioned those daydreams even to Teo; they were
another secret he sensed he had to keep.

As he neared his house, he saw that Eleta was kicking a
stone along the path; one of the household's adults must
have brought her home from the nursery. He sighed, hoping no one had looked into his messy room. Eleta spun
around and ran toward the trees; Chimene was sitting
there, watching the child.

Eleta nestled next to her older sister; Chimene smiled
as Dyami approached. "Chen's inside," she said, "finishing
that carving for me. He's asked me to stay for dinner, and
he said you helped Kolya make the bread this time—I'm
sure it's delicious."

He tilted his head. Over the past months, Chimene
had gone out of her way to be pleasant, and yet he still felt
uneasy during her visits. "You shouldn't come here," he
blurted out.

She continued to smile. "What a thing to say."

"Risa doesn't like it."

"She hasn't said so to me."

"That's only because everybody else keeps saying she
should be nicer to you, but she still doesn't like it."

"Well, I guess I understand that," Chimene said.
"Mother's a proud woman—she doesn't like to admit she
was wrong." Dyami disliked it when Chimene called Risa
Mother. She drawled the formal term, and her voice was
colder when she used it. "But she knows how much I care
about all of you, and I think she feels a little warmer toward me now."

He studied her face. Everybody was always saying
how beautiful his sister was, but her composed expression
made him shiver.

Maybe, he thought, there was something wrong with
him. He had only hazy memories of the last time Chimene
had lived with them, before she had finished her studies on
Island Two and gone to live in ibn-Qurrah; he could not
recall much about the preceding years. But during her last
stay, she had often helped him with his lessons, played
games with him, and acted as an older sister should. He
could not think of anything to hold against her, so why did
she make him feel strange, as if she were someone he did

not really know and around whom he had to be on guard? Maybe it was only that she had been away from this household so much, and he hadn't been able to feel as close to her.

"Mene," Eleta said; she had trouble pronouncing her sister's name. "You said we were going to play a game."

"And we shall. Why don't you go inside and find the one you want to play and bring it out here?"

Eleta stood up; Chimene gave her a hug, then gently propelled her toward the door. She turned back to Dyami. "You don't like having me visit, do you?" she asked. He did not answer. "You can be honest with me, Dyami—you don't like having me around. Believe me, I won't get upset if you admit it. You were so young during most of the time I was here, and I was away a lot, and we didn't have the chance to be as close as we might have been, but maybe when you know me better, we can be friends." Her words made him think she could read his thoughts. "I want you to feel that we will be friends."

"You're in Ishtar," he said. "Risa says that all those times you were living here, you were in it and you didn't tell her—that's why she got mad at you. You lied to her."

"I didn't lie. I just didn't tell her everything I was doing. Surely you see why I had to keep it a secret—she wouldn't have understood. But I knew she'd find out someday. It wasn't as if I were going to hide it from her forever —that would have been wrong." She smiled, showing her perfect teeth. "I'm sure you must have a few secrets of your own you don't share—most children do."

He looked down, wondering if she knew anything about the volunteers who had confronted Lucas Ghnassia and what they had wanted with him.

"Don't you know why I joined Ishtar?" she continued. Her voice sounded gentler; Dyami lifted his head. "I want a world that's better than the one we have now, where no one ever has to feel lost and alone. I want a world in which the barriers that separate people have fallen away, where we can love one another and share what we have freely. Wouldn't you like to live in such a world, one where you'd be at peace with all your brothers and sisters, where you could trust everyone?"

"You're not supposed to talk about Ishtar here," Dyami said.

"I was only trying to explain—I understand your feelings, and Risa's, too. I've had my doubts and I still struggle with them. I wonder whether Ishtar can bring us to something better. But where else can we turn? So many of us have lost sight of what the Project was meant to be. The Island specialists see it as a kind of laboratory—they can't see beyond their own narrow goals. The settlers here think only of giving their children more than they had, even if that means someone else might have less. Surely—"

Dyami felt the jolt then. He stood still for an instant and then the ground lurched under him, throwing him onto the grass. The trees above him swayed wildly; his hands clawed at the dirt. He heard a sharp crack; Chimene threw herself across him as a branch struck the path. In the distance, someone was screaming.

He peered over his hands. Across the way, houses swayed, as if they were vessels riding on a sea. He was afraid to look up at the dome, fearing it might begin to crack. Terror welled up inside him; he covered his head.

The ground was still. He clung to Chimene, then managed to sit up. A wing of one house had collapsed; people were already running toward the wreckage.

Chimene stumbled up and pulled him to his feet. "Are you all right?" He nodded. His own house was standing; she spun around and hurried toward the door.

He raced after her. The door opened; apparently it still worked. Chen lay on the floor, his hand around one of his chisels; blood streamed from a gash in his head. Eleta was wailing; he found her in the corridor just outside her room.

"Dyami!" she cried out. He held her, stroking her hair until her sobs subsided.

"Are you hurt?" he asked. She shook her head. "It's all right, it was just a quake. We knew it was going to come." Eleta pressed her lips together and squeezed her eyes shut. "You're safe now."

He led her into the common room. Chimene emerged from Bettina's examination room and knelt beside Chen to clean his wound and bandage his head. "Can you walk?" she asked when she was finished.

"I think so."

"You should rest until Tina gets back. I'd better help you outside—there may be an aftershock before long, and you'll be safer there until we know how damaged the house is."

She helped the old man up; he leaned against her as they walked toward the door. Dyami followed with Eleta. He glanced at the greenhouse as they moved down the path; cracks marred a few of its panes.

Chimene settled Chen on a grassy spot away from the trees. A member of the patrol was near another house, tending to a man who seemed injured. "Dyami," Chimene said, "you have to look out for Chen and Eleta. Somebody else may need help."

She left him and hurried up the path. Alarms were wailing. He could see more of the damage now. A tree had fallen onto the roof of one house; another house, only partially built, lay in ruins. Eleta began to cry again; he reached for her.

During the days that followed the quake, Dyami was too busy to dwell on his new fears. Members of the patrol were organizing the settlers; injured people had to be tended and damage to many of the buildings repaired. Two members of the patrol met the children in the west dome's school; the teachers were needed elsewhere. Some of Dyami's friends, including Teo, were asked to assist the adults who were checking the school to make certain the structure was safe. Others, Dyami among them, helped in clearing away broken tree limbs, rubble, and salvaging anything that could be repaired.

Two aftershocks shook the dome two days after the quake; the first seemed nearly as severe as the quake itself. Dyami found himself moving over the ground tentatively, expecting it to buckle under him at any time. Most of the houses had been left standing, but a few near the lakeshore had been flooded by water overrunning the banks.

The screens were filled with statistics about damage and deaths. All of the settlements had felt the quake, but Hasseen, Lyata, and Mtshana, the communities in the south of the Maxwell range, had sustained the most damage; nearly one hundred people had died in those three dome clusters. Oberg, Dyami supposed, had been lucky, with only twenty deaths, while the two domes in the Freyja Mountains were practically unscathed.

Chen recovered from his head injury after two days of

bed rest; only the most severely injured had been taken to
the main dome's infirmary. Some of Dyami's neighbors
had taken to sleeping outside in tents or unsheltered on
mats, but Risa told Dyami there was no need for this.
Nikolai and Emilia had checked the house thoroughly, and
there would be no danger in staying inside; she explained
this very carefully in a calm, measured voice. She did not
want her children to give in to their fears, which would
only make it harder for them to readjust. They reached a
compromise; Sef would stay in Dyami's room for a couple
of nights, while Eleta slept with Risa. Dyami gave in,
mostly because he did not want Irina mocking him for
being afraid.

Irina and her father Nikolai seemed relatively unaffected by the quake and its aftermath; they were simply
grateful that everyone in the household was all right. Some
of the other children Dyami knew, after the first shock had
passed, seemed almost to welcome the break in their routine and were soon exchanging stories about the adventure. Dyami mimicked the others when he was around
them, but when he lay on his bed trying to sleep, all his
fears returned. Sometimes he started from his sleep, suddenly terrified that the walls of his room would fall in
around him.

He had always felt safe inside the domes, whatever lay
outside. The domes had been built at some distance from
the nearest cliff, where boulders might be loosened, but
they could withstand falling rocks in any case. Bartai had
taught him enough about the domes for him to know that
they would remain secure even during the most severe
quakes. None of this kept him from imagining that the
west dome might be breached, leaving the settlement vulnerable to Venus's deadly air, sulfuric acid rain, and crush-
ing atmospheric pressure.

The patrol volunteers did their best to reassure the
children. The deaths and most severe injuries in Oberg
were largely, so they claimed, the result of human carelessness. Heavy equipment had been improperly secured, or
people had not pruned potentially dangerous tree limbs
near their houses, or neglect during construction had re-
sulted in the collapse of a wall or roof. It was a lesson for the
children to heed. Their lives depended on maintaining
what was around them and anticipating possible hazards.

Everyone, even the children, had to be alert to anything out of the ordinary. The volunteers implied that this meant paying attention to anyone who might be acting strangely, as well as to installations and equipment.

The volunteers encouraged the children to talk about any lingering fears, but Dyami refused to confess any of his. Ishtar's people seemed to be everywhere. Someone wearing the sash always seemed nearby to reassure a household about an injured family member or to help out in other ways. Those in Ishtar moved through Oberg, secure in their faith, untouched by fear.

A private message from Bartai arrived ten days after the quake; Dyami decided to view it in his room. He found out then why he had not seen her anywhere; she had gone to Island Three the day before the quake, without telling him.

"Please understand, Dyami." The strong-boned face that reminded him of Risa's wore a look of concern. "You knew I was leaving, and I thought it'd be best this way. Saying farewell in person might have been more upsetting to you—farewells can be hard. Your family didn't want you to get too attached to me, and I have to respect that—I also didn't want to cause you trouble by having you visit or by coming to your home."

You don't want to cause yourself trouble, he thought; that's what you really mean. You couldn't even make a call, you had to send a message.

"But I'll remember you," she continued. "I'll remember that a boy in Oberg tried to be a friend to me, at least as much as he was allowed to be. Maybe someday we'll be able to meet as true friends. Farewell."

The screen went blank. He should have expected it; Habbers, after all, weren't people like him. Chimene claimed that Habbers had hidden designs on their world. He doubted that any of them cared enough about Cytherians to engage in such plots. They could always leave; he would be here forever.

He left his room and wandered down the corridor. Irina, her brown braid down her back, was sprawled on the floor of the common room, reading a book on her screen. "Bartai's gone," he said. "I just looked at her message."

Irina looked up. "From the Platform?"

He shook his head. "Island Three."

"I guess she's still waiting for a ship then."

"Unless she already left," he said bitterly.

"You knew she was going. You shouldn't spend so much time with Habbers anyway. Chimene says—"

"I don't care what she says."

Irina scowled. She seemed ready to start one of her arguments with him when Risa entered the house with Eleta. "You're home early," Irina said.

"Keep an eye on Eleta," Risa replied. "I have to call Tina."

"Anything important?" Irina asked.

"I don't know yet. It might only be rumors." Risa frowned. "I don't want any of you children to leave the house right now."

She went to the wall screen, sat down, and pressed a button on the console near the floor. "Bettina Christies," she muttered, "at the infirmary. If she isn't available, leave a message telling her to call me as quickly as she can."

Dyami moved closer to his mother. Her voice was that low and deliberate only when she was worried. The screen lit up; a large image of Bettina gazed into the room.

"I hear there's been an outbreak of some kind," Risa said quickly. "Alasid said something about it at work."

The physician nodded. "I may as well tell you now. Gupta and a couple of the other physicians are speaking to the Council, and they'll be making an announcement before dark. We don't want panic, but we have to act."

"What is it?"

"Some of our patients are displaying a disease something like pneumonia, but it's much more severe and rapid in the way it progresses. The Island physicians have already told us that a few pilots on the Platform have come down with the fever, and it's spread to at least two of the Islands."

"But how—" Risa began to say.

"Two of our patients here were among the most recent group of immigrants from Earth. They were the first to show the symptoms. That group of immigrants was small—a few of them are here, and the rest went to Tsou Yen and Kepler. The physicians there have already reported other cases among those settlers and a couple of the pilots who transported them."

"It doesn't seem possible," Risa said. "They would have been scanned before they left Earth. Surely—"

"I doubt they were scanned on the Platform," Bettina responded. "Maybe Earth's become as careless as we are, or maybe they picked it up somehow aboard the Habber ship that brought them to Anwara—there are a couple of cases there, too."

"Are you saying that the Habbers—"

"I'm not saying anything—there are enough wild rumors already. I'll stick to the facts. We're dealing with a myxovirus—we found that out almost immediately, after checking some blood samples. It's a particularly vicious myxovirus—the earliest symptom is a slight feverishness, followed by difficulty in breathing and fluid in the lungs. The patient barely has time to become aware of the symptoms before the body temperature rises and it becomes nearly impossible to breathe. To put it simply, the body's literally burning itself up and the patient can't get enough air. Before we can even make an opening in the trachea and get the patient on a breather, it's nearly too late, even if we had enough breathers for everyone. The disease runs its course in a day or two."

"It can't be," Risa muttered. "I've never heard of such a thing."

"Well, we've got it now." Bettina's thin face sagged; she rubbed at her eyes. "Two patients are dying already—we can't replace what their bodies are burning up. Our facilities were already strained by patients injured during the quake. We've got one patient who seems to be fighting it so far—he might recover. But this virus is a mutation the medical researchers haven't seen before, and it's deadly—it's almost as if it were designed to be as deadly as possible." The physician brushed back a lock of her disorderly gray hair. "I shouldn't say that, I suppose—I've been hearing too much wild talk about those who might be interested in attacking us this way."

Dyami glanced at Irina. Her pale eyes were wide.

"Surely you can stop it," Risa said.

"Oh, yes. The medical people down here and on the Islands are already trying to produce enough RNA and interferon to vaccinate everyone—anyone who hasn't been exposed would be protected then, and some people are bound to be immune or have a higher resistance. The

researchers are also working on an antibody that could
help those already infected. Oh, we have the means. The
trouble is that we don't have the time. We have over eighteen thousand people in Oberg alone to deal with, and no
way of knowing who's been exposed already without scanning them all right away. We've traced the infection's
probable path, but we can't know about everyone who
might already have had contact with someone who's infected."

Dyami sank to the floor. This was something he could
barely comprehend; such a disease belonged to older
times, eras he had heard about in school or read about on
his screen.

"The Administrators ordered a halt to travel," Bettina
continued, "so we're going to be on our own for a bit. You'll
hear more when the announcement's made later. I don't
know—we never expected to have to handle anything like
this." She wiped at her face. "Paul and Grazie were so
annoyed with Patrick for volunteering to work on the Bats.
Now I'm glad he's there—at least he'll be safe. It doesn't
appear that anyone there's been exposed."

Risa turned and stared at Dyami. He had never seen
such fear in his mother's eyes. She gazed past him at Eleta,
then suddenly pulled her daughter to her side.

Twenty-two

Chimene wandered into the common room, unable to sleep. Only a day after the announcement, the household had seen the flush of fever on Kichi's cheeks. Lang Eberschild had quickly taken the Guide to her room, insisting that he should be the one to stay with her. He was, next to Kichi, the oldest one in the household and had been with her the longest; he would take the additional risk.

It did not matter, she thought. There was little Lang could do for Kichi except to give her what little nourishment she could take and pray that she might be one of those who survived the illness. He would not have long to wait if the disease took its expected course; they would know one way or the other by tomorrow before dark.

They might all be harboring the virus. A pilot later found to be afflicted had been here for their last meeting. Chimene thought of her pupils in the southeast dome's school, of all the times she had hugged a child needing comfort or had shared the midday meal with others. She sat down. She was afraid to go to the screen and call their families, to ask how they might be. She could not bear to think of the men who had recently shared the rite with her.

Kichi should have been in the infirmary, on a breather, with a tube to nourish her; aged and weak as she was, she might still have had a chance then. But the infirmary was already overburdened with people injured during the quake and an ever-increasing number of infected patients. The physicians were being forced to make painful decisions, judging who might have a chance to survive

373

on one of their few breathers, who seemed healthy enough to be able to fight it off, and who had almost no chance at all. Even her housemate, Galina Kolek, who was a physician, could do little for the Guide now.

Galina, along with every other physician and paramedic in Oberg, had been summoned to the main dome's Administrative Center just before the announcement. She had not returned since then but had left a message for the household. Her med-scan was negative; she and her colleagues had been vaccinated. She would have to treat patients and would be living in one of the tents set up around the infirmary until the quarantine limiting everyone to their houses had been lifted.

Galina had not asked, in her message, if anyone in her household was ill, and there was no point in begging her to come here now. If the outbreak was to be controlled, according to the Council's announcement, the necessary measures were clear. The physicians and medical researchers, who were the first line of defense and therefore most likely to be exposed, had to be vaccinated. Next came the patrol volunteers scheduled to be on duty at this time; they had to keep order and make certain that the quarantine was not violated. After the patrol, essential personnel needed to maintain the settlement's installations would be vaccinated so they could return to work as soon as possible. Only then could the physicians deal with the thousands of others who had to be protected.

Yakov Serba had spoken for the Council. "We need your cooperation," he had said in his steady voice. "I know that many of you are frightened, but I urge you to be calm. Some of you will be tempted to violate the quarantine, seek out a friend or relative who is a physician, and beg for help right now. Such pleas will only interfere with our efforts, and I must tell you that anyone who engages in such actions will be brought before a hearing when this crisis is past, and that the penalty for putting one's own welfare above all others will be severe. Any physician or paramedic who doesn't follow the procedures we've outlined will also be brought before a hearing. The patrol has been given the authority to use whatever means are necessary to restrain anyone who violates the quarantine, and offenders will be the last to be vaccinated."

Yakov had followed his warning with words of reassurance. The infirmary's laboratory could, within a week, have sufficient supplies of both a vaccine and antibodies for those already incubating the virus. The quarantine would protect those who had not yet been exposed, while others were probably immune or capable of surviving the illness. He ended with a warning to everyone to avoid close physical contact with others in their households as much as possible.

Gupta Benares had spoken then. Human beings, he pointed out, lived in a sea of microbes that were capable of mutating, of trying to breach the defenses medical technology had erected. Carelessness born of a false sense of security had led to this crisis; to spread rumors that the epidemic might be deliberate would only keep them all from drawing the proper lesson from this event.

Gupta would say that, Chimene thought. Like most physicians, he preferred to believe that almost anything except the ailments of advanced old age or accidents could be averted by medicine and common sense. His words had not convinced her.

A few recent immigrants had brought the virus here; that much was evident. Earth's Guardians would have scanned them before allowing them to leave; they had been brought to Anwara aboard a Habber ship. The infected immigrants had come to Venus from the camp outside Tashkent; why was there no word of a similar outbreak there or at the Wheel, where the new settlers had boarded the Habber ship?

She was sure of the answer; others had seen it, too, before Yakov's announcement. The Habbers had done this. They would not have to use force to bend the Cytherians to their will; they had other means. This was an early experiment, and a warning.

How foolish the Habbers were! Did they really think they could frighten Cytherians in this way? Did they believe people might be cowed into granting the Habbers whatever it was they wanted? The Cytherians would only be more suspicious of them; Habbers still had a lot to learn about her people. Matthew, in spite of his concern for Kichi and others who were stricken, had even pointed out that the epidemic had presented Ishtar with an opportunity. Hadn't they warned people about the Habbers' possible intentions, and didn't this event prove that they were correct? Perhaps Ishtar had been too patient in waiting for people to come to the truth.

But what would Ishtar gain if they lost the Guide? Chimene twisted her hands together. Her face burned with rage at her helplessness; she longed to strike out at the Habbers who had done this and at all of those who had so easily tolerated their presence here.

The air felt cold; she hugged herself with her arms. She knew she should be sleeping; waiting here would do no good. She was about to get up but felt too weak to stand. She heard the soft sound of footsteps as someone entered the room from a hallway; she tried to lift her drooping head.

"Chimene, why are you—" It was Josefa Huong's voice. "Chimene!" A cool hand touched her face.

"I've got it, don't I?" Her throat was dry; the words came out with difficulty. Chimene sank back on a mat and closed her eyes.

Twenty people had died in Oberg, fifteen in Kepler, twelve in Tsou Yen. Anwara reported ten victims; six were dead and four were recovering. Two cases had shown up in Lyata; apparently a pilot had carried the virus there. Ibn-Qurrah had one case, Galileo three, and five of the Islands, including Island Two, reported deaths.

The low figures did not reassure Sigurd. The Island cyberminds had more data now, and he had studied their estimates. A thousand people might die before the epidemic was stopped, perhaps more.

Sigurd stood on the platform that circled Island Two and gazed through the dome at the darkness below. The quarantine here had been lifted earlier that day, but he could see no one else on the platform. The last of Island Two's residents had been vaccinated, but they had lost twelve people already and were likely to lose at least twenty more. Several of the dead had been pilots or workers on the Platform port; the loss of these people could only slow the Islanders' efforts to get additional supplies of the vaccine to the domed settlements.

His Link was silent. The Link would alert him to any unexpected turn of events that required his attention, but for the moment, he welcomed the silence.

He was aware of the rumors; even a few of the medical

personnel here were giving some credence to them. Habbers had done this; they were afraid that they might be losing their chance to gain more influence over Venus. The Habbers had seen that more people, even among the Islanders, were growing more sympathetic to Ishtar. What better way to decimate the cult than through the pilots who had to convey new settlers to the domes? Most of the pilots belonged to the fellowship, and a disproportionate number of Ishtar's adherents were among the disease victims. The epidemic would be both a warning and a way to get rid of a few enemies. The Habbers here had unwittingly added fuel to such suppositions by offering to help the medical teams in their laboratories and in tending to the ill; Tesia had pointed out that Habbers were able to resist the contagion. The offer was refused, amid talk that the Habbers might only be trying to infect even more people.

Sigurd did not believe the rumors. Most of his colleagues did not believe them either but were waiting to see if they could make use of them. The situation on Earth was changing once again; a Guardian Commander was becoming a more powerful rival of Ali Akar's on the Council of Mukhtars. Alim ibn-Sharif was one of the Island Administrators who was saying that it might be time to yield more authority to Earth now. Alim had been cultivating the Guide; he knew that Kichi Timsen's followers might put up with more control from Earth if that meant being rid of the Habbers. Alim was also thinking of his own ambitions. Sigurd, who had been so friendly with the Habbers here, might no longer be a suitable Liaison with the Project Council.

All of this musing was bringing Sigurd to a suspicion he was reluctant to face. Only Earth had anything to gain from an epidemic that might drive a wedge between settlers and Habbers. The Guardians might have planned this in secret, but the Mukhtars would also have to conceal whatever evidence they had about such a plot or risk losing a chance to regain control of Venus.

It did not matter that he had his suspicions; he would find no evidence in any records. Perhaps the epidemic was also meant as a warning to him.

"Salaam, Sigurd."

He looked around. Malik Haddad was climbing the

steps toward him. Except for a slight hollowness in his cheeks and a touch of silver in his dark hair, the historian looked much as he had years ago.

Malik leaned against the railing. "I just got a message from one of Chimene's housemates," he continued. "My daughter's ill. They don't give her much of a chance—the doctors may be too busy to get to her in time."

Sigurd bowed his head. "I'm sorry to hear it."

"Sorry?" Malik lifted his brows. "After she moved to that house, when I learned she'd been seeing that woman in secret for years—" He paused. "I wouldn't put it past Kichi Timsen to have used my daughter as a spy—a young, impressionable, lost girl who'd be happy to tell the Guide any Island gossip that might prove useful. Maybe you shouldn't be sorry."

"I'm sorry because it grieves you."

Malik sighed. "I suppose Ishtar will have a few martyrs now. It ought to help the surviving members to bring in more prospects."

Sigurd thought of the first time he had met Malik, at Pavel Gvishiani's funeral, and of how he had pitied the former Linker. Malik's disgrace had been caused, in part, by the suggestion in some of his work that human history was marked by a series of discontinuities akin to sudden evolutionary leaps, and the implication that humanity might be on the verge of another such leap. It was a vision at odds with the outlook of the Mukhtars, who viewed human history as a falling away from the perfect state outlined in the Koran.

He felt more pity for Malik now. The man had come to a world where it seemed that people would never escape what they were. Malik was also the victim of his own nature and carried the burden of history inside himself.

Sigurd stared at the dark clouds outside. Before the quake, he had been preparing an announcement; he had been planning to say that more Habbers would arrive to work in the Freyja Mountains and that the pace of construction there would be increased. He would be lucky if the settlers did not demand that all the Habbers be expelled. He should be back in his room, thinking of ways to put a stop to the rumors and to find allies among the settlers who might help him in that.

This was the struggle in which he was trapped—a

battle between those who embraced a human nature they believed could not be changed and those who were seeking to transcend it. Yet Earth, even though wedded to the past, had seen the need for a Project that might revitalize the old world with a new vision. The Habbers might have freed themselves from the old world, but they had not reached the point where they could sever their bonds to it completely. If they did so now and abandoned those they might have helped, their society would be rooted in two of the more ignoble parts of human nature—selfishness and the desire to protect oneself.

Each culture was a cell, with Venus as the membrane through which molecules from each cell could pass. Without such an exchange, the cells would die.

The Project, although it would strain Earth's resources to do so, could go on without the Habbers. Earth had tolerated them, almost as if dimly sensing that contact between the two strains of humanity was necessary, something the Habbers already knew. Tesia had shown him that with her love. She and her fellow Habbers had been waiting patiently to press on with this next stage of the Project. To give the Cytherians an industrial capacity that would make them more independent was important; the settlers, freed of being so dependent on others, might then be able to reach out to the Habbers as friends and to Earth as a viable, thriving culture.

The Habbers might decide to abandon Venus now. They would not force their presence on the settlers, since this would only poison what they hoped to create. He had deluded himself by imagining that he could bring closer ties between Venus and the Habbers. He had deceived himself by hoping that there would be enough time for Earth to understand that the Habitats were not a threat.

This current epidemic might pass, but another might take its place; Ishtar was already incubating the disease. The cult's vision of a perfect society was no more than a longing to embrace the prerational state of mind that had existed long ago. Sigurd did not have to study any sociological projections to guess at how far that contagion might spread now. He had been as careless as anyone else by assuming that the mutated descendants of humankind's biological and ideological past could not thrive here.

* * *

A physician named Arne Kenner met Risa outside her house, a female patrol member at his side. He scanned her quickly, then studied his small screen for a long time.

"You're not harboring the virus," he said at last. He stood up and thrust the med-scan console into his bag before pulling out an injector. "Either you weren't exposed or you have a natural immunity." The injector hissed against her upper arm.

She wanted to beg for the rest of her household but forced herself to swallow her words. Alasid had decided that she was one of the essential members of his team; she was being immunized only so she could go to work. Arne Kenner would have other people to see; if all of them wasted his time with useless pleading, that would only delay his progress. Her scan had been negative; maybe that meant that her household was safe.

Both the physician and the woman bore large red stains on their foreheads; the woman pressed a stamp against Risa's skull. "Keep your hair brushed back," she said to Risa. "You want the mark to be seen." The patrol would be able to see at a distance that she was not violating the quarantine.

The two hurried off before she could say anything more.

Risa kept her band on for much of the day, without a break. Her team, during the days following the quake, had spent most of its time repairing minor damage to the bunkers that provided the dome with air. Now a cooling unit was beginning to fail, and there were still rocks and boulders, loosened by the quake, to clear away from the small mines beyond the bunkers.

Alasid tapped her on the shoulder at the end of her shift. She removed her band; two people had already arrived for the darktime shift. "They say that the damned thing can incubate for weeks before symptoms develop," one of the men was saying to the other. "Makes you wonder how many will come down—" His eyes met Risa's. "I'm sorry about your daughter."

She lifted a hand to her throat. "My daughter?"

"Chimene." The man pulled at his red and black sash.

"A friend of mine who knows her housemates fairly well got a message earlier. I thought you knew or I wouldn't—"

"Tell me," she whispered.

"Chimene's ill. So is the Guide. They're pretty badly off. I'm sorry—"

She hurried out of the room. As she left the building, she saw a passenger cart, empty now, continuing on its route around the west dome's perimeter. The cart rolled toward the External Operations Center; Risa stepped into the main road. The cart slowed to a halt; she climbed aboard.

Chimene might die. She suddenly regretted all the harsh words that had passed between them; her daughter might die before they could be reconciled. But even that possibility didn't frighten her as much as the likelihood that Chimene had exposed Risa's household to the disease. Chimene had been in Risa's house just before the quake; Chen had told her that. She had bandaged his head before going off to aid other victims; she might have been infected even then.

No, she told herself, I'm well, and maybe the others are like me.

The cart rolled toward the Habber residence that bordered the road. The Habbers had offered to nurse some of the afflicted, but the Council had decided against that. Some people resented the Habbers already; allowing them to leave their residence to help others would only present the patrol with another problem.

Whatever she felt about Habbers, she was certain this epidemic was not their doing. Once this was past, even Ishtar would see that this was hardly a way to win goodwill among the settlers or to make them more trusting of Habbers. Earth's history was filled with stories of plagues that appeared unexpectedly, with entirely natural and understandable causes; she had learned that much from Malik.

The cart passed the tunnel leading into the southwest dome; she peered through the trees at residences until she spotted her own house. "Stop," she said.

She was out of the cart in an instant; she raced toward the house. A man was on patrol near the tunnel that led to the main dome; he lifted his wand. She shook back her hair so that he could see the mark on her forehead, then turned to cross the land in front of the house.

The door opened. Nikolai was leaving the kitchen with a bowl of soup; he tensed as he saw her. "Chimene's ill," she said. "I heard it at the Center."

"I know. Paul called from the infirmary—he and Tina heard it from a physician there—one of her housemates." Nikolai lowered his eyes for a moment. "I don't know how to say this. Chen's got it—so has Eleta. Emilia and Grazie are with them now. I sent Dyami and Irina to their rooms."

"Give me that." She took the soup from him. "I'm vaccinated—I'll take care of them. I don't want the rest of you taking any more risks."

"But—"

She hurried toward her daughter's room.

Iris was near. What could have brought her to his side? Chen moved his lips as he tried to call out to her, then felt a cool liquid trickle into his mouth. He swallowed, but the water did little to ease his parched throat.

"Chen," she murmured. He could not answer; he gasped for air. Something was wrong with the light; Iris's hair was longer and darker, and her eyes were brown, not the familiar green he remembered. She pressed a cold cloth to his head.

He had to tell her about the carving he had made as a model for her monument. She had chided him so often for carving others and not her; he had replied that he had no need for a carving, with the original at his side. Once he had admitted that he did not want to imprison her soul in a piece of wood.

Was she here to tell him that she had forgiven their son? Did she know about the message Benzi had sent him so long ago, saying that he would not forget them?

His mind drifted. He was once again on Island Two; he stood in front of a wall screen, with other workers pressed in around him. On the screen, a vast black pyramid trembled in the center of a lightning storm as lava flowed from its base. The workers had gathered to view images of this phase of the Project; Venus, shaken by this powerful antigravitational pulse, was beginning to turn more rapidly. They had waited a long time to view this event.

The images of awakening volcanoes and crumbling massifs filled him with awe, carrying him out of himself. He could forget the bondmate who no longer loved him, who had been swept away from him by her dreams and ambitions; only the new world mattered, the world their labor would bring into being. That world was heaving below him now, torn by the pangs of birth.

But Iris was with him. He recalled that she had come to him later, weeping over the son who had betrayed them by fleeing to the Habbers. The loss of Benzi had brought them together again, at first only because they needed each other's comfort, and later because they had managed to recapture their former love.

He had to tell Iris about the daughter she had never known and the grandchildren who now lived on Venus. He let out a sigh, but lacked the strength to speak.

"Father," Iris said. Why would she call him that?

The room vanished. The heat and black air of Venus pressed in around him, an atmosphere he could not breathe, one that would crush him. Iris was still at his side. She beckoned; she wanted him to come with her now.

"Iris," he whispered as the darkness closed in around him.

At first, Chimene felt only a deep lassitude, a weariness so intense that she could not even open her eyes to see who lifted her head, fed her water and soup, and bathed her face with cold cloths.

Her face was burning; her body ached and her lungs were filled with fluid. She struggled to breathe. Someone leaned over her; she closed her eyes.

"I've had my doubts." Kichi was speaking to her now. "I thought I might never find my faith, but it came to me when I needed it most."

I'm dying, she thought, I'm dying because I don't have enough faith. Forgive me—don't let me die alone.

Don't you know that you cannot be alone, that I am always with you, that even space-time presents no barrier to the Spirit?

She drifted, but a Presence was still with her, One that felt her suffering as Its own. The Spirit of Ishtar was inside her, lending Chimene her strength. She was Venus, burning with the heat of this world, longing for her transformation.

How could she have doubted? The Spirit was with her, sweeping away the clouds, easing the weight that pressed against her chest. The Spirit would not let her die; already, dimly, she could glimpse the light that would shine upon this world.

"Can you hear me?"

Chimene opened her eyes. A spasm seized her; she coughed, spitting up fluid. Matthew held her head, wiped her mouth, then eased her back on the bed.

She slept. When she awoke, Matthew and Eva were sitting on the bed watching her. "You're going to be all right," Matthew said. "You fought it for three days, but you'll get better now." Her sheets felt soiled, but she was too weak to move. Matthew came to her, picked her up, and settled her on a mat.

"We have to change your bedding," he murmured. "Don't worry about us. A physician came here to vaccinate us just an hour ago—we're clean."

She lay there passively, listening to the rustle of the sheets. The Spirit had reached out to her; she should have known that death could not touch her as long as she held to her faith. Kichi had been right; faith had come when she needed it most.

"I saw the light," she tried to say; her voice cracked. "I heard the Spirit." The words were inadequate; they could not convey the perfection of that moment, the loss of all barriers, the instant when the Spirit had filled her and purified her. Even the rite had never given her such a moment of joy.

Matthew lifted her to the bed and gave her a sip of water. Chimene fell back against the pillow. "Eva's gone to get you some soup," he said.

"Kichi," she said. "The Guide was right. I—"

Matthew sat down and clasped her hands. "I kept telling myself you couldn't die," he said. "I was watching over you. I nursed you and I prayed for you. I think you're strong enough to hear what I have to say now."

"What is it?" she rasped.

"Kichi's with the Spirit now. The patrol came for her body a day ago. You know what this means. The Guide made a record of her choice, to be revealed to everyone after her passing, and all our brothers and sisters will know of it soon. You're our Guide, Chimene."

No, she thought, it's too soon; I'm not ready. Would the

Spirit abandon her again? She clutched at Matthew; he rested his blond head against her chest.

"You mustn't fear," he whispered. "I know you're young, but Kichi was led to you by the Spirit—she saw what was in you. I'll be with you, and so will the others. Kichi is gone, but the Spirit has left us our Guide."

Surely the Spirit would touch her now. She listened but heard only the sound of Matthew's breathing. The transcendent moment was past; the struggle she had not expected for years would now begin.

Gupta Benares walked toward Risa with his bag, then halted on the path outside her house. "You're too late," she said.

"Risa—"

"You're too late for my father and my daughter, and you're too late for Emilia. They came for the bodies before first light."

"But no one else is showing symptoms?"

She did not reply. He touched her arm; she struck him away. He stepped back and hurried inside.

She continued to sit under the trees until he came back outside. "Let me give you something to help you rest," the physician said.

"I don't want your fucking remedies. Go on—there are still others you can save."

Gupta hurried away. The door opened again; Sef and Nikolai walked toward her. "Risa," Sef said, "I just got a message about Chimene. She's recovering—she'll be all right."

Risa said, "She brought death to this house."

"You mustn't blame her for that—she couldn't have known."

"She brought death here. She shouldn't have been coming to see us in the first place, but the rest of you just had to be soft-hearted about it."

"Come inside—you need to rest." Sef's eyes were red; his broad shoulders sagged with grief and weariness. "We all need rest." He held out his hand; she shrank back. He gazed at her for a few moments, then went back inside.

"Irina's asleep," Nikolai said. "With the antibody treatment, her symptoms won't get any worse, and Gupta says she'll be almost recovered by tonight." He paused. "At least you still have Dyami and Sef."

She looked up, then got to her feet. The lines in his broad face had deepened, and shadows darkened the hollows under his blue eyes. She gripped his hands. "Kolya—"

"Irina will be all right. I might have lost them both. I—" His throat moved as he swallowed. "Let's walk. I haven't been outside in days. I don't want to be in the house right now."

They walked toward the path. Gupta was already leaving the house next door; another physician was entering Thierry Lacan-Smith's house. The door to Lucas Ghnassia's home opened; two members of the patrol carried a body outside and laid it on a litter. Risa heard a wail before the door closed. She kept her eyes on the path, afraid to look at the other houses.

They continued on their way in silence until they reached the lake. The surface was smooth, almost glassy, undisturbed by any wind.

Risa said, "I would have traded Chimene's life for Eleta's."

"You mustn't say such things."

She began to weep. Nikolai held her; his body trembled, and then she heard his choked sobs.

Twenty-three

A third memorial pillar had been erected only a week before in Oberg's main dome; the images of some of those who had died of the fever filled the spaces on the other two. Oberg had lost nearly a hundred and fifty people, half of them residents of the main dome. The other three domes had been more fortunate, Risa thought; everyone said so, although most were careful not to speak of their luck in her presence.

She stood with her household, waiting for Yakov Serba to speak. They had waited until Patrick was home from his shift on the southern Bat to hold this dedication; Yakov had offered to say a few words. It was one of the duties of the Council members to speak at such ceremonies; at least one Councilor had been present at all the others.

This would be the last ceremony honoring those dead of the fever. Risa glanced at her household. Paul and Grazie stood together, hands clasped; Bettina leaned against Patrick. The physician seemed weak and fragile, as if, without her grandson's supporting arm, she might crumple to the ground. Nikolai's head was lowered, and his hand rested on his daughter's shoulder; Irina's eyes filled with tears as she looked up at her father. Sef's jaw was tight with tension. Risa had not seen her bondmate cry since the death of their daughter. Sef did not give in to tears; he had explained to her once that his people on Earth were like that, shunning open displays of such emotions. The strain of holding himself in was beginning to show on his face. Dyami was also restraining himself. His body was still, his brown eyes blank, but his lips were raw where his teeth had bitten into them.

Chimene stood a little apart from the others. She was wearing a black tunic and pants, with her sash around her waist; her head was bowed. Perhaps she was praying to her Spirit. Risa's anger flared and then faded. Chimene's household, including a man named Boaz Huerta who had recently joined them, had sent individual messages of condolence; Risa had feared that they might also come to this ceremony. She could not have endured that in silence, seeing her daughter here with some of those who had corrupted her and turned her into the Guide's successor. At least Chimene had the grace to arrive alone.

No one else had come. Noella had offered to attend, but Risa had dissuaded her old friend and had made it clear to others that she did not expect them to be here. She had not even listened to most of the messages of condolence; she could not have borne hearing such sentiments in person.

She searched the pillar. Emilia Knef's placid, smiling face had been set next to Eleta's broad one; carvings done by Chen had been used as models for the images cast in metal. Chen was commemorated with the standard holo portrait; during all his years in Oberg, he had never made a carving of himself. His face was serene; his eyes stared past her in the direction of Iris's monument.

Risa's eyes stung; she blinked back her tears. Chen would have told her that he'd had a long life, spanning over a century; he would not have wanted her to wallow in grief over his death. Perhaps it was a mercy that he had never known of his granddaughter's passing.

Yakov stroked his short beard; he was about to speak. He suddenly lifted his hand; Risa turned her head.

Malik was hastening toward them, a small duffel slung over his shoulder. He came to Risa and embraced her; she pressed her face against his chest. "I didn't think—"

"I had to come," he replied. "I had to be here—a message didn't seem enough. I'm sorry, Risa." He released her and gripped Sef by the elbows, then stepped back. Chimene was watching her father; Malik looked away from her.

"We have come here to commemorate three Cytherians," Yakov began. "Liang Chen was one of the earliest members of our community. He never claimed to be more than a humble worker, but many would say that without the courage he showed in the past, when the Project itself was threatened, we might not be standing on this world. Chen helped us build what we have now, and he added his own touch of beauty to it."

Yakov paused. "We also come here to remember Emilia Knef. Emilia was also one who would claim little for herself, but her steadiness and practicality were always a source of support for those closest to her. People like Emilia are the bedrock of our world." He lowered his voice. "And we mourn Eleta Liang-Talis, one who was born here and who knew no other place. Her death may be the hardest to bear, for her life was brief and she was robbed of the chance to make her own contribution."

Risa's throat tightened. She thought of how she had nursed Eleta, of the time the little girl had taken her first small steps, of the way the nursery workers had praised her for her good behavior under their care, and of how quickly Eleta had taken to her first screen lessons and games. She closed her eyes for a moment, nearly overcome with grief; part of her own future had died with her child.

"We mourn those who are gone," Yakov was saying, "but our community survives. We must remember the dead while we go on with the work of the living. May their spirits watch over the world they helped to build."

Risa bowed her head. When she looked up once more, Yakov had gone to Bettina; he took her hands as he murmured to her. Chimene's lips moved; she seemed to be whispering a prayer.

"I'm sorry," Malik murmured to Risa. "It's all I can say, but it doesn't seem enough."

Chen had been so happy to have a scholar in their house; he had taken even more pride in seeing Malik become her bondmate. It all seemed so long ago, part of a brief interval during which Chen had believed that his daughter's future happiness was ensured. She swallowed hard.

The other members of the household were clustered around Yakov; Patrick was closer to the glade, speaking to Chimene. "You're welcome to stay with us until you go back," Risa managed to say, "unless Chimene—"

"I'll stay with you," Malik said quickly. "It'll just be for a couple of days. There's no reason for me to stay with Chimene." His voice sounded cold. "Risa, I have to say this. Maybe you could come to one of the Islands to live, you and Sef and your son. I could speak to Sigurd, see if there might be a place for you. It might be easier than staying here, with your memories."

"This is my home. I can't leave it, not now, and I don't want any special privilege. Chen wouldn't have wanted that—he'd expect me to stay and go on, the way he did when he lost my mother."

"I only thought—I worry about what might happen here now." He was gazing at Chimene. "Even on the Islands, more people are giving credence to those baseless rumors about the Habbers, and Ishtar's benefiting, saying they were right all along."

"It'll pass."

"I'm not so sure. Sigurd thinks he can stop the talk by reasoning with people and demanding stricter procedures with new arrivals at Anwara and the Platform so something like this can't happen again. He believes people will be reassured if he points out that we could have prevented this. I don't know if he's being naïve or if he simply sees no alternative."

Yakov approached them. Malik touched her arm. "I should speak to Kolya." He went to the others as the Councilor took her hands.

"My sympathies, Risa," Yakov said. "Your household suffered more than most. I'm sorry I couldn't be more eloquent."

Her sorrow welled up, mingled with rage at the useless words and pointless deaths. There had been no prayers for her loved ones; Chen had put no faith in prayers. Maybe it would have been easier for her if she had found a faith of some kind.

"You spoke very well," she managed to respond.

"I also wanted to talk to you." His voice was lower; she had to strain a little to hear him, even standing so close. "I know this isn't the place, but there isn't much time. Another election comes up in a month, and Ishtar's certain to get at least one of its members on each of the dome Councils. It's not likely I'd win now. Ishtar knows I barely tolerate them, while some of those who dislike the cult think I've shown weakness in dealing with them. Maybe I have, but I didn't think they'd get a chance to get stronger. You could run in my place."

"It wouldn't work."

"Do you think they'll still hold a past mistake against you? Many have already forgotten about that. Some probably think you did the right thing every time they pass that detention center and see members of Ishtar trying to save and forgive those wretches. You'd have support, and even Ishtar might have problems working against you, since you are the mother of their new Guide."

"I suppose you've done some sort of projection," she said, "to see what my chances are."

"Projections of a vote can be wrong."

"They haven't been yet."

"Times are more uncertain now," he said. "There are new factors that can't be as easily assessed. What do you want, a guarantee? We'll have to stand against them sooner or later."

"I know that, Yakov," she said softly, "but engaging in futile efforts won't help." That was what it came to, she supposed; she could not let Chimene see that Risa might be her enemy if she was to work against her. She might have to deceive her own daughter in order to fight Ishtar's influence. She felt as though the cult had already poisoned her. "We'll find other ways."

He bowed a little, then walked away. Risa took a breath, and began to move toward her daughter. "—with the Spirit now," Chimene was saying to Patrick. "I have to believe that. Even death is no barrier to Ishtar."

"They weren't believers," Patrick answered.

"All it takes is one leap to a faith that might have come at any time. Perhaps it came to them in the end. The Spirit doesn't seek to punish but to unite, and feels only sorrow when a soul is lost to Her."

Chimene would try to infect them even here. Risa gritted her teeth, then extended a hand to her daughter. "I hope you can be with us tonight," Risa murmured. "Some of our neighbors will be coming by to pay their respects."

"Then I shall," Chimene said. "I can attend a meeting near your house and come there afterward. Risa, I—" A troubled look came into her dark eyes, then passed. "I love you. You know that, don't you? I wanted so much to have you see that, but it pains me so deeply that this is what brings us together."

"You're my child." A bitter taste filled her mouth. "Nothing can change that."

Chimene's eyes glowed; a blush rose to her cheeks as Sef led Dyami over to them. Her face was serene now; for a moment, Risa felt as if she were with Kichi Timsen again. She looked away as the Guide clasped Sef's outstretched hands.

THE CAULDRON

Twenty-four

Two women on patrol were standing next to the main road as Chimene left the tunnel, their forms shadowed in the dim light. One of them moved toward her, then hesitated.

"Excuse me," the woman said. "I didn't realize it was you."

"Don't apologize," Chimene responded. "You have every right to wonder why I'm out so late. I was visiting with the parents of a few of my students, and I'm afraid I lost track of the time. I didn't run into anyone on patrol or I would have told them I was heading home, so you could have been informed. You must treat me the same way you would anyone else."

"Of course." The woman glanced toward the trees just beyond the road. "Maybe we can walk you home."

"That won't be necessary. Good evening."

Chimene crossed the road. As she hurried through the small forest, she heard twigs cracking behind her; apparently the two women had decided to follow her anyway. They were thinking of her safety, she supposed; a woman had been attacked not far from here a few weeks earlier. At the offender's hearing, the man claimed that his victim had enticed him, a statement that had particularly disgusted Chimene. She hated such crimes, infrequent as they were, since they only debased the act through which people showed their love for one another and the Spirit. The man would be in detention for many years now, and he would have to wear an identity bracelet with a tracer.

Already he had paid a lot of credit in reparations, but his punishment seemed too mild.

Yet even someone that base could be led to the truth. She had encouraged others to speak to the man about Ishtar, in the hope that he might find enlightenment. When he saw the truth, he would be overcome with remorse for what he had done; that might be a fitting punishment, one he would endure for the rest of his life. She dismissed the man from her thoughts; such offenders troubled the settlements only rarely.

She came to the creek and followed it toward her own house. A neighbor leaving a greenhouse waved at her as she passed. In the eleven years Chimene had been the Guide, Ishtar had achieved more than even Kichi had envisioned. Nearly half of the people in Oberg had joined the fellowship, and the same was the case in the other domed settlements. They had even won a fair number of adherents among the Islanders, although she suspected that some of them were less than fervent in their faith and only thought it was to their advantage to join. That did not matter; they might come to the truth in time. Those not part of the fellowship seemed content to live with Councils dominated by Ishtar's members, and why shouldn't they? The patrol protected them, and many of them sympathized with Ishtar's dreams of peace and freedom.

The Cytherians had also not forgotten the unhappy events of 615 and the fever that had taken so many lives. Chimene's first important act as the Guide had been to pressure Administrator Sigurd into removing all Habbers from the Maxwell Mountains, an action he had agreed to out of concern for the safety of the Habbers there. The only Habbers remaining on the surface were in Turing, the two-domed settlement in the Freyja range.

Sigurd probably saw this as a temporary concession, but it was only a first step. She was determined to see Habbers expelled from Turing and the Islands and to rid her world of their insidious influence. They thought they could rule here; they would learn better. Then it might be necessary to deal with Sigurd, who believed Chimene could be appeased with a few kind words and favors. Perhaps he was still so besotted with his Habber woman that he could not see how Tesia's people were using him while pretending to be his friends.

Chimene pressed her lips together. Sigurd spoke to her as though she were a child to placate and dismiss. He thought he could control her; he would learn.

But such musings were unworthy of a Guide. She should be thinking of what was in the interests of her people, not of personal resentments. Sigurd was useful; when he no longer was, and another held his place, maybe the loss of his power would leave him more able to find the right way.

She walked up the path to her door. A few neighbors or some of the pilots from the dormitory usually visited in the evening, but they would be gone by now. She did not expect to find anyone in the common room, but Matthew and Boaz were still up, reclining on mats in the center of the large room, a pot of tea between them.

"You're late again," Boaz said with a smile. "Everyone else, except for Eva, is already asleep."

"I had to speak to some parents. They wanted to know about some additional tutoring for their children."

"I hope one of your colleagues can handle it," Matthew said. "You work hard enough as it is."

"No more than anyone else."

Eva entered the room with a small tray of fruit; Chimene seated herself on a mat. Boaz handed her a cup of tea; she sipped, savoring the taste of the mint and herbs.

"I've been thinking," Boaz murmured. "Maybe you should consider giving up your work as a teacher. It wouldn't be that difficult to find another to take your place."

"I couldn't do that," she said. "We all have to work. What kind of an example would that set?"

"I'm considering what's best for Ishtar. You have to get up early if you want to see any of your pupils before school, spend time on your own screen lessons, and see the children or their parents afterward, in addition to assessing their progress and recommending what they might pursue later. It might not be such a strain if you didn't have your duties to Ishtar as well."

"I'm a teacher," Chimene said firmly. "I was told I had the aptitude, and I chose the work—I made a commitment."

"You also made a commitment to your brothers and sisters. If you weren't teaching, you'd have more time to travel to the other settlements and the Islands, to speak directly to our members there—they value such contacts with the Guide. You could devote more attention to Council matters when we Councilors need your advice. You could make more efforts to win others to our fellowship."

"I can't give up my work."

Boaz sighed. "You wouldn't be giving up work—you'd be doing other work. You can always join one of the community greenhouse teams—that would satisfy your obligation to the Project and leave you with more time than you have now. With what the rest of us earn and the contributions we're given, our household would have enough credit."

Chimene shook her head. "I can't see how it'd benefit Ishtar if people see the Guide ignoring some of her obligations."

Boaz touched her arm lightly. "I was only thinking of you, Chimene."

He was thinking of her; he said that so often, usually when he was telling her what to do. He advised her on what to say to Sigurd, which people should be seen more often, and whom to avoid. As one of Oberg's elected Councilors, Boaz often settled some problems without consulting with her; that too was allegedly in her interest, so that she wouldn't be unduly distracted. She had grown to rely on both him and Matthew, who almost always agreed with Boaz; they had eased her insecurity during her first years as the Guide.

At times, however, their solicitude seemed a barrier separating her from others. She was beginning to wonder if she depended too much on their advice.

"It's your decision," Matthew said. "Anyway, that isn't the only thing we wanted to discuss with you now. We've been biding our time long enough about those Habbers on the Islands and in Turing. Some are saying that by continuing to ignore what they did in the past, we make it more likely that they'll tighten their grip on our world. We should rid ourselves of their presence once and for all."

"I spoke to Administrator Alim ibn-Sharif just a little while ago." Boaz's dark eyes narrowed as he spoke. "He says more of the Islanders are getting impatient. They know things can't remain this way, with the Project stalled and Sigurd hoping that we'll eventually forget what an affront the presence of Habbers here is. Habbers are cowards—they can work only through guile and deceit, not with force. If they see they're no longer welcome anywhere here, they'll retreat quickly enough."

Eva set down her cup. "I'm not sure we should be so anxious to expel the Habbers soon."

"Their agreement with the Project states that they can remain here only as long as they're welcome," Matthew replied. "If we held any kind of a referendum now, a majority would vote to be rid of them, and even Sigurd would have to abide by that or else show himself to be one of their minions openly. Do you think the Habbers would stand against such a decision? They haven't shown themselves to be all that brave in the past, and if they tried to defy us, a few threats against those here would change their minds. Their unnaturally long lives have made them weak—they cling to all those years stretching ahead of them."

"I wasn't thinking of what the Habbers might do," the blond woman said. "Having them in Turing serves our purpose for the moment."

That was true, Chimene thought. Boaz and Matthew had seen the possibilities the domed settlement in the Freyja Mountains presented. Even with the delays that had slowed work there, the mining and refining center was providing the other settlements with some needed materials, and another facility was producing ceramics that would be an improvement over the ones now used in various installations.

Yet this was less important than what Turing had come to represent. Some settlers still welcomed the prospect of working with the Habbers. Turing was a place without patrols, a settlement that attracted those who found Ishtar's growing power burdensome, and several people had applied to be sent there.

Chimene had not been pleased by this state of affairs, but Boaz had convinced her of the wisdom of leaving Turing alone. "Let the discontented gather there," he had argued. "Let them imagine that Habbers can be their friends. It'll lull the Habbers, and also show us exactly who the most recalcitrant people are—people who would otherwise be here to spread their discontent. Let them think they're safe there, and when the time comes to do something about them, we'll know exactly where many of our potential enemies are."

She had conceded the point, although she had not cared for the reference to other settlers as their enemies. Habbers were enemies; other Cytherians were simply people who had not yet seen the truth. Allowing some of them more contact with Habbers was only a temporary measure; when they lost their Habber friends and saw how easily they would be abandoned, they might grow more receptive to Ishtar.

She frowned. It had been easier to consider the matter objectively before Dyami had gone to work in Turing. That her own brother could wound her in that way—

Chimene steadied herself. Dyami had never warmed to her even after the rest of Risa's household had made their peace with Chimene. Risa remained somewhat distant, but at least she was polite; she had even tolerated Sef's becoming a member of Ishtar. Chimene sensed that Sef was not terribly devout, but he and Nikolai had taken that first step, and the others in the household were always friendly to her when she visited them. Only Dyami insisted on carrying an unspoken and unspecified grudge against her.

"You know," Boaz was saying to Eva, "that we never intended to leave Turing alone indefinitely."

"If and when the Habbers leave," Eva said, "Earth may see it as a chance to act, and we'll need Earth's help then to push forward. The Mukhtars are not going to aid us purely out of the goodness of their hearts, especially now that a Guardian Commander has a place among them. They'll demand more control over us. Our people won't be very happy about that."

"Eva's right," Chimene said, "much as I hate to admit it. I want the Habbers expelled, but not at the price of bowing to Earth later."

Boaz lifted his head. "It's possible to deal with Earth. The Habbers may seem indifferent to us now, but you know what they think of Ishtar. We mustn't allow them to subvert misguided Cytherians and try to win them over to their inhuman ways. Kichi knew that we might be forced to deal with Earth eventually, repugnant as that is. The Spirit isn't well served by pointless acts of defiance. Coming to some sort of arrangement soon may help us keep what we're trying to build, and it would be only a temporary agreement until we have the power to stand alone. We could make a few concessions to Earth as long as the Mukhtars don't interfere with our fellowship. We have enough influence now to convince most Cytherians that Earth is no real threat to our eventual goals."

Boaz had never stated this view so baldly before. Chimene looked into Matthew's gray-green eyes; the blond man seemed untroubled by Boaz's words. She wanted to protest; such an agreement would make their talk of free Cytherians a lie.

She knew what Boaz would say to that. "Your faith does you credit." He often told her that. "But to serve the Spirit sometimes requires that you temper your faith with practicality. You can't be wrong if the means you use serve our ends."

She set her cup on the floor. "We may have other alternatives," she said. "The Council of Mukhtars is still far from being united. Maybe Earth will be so grateful when the Habbers are gone that they won't ask us for anything in exchange for more of their aid, since we will have eliminated their rivals here." She got to her feet. "I must sleep."

She went to her room. Kichi had slept in the large bed, had sat at the desk in the corner, had rested on the cushions while speaking to Chimene about her faith. She suddenly wished, as she so often did, that Kichi were still alive and here to advise her. Kichi had promised Chimene that she would find her own faith, but she hadn't told her how precarious that faith might be. Moments of enlightenment, of sensing the Spirit inside her, came only rarely before slipping away. Chimene often had to struggle to recall how such moments felt. Kichi had died too soon, before Chimene was ready to replace her.

She undressed and got into bed, huddling under the sheet. She had thought that, after she became the Guide, she would escape the need for deviousness and actions that seemed contrary to the right way. That had been a foolish hope. She might soon have to deal with Earth, and some deviousness in working around Sigurd was already required; more secrets would have to be kept.

This was one of the paradoxes of being the Guide or one of those closest to her; while leading as perfect a life as possible, one also had to accept necessary evils in the furtherance of Ishtar's aims. She would have to engage in repugnant actions in order to bring her perfect world into being and yet keep her own faith pure. She would not be able to avoid certain decisions, but she had ways in which to reason about them and come to the proper conclusions. Kichi had tested her mind with paradoxes, mental puzzles, and apparent contradictions often enough to prepare her for that.

Her door hissed softly as it opened; she heard the sound of footsteps and then the rustle of clothing. The bed shifted slightly under her; she felt a hand on her head.

She caught a glimpse of Boaz's brown-skinned face before she closed her eyes once more. He stroked her hair, apparently sensing that she wanted only to be held. She had never admitted it to him, but Boaz had to know how difficult it had become for her to take pleasure with a lover alone; he had tried often enough to please her. Only during the rite could she give herself freely.

"You do love me, don't you?" he said.

"You know that I do."

"As you love all your brothers in Ishtar. I still hope that you love me just a little more than that, even though I know you must love us all." He was silent for a while. "I can still long for your child."

He had been pressing her about this for some time now. "Is that why you want me to give up teaching, so that I'd have more time for a child?"

"Of course not. There's the nursery and the rest of the household to help out. The child wouldn't be ours alone, but Ishtar's. We have no children in this house, and we've been content with that, but I can't help thinking that a child might draw us all closer to the Spirit. She could know a nearly perfect love—she could grow up to be an example of what we hope all Cytherians will become."

She nestled closer to him. "Why would she have to be ours? Any child would do. Our love should extend to all children. Whether a particular child is mine or not shouldn't matter."

"I know what you're thinking. You're afraid that if you had your own child, that might inhibit your love for others, that you'd fall into error by feeling that your child mattered above all others. It doesn't have to be that way. You could see her as a gift to Ishtar, one who will give more love to others, who will never know the barriers that hold people back from the truth."

The temptation was too great; she did fear that too much of her love might go to her child. Perhaps if her faith were as strong as Kichi's had been, she might have risked it.

"You want a child," he went on, "but you're afraid to have one. I want one with you because I know that then there would always be that bond between us, apart from the love you'd give to any of your brothers. Shouldn't we confront this temptation and overcome it instead of shying away from it? There's virtue in struggling with one's flaws and conquering them. There's nothing praiseworthy in trying to pretend they don't exist and refusing to confront them. Do you want to go through life always wondering if the love you have for others is no more than a substitute for the love you couldn't give a child? Kichi knew that love for all often begins with love for one."

Boaz could be so persuasive. She might have more learning than he did, but she often felt helpless during their gentle, restrained arguments. Both he and Matthew, in spite of being only two mechanics who had found their way here from Earth's camps, often seemed more learned than most such people. But then, they had always been quick, and they had also had Kichi to instruct them.

"I feel that the Spirit may be preparing you for this child," Boaz said. "I've thought about this deeply, and never once have I had the feeling that this is merely a temptation and no more. I think the Spirit wants this child. It may even be that someday she'll take your place as the Guide."

She tensed. That was too great a temptation, one even Kichi had avoided by choosing to have a son. She wanted to tell Boaz that he was wrong, but the words did not come.

"I'm still young," she said at last. "We have many years ahead of us to consider this. I can't think of it now when there's so much else to worry about."

"I'm not saying we should have this child right away. But we could at least store our genetic material. Plenty of people do that, just in case—"

That was true enough. Those who were certain they wanted children, but who wanted to wait, sometimes

Pamela Sargent

stored their sperm or eggs in the medical laboratories. If
an accident befell one's bondmate in the meantime, the
surviving partner could then petition for a child created
from the stored material. If the survivor was a male or a
woman too old or otherwise unable to carry a child safely,
an embryo could be brought to term in an ectogenetic
chamber.

Such practices were more common among the Islanders, who had somewhat more advanced medical facilities
than the dome-dwellers, but even Islanders did not want
to rely too much upon these techniques. Most people in
the settlements had their children while still young, with
only basic scans and whatever gene transplants might be
necessary to repair any defects. But lately, more dome-
dwellers had taken to preserving their genetic material;
they remembered the casualties that the quake and fever
of 615 had brought.

It was also possible to store an embryo or a fetus cryon-
ically, but this was resorted to only in special circumstances; neither the Islanders nor the surface settlers
wanted to overburden their medical facilities with such
additional responsibilities. Chimene had other reasons for
looking askance at this practice; unlike other medical procedures, it did not further natural ends and was too close to
the kinds of things Habbers did.

She could not find any theoretical objection to Boaz's
suggestion. Until the time Cytherians would be free of
their dependence on such technologies, when the Spirit's
power gave them control over their minds and bodies,
they could make use of tools that furthered the natural end
of having young. She could, however, see practical problems. The laboratories were still limited in how many they
could aid. Those who had lost a child, who were exposed to
the more hazardous work on the Bats, or who did not yet
have children but were committed to having them with a
particular partner would have their requests to store their
genetic material granted. Others without compelling reasons were usually turned away.

Chimene sat up. Boaz was slouched against a pillow,
his muscular arms folded across his bare chest. She
glimpsed a distant, icy look in his dark eyes before they
warmed with his familiar concerned expression.

"I wonder if we have the right to ask for this," she said.

"I don't see why not. You're thirty, older than most are before having children. I'm a few years older, and I'm childless. You also leave this settlement more often than most people, and one can never discount the possibility of an airship accident. And even if those reasons aren't enough by themselves, you're also our Guide. Several physicians are part of the fellowship, and Galina would plead your case with them."

"Being the Guide doesn't give me special privileges—that's contrary to everything we believe. Anyway, the physicians would have to know that we're both committed to having this child. Taking this step is tantamount to saying we've already made that decision, whatever happens and however long we might postpone it—we can't have people burdening the infirmary's lab for capricious reasons. What kind of example would I set as Guide if I do this without being sure?"

"You want a child," he said. "I see it even when you try to deny it. I've waited and I've hoped—" He leaned forward, draping one arm across his raised knees. "I'm thinking of what's best for you as the Guide. You want a child, but you're afraid to have one because you worry that such a particular love will outweigh the love you should have for all. You'll go on postponing any decision, and then one day you'll realize that you made a needless sacrifice to duty, when it may be too late to change your mind. How much love will you have for your sisters and brothers then? You may only resent them because of what you gave up. How will that make you a better Guide?"

"A Guide must live in a way others can't," she replied. "This isn't even something I have to decide now. Later, when I'm—"

"You may wait too long—until more medical intervention is required. The physicians might decide it isn't worth the use of their resources to help one who couldn't make up her mind earlier." He took her hand. "Chimene, making this decision now, knowing that you had committed yourself to having our child, would force you to confront your fears and work through them. When she's with us, you'll see how groundless your worries were. You'll be stronger, and you'll have more love for others growing out of that love. Your child will be one of your contributions to Ishtar's future."

She slipped her hand from his. "Those aren't your only reasons. You can't just be thinking of me—you want this child too much. You must be thinking of yourself, too."

"I want this bond between us—I'll admit that. I'm not yet so close to perfection that having a child with the woman I love most wouldn't mean more to me than the rest of Ishtar's children. But that isn't the only reason. If anything happened to you—"

He pulled her gently toward him. "I couldn't bear it," he continued. "I love you too much, Chimene. I tell myself nothing will happen, and then I think of how I felt when I learned you were ill with the fever. I knew I loved you the first time we shared the rite together—I always prayed you'd choose me after that or that I could be with you every time you showed your love for others. I knew that, if you died, any love I bore my sisters in Ishtar would die with you. I couldn't stand living in a world where no part of you was left for me. Can't you show some love for me by saving me from that sin—hating instead of loving? Can't you assure me that something of you would remain with me?"

She could not reply.

"If anything happened to you," he said, "all of Ishtar would rejoice at knowing that at least a child of yours would live. But that won't come to pass, and you can help me put aside my fear. We'll prepare for this child, and when the time comes, when you know you're ready—" He swallowed. "Maybe you'll be ready sooner than you think, and we may never have to use what we've stored. But it would give me such joy to know that our child will exist, however long you wait. When it's done, you'll feel the same way."

Boaz wanted her child; he knew her well enough to see that, regardless of her worries, she wanted one as well, if only to fill the void she still sensed inside herself. That was the problem, that emptiness, a sin she would have found hard to confess even to Kichi. The love for her brethren that should have satisfied her was tenuous and unfocused, already a struggle to maintain. Having a child might drag her further back into an imperfect state, where an individual love mattered more than anything else, and make her unworthy to be the Guide.

Yet Boaz could be right. She might have to face this

possible obstacle to her faith and overcome it. Could there be anything so wrong in having the child they both wanted? Boaz had admitted that his love for her meant more to him than any other; he was facing a problem not unlike her own. She might not love him any more than she loved the rest of her brothers, but she did not want to lose him and depended on his advice. Refusing him now might only raise a barrier between them and drive Boaz further from the Spirit's love. Surely that was not a desirable end.

She pressed her cheek against his chest. "I'll think about this," she whispered. "I can't decide it now."

"At least you haven't dismissed it. You'll see I'm right." He eased her down beside him and held her until she drifted into sleep.

Sef was up. Risa lay in bed, watching him as he dressed. His body had changed very little; from the back, with his slim hips and long, muscled legs, he still looked much like the ardent boy who had come to her room nearly twenty years ago.

Sef pulled on pants and a gray tunic, then tied his red and black sash around his waist. Risa sat up and stretched. "I hate to see you wear that thing."

"Every time I don't, somebody's always ready to make a remark about it."

She did not pursue the topic. He had joined Ishtar partly to protect her, and Nikolai had joined so that Sef would not have to attend meetings alone. Neither of them thought any more of the group's tenets than she did.

She had once thought her household might need such protective coloration, back when she, Yakov Serba, and a few others had first begun to meet, trying to think of ways to combat the cult's growing influence. They had spent a lot of time devising elaborate passwords and ways to send coded messages to sympathizers in the other settlements, but their plotting had been largely fruitless.

Ishtar now had more followers, the Councils, and the patrol, and they had always claimed the loyalty of most of the pilots. Grief during the fever's aftermath had brought some to a faith that promised to ease their pain; anger at the Habbers had led others to the cult. Some had joined out of self-interest. Andrew Dinel, as a member, might now have to contribute more of his profits to supporting less prosperous members, in keeping with Ishtar's belief that more should be shared, but he had also increased the sales of his whiskey to people in the cult. Many others were simply passive bystanders, content to live with Ishtar as long as it left them alone.

Risa and those who felt as she did could plot all they liked, but there was little they could do. Violence against individual members of Ishtar would only bring retribution and more sympathy for the victims. Acts of sabotage that might be blamed on Ishtar could endanger too many lives, even threaten the domes themselves.

Some in Ishtar might already have guessed that others gathered in the hope of finding ways to stand against them, but they could probably afford to be indifferent. They had little to fear from disgruntled former Councilors, restless young people, some specialists who considered themselves intellectually above the cult, the few devout Muslims and Christians who muttered about infidels, and an occasional member of Ishtar itself who had trusted Kichi but had doubts about Chimene. Risa and her allies had no weapons other than malicious rumors, lies sometimes told to the patrol to protect someone else from an unnecessary hearing, jokes about the cult, and obscene or mocking inscriptions that appeared in the tunnels only to be covered quickly by the patrol or a team of workers.

More people should have seen what Ishtar was. An intellectual disease—that was what Theron called it. The cult was a drug that twisted emotions and lulled thought. Terraforming Venus was to have given part of humanity a chance to begin anew; Ishtar dreamed of returning to an unthinking earlier state. The sun might eventually shine on the Venus Ishtar wanted to create, but shadows would darken the souls of its people.

Reason was one of Risa's weapons, but it was one few people chose to wield. A cold blade that could cut through comforting illusions was no match for the mindless acceptance of a so-called truth that required little thought. It was enough to bring even Risa to think that the Habbers might be right in trying to alter part of their human nature.

"You'd better get up," Sef said. "You'll be late."

"I have today off, remember?" Risa got out of bed and

pulled a shift from the clothes rod. "Maybe you can come home early."

He shook his head. "Not tonight. They want a couple of us over in the airship bay to repair two crawlers, and apparently the team there asked for me. I ought to go to the meeting later, too—I haven't been to one for a month. Maybe I'll go to the one at Chimene's house. It usually draws a crowd, so I should be able to lose myself when it's over."

She looked up at his open, honest face. Sef's attitude toward Ishtar was simpler than hers. Metaphysical speculation bored him, and he was suspicious of anyone who claimed to know the truth. He disliked the cult but persisted in thinking that its adherents would eventually come to their senses. Chimene might have been misguided by her companions; he could not believe that Risa's daughter would knowingly be cruel or unfair.

He attended the meetings as little as possible and avoided the rite whenever he could. He offered the excuses others gave—that he felt unworthy, that he was still far from the right way and could not yet shed some of his ties with his bondmate, or that his thoughts would be with the Spirit when he went to Risa's bed. On the few occasions when he could not avoid the rite, when he was approached by a woman in the throes of religious fervor, he shared it with her apart from others.

Risa had learned not to ask about those encounters and was happier not knowing the specifics. They would mean nothing to any of the women, who might have shared themselves with other men as easily. They meant little to Sef; the rites and the meetings were events he tolerated so that Ishtar would not see him as an enemy and would leave his household alone.

The rites revolted Risa; she felt a bit ill whenever she thought of the number of times her daughter must have participated in them. People could so easily use their faith to justify deeds that would have repelled them otherwise; it had happened often enough in the past. Professions of faith could rationalize cruelty, persecution, even murder —or, in this case, the rutting of Ishtar's believers.

She could have understood it if Chimene had been more like a Plainswoman, someone who needed more than one man. But even Bettina had spoken scathingly of the rite; there was a difference between taking a new lover for a while and throwing oneself indiscriminantly into the arms of various men with other people present. One was an expression of love, although an admittedly temporary one; the other was hardly more than a perversion.

Chimene, of course, did not see things that way. As far as Risa knew, her daughter did not share her bed with anyone except Boaz Huerta or, less frequently, one of the other men in her household. Perhaps Chimene thought of herself as being virtuous by saving more of herself for the rite.

"I still don't like it when you go to meetings there," she said. It was hard enough for her to pay an occasional visit to Chimene's home, and she usually tried to pick a time when most of her daughter's housemates were elsewhere.

Sef cupped her face in his large hands. "Wouldn't it be better to have her see that we're concerned for her? She might need us sometime, you know. There's always a chance she might come to her senses. I want her to see that she can turn to us instead of just leaving her to those friends of hers."

"She might have had a bondmate by now and children." Risa sighed. "This house seems so empty sometimes. I wish Dyami were home."

Sef's arms dropped; he frowned for a moment. "He's safer in Turing for now."

"He should be here. He's nineteen—he ought to be thinking about a bondmate himself."

"Don't concern yourself with that, Risa. You waited before making a pledge yourself. He'll visit before too long, and you shouldn't pester him about pledges—that must be his decision." His troubled expression passed as he smiled. "I have to go."

By the time Risa had bathed, dressed, and gone out to the common room, Sef was gone. She began to gather the breakfast bowls and cups, piling them onto a tray. The house was quiet; Paul had said something yesterday about going over to the school to examine some of the children. Grazie and Nikolai would be at the community greenhouses today. She heard the sound of movement in the kitchen; Noella, she recalled, was on a darktime shift at the External Operations Center and would be home today.

Theron and Noella had become part of this household a few years ago. Noella had, after all, lived here for a while before she and Theron built their own house; she had decided to leave that house to her children and their bondmates. Risa had welcomed the couple, but even now the house often felt empty.

Bettina's face was now next to Chen's on the memorial pillars. She had weakened rapidly after his death, as though she no longer had the will to live; her inability to do anything for Chen had haunted the physician. Patrick was living in Kepler with his bondmate, whom he had met on the southern Bat, while Irina had moved in with her bondmate's family in ibn-Qurrah.

Noella, who was a little unconventional, could say what she liked about the wisdom of parents keeping some distance from their adult children, but her children and grandchildren were still here in the west dome; she had only to walk down the path to see them. Risa had once envisioned a house with more rooms and grandchildren to fill them, but only one generation lived in this house now.

She lifted the tray. Dyami would be visiting in a couple of months, and maybe one of his former schoolmates would hold more of an attraction for him now. She knew of at least three young women who asked her for news of her son; she would invite them over while Dyami was here. Sef might say that she shouldn't pester the young man, but she had seen him look a little worried when he spoke about Dyami; he was probably as concerned as she was.

They might have had another child together, but she had grieved too much over Eleta's death to consider it. Later, she had consoled herself by believing that there would be grandchildren. Perhaps she had made a mistake, and it was not too late to change her mind. She might petition the physicians to allow her the use of an ectogenetic chamber if she proved unable to carry the child herself, although at fifty-six, with over a decade of rejuvenation treatments behind her, there was still a chance she could.

Maybe she was simply too tired to take on a parent's responsibilities again. Perhaps she did not want another child of hers to grow up in Ishtar's shadows.

She went to the kitchen, set the tray down, and began to stack the dishes in the cleaner. Three large ceramic pots were atop the convection oven; she sniffed at the aroma of cooked fruit. Noella was stirring one pot.

"You didn't have to do this now," Risa said. "You could have slept late."

"I can get some rest later." Noella handed her a spoon. "You'll have enough to do with preparing the dried beans."

Risa leaned against the oven. "Things don't change all that much, do they? My grandmother's household on the Plains might have spent a day like this."

"Not very often, I expect. They probably had some sealed provisions and a dispenser."

Risa stirred a pot of berries. "Sometimes I think I made a mistake," she murmured.

The blond woman raised her brows. "You say that a little too often, Risa. Maybe you'd better have Paul scan you and see if your rejuv treatments are working. What mistake are you wondering about now?"

"Not getting more training—telling myself I knew most of what I had to know. I try to read when I can, but it isn't the same. I know a lot of things but not how to think about them." She paused. "Too many of us are like that. We do our work and tell ourselves we're building a new world, but we don't really think about what that requires. We think the work is enough, that we don't have to think of things differently. It's what makes something like Ishtar possible, with its easy answers and assurance that everything will be all right."

"You remember what happened when Theron tried to enlarge the curriculum a bit," Noella said. "He just ended up with parents telling him he was trying to turn their kids into dreamy scholars."

"Well, he was right to try," Risa responded, "even if I had my doubts at the time. A lot of the specialists get so caught up in their specialties that they've almost lost sight of any larger purpose in their work. Some of them probably wouldn't care about the settlements as long as the Islands remained and they could go on with what they do. And we learn less than we should about what they know, or what the Habbers might have added to their knowledge."

"People have a chance here. It's their own fault if they don't take it. Most people here mastered more than their parents did, and their own children—"

"—might decide it's easier to let others make their decisions for them." Risa put down her spoon. "Malik told me once that these settlements were an experiment. Terraforming Venus could have continued with only Islanders, but Earth wanted people to believe that even ordinary sorts had a stake in this Project. I suppose the Mukhtars thought it might dampen some discontent—even if somebody's own life seems pointless, there's a little consolation in thinking that some other simple souls elsewhere are capable of a greater enterprise. Now the results of the experiment are becoming clearer. We're showing that we can fall into the same traps Earth's people did. Maybe the Mukhtars expected that."

"I know," Noella said. "Maybe it was foolish to hope for more."

"I can't accept that. My parents didn't come here and give up their lives so that people trying to rid themselves of old bonds would decide to hobble themselves with new ones." She poked at the stewed fruit with her spoon. "Sigurd was trying for more. I didn't quite see that either until recently. It's why he wants the Habbers here. We could gain a lot from contact with them without becoming like them—that's what he thinks."

"I doubt he's thinking much about that now," Noella said. "He'll have all he can do just to maintain his own position."

That was true enough. Grazie had heard rumors that Ishtar's inner circles were growing more discontented with Sigurd. Risa did not discuss her meetings with Yakov and other troubled settlers with Grazie and Paul. Grazie gossiped enough to acquire some interesting information, but she was also too likely to say things she shouldn't to others. She and Paul were like too many people, content to let things be as long as they and those closest to them were secure.

This was what her life had come to—keeping a few secrets from two of her housemates and fearing her own daughter. At least Sef had never failed her, nor had her son, although she had been disappointed when Dyami chose to leave for Turing. She would forgive that when he came home; whatever she did was for Dyami and the children he would have someday. The situation would change again and perhaps present her with some way to strike out at Ishtar. She would not have her descendants live in the irrational darkness cast by the cult.

"We welcome all who are true Cytherians," Chimene said, "all who see that the shadows of doubt and despair must be swept away before we can become what we must be. We welcome those who sense the Spirit of this world, the one we must appease and embrace with both our strength and our love."

The room grew dark; then the screen behind her illuminated the gathering. Several people were gazing at the familiar sequence of images, still capable of being awed by those visions of Venus; others bowed their heads.

Her talk had gone well tonight; she had held their attention, as she usually did. Boaz might occasionally resort to more screen images to enliven his speeches, but she had never felt the need for many of them during her own talks. Words were enough; she had learned how to cast her spell, to caress her sisters and brothers with her phrases.

This talk had been a little different. She had hinted that Earthfolk, however benighted they were now, were not incapable of apprehending the truth and of living in peace with their own planetary Spirit. A few historical examples from the works she and Malik had once read together had proven useful, even though her father would not have cared for the use she made of them. She had worried before giving her talk that this group might be troubled by gentler words about Earth. Her worries had been groundless. These people loved their Guide and would accept whatever she said.

The ceiling light panels brightened. Her talk, as usual, had been captured by two tiny recorders on either side of the room. Eva and Lang would look at the recording later; if it worked as well on the screen as it had here, they would put it into the system so that others could view it.

She surveyed the crowd. She did not notice any new faces in the group of more than one hundred, and doubted that anyone would be coming forward to join, but she waited, just in case. She heard sighs as people began to stir. Sef was to her right, sitting against the wall. He had arrived late, just as the meeting was about to begin, but some people had made room for him there. He looked around restlessly, then caught her eye; he smiled. He often looked at her that way, as if she weren't the Guide but only the child who had lived for a time in his house.

One knot of people moved toward the door; others were beginning to stand. "You were so inspiring," a woman said to Chimene. Several people were lingering nearby, clearly hoping that the Guide or someone in her circle might invite one of them to join them in the rite. She often welcomed unfamiliar participants; leading a different man to shed a few more of his barriers always made her feel closer to the Spirit. She could recapture that all-encompassing moment of joy that eluded her at other times.

"I feel such love," a dreamy-eyed young man said. Chimene murmured a few words absently, then retreated to a corner near the screen. A few couples, arms around each other's waists, were moving toward the door. Chimene gazed in Sef's direction. He had not come to a meeting here for a while; surely he would stay for a few moments and share any recent news of his household. But he was already trying to push past those near him, as though anxious to leave.

She suddenly knew what she had to do.

Chimene beckoned to Eva. "Lang isn't with us tonight," she murmured; the gray-haired man was attending another meeting. "Sef will take his place. Ask him if he'll join us in the rite."

The pale-haired woman frowned. "Are you sure of that?"

"Yes. I feel it."

"Everything I've heard tells me he still has some inhibitions," Eva said. "I don't know if he's ready for this."

"I have faith that he is."

"Don't question our Guide," Boaz said behind her; Chimene turned to face him. "She sees deeply into the hearts of others. Ask the man to join us."

Eva walked toward Sef. Matthew came to Boaz's side, then took Chimene's arm. "He's still a barrier for you, isn't he?" the blond man said softly. "You haven't yet been able to see him as your brother in Ishtar but as your old love, one you couldn't have. That will pass when he joins us."

Sef tensed as Eva spoke to him. Chimene was afraid

that he might refuse. But he couldn't refuse; a few of the people next to him must have heard Eva's invitation. No one could turn away someone so close to the Guide; there was no possible excuse he could offer. None of those closest to her would ask anyone who was not ready; for Sef to reject this sign of their love would be the same as turning away from the Spirit. Others would wonder at his refusal; he would only shame himself by admitting he could not make his offering to them. That was why she was always so careful about those who were asked; she did not want to risk driving hesitant souls further from the truth by shaming them.

But he would not refuse. She knew what to say to him.

Chimene freed herself from Matthew and made her way to Sef. She gestured at Eva; the other woman left them.

"Your friend honors me." Sef's voice was strained. "But I don't know—"

"Eva longs to share her love for you," Chimene said quickly. This wasn't entirely a lie; she had heard Eva and Josefa whispering admiringly about Sef after other meetings. "I'm speaking to you as our Guide now. You wouldn't hurt a sister I love so much by retreating behind a barrier."

Sef's face reddened; he seemed embarrassed to be talking of this in the presence of others. His tall body slumped; his expression showed the uncertainty of a boy. "It's only that I feel unworthy."

"Eva wouldn't have spoken to you if you were," another man said. "She wouldn't make such a mistake. Surely you don't doubt her wisdom—or the Guide's."

"I know this is hard for you," Chimene said, "as it once was for me. The Spirit doesn't withdraw from those who might fail, only from those who don't make the attempt."

Sef's throat moved as he swallowed. She felt a little pity for him, and then it passed. He would learn that she was right and be grateful.

He nodded, silently assenting. The crowd was thinning; he stared at the floor. Galina and Yusef removed the tiny recorders from the walls; Matthew and Boaz walked toward the door, saying their farewells to a few of the worshippers.

"If I were alone with her," Sef said, "I could manage it then. You see, I haven't—"

"You musn't fear. There will be only a few of us. Do you think I would have allowed Eva to approach you if I had any doubt? You mean too much to me for that. You know that, don't you? Out of everyone in my mother's household, you were always the kindest to me."

He lowered his head; his eyes met hers. Those words had moved him—not the words of the Guide but of the girl he had treated as a daughter. For an instant, his gaze was more intense; he was not looking at her as a child now. The light in his eyes faded, but he had already told her what she longed to know.

He wanted her. Perhaps he had all along but had refused to acknowledge it to himself; maybe he had only just realized that he did. A barrier had fallen for a few seconds; now he was turning away, as if already denying what he had felt.

The Spirit had led him here tonight; she hadn't been wrong about that. Kichi had said she would lead Sef to Ishtar. Her heart pounded; her soul warmed with love.

Chimene stood with her three shrouded companions. The other men had given Sef a robe; he stood next to Yusef, his head bowed.

She went to him quickly, knowing that the Spirit guided her now. Her hand touched his lightly; she led him to a mat near the screen, away from the others. Usually she joined with other brothers during the rite's aftermath, when all barriers were gone, but she wanted this night to be theirs alone. This way of celebrating the rite was new to Sef; later, when he had accepted her love, he would be able to reach out to her sisters more easily.

They lay on the mat; his robe fell open. His hands groped awkwardly at her body through her shroud; he seemed uncertain of what to do. Was he imagining Eva? Was he hoping he would find Chimene? His hands slipped under the shroud, searching her.

Men had to appease the Spirit, but some needed more guidance. She had been with others who had shared themselves with only one woman in solitude or who were older and needed to be roused. She lowered her head and spread her shroud over him, careful to keep herself hidden, and felt him stiffen as she gripped him with her hand.

Her lips found him; she circled his shaft with her

tongue and felt him move under her. He moved inside her mouth; she caressed his testes gently with one hand as her tongue slid over him.

Ishtar had given him to her. She lifted her head, knelt with her knees on either side of him, and opened herself to his touch before guiding him into her. His back arched; he clutched at her hips. Her inner muscles tightened as she rocked on top of him; she lifted her shroud and let it fall.

Sef let out a cry. His face was distorted by horror; for a moment, she feared he might throw her from him. The screen image of a future Venus illuminated him with its dim greenish light. He twisted under her, and then his arms were around her, pulling her down to him.

"I love you," she whispered, feeling the soft hairs of his chest against her cheek. "I've always loved you, and now you'll love me, too."

The barrier between them was gone; he would appease the Spirit through her. A dart of pleasure stabbed inside her, then blossomed as her cries mingled with his.

Twenty-five

The airship rose above the peaks of the Freyja Mountains, then hovered a bit before it slowly moved southeast. Turing was now only two small glowing spots on an open plateau surrounded by walls of rock. As the domes disappeared behind the mountains, the image on the screen above the two pilots changed. A rust-colored stagnant mist hung over black barren slopes as yellowish droplets sifted down from above. The screen was showing an image of what people might have seen had there been any light to illuminate this dark landscape.

Dyami rested his head against the back of his seat. The image, there primarily for the diversion of any passengers, did not interest him; the mechanisms that were creating it did. The ship's sensors gathered data about what lay outside, but its lenses alone could not have produced this image. Fractal geometries were the lenses through which this landscape was glimpsed; using the data the ship collected with its sensors, the vessel's computer could calculate exactly what light would have revealed, down to the smallest detail. The image was a model based on the symmetries that underlay the rocks outside, the thicker pockets of mist, the movement of the atmospheric winds high overhead, the position of Venus in relation to the sun. The image was a picture built up from millions of parallel calculations; had the sun been shining down on Venus now, the world would have looked exactly like this. Mathematics could pierce the shadows and illuminate what might otherwise remain hidden.

Mathematical formulas were a tool, a way to find order, view the invisible, plot paths, discern what was possible, and describe chaos and disorder—the points at which a system began to break down or where a small variation might have a great effect on the whole. To Dyami, mathematics reflected a beauty and truth he longed to glimpse more often; his world seemed an imperfect shadow that had fallen away from their light.

He had never spoken such thoughts aloud to Balin, but the Habber clearly viewed the universe in a similar way. Yet he and the other man differed in some respects. To Balin, the technology with which he worked seemed almost incidental and was of interest only when it furthered his speculations. For Dyami, it was almost the reverse; he looked for ways to apply what he glimpsed. Mathematics provided a bridge linking him to Balin, the purest expression of the love Dyami felt, the only way, it seemed, that he would ever be able to express it.

The female pilot took off her band and turned to face him; her copilot continued to monitor the ship's panels. Dyami tried to ignore the sashes around both pilots' waists. "You must be glad to be going home for a while," she said.

"I suppose I am." He was the only passenger on the airship; some of the seats, and the aisle between them, held secured cargo—crates of refined metals used in circuitry and ceramics with a variety of purposes.

"It's odd that you, of all people, wanted to work in Turing. You are the Guide's brother, after all."

Dyami shrugged. "My sister has never offered an opinion about that. The Habbers wanted some of us to work with them there, and surely that makes more sense than leaving Habbers to themselves. It wouldn't serve our purpose to have them in control of Turing."

"Still—" The pilot rested her arms on the back of her seat. "There are dangers in being around Habbers too much, especially for those who lack faith. You can come to believe they're friends, and they can never be that."

"Seems to me we're being of service to Ishtar. True believers don't have to endure constant contact with Habbers or contamination by their thoughts, and you'll have a group of Cytherians who can eventually make use of what those Habbers teach us."

"Even so—" The pilot paused. "I've always wondered

why the Guide's own brother didn't choose to join our fellowship. That must cause your sister some sorrow."

"Chimene knows we must all find faith in our own way," Dyami replied. "Her love for our mother isn't lessened because Risa never joined. Don't you say that the Spirit must be embraced willingly and without coercion?"

"Yes, but sometimes one must be guided to make the effort. Some people are like children—they don't always know what's best unless you're a bit firmer with them. The Guide has been patient. I don't question her wisdom, but—" The woman smiled. "You should attend some meetings when you're back in Oberg. You may find that you're ready for enlightenment now, after being among our enemies for some time."

"Perhaps I shall." He lapsed into silence, keeping his eyes focused on the screen above her. At last she turned back and put on her band.

He did not like to think about Chimene. Her beliefs and obsessions were at the center of a system whose branches were distorting his world, threatening it with disorder. She would be a threat to him if he was not careful.

Already, he longed to be back in Turing, where he could pretend for a while that Ishtar could not touch him. No members of Ishtar, except for the few pilots who stayed there temporarily between trips, were inside Turing, and the pilots generally kept to themselves. The two hundred Cytherians there and the fifty Habbers who worked with them met freely, as they could never have done elsewhere. No patrol existed to question them about their actions; no one looked askance at their friendships.

Turing had, in fact, become a kind of school; perhaps the Habbers had intended that all along. Much of their actual work was done by machines and cyberminds; Dyami's work in engineering left him enough time to enjoy discussions with Cytherians and Habbers. No one called such sessions seminars, although that was what they were. Dyami had planned to stay in Turing only for a short while before going to an Island school that had accepted him. Now he felt that he might learn more by remaining where he was.

How long would Ishtar tolerate the situation? That depended on factors he could not control and had no power to engineer. Having the Habbers here served to keep Earth at a distance, but their presence was also an affront to the cult that despised and feared them.

An affront to Ishtar . . . an offender against the Spirit —he had heard such words several times, whispered not about Habbers alone but about a few settlers as well. He was an offense to Ishtar. He had always known that, even before Teo had discovered his secret.

Dyami had been fourteen, sprawled on his bed with Teo. They had been going over a geology lesson before setting aside their screens to gossip about a few of their schoolmates; Teo often spoke scornfully about how some of the boys had begun to behave in the presence of the girls they knew. He could not recall exactly when they had stopped talking, when he first realized that Teo was looking at him with more intensity. His friend's affectionate grip on his shoulder had suddenly become an embrace.

They groped at each other awkwardly. Teo loosened Dyami's garments and gripped him with his hand before Dyami could protest. Then he was suddenly growing hard, holding the other boy's hand as he shuddered and spent himself. The spasm of pleasure made him reckless; he pressed his mouth hard against Teo's and held him firmly, delighting in his friend's response when the dark-haired boy spurted against his belly.

The fear came then, a terror he had rarely felt. One of the household might have come to his door; he had carelessly revealed what he was to his friend. He could no longer pretend that the urges he felt could be kept hidden.

Teo said, "You *are* like me. I knew you were, I felt it for a while."

Dyami sat up and fastened his pants. "How did you know?" His fear was growing; how had he given himself away?

"Little things. You don't go off with some girl to her house to fool around. You never really look at the other boys in the bathroom at school or join in when a few of them start showing each other how they do it alone. They just think we're shy, but I guessed—you're my friend, so I can guess how you think, and I figured you might be like me. You didn't want to watch them at it because you knew you'd enjoy it too much." Teo leaned back against a pillow.

"Don't look so worried—they can't know. They probably think you don't want to do anything like that if it might get back to your sister. She might think it's an offense, even if it's just guys fooling around."

"Does anyone else know about you?"

Teo shook his head. "I'm not stupid. I was pretty sure about you though, and if I'd been wrong, at least you wouldn't have told anybody else—I knew that." He nudged Dyami gently in the ribs. "I kept thinking about you. There must be someplace we can go, where we don't have to worry about anyone seeing us. Or we can always lock our doors and tell our parents we have to concentrate on our lessons." He laughed. "You want to be with me, don't you?"

Dyami nodded, but his fear was still there, threatening to overpower him. He wondered if the pleasure he longed for so much was worth enduring that fear. Teo did not seem afraid; he almost seemed to welcome the danger involved.

"How long have you known?" Teo asked. "I mean about yourself."

"I think I always did. When I was younger, there was this teaching image—I used to daydream about him a little without really knowing why. I'd look at certain men and start wondering about them, and then I'd try to put it out of my mind. Whenever I touched myself, I'd think about a man. It never worked if I thought about a girl." Dyami closed his eyes for a moment. "I kept hoping it would go away. Now I'm pretty sure it won't. Even physicians and Counselors might not be able to do that much for me—it's too complicated. I looked up some research. They'd probably have to play around with my hormonal levels and work on my behavior for years, and even then I might not be that different. Makes more sense to leave it alone—there are places where people don't care, but I guess none of those people decided to come here. Besides, it'd cost too much anyway, and I knew I couldn't tell anyone—I didn't want anybody to know." Dyami bit his lip. "An affront to Ishtar—that's what Chimene would call me if she ever knew. She'd have somebody dragging me to meetings and harping at me about appeasing the Spirit and how Ishtar will love me and forgive me only if I spend my whole life pretending I'm something I'm not."

"You don't feel guilty about it, do you?" Teo asked.

"No." He could not feel guilt at having desires he had not chosen to have; it could not matter to others what he imagined when he was alone, pleasuring himself. Fear was what he felt—fear of discovery, combined with a feeling that to protect himself he could never give in to what others called love, that he might always be lonely. Knowing that Teo shared his desires was a small consolation, but now he would have to fear for his friend as well.

Dyami looked up at the airship's screen; the flatter land of the Lakshmi Plateau stretched before him. He and Teo had shared other moments alone after their first encounter, but Dyami had never been able to shed his fear; it was always there, waiting to make him pay for a moment of joy with hours of despair and dread.

He had never admitted his fear to Teo, who took his pleasure without inhibition and felt only contentment when it was past. But Teo must have sensed something was wrong; he had never been able to ease Dyami during his brooding silences afterward. He had not been surprised when Teo began to hint that he had found a couple of other companions; Teo had wanted to give him some joy and had failed.

Since then, except for an infrequent meeting with Teo when his desire had grown too great, Dyami had lived without love. Even in Turing, where he knew there were a few others like himself, he had never betrayed what he felt. Turing might not always be the refuge it was now; his fear had not left him even there. He was safe only if he hid what he was. If he reached out to anyone else, he risked an interaction that might create its own pattern of disorder, one he could not map mathematically or control, one that might lead to shame and disgrace.

He thought of Teo, whom he might have loved, and Balin, the Habber he knew he loved now. He wished that the communion of thought he shared with Balin were enough to ease the aching inside himself.

Teo was waiting for Dyami just outside Oberg's bay. The dark-haired young man shook his hand lightly, but the warmth in his eyes was that of a lover. Dyami's eyes narrowed as he stepped back; under Teo's open dark vest, barely visible against his gray tunic, he saw the black and red sash of Ishtar.

"You didn't have to meet me," Dyami said.

"It's no trouble. I'm working in the main dome now with a team of lab technicians, tending to all those little details so that the chemists aren't unnecessarily distracted. Didn't I tell you in my last message?"

"I don't think so." Dyami was silent until they were past the pilots' dormitory and near the greenhouse complex. "I never thought I'd see you wearing the sash," he said in a lower voice. He felt a twinge of fear; maybe Teo had changed.

"You don't think it means anything, do you? My parents decided to join. It would have looked strange to them if I hadn't, especially since I'm not living with them now. This way, they can rest assured that the son they have their doubts about is safely part of the fellowship."

"You didn't tell me you'd moved either."

"Didn't get a chance—I only moved about a month ago. I put up a small house in the southwest dome. I had to set up another household—hiding some of what I do was getting to be troublesome."

"A household?" Dyami asked.

"A friend who's like us—he's not my lover, but at least I don't have to hide anything from him—and two women who are lovers and don't want anyone to find out. It's a convenient arrangement for all of us."

Dyami's hand trembled a little as he adjusted the duffel hanging from his shoulder. He could not imagine trusting others that way, even people who were like him. A sudden surge of guilt, or shame, or anxiety over being found out could lead one of the others to betray his friend.

"You can meet them while you're here," Teo continued. He glanced up at Dyami's face. "Don't look so nervous. They don't know about us, and I won't be the one to tell them. They think you're only my close childhood friend, and they'll be happier if they think you don't know about them."

"Then maybe you shouldn't have told me."

"I can trust you," Teo said easily. "People like us have to be damned sure about who's trustworthy. Anyway, we've all joined Ishtar, so we're quite respectable. We can go to meetings and tell anyone who approaches us that we prefer to share the rite among ourselves, and if it can't be avoided—well, I've found I can steel myself and pretend I'm with a man." He laughed. "It isn't too bad once you get used to it. A couple of women have even complimented me on my vigor. If they only knew—" Teo chuckled again. "My parents have been quite pleasant to me since I moved out, even though they were somewhat disappointed that I did. They can be happy believing that either Haru or Sharla will eventually become my bondmate or thinking that my housemates and I will move closer to perfection and live the way your sister's household does." Teo was smiling, but Dyami caught the bitterness in his tone. He had chosen denial; Teo had chosen deception.

"Speaking of your sister," Teo went on, "I suppose you must know about the child she's planning to have."

Dyami raised his brows. "No, I didn't."

"I know you don't have a fellowship in Turing rushing to spread good news about our Guide, but I thought one of the pilots might have told you on the way back. Chimene and Boaz Huerta have stored their genetic material so that they can have a child together. Our Guide's precious genes will be preserved."

"Why didn't they just have their implants removed? They're young enough."

"Apparently they want to wait," Teo replied. "Maybe Chimene thinks a pregnancy now would unnecessarily deprive her of her enjoyment of our rite. Of course, we're all overjoyed that, whatever happens to Chimene or Boaz later, they've made that commitment to leaving a child among us."

Dyami's mouth twisted. "How delightful—a potential relative who's Boaz's child." He had met the man only a few times; he had noticed how Chimene occasionally glanced at him, as if she were uncertain of herself without him. Whenever he thought of Boaz Huerta, he felt fear.

"That reminds me," Teo said. "Maybe you haven't heard this joke in Turing. The Guide and her housemates are sharing the rite, and they get carried away with their exertions, and by the time they're finished, they've worked up quite an appetite. So they go to their kitchen but find out they're practically out of food. Well, that's not a problem, since they figure someone else can feed them, so they go over to another house."

"Go on," Dyami said. "I haven't heard this one."

"This household's in Ishtar and you are supposed to share, so they get out a gigantic repast for the Guide and her friends. After they're finished, they realize they're very thirsty, so they go to another house and drink up most of the liquor in the place—but that's all right because they're with brothers and sisters, and you are supposed to share."

Teo took a breath before continuing. "All that drinking just gets them all hungry again, so they go to a third house, get everyone out of bed, and have another meal— some imports from the Islands and just about everything you can imagine, and they wash that down with some wine. Then, as they're staggering home, the Guide says, 'It's a wonder everyone doesn't join Ishtar! See how much better off we are when we share?'"

Dyami laughed a little. They were near the Buddhist temple, not far from the tunnel to the west dome. Teo suddenly pushed him toward the trees and groped at his groin; Dyami gasped. "Not here," he whispered.

"You're already hard." Teo fondled him; Dyami was afraid that in a moment he would be unable to control himself. "You'd think you hadn't had any in a long time."

Dyami managed to push his friend's hand away. "I haven't—not since I left."

"A year and a half?" Teo's eyes widened with astonishment. "But you've been in Turing. The Habbers probably wouldn't care, and I doubt anyone else would bother you. I know there are a few people like us there—it's one of the reasons some of them wanted to work up there."

"I guess I haven't seen anyone I wanted that much." It was easier to say that than to tell the other man about his fears.

"Well, we'll have to do something about that." They left the trees and walked toward the main road and the tunnel. "Your parents will want you to themselves tonight, but I'll come by tomorrow—I've got some time off."

"Not there. We shouldn't—"

"No, not there. I know a place—well, you'll see."

The household welcomed him effusively, but Dyami quickly saw how strained Sef's greetings were. His father had changed; Sef's face was thinner and he poked at his food; he had lost his usually hearty appetite. His gold-flecked brown eyes had a wary expression; Sef was clearly troubled.

The rest of the household listened as Dyami spoke of his work, but Risa kept glancing toward her bondmate. Sef had always been so open; what could he be hiding now?

Dyami did not get a chance to speak to his mother alone until the others drifted off to bed. He led her outside, then stopped in front of their greenhouse.

"I have to ask you," Dyami said. "How long has Sef been like this? Something's wrong."

"I know that."

"Hasn't he said anything to you?"

"No." Risa's face was hidden in the darkness. "I've tried to ask, but that just makes him more unhappy. The past couple of months—he's been moody and he's home later from the meetings. I think he's been staying for the rite all those times, but I promised myself I wouldn't question him about that. I keep telling myself it doesn't mean anything to him."

"Do you think he's started to believe in it?" Dyami asked. "I thought that was just a ruse."

"It isn't that—I'm sure of that much. I thought having you home might cheer him a bit, but it doesn't seem to make any difference."

A woman, Dyami thought. An encounter during the rite might have grown into something more. Risa might refuse to admit it to herself until she was confronted with the fact, and Sef was incapable of hurting her in that way. He could understand his father; he had hidden his own secret long enough. But Sef, unlike him, was not accustomed to years of secretiveness and deception.

"Maybe you can speak to him," Risa said. "He might find it easier to talk to you. I just wish—"

"I'll see. Maybe he just needs to work through whatever it is by himself. He loves you enough not to want to burden you with his troubles." He was beginning to wish he had never come home to this mire of emotion, to people who claimed to love him without really knowing him.

Dyami left the house with Teo just as the light was beginning to fade. Risa and Noella had come home only a little while earlier; as far as they knew, he was having supper at Teo's house and would sleep there so that he would have more time to reminisce with his friend. He had been apprehensive about accepting Teo's mysterious invitation; the other man had still not told him where they were going. Now he felt a little relieved at escaping his mother's troubled gaze.

"What's it like being home again?" Teo asked.

Dyami shrugged. "I must have been given the name of every eligible young woman in Oberg at breakfast. Risa seems convinced that they're all just waiting to throng around me."

Teo grinned. A conspiratorial look was in his eyes, as if he and Dyami were off on yet another boyish adventure. They walked along the main road, stepped aside as a cart passed, then turned toward the tunnel to the southwest dome.

"Well?" Dyami said. "Where are we going?"

"Patience." The smaller man nodded at five people leaving the tunnel; inside, two patrol members were already on duty. Teo smiled at them as they walked by, but his dark eyes were grim. He did not speak until they had entered the dome.

"We'll wait for a cart." Teo stepped into the main road. The southwest dome seemed larger than the others, but that was because fewer houses had been built here so far. Clusters of houses stood at the edge of a wide grassy plain, a few of them still under construction; the slender trees bordering the road were hardly more than saplings.

"Where are we going?" Dyami asked again.

"To a friend's. I told you I'd take care of you. You'll meet other men there, ones like us."

Dyami tensed. "What do you mean?"

"I told you. You won't be deprived for long. At least one of them's sure to take a liking to you."

He clutched Teo's shoulder. "You must be mad." Teo shook off his hand. "What kind of risk are you taking?"

"It isn't a risk. You can trust these people, and if you're with me, they won't have any suspicions about you. Do you really think I wouldn't be careful about something like this?"

"But the patrol—"

"No one will see us enter the house," Teo said, "and you can either stay there for the night or find someone who can guide you to the road when the patrol's not in the vicinity. It's not hard to dodge them—I've done it often enough. The worst that can happen is that the ones back at the tunnel will ask where you were and where you're going, and you can say you were at my house—it's not far from where we're going."

"And what happens if they call your housemates to check on that?"

"They know you're my friend. They'll cover for you. They'd lie to the patrol anyway on general principles."

"You told them about me!" Dyami said.

"I didn't tell them anything. They can guess where I'll be, but they won't know you're there. It probably won't even come up—that pair saw us in the tunnel just now, so they'll assume you were visiting me." Teo folded his arms. "What's the matter, Dyami? Scared?" He sounded the way he had whenever he had dared Dyami into an exploit. "Do you think you can just keep it all inside and get along without it? You'll just get more frustrated, and then you're a lot more likely to try something foolish."

"I thought maybe we—that you'd found a place where we could be alone."

"We'll have our moments, don't worry, but I've gotten to the point where I need more excitement once in a while. Once you're there, you might like it more than you expect." Teo moved to the cart as it came toward them. "Just think of it as your way of striking back at Ishtar."

But this wasn't a blow against Ishtar. Teo and his friends could probably accommodate themselves to the cult's presence as long as nothing happened to them. Ishtar would do better to ignore such people altogether, but he supposed many in the fellowship were too fervent in their faith to be practical.

Teo greeted the few passengers aboard the cart and was soon talking to one young couple. Dyami looked away as he tried to compose himself. His fear was still with him, but it was now tinged with anticipation. It had been too long; he could never have been so reckless otherwise.

They passed two large greenhouses. An older woman outside one waved and called out his name; Dyami started before recognizing Jeannine Loris. He lifted his hand; she could not know.

Ahead of them lay a more densely wooded area; two

more members of the patrol were strolling near the road.
They left the cart and walked toward the woods. It was
already growing dark; Dyami squinted when they were
among the trees, waiting for his eyes to adjust to the darkness. He looked around and saw no one nearby, then said,
"This place—is that where you always go?"

"Of course not. There are other houses in all the
domes. We have ways of leaving messages for one another,
saying where we'll be or which houses are welcoming
guests on a particular evening. The place we're going usually draws men whose tastes aren't too odd—I didn't think
you'd want anything too extreme."

It reminded him of his parents' useless meetings with
others who hated Ishtar, where they consoled themselves
by sitting around and believing they could find a way to
fight. But he had no right to be critical. He had gone to the
Freyja Mountains, where he could pretend that Ishtar did
not exist.

He glimpsed the lights of a few houses beyond the
trees; Teo pressed on until the lights disappeared and they
were surrounded by darkness again. Dyami's mouth was
dry. I should turn around now and go home, he told himself. Teo would mock him for being a coward; maybe he
would even begin to worry if he could trust Dyami after
all, if he could shrink from this so readily.

They were nearing the edge of the woods; a small lake
was ahead. Several houses stood along the shore in the
distance. "My house is over there," Teo said, motioning at
the distant dwellings. "Our destination's straight ahead."
He pointed at a house no more than a few paces away; the
structure sat on a small rise just above the shore. Only one
other house was near it; a woman stood in the doorway,
calling out to three children playing on a dock. Teo leaned
against a tree trunk. "We'll wait until she goes inside. It
wouldn't matter even if she saw us, but I guess I should be
cautious for your sake."

"How can you be so sure you won't be betrayed?"
Dyami murmured.

"How can anyone give us away without betraying
himself? He'd have to explain what he was doing there."

"Somebody could have a change of heart and decide
to repent."

"And we could say he was lying and trying to impli-

cate innocent people in his deeds. You worry too much,
Dyami. There are a few on the patrol who can be bribed,
and if anyone really started coming after us, Ishtar would
have more trouble than it needs. There are a lot of people
like us—they don't need that much of a fight."

But there would be no fight. Many would be like Dyami, hiding what they were without meeting with others;
they would not be likely to come out in the open to defend
offenders against Ishtar. Many would keep silent out of
gratitude that their own deeds remained unknown. Ar-
rayed against them would be not only Ishtar's true believers but also other Cytherians, people who disliked the cult
but also despised what men like Teo did.

Ishtar talked of love and sharing, but its inner circles
wanted control. They would not stop until they had power
even over everyone's most intimate and private thoughts.
This was their way of controlling people like Teo and him
—forcing them to be furtive, so fearful of discovery that
they would not risk standing against Ishtar openly.

The three children ran toward their house; the door
closed behind them. Teo beckoned to Dyami; they left the
trees and went rapidly along the bank toward the dwelling
ahead.

The door opened; a stocky young man with Japanese
features ushered Dyami and Teo inside. He did not introduce himself to Dyami or ask his name; perhaps it was
better not to give it.

He might have been at any gathering of friends. Five
men sat on cushions around a table, sharing food and herb
tea as they talked. In a corner near a large screen, two men
were throwing dice. One blond man sat alone, his back
against the wall, his head bowed.

Dyami looked around the dimly lit room. A couple of
faces were vaguely familiar, but he did not know anyone
here. He felt a wave of relief before his fear returned;
someone might still have recognized him. He was the
Guide's brother; any of these men might be aware of that.

"Will anyone else arrive?" he murmured to Teo.

"I doubt it. We don't like too much of a crowd at any
one place, even here, where there aren't many neighbors
nearby. Why—haven't you seen a likely prospect?"

He was being watched. The men around the table

were studying him quite openly now; one mustached man whispered to another. The two men near the screen picked up their dice, then disappeared into a hallway.

Teo walked toward the table. He stood there for a moment before he leaned toward a bearded man. The other man laughed, got up quickly, then slipped an arm around Teo's slender body as they moved toward the hallway where the other two had gone.

Dyami felt dizzy; he wanted to flee. He was limp, totally devoid of any desire. He shouldn't have come here, but it was too late to leave. The others had seen him already; if he left so soon, he would only arouse suspicion. They might even think he was his sister's spy.

A hand touched his arm; he looked down into the face of the stocky young man who had greeted him before. "Someone new," the man said. "Welcome to our fellowship." He began to stroke Dyami's arm, then let his hand fall to his hip. Dyami flushed. The knot inside him uncoiled as he felt himself stiffen; his will seemed centered in his member, a thing apart from his fears.

"We can go with the others." The man motioned with his head toward the hallway where Teo and the others had gone. "Or would you rather be alone?"

"Alone," he managed to say.

The man led him to the other narrow hallway; they entered a room. The light panels above them flowed on, then dimmed as his companion muttered a command. They shed their clothes quickly and went to the bed.

They stroked each other in silence. The man's hands both demanded pleasure and gave it; there were no whispered endearments or gentle kisses. They slowly sought each other out with their hands and mouths, moving closer to that moment when nothing outside existed. Dyami throbbed, aching with all he had held back for so long, and then his pleasure rushed from him, a bright stream sweeping him forward to an intense, transcendent joy.

The moment was gone too soon. He lay lost in a stranger's arms, alone once more, his fears drumming inside his mind.

His companion sat up. "Enough for you?"

"Yes."

"Maybe just for now." The man slipped off the bed and picked up his clothes. "You can stay in this room if you

like. I imagine that at least one of our friends will look in on
you in a bit." He smiled as he gazed at Dyami's body. "And
if you're willing—" He left the room without bothering to
dress.

Dyami stood up hastily. He was trapped with his fears
again; the thought of another anonymous encounter repelled him. He had risked too much for such a brief pleasure. The moment was gone, swept away by the current,
leaving only loneliness and disgust with himself in its wake.
He had never felt disgust with Teo; there had been love for
someone he knew.

He pulled on his clothes and left the room. Only two
men remained in the common room, the blond man and
an older dark-skinned man. The fair-haired man was
standing; he was taller than Dyami, nearly as tall as Sef. He
shrank back against the wall as his companion edged closer
to him.

"I brought you here," the swarthy man was saying. "I
thought you wanted to come, but you're not being very
cooperative. I know what you need—you're acting like
one of those who likes to display himself without admitting
what he is."

Dyami moved toward them; the blond man looked at
him with frightened dark eyes. His height was deceptive;
his handsome but slightly rounded face was a boy's. "Let
him be," Dyami said. "Can't you see he doesn't want
that?"

The dark man's eyes narrowed. Dyami noticed now
that both were wearing Ishtar's sash. "I guess you think
he'd prefer you."

"Maybe he doesn't want anyone right now. Leave him
alone. Enough willing men are here."

The man tilted his head. "You wouldn't like to—"

"I've had my pleasure. At the moment I need some
food."

The man stared at Dyami for a bit, then walked toward the hallway where the other men had gone. Dyami
went to the table, cut himself a piece of bread, ate it hastily, then poured himself some tea. The tea was tepid; he
put down the cup and looked back at the boy. "How old
are you?" he asked.

"Almost fifteen."

Dyami let out his breath. "Then maybe you shouldn't

be here. This isn't a place for a boy, whether he has a man's body or not."

The tall blond boy sank to the floor. "I know."

Dyami kicked over a cushion and seated himself next to the boy, who shook back his hair as he glanced warily at him. "Don't worry," Dyami said. "I don't want a bed-partner now. I'm not used to this either—I wasn't sure what to expect."

The boy closed his eyes. Dyami studied his face, admiring its boyish beauty, the strong, well-shaped bones under the youthful chubbiness; he would be a beautiful man someday. "Kinsu was lying," the boy said. "I didn't want to come here. I only said that because I didn't know how to refuse. He's always been able to make me do what he wants, ever since he became my lover."

"And how long has that been?"

"Over two years. He said he'd been watching me, that he guessed about me. My family thinks I go to his house just to talk—at first, that's all it was. They feel sorry for him because he and his bondmate don't have a child—they don't know he never wanted one. They think it's so nice that he has somebody who's like a son."

Dyami's gorge rose. The boy must have suffered enough when he realized what he was; the thought of a man preying upon one so young angered him. The boy should have had a companion of his own age, someone less predatory and more innocent. Any man who treated a girl so young in this way would have risked a family's anger, perhaps even disgrace in a hearing if his attentions had been forced or coercion was used. But this boy could not have complained to anyone without shaming himself and admitting what he was.

"He shouldn't have brought you here," Dyami said. "If the others knew you were so young, they'd probably feel the same way. He should have waited until you were older before he—"

"What difference does it make?" The boy turned his head; his black eyes filled with tears. "It's horrible, what I am. I hate myself—it doesn't matter what he does to me."

"You mustn't say that. You shouldn't hate yourself just because a lot of people are too ignorant to understand. There are places where no one would care, where we'd be accepted, or at worst mocked only a little. You mustn't

believe that your way of showing love to someone else is
any less worthy than what others practice. I know how you
feel—I'm often afraid myself. There's torment enough for
people like us without adding guilt to it."

"It's wrong—what they're doing now in this house."

Dyami shook his head. "It may not be what I'd choose,
but you shouldn't judge them too harshly. Need and loneliness and having to hide what they are brings them here. Is
what they do so different from the rite many in Ishtar
practice openly?"

The blond boy recoiled. "How can you say that? The
rite appeases the Spirit. What they do is hateful to Her—
the Spirit reaches out through Her daughters, who carry
life, to Her sons, who make life possible. Those men refuse
to honor the Spirit." He shuddered. "I know that, I pray so
often, I want to change, I don't want to be this way, but I
can't stop. The Guide says that the right way is a struggle,
but why does it have to be so hard for me?"

Dyami felt cold. This boy was even more troubled
than he had suspected; he believed in Ishtar even while
engaging in what the cult called a sin. If his guilt grew
great enough, it might destroy not only him but others as
well. His pity for the boy turned to fear.

He tried to calm himself. "I didn't intend to mock
Ishtar," he said. "But the Guide speaks of love, and I can't
believe that any Spirit would hate a boy who can't help
what he is. I can't believe that creating barriers between
us and other people, or making you feel that you must hate
yourself, is what the Spirit would want." He tried to think
of what else to say; calling the cult's beliefs misguided and
false might only provoke the boy further. "Other faiths
have come to see that things they once thought were
wrong aren't evils. Ishtar may change, too—even the
Guide would say that mistakes are possible and that we
may have an imperfect grasp of the truth."

"Ishtar has the truth," the boy replied. "The truth
can't change. I can't change." His voice was weaker.
"Maybe the Spirit will always hate me. No one could love
me the way I am now, not if they knew."

"That isn't so. I don't hate you."

"But you're just another one like me."

Dyami gripped the boy's shoulder. "Listen to me.
Some in Ishtar live without bonds, but they don't condemn

those who can't and who practice the rite only with a bondmate. If you're trying to live in the way you think is right, even if you fail sometimes, you can't be condemned for that." This was the only consolation he could offer if the boy was unable to give up his beliefs. He clenched his teeth, silently cursing Chimene and those who followed her.

The boy shook off his hand. Teo suddenly entered the common room, pulling up his pants, a broad grin on his face; he halted as he caught sight of Dyami.

"Wait here," Dyami murmured as he stood up and went to his friend. "I think we should leave," he said softly.

"So soon? I was just going to check up on you." Teo draped his tunic over one bare shoulder. "Our host was quite pleased with you—he felt your passion more than made up for your relative inexperience. Don't you want more than a few preliminaries? He wouldn't mind another session later, and there's a roomful of men who'd enjoy showing you a few things."

Dyami jerked his head toward the boy. "We should get him out of here. He shouldn't have come. He's only fourteen years old."

Teo's smile faded. "I wouldn't have guessed," he whispered. "His escort didn't say he was bringing a boy. He may no longer be welcome himself if he tries that again."

"You said you can dodge the patrol," Dyami muttered. "I assume I can trust that statement. You were apparently mistaken about how cautious your friends here are—one of them, at least."

"I can get you to the road." Teo slipped his tunic over his head. "I'll get him to his house, wherever it is—we can come up with some sort of story."

They went to the boy. "We're leaving now," Teo said. "Maybe you'd like to come along. Where do you live?"

"The southeast dome." The boy's face paled. "But Kinsu might wonder—"

"Forget about your friend. We'll have a few words with him another time. Wait two or three years before you even think of meeting with others like this again—we have quite enough grief without having people think we're trying to ensnare children." Teo's mouth twisted. "You're young. Maybe you'll be lucky later and discover you're one of those who can function fairly often with the opposite sex and take some enjoyment in it. You might be able to give this up then. Did anyone on patrol see you coming here with your friend?"

"No. I came as far as the woods alone, and it was still light then. He told me to meet him there."

"Good," Teo said. "That makes it easier. I can get you as far as the tunnel. If the patrol asks you why you're wandering around, you can say you were trying to make the rounds at night or something. I used to try that a lot myself."

The boy got to his feet. He moved awkwardly, as though his body were an obstacle he wanted to push aside. Dyami glimpsed the despair in his eyes.

Dyami busied himself around the house the next day, replacing a faulty component in the kitchen's recycler before washing some of the household's clothing. Except for Paul and an occasional visitor who came by to see the paramedic, the house was empty. Dyami had volunteered to do the chores; he had muttered an excuse about wanting some time to himself when Risa and Grazie suggested he pay a call on an old schoolmate, a young woman who worked in the nursery. "Shy, that's what he is," Grazie had murmured to Risa as the two women left the house. "Think he would have grown out of it by now."

He was in the greenhouse, checking the tiers of crops and selecting some ripe fruit for the evening meal, when he saw Teo walking up the path. He went to the door and beckoned his friend inside.

"My housemates tell me the patrol didn't call them," Teo said, "so you must have gotten home without much trouble."

"They asked me where I'd been. They didn't bother to check. What about the boy?"

"No problem. He got to the tunnel, and the patrol didn't see us together. They didn't spend more than a few seconds with him before letting him pass."

"That boy is troubled," Dyami said. "He really believes what Ishtar says about people like him."

"A pity he's so young." Teo leaned against a tier of soybean plants. "I wouldn't have minded an encounter with him if he were older."

"I'd avoid him if I were you. His feelings are so twisted

up with guilt you can't tell what he might do." He spied a tiny shoot, saw that it was the beginning of a weed, and plucked it out.

"You must come to my house tomorrow," Teo said. "We'll have the place to ourselves—we can indulge ourselves completely. I'd invite you for tonight, but I'm forced to endure one of those wretched meetings." He paused. "When are you going to come back to Oberg for good?"

"I don't know."

"The Habbers won't be up north forever. Too many still blame them for that fever, and the word is that even Sigurd Kristens-Vitos is under pressure from some of his colleagues on that score. Ishtar doesn't lack for allies among the Administrators now."

Dyami thought of Balin and felt a pang. "Even if the Habbers leave, we'll still need people in Turing."

"It might be better for you if you left sooner," Teo said. "Some say that the people in Turing are forgetting that they're Cytherians. Ishtar wonders just where their loyalties lie. Listen—you could live in my house if you came back. We can easily add another room. Don the sash and get on with your life. There's nothing we can do about Ishtar—we have to live with it however we can."

"I don't think I can live that way, Teo."

"You may not have any choice."

"At the moment, I do—I can go back to the Freyja Mountains."

"Will you visit me tomorrow?" Teo asked.

"Yes." He could lose himself for a little while anyway, escape his fears in the other man's arms. He turned back to the plants. When he looked up, Teo was gone.

Dyami excused himself from supper early and retreated to his room. He knew what he would see if he stepped outside—groups of people in sashes going to one house or another for their meetings, where they would hear fine words about the world Ishtar would bring into being. It would be a world without doubt, without secrets, built on knowledge that might eventually be forgotten by future Cytherians. It would be a world without people like him.

He tried to sleep. When he could not, he got up, pulled on a pair of pants, went outside, and sat down under

the trees. Across the way, people in sashes were leaving
Thierry Lacan-Smith's house; Nikolai was among them, his
arm around a woman. Dyami watched the pair walk away;
apparently Kolya would not escape the rite this evening.
Perhaps, in spite of his feelings about the cult, the Russian
had learned to enjoy that ceremony. The group dispersed;
he did not see Sef.

He looked up. The dome was invisible in the darkness;
the dim, pale disk of light might have been floating in a
night sky. His people were protected from the dark world
outside but not from the poisonous clouds and shadows in
their own minds. The domes were cauldrons, boiling under the oppressive atmosphere as old hatreds and needs
bubbled to the surface.

He sat under the trees for a long time, until the paths
were empty. Two men on patrol, who had been watching
one meeting on a screen inside the tunnel, paced along the
main road. A man left the tunnel; Dyami recognized his
father.

So Sef had gone to the main dome instead of attending
a meeting here. The tall man strode rapidly to the house
and entered without speaking. Dyami was about to rise
when the door opened once more. His father's broad-
shouldered form was outlined against the light; he was
holding a bottle. Sef came back outside and seated himself
a few paces away.

"Sef," Dyami said.

His father started. "I didn't see you."

"I couldn't sleep." Dyami heard the sound of gulping;
Sef rarely drank alcohol. "What are you drinking?"

"Some of Andy Dinel's finest, of course. Want some?"
Sef's voice was even huskier than usual.

"No."

"It's quite good. I've come to appreciate it more
lately."

"Sef, what's wrong?"

"Why, nothing."

"I know something's troubling you," Dyami said.
"Risa's worried about you—she told me so." He moved
closer to his father. "Can't you talk about it?" Sef did not
respond. "What is it?"

"I should be honored," Sef said; his breath smelled of
whiskey. "I should be grateful that the woman who's the

embodiment of Ishtar to so many is so willing to accept my offering. I should rejoice that the Guide has chosen me so often."

Dyami tensed in shock. In all his darkest thoughts about his sister, he had never imagined that Chimene might be capable of this.

"Her friend Eva asked me to stay the first time," the older man continued. "Others heard her—I couldn't refuse. I told myself it didn't matter, that I didn't want them wondering about a refusal. I didn't know Chimene would choose me, but she did, and when I realized who I was with—" He heaved a sigh. "I wanted her. I didn't care that she was Risa's daughter or your sister. And I can't stop—I keep going back and hoping she'll choose me again, and she always does. Maybe I always wanted her, and she saw it before I could. I tell myself it isn't so, but I can't rid myself of the thought."

"How can she do this to you?"

"What is she doing, Dyami? She believes it all, she doesn't think she's doing anything wrong. It doesn't matter who the man is—it's the rite that's important. I'm the one to be blamed. I don't have any faith, and I don't care about the rite. I go there for her. She talks of love, but what I feel has nothing to do with love—it's just a need, a kind of craving I can't give up. Maybe I could if she left me alone, but I keep going there, and I'm always asked, and I always find her under the shroud."

"If Risa finds out—" Dyami began.

Sef groaned. "I know. She'd never let it pass. Even if she forgave me, she'd never forgive Chimene. All these years, she's tried to protect us all by letting Chimene think we're reconciled with her, but if she knew about this, there's no telling what she'd do."

"All it would take is one careless word," Dyami said. "How long has this been going on?"

"A couple of months. I never thought anything like this could happen to me. I loved your mother—I love her now. I didn't think anything like this could ever touch me."

Poor Sef, Dyami thought. There were times when his father still seemed like a boy. "It'll pass, you know," he murmured. "Those feelings always do. You're still in the early throes of passion—it does go away eventually."

"I wish I could believe that, but you don't know what it's like, being with her."

"I know what it's like to have feelings that can only bring trouble."

"I guess you do." Sef cleared his throat. "I'm not the only one with a secret I have to keep, am I? The only difference is that yours is something you shouldn't have to feel shame about."

Dyami's chest constricted. He was very still, unable to speak for a while. He caught his breath. "What do you mean?" he whispered.

"I knew a while ago. I saw how you'd look at your friend Teo sometimes. Believe me, no one else suspects. You've covered yourself fairly well. I probably wouldn't even have noticed if I hadn't had a couple of friends like you on Earth, though they could be more open about it there. You're my son—do you think I'd love you any less? I've been sorry you couldn't confide in me. I wanted you to think you could come to me with your troubles."

"If Risa ever knew—"

"She'd cry a little," Sef said. "She'd be sorry if you never had a bondmate. But her main worry wouldn't be what you are—it'd be how others would treat you if they knew. I never told her what I thought. I figured she had enough worries without having to fear for you. But it must have been hard for you, having to hide this even from the people closest to you. I can see exactly how hard now."

Sef closed his bottle and set it down. "I had such hopes when I came here," he continued. "Being part of something worthwhile, helping to build a new world. I wanted to leave my children with more than they would have had if I'd stayed on Earth. I wanted them to have some hope. But Eleta had only about three years, and you would have been freer somewhere else."

"I can go back to Turing," Dyami said. "I've been happier there. It's what the Project might have become, what it could still be. The Habbers don't want to rule us, and we can learn much from them. If Ishtar closes us off and claims the future of Venus for itself—"

"And have you found someone there?" Sef asked.

"No. It isn't that I couldn't, but I went through too many years of being afraid to feel that free, even there."

Sef's strong hand gripped his shoulder. "I'm sorry, son.

Now that I've told you what I've done, I feel disgusted with myself. I almost think I could give her up, just so that you wouldn't think less of me." He coughed softly. "And then I remember what she's like with me. If she'd only leave me alone, I'd have the strength. But I know that, next meeting day, I'll be going to her house, and one of her friends will ask me to join them once again, and I won't be able to refuse. I don't think she'll let me go until she knows I'm hers, and Ishtar's."

"You mustn't torment yourself," Dyami said. "Few men could resist Chimene. It's probably one reason she hates my kind so much—not because they offend the Spirit but because they're immune to her beauty."

"Every time I come back here, thinking that I've betrayed Risa with her own daughter—"

"She doesn't know, and maybe she'll never find out. She might not believe it even if she heard about it. I told her that whatever was troubling you, you loved her enough not to burden her with it. You should go to her now and hold her, and try to remember that you do care about her. This will pass—I promise you that."

The southern half of Oberg's southeast dome was divided by a small river that fed two small connected lakes bordering a wooded park. Dyami left the main road, crossed a wooden bridge, and moved past a long row of houses along the bank. He finally spotted the school, which stood under the center of this dome, just beyond the square windowless building that served as an External Operations Center here. He sat down in the grass and waited until the children began to stream from the school's main doorway and side exits.

Chimene came outside, accompanied by a gray-haired woman who was probably another teacher; they continued to speak until Chimene caught sight of Dyami. He got up and lifted his hand; she murmured to the other woman and then walked toward him.

"Greetings," he said as he clasped her hands.

"What a surprise." Her full lips formed a smile; she lifted her chin as she gazed up at him. "What brings you here?"

"A chance to see my sister, of course. My visit will be all too short, and you can guess how it's going—old schoolmates to see, doing my share around the house while I'm here, meeting every young woman Risa sees as a possible incubator for her grandchildren." He forced himself to keep smiling. "I decided I'd better make time to see you as soon as possible. I've been here five days already and not a word from you."

"I would have come by at least once," she said. "You know how it is—there's so much to do. But you're always welcome at my house—you know that."

"Yes, but you're often distracted there—brothers and sisters coming by to seek your advice, meetings to plan, all of that. We can visit while I walk you home and have more of a chance to talk."

She slipped her arm through his. "You should come to a meeting while you're here." They strolled away from the school and skirted the Operations Center. "It's been a source of some unhappiness for me, the fact that my own brother hasn't yet become one of us."

"I may not be entirely immune to Ishtar's call. You say yourself that some of those who resist the longest become the most fervent followers." Dyami tried to keep a tone of sarcasm out of his voice. "The Spirit can respect those who resist, when they finally come to Her."

She glanced toward him; her dark eyes glowed. He saw no doubt in her face; doubt would have reassured him. He would have been happier to think of her as someone who was using the cult and her position for her own gratification; that would have meant that she could still be reached through reason.

"It would give me such joy," she said, "if you came to us. I know you have to be free to find your way to us, but I've worried about having you in Turing. I can't understand why you'd want to consort with people who very likely brought about the death of our sister and grandfather. Some may say it isn't true, but I've seen no evidence against it."

"The Habbers are still useful," he replied, "and that's all that concerns me. I appreciate what you have here more now—all those people secure in their faith, knowing that their Guide is leading them along what they call the true path. Perhaps their faith will touch me before too long. I'm not one who finds such beliefs easy to accept, but—"

"I sympathize. It was often a struggle for me."

Teo thought that because Dyami was Chimene's brother, that gave him some protection. Dyami did not believe it. If Chimene ever learned what he was, what he had done with Teo in his friend's house, protecting him would be the last thing on her mind. She would never allow her own brother to be such an affront to her. His fear uncoiled coldly within him. He swallowed; he had already considered what to say to Chimene.

Between two rows of houses, a long path stretched past a row of trees towards the tunnel in the distance. "Still," he said, "some in our mother's household have found their faith—Kolya and my father." He paused for a moment. "I spoke to Sef the other night, alone. He tells me that you've shared the rite together."

Her fingers tightened on his arm, then relaxed. "And you disapprove. I'm not ashamed of what I do, and Sef is my brother in Ishtar."

"It doesn't trouble me particularly." He tried to sound sincere. "As you say, he's part of the fellowship, and for you to withhold your love from a man who's been so close might not be right. You've given him some joy. You see, I have grown to understand your faith a bit more." He lowered his voice. "But Sef is perturbed. Not because of you, needless to say—he has a great love for you. He's worried about Risa. He's hoped that she might be led to Ishtar, but she's much too far from your way still to see what your love for Sef means. He feels he must keep the truth from her, and that troubles him. He thinks he's straying from the right path."

"Did he tell you to talk to me?" Chimene asked.

"Not at all. He loves you very much, Chimene. I must admit I was a little startled, but he would be an unusual man if he could resist you. But he is concerned for our mother and what she would feel if she knew, which is hardly likely to bring her to your faith. Isn't that a wrong in your eyes—creating an obstacle to someone else's potential belief?"

She said, "I love him. I always have. I knew he would come to me."

"And he has, and he shares your love." He fought back the disgust welling up inside him. "Perhaps he loves you too much. He can't stop himself from going to you and praying that you'll choose him again. He tells himself that you are his Guide, and yet he suffers because of Risa. But I'm also concerned about you. Many of your followers would understand, but others might wonder why the Guide, who has the love of so many, has to choose her mother's bondmate. Surely you don't want any of your followers to doubt your wisdom. They might not see this as an act of love but as an affront to the woman who bore you."

She halted; her eyes widened, as if this were a new thought to her. Perhaps it was. She had lived among people who served her for so long that maybe she could not believe that anyone would find fault with her. "I'm the Guide. What I do is right as long as it serves my faith."

"But this may not serve it," he said. "Your love for Sef may keep you from sharing yourself with others. His love for you may drive a wedge between you and Risa. There are many who would take her side against you if they knew, regardless of their faith. They might think that their Guide had slipped into error by sharing love with a man before his bondmate could welcome its expression. I know you're aware of the ties that still bind others who haven't reached your state of perfection and that you don't seek to loosen them before such people are ready to shed them. It's one of the reasons so many love you. How unfortunate if you gave them cause to doubt you."

"And just what would you have me do?" she asked.

"Perhaps you should stop inviting him to share the rite with you. His love won't lessen—you have that now. Let him share himself with others, knowing he'll always have the love of his Guide. Isn't that what you want, to make him more capable of that? Choose others, and allow him to make his offering elsewhere. I suspect his thoughts will always be on you even then."

They approached the tunnel. She absently greeted a few people entering the dome; the frown on her face told him that his words were having an effect. He thought of the ceramics made in Turing, how stresses and resiliency had to be assessed, what would strengthen them and what might shatter them altogether. Chimene's thoughts were other material to be handled and shaped; his tools were words, drawing on her faith, her fears, and playing on her vanity. He longed to tell her the truth, how Sef's need for her was filled with self-loathing, that he could never love her as he loved Risa.

She did not speak for a long time, until they were inside the main dome and crossing the road. "I may have slipped from the right path a little." She let go of his arm as they moved under the trees. "I share myself with Sef, and yet I don't share him with others. Sometimes I almost wish I could be one of those who live a more flawed life, and have Sef's love for myself." She paused. "Kichi might have told me what you've said. Maybe I needed my brother to say this to me, but it'll be hard to let Sef go."

He nearly sighed with relief. Sef, regardless of his desires, was not likely to go to her without her encouragement. "Don't be too downcast," he murmured. "You still have his love, and maybe in time, if Risa's able to accept it, he can come to you again. You can always hope for that, and in the meantime you'll be able to give your love to others. There must be many who are waiting to move closer to the truth in your arms."

Birds sang above them; a pale yellow light shone down through the trees. "I thought you didn't feel close to me," she said. "There's always been some distance between us. I'd always hoped you'd come to care about me more, and now it seems you have. I've wanted to be a real sister to you, but you always shied away."

"I was still a child when you went to live with Kichi. We didn't have much opportunity to be close."

"And then I was the Guide, and there was so much to do—" She stopped and leaned against a tree. "I should have gone out of my way a little more, and maybe it wouldn't have taken you so long to begin to see what Ishtar means. I see that I do mean something to you." Her hand closed around his wrist. "Why do you have to leave Oberg?"

"What I learn from the Habbers may be useful. You needn't fear they'll subvert me."

"I suppose not. You were always one who kept his own counsel." She gripped him more tightly. "But maybe I need you here now. You're my brother—you could be one of those closest to me. You could become my brother in Ishtar, and nothing could separate us then." She moved closer to him. "You're so much like Sef—you have his face and his eyes. You look almost the way he did when I first knew I loved him."

His fear nearly overwhelmed him. A bitter taste filled his mouth; he swayed, afraid he might be sick. Her hand was a vise; her dark eyes held his gaze.

"Why do you look so pale, Dyami?" Her fingers were warm against his cheek. "If you become my brother in Ishtar, do you think there can be any barriers between us?" His chest tightened as he struggled to breathe. She released him and stepped back. "But you're still far from the truth, still trying to grasp it. You'll see it someday." She paused. "Aren't you going to walk to the house with me?"

"I've come far enough." His throat was so tight he could barely speak. "I must start home—it'll be growing dark soon."

"Give everyone my greetings. I'll be sure to stop by the house before you leave."

He watched her go; her cloud of soft black hair swayed against her back as she walked. He felt soiled, as if something unclean had touched him. He longed for the purity of Turing, the light that shone from the domes of that settlement, the clean, open land, the clear and unsullied rationality he glimpsed in Balin's eyes.

Another passenger was on the airship when Dyami boarded; one of the pilots mentioned that his fellow traveler was from ibn-Qurrah. The woman had slept throughout the trip, reclined on a seat near the back; she was still sleeping, her blond head resting against one arm.

He got up, wound his way among the crates secured along the aisle, and entered the lavatory. When he came out, the woman was awake; she stretched, then adjusted her seat as she sat up.

He motioned at the seat next to her. "Mind if I sit down?"

"Go ahead."

He seated himself. The steady, calm gaze of her large blue eyes made her seem older than she had looked at first. "Are you going to Turing for the first time?" she asked.

"No—I've been there for a year and a half. I was just home visiting my family."

"It's the first time for me. I haven't seen many images of the place, so I don't really know what to expect."

"Maybe you should have prepared yourself," he said.

"It has to be better than what I left. You're still rough-ing it a bit, aren't you?"

"You can say that," he replied. "Our temporary shel-ters have become more or less permanent. The people who were there early put most of their effort into the mining operation and the ceramics plant, so there wasn't much chance to put up houses."

"And later, they didn't want to make too many de-mands for the necessary materials because Ishtar might have given them trouble, I suppose. Ishtar wouldn't want too many others tempted to go there and risk so much contact with those devious Habber folk. Too many enjoy their hard-won little comforts to want to give them up for Turing. It doesn't matter. I'm glad I'm going, anyway."

He looked toward the female pilots. Both wore their bands and seemed intent on monitoring the airship. "What kind of work do you do?" he asked.

"Metallurgical engineering. I knew I'd need a skill like that to get to Turing, but it's not what really interests me. I heard about a couple of Habbers who have some intriguing speculations in astrophysics—I wouldn't mind exchanging some thoughts with them."

"It's that way with most of us," Dyami said. "Being free to talk with Habbers whenever we want, apart from our work—it makes you come up with ideas you might not have had otherwise, and it's the same with them. I wanted to do more in mathematics—I figured I might learn more in Turing than on the Islands."

"You're right about that." The blond woman folded her arms. "Ishtar's just about as strong there as on the surface. I went to an Island school for a couple of years. Appropriate knowledge—that's all we're supposed to care about. Learn what you need to help build the perfect society, and everything else is extraneous. You'd think more of the specialists would chafe at that, but few do. Basically, they want to be left alone, and they think the cult's just a temporary inconvenience and that they can benefit themselves by going along with it—or they really believe all that nonsense. It's sad—how few people there are who can be content without surrendering themselves to some ideological irrationality. You'd think just being part of the Project would be enough for them, but it's not."

"The goals are too distant from them," he said.

"So they fall into Ishtar's arms and pretend that the future's already arrived. Makes you wonder why the Habbers still bother with us."

The woman was being very frank with someone she'd only just met. Perhaps she assumed that since he was going to Turing, he would almost certainly sympathize. He glanced toward the pilots warily, but they could not have heard the woman's low-pitched voice.

"I ought to introduce myself," she went on. "My name's Amina."

"Just Amina?"

"Don't laugh too hard—it's Amina Astarte." Dyami grinned. "My parents decided to change their family names when they settled in ibn-Qurrah, and ancient mythology was something of a hobby for my mother. She thought it might be charming to use a goddess's name, one of the old names for this world. I find it ridiculous myself but never took the trouble to change it—that would have hurt my parents' feelings."

"I'm Dyami."

She peered at him through her long dark lashes. "Just Dyami? Don't tell me your parents decided to be creative with your name, too."

"Dyami Liang-Talis. I'm Chimene Liang-Haddad's brother." He had to admit it now; she would find out anyway.

Amina drew back a little; her blue eyes were colder. "I see. I knew she had a brother, but I never paid much attention to that. The only relative the Guide seems to publicize widely is her martyred grandmother, Iris."

"We were never very close. Her father and my mother separated and didn't renew their bond, so she lived with him part of the time on Island Two."

"So I've heard." She was still looking at him with suspicion.

He said, "I'm not a member of the fellowship, and the people in Turing will vouch for me." Gaining their trust had taken some time. That was another reason he had kept to himself, waiting for people to seek out his friendship instead of reaching out to them. He had not wanted anyone to think he was prying, serving his sister's ends. The others had finally come to trust him, largely because Balin had become his friend, but they rarely confided in him. He had hidden too much of himself for them to share more with him.

Yet Amina was willing to risk honesty with a man she hardly knew. She might become a friend if he were equally honest with her. His fears had ruled him for too long; perhaps his visit to Oberg had finally shown him that. He had carried his prison inside himself to a place where he could have been free.

"I went to Turing," he said, "because I also wanted to be in a place where I didn't have to see people wearing that damned sash." He motioned toward the pilots. "I loathe everything Ishtar stands for."

"The Guide does have a way about her," Amina said. "I looked at a couple of her talks on the screen once—I even felt a little moved myself. I can imagine the impression she must make in the flesh. That beautiful face, those eyes so entranced by her vision, that voice so resonant with strength as she demands your love and then almost singing as she pleads for it and tells you how perfect we can all be. It makes you want to surrender to her and comfort her at the same time."

"She repels me."

"Well, I guess I know where you stand, Dyami. It must be an embarrassment for her, having a brother in Turing."

"Perhaps less of an embarrassment than having me in Oberg, where her followers can see the brother who refuses to join. She thinks I'll eventually see how hateful the Habbers are and admit that she was right about them. I'm content to let her believe that she'll have her triumph over me in time, as long as she leaves me alone. I'd rather not talk about Chimene."

Amina straightened in her seat. "Seems our trip is nearly over."

He looked up at the large screen. The two domes were already visible; he could dimly see the high cliffs that surrounded Turing. Lights secured against the escarpment illuminated the dark rock; diggers moved over a wide, flat surface at the top of the cliffs to the east, uncovering the iron and copper ores that lay under the rock. Carts carrying the mined materials rolled toward the edge of the cliff and onto the vast platforms that would lower them to the ground below. There, other carts carrying ore moved past

the airship bay in the south to a smaller bay on the east side
of the main dome. Empty carts were leaving the bay, rolling on their sturdy treads back to the platforms awaiting
them.

The mining was automatic, although a few people
monitored the operation in case human intervention was
required or a quake forced them to halt the machines
temporarily. Inside, the ore would be refined and the slag
broken down into its constituent elements, some of which
were used to feed the dome's power plants. This undertaking had been far more demanding than the small-scale
mining that went on around the other settlements, and the
Habbers had helped make it possible.

The roof of the airship bay was opening; the airship
slowly began to drop toward the cradles. Other domes
should have risen around the two now there; other mines
and settlements should have been built in the mountains
beyond.

Dyami suddenly sensed how temporary this refuge
might be. He had lived here clinging to his hope that
whatever happened outside, life in Turing would go on
much as before. Ishtar might hate the Habbers, but he had
thought removing them from the Maxwell Mountain settlements was enough to placate the fellowship. Now he
recalled Teo's warning and the wild, mad look he had seen
in Chimene's eyes. He might lose what he could have here
before he even had a chance to seize it. He had imprisoned
himself for too long.

Suleiman Khan and Allen Sirit were in the bay, standing next to a cart. Dyami waved at them as he descended
the ramp behind the pilots.

"Welcome back," Suleiman called out. "As you can
see, we have the privilege of loading this stuff into the cart
today." He gestured at the crates rolling down another
ramp. "On the other hand, we won't have to walk to the
north dome." The dark young man pulled at his worn gray
shirt. "I'm looking forward to some new clothes."

Dyami turned toward Amina and introduced her to
the two men. "Amina Astarte," Allen said as he rubbed his
short brown beard. "I must admit that name gave me
pause when I first heard you'd be joining us."

"No jokes, please." Amina smiled as she raised one hand. "I've heard them all, believe me."

The pilots stood to one side, near another cradled airship, pointedly ignoring the group. They would stay in the pilots' dormitory just outside the bay with any others who were here and avoid Turing's residents as much as possible. There were usually no more than ten pilots in Turing at any one time, and all of them had permanent residences elsewhere. If these pilots were like the others, they would keep to the area around the dormitory while impatiently awaiting the day they could leave.

Dyami adjusted his duffel. "Need any help?"

Suleiman shook his head. "You go ahead and show Amina around."

The woman lifted her duffel to her shoulder. "Good to have you with us," Allen said before bending down to pick up a crate.

The main dome was already darkening as Dyami and Amina left the bay. A wide road bisected the settlement; the land was so flat that the entrance to the tunnel on the other side was dimly visible. The refinery, a long, low, thick-walled metallic structure, stood on the right side of the road; to the left was the large glassy dome that housed the ceramics plant. The two buildings dominated the landscape, dwarfing the people who were leaving them and making their way to the main road.

"I've seen images of those buildings," Amina said, "but they seem a lot more impressive when you're actually standing in front of them. We ought to get someone to make a mind-tour of this place."

Dyami gazed to his right, where a door in the wall below the dome was opening; carts began to roll out of the small bay up a ramp toward the refinery. He pointed at a square structure just beyond the door. "External operations," he said. "We've got a couple of teams who tend to that, but a lot of us have learned enough to take over once in a while."

A small wilderness of trees covered the land behind the ceramics plant. A cat scurried across the path, moving toward the forest. Dyami took a breath. He had begun to take Turing's spaciousness for granted before his return to the more crowded environs of Oberg; he welcomed the

454 *Pamela Sargent*

scent of grass and the silence broken only by the distant twittering of birds.

"We all live in the north dome," he told Amina. "Originally, the idea was to leave this dome for industrial installations and build houses elsewhere."

"So I heard."

"No passenger carts here. We can wait for Allen and Suleiman, or we can walk."

"Let's walk."

They strolled the long distance between the refinery and the ceramics plant. Amina studied the buildings in silence as they passed, then said, "No one told me where I was to live, and I don't know anyone here. I asked if I should bring a tent, but was told there'd be room for me somewhere."

"We're kind of informal about arrangements," he responded. "You can use one of the tents here until you find something else, or you can go to the women's shelter—they'll have at least a couple of empty rooms. You'll be meeting people in the dining hall, though—maybe one of them will offer you another place to stay."

"I see." She sounded a little worried. He looked down at her; Amina's pretty face was set in a frown. Maybe she shared some of his shyness, in spite of her open manner during their journey. He recalled how he had felt when he first arrived in Turing. The people he met had been friendly enough, but he had sensed that they wanted to assess him before offering him a place in one of their residences. He had lived in a tent for a while; in the end, he had decided it might be best to live alone.

"Maybe you can stay with me, just until you decide where to go," he said. "It isn't much—just a small room where I sleep and a slightly larger one to entertain any visitors. But I don't have many guests, so you can have that room to yourself."

Her steps slowed. "I'd better make one thing clear," she murmured. "I'm an affront to Ishtar. I've tried to offend the Spirit whenever I've been lucky enough to have the opportunity. I'm not interested in men—that's another reason I came here. I was told people here don't care about that, whether they share my inclinations or not, and that Habbers are indifferent to such things."

"You're being very honest."

"If I can't be honest here, there's no hope. If this is just another place where I have to sneak around and lie, then there's no freedom for Cytherians anywhere. I can't live that way anymore—I'd rather not live at all. I have to believe there are some sane people left who can reclaim our world when this madness is past."

Dyami was silent.

"I'm not wrong, am I?" she asked. "It *is* different here, isn't it?"

"Yes, it's different." He stepped in front of her, forcing her to halt. "You don't have to lie, and you don't have to worry about me. I'm an offender against Ishtar myself. Women are friends to me—no more."

He felt as if a weight had been lifted from him, one he had carried for so long that he had forgotten it was there. Even his fear had receded; he would live as he wanted to, for as long as he could remain here.

Amina gaped at him, then threw back her head and laughed. "And you the Guide's brother! No wonder you came here. But I shouldn't laugh." She hooked her arm around his as they walked on. "It must have been even worse for you."

"It was. Until right now I couldn't have said that to you." He lifted his head, inhaling the clean air of Turing.

"No patrols!" she said, and laughed again. "No sashes, no meetings, no obnoxious believers trying to convince you of the truth!" They went down a slope and entered the tunnel.

Dyami was home. This was his home—not Oberg, not the house where he had grown up and had learned to be wary and distrustful. Here the land sloped gently, flattening out around the large lake in the center of the dome. Ahead of him, in a wide hollow between two small hills, a few tents and several tidy square structures that were little more than shacks were clustered around the large dining hall. The men's and women's dormitories lay a little to the east, on flatter grassland bordering a creek; a pale gray building near them housed a lavatory.

He pointed them all out to Amina. "You can't see it, but there's a smaller lavatory just past those tents, behind the hill."

"I guess they weren't exaggerating when they called this place primitive."

"Sorry you came?" he asked.

"Of course not."

A group of people entered the dining hall; he heard a snatch of music before the door closed. "What was that sound?" Amina asked.

"Music. A few people set up a system so we could enjoy music during meals. Some of it's composed by people here. We use the wall screen in the hall to display landscapes or for the more artistic among us to show off their graphic designs. That's the only wall screen we've got over here—the others are in the main dome's buildings. A lot of the shacks don't have toilets, and the doors don't have palm-print locks or any locks at all, and the rooms in the shelters won't hold much more than a mat, but we have music and graphics in the dining hall. Never let it be said that we don't take care of the necessities."

He led her toward the creek, past the dormitories and the lavatory. A few more shacks had been built just above the creek, near a flat wooden bridge that led to the other side. Dyami gestured at two large buildings that sat above the opposite bank. "The Habbers live there."

"They look the same as your dormitories."

"They are, and we all share the dining hall. The Habbers take their turns preparing meals, working in the greenhouse, and cleaning the lavatories just like the rest of us."

"Seems to me Ishtar might profit by your example."

They walked along the creek until they had reached the last shack. Dyami lifted the latch and pushed the door open. "My home." The term came to him easily now. "I've put in a toilet, and a pipe brings water up to my sink from the creek, but you'll have to shower in one of the lavatories —the Habbers won't mind if you use one of theirs. You can clean your clothes in the laundry of the women's dorm."

"You might have provided yourselves with a few more conveniences."

"We do have our priorities," he said. "Music for the dining hall and setting aside time to discuss stellar evolution are clearly more important."

Amina entered the shack. He followed, leaving the

door open, then knelt to turn on the small light resting on the floor. The globe illuminated a space not much larger than his old room in Oberg; a curtain concealed his toilet and sink. Another curtain hung in front of the space where he slept; a rolled-up mat was near the door. "You can use the mat if you like," Dyami said, "but now that you've seen this, you may prefer the dormitory."

"It looks roomy to me. I had to share a room with my sister for quite a few years." Amina looked toward one corner. "What's this?" She sat down, leaned over, and picked up a small metal bust that showed the head of a man. His cheekbones were a sharp ridge below his wide-set eyes; his short hair curled softly over his forehead. She touched the narrow nose lightly. "Where did you get it?"

"I made it," he replied. "I made the mold and cast it over at the refinery after a shift. It's a hobby I took up after I came here—a couple of friends showed me how—but it was months before I could manage anything that looked the way it was supposed to. I've done a few, but I gave the others away."

"Is he someone you know?"

He looked down. "A Habber named Balin."

"Dyami!" Luinne Mitsuo was standing in the doorway, holding a light wand; he beckoned the small woman inside. "And you must be Amina Astarte."

"Greetings," Amina said as she set the bust down.

"I'm Luinne Mitsuo—I'm one of the geologists. Are you going to be staying here?"

"For a while—at least as long as Dyami wants to put up with me."

"I'd offer you a place in my shack, but he's got more room than I do. I was just on my way to the dining hall—I assume you two haven't had time to eat yet."

"No." Amina stood up, leaving her duffel on the floor. "And I'm starving."

"You two go ahead," Dyami said. "My mother and her housemate Kolya insisted on plying me with a feast before I left. If I get hungry, I'll go to the hall later."

"How long will you be up?" Amina asked.

"You won't disturb me even if I'm asleep, so come back whenever you like. No patrols, remember?"

The two women left. Dyami sat and stared at the bust.

Balin would not be at the dining hall now; he usually ate early or else made a meal of some leftovers before going to bed. He got up and went in search of his friend.

A Habber at one of the dormitories told him that Balin had gone for a walk by the lake. Dyami headed in that direction, following the creek past the large greenhouse.

A mower was moving over the grassy plain, followed by a weeding machine. Dyami marched rapidly; his heart was beating more quickly against his chest. He passed another bridge where the creek widened a little, climbed a small rise, and looked out over the lake.

The silence was broken only by the low hum of the mower behind him. The lake was black where it met the shore and silver where the dome light shone down on the water. To the east, near the wood that bordered the lake on that side, he saw a man walking and recognized Balin's slender form.

He hurried over the rocky shore, nearly losing his footing a couple of times before he reached the softer ground under the trees. "Balin," he called out.

The man turned, then walked toward him. "Dyami?"

"I just got back a little while ago." Maybe Balin was not particularly anxious to see him; perhaps he wanted to be by himself. "I was told you'd come here."

Balin clasped his hands. "I'm pleased you came back. I was wondering if you would."

"And why wouldn't I?"

"You might have asked for more time off or asked the people here to find a replacement. Others have done so, to make their peace with the people they left."

"That isn't what I want," Dyami said. "I kept wishing to be back here."

Balin seated himself under a tree. "And how was your visit?"

Dyami hesitated, then sat down next to the Habber. "Not what I expected. My parents were having a problem, but I think they're on the way to resolving it. I managed to avoid my sister for the most part. I saw some old friends. I'm sure I must have mentioned my old schoolmate, Teo Lingard, to you. He wanted me to stay and become part of his household."

He could not see Balin's face in the shadows. He thought of how he had shaped the mold for his bust, how he had imagined his hands on Balin's high cheekbones, cupping his face, touching his narrow lips. "And did he tempt you to stay?"

"No, not really. Teo has to hide what he is there. I didn't tell you that about him before. He loves men, but he's found a way to live with that and conceal it while doing as he likes. I knew I couldn't do the same."

"Why would you—"

"Because I'm like Teo." He shuddered and caught his breath. "I've always been that way." It was easier to admit it in the darkness, clothed in shadows. "I think Teo loved me once, but I was too frightened to accept anything more than some sex when my need grew too great. I told myself it was better if I didn't love anyone."

"And you were afraid to tell me this? But my people have never felt the way yours do about such things."

"I didn't want your pity," Dyami said. "I didn't want to lose your friendship when I knew that was all I could have, and I couldn't risk driving you away by wanting more. I love you, Balin—I know that now."

He was about to rise, then felt a hand on his arm. "Don't go, Dyami."

"You needn't worry. I'll never say it again."

"But didn't you ever think that I might feel the same way?" Balin asked. "I've wanted to be closer to you, but I also thought I might sacrifice our friendship if I admitted it. I didn't want to make a mistake. Even Cytherians who show some friendliness to us might reject such advances."

Dyami swallowed. "Your people—you could have changed yourselves so that none of you would be like me. I used to wonder if you had and pitied us because we couldn't. I thought all those stories about how Habbers would practice any vice were all lies."

"Why would we change anything like that—a natural variation in behavior and response? We never felt the need. The longer we live the more aware we become of the range of responses any individual might have. Many of us here have come to prefer the satisfactions of thought and contemplation, but I find I need others as well. When I feel love, should I welcome it only for a woman and not a man?"

Balin's arms were around him. His fear was gone. Dyami lifted his hands and touched the face he had molded as Balin's lips found his.

Twenty-six

The door closed behind Chimene. She glanced around the empty common room of her house, trying to recall the last time she had been alone. Someone was always with her —a fellow teacher, her students, housemates, members of the patrol whenever she wanted to walk at night, people seeking her advice or simply wanting to be near her. Even when she slept, Boaz or Matthew was always at her side.

She had gone to her mother's house to wish Risa a happy new year before returning to the main dome to put in an appearance at the largest of the celebrations. She had planned to visit the other two domes as well, but a sudden listlessness and urge for solitude had driven her back here. Two volunteers from the patrol had followed her, but she had dismissed them at the door.

Now she was beginning to regret being alone; it allowed disturbing thoughts to enter her mind, doubts about her faith and worries over whether she was doing what was good. Was the Spirit still guiding her? She could no longer tell; lately, the Spirit seemed to speak to her with the voices of Matthew and Boaz. The two men heard Her clearly; she wondered why she could not.

Solitude also brought too many thoughts of Sef. He had continued to come to meetings at her house for a while even after she had stopped inviting him to share the rite there. She had told herself that her love for him was inhibiting her love for others; instead of bringing him closer to the right way, she had dreamed of having him to herself. She had kept away from him, certain that once her struggle with herself was past, his love for her would bring him

461

to seek her out. But he had not come to her, and then he had stopped attending her meetings. Every time she visited his household, Sef spoke with her impersonally and even seemed relieved when she was leaving.

Perhaps he no longer loved her. Maybe others she thought she had won did not love her any more, in spite of all her efforts. She sank onto a cushion and bowed her head.

The door opened; Matthew walked toward her. "I saw you coming back here," he said. "Is anything wrong?"

"Just tired, that's all."

"Too tired to welcome the year of 628?"

She shrugged. "It's Earth's calendar, not ours. It's merely a convention until we devise our own. There's no need to make more of it than it is."

"Ah, but people do enjoy an excuse for a festival." The blond man sat down next to her. "Besides, this won't be just another new year—it marks the beginning of a new phase in our history, when some of our efforts will come to fruition."

It was so. They would be rid of the Habbers at last. All of the settlement Councils were in agreement—not surprisingly, since members of the fellowship held those positions. The long-awaited referendum would be called, and there was no doubt that a large majority of the settlers would vote to expel the Habbers from the settlement in the Freyja Mountains. The pilots who traveled to Turing had been useful in spreading rumors about the growing friendliness and closer ties that were forming between the Cytherians and Habbers in that settlement, and this had fueled the suspicions of many. Others would vote for expulsion only so that they would not be on record in support of this world's enemies. Secrecy in voting, as in other things, did not serve Ishtar.

The Habbers would go. Their agreement would compel them to leave if they were no longer welcome; Turing would be left to Cytherians. The Habbers on the Islands would be next; Alim ibn-Sharif had cultivated allies among his fellow Administrators and with the Project Council on Anwara. Sigurd Kristens-Vitos would be asked to resign as Liaison to the Council. If he gave in gracefully and admitted that the Habbers had led him astray, perhaps he could continue as an Administrator. The Habbers would lose their most powerful ally. If their past history was any indication, they would depart from the Islands rather than risk a confrontation and show themselves to be the cowards they were. They would have to leave or admit that all their talk of only wanting to help Cytherians was a lie.

She almost hoped a few would resist; individual Habbers had occasionally shown a little courage in the past. Some people on the patrol would enjoy demonstrating exactly how futile such actions would be. They were Habbers; she did not have to love them.

"A new era is dawning," Matthew said. "You've worked for this, and yet you seem troubled. In just two days, once we're past these celebrations, the Habbers will see that they no longer have a place here. Are you afraid that they'll try to stand against us? They wouldn't have only Cytherians to contend with but Earth as well."

"Maybe that still troubles me," she said. "With the Habbers gone, there would be little to prevent the Mukhtars from reasserting their control over this Project. It's the reason we've been as patient as we have."

"Now you're sounding like Eva. How many times do I have to tell you that our interests coincide with Earth's at the moment? We want to be rid of the last obstacle to our progress, and the Mukhtars want to look as though they've regained control here. Let them appoint a new Liaison with the Project Council—it's likely to be Alim, and even if it isn't, any Liaison will be forced to work with us. Earth won't interfere—they'll be happy to let us do the work of subduing the recalcitrant and bringing them around to our truth. We'll have an interim during which we can strengthen the fellowship before the Project proceeds with more settlers. This world will be ours, Chimene."

"If the Mukhtars behave as you say they will."

"They have no reason to do otherwise," he said. "They want only the appearance of control—trying for more would cost them too many of their resources, and they'll already have to make up for the help the Habbers won't be able to provide. Let the Mukhtars believe we're their allies. Eventually, when everyone here is part of our fellowship, when we're strong and thriving—that will be the time to break with Earth."

Chimene did not respond.

"It's only a temporary necessity," he went on, "one

that will bring about our perfect society in the end. You'll be the Guide who made that possible. Generations of Cytherians will remember you and bless your name."

She frowned. "Some may say we expelled the Habbers only to bow to Earth."

"No, Chimene. They'll see how wise you were when this world is ours. Don't you know that they love you enough to understand that you wouldn't lead them into error? Do you think they won't trust their Guide? Let the Mukhtars tell their people that Venus is their achievement. Every Cytherian will see that you are the true authority here."

"I have only a Guide's authority," she said, "and the love others choose to give me."

"Sometimes one must make difficult and painful decisions in order to demonstrate one's love. You won't be alone. You'll always have the counsel of those who love you most."

She got to her feet. Matthew rose and took her hands. "Will you return to the celebrations now?" he asked.

Chimene shook her head. "I must rest."

"Then I'll stay with you. You've been under a strain, I know. Perhaps you've waited so long for this time that you can't yet believe that it's nearly upon us."

Dyami did not have to view the results; he already knew what they would be. The Councils Ishtar controlled would not have allowed this referendum without knowing how it would go. The two hundred or so votes of the Cytherians in Turing would not outweigh the thousands of others.

The people standing around him gazed at the large wall screen in silence. He stepped back and looked at those who were seated on the floor around the dining hall's tables. One man pushed his breakfast away, then bowed his head; Luinne Mitsuo lifted a hand to her mouth. No one else seemed surprised.

"We will make arrangements for the Habbers who will be leaving Turing within a week," Boaz Huerta was saying now; the dome Councils had designated him as their spokesman. "We were told that if it was our will that they leave, the nearest Habitat would send a ship for them. Since their presence is not required on the Islands, they will be returning to their home. We have capable people in Turing who can continue working there."

Dyami heard a few sighs. They had been granted that much, at least.

"We Cytherians have spoken," Boaz continued, "and our voices will be heard. Those who share our goals and our vision are welcome here. Those who seek to deceive us and use us in some hidden plan of their own are not."

Dyami could listen to no more. He walked toward the doorway, where Balin was waiting. Music still filled the hall; no one had bothered to turn it off. Allen Sirit had engineered this piece, blending the sounds to reproduce his own composition. Stringed instruments rose to a crescendo and broke against the deeper, more threatening sound of percussion.

The two men left the hall and walked toward the creek, ignoring those they passed. Amina was sitting outside the shack she had built next to Dyami's, her blond head on the shoulder of Tasida Getran. The brown-haired physician looked up at Dyami and said, "I don't have to ask, do I."

He shook his head. "The vote might have surprised them a little. Almost a quarter of the people in Oberg and Curie voted against expulsion. In Mtshana, it was nearly a third."

"But it doesn't make any difference, of course." Tasida's freckled face contorted. "And things will be a little harder for the ones who voted no."

He walked on with Balin. They did not stop until the greenhouse and the bridge leading across to the glassy building were behind them. Balin settled himself on the bank; his eyes were empty, his thin lips pressed tightly together.

"You're going to leave," Dyami said.

"I have no choice."

"You could refuse—all of you could say you won't go. Your people could insist—"

"And what would that accomplish?" Balin asked. "Your people would then say that what Ishtar believes about us is true—that we abide by your wishes only when they don't conflict with ours. Oh, we could bring more ships here and force you to accept us, but will that bring our people closer together? It would only destroy what little goodwill is left for us."

"You think you'll keep it by running away?"

The Habber touched his forehead, where his Link was hidden. "Your people have spoken. So have ours—those who dwell in the Habitats out near Mars. They are saying that we cannot hold out a hand to people who refuse it. This will pass perhaps, and then our people may meet yours again."

"When?" Dyami asked. "But that doesn't matter to you, does it? You may still be alive when everyone now living here is dead. What about those of us in Turing? Doesn't what we want count for anything with you? What about the others who reject Ishtar's dream?"

"That must be your struggle, not ours. You must decide this world's fate. Your people have asked us to leave this planet's surface. Should they ask us to return in the future, we'll do so gladly."

Dyami stepped back. Balin had been his lover for only a year and a half, but that time now seemed to encompass most of his own life. The years before had been lived in the shadow of fear; the boy who had concealed part of himself, who had felt that he would always be alone, was not the man who lived now. He could not have hidden what the Habber meant to him even if he had wished to do so. His openness about his feelings had not only brought him Balin's love, but had also dispelled the lingering doubts some of his colleagues held about him. He had at last been honest with the people here; after their initial surprise, some had come to be true friends. His true life, one without loneliness, had begun.

He should have seen that it could not be the same for the Habber. Balin's life had begun decades before his, and it would continue when his was over. He was no more than a brief interlude. The microscopic implants in the Habber's body would go on maintaining his youth and vigor, replicating new cells to replace the old, when Dyami was no more than a face on a memorial pillar. Balin might have hoped for more years with him, but he had loved others before and would undoubtedly love other people again. Dyami had always known there could be no true bond between them, that this love would pass, yet he had hoped it might endure for longer than this.

"I should have known better than to love a Habber,"
he said. "Once you're with your own people again, you'll
forget me soon enough. You'll tell your friends a few amusing stories about the Cytherian who was foolish enough to
love you, and then you'll forget."

"Do you think this is easy for me? Do you think I
wouldn't stay if I could or take you with me if that were
possible?"

Dyami stared at the ground. "I couldn't go, even if it
were. I'd be giving up on my own world, saying it'd never
be anything better."

"Maybe it will be. We found each other, didn't we? It
didn't matter that I was a Habber and you were a Cytherian. Don't let me leave here thinking that you'll come to
share your people's distrust of us. I have to be able to hope
we can meet again."

"You're abandoning us," Dyami said.

"We're leaving you to decide what your world will be.
You wouldn't have that choice if we remained against the
will of most of your people." Balin reached up and took his
hand. "We'll still have a little more time together. We can
forget the demands of both our worlds for a little while."

Dyami sank to the ground. He would be alone. Easing
the demands of his body with other men later would not
make up for what he was about to lose. Balin would be
gone; he would have to live in shadows again.

Sigurd felt his world slipping away from his grasp. No
Habbers remained in Turing; they were gone now, departing from Anwara in the Habber vessel that had come there
for them. Tesia had summoned him to her room; he had
already guessed what she would say.

He had been wrong in thinking that he could appease
Ishtar, in believing that the wretched cult would never
grow strong enough to challenge him. He had ignored the
plotting of Alim ibn-Sharif and his allies, certain that they
could never gain support for their ambitions from Earth.
He had counted on having the Habber presence here as a
shield; he had expected to have time enough for people to
come to their senses. He had hoped that the people he
served would see reason and remember the true goals of
the Project. Perhaps he had been in power too long to
remember how easily it could be lost.

As usual lately, a patrol volunteer was standing outside the Habber residence, hands hooked around his sash. He glanced at Sigurd briefly, then allowed him to pass. Tesia had been asking him to come here more often, and he knew why; she was convinced, despite his protests, that Alim and his friends had ways of finding out what they said and did in Sigurd's room.

Tesia, wearing a long blue robe, was sitting on her futon. Had he been her lover for over thirty years? It did not seem possible. His waist had thickened a little, and the skin of his once-youthful face sagged a bit more, but Tesia still had the body and face of a girl.

She lifted her chin as he sat down. Her reddish hair was pulled back, making the angularity of her face more evident. "I have something to tell you," she said. "My people have decided to withdraw from Venus entirely. We will be gone in twenty days."

"Aren't you even going to wait until you're asked to leave?"

"There's no reason to wait," she responded. "We know how things will go."

"Maybe you didn't look at the results of that referendum too closely," Sigurd said. "Ishtar's victory wasn't quite as overwhelming as I expected—just a good solid majority. It means that a sizable number of settlers aren't quite so willing to see you go."

"That gives us some hope, but as long as we're here, Ishtar can unite more people by focusing their hatred on us. When we're gone and they see they're rid of us, they'll have to find other outlets. Maybe then, more of your people will be moved to stand against them. To put it another way, it's time to allow this particular kettle to boil."

She was speaking so calmly about possibilities that might bring suffering to many. Habbers, of course, could not bear to witness suffering of any kind. They would rather retreat and let others inflict such wounds on themselves, while Habbers stood aside and told themselves they were blameless.

Tesia could wait. She probably saw his struggles and those of his people as he might view the lives of a short-lived insect colony.

"And when it's boiled over?" he asked. "Maybe Earth will lower the fire. Didn't you think of that?"

"If Earth acts overtly, your people won't give in easily. The Mukhtars would find it difficult both to subdue them and to proceed with this Project without our aid. I think we can expect that our departure will be a temporary one."

He could not even feel angry. She was now viewing his life in the same way he had seen the lives of others— pawns in a game, pieces to be moved in ways that would make his goals for this Project a reality.

"I suppose your people want me to make the announcement," he said. "Maybe you think that if it looks as though I ordered you away, it'll shore up any lingering support I might have. I could give quite a speech, but I'm sure my colleague Alim and his friends will find a way to force me to resign. I may be lucky if I stay on as an Administrator's aide. How gratified Ishtar will be. That bitch Chimene Liang-Haddad will no doubt give a stirring speech of her own about how the new age is beginning to dawn for us."

"One of our ships will head for Anwara," she said. "Because of our respective orbital positions, it can make the journey in less than three days if it leaves sixteen days from now. We'll leave the Platform in your shuttles and meet our ship at Anwara." She paused. "There are only a hundred of us on all of the Islands, so two shuttles should be enough for us—perhaps three, if our closest friends among the Islanders choose to travel with us to Anwara to say their farewells to us there. Surely you won't deny such a request to any Islander who asks."

"Oh, of course not," Sigurd replied. "If anyone's foolish enough to want a few additional moments with those we once thought of as friends, I'll grant them. Even Alim wouldn't object to that, since it will show him exactly who might be most untrustworthy. Some of those people may pay a price for their farewells."

Tesia took a breath. "Those can be the official arrangements anyway." Her face was paler; her hands fluttered nervously.

"What do you mean?"

"They won't be saying farewell to us but to the Islands. Some of us have lovers here or close friends whom we can trust. We'll offer them the chance to come to our Habitat with us. Some will take it, and those who don't won't be people who would betray us. I pleaded with my people for this, and they agreed."

"And exactly how do you expect to accomplish this?" he asked.

"Your pilots will be disabled when they're aboard. There will be Habbers aboard each shuttle capable of piloting it, should the automatic systems fail. When we're in orbit, we'll set course for the Habitat. Our own vessel will never dock at Anwara. Once we're in orbit, the pilots in that ship will go into a high orbit and follow us back. We won't be pursued. You have no vessels docked on Anwara with weapons capable of disabling us at the moment."

Sigurd did not speak.

"We'll return the shuttles, needless to say. I imagine the distaste of your pilots for us will outweigh any fears they might have of reprisals for their carelessness. We know we can reach the Habitat in your shuttles. After all, it's been done before, when our world was close enough to be reached that way. We have those pilots who joined us long ago to advise us."

"And you expect me to see that anyone who chooses to go with you gets aboard those shuttles? That's hardly going to help me here. Alim will never believe that I was unaware of your plans, not after all the years you and I have been together."

She said, "Sigurd, I want you to come with us." She pulled at his arm. "Why do you think I begged my people to allow this? I don't want to leave you behind."

"Some of your people had friends in Turing," he said. "You didn't try to bring along any of them."

"If it had been possible—" Tesia closed her eyes for a moment. "I wish it had been. I had to plead just for this much. You must come."

He gripped her hand tightly, then let go. "I can't."

"Why not? You've done all you can—don't you deserve a life for yourself? You know your position will be precarious when we leave. When it's time, if you and the other Islanders want it, you can return here and rejoin—"

"I might not be a Cytherian by then, but a Habber. No, Tesia. If I leave now, I'll be abandoning my world. I'd be deserting all the people who understood what I was trying to do. I can't do it. I shouldn't even allow others to run away. I'd be wiser to reveal your little plot before you go—that might convince Alim he can trust me a bit more."

"I knew there was a chance of that before I spoke," she said, "but I can't believe you'd do it, and I couldn't hide our plans from you. Sigurd, I was pleading for you—I can't lose you now."

"Would you give up your people for mine?" He did not wait for a reply. "You know the answer to that."

"Sigurd—"

"I'll see you off safely. If I'm reduced to being just a Linker on a team of specialists, I think I can live with that. If some Islanders choose to go with you—well, maybe it's better to be rid of people whose commitment to this world is so weak. You'll forget me, Tesia. You'll have a Habber's long lifetime in which to forget."

"Yes," she whispered. For the first time since he had met her, he saw her weep.

Boaz Huerta arrived at Risa's house just as she and her household were preparing to eat supper. Risa greeted him at the door, then ushered him into the common room while his two male companions waited outside.

"To what do we owe this unexpected pleasure?" Theron asked.

Boaz waved a hand. "I'm not here to dine with you. Sit down with the others, Risa. I have something to say to all of you."

Risa seated herself at the table. Boaz continued to stand, glancing from her to the others. Sef tensed; Theron stroked his beard. Noella moved a little closer to Nikolai; Grazie and Paul kept their eyes lowered.

Boaz said, "Every one of you voted against expelling the Habbers. Frankly, I was a little disappointed to hear it, but perhaps you've been misled by Dyami. Maybe he's told you in his messages about his fine Habber friends and made you think they're not the wretches they are. It hardly matters now. His friends left quickly enough, and soon the ones on the Islands will be gone. This world belongs to us at last."

Risa hated the man; he spoke as if he were Venus's ruler. She struggled to keep her composure. "I have no particular fondness for Habbers," she said. "It only seemed to me, and to my household, that it was unwise to expel

them when we can still make use of their help. We should
have been building more domes by now—being without
the Habbers will only set us back."

"We can go on without them."

"Not easily."

"All things are possible for Ishtar." Boaz smiled; Risa
longed to hurl a plate at his handsome face. "A great deal
of work lies ahead for our Guide during this new era. We'll
all share her burden, of course, but between her spiritual
duties and her consultations with both dome Councilors
and Island Administrators, much will be asked of her. She
is reluctantly giving up her position as a teacher in order to
be better able to serve us all."

"So I've heard," Risa said.

"We also see that it's time for some changes in the
patrol," Boaz said. "Several have shown how valuable they
are in that capacity and should no longer be distracted by
other work. They will become permanent members of the
patrol, although volunteers will continue to work with
them. That will mean others will have to take on their
former duties, but with a few adjustments, that additional
burden shouldn't fall too heavily on anyone."

"What a striking innovation." Risa's mouth twisted.
"For the first time, we'll have people among us who contribute no real labor to the Project."

Boaz lifted his brows. "That comment is unworthy of
you. The patrol guarantees our safety, and the Guide
serves all of us. Surely that is as important as tending our
crops or working a shift in external operations, or anything
else we have to do. It is true that these people will lose the
credit their other jobs gave them. Their allotments must
come from elsewhere."

"Indeed," Theron muttered. "From the accounts of
others, no doubt."

"Can any of us really call what we use ours?" Boaz
asked. "In the end, doesn't everything we have belong to
every Cytherian? Clinging to possessions only makes us
unable to share as we should."

Tell that to my daughter, Risa thought; see how willing Chimene would be to give away the clothes others
make for her, the jewelry Kichi Timsen left her, the provisions her followers bring to her.

"You will make your contributions to the patrol and to

our Guide," Boaz continued. "You'll be asked for only a small percentage of what your household has, to be used for sustaining the permanent members of our patrol and maintaining our Guide. I know I can count on your cooperation. Anything in excess of their requirements will go to those who have less than others."

"A tax," Risa murmured. "It's called a tax. They used to have them on Earth before the Mukhtars devised other ways to distribute resources, before the cyberminds were able to keep records of—"

"Spare me the history lesson, Risa. It isn't a tax, it's a contribution."

"And will we all have to make these contributions?" Noella asked.

"Those who are members of the fellowship have always made their contributions to Ishtar—some more willingly than others." Boaz focused on Nikolai, then Sef. "They are already doing what they can to follow the right way. But others, I'm afraid, must be persuaded—namely, those of you who unwisely voted to keep our enemies on Venus. It's time you learned how to share, and maybe by doing so, you'll be moved to see how much pleasure there is in giving to your brothers and sisters. You will provide a record of everything you hold, including what you make or produce for your own use or for trading. You'll be told what to contribute after that. I've always felt that allowing households to keep such records private only furthers avarice."

Risa clenched her teeth. People knew approximately how much others owned anyway, without having access to such records. Each child had an allotment of credit, to be repaid with work later on. The more unpleasant, tedious, or dangerous one's work was, the more credit one earned, but the credit was useful only as another medium of exchange, to be traded for goods or services; there was little point in accumulating much of it. She knew what others had to offer every time she engaged in trading some of her goods for theirs, and this was not a place where large discrepancies in what people owned had yet developed. Chimene's household, which chose to be more open about such things, claimed to own nothing. Their credit was Ishtar's; their possessions only items that they used or that were given to them without payment being asked—so

they claimed at any rate. In spite of that, they did not lack
for more than their share.

"And if we don't contribute?" Nikolai asked.

"Then you'll learn the joy of sharing by having even
more taken from you. You'd have your house—we mustn't
leave people without a place to live. You'd have to hope
that others aren't as selfish as you and that they'd willingly
share what you may require."

"Too many people will object to that," Risa said.

Boaz shook his head. "I wouldn't go to the trouble of
testing that hypothesis. You'll make your contribution. I
assure you that you won't find it excessive." He turned
toward the door. "I must leave you now."

"To speak to other potential contributors, I suppose."

"Messages will be sufficient for most of the others. All
of the dome Councils are preparing them now. I thought
you deserved a personal visit, Risa—you are the mother of
our Guide."

The door closed behind him. He had not come here as
a courtesy but only to display his power. Risa pushed her
plate of beans aside. "He's a fool," she said. "My daughter
and all of her friends—they're fools. The Habbers haven't
even left the Islands yet, and already they're overreaching
themselves. People won't stand for this."

"You've said that many times," Noella said, "and yet
they always do stand for it, don't they? Anyway, it's only
the people who voted against Ishtar's wishes who will be
affected, and we're a minority here."

Risa got to her feet. "I'm going to my room." It was
time to arrange another meeting with Yakov Serba; maybe
they would finally find a way to act.

Malik waited in the hallway just outside the shuttle
docks, at the edge of the crowd of Habbers and Islanders
who had gathered inside the Platform. The people were
silent; the dark-haired Habber woman next to him
touched his sleeve, then turned away.

Why was he going? He was not acting out of love for
the woman with him; Kyra was only the most recent of
those who had shared his bed. He might gain a Habber
Link, but he had grown used to living without one. He
might be granted a Habber's long life and accomplish no
more with that life than he had here. Yet when Kyra had

asked him to come with her, he had accepted without hesitation.

He could still turn back and say farewell to her here. He surveyed the other Islanders who would soon be exiles on the Habitat. Nearly eighty of them had gathered here, most of them scientists, many of them Linkers; he could understand their reasons for leaving. They could tell themselves that their obligations to their disciplines outweighed their duty to the Project now, that they would betray themselves by remaining in a place where certain kinds of inquiry would be discouraged and their knowledge used for the cult's ends. Some could cling to the belief that they might return here eventually. The Project would be losing some of its most gifted people, but he could see why they had made this choice.

He might have shared their feelings once, but he no longer did. He was a historian trying to escape this world's history and his own past. He wanted to be free of his daughter and her mad dream, the child who had failed him and whom he had failed.

A door to one room opened; a pilot entered the hall. The man shook back his graying sandy-brown hair as he glanced at the crowd. The pilot's name came to Malik then —Evar IngersLens, a former lover of Risa's and a devout member of the cult. He had sought Malik out a few times during short stays on Island Two, apparently feeling that it was his mission to bring the Guide's father closer to Ishtar. Malik had not seen him for nearly three years.

Evar beckoned to him; Malik walked toward the pilot. "So you're saying good-bye to the Habbers," Evar said. "Kind of an inconvenience for you, and one that may prove embarrassing. This isn't exactly a time to show how much feeling you may have for such people."

Malik gestured toward Kyra. "The woman's been a close friend. Since I'll never see her again, I wanted these last moments with her."

"I hope you can tolerate your quarters in Anwara if a shuttle isn't available to bring you back right away. With this group, they'd have to crowd you in. I'm surprised Administrator Sigurd is allowing this, but then he's been all too close to a Habber himself. It won't do him any good when they're gone."

"Are you going to be one of our pilots?" Malik asked.

Evar shook his head. "I'm just getting ready for the run to Oberg. I'll be attending a meeting at the Guide's house when I'm back. I'll give her your greetings, though she won't be happy to know you came here."

"My sins can't touch my daughter," he said. "After all, she has the consolations of her truth. She proves her virtue by refusing to let even her own father lead her into error."

The pilot frowned. "I feel sorry for you, Malik, you and those others. It's hard to say farewell to friends, knowing you won't be with them again."

"But of course Habbers can never be our friends. My daughter, the Guide, is always saying so. Maybe when they're gone, we'll be more receptive to the Guide's wisdom."

"The Guide is wise," Evar said quickly. "Even so, I wonder what will happen now." He lowered his voice. "I've never believed that story about the Habbers loosing the fever on us. I've examined it, and I always come to the conclusion that they had nothing to gain. That they might subvert us with friendliness—that I could believe—but provoking our hostility would be useless. They were useful, whatever reasons they had for being here. Administrator Sigurd might have favored them a little too much, but he kept them in check, and Earth at a distance. He kept us freer than we might otherwise have been."

"You sound as though you're sorry they're going."

"I'm only saying that Ishtar may not be served by this. If the Guide and those close to her had waited, maybe—" Evar sighed.

Malik looked away from the man. If Evar, whom Risa had rejected because of his dogged adherence to his faith, was saying such things, others had to be thinking them as well. But maybe this was only a ploy designed to ferret out what Malik was thinking. Ishtar's believers were like that, eliciting confidences from others on the grounds that all should be shared and no secrets kept, and then using the confessions against those who had made them. It did not matter; he would not be here to suffer the consequences for anything he said to the pilot.

"Driving the Habbers away is a mistake," Malik said softly. "Earth is probably welcoming this development, even though it will now cost them more to keep the Project going. They'll be able to reassert themselves, and Ishtar may not be strong enough to prevent that. One might almost think that Earth had a hand in bringing this about."

"The Guide wouldn't—"

"The Guide is my daughter. She may talk of being open and honest, but she learned how to hide a great many things from me when she was growing up. She had her reasons, of course—she was preparing to serve a higher truth by sneaking off to see Kichi Timsen. Maybe she has similar rationalizations now for whatever she does."

Evar glanced at the timepiece on his finger. "My airship is waiting," he murmured. "Perhaps we can talk again, when I come back to Island Two. I've been seeing lately that even an unbeliever can sometimes shed some light."

"Even if it means questioning your Guide's judgment?"

"I can't doubt her, but those around her—" Evar paused. "A few near our Guides in the past sometimes strayed from the right way, though never in matters as important as this. Farewell, Malik. I'll hope to see you when you return."

The pilot hurried away; Malik returned to Kyra's side. She looked up at him as she motioned in Evar's direction; Malik shook his head. "An old acquaintance," he said, "trying to tell me I wasn't wise to be here."

"You aren't regretting that you are?"

"No."

A cart was rolling toward them, carrying eight pilots, Tesia, and Sigurd. The Administrator had not confided in Malik, but he was convinced that Tesia had told Sigurd everything and that the Linker was planning to join them. That had to be why he was allowing all these people to board the shuttles; he was going to leave with Tesia himself.

The cart came to a stop; the blue-clad pilots climbed out and began to station themselves in front of the four nearest dock entrances. Sigurd helped Tesia down, then gripped her arms for a moment.

People turned toward the Administrator. "We can all be grateful to the Habbers here," Sigurd called out, "for seeing that it was our will that all of them depart, instead of staying here and trying to work against that decision. Because of that, I am allowing you to make this journey to-

gether and to share these final few moments. God go with
you. I shall await the return of you Islanders, when we'll
redouble our efforts on the Project's behalf."

The crowd stirred. Tesia trembled as Sigurd released
her. Malik shot the Administrator a glance; Sigurd stared
directly at him as he climbed back into the cart, then
bowed his blond head. The cart turned and rolled back
down the wide hall. Tesia leaned against another Habber
woman, her face pale.

Malik was suddenly afraid. How could Sigurd remain
behind? Would anyone believe that he didn't know what
was about to happen, that his Habber woman would conceal that from him? Even if others imagined that Sigurd
had been deceived, that would hardly strengthen his already shaky position. No, Malik thought, Sigurd would betray them all first. He could demonstrate his loyalty by
revealing more Habber perfidy and punishing the Islanders who had rashly hoped to escape. Perhaps he was already summoning others through his Link, people who
would come for the Islanders and then release some of
their anger against the Habbers before allowing them to
leave.

He waited, expecting to see other carts move down
the hall toward them, carrying people who would drag
him away to certain punishment. But the doors to the
docks were opening; people began to file inside. The two
pilots by each entrance stared at their pocket screens,
checking the names.

Malik and Kyra were soon at one entrance. They murmured their names; the female pilot seemed surprised as
she peered at Malik, but did not speak. They entered the
wide cylindrical dock and moved toward the ladder that
led to the shuttle's entrance. Kyra climbed up first; Malik
followed. Perhaps Sigurd was only waiting to give one last
chance to anyone who might have second thoughts. Malik
could still turn back. The familiar weariness settled over
him, the same lassitude he had felt when he decided to
travel to the camp near Tashkent. He no longer had the
strength to resist whatever happened to him.

The other passengers were already strapped into their
seats. Malik and Kyra climbed to the front of the shuttle
along the handholds and rungs jutting out from each seat
until they found two empty places. He waited until Kyra

had settled herself, then eased into the seat next to her and stretched out, his feet against the wall.

He wondered if life was truly different among the Habbers. Did they oppose one another, or struggle and quarrel among themselves? Was their history more than the merry-go-round he knew so well? Had they found a better way?

The two pilots climbed toward the front of the ship. Malik watched as two Habbers in seats across from his loosened their harnesses and crept out onto the rungs. The pilots were just below the door leading into their cabin; Malik's mouth was dry.

The male pilot looked down as a third Habber began to leave his seat. "Get back," the pilot shouted; the Habber just below him suddenly pressed a metal cylinder against his calf. The pilot fell backward; one Habber man caught him and pushed him into one of the empty seats.

The female pilot was trying to get inside the cabin. The Habber nearest to her lashed out with his cylinder and missed. She grabbed at a rung and lost her grip; her body twisted to one side as she fell across Malik. Her hands clawed at him; the Habber man pressed his cylinder against her spine. She sagged into unconsciousness; her fingers loosened their grip on Malik's arm. Someone pulled her away and dumped her into another seat as the two Habbers in the front of the ship disappeared behind the door of the pilots' cabin.

Malik trembled; they still might not be safe. If the female pilot had been able to reach the cabin, she might have had just enough time to send out a warning; a pilot in one of the other ships could already be doing so. He stared at the small screen in front of him, his body tense. Kyra brushed his hand lightly, then gazed at the other small screen, which also showed the inside of the dock.

A message would come now; someone was probably already preparing it. They would be told that they would have to leave the ship and return to the Islands for certain punishment. No one would believe that the Islanders aboard these shuttles were ignorant of the Habbers' plans.

"Prepare to launch," a voice said over the shuttle's comm. The dock was opening above them; the shuttle began to rise on its lift toward the Platform's surface. On the screen, he saw the vessel resting inside a circle of light.

Malik's hands dug into his armrests. A weight suddenly pressed him against his seat as the Platform fell away. He glimpsed the glow of an Island dome before everything was lost in the darkness.

He struggled for breath. At last the pressure eased, and then he floated up against his harness as the ship fell into orbit. The screen revealed only a black expanse; Venus was hidden. Voices murmured over the comm. A curving band of light shimmered at the edge of the Parasol, then blossomed as the vessel emerged from the umbrella's vast shadow and was caught in the light of the sun.

"Respond." The voice over the comm sounded urgent. "Can you hear me? Do you have a malfunction? Can any of you hear me? Please respond. My screen shows that your orbital path—"

The comm was silent. The southern Bat was now visible. Its winged panels gleamed with sunlight; the tiers of the satellite's docks were a jeweled latticework twinkling in the shadow cast by the Parasol. An aurora's colorful curtains of light danced below the Bat.

Malik gazed one last time at the planet below and thought of Sigurd, who had chosen not to escape, who was now trapped in the darkness. The shuttle hurled itself out of orbit toward the nearest Habitat.

Sigurd waited in his room. His Link was silent, as it had been for the past few days, ever since the four shuttles and their pilots had returned to Anwara from the Hab. The Project Council had demanded his resignation as Liaison, and had appointed Alim ibn-Sharif in his place. He had expected it.

He had not expected the silence. Every channel was closed to him; his Link opened only when there was a message for him, and there had been few such messages lately. The Project Council had not told him what would become of him now; perhaps they would leave that to Alim and his allies.

He might have escaped whatever lay in store for him. He had thought that by staying behind, he might still have some power to influence events, that he would be showing others he had not given up his hopes. Even some of Ishtar's own believers were beginning to see that the absence of the Habbers made the future more uncertain; those nearest the Guide were trying to tighten their grip too quickly. Sigurd had imagined that in time the Project would turn to him again.

He thought of Pavel Gvishiani, as he had so often lately. Perhaps the most he could hope for was to be honored after his death, as Pavel had been, when people would realize that he had tried to preserve his world. Maybe he would not even have that; the minions of Ishtar might erase his memory. The Mukhtars would be tempted to exert more authority over Venus now, but wiser heads might prevail, allowing Ishtar's inner circles to consolidate their power before Earth reasserted itself here. Perhaps they would let Chimene Liang-Haddad believe she had won before she was forced to bow to Earth, as she eventually would if the Project were to continue. By then, there might be no one left to object to Earth's rule, especially if the Mukhtars wielded their power subtly and granted some concessions to the Guide.

He no longer believed what Tesia had told him. The Habbers would never return.

His door chimed. Sigurd knew who was waiting outside even before his visitors were announced. The airship carrying Chimene to Island Two would have arrived by now, and he was sure Alim had met her.

"Chimene Liang-Haddad," the door announced. "Alim ibn-Sharif. Boaz Huerta. Eva Danas. Matthew—"

"Let them all enter," Sigurd muttered, cutting off the voice. The damned woman must have brought her whole household to confront him here.

The door opened. Alim, wearing his formal white robe and headdress, ushered the group inside, then settled his plump body on a cushion. Eva Danas and Yusef Deniz sat down behind Alim as Chimene entered with Boaz Huerta and Matthew Innes. Sigurd caught a glimpse of one of Alim's aides and two sashed men carrying wands before the door closed.

"Salaam," Sigurd said. Boaz and Matthew seated themselves; Chimene continued to stand. Her arms were folded, her fingers claws digging into the sleeves of her red tunic. "You honor me with this visit. I didn't expect to have the pleasure of greeting all these others in your household as well."

"My other housemates were sorry they couldn't

come," she replied. "They knew we weren't coming here
to honor you. They wanted me to tell you how deeply they
regret not being able to see you now." Her dark eyes
narrowed. "You're wearing your formal robe."

"In your honor."

"You no longer have the right to wear it."

"This is the robe of a Linker." The wretched woman
probably could not tell the difference. "As you can see, the
material isn't quite as fine. I've set aside my Administrator's robe until I discover what God has ordained for me."
So he would no longer be an Administrator; that was
hardly a surprise.

"The Guide is saying," Alim murmured, "that you are
no longer entitled to wear *that* robe. Your Link has been
closed, Sigurd. A physician will soon be summoned to remove it."

Sigurd drew in his breath. "That hardly seems wise,
when we've lost a number of Linkers already."

"Some have proven themselves unworthy of that position," Alim responded, "not only those who betrayed us by
fleeing to that Hab but also several who have remained
behind. A couple of them have already been brought to
admit that they knew what the Habbers were planning
and didn't tell us of that. They were foolish to think they
could keep that secret. It's pitiable how they ask for forgiveness because they chose not to go. Others will lose
their Links—those who were too close to the Habbers and
the ones who were too loyal to you."

Sigurd leaned forward. "You're mad. That's not going
to serve the Project."

"The Project is best served by Linkers whose loyalty is
unquestioned. People can be trained to replace the others,
and in the meantime—"

"You're not fit to be Liaison," Sigurd said. "You're going to create more enemies than you have now. The Project Council—"

"—is not objecting," Alim finished. "They are leaving
such matters to me and the Administrators here." He
touched his forehead as he nodded toward Chimene. "And
the Guide is generously offering to consult with me."

"What a fine prospect," Sigurd said. "I think you could
manage enough mistakes in judgment on your own."

"You cursed man." Chimene took a step forward. "I'm

finding it very hard to feel any love for you now. You knew what the Habbers were planning—you had to know. That woman of yours would have told you. You knew and you let them go."

"I knew nothing." He no longer expected anyone to believe that.

"Oh, you knew. I should have seen something was going on when I heard you were going to allow them all to travel to Anwara together—such compassion is uncharacteristic of you. You wanted to hurt the Project—that's why you let them go."

Sigurd's lip curled. "I'm surprised you feel that way, Chimene. You've only lost people who've shown they weren't that devoted to the Project anyway."

"You wanted to wound me!" Her voice had risen; her face was flushed with rage. "My father was with them! You made it possible for my own father to join them! They played on his weakness—they lured him to their beds for whatever perversions they practice, and then they stole him from me! How can I ever forgive you for that?"

He looked away, thinking of the little girl who had once dwelled on this Island, the one who often seemed to be searching her father's face for a sign of his love. Malik had cared for her once; perhaps he had cared too much. He had been wounded all the more when Chimene had dashed his hopes for her by joining herself to Ishtar. She had lost his love and would never have it again.

"But I must forgive you," she went on more calmly. "You've been so misled by the Habbers that you may not have comprehended what you did. You will be brought to repent of your actions, and maybe then you'll glimpse the truth. Maybe then I can come to love you as the Spirit demands. I'll try to believe that something good inside you made you stay behind."

"I made my share of mistakes. I felt it was appropriate to pay for them. You may have more sympathy for me should you ever have to pay for your own."

"You'll pay," she said. "You'll lose your precious Link, and we'll find ways for you to aid the Project."

Boaz got to his feet and went to her side. "You shouldn't have had to endure this," he said softly as he took her arm. "Your father may already be regretting what he did, what this man allowed him to do. But our world is rid

of the Habbers and belongs to Ishtar now." He turned back
to Sigurd. "Eva and Yusef will be returning to our household in a few days, but the Guide will remain here somewhat longer, with her brother Matthew and me. These
quarters look comfortable enough for us. One should
never grow attached to possessions, but you'll be allowed
to take whatever items you can carry in a pack."

"And where will I go?" Sigurd asked.

"I think the former Habber residence here would be
suitable, at least for the time being. You'll be able to
recuperate from the loss of your Link there, and you probably won't be alone for long—others whose loyalty is
doubtful should be joining you. You'll have time to think
about the so-called friends who were willing to abandon
you and who could not stand against us. You will have time
to hear of Ishtar." Boaz bowed a little toward Alim. "That
is, if our new Liaison with the Project Council has no objection."

"Of course not," Alim murmured.

"You may gather your things now," Boaz said. "We'll
be with Administrator Alim in his quarters. Two members
of the patrol will be here to assist you."

The others stood up. As they left the room, two men
with wands entered and took places on either side of the
door. Sigurd gazed at them absently. What a pointless gesture he had made; how mistaken he had been to assume
that even Alim would not allow Sigurd to be disgraced so
completely.

"Get your things," one of the men said. Sigurd stood
up slowly and took off his robe.

Chimene released Alim's arm as they neared a small
flight of steps. The Administrator had asked her to walk
with him, but he was already panting a little; he wiped at
his round face with the edge of his headdress. She had
been a little surprised at the invitation; at dinner, she had
noticed, he seemed more interested in talking to Matthew
and Boaz.

Her housemates had not accompanied them here;
they were trailed only by two female members of the
patrol. She climbed the steps toward the curved platform
that circled Island Two; Alim wheezed a little as he followed. During dinner she had feared that the man might

show a more intense interest in her, but his food had preoccupied him then, and the walk had clearly drained more
of his energy. She felt relieved; it would not be necessary
to discourage his attentions. She had to work with him, but
as long as he was not her brother in Ishtar, she did not have
to share more of herself with him.

The women on patrol waited at the bottom of the
steps. Alim leaned against the railing with a sigh. "A new
era," he said somewhat breathlessly. "Even if I can't share
your faith, our goals are the same. You do understand—I've
always tried to be tolerant of the beliefs of others. Many
roads can lead to what is right, and God's will governs us
all."

"The Spirit seems willing to work through you. She
asks only that others be open to the truth. I can pray that
you may come to accept it."

She curled her fingers around the railing. The dome
overhead was dark, with a pale silvery disk at its center.
She and her housemates had dined with Alim at a table
near the path outside the ziggurat, in full view of the
passers-by; she had walked with him here to the edge of
the Island past people sitting outside their residences. She
had recognized a few old schoolmates, people who had
once called her a grubber, who had sneered while saying
that she did not belong in their school, that she was there
only because her father was a favorite of Sigurd's. She had
enjoyed letting them see her on such friendly terms with
Alim; maybe they now regretted their mockery. But such
thoughts were unworthy. Some of those people now wore
the sash; even those who were not her brothers and sisters
would have to honor her now. She could bring herself to
love them, since they would see how mistaken they had
been.

Perhaps they were whispering about her father, who
had fled from her. Chimene's hands tightened on the railing; she had to put aside thoughts of Malik's treachery. He
had been only another obstacle in recent years, with his
infrequent sardonic messages that upset her and caused
her to doubt herself. He would be sorry when he was living
among Habbers and saw how easily he had been misled.
The Habbers had deliberately enticed him in an effort to
strike back at her; that probably showed how much they
feared her. Did they expect her to lash at herself in agony

because her enemies had taken her father? She would prove herself stronger than that.

Alim dabbed at his damp face with a sleeve of his formal robe. "Our walk seems to have tired you," Chimene said. "Perhaps I should have refused your kind offer to walk with me."

"Oh, no, my dear. I should keep myself more fit and stronger for my new responsibilities."

"Maybe you need a metabolic adjustment."

"I've had a couple. I only end up eating more, and I'm also too much in the habit of using carts. Any more metabolic tampering, and I'd turn into a wisp if we ever had food shortages. No, I simply must discipline myself—more walking and less food." He looked mournful at the prospect. "Anyway, I wanted to speak to you alone."

She felt a qualm. "Oh?"

"I felt you might need some reassurance," he said. "You didn't seem happy with some of what Boaz and Matthew said at dinner."

"My brothers are wise, but I also worry that they dismiss possible difficulties too easily. We are embarking on a new era, but I still fear what Earth may do. I wouldn't want the Mukhtars to think that with the Habbers gone, they can have a freer hand here. It's true that we have less to fear from Earth than from Habbers, but surely Earth is better served by allowing us more control of our own affairs. Boaz often seems indifferent to the Mukhtars' possible reactions."

"That's exactly what I wanted to reassure you about," the Administrator responded. "I know how to deal with Earth. As long as I'm Liaison, you needn't concern yourself with the Mukhtars. Leave the Project Council and the Mukhtars to me. I can grant them enough small concessions to keep them from wanting larger ones, and none of it will affect us in the least. In fact, I had a message from the Project Council today."

Chimene raised her brows. "You didn't mention it at dinner."

"I wanted you to hear about it first. The Mukhtars are gratified that the Habbers are gone, and they're not about to offend the Guide who made that possible. They'll aid us in whatever way they can, and all they'll ask is that we go on with our service to the Project. They're aware of your great love for your people and the love they bear you. They have no desire to interfere with anything that can only further the progress of the Project."

She smiled a little.

"The Mukhtars were upset by Sigurd's recent actions," he continued, "but he will be punished, and the Project is now on its proper course. What he did only shows how far he forgot his duty, and his fate will be an example to others. The Mukhtars may choose to believe that I have their interests at heart, but you and I know that we both serve Venus in the end. I'll intercede for you, and you and your followers will have a free hand here."

"Only so that others can be brought to our way."

Alim placed a hand over his heart. "I'm moved by the love I see for you in the eyes of those closest to you. It only makes me admire you more, that you can elicit such devotion. I can even—may God forgive me—feel a little envious. All of us will serve you. Even I, who am not your brother in Ishtar, only want to share the burden you bear as the Guide." He was silent for a moment. "Someday, you may even meet the Mukhtars as an equal, as the ruler of our world."

"I'm only the Guide," she said, "not a ruler."

"But you must guide your people. That may require acting as a ruler would, but only to bring the society you want closer. Won't you help your people more by accepting any power that's given to you? You can set it aside when your goals are achieved. I've spoken highly of you to the Project Council. Word of that should reach the Mukhtars in one of the Council's reports."

She turned toward the dome wall just beyond the railing. Her world was below, hidden by the dark and turbulent clouds. Centuries of effort had made it possible for people to live here, and now their fate was in her hands. Could she turn away now and say that a Guide's duty was only to persuade and set an example but not to rule? She had accepted other necessary evils to further Ishtar's aims and had accomplished more than Kichi had envisioned.

I am Ishtar, she thought; I carry the dreams of all my people. I could not have won this much unless the Spirit had guided me and had spoken to me with the voices of those around me. With every step along this path, more obstacles to the truth have vanished. The Spirit is with me. Even Earth's Mukhtars will see that now, and all they understand is power—seeking it and keeping it. They have to see me as one with the power to stand against them, and when we are stronger, I can share my power with all of my sisters and brothers. Perhaps I must rule now, as the Spirit rules me . . .

Twenty-seven

Three members of the patrol were walking past Risa's house when she came outside. One man lifted a wand in greeting; Risa forced herself to smile as she waved back.

Theron was sitting under a tree with Yakov Serba; she went toward the two men. Risa had been careful to alert the patrol that some of her friends and neighbors would be gathering there tonight and that they needn't trouble themselves about any visitors who left her home late. Just a small party, she had told them, while Irina Burian was visiting with her son from ibn-Qurrah. She had even invited Andrew Dinel, although he and his bondmate Grete had stayed only long enough to greet Irina and share a drink with her and Nikolai. It did not matter; Andrew's respectable presence, however brief, had probably also reassured the patrol.

She sat down next to Yakov. Theron held out his cup of whiskey; she shook her head.

"I had a message from Dyami yesterday," she said. "In his customary roundabout way, he let me know that the people in Turing would support us in whatever we do." Lately, she preferred to discuss such matters outside. She could not escape the feeling, irrational though it might be, that otherwise someone might be listening in to whatever she said. She inspected her house often, searching for any small eavesdropping devices a visitor might have planted, but she had not yet found anything. She used only private channels to speak to her son but remained cautious in what she said, as he did.

489

"I expected they'd feel that way," Yakov murmured. "Unfortunately, there's not much any of us can do."

"I've been hearing more complaints lately," Theron said, "about the patrol, about the months the Guide has spent on Island Two."

Risa had heard similar complaints. The patrol had grown more heavy-handed, even restricting the movements of people they distrusted. There was some divisiveness within the patrol's ranks; the volunteers were beginning to resent the permanent members, who seemed to think all decisions should rest with them. Other people worried about the specialists and Linkers the Project had lost—those who had fled with the Habbers and those who had been detained and deprived of their Links. Even among the pilots, who as a group had always been strongest in their devotion to Ishtar, there was muttering about the Guide who might have forgotten her duty to the fellowship and who spent more time with Administrators than with her brethren. All of this free-floating discontent might be useful to Risa and those who felt as she did, if they could find a way to harness it.

But they had not. The domes on which their lives depended had to be maintained, and this required their cooperation, regardless of their feelings. Some had spoken of trying to poison food taken to the Guide's household or of using more discontented members of the patrol against those they resented, but such actions could also bring reprisals that might destroy any chance for change. A few wilder ideas had also been entertained—refusing to work, threatening one settlement or more with destruction if Ishtar and the Administrators did not give in to certain demands, even seizing the Platform. Risa had done her best to put a stop to such speculation; it was not likely that they could succeed, and such attempts would give the cult more excuses to tighten their control. Even if they could succeed, she was not about to encourage anything that could only threaten the world they hoped to save.

"Irina says things are a little worse in ibn-Qurrah," Risa said.

"So I've heard," Yakov responded. "More people are being asked for larger voluntary contributions."

"Contributions!" Risa cursed under her breath. "It's a good thing Andy so kindly brought us two bottles of whiskey—otherwise, I doubt there would have been enough for all our guests."

"We have to hope things do get worse, you know," Yakov continued. "That would mean more people would be likely to side with us."

The engineer, unfortunately, was right. If things got worse, they would have a chance to make them better. They could not possibly succeed against Chimene and her inner circle unless more of the settlers, including members of the cult, came over to their side.

The door to the house opened. Carlos Tokugawa walked down the path, carrying his small son; his daughter clung to his other hand. Lena Kerein followed her bondmate and children outside. "Thanks for the hospitality," Carlos said as he passed. "Nice seeing Irina again."

"Going so soon?" Risa asked.

"Carlos wants to take the children home," Lena said, "but I'll stay for a bit." She kissed Carlos, then settled herself in front of the globe of light next to Risa.

Risa eyed the younger woman warily; she had never been sure of how much she could trust Lena. "It's too bad Chimene couldn't be here to see Irina," Lena went on, "but I suppose she's getting too grand to bother about a little get-together like this."

There, Risa supposed, was the source of some of Lena's discontent. Chimene did not often see her old friend, and lately their exchanges had been limited to an occasional message.

"It might be just as well," Risa said. "Chimene and Irina were never especially close."

"Still—" Lena gestured with an arm. "It's those people around Chimene. I can't tell you how many times I've called or gone to her house, only to have Matthew or Eva or that old man Lang tell me that she's too busy to see me. She listens to them too much, especially Boaz."

Risa pursed her lips. "You're speaking of the prospective father of my grandchild—that is, if my daughter ever finds the time in her busy schedule to give birth."

"Too bad for you. Frankly, I never liked Boaz. Oh, he probably serves well enough as a bed-partner, but I think he lost sight of our ideals long ago—sharing goes one way with him. If Chimene didn't love him so much, she'd see what he is fast enough, but she's the Guide, and she probably can't believe that anyone so close to her might give her bad advice." Lena's mouth twisted. "Let's hope the Spirit opens her eyes soon and brings her back to the right path."

Lena might believe that Chimene had only been misled by her companions; Risa was not sure that she shared that belief. It would have been easier if she could, if she could hope that some sort of reconciliation might be possible.

"I think she made a terrible mistake in calling that referendum," Lena continued.

"Our dome Councils were responsible for that," Theron said.

"But we all know they would have sought the Guide's advice or Boaz's, which amounts to the same thing nowadays. She might have used her influence to postpone it or to point out what a bad idea it was."

"You didn't seem to think," Risa said, "that expelling the Habbers was a bad idea at the time." She knew how Lena and her household had voted then.

"Maybe I've changed my mind." Lena brushed at a loose strand of brown hair. "This wasn't the time to get rid of them, not when we still need their help. We could have been building more settlements in the Freyja Mountains by now, and it's not going to be easy to do that alone. People may wonder about the wisdom of their votes when they're told there's no room to build new houses or that there'll be even more restrictions on the number of children they have. A couple of my friends—fervent believers, I assure you—are even saying that things were better when the Habbers were here and Sigurd Kristens-Vitos was the Liaison."

Risa frowned. She had heard no news of Sigurd since his disgrace. Maybe he was regretting that he hadn't fled with the Habbers; perhaps he was no longer alive. She wondered if Chimene and those around her were capable of ridding themselves of Sigurd once and for all.

"You're certainly being blunt," Theron said.

"I wouldn't talk this way to just anyone," Lena replied. "But I don't think any of you will think unkindly of my words." Theron stared at her blandly; Yakov was trying to look unconcerned. "I'm even more worried after the message I got from Chimene earlier."

"Oh?" Risa arched her brows.

"She does still occasionally send off a few words, usually when she's got something to brag about. It wasn't anything specific this time, just hints about the Mukhtars taking a greater interest in our affairs and consulting with the Project Council about how to proceed. She seems to think this growing interest is a sign that even the Mukhtars are willing to work with her—and Administrator Alim, of course—out of gratitude for the fact that the Habbers are gone. Well, when Earth starts getting more interested in us, I begin to worry."

"I expected that they would," Yakov said. "We will be more dependent on them now, but since Earth doesn't have to worry about Habbers trying to subvert us any more, chances are—"

"You hope," Lena said. "Anyway, I thought you might be interested in what she told me, vague as it was." She stood up. "I'd better get home. Do tell Sef I thought his berry wine was delicious."

Risa was silent until Lena was out of earshot, then said, "I wonder why Lena dropped that tidbit our way."

"Maybe she suspects that we'd all like to do more than complain," Theron answered. "It might be her way of saying that she's with us. If she spreads news of that message around, it could sow doubt about what Earth's intentions are, and that could help us."

"Do you think she can be trusted?" Yakov asked. "You know the woman better than I do."

"She's an old friend of Chimene's," Risa said. "Her faith in Ishtar isn't a fanatic's, but she admires its ideals. Lena probably believes that if she went and had a stern talk with her old schoolmate, Chimene would suddenly see reason."

"Well." Yakov sipped from his cup. "We certainly wouldn't want her betraying any of our plans in an effort to convince the Guide to mend her ways."

"Our plans." Risa shook her head. "Even if we came up with some, they won't mean much if Earth decides to reclaim the Project entirely. Almost everyone would be on our side then, but it would be too late." Their dream of a new world would die, one where people might reach for more instead of clinging to what they had. They would become only another Nomarchy used to display the power of the Mukhtars while Ishtar filled their minds with illusions. Earth's stagnant, dying culture would strangle them.

Risa got to her feet slowly. "I must go inside," she said, "and be more hospitable to our guests." She turned toward the house. Was she nearly sixty already? Once, she would have found that unbelievable; now, she felt even older, weighed down by her burdens. She had many to carry now —a dead child she still mourned, a former bondmate who had shown his lack of faith in this world by fleeing to a Hab, a daughter besotted with a mad dream, who had become her enemy.

Chimene awoke late. For a moment, she felt disoriented, then recalled that she was back in her own room, having returned to Oberg the day before. Boaz and Matthew had gone back to the settlement a few weeks earlier and had assembled a group of nearly one hundred people to greet her outside the bay. The crowd had cheered when they saw her; two children had presented her with a garland of red flowers. She might have been more moved by the display if she hadn't felt so tired.

She longed for rest, for a few quiet weeks with her friends, but Boaz was already making plans for her to begin a tour of the other settlements. He had pointed out that the other dome Councils would appreciate seeing her after her sojourn on the Islands and that her presence at meetings in the other communities would inspire her followers now. He had talked of little except the trip after her return; she felt tired just thinking about it. There would be more months away from her home, more speeches to prepare, more people asking for spiritual guidance or inviting her to their houses. But Boaz would come with her and ease her burden however he could.

She forced herself to sit up. Her bed was empty; Boaz had gotten up without disturbing her. She glanced at the timepiece on the table near the bed; the others would be finished with breakfast by now.

By the time she had washed, dressed, and entered the common room, she found the rest of the household still seated around their trays of dishes. Two guests were with them, a blond young man, who seemed familiar, and a slender dark-eyed girl she did not know.

Before she could greet them, Lang Eberschild got to

his feet. "I'll fetch you some breakfast," the gray-haired man said.

"And I'd better be on my way," Galina Kolek murmured as she stood up. "I've got two patients at the infirmary to see. It's good to have you back, Chimene—too bad you won't be staying that long."

"I wish I could." Chimene seated herself on the floor. "But it will give me joy to see brothers and sisters I don't often have the chance to visit."

Galina picked up her bag and hurried out the door; Lang returned with a bowl of grain soup, herb tea, and some fruit. "You know at least one of our guests." Josefa Huong gestured at the young man. "Maxim Paz—he says he was one of your pupils."

The blond man gazed at her with his black eyes before lowering his head. She remembered him now—an attractive but sullen boy, who did not have many friends and who had displayed no particular intellectual prowess. He had left school at twelve to apprentice himself to an airship mechanic.

"I'm happy to see you again." She was a little annoyed that no one had told her there would be guests. "Still working in the airship bay?"

The young man nodded. "I'm a patrol volunteer, too."

"That's recent," Boaz said, "but he seems to be working out well enough. Maxim has been visiting us from time to time while you were away, and I've been giving him some guidance, but it's my hope you'll make time to speak to him before we have to leave."

Maxim kept his eyes down. He had been tall even as a boy; he looked like a man now, although he had to be only sixteen or seventeen. "Of course," Chimene said, wondering why Boaz wanted her to speak privately with this boy.

"Maxim has a few problems," Boaz said. The young man flinched; his cheeks were reddening. "But we needn't discuss that now. He has been making the effort to overcome obstacles to his faith. I assured him that you bear only love and forgiveness for anyone who tries to walk the right path, whatever his failings."

"That is true." Maxim was refusing to look at her; his teeth dug into his lower lip. "I've struggled with my own faith," she went on, "and committed my share of sins, I suppose, especially when I was your age. No one is condemned for trying to follow the right way. Please feel free to visit me tomorrow evening, if the patrol can spare you then."

"All right." He did not sound as though he welcomed that prospect. "I'm honored." Maxim rose. "I have to get to work."

"Which reminds me," Josefa said as she got up. "I'd better get to the lab. Come along, Maxim—we can walk part of the way together." She slipped her arm through his and led him from the room.

"And this child," Matthew said, "is Lakshmi Tiris."

The girl looked up. Her long black hair hung in a thick braid to her waist; her pale brown skin was flawless. Chimene saw her beauty then; the child almost reminded her of herself.

"I wanted to meet you so much," Lakshmi said. "I saw you a couple of times at meetings in our dome, but you probably don't remember me. When Boaz invited me here—" She turned toward Boaz. A flush darkened her cheeks; her brown eyes warmed as she gazed at him.

"I should have remembered anyone as beautiful as you," Chimene said.

"Lakshmi's taken to following Boaz around," Yusef said. "He attended a meeting at her parents' house while you were away, and he was moved by the interest she took in his talk. He's visited with her family since then and told them she'd have a chance to meet you."

"I'm delighted," Chimene replied. The girl was still staring at Boaz. "Are you in school?"

"Oh, yes." Lakshmi focused on Chimene. "In the southwest dome."

"And quite a good student, I'm told." Boaz put a hand on Lakshmi's shoulder; her blush deepened. "I'm sure her teacher will forgive her for being late today when she knows Lakshmi was here, but we've detained her long enough. She and her household will be joining us for dinner after dark."

"I'll look forward to meeting your parents," Chimene said.

"Now be off with you," Boaz said. "We'll see you later." The girl hurried toward the door and shot Boaz one last look before she went outside.

Chimene sipped her tea; Lang gathered up the empty

trays and retreated to the kitchen. "Charming child," Eva said. "She's so taken with Boaz—you'd think he was another father."

"I wanted to ask you about Lakshmi." Boaz reached for a berry on Chimene's tray. "I've discussed this with the household, but I haven't said anything to the girl or her parents yet. I wanted to speak to you first. You needn't decide right away, until you've had more time to talk with her, but I think she should live here with us. We'll have a couple of weeks before the trip, and I think you'll warm toward her as quickly as we all did. It'd be good to have a child in the house, and Lang's already offered to give up part of his room space so we can add a room for her. Josefa's willing to share her room with Lakshmi until we leave on our tour—she's quite enthusiastic about having the girl with us."

It seemed the others had already settled this and expected her to go along. "Her parents would have something to say about that."

"They would be honored to have her in the Guide's household," Boaz responded. "They're quite devout—I doubt they'd object. On the contrary—they'd be delighted that we think so highly of her."

"How old is she?"

"Twelve—old enough so that her parents would be willing to let her go."

She could think of no other objections and wondered why she felt uneasy about having the girl in this house. Lakshmi was too young for the rite, and she did not want the child startled by seeing things she was not yet ready to view, but that small difficulty could be solved. Lang could always stay with her then; the older man often lacked the strength for the rite.

"You seem quite anxious to make her part of this household." Chimene looked directly at Boaz; he gazed back steadily. "Surely it isn't just because you want a child here."

"No, it isn't. I think the girl may have the makings of a Guide. I can't be certain—the Spirit will have to reveal that to you if such is the case. But if it's true, think of how much she would gain by being here, growing up with this household to guide her. She could be at your side, learning from you. If it turns out that she won't be the Guide, she will still be closer to the truth."

"She's awfully young for you to envision such a future for her," Chimene said.

"Older than you were," Matthew murmured, "when Kichi chose you."

"And I'm not so old that I have to worry about a successor."

"But that's the point," Boaz said. "She'd have years with you—decades to master what being a Guide demands. By the time she became the Guide, she would know almost as much as you do, and she'd be prepared to see the fellowship into the new era you've made possible. And if she isn't to follow you, that experience will still make her a valuable teacher to the one who does, when you're no longer with us." Boaz gestured with one hand. "How it pains me to speak of that—I'd have you live forever if I could, I can't imagine our world without you. But we must prepare for that eventuality, and it would give me joy to know that your wisdom will live on in another."

She could not bear to think of death or of the aging that would precede it. Occasionally, she thought that Kichi had been fortunate to die before she lost all her beauty. At other times, she had almost wished for a way to gain a Habber's long life, with a body that would have remained unchanged. It was a sinful thought at best.

"If you want a child here so much," she said, "we could have the child you want ourselves."

"As we shall, in time. But you see how much lies ahead for you now. You have other concerns, and I fear that our child will have to wait, but there's no reason we can't share what we have with another of Ishtar's children in the meantime. You'll grow to love Lakshmi, and our child will have one who will be like an older sister to her."

"Lakshmi will be devoted to you," Matthew said. "For the past days, almost all she's talked about is having the chance to meet you and talk with you."

Chimene set down her bowl of grain. "I suppose I must consider this, since those so close to me recommend it."

"Well, then." Matthew reclined against a cushion. "We can set that matter aside for now. We have other things to discuss. Boaz has spoken to the other Councilors here and communicated with the other settlements. The patrols in all of our communities are already looking for members who are trustworthy and willing to go to Turing."

She frowned. "Turing?"

"We've left them alone quite long enough," Boaz said. "I don't like the rumors I hear about the place—that the people there imagine they can find a way to summon the Habbers back, or that they're trying to plot with others against us. It's time we tried to lead those misguided souls back to the truth. They need the patrol to persuade them to contemplate the right way. They need a firmer hand."

Chimene glanced at Eva and Yusef; they seemed as surprised as she. "If you feel they need to hear the truth," she said, "we can always call them back and find others to work there in their place. Surely they'd be more receptive to our teachings once they're back among their families and friends."

"Your faith does you credit," Boaz said. "When I see how it lives in you, it's hard to believe that anyone can resist its beauty. But some people cannot be won with gentle words and persuasion. Oh, some of them might reach out to us if they were brought back, but many would only spread discord here. Any seeds the Habbers may have planted in their minds must be torn out before they come among us again."

"And you decided this without consulting me?" she said angrily.

Boaz pressed his fingertips together. "I was acting for you, Chimene. I was sure you'd agree once you were back. It would be wise for you to show the Project Council and Administrator Alim that you are capable of handling this potential source of trouble." He smiled. "And how can it possibly be wrong to bring those people in Turing closer to Ishtar, even if that means we may have to be a bit harsh with them?"

She said, "My brother's there."

"All the more reason you should be supporting my decision."

"Really? The last time Dyami visited, he led me to believe that he wasn't entirely unsympathetic with our fellowship."

"That was some time ago."

"He hasn't told me anything in the few messages he's

sent me to indicate he's changed his mind." Chimene finished her tea. "He has some of our mother's skepticism. It may take him longer to reach the truth, but I think he's trying. It's true that he spoke kindly of some of the Habbers there, but by now he's probably seen that they were never really his friends. I wasn't happy that he chose to work with Habbers, but he was young when he decided to go to Turing, and it's natural to want a little more independence at that age. I'm sure many of the others there are not unlike Dyami. It'd be foolish to be hard on people who might turn to us freely in time."

Boaz glanced at Matthew; the blond man's lip curled slightly. She could tell what they were thinking—that she was being too lenient, that her love for her people left her a bit more tolerant than she should be. They did not understand. She knew Dyami would come to her eventually, that the barriers between them would fall, as they once had with Sef. He would come to love her; she felt that the Spirit had promised this to her, that her moments with Sef were only a shadow of the love his son would give her.

Sef, of course, had retreated from her, but only because he was still so bound to Risa. Dyami had no such ties. He would be struggling with his feelings, telling himself they were wrong; she had seen how he had shied away from her. Perhaps he had remained in Turing because he feared what might happen. When he became part of Ishtar, however, he would see what had to exist between them. They would have a perfect love, one that would shatter yet another barrier.

Boaz said, "I have other things to tell you. I think we'd better speak alone in your room."

"More secrets, Boaz? More matters you've decided without my advice? Can't you speak freely before our housemates?"

"I think you'd prefer to hear this alone." He stood up and held out his hand.

"You'd better sit down." Boaz settled Chimene on a cushion near her bed, then began to pace. "I didn't have an opportunity to tell you about young Maxim Paz before. The boy has been quite tormented, but he came to me freely to confess his sins. Since he's desperate to atone for

them, I saw no need for him to admit them publicly. I'm
sure you'll agree when you've spoken to him privately."

"What has he done?" she asked.

"He's an affront to Ishtar. He's struggled against it, but
his wants sometimes drive him to the beds of men."

"How pitiful."

"But he knows he's offended the Spirit, and he deserves our compassion. An older man seduced him when
he was a young boy and apparently used him quite bru-
tally. That man will have to atone for that, but I think it
would be kinder to Maxim not to drag that out in a meeting yet, since he'd be shamed along with the man. He
needs time to find the right way and to practice it before
he confronts his corruptor."

Chimene struggled against her distaste; anyone who
would use a child that way deserved no love.

"The young man still has his lapses," Boaz continued,
"but we can inspire him to resist his urges. He's also been
open with me about some of those who share his particular
desires. When he's ready, we'll see that they're brought to
repent. The thought of leaving them to practice their offenses disgusts me, but it might be a greater evil to shame
Maxim now—it might only drive him further from the
truth." He stopped pacing and leaned against the wall.
"The men he told me about aren't a threat to us. Most of
them are so frightened that their secret will be discovered
that they go out of their way to look respectable. Some of
them have reputations as our strongest believers."

"But that's worse than not believing at all," she objected. "If you know who some of them are, how can we
allow them to go on offending the Spirit? Surely we should
be finding ways to bring them to confess and atone."

"And we shall, but not right away. Some may be
moved to confess by themselves, and others are probably
struggling with their urges, as Maxim is. You must be patient, Chimene. Dealing with Turing is more urgent now.
Some there have practiced similar evils, while those who
haven't have tolerated them. They've not only mocked
what a woman and man must share together, but they've
also practiced their filth with Habbers—of that you may be
certain. When they've given up their sins, perhaps others
in these settlements who need more persuasion can be
sent there."

"You speak of Turing," she said, "as if you want to make it a prison."

"Not at all. It can be a place of atonement and a place where evildoers won't infect others with their deeds. Perhaps Sigurd and the others who thought they could give our world to Habbers can labor there—we can't keep them under detention indefinitely, and in Turing they'd be of some use."

"You seem to have thought about this quite a lot."

"Matthew and I," he continued, "have also discussed sending some of those under detention here to Turing—those who are nearing the end of their punishments and who might prove their worthiness to reenter our society by aiding the patrol there. That would relieve our patrols of some responsibilities, and we don't want to strain our resources too much."

"Dyami's there," she said. "Why should I alienate him now, when I know—" She swallowed. "Anyway, what can those people do? They have to realize we've won, that they can't stand against us. I have no objection to sending brothers and sisters there to live among them and profess the truth, but—"

Boaz came toward her. "Perhaps your concern for your brother is preventing you from seeing your obligations to others." He sat down in front of her. "You know Teo Lingard."

"Of course. He was Dyami's closest friend."

"And I know what kind Teo is. Maxim told me. He's seen Teo in certain houses, offering to men what should be offered only to women, through whom men commune with the Spirit. Teo fucks men—that's the kind he is. That's the kind your brother Dyami is."

She struck at his face; he seized her by the wrists. "I don't believe it!"

"What do you think he and Teo did all the times they were alone? Why do you think they were so close? I showed Maxim an image of your brother—he recognized him quickly enough. He'd seen Dyami before, at a place where his kind gather. He saw him go to a room with another man. He spoke to Maxim and didn't trouble to hide what he was—he even told the boy there was no evil in what he did."

She tried to pull away; Boaz gripped her more tightly.

"I didn't want to tell you this, but your love for your brother has blinded you to the truth about him. He mocks Ishtar and he mocks you. He satisfies his lusts with no thought of the communion that must exist between a man and a woman, that binds us to the Spirit. He raises barriers between himself and any hope of appeasing Her. He thinks he can practice his offenses without suffering the retribution nature has inflicted on them in the past."

"I won't listen to this!" she cried.

"You must. Shall I summon Maxim here and have him tell you what he knows? Should I tell you about a pilot who told me about the warm glances and sighs he saw pass between Dyami and a Habber man in Turing's bay? Maybe he even lay with the Habber—that's worse than what his friend Teo does. How long do you think the Spirit will remain with you if out of misplaced feeling for your brother, you allow him to keep affronting Her?"

Boaz let go; her wrists felt bruised. How could her hopes have been so mistaken? She feared that the Spirit might already be abandoning her.

"I didn't want you to bear this wound," he said more gently. "I didn't want to believe it myself. I warned that gossiping pilot not to spread his rumors because I thought he must be mistaken. But Maxim has told me much, and I know that he spoke the truth. Teo told him about his boyhood love, and though he didn't tell Maxim his name, we can guess who that love was, can't we?"

"I can talk to Dyami," she whispered. "I can make him listen. I can be patient if I know he'll give this up."

"You were just telling me that his kind shouldn't be left to pursue their practices. You're putting Dyami above your responsibilities as our Guide." He reached for her wrists again; she winced in pain. "Your family has set many bad examples, Chimene—an uncle who fled to a Hab long ago, a father who was seduced by Habbers, a mother who pretends to love you but steadfastly refuses to join us, and now a brother who engages in vices that can only condemn him. I can just see him laughing with one of his lovers about the sister he was able to fool so easily."

He released her. She crumpled to the cushion, sick with shock and shame. Dyami had not retreated from her because he feared surrendering to her love but only because the thought of women disgusted him.

"Ishtar is testing you," Boaz said. "You can only show your love for Dyami and those like him by forcing them to turn from such evils. You mustn't give people any reason to doubt their Guide, especially now when another sign of our triumph may be near."

She raised her head.

"I spoke with Administrator Alim earlier, before you were awake," he went on. "There's talk that Commander Kaseko Wugabe is now completely in control of the Council of Mukhtars. Naturally, given how his Guardians have always regarded the Habbers, he's pleased that they're no longer among us, and he knows Ishtar was largely responsible for that. It's also strengthened his hand against those who had their doubts about us."

She sat up, unable to care about what a distant Earthman thought. "Alim might have asked to speak to me," she muttered, "or said something to me before I left."

"But he knows that communicating with me or Matthew is nearly the same as speaking to you, doesn't he? Anyway, that's not all he said. A final decision hasn't been made, but a delegation from the Council of Mukhtars may visit us sometime in the future. A Mukhtar may even be among them, and they would be coming here to mark this new era and to show their gratitude. After all, with the Habbers gone, they have nothing to fear by granting us more freedom, and they can still claim part of the Project's glory for themselves. They would be dealing with you and Alim as the rulers of one world would treat another. Think of how every Cytherian would honor you then, seeing the Mukhtars treat you as an equal. This will truly be our world at last."

Chimene clutched at her robe. "They would come here?"

"To honor you, to show that the time for our freedom has finally come. They began by guiding the Project, but in the end it may be we who guide them, who renew their dying civilization with the power Ishtar lends us. It's what every Cytherian has hoped for. I want those visitors, if they come, to see the light of faith that shines from you."

"My faith," she said sadly. "It's still an effort, isn't it? My faith didn't show me the truth about Dyami."

"You're being tested. Your brother is only another obstacle, one who can never live in harmony with the Spirit if he remains as he is now. You know what the Spirit demands, both from him and from you. His actions prove how steeped in error he is. You can only show your love for him by trying to help him now."

Boaz drew her to him. "I've told you what I plan to do, but I must have your assent. You are still my Guide, Chimene."

She steadied herself. Dyami had separated himself from the Spirit that embraced all men through women. He refused to make the offering all men had to make and that all women had to accept, the act that made life possible and that lay at the very root of what they were as human beings. He refused Ishtar's gift, which united all people with Her. His acts showed that he believed he could escape his human nature, shrug it off as though it were no more than an accident instead of what had been ordained. He had been among Habbers too long, those creatures who thought they could change or escape what they were. But he would be brought to repentance, and then he would come to her. She could not be mistaken about that; she had felt it too strongly before finding out the truth about her brother. She had to rid him of this obstacle to her love; that was what the Spirit was saying through Boaz.

She closed her eyes. "Carry out your plans."

Twenty-eight

The wood bordering the north dome's lake was becoming overgrown. Dyami trailed after one of the gardening machines as it sucked deadwood into its maw; the square machine shook a little on its treads as it chewed up the wood. He wondered if it would break down again.

They needed either more machines or more people. As a child in Oberg, he and his schoolmates had been taken to the forested areas to clear away deadwood and underbrush. Here in Turing, they had been neglecting the work recently and the woods were becoming more wild. He would recommend to the others later that they all come here and clear away what they could before the task became even more difficult.

More people would arrive in Turing soon; he was sure of that. They would not be left to themselves much longer. The new arrivals were not likely to resemble those here now; his refuge would be transformed into another domed settlement. Those people would want real houses and a school for their children, and believers in Ishtar were likely to be among them; perhaps there would even be a patrol. Some of those here might have to return to their old homes. He wondered which he dreaded more, going back to Oberg or staying to witness the changes in Turing.

He would be forced to hide once more; he would reacquaint himself with his old fears. A few of his friends, contemplating the changes that were sure to come, had suggested that they override the airship bay's systems and prevent any ship from landing there. Such an act would be futile. They could not make everything they needed for

506

themselves; sooner or later, an important installation
would fail, and they might be without the tools or components to repair it. Their existence would be precarious at
best, and Ishtar was hardly likely to tolerate such an open
act of rebellion.

Even so, he wished that more of his colleagues here
could be persuaded to make the attempt. Such a gesture,
even if it failed, was preferable to waiting passively while
others decided their fate.

He moved toward the lake; he was near the spot
where Balin had first made love to him. Longing filled him;
had the Habber forgotten him already? Balin would not
want to forget, but if his memories grew too painful, he
might give in to the temptation to have them erased. They
would not disappear entirely; the Habitat's cyberminds
could preserve them. Dyami would become another bit of
information, to be called up through a Link if Balin ever
wanted to relive part of his past.

He had once thought of Habbers as being much like
Linkers, but Balin had told Dyami a little more about his
people. His Habitat's cyberminds, like Earth's, were complex machines that had achieved self-consciousness—so
everyone assumed at any rate, since the cyberminds' responses were indistinguishable from those of a conscious
being. They were societies of mind, built up from smaller
bits of data and simpler functions into minds that could not
only mimic human thought but even surpass human minds
in the amount of data they could store and analyze.

Linkers, however, treated their cyberminds as little
more than servants or useful tools; they took only what
they wanted from them while ignoring whatever con-
flicted with their aims. Habbers did not see their minds
in that way, but rather as partners, beings whose judgments at times might be superior to theirs. Balin had
claimed that, in many instances, it was impossible to tell
whether his people or their cyberminds had decided on a
given course of action, and it was a distinction that did not
really concern the Habbers. Human minds, as he saw it,
were other cellular automata interacting with their cybernetic children. A human mind and a cybermind were both
marvelous and complex machines that grew, matured,
taught, learned, reasoned, and felt. Through a Habber, a
cybermind could act after perceiving that a particular ac-

tion might be necessary. Earth's cyberminds might also possess volition, but their Linkers had given them no power to act, reserving that for themselves.

Would Earth's cyberminds grow discontented with this state of affairs? Balin had playfully suggested that they might. "How many times," he had murmured, "do those cyberminds see what seems to them a rational and constructive course of action rejected for one that only furthers the limited aims of a few people? They might begin to wonder if that power should be left in the hands of human beings."

"Linkers set the goals," Dyami had replied, "and they're not likely to surrender that power. They wouldn't allow things to get to that point. At worst, to use a very old expression, they'd try to put the *djinn* back into the bottle."

"But your people couldn't get along easily without them. It's no wonder they refuse any direct communication with our worldlets—their cyberminds might begin to exchange information with ours and see how matters could be ordered otherwise. As it is, they've learned what little Earth has allowed about us. They might wish to learn more in time—they are, after all, designed to gather and assess data. They might want to reach out to their cybernetic siblings."

Dyami could almost wish that were possible. Some Linkers irrationally feared that if they allowed cyberminds to make more than trivial decisions, the machines would rule. The Habbers had shown, however, that human capabilities would only be enlarged by such cooperation. At least that was what Dyami assumed; he had known Balin as well as he knew anyone, and his lover's humanity was not diminished by his Link with his own cyberminds. But Balin's Hab, as he had admitted, was not like the ones near Mars and beyond; his people had chosen to retain much of what human beings were. They did not want to lose their ties with other human beings, but perhaps they would also guide both Cytherians and Earthfolk to that larger community of minds eventually.

If they ever came back, he thought. Chimene and her associates knew little about what Habbers really thought. She preferred to imagine plots and designs on Venus, and yet her fears were not entirely groundless. Closer ties with

Habbers would inevitably clear away the deadwood that rotted in the minds of those like his sister, that created a decaying mass of hatreds, fears, and irrational longings. She spoke of embracing human nature, while rejecting the most beautiful aspect of any human mind—reason, the spirit of inquiry, the ability to discern the patterns that could open a universe to them. She talked of a fellowship with no barriers; what she wanted was a world where every mind was a reflection of her own poorly examined self.

"There you are."

He turned; Amina was walking toward him. "My gardener has surrendered to the inevitable," she said. "It stopped dead in its tracks. We're going to have to get everyone out here and let other work wait for a bit." She peered into his face. "You're missing Balin again, aren't you?"

"Yes." She could often tell what he was thinking.

"Suleiman wouldn't turn you away."

"I know, and I'd probably enjoy it, but it wouldn't be the same."

"Poor Dyami." She put her arms around him and rested her curly blond head against his chest. "I do love you just a little. It's too bad you're not a woman."

"I'm sometimes sorry you're not a man." He smoothed back her hair. "Maybe we ought to try it together sometime. We wouldn't have to go through the whole business anyway, just the preliminaries, and we could close our eyes and pretend."

"Your heart wouldn't be in it." She released him and stepped back. "What problematic machines we are."

"Only when others insist we're not working properly." He took her hand as they walked along the shore. "When more people come here, we may have to pretend that we do."

"That reminds me. Tasida had a message this morning, before she went to the plant. A friend in Mtshana said something about a few people on the patrol getting ready to come here. It's all very vague—nobody seems to know exactly who's coming or when."

"I imagine they'll let us know," he said. "We don't have to let them land."

"You're still thinking about that? I'd go along with you, but you'll never get most of the others to agree."

"At least that would show Ishtar exactly how we feel."

"It wouldn't do us any good," she said. "That's what our friends would say—most of them. We're stuck here and we have to get on with our lives, just like everyone else."

"That's the attitude that made that wretched cult get as far as it has." Dyami sighed. He had not gone out of his way to be openly antagonistic himself. He had hidden away here, thinking he could live untouched by Ishtar.

"When I heard that Malik Haddad had fled with the Habbers—" Amina chuckled. "I can still laugh about it. Oh, that must have been a blow to the Guide. I'm sure it tarnished her little triumph for her, seeing her own father repudiate her beliefs so thoroughly."

"Malik was a coward to leave."

"No, he was wise. If he was that close to Habbers, he would only have been disgraced along with Sigurd Kristens-Vitos and those others. Or else his dear daughter would have been after him until he confessed his sins and donned the sash."

Dyami felt a flicker of fear. Maybe now Chimene would insist on dragging him back to Oberg, where it would be much more difficult to placate her with only a few vague words about how his thoughts sometimes turned to her teachings. The deception sickened him; he recalled again how she had spoken to him during his visit, how her hands had clutched at him.

"I'm going to try once more," he said, "to talk some sense into the others here. If we refuse to let any more ships land and let the other settlements know we want nothing to do with Ishtar, it might be just the sort of action that could inspire others to act."

"You won't convince our friends," she said, "and people in the other settlements would just say the Habbers had subverted us, or worse. We might as well give in gracefully. Anyway, it can't be any worse than the way we all lived before we came here."

They halted by the shore. The smooth surface of the water stretched before them, undisturbed here by any currents. Dyami picked up a pebble and threw it. The stone dropped into the water and a pattern of circles fanned out over the lake.

* * *

Dyami waited inside the bay. The thick wall that closed off the cradle area during landings was down; the airships carrying new settlers to Turing would be descending by now. Turing had been given no more than a day's warning, and the four remaining pilots in the south dome had been ordered to leave in their ships earlier that day, since they would be replaced by pilots coming with the settlers.

"Let's hope they brought enough tents," Allen Sirit muttered.

"They know what it's like here," Luinne Mitsuo said. "They'll probably want to build houses right away. We may finally have a few comforts."

Allen ran a hand through his thinning brown hair. "You'd think they would have given us a list of names. The Oberg Council didn't even reply to my last message when I asked if we should make any provisions for small children."

"I doubt they'd send children with the first group," Suleiman Khan said. "They'd wait until they're settled first."

Dyami moved to the edge of the small group. Allen had suggested that a few of those who did not have pressing work today gather to greet the new arrivals; it could not hurt to look as though they welcomed this group. Dyami frowned. Somehow this whole business felt wrong. He had asked Risa what she knew about the people coming to Turing, and she had not been able to tell him a thing.

He had sent her a message just that morning on impulse. He had phrased it carefully, but his mother had practice in discerning exactly what he meant. He had told her that he was looking forward to meeting whoever arrived and that he would be speaking to her again within two weeks to let her know how they were getting along. She would know what he was really saying—that he was worried and that if she did not hear from him by then, something was wrong.

His fears were probably groundless. He would tell himself that and then remember that Chimene had not replied to any of the three messages he had sent to her during the past month and a half. That wasn't like her; she had always replied to the others within a day, even when she was away from Oberg. He knew her usual patterns; something had altered them.

The lights on a large console near the wall lit up, signaling that air had cycled into the bay beyond. Dyami stepped back as the wall slowly began to lift.

The pilots were the first to descend the ramps leading up to the three airships. They strode quickly toward the waiting group and passed them without a word; their faces were grim. Then others were filing down the ramps, all of them wearing Ishtar's sash, each of them carrying a wand. More than half of them were men; they all seemed to be members of the patrol. Dyami tensed. He had expected that some would be part of the patrol; he had not anticipated nearly sixty of them.

The strangers came toward them; those in the front had their wands pointed directly at the group, as though they expected resistance. "Greetings," Allen said faintly.

A short, stocky man stepped forward, keeping his wand aimed at Allen's chest. "I'm Jonah Kanmer," he replied. "I'll speak for my associates. The Guide and those closest to her have been worrying over what to do about you. People who have lived so long among Habbers, without believers who might have guided them, may not yet be fit to live among the rest of us."

"Let me reassure you," Allen responded. "The Habbers are gone, and we wish only to continue with our work for the Project. You needn't fear—"

"Be quiet. We'll soon see how fit you are. I'll tell you what I've heard—that you plot against Ishtar, that you dream of seeing the Habbers return so that you can rule over us with them, that some of you have practiced offenses against the Spirit. Everything will change now— you'll be brought to see the right way and to follow it."

Dyami moved closer to Allen. "Perhaps so," he said, "but the Guide has always claimed that people must search for the truth in their own way. After all, if she's in possession of the truth, that truth will eventually impel all to believe, and—"

A hand struck the side of his head before he could react; Dyami staggered, then righted himself. He blinked, trying to focus on Jonah's broad face.

Jonah said, "As I told you, things will change. Those who cannot yet come to Ishtar, but who are willing to hear something of the truth, can be left to search their souls, but others need more persuading. You'd better get this straight now—we have authority here, granted to us by our Guide and the Councils that serve us all. We will bring you closer to the Spirit in whatever ways we choose, and you will listen to us until we see the light of truth in your souls. All of us here have volunteered for this mission—it is our way of showing our love for you. Some might say that the Habbers have corrupted you too completely for you ever to be part of the fellowship, but I can't accept that. You will see our love, but sometimes love requires firmness and discipline."

"You have no right—" Dyami began.

"I have every right!" Jonah raised his wand again; Dyami recoiled. "Did you think this settlement was yours alone? I see you'll have to learn about sharing as well. Let me tell you what this place will be now—a place of repentance, a place where people will be brought to the truth who cannot reach it in any other way."

Jonah motioned to a few of his companions. "Take these people to their dining hall and keep them under guard, along with anyone else who's in the north dome." He gestured at another group. "Thomas, go to the plant and the refinery, and bring out everyone there. If anyone resists, use whatever force is necessary. Leave a few of our people there to monitor the systems. We'll unload the supplies and join the rest of you in the north dome."

A man shoved Dyami. He turned and followed his companions from the bay.

In the dining hall, Dyami and his companions were told to push the tables to one side of the room, then to sit down near the opposite wall. One of their guards motioned at a square component that had been placed on the wall near the screen. "What have we here?" he asked.

"A sound system for music," Allen answered. "That way, if someone's using the screen for something else, the music needn't be interrupted, or—"

"Well, you won't need it now." Others began to dismantle the system. By the time others were being led into the hall, their guards were already disconnecting the screen.

Their guards—that was how Dyami was already thinking of them. The new arrivals had a hard look about them; he supposed that many, perhaps most, were people who had no other work except their patrol duties. He wondered what inducements they had been given to come here; surely Jonah had exaggerated when he said they were volunteers. But perhaps not; maybe they were such strong believers that they really felt they had a mission here. He would have preferred to think that they had been bribed or threatened in some way; that might have given him and his friends a chance to come to some understanding with them.

Prisoners, he thought. He was already thinking of himself and his colleagues in that way.

No one spoke. A couple of men had made an attempt at some conversation; the guards had silenced them with glares and lifted wands. Other people were led inside; he noticed a bruise on the cheek of one woman, while another man looked dazed as he clutched at his chest.

When everyone had been collected and the guards had eaten from their packets of provisions without offering any food to the others, Jonah stood up. "We've noted your names on our list," he said. "We're now going to attempt to bring some order here—it seems you've been living in a somewhat disorderly way in your tents and little shacks."

"We had to make use of what we were given," Amina called out; she was sitting with Tasida near the door. "We didn't want to build houses until they could be properly planned, and we didn't care to ask for additional materials when the other settlements might have needed them more."

"How thoughtful of you. Have any of you moved to the dormitories that housed the Habbers since they left?"

"No," Dyami said. "We thought we'd leave them free for those who might be joining us here."

"I doubt that very much," Jonah said. "You were probably just hoping that your Habber friends would return before long. They won't, you know. Get that through your heads. They don't care what happens to you now. You'll learn who your true friends are."

Jonah thrust his wand under his sash, then folded his arms; those standing to either side of him kept their wands aimed at their prisoners. "We're going to search those dormitories, and then we'll be accompanying all of you to your residences. You'll be given a chance to collect whatever you may need. Then you'll be housed in the Habber dorms. We'll dismantle the other dwellings and use your dorms ourselves for the time being."

Allen stood up. "May I speak?" he asked.

"Ah, you're learning some manners. Go ahead."

"Wouldn't it make more sense for you to use the Habber dorms and for us to stay in the others? The Habber dorms can house only about twenty-five people each, while the men's and women's dorms can each house nearly fifty. There are about sixty of you, and some two hundred of us."

"You'll live where we tell you to live." Jonah turned to the man standing at his right. "Start searching the Habber dorms."

The rest of the day was spent in waiting. When the Habber residences had been searched, those who lived in the other dormitories were led outside in small groups. They returned carrying packs; from whispered comments, Dyami learned that they had been allowed to have no more than a mat and a few clothes. He supposed that this was part of teaching them to be more indifferent to possessions.

When the dormitories had been searched, the people of Turing were allowed to line up near the kitchen, where they were given what food remained; apparently their guards would not let them prepare more. Dyami made do with a piece of bread, water, and a spoonful of bean soup. Guards led them in small groups to the lavatories in the dorms, then back to the hall, where they were to sleep. Those with packs used them as pillows as they rolled out the mats they had been allowed to keep; the others stretched out on the floor.

Dyami slept restlessly on the hard floor. Their guards, watching them in shifts, refused to dim the lights. Once, he started up out of his sleep only to see a hard-eyed young man standing near him, toying with his wand as if he were trying to decide whether or not to stun Dyami with its beam.

They were given no food at first light. More people were led outside, to return with packs and mats. Dyami was aching with weariness by the time Jonah's people be-

gan to summon those who lived in the shacks along the
creeks. He, Amina, and Tasida were the last to be brought
outside.

The tents in the hollow around the dining hall had
been taken down. Jonah was standing near a cart heaped
with various items; Dyami could see a few microdot library
holders, graphic compositors, personal ornaments, and
several pocket screens.

Jonah came toward them with five of his men. "I'll
accompany these three myself," he said, then glanced at
his screen. "Dyami Liang-Talis. Yes, here's your image,
hard as that is to believe. What a burden it must be for the
Guide, having a brother like you. Don't think that relationship will earn you any special privileges. And you two must
be Amina Astarte and Tasida Getran." He looked up.
"Amina Astarte. Unusual name—easy to remember. There
are a few volunteers here from ibn-Qurrah who spotted
your name on the list. Not much escapes the patrol's notice. They'd heard some unpleasant things about you and
certain of your female acquaintances there, but you'll be
making a new start now."

Dyami moved closer to the women; one of the men
prodded him in the back. "Let's go," Jonah said.

They followed him toward the creek. Another cart
had been driven up to the bank. On top of one of the seats,
Dyami saw a sculpture he had cast for Willis Soran, one of
the young men who lived in a shack near his. The group
halted in front of Dyami's shack. "Which of you lives
here?" Jonah asked.

"I do," Dyami said.

"Then you two must share the other." Jonah looked
toward the shack next to Dyami's, then back at the two
women. Tasida's freckled face was very pale; Amina's blue
eyes were angry. "Kind of close quarters. But maybe you
two like it that way." His lip curled. "I'll tell you what I've
told some of your friends. There won't be any more offenses to the Spirit practiced here. Any of us might enter
your new residence at any time, and if we see anything we
shouldn't, you'll be very sorry." He turned to Dyami.
"Let's see what you've got."

Dyami went inside as three of the men pushed the
women toward their shack. Even with the light outside,
the room was still dark; he bent to turn on his light globe.

"I haven't got much," he said, "just a pocket screen and a few books on microdot, and my mat and clothes, of course." He straightened as Jonah came inside. "You see, I have learned something from my dear sister about how meaningless possessions are."

The stocky man scowled. "Don't mock the Guide. You won't be needing the books or the screen."

"What about messages?" Dyami asked, although he could already guess the kind of answer he would get. "I do send them when I can, and the people I know will surely be sending more to me. They might wonder if they don't hear from me."

"Whether you get to view any of your messages is going to depend on how you conduct yourself. If you behave, you'll be allowed to view them in the presence of one of my volunteers, and even to send one if we choose. One of us will be with you when you do. We must try to free ourselves from the temptation to keep secrets."

Dyami sighed. There were screens in the south dome's installations, but he was sure they would all be watched while they were at their work. His last link with the outside was gone. He trembled a little, then tried to steady himself. If Risa did not hear from him in the next two weeks, she would know that something was wrong. He had to hope she could find a way to help him.

The other two men came inside. One of them pulled aside the curtain concealing the place where Dyami slept, then stooped to pick up a metal object next to the mat. "What's this?" the man said.

Dyami felt the blood drain from his face. The man was holding a sculpture he had cast of Balin. He had given the bust to his lover but had kept this piece for himself, one he had made only a little while before the Habbers were told to leave. The sculpture showed a nude Balin in repose, his head resting on one hand, his other arm draped over one raised knee.

Jonah reached for the sculpture. "Our friend here's quite artistic. We found some of his work in a few other residences. I asked who had made the stuff." He hefted the image of Balin, then looked up. "I assume you made this one."

"Yes," Dyami managed to say.

"Who is it? I don't recall seeing anyone here who looks quite like that."

"It's one of the Habbers." He might as well admit that now; Jonah could find it out from anyone here.

"A Habber? Did you use your imagination, or did you have him pose like that?"

"It's hardly unusual, doing a nude." Dyami struggled against the fear that was rising inside him.

"Hardly unusual? Having a man take off his clothes for you? Having a Habber strip so that you can make a nice image of him?" Jonah peered at the sculpture. "He looks well equipped. Maybe you liked seeing that."

One of the other men laughed. "Get your clothes and your mat," Jonah said. "You won't be needing this."

Dyami gathered his few clothes quickly and put them into his pack, then rolled up his mat. He followed Jonah outside; the other two men were walking toward the cart with his screen and the sculpture.

Amina was standing on the bank, her pack on her back. "Please," he heard her say to the dark-haired man standing near her, "surely you can let me keep that. It was a gift."

The man lifted his hands. He was holding a delicate crystalline globe on which the stars in this region of the galaxy were represented by tiny gemlike points and clusters. "Who gave it to you?" he asked. "It doesn't look like anything I've ever seen."

Amina was silent.

"I'll bet it came from a Habber. It did, didn't it? I don't see what use you have for anything like that." The man lifted the globe, then hurled it toward the creek. The crystal shattered against a rock; glinting shards pierced the water.

Twenty-nine

Eva Danas greeted Risa at the door. Risa had expected the usual courteous and cool greeting, but the blond woman seemed genuinely happy to see her. "It's been a while," Eva said as she clasped Risa's hands. "Chimene will be delighted to see you."

Risa was not so sure about that. Chimene had returned to Oberg almost three weeks ago, and it had taken that long to arrange this visit. Risa had left several messages, only to get brief responses from either Matthew or Boaz: The Guide is resting from her journey; she's preparing a speech; she's having a conference with the Council; she's counseling a brother or sister; she's conferring with members of the fellowship in other settlements over the screen. She had expected a similar answer this time, but Eva had called back to say that Chimene would welcome a visit.

"I'm pleased she was able to make some time for me," Risa said. "Boaz and Matthew had led me to think she might not really want to see me."

"My brothers are sometimes a bit too solicitous." Eva's eyes narrowed; her expression was a little colder. "Anyway, they're not home at the moment." She released Risa's hands. "When Chimene heard you wanted to see her, she was quite anxious that I call you back. She's with some students now—Lakshmi Tiris and a few of her young friends—but they should be just about finished with their instruction."

Risa had heard about Lakshmi, the girl who had come to live in this house. "Well, I'd better go to her room."

"Oh, she isn't in her room. There's a place outside where she likes to go lately. I'll take you to her."

Eva turned to her right and led Risa down one corridor. The doors to all the rooms were open, as they often were whenever someone was visiting. She glanced into Chimene's room and noticed that several new garments were hanging on the clothes rod; for a woman who owned nothing, her daughter certainly did not lack for things to wear. The exit opened; she followed Eva through the trees bordering the house until they came to a small clearing in back of the dwelling.

Chimene was seated on a reclining chair in the center of the grassy circle; a screen rested on her lap. She wore a long red robe; a shiny black stone hung from a pendant around her neck. Her shoes were only thin soles with slender straps, useless for walking, no more than ornaments for her feet. Lakshmi Tiris and several other children sat on the ground, gazing intently at the Guide. Teaching was what Chimene called it, the process of filling the heads of these children with Ishtar's twisted reasoning and tales of the world to come.

"Greetings, Mother," Chimene murmured. Risa winced a bit at this expression; its formality only seemed to increase the distance between her and her child. "Lakshmi, you and the others may go into the house with Eva, and she'll give you all a treat. I must visit with my mother now."

The children got to their feet. The beautiful dark-haired girl with the long braid had to be Lakshmi Tiris; she already had some of Chimene's poise. "I'm so pleased to meet you," the girl said. "The Guide was telling us all about your mother Iris today and how she gave up her life for Venus. It's one of my favorite stories."

"Indeed." Risa's mouth twitched. Chimene often invoked Iris's memory, making it seem as though her ancestor would have sanctioned the Guide's aims.

Eva beckoned to the children. "Come along now." She led them toward the house. Risa gazed after them; she had heard all the rumors about Lakshmi. She was like a daughter to the Guide; some claimed that she might eventually become the Guide herself. Chimene would be filling the girl's head with dreams of her destiny, as Kichi Timsen had done with her.

"Do sit down," Chimene said. Risa seated herself near the chair, feeling at a slight disadvantage as she looked up at Chimene. The younger woman was thinner, as if she were still recovering from the rigors of the tour of the other settlements. Any other woman would have looked too drawn or unattractively bony. Chimene only seemed more beautiful; she was a fragile object one might want to treasure, a being so perfect that she hardly belonged in this world.

Risa could barely glimpse the house through the trees. They might have been in the middle of a forest on a garden world. "I enjoy coming here," Chimene said. "It was Boaz's idea, clearing this little spot, and a few of the fellowship donated their labor to do so. I've spent many happy hours here lately. One can feel so enclosed—by rooms, by walls, by the domes around us."

"I suppose it's refreshing after your tour."

"I enjoyed seeing so many of my sisters and brothers, but I'll confess that it was tiring."

Risa tilted her head. "Some say the tour seemed as much Boaz's as yours. A few even say that he sees himself as your Guide."

"He's closest to me. There are no barriers between us, and I've chosen him to be the father of the child I'll have someday. The Spirit has often spoken to me through his lips."

"And he loves you," Risa said.

"Of course."

"And you love him."

"As I love all my brothers." Chimene fingered the stone at her neck. "Did you come here to speak of Boaz? Has your heart finally warmed a little to him? It would give me such pleasure if my mother and the man who will give her a grandchild were friends."

"I came here about another matter," Risa responded. "My thoughts have been very troubled lately. I hope you'll listen to what I have to say."

"But I always do."

"No, you don't. You let me talk, and then you dismiss me from your mind. Let me speak plainly. I'm appealing to you not only as your mother but as a citizen who knows you have the power to help me, and I also have your own interests at heart."

Chimene turned her head toward Risa. "What is it?"

"I'm very concerned about Dyami. I haven't had a message from him for nearly two months, and that isn't like him. I've sent him messages, and he never replies."

"I don't see why you're worrying about that. There's more work to do in Turing now, and Boaz tells me that the new people there think it's best not to have too frequent an exchange of messages or conversations with people outside Turing. Some of the people in Turing have unreasonable resentments against us, even though all we're doing is showing them where their duty lies. At the moment, some of them would be tempted to spread discord here. When they come to accept their situation, they'll be free to send whatever messages they like."

"Chimene, I found out about the kind of people who were sent there," Risa said, "permanent members of the patrol and volunteer members who generally have a reputation for being a little too quick to impose their authority on others. I've called up the names, and I've asked a few people in the other settlements about those who were sent to Turing from their domes. They're the same kind of people, and I don't like the idea of their being up in Turing with little to control them."

"They're my brothers and sisters," Chimene responded calmly. "They'll do nothing of which I wouldn't approve. Unfortunately, some of the people in that settlement need a firmer hand—they were among Habbers too long and deprived of our guidance. But Boaz assures me—"

"Listen to me, daughter. I'm not the only one who's worried. This isn't like detaining someone who's committed a violent crime—it isn't even like depriving several Linkers of their Links and shutting them up somewhere. People can let that pass and tell themselves that Sigurd and his allies are only paying a price for letting Islanders leave with the Habbers, and that there's some justice in that. But the men and women in Turing have families and friends here, all of whom are going to be worrying about them. Do you really want all those people to be wondering about how their loved ones are faring? They might begin to question your judgment, even those who believe in you."

"I'm telling you that there's nothing to worry about."

Risa gazed into her daughter's face. Chimene seemed sincere; her dark eyes were filled with compassion, yet it seemed that her daughter was looking at her from the center of a complex web. "A few pilots are talking," Risa said. "They're saying that recently, whenever they deliver anything to Turing, they're asked to stay in the bay. They sleep aboard their airships before they leave, and there are always a few members of the patrol inside the bay while they're there. They never see the six pilots who are stationed there permanently, and any of the people who help them unload their cargo seem afraid to talk to them. It makes them wonder if there's something to hide."

"Foolishness," Chimene said. "The pilots were never terribly eager to mingle much with the people in Turing before, and surely there's no reason for them to do so now. As I told you, some of those people wouldn't be above spreading false tales in an effort to sow discontent. Boaz tells me that when things are more settled—"

"I'm tired of hearing what Boaz says. Maybe he doesn't tell you everything and thinks that you'd restrain him more if he did. Aren't you concerned about Dyami? Don't you care what happens to him?"

"I care very much."

"Then do something!"

"There's nothing else to do." Chimene swung her feet to the side of the long chair and sat up. "I'm afraid you simply don't understand what Turing has to be now—a place where people must be brought to remember their obligations. You have no idea what some of them have done—plotting with Habbers against us, engaging in every manner of offense against the Spirit. It pains me that Dyami is among them, but I can't put my feelings for him above my duty to others or, for that matter, above my true duty to him. He will come to repent of his actions, and then—"

"What could he possibly have done?" Risa cried.

"He has offended Ishtar," Chimene replied. "I'll be blunt—he's gone to the beds of other men. You may not be a believer, but even you must be repelled by such actions, which pervert and degrade the act of love that binds us to nature."

Risa said, "Someone's been telling you lies."

"Oh, no. There's no doubt of it—I've heard about his

deeds from a witness. Dyami admitted what he was to
him."

Chimene was telling the truth. Oddly enough, Risa
did not feel surprised at realizing that, or as sorrowful as
she might once have been; she was only more afraid for
her son. He couldn't come to me, she thought; he kept his
secret all this time. How fearful and lonely he must have
been.

"You see why we must be firm with him and the others
of his kind," Chimene continued. "We have to rid them of
that evil. I'm sorry that I had to tell you this. When I first
learned what my brother was, I wanted to hide it from
everyone, convince myself it wasn't true. But I won't hide
the truth any longer. If others happen to learn what those
people in Turing really are, they won't be so concerned
about them. They'll know we have to free them of what's
inside them." She leaned forward. "You don't seem terribly shocked. Maybe you knew what Dyami was all along."

"No, I didn't know."

"You see why I must show my love by bringing such
people to give up their offenses."

"Oh, yes." Risa took a breath; she had thought she
might still be able to reach her daughter. Now she saw that
no mercy remained inside Chimene. Very well, she
thought; this would make her task easier. She would no
longer have to be troubled by guilt while working against
the Guide's ambitions. "I know why you have to force
them to change. You and those creatures around you can't
bear the thought that there are things you can't control,
that there are parts of people over which you have no
power. You won't settle for power over what we do or
think—you'd control our deepest feelings as well. You're
not grieving over those people because they offend your
Spirit—you're angry with them because their most intimate acts defy you and the power you seek over them.
They're a sign that they still claim some freedom for themselves."

Chimene's cheeks reddened. "That's how you see
what your son has practiced?"

"Maybe he found some love in such deeds. Perhaps he
found more than you have, with all that rutting you call a
rite. What you do sickens me more than anything he might
have done. What did you think—that you could destroy me

by telling me this about Dyami or that the shock of hearing it would bring me to see things your way?"

Chimene got to her feet. "I've been patient with you, Risa. I believed you'd come to the truth if I waited. I can wait a bit longer, but you'll live to see Dyami accept the right way, and then you'll be brought to it by whatever means are necessary—I promise you that." She smiled. "But we mustn't part with such angry words. I'm pleased you came to visit, and perhaps you'll ponder what I've said. Do give Sef my love. I've missed his presence at our meetings here and the offerings he once made to the Spirit through me at our rite. It gave me joy to see how much he loved me. You must tell him that I long to share such moments with him again."

Risa flinched as her insides knotted; she was afraid she would not be able to get up. Chimene stared down at her, still smiling, then walked toward the house.

Risa waited until the pain began to ease, then slowly stood up. Chimene's revelation could be a lie, designed only to poison her love for Sef. It might be the truth; in that case, Sef had probably regretted his weakness some time ago. Chimene had as much as admitted that he had given her up. Her confession had only been another weapon to use against her mother, and Risa did not have to let the blow strike at her heart. What her bondmate had done was past; she would not risk driving him back to her daughter with pointless accusations.

Even in her numbed state, she felt a sense of relief. She now had another just reason to hate Chimene.

Dyami was keeping track of the days. He marked them off with a stylus on the wall of the tiny room he shared with Allen Sirit, Suleiman Khan, and Helmut Renas-Korbs. The patrol had been in Turing for exactly one hundred and twenty days now. He made his mark, then dimmed the globe of light next to him before stretching out on his mat.

He had grown used to sleeping with his long legs slightly bent so that they did not touch Suleiman's feet in the tiny crowded room. He had grown accustomed to Allen's soft snore and Helmut's occasional nocturnal murmurs. Sometimes he was startled by how quickly he had habituated himself to his new life; he would never have guessed that being a prisoner was, for the most part, boring. Tedium was, however, easier to endure than hope, which only led to despair. He could not allow himself to think about how much of his life might slip away here. He could not dwell on those outside and whether or not they had resigned themselves to his fate.

The first month and a half had been more eventful. They had dismantled all the shacks under the supervision of their guards. They had been ordered to tear out all the partitions in the lavatories of the former Habber dorms, since their guards seemed to think offenses against Ishtar might otherwise be practiced there.

A neat row of simple houses, with plumbing and light but no screens, now stood in the hollow near the dining hall and the two dormitories where the patrol lived. The guards took turns living in the houses; even with the more than ample space of their dorms and their belief that no barriers should exist between members of Ishtar, they apparently felt an intermittent need for more privacy.

Now, for over two months, the days had passed in normal routines; at times Dyami could almost imagine that things were much as they had been. He had his two weeks on duty at the refinery, his week on an external operations shift, and a week spent working in the greenhouse and preparing meals with others in the dining hall's kitchen before the cycle began again. He no longer took a turn on darktime duty; members of the patrol monitored essential operations then. He and his companions were given no days off, but in a way that was a relief, since it meant less time to brood on his situation.

During the past month a new custom had been added. Once a week the prisoners were required to remain in the dining hall after dinner for a meeting. Usually, one of the guards gave a dull speech about the cult's teachings, but sometimes the proceedings were enlivened by a recorded lecture of the Guide's. A large screen would be set up; the room would be filled with his sister's dulcet tones as she pleaded with them to accept the right way. At the meeting's conclusion, the screen was taken outside and carried back in a cart to the south dome; since the tunnel was always patrolled, this ensured that the prisoners would have no way of communicating with the outside.

The guards always waited at the end of meetings to

see if anyone was willing to don the sash. Jonah had made it clear that new adherents would have not only the benefits of the truth but also a little extra food, perhaps new clothes, and a chance to view more messages from home. So far, the captives had resisted such temptations, some out of pride, others out of fear that they might lose the respect of their fellow prisoners.

Dyami had his own private names for the guards; it did not matter to him what their actual names were. The black-bearded man who seemed to serve as Jonah's aide was the Puncher because he was so quick to deliver such blows whenever a prisoner did not reply to his questions immediately. A skinny red-haired man was the Peeper, since he was always entering the prisoners' dorms unannounced with other guards in the hope of catching some unwary souls committing offenses against the Spirit—not that this was likely, since their doors had to be left open and the lavatories were now in full view at the end of the halls. A plain mousy-haired woman was the Ogler, since she often found excuses to be inside the dorms when a few of the men were showering. There were others—the Conductor, who wielded his wand like a baton, and the Hawk, a beady-eyed man with a prominent nose, who swooped down without warning on anyone caught lingering near any of the refinery's screens.

The prisoners had learned how to obey. Dyami had cursed at one particularly obnoxious guard during the first month; the man had answered with a beam from his wand. The weapons only stunned, but Dyami had come to with the worst headache of his life; he had also been told that because of his recalcitrance, his roommates would have no food for a day. A few similar displays on the part of his companions had brought other such punishments—beatings given to others besides the offender or no food for any of the prisoners. Being obedient was wiser than having others suffer for one's misdeeds.

They had learned that their guards were capricious. The Puncher might deliver a blow for no reason at all; the Peeper would browbeat a couple of women or men for doing no more than exchanging what he saw as an unusually affectionate glance. Perhaps the guards were as bored as their prisoners and sought ways to enliven the passing weeks. Maybe they had come to realize that they could do as they liked, with no one to restrain them. They had to lead their prisoners to the truth and could probably justify any of their somewhat primitive techniques.

Dyami had heard no news from outside Turing; no one had yet deemed him worthy of receiving a message. He wondered if any had been sent or if his household and friends had been given a story to explain his silence. Of his roommates, only Suleiman had been allowed to view a message from his father, but the dark-haired young man believed it had been edited. In the presence of two guards, Suleiman had been limited to replying that he appreciated the news of his family and that he would send a longer message when he had more time.

Their guards, of course, could have saved themselves this extra trouble by using holographic images of the prisoners. A specialist, working with a cybermind to construct such an image, could produce one almost indistinguishable from the person himself. But Dyami could guess why the guards had not bothered with such a deception, even though they could probably have found someone capable of the work. Those outside to whom the images would have replied had been too close to the prisoners, and they already had reason to be concerned about them. An image might lack certain subtleties—a particular facial expression, a peculiarity of speech, certain gestures or private jokes.

He could still hope that he might be allowed to send a message to Risa. Even in front of guards, he would be able to give her some indication of how bad things actually were. On the other hand, maybe he should not be so anxious to let her know. There might be little she could do; he might only bring more trouble to her household.

Dyami folded one arm under his head, trying to get more comfortable. The time just before sleep was dangerous, when his despair could easily deepen or his rage rise to the surface to distract him with wild and hopeless plans. He tried to keep his feelings at bay. He could look forward to a break in his routine tomorrow. The guards would be putting him and a few others to work building a wing that would connect the two dorms that housed the captives. That had to mean they were expecting new prisoners. The work would be a change; the next arrivals might have some news.

* * *

"Ishtar welcomes all who are willing to accept the truth," Jonah said. Dyami, sitting among the other prisoners, kept his eyes on the floor. This meeting had been even more tedious than usual; Jonah, who was not unduly eloquent, had given a less-than-inspiring lecture. "Surely some among you must be moved to embrace the Spirit."

No one stepped forward. Dyami looked up; several of the guards were seated next to Jonah. The others were behind the prisoners, near the door, their wands ready.

"You insist on making things harder on yourselves," Jonah said. "Don't you want to set a better example for the penitents who will be joining you tomorrow? Fifteen of them will be arriving here, along with a few more volunteers, and I'd hoped they'd all see more cooperation on your part."

If we joined, Dyami thought, you'd eventually expect us to share the rite with your people, and surely even a sinner doesn't deserve to suffer that much. It was the kind of remark he wanted to make aloud but one which would only bring a reprisal.

"Very well," Jonah muttered. "I'll pray for you and hope you see the light."

The prisoners got to their feet. Dyami was just behind Amina when he reached the door; a young man pulled her roughly aside. "I've got a message for you," he said. "I'm sure you'd like to view it."

The blond woman glanced at Tasida, then Dyami; she had, he knew, been given no messages before. Dyami filed outside with the others, then followed them toward the creek as their guards walked at their sides. The dome was nearly dark, but flat panels of light had been placed on the ground along their route. No one spoke. The prisoners, acting together, might have overcome the people herding them along, but they could not escape. If they made for the forest, the others would hunt them down and probably summon aid from outside to do that. If they ran toward the bay, they would have to force the pilots in the south dome to take them out in the airships, and even then, where could they go?

It might still be worth it, if only to show their captors they were not completely cowed. He pushed that thought aside. Better to wait until any plan had a chance of working.

We have perfect prisons, he thought. There was a kind of logic in using a settlement in this way.

They crossed the wooden bridge, a few people at a time, then entered the building on the other side. The two dormitories were one structure now, joined at the opposite ends by the addition the prisoners had completed a few days ago. Guards were always posted near the two doors that were the only way out.

Dyami went to his room, which was the first one on the right of the corridor. People murmured to one another as they entered their own rooms; others were moving toward the lavatories in the back. Women and men shared both wings of the building; the Peeper had explained why they were not housed separately. "That might tempt you to commit offenses," he had told them. "Maybe you'll mend your ways if we keep you all together." The Peeper, as did most of the guards, assumed that they were all potential offenders against the Spirit; he undoubtedly thought that those who had tolerated such practices were as bad as the offenders themselves.

Dyami settled himself on his mat but did not lie down. He would wait until his roommates returned from the lavatory before going himself. At least the new addition would solve one problem; men and women would no longer have to share the lavatories, since they could now move freely between the two wings. Perhaps that would restore a little of their lost dignity; the guards were sometimes amused by their efforts at preserving some modesty.

He took out his stylus and marked off another day. One hundred and thirty-five, he thought as he put the stylus back into his pocket. The walls suddenly rattled a little, then were still—a minor quake. A major one might give them an opportunity to overpower their captors; he filed that notion away.

He might die here. If that was what lay in store for him, then he would have to find a way to fight before he grew too weak to make the effort.

Dyami waited until the corridor was silent, then wandered down to the lavatory. Ten toilets without partitions lined the wall to his left; ten sinks with small mirrors above them stood to his right. The showers were at the other end of the room, small nozzles that now yielded only cold water.

He relieved himself, then went to a sink to wash. The stubble on his face prickled against his hands. He gazed at his slightly haggard visage; his thick chestnut hair, in spite of his efforts, was becoming an unruly mass. He had begun to notice that more of his fellow prisoners were failing at their grooming. He pushed at a dispenser panel and slapped some depilatory cream on his face, deciding to tend to himself now. Grooming was one way of keeping a little of his pride.

To his left, an opening led from the showers to the new addition. He walked toward it and stared down the hall, seeing the showers at the other end. Jonah had said fifteen more prisoners would be coming, but this addition could house more than that. He wondered how many other prisoners would follow them and how many more dormitories they might build.

He had to stop thinking of himself and the others as prisoners. Seeing himself in that way only added to his sense of helplessness. A resister—that was a nobler term. He could still resist the teachings with which his captors wanted to cloud his mind.

He heard footsteps in the distant lavatory. Dyami flattened himself against the wall; some of the guards might be making their rounds. The footsteps stopped; he heard a queer retching sound. This could not be any of the guards; he had heard only one set of footsteps, and no guard, even with thoroughly intimidated captives, ever entered the building alone.

A naked woman suddenly stepped under one of the shower heads in the other lavatory; he recognized Amina. The water poured over her head as she scrubbed with the harsh soap. When the water stopped running, she stumbled toward a rack holding several worn and stained towels, then disappeared from view.

Something was wrong. Amina had seemed distracted, her movements jerky and awkward. Before he could decide whether or not to go to her, she entered the new wing and went into one of the open rooms.

He hastened toward her and peered into the room. She was sitting against one wall, barely visible in the pale light that shone from the ceiling of the hall. Her gray shirt was torn at the shoulder; her wet hair was plastered against her head and back, wetting her garments.

"Amina," he whispered.

She started, then shrank back, raising her hands. As he came inside, she pulled up her legs and pressed her forehead against her knees.

"What is it?" he asked. "Was it the message? Is there something the matter back home?" That, he supposed, would be characteristic of the guards—offering to show a message that might bear only sad tidings. "Do you want me to stay?"

"If the guards come in to check up, it'll just mean trouble for you." Her voice sounded hoarse. "You should be in your room. You'll need your rest for tomorrow's labors."

"I don't have much to do tomorrow. They're allowing me the great privilege of unloading some of the cargo in the bay when the new people arrive." He sat down.

"You'd better go away," she said. "They wouldn't like it if they found us sitting here."

"Maybe they wouldn't mind that much. If I'm with a woman, at least they can't accuse me of trying to offend the Spirit."

He heard her choke; then she was sobbing softly as she clawed at her legs. He reached for her; she struck his hands away. "Amina, what's wrong? I can't leave you alone like this."

"There's nothing you can do for me."

"I can listen, can't I? What happened? Was it bad news about your family?"

She was silent for a long time. At last she said, "There wasn't any message, not one he would show me anyway. He took me to one of the houses—he's been staying in one. All the way over, he kept asking me if I could guess who the message was from. When we got there, he said a friend of his would be joining us, and then he went on and on about Ishtar and how sorry he was for me until the other man arrived."

She lapsed into silence once more; he heard her gasp for breath. He reached for her hand; she recoiled. "They raped me," she said in a toneless voice. "They took their time. One of them would hold me down while the other one worked on me. They were only trying to make me more receptive to the Spirit—that's how they see it. I'm an offense to Ishtar, and they don't want me to be that any more."

Rage welled up inside him; he gritted his teeth.

"They wanted to force me to respond," she continued. "Maybe I could have faked it so they'd leave me alone— they wouldn't have known the difference—but I didn't. I still have some pride left, for all the good it'll do me."

"I won't let it happen again," he muttered. "We'll make them pay."

"How? Going to Jonah with the story? Maybe he knows and doesn't care—maybe it's already happened to somebody else who's afraid to talk about it. Even if he doesn't know, it'd be my word against two of his men, and you know who he'd believe."

"If Chimene knew about this," he said, "she'd put a stop to it. Whatever she is, she's always hated such crimes. She'd never allow—"

"And how will she ever find out?"

"I'll think of something," he said. "If our friends knew what happened to you, maybe they'd finally decide to fight them."

"Dyami." Her voice was very cold. "There's nothing you can do that wouldn't make it worse for me, and you'll bring trouble to yourself. They'd probably take it out on me for telling you what happened, and maybe some of my friends as well. You know what they're like—they'd make others suffer if anyone tries to protect me. Maybe I shouldn't have said anything to you."

He gazed at her, hating his helplessness.

"I don't want you doing anything stupid," she said. "I'll get through this. They didn't touch anything inside my mind, and I won't let them break me. They think they can make me enjoy what they do, but they've only made me hate it even more than I did. It'll help me, hating them more. It'll keep me alive until I can find some way to strike back."

"Amina—"

She got to her feet. "I'm going to my room. I don't want anyone to know. Promise me you won't say anything to the others."

"If that's what you want, but—"

"Promise me."

"I promise."

She left the room. Her body was slumped, her back bowed. She claimed they had not touched her, but they had; some of her spirit was already gone.

"You, there." The guard named Thomas beckoned to Dyami. "Load those crates."

Dyami moved toward the side of the cradle, where several large crates stood at the bottom of a ramp. Jonah had decided earlier that only Dyami could be spared for this work. "You look strong enough to handle it alone," he had said, "and if it's too much for you, the new people can help you with it." Jonah had clearly been in a playful mood. If Dyami strained too much and injured himself, he could be punished for being careless. If he asked Thomas for some of the new captives to help him, the guard would have some amusement mocking him for weakness and find an even more unpleasant task for him. It was another of the choices the guards occasionally liked to offer.

Thomas climbed the other ramp toward the entrance to the cabin, trailed by two other men. The passengers aboard the airship had not yet come out. The two pilots, both men this time, were standing near the crates. One of them, a man with graying light-brown hair, looked familiar, but Dyami could not recall his name.

Three other guards were standing several paces away. One of the female guards had her wand casually pointed in his direction but did not seem to be paying much attention to him; her companions were murmuring to each other. The pilots moved back a little as he approached; he wondered what they were thinking. They would have little pity for him; they probably believed what Jonah said they had been told—that those in Turing would have to be guided by members of the patrol until they were fit to live among others again. The pilots might suspect that the patrol here was occasionally firm but would assume that their charges were being treated fairly. Even if they heard the truth from Dyami, they were not likely to believe it; he would be only another liar attempting to sow discord. The two men would not have been here in the first place unless they were strong believers, who would not question their Guide's wisdom.

He put his arms around one of the crates, testing its weight. If he lowered one side of the cart, he could probably heave it in by himself.

"Dyami." The voice was so low he barely heard it. "Don't turn around. I've been told your household has had no messages from you. They're well—I'll let them know somehow that you are, too."

Dyami moved to the cart by the ramp and began to lower its side. As he bent over, he glanced around quickly at the pilots. The brown-haired man was staring at him; he was sure he had been the speaker. He searched his mind. Evar—the pilot who had once aspired to becoming Risa's bondmate. He had come, apparently uninvited, to a party of his mother's when Dyami was a boy. Risa had gone on at length after he left, poking fun at her former love's faith. He had visited only a few times after that.

He slid the crate over, slipped one arm under it, and heaved it into the cart. Helmut had tried to speak to a pilot in the bay once, but the woman had not believed his stories and had mentioned them to one of the patrol. The guard had made light of the stories; he had even looked a little hurt that Helmut could utter such accusations. Helmut had been given his beating later.

Evar wasn't any more likely to listen. He and his companion would stretch their legs, then board the dirigible to rest before they left Turing. He might have been moved to make one small gesture, but he probably thought Dyami belonged here. He would go back and tell Risa that her son was safe and that she needn't worry. Maybe that was best. She could do little for him, but she might at least have some comforting news.

The three patrol members now had their backs to him. He would not get another chance. He went to another crate, then edged a little closer to the two pilots. "We've been beaten," he whispered, keeping his lips as still as possible. "We're often deprived of food. One woman has been raped, and there may be others I don't know about. It's been getting worse. They have the power to do whatever they like to us, and they're using it. They're only teaching us to hate the Spirit." He pushed at the crate; one of the guards was turning in his direction. He could not risk saying any more. The two pilots walked slowly away. They did not believe him; he could only hope they would not speak to the patrol.

Thomas was descending the ramp. "Let's welcome our new residents," he called out. "I've told them that we've been looking forward to their arrival, and I know that having people with their expertise will benefit us all. They're quite drained after their trip from the Platform, so when they're settled, they'd probably like to rest."

Dyami looked up. Others were coming down the ramp; he gazed into the eyes of one man and nearly gasped in surprise. The man's blond hair had gone completely gray, and the skin of his face sagged, but Dyami had seen his image too many times not to know Sigurd Kristens-Vitos. No Linker's jewel gleamed on his forehead now; a thin, almost invisible white scar marked his brow and those of his fellow passengers.

"We'll walk over with them," Thomas said affably, "give them the tour." He tilted his head as he looked toward Dyami. "My, my—don't you think you'd better get those crates loaded? It isn't like you to stand around being idle." Thomas said the words gently. Dyami sighed. The mild reprimand would probably cost him his supper later.

He was about to move another crate when he saw five sashed men leaving the cabin. More patrol members, he thought bitterly, just what we need. One man suddenly halted on the ramp and looked directly at him.

Dyami felt faint. He knew this face, too, and now he realized that the man had recognized him. As he had expected, the unhappy boy he had once tried to console had become a handsome young man. His youthful chubbiness was gone; his black eyes were stony. He smiled a little as he gazed at Dyami; he did not seem like the boy tormented by guilt over his sins, the one Teo had guided home from that house three years ago.

Dyami bent toward a crate. His heart was pounding; his ears throbbed.

"Welcome to hell," Suleiman muttered as Sigurd and the people who had arrived with him sat down on the lavatory floor. "That's where you are, you know. I would have thought someone like you would have found a way to avoid this, but maybe you deserve it. You failed us all in the end, thinking you could keep Ishtar—"

"Steady." Dyami put a hand on his friend's shoulder. "He's one of us now."

People had crowded into this lavatory; others sat in the hallways that led to it. Sigurd and the other former Linkers had been taken here earlier, before the other prisoners were brought back after supper, and no one had yet had a chance to speak to the new arrivals. Their curiosity was now overriding their fear of punishment, should the guards enter and find them gathered here.

"Where were they keeping you all this time?" a woman asked.

"In the Habber residence on Island Two," Sigurd replied. "Some of the others they were holding with me have been released, although they've lost their Links. The ones here are those who were closest to me or people Ishtar has doubts about. No one's told me much these past months, but I did hear some talk on the Platform."

"Are people finally coming to their senses?" Orban Szekely called out. "Isn't anyone wondering what might be happening to us?"

"I can't answer that," Sigurd said. "Some people must be, but I can't tell you what's being said about you. They'll learn I'm here, of course—I was seen by many on the Platform." The former Administrator rubbed his chin. "I can tell you what I did hear, but you won't welcome the news. A delegation from Earth will be arriving on Anwara within a couple of months to meet with Administrator Alim and the Guide. The talk is that Earth is prepared to leave us with almost completely autonomy now that the Habbers are gone. It seems quite a triumph for the Guide, a Mukhtar dealing with her as an equal."

"A Mukhtar?" a man said.

"Mukhtar Kaseko Wugabe will be with the delegation. You see what an event that is, having a Mukhtar visit our world for the first time. Earth will aid us in whatever ways are necessary but will leave us free—even the Project Council will have less power, or so it's claimed."

"Then we're lost," Suleiman said angrily. "The Guide will be even more powerful than she is now."

Sigurd sighed. "It seems an uncharacteristic move on the Mukhtar's part, given what little I know about Kaseko Wugabe. He's also a Guardian Commander, the type who might have welcomed an actual battle with the Habbers,

costly as that would have been for Earth. But maybe he's
satisfied with simply having them gone from here. It's
probably wise for the Mukhtar to conduct himself this way.
Earth has had some of its pride restored, and it doesn't
have to worry about Habbers influencing events here. It
can grant us some freedom and convince us Earth is our
friend."

"Freedom," Allen said. "That's what you call it. The
Guide's followers will love her all the more now. We'll be
free of both Earth and the Habbers. The only one we'll all
have to bow to is her. How delighted she must be. She's
pulled off something even you couldn't manage, and now
she'll have a Mukhtar courting her. I don't believe it."

"I can hardly believe it myself," Sigurd said, "but I've
been isolated for a while, and maybe circumstances have
changed. Earth may simply want to lull us for a while until
it can tighten its grip again."

"People would resist that," Allen said. "They couldn't
passively surrender our world to Earth, no matter what it
cost to resist. And Earth doesn't have the resources to give
us the aid the Habbers might have provided. People would
see that we were better off when the Habbers were here,
helping and asking nothing in return except a little understanding."

"People might try to resist Earth now, if they felt
threatened," Sigurd replied, "but they may not later, with
Ishtar to dull their minds. I've failed you—I can't deny it. I
wanted our world to be free of the old world's mistakes
and become a bridge between our people and the Habbers. I thought I could buy enough time to make that
possible. Instead, my mistakes in judgment have delivered
Venus to the Guide and her friends, and to my colleague
Alim, who would probably bargain with anyone to keep
the power he has now."

Sigurd paused. "I haven't been allowed to see anyone
for some time, except a few wretches who talked to me
about their damned cult, and the Guide before she left the
Island. She and Alim found it hard to resist the chance to
gloat. They're intoxicated with themselves and their new
power. I suspect they're going to overreach themselves
sooner or later or make some mistake that may turn others
against them. I have some experience with what power
can do to a person and how foolishly one can act when one

feels things are going one's way. Their hold on our world may be more tenuous than they realize."

"And none of that," Suleiman said, "does us any good."

"We could fight," Sigurd said. "If things are as bad here as you say, we wouldn't have much to lose."

"Fighting's no use," Luinne Mitsuo replied. "Making trouble just makes things worse for others besides the troublemaker. You'll understand that when you've been here a while."

"So you'll just give up?"

"You still think you're an Administrator," Suleiman said. "Who are you to tell us what to do? Haven't you made enough mistakes?"

Sigurd held out his hands. "I don't know much about your situation yet, but I've already seen that we outnumber them, even if they're armed. We could come up with something that might work. You wouldn't have to disable them completely, just long enough to get to a screen and tell others what's going on here. I saw how they were acting today—I saw a man punched several times for no reason at all. Many people would be appalled to know that you're being treated that way. At the very least, you could cause the Guide a lot of trouble in trying to subdue this settlement, and that might inspire some to—"

"They've all forgotten us outside," Suleiman shouted. "Either they'll believe what they're told, or they'll keep quiet so that the patrol doesn't come after them. No one cares about us anymore, and they wouldn't listen to anything we'd say even if we got a message out. Even our families will forget—some of them weren't too happy when we came here to work with Habbers in the first place."

"You may be wrong," Dyami said. "I managed to speak to a pilot today."

Heads turned toward him. The room grew quiet. Maybe some of them were recalling his earlier pleas, when he had tried to convince them not to let any airships land here until they knew who would be joining them.

"Actually," he continued, "the pilot spoke to me first. He was careful, and the patrol didn't notice. He said my family was wondering about me. I told him a little of what's

going on here. He didn't say anything, but he didn't give
me away to the patrol either."

"Probably didn't believe you," Luinne murmured.

"Maybe, maybe not. But I've been thinking about that
encounter all day. He was very cautious. Why would he act
that way unless he was already worried about what things
are really like here? And if he didn't believe me and
thought I was trying to spread lies, why didn't he do something about that? Why didn't the other pilot speak to the
patrol? Don't you see? If someone trusted enough to bring
an airship here is worried, a lot of other people may be,
too."

"That's a slender thread to hang hopes on," Allen muttered.

"Maybe. But it's more than we've had so far." Dyami
looked down. Perhaps he was hoping for too much; recent
events had disoriented him. He wondered if he could still
trust his perceptions. Too many emotions had jarred him
in too short a time—rage over the assault on Amina, hope
at hearing Evar's words, shock at the sight of Sigurd, and
fear when he saw the young blond man. Maybe he would
grasp at anything now.

"I have something to say." He raised his head; Amina
was getting to her feet. "It's going to get worse here—all of
you must know that," she continued. "We can't count on
any help from anyone else, and that means we have to act.
But we can't throw ourselves away doing something that
has no chance at succeeding, or the patrol will have more
excuses for treating us badly. We have to plan, and while
we're waiting, we have to lull our guards by behaving
ourselves and doing what they want. They have to believe
they have nothing to fear from us, that we're already
beaten. I can endure that if I know we'll get a chance to
fight."

"And what if we do succeed?" Fadil Fedorson called
out. "We'd be entirely dependent on our installations,
even if we keep other ships from landing, and if we lack
the equipment to repair the life-support—"

"Then we'll just have to ensure that nothing fails for a
long time," Amina interrupted. "Anyone working in external operations will simply have to be even more alert to
problems that might develop and tend to them immediately while we're making our plans. We have no other

choice." She paused. "Or would you rather go on living the way we are now?"

"Bad as it is," Fadil said, "it could get a lot worse if we try to fight them."

"It'll get worse if you don't," Sigurd said. "Take a good look at me. What do you see now?"

Dyami knew the answer just before Tasida responded to the question. "An old man," the physician replied, "someone older than your years, Administrator. Someone in need of rejuvenation therapy."

"Which I haven't been getting since my Link was removed." Sigurd looked around the room. "Somehow I doubt that Ishtar intends to waste many medical resources on people who are troublesome to them. Most of you look fairly young, but you won't always be. Maybe you should think about how quickly one's youth can vanish if life gets hard enough."

Dyami glanced at the people closest to him; their faces were grim. "We have to discuss some possibilities," Sigurd continued. "I'll want to know everything about the patrol here that might help us—their lapses, their individual weaknesses, their procedures, and where they might be vulnerable. Once we've decided on a course of action, we're all going to have to work together. We'd better go to our rooms now, in case the guards decide to check up on us."

Dyami could not free himself of his fear. During his week-long shift at the greenhouse, the young blond guard often seemed to be nearby, watching him at his work. His presence was unnerving; Dyami had to force himself to concentrate on the tiers of crops and had nearly flooded one level with too many nutrients. The guard occasionally spoke to others in the greenhouse but not to Dyami, yet the blond man was always watching him as a smile played about his lips.

The young man's name, Dyami had learned, was Maxim Paz. Had he told the other guards about his first encounter with Dyami? So far, Jonah and his colleagues had only suspicions about Dyami's inclinations. Would Maxim try to use what he knew against him? It was pointless to speculate, and the worries only kept him from trying to come up with ways to fight his captors.

Dyami had helped in building the new addition to his living quarters; no eavesdropping devices had been added to the walls, and all of the prisoners had searched their rooms thoroughly. The guards, he supposed, had too much contempt for them to believe they were capable of any plotting. They could, however, still be betrayed. A prisoner, in a moment of weakness, might reveal their hopes to a guard in an effort to gain better treatment for himself. Maybe they would never get further than discussing plans to which someone could always find an objection.

Now, after supper, a few prisoners were usually summoned to the residences of the guards. Occasionally, they returned to their own dormitory with tales of messages they had been allowed to see. More often, they were silent, and kept their eyes averted. More of the women had Amina's haunted, listless look; more of the men bore the marks of beatings.

Three weeks after his arrival, the blond man pulled Dyami aside as he was leaving the dining hall. "I have a message for you," Maxim Paz murmured. "Come with me."

Dyami followed the young guard to one of the houses near the hall. Maxim ushered him inside, then gestured at the floor. "Sit down."

Dyami seated himself. Through the entrance to a tiny adjoining room, he could see a mat. Maxim disappeared into the other room for a moment, then came out; he was holding Dyami's sculpture of Balin. "I was told you made this," he said. "I rescued it from what was confiscated here, and Jonah said I could keep it. I admire your skill."

Dyami looked up warily. Maxim was smiling down at him. Could it be that the guard pitied him or had some sympathy for one of his own kind? Had Maxim volunteered to come here in order to find some way to aid the captives? He would have to be careful; he knew too little about the young man.

Maxim was even taller and more muscular than he had been as a boy; his body seemed almost to fill the small room. He set the sculpture on the floor, then sat down. "Aren't you curious about the message?" Maxim asked. "Don't you want to know who it's from? Shall I fetch a pocket screen so that you can see it?"

"Please do," Dyami said.

"But you have to guess first. Who do you think it's from?"

"It could be from any number of people."

"Oh, yes. Maybe your parents sent it, or a neighbor. Maybe there's a message from your old friend, Teo. Do you think it might be from him? I don't know how much he'd have to tell you—it might be embarrassing or even danger- ous for him to touch on certain things. It might not be a good idea for you to see any messages from him. It could only stir up old memories that are best forgotten, don't you think?"

"Perhaps."

"Teo tried to seduce me once," Maxim said. "He shows no remorse or repentance over the kinds of things he's done. He thinks he can go on as he has, but he'll regret that. Even the Guide's patience will wear very thin. It would also grieve her to know that none of the penitents here has accepted the truth."

Dyami did not reply.

"There are a few people under detention now who may be sent here soon to finish out their sentences," Maxim continued. "They would assist us, of course, in an effort to make some recompense for their earlier deeds. I'm sure they'll be grateful for the opportunity to prove their worthiness of our trust."

That, Dyami thought, was useful information. When his fellow captives learned this, they might be moved to act more quickly. "I would like to see whatever message you have," he said.

"Perhaps another time."

Dyami kept his face still. "You said—"

"Oh, I do have another message of sorts, but it isn't recorded. It's from your sister. She's very concerned for you. I've spoken to her often, and when I volunteered to come here, she honored me by including me in the party sent to the Platform to bring those former Linkers here. I told her that I would do my best to guide you to the right way. She knows that you and I have been guilty of offenses against the Spirit."

Dyami's heart fluttered. He had clung to a faint hope that Chimene, if she discovered how the prisoners were being abused, might be moved by some concern for her brother. If Maxim spoke the truth, she knew what he was now; that was something she would never forgive.

"I confessed my sins to Boaz," Maxim said, "and he brought me to the Guide. Her kindness to me was more than I expected. She saw how I hated my deeds, how I fought against what was inside me. She told me that I would be forgiven, that there is great virtue in overcoming great obstacles to reach the truth. I wanted to say that to you. You see that she loves us, don't you? She awaits the day when you'll make your peace with Ishtar."

The blond man reached behind him and handed Dyami a bottle. "Go ahead," Maxim said. "It's just some whiskey. Maybe you've missed it. I can show you a little hospitality."

Dyami took the bottle. He could bring it down on the other man's head; he might have just enough time to find Maxim's pocket screen and get some sort of message out before— He dismissed the wild idea. Maxim was holding his wand now; he would fire before Dyami could move. He lifted the bottle, drank, then set it down.

"I didn't know who you were that night we met," Maxim said. "I didn't find out until I spoke to Boaz. I couldn't believe that the Guide's own brother could be guilty of such affronts, that you, of all people, could have sat with me and told me there was no evil in what your kind does. What sorrow the Guide must have felt when she knew."

Dyami's head swam; his arms felt heavy. He took a breath, afraid he might faint. The room seemed to be spinning slowly. He tried to move, then closed his eyes for a moment.

"But you will repent." Maxim's voice surrounded him. "I'll see that you do."

A blow caught Dyami on the side of his head, knocking him to the floor. He gasped, struggling for air. He could not move; his limbs felt weighted to the floor. He had been drugged; he was sure of that now. Maxim continued to strike him, then pinned him.

"You're going to learn to hate this," the young man murmured. "You're going to be taught to give it up." He pulled at Dyami's clothes. "You won't be able to think of it without hating the evil inside you. I'll show you how much

I love you by making you hate this." Maxim held him face down, then thrust inside him painfully.

Dyami lay in the darkness, his face against the ground. Pain shot through his chest as he took a breath; his back felt bruised, his insides torn. He was certain he was bleeding, and felt that something had ruptured inside him. He had lost consciousness at least once, only to awaken to the horror again. He wondered how many times Maxim had assaulted him, whispering of his love as he entered, groaning as he spent himself.

"Get him back to the dorm," someone was saying.

"Acting up, was he?" another man said.

"He got a bit out of line." Dyami recognized his tormentor's voice. "I was forced to take steps to restrain him."

"I hope he's able to work. He won't get fed until he is. Next time, try not to disable them too much—it just means more trouble for us. There are plenty of ways to hurt them and leave them fit enough for work."

He was picked up by his arms and legs. He nearly groaned aloud. His battered muscles contracted in pain as he was carried through the darkness.

"—really worked him over," one of the guards was saying. "Maybe it's just as well—kind of a warning to his friends not to step out of line."

The darkness swallowed Dyami. When he came to himself, he was lying on his stomach, his cheek against a mat; a hand was on his head. "Tasida's coming." That was Suleiman's voice. "Who did this?"

"Maxim Paz."

He heard Allen curse. "What is it?" a woman's voice called out from the doorway. "Oh, no." Tasida knelt at his side; Dyami squinted at her. She gripped his hand as someone else removed his clothes; he heard a gasp. "Oh, Dyami." The physician clutched his hand more tightly. "What have they done to you?"

"Is he going to be all right?" Allen asked.

"Get one of the guards outside," Tasida said. "Tell him I need my physician's bag. You know what to say—that we want to be sure that he's able to work as soon as possible. Look meek, apologize for the trouble he might have caused if you have to, but just get me my bag. Helmut, you and Suleiman can go to the lavatory, find a couple of relatively clean towels, soak them, and bring them back here."

Tasida's freckles were tiny dark spots on her white, angry face; Amina was peering over her shoulder, tears in her blue eyes. Dyami moaned as the physician touched his back.

"I'll be all right," he managed to say, "—have a lot of time to think while I'm recovering, come up with a plan that'll work."

"Dyami," Amina said, "you mustn't—"

"That'll work," he muttered, "and soon, because if we don't act soon and I have to go through that again, I'll kill him. I won't care what they do to me—I'll kill him." He closed his eyes, welcoming the darkness.

Thirty

A Guardian and a Linker had come to Chimene's room to present gifts from Kaseko Wugabe. There were other Guardians in the hallways of Anwara; Chimene had seen them the day before, after leaving the shuttle dock. The sight of the stark black uniforms made her uneasy; there was no need for the Mukhtar and his delegation to bring Guardians to Venus's satellite. But Mukhtar Kaseko was also a Guardian Commander; perhaps he felt more at ease with other Guardians around him.

Boaz hefted his present, a hand-made spear from the African Nomarchy of Azania, where Kaseko Wugabe had been born. Chimene's present was a small silver dagger with Arabic lettering engraved on the blade; Eva had also been given a dagger.

"Maybe we should wear these to the meeting," Chimene said. "The Mukhtar might expect that." The presents struck her as odd but perhaps not out of keeping for a Commander.

"Boaz and I are hardly going to be able to carry spears into the meeting." Matthew stood his spear in a corner, then sat down on a cushion. The room, like most of the residential quarters on the space station, was small, and Chimene would be sharing it with Boaz while they were here, but the minor discomfort was a small price to pay for what the Mukhtar would grant them.

She glanced at Eva, who was studying her own dagger. Maybe after they had met with Kaseko, there would be no more complaints from her friend. Somebody had been filling Eva's head with foolish stories—rumors about

547

possible brutalities in Turing, tales of the patrol calling on households Boaz held grudges against, discontented pilots, complaints about requested contributions, restlessness among workers on the Bats, grumblings that the Guide was losing touch with her followers. Idle talk, she thought, clearly designed with only one aim—to sow discord in her household and to make her distrust those who had been of such value to her. She had not deigned to discuss such matters with Boaz or Matthew, since she had been preoccupied with preparations for the Mukhtar's visit. Her people still loved their Guide; they would love her all the more when their freedom was upon them. That would be her gift to all Cytherians.

"What does it say?" Eva asked. She held out her dagger; Chimene studied the calligraphy. Her Arabic was a bit rusty, being a legacy from her father that she preferred to forget.

"His is the kingdom of the heavens and the earth," Chimene translated. "He ordains life and death. You have none besides God to protect or help you." She gazed then at her own dagger. "Believers, make war on the infidels who dwell around you. Know that God is with the righteous."

"Well." Eva put her dagger back into its case. "They hardly strike me as appropriate sentiments."

"I think they're quotations from the Koran," Chimene replied. "God's Revealed Word is full of such sentiments. I'm sure the Mukhtar doesn't mean anything by them."

"Chimene." Boaz took the dagger from her. "We meet with Kaseko Wugabe and his delegation tomorrow. Matthew and I have to speak to you and Eva now. Administrator Alim would be here to discuss this meeting with you himself, but I urged him to allow me to speak to you first."

His face was solemn, his large dark eyes filled with apprehension. Boaz was probably as nervous about meeting the Mukhtar as she was, and perhaps even more worried. She, after all, had prevailed upon their housemate Galina for an implant that would keep her calm during her sojourn on Anwara. The physician had somewhat reluctantly, after Boaz had requested it, provided one; its carefully timed doses of hormones and enzymes would block any surges of adrenaline while keeping her mind clear. Chimene did not like depending on the implant, but Boaz had pointed out that she was using it in service to Ishtar. She did not want to shame herself by betraying her nervousness when meeting the Mukhtar.

"Alim's already explained a great deal," she said, "what to say, how proud the Mukhtar is. I think I know how to conduct myself."

"Alim had more to tell us during our consultations earlier," Boaz said. He and Matthew had been in the Administrator's room before, supposedly to settle small details that did not have to trouble the Guide. "I don't quite know how to tell you this, but you must listen. I found it difficult to accept myself, but Alim has convinced me that we must. He was very worried about you—he knows how strong your faith is and about the hopes you were bringing here. Please hear me out and understand that the Administrator has only the interests of our fellowship in mind."

She looked at him steadily, unable to summon up too much concern. "What is it, Boaz?"

"The Mukhtar is not prepared to grant what you wish. He isn't here to give us autonomy but to reassert Earth's control over this Project. Kaseko may be a Mukhtar, but he's also a Guardian, and he's never lost sight of what happened during Pavel Gvishiani's time, when it seemed Earth might lose control of this world to the Habbers. The Guardians wanted to force a surrender from the Islanders then, even battle the Habbers, but the Mukhtars refused to unleash them. Kaseko has always seen this as an admission of Earth's weakness, even though the matter was settled peacefully and the Mukhtars were able to save face. He still sees it as a stain on the honor of the Guardians."

"But the Habbers are gone now." She was still calm but also numb, as if her mind could not yet grasp the import of Boaz's words. "Isn't that enough? Can't the Mukhtar see that the Habbers no longer have any influence here and that allowing us freedom poses no threat to him?"

"That isn't the point," Matthew responded. "With the Habbers gone, Earth will need to do more to keep this Project going. They're not willing to do that unless it's made plain that we're subject to their will. Kaseko controls the Council of Mukhtars now, and he's tired of the ambiguity in our status. He wants Venus to become another Nomarchy. Treating us as equals or as a sister-world with its own

autonomy—he would see that as only another humiliation."

Eva bowed her blond head. "I feared this," she said.
"If the Habbers were still among us, the Mukhtar would
have had to be more cautious. Maybe the Habbers even
guessed that Earth might make this kind of move, and
that's why they left so willingly. They knew Earth might
be ready to fight them—that's why they left without even
trying to hang on for a bit in the hope things might
change."

"You sound," Matthew said, "as if you regret their
departure."

"Oh, no." Eva looked up. "I can't be sorry about that. I
can be grateful for their cowardice. At least it may have
kept us from becoming their battleground with Earth.
Alim must have seen this coming all along. He'd bow to
Earth to keep what he has—maybe he's even dreaming of
becoming the Mukhtar of this new Nomarchy."

"Alim has also been working for us," Boaz said. "You
must believe that. He convinced Mukhtar Kaseko that his
original plan was unwise."

"What plan was that?" Chimene asked.

"The Mukhtar was going to tell us he would meet with
us on Island Two. After his ship landed here, shuttles were
to carry a Guardian force to the Platform. We wouldn't
have known that, of course—we'd have been thinking they
were only the delegation bound for Island Two. Our people couldn't have prevented a well-trained force from taking control of the Platform, and you know what that would
have meant. We'd be completely cut off from the outside,
with no shuttles able to land on the Platform unless the
Guardians allowed it. No airships would have been able to
carry supplies from the Platform to the Islands or the surface, unless we gave in to all of the Mukhtar's demands."

Boaz did not have to explain that to her. The Islands
and the domes would have been entirely dependent on
the supplies they had now. They could survive for quite
some time, but eventually an important installation for
which they lacked replacement parts would fail, and
threaten an entire community. The Cytherians would
have had to surrender, or else wait for the slow and inevitable end.

She lifted her hand a little, surprised at how steady it

was. "Alim," Boaz continued, "convinced the Mukhtar that such actions were both needlessly provocative and unnecessary. He said it was possible for Kaseko to achieve his aims peacefully, but for that, he needs us. Alim has persuaded him that we're reasonable people who know that we can gain nothing by taking a futile stand against him."

"Giving in to him can't serve the Spirit," Chimene said. "It makes a lie of everything I believe."

"It won't serve the Spirit to defy him," Matthew said, "and bring suffering and death to our brethren. Let him call Venus a Nomarchy, let him bring in his own people to serve on the Project Council and as Administrators. We'll still have the Project, and you'll be the Guide. Alim will see that you're consulted. Which is more important—preserving our pride, or keeping our people safe? Your brothers and sisters won't thank you if you defy the Mukhtar and put them all at risk."

"Ishtar will go on," Boaz murmured. "Our people will still be free to find the truth. We can live for the day when Earth will have no power over us, when we're strong enough to stand alone. Kaseko's grateful that we persuaded the Habbers to leave, and Alim has convinced him of the wisdom of working with us. You may see this as a defeat now, but we'll be victorious in the end."

His advice had led her to this, having to surrender her world to Earth. She had thought that the Spirit spoke through Boaz and Matthew; now it seemed as though their words had always been Earth's. Maybe they were only two men who had acquired a taste for power, or perhaps they had been Earth's minions all along.

She was grateful for her implant. Perhaps Boaz had thought it would keep her passive as well as calm. She would deal with the rage, shame, and despair that were likely to overwhelm her at another time, but at the moment she was free to consider what Boaz and Matthew had told her.

She did not believe that Mukhtar Kaseko had actually planned to seize the Platform, now that she could reflect on this threat. A siege of that sort would have cost Earth too much. The Mukhtar had probably only been trying to impress Alim with his ruthlessness before agreeing to what might have been his own plan all along—letting Alim's people and those closest to the Guide prepare the Cytherians for the new order. She would have to assess this Mukhtar when they met and try to see exactly what he might be willing to do.

She was sure of one thing. If the Mukhtar found reason to distrust her or felt that she was unwilling to cooperate, she would probably not live to betray him. A way could be found to explain her death; a more malleable Guide could take her place—perhaps Lakshmi, a young girl who could easily be guilded by Boaz. Many people already assumed that Chimene was training the girl as a possible successor.

She felt a queer, disembodied fear; it hovered above her, unable to grip her yet with its icy talons but ready to pounce. She was thinking of how Boaz had brought Lakshmi to their house, of all the discussions with Alim that Boaz had mentioned to her only afterward, of all the duties he had so willingly taken upon himself so that she would not be troubled. Perhaps he had been preparing for a time when she was no longer necessary.

She gazed into Boaz's eyes. He was an obstacle now, but she could not let him see that she viewed him that way. "You've loved me," she said. He would expect her to seem grieved and despairing. "You've advised me when I was unable to see what might bring our people closer to the right way. You've told me things I had to know but didn't want to hear, and then you've consoled me and given me back my strength. But I don't know if I can face what you've just told me." Her reluctance was something else he would expect. "The Spirit is silent in me now. I cannot know Her will. I am trying to see how what you've told me will lead to the perfect state that awaits all Cytherians, and I don't know if I can."

He took her hand. "Let me help you now," he said. "This is as hard for me to bear as it is for you—perhaps harder because I feel I may have failed you. I knew some of Alim's fears about what the Mukhtar's visit might indicate, and I didn't share them with you—I kept telling myself he was mistaken. I think I sense what the Spirit would have us do now. We must preserve our world however we can. We will be stronger later."

"When our people learn what the Mukhtar intends," Eva said, "they may take this matter into their own hands.

They'll feel betrayed, and they may resist even if they know they can't win. They may turn against us."

"That's why they mustn't know of this yet," Matthew replied. "All they'll hear for now is that Earth will be aiding us more, and that Mukhtar Kaseko is concerned about the Project's progress. We'll have time to prepare them by pointing out the possible benefits of closer ties to Earth so that hearing they're going to be part of a new Nomarchy won't come as too great a shock."

"We'll also root out any potential troublemakers," Boaz added. "The patrol has questioned some in a few of the settlements, people who enjoy gathering in secret to murmur against us. Our patrol hasn't learned much, but others are clearly directing those malcontents and looking for ways to strike out at us. We'll find the ones behind it all, and they will regret their lack of faith with those others in Turing."

"I see," Eva said. "I suppose there's nothing else to be done. We can't stand against Earth alone. We can quiet any grumbling by removing the most troublesome—the others would fall into line then. If our sisters and brothers know that Earth will allow us to practice our faith and keep our dream of being freer in the future, they'll see that their Guide acted wisely. And perhaps the Mukhtars' representatives here will be so moved by our faith and by Chimene's future efforts on our behalf, that we'll win some of them to the right way. After all, we can be free inside ourselves. It doesn't matter if Earth calls us their world." The blond woman's face was composed. Chimene could not tell if Eva's words were sincere, or if her friend was also cloaking fear and anger.

"Leave me," Chimene said. "I want to be alone with Boaz now." Matthew got up, reached for his spear and helped Eva to her feet. Chimene caught a glimpse of a Guardian in the hall before the door slid shut behind them.

"Hold me," she said to Boaz. He would expect her to seek his comfort now, to cling to him, question him, and then allow him to persuade her that she had to give in. By depending on him, by sharing her doubts and fears with him, she had let him see her as weak and easily led. She had needed him after Kichi's death; she should have freed herself of him long ago.

His arms were around her. She would let him make

love to her before she told him she would heed his advice.
Strangely enough, she felt more love for him now that she
understood how deeply he had fallen into error. She was
still his Guide; she would find a way to bring him back to
her truth.

Two Guardians stepped aside; the door to the meeting
room opened. Chimene was wearing her dagger under her
sash; she was expecting this meeting to be somewhat anti-
climactic, now that she knew why the Mukhtar was here.

At the far end of the room, several Linkers, all clad in
their formal white robes, sat on red cushions. The men
wore their headdresses; the women had covered their hair
with long white scarves. Kaseko Wugabe was sitting in a
chair in the middle of the group; his broad face was nearly
as dark as the black uniform he wore under his open white
robe. Two uniformed Guardians stood at his sides; a slim
golden-haired woman, also wearing a Guardian's uniform,
sat in a chair near his. Behind them, a wide screen displayed an image of Venus's Parasol. The planet was hidden; the umbrella's vast panels reflected the light of the
sun.

"Salaam, Mukhtar Kaseko," Administrator Alim said,
then bowed, touching his forehead; Chimene and her
companions did the same. The Mukhtar touched the Linker's jewel on his own forehead but did not speak. "It is my
hope, God willing, that your stay will be most pleasant. It is
a great honor for us to have you here, and we hope that you
will take pleasure in being so near the world that is, after
all, the fruit of an Earthman's dream."

"Salaam." Kaseko waved one hand languidly. "Come
forward."

Alim led the group toward the empty cushions in front
of the Mukhtar, then bowed again as Chimene and the
others seated themselves. "In the Name of God, the Compassionate, the Merciful," the Administrator murmured,
"Whose Hand guides us all." He lowered his plump body
to one of the scarlet cushions. "May He guide us now."

"I invoke the Spirit," Chimene said then, "Whose love
encompasses all who dwell on Her world, Who reflects
their dreams and is Herself a reflection of them."

"God's will be done," Kaseko said. He stared down at
her coldly with his dark brown eyes. "We shall dispense

with more formalities." He gestured at the people closest to him. "I won't introduce the new members of the Project Council here—you'll be learning their names soon enough." He held out a hand to the uniformed blond woman. "This is Commander Johanna Wulf, my aide, my companion, and my closest adviser. She is also in command of the Guardians who have accompanied us—I trust her patience will not be tested. I've viewed the records of these people, Administrator Alim, so you needn't introduce them either. I'll be speaking for my people. Much as I would prefer the subtleties of Arabic, Anglaic is more useful for precision, and I do not want to be misunderstood. I should also use a language your companions can understand."

Chimene tried to ignore the comment, which seemed intended to mock their lack of learning. "The Guide has some familiarity with Arabic," Alim said.

"Learned from her father, no doubt, disgraced scholar that he was." Another insult; the man seemed intent on belittling her. Kaseko smiled. "But his daughter, I am sure, will erase any memory of his shame." He leaned forward. "Very well, Chimene Liang-Haddad. You know why I'm here. When I joined the Guardians, and learned the true reasons Earth had backed away from a battle here, I knew that my mission was to restore our honor. I did not come here to heap further humiliation on Earth and its people by telling you this world will be yours. But Alim has told me that you are a reasonable woman, and that your people have great love for you. If God wills, it is my hope that we can work together. I remain grateful that your influence with your people led the Habbers to depart, even though you were thinking of your ends and not mine. I do not intend to interfere with your duties as Guide of your cult or with the spiritual life of your followers—that is, if you are actually as reasonable as Alim claims." His deep voice was so resonant that he might have been using an amplifier.

"I must be honest," Chimene replied. "I was sorrowful when I learned your true reasons for coming here. I had believed that the Spirit—" She paused deliberately, forcing herself to keep her eyes on his face. "But I won't speak of the Spirit. As real as Her presence is to me, you do not share my faith. I'll speak of my people. We need your aid even more, now that the Habbers are gone, and must accept your conditions for giving it. Those closest to me have convinced me that we must bow to you, much as I struggled against that. I'll do what I can, but—" She waited.

Kaseko tapped his fingers against the arms of his chair. "But what?" he said at last.

"My people may not give in easily. Many will want to fight this, even if they know they must lose, and it will cost you much to subdue them."

The Mukhtar leaned back. "You're constantly bombarding them with your inspirational little talks. You supposedly have a patrol that answers to you. You have ways to bring them around to an acceptance of the new order."

"Even many on the patrol would object to this."

"Then you had better see that they don't. If you can't serve my interests, I'll be forced to find someone who can." He folded his arms. "Let me tell you what lies in store for your people if they resist—it will give you an additional incentive to do my bidding. If they resist, we'll disable or destroy the Platform. That will be the end of anything your people can do against us."

"You'd be condemning a whole world," Chimene whispered. "You'd just be throwing the Project away. That would gain you nothing."

"But the Project would not end. The atmosphere could still be seeded with algae, and Venus would continue to cool in the Parasol's shadow. The geological processes begun by our terraforming efforts would go on. All that would end is one phase of the Project, a perhaps misguided attempt to settle this planet at an earlier stage. We would retain the knowledge we've gained about terraforming, and we could then direct our resources to using that knowledge for Earth's benefit, which was one of the reasons for beginning the Project in the first place. Venus would be settled again eventually but only by people who will bow to us."

"Earth may not stand by and let you watch a world die."

"Do you care to test that?" Kaseko's voice had risen a little. "Earth is subject to my will now. What the people there think depends on what they learn, and I am in charge of that. They can be told it was your people who destroyed the Platform in a suicidal gesture of defiance, that it was those you call Cytherians who condemned their fellows to a long wait for a prolonged death. I think we can make them believe that—your own grandmother died trying to prevent a similar action. Earth will feel pity for those sorry multitudes, and disgust for the leaders who failed them. We will of course make an effort to rescue those we can, but it may be too late for many. That will be your legacy—death, and exile from this world for the few who might be lucky enough to be saved."

He could not mean it; he was only trying to frighten her. His gaze was steady; she saw no mercy in his eyes. A man who made too many empty threats would not be in his position; she wondered how many he had pushed aside during his climb to power.

"It won't come to that," Chimene said softly. "I wouldn't wish such a fate on my brothers and sisters."

"I'm pleased to hear it. I'll give you a couple of months to prepare your people for the inevitable and to point out the benefits of closer ties with Earth. I advise you to silence as many potential dissenters as you can by any means you choose in the meantime. After that, you will announce my intention to visit your Islands, at which time my aide and her Guardians will secure the Platform. We'll make the nature of our agreement public then, and you will keep it a secret for now. The new Project Council, with Alim's Administrators, will make all decisions regarding Venus, and our Guardians will supervise your patrols. Alim will be free to consult with you, and you may keep your little cult. Are we agreed?" Kaseko's smile widened. "But of course we are. You have the look of a woman who's used to comforts and the idolatry of those who adore her. You're not the sort who would martyr herself in a hopeless cause."

"We're agreed." She bowed her head. Her right hand was near the dagger under her sash; she might be able to get to him before she was stopped. He could pay for his arrogance with his life, and all Cytherians would see her as a heroine. No, she thought; that wasn't the way. Such an act would win no victory for the Spirit.

The Mukhtar was speaking to Alim now. Kaseko had underestimated her. He was counting on an easy victory; she would see that he had no victory at all. She did not have to keep his plans secret; the Platform could be secured before his Guardians landed. He would lose some of his power over the Council of Mukhtars if others on Earth saw that he was leading them into a costly battle; he might be forced to withdraw. If he did not, then surely it was better for Cytherians to die fighting; the Spirit would expect that sacrifice. The defiance of a world could bring down the Mukhtar. The martyrdom of the Cytherians would unite all of her people with Ishtar.

Thirty-one

One line, written in crude black Anglaic letters, had been added to the inscription on the monument to Iris Angharads and Amir Azad. Under "They rest forever on the world they helped to build," someone had written: "Where the Guide and her followers now trouble their long sleep."

Chimene glared at the monument, trembling with fury, then turned toward one of the three patrolwomen trailing her. "I want this removed immediately," she muttered, "and I want you to find out who dared to deface this pillar." Eva reached for her arm as Josefa moved closer to her. The patrolwomen stared back at her uncertainly. "Now!"

"We'll have to summon a maintenance worker," one woman replied. "Those letters won't come off easily, and we wouldn't want to mar—"

"Then summon somebody." Chimene glanced toward the other memorial pillars, where five people were laying a wreath at the base of one column. "In the meantime, you can search that group and find out if any of them has materials that might have been used to do this."

One woman spoke quickly into her wrist communicator; then the three moved toward the five mourners. Chimene led her two housemates toward the nearby wall.

"We'd better stay within sight of our guards," Eva said. "They are supposed to be protecting us."

"Protecting us!" Chimene shook her head. Ever since she and her party had returned to Oberg a week ago, members of the patrol were almost always at her side

559

whenever she left her house. They waited by her door and
outside the houses of those she visited; they even stood at
her side during meetings to watch the crowd of worshippers. It was Boaz's doing; he claimed that he wanted her
safe from the few malcontents who might threaten her.
Instead, she felt as though she was being watched.

"For all we know," Josefa said, "a member of the patrol might have defaced the monument. You'll probably
never find out who did it."

Chimene gazed through the dome at the darkness
outside. Walls surrounded her now, separating her even
from those closest to her. Most of her household seemed
afflicted with ennui as they passively went about their duties. Boaz and Matthew, on the other hand, were notably
more energetic. They spent their days with her drawing
up lists of Councilors and permanent patrol members who
could be trusted to subdue any who might resist Mukhtar
Kaseko's new order. Other lists included people Boaz particularly distrusted and whom he suspected of being organized into a group of conspirators against Ishtar. A few of
those people had been interrogated, and Boaz had learned
a little about the group's organization. Each person had
contact with only a few other conspirators; none of those
who had been questioned seemed to know who was at the
heart of the group.

Under other circumstances, they might have ignored
these malcontents, who had so far limited themselves to
spreading scurrilous rumors, telling stories of injustices at
the hands of the patrol, attacking and temporarily disabling a few patrol members under the cover of darkness,
protecting wrongdoers, and defacing tunnels and buildings with mocking graffiti. But these people might win
other supporters when the agreement with Kaseko
Wugabe was announced; they had to be rooted out before
that. Boaz was prepared to be harsh; every person who
broke down under questioning would lead him to a few
others. He would trace the chain to its center. He already
had a few suppositions; Chimene knew Risa's name was on
his list. Boaz would even move against the Guide's mother
when he had more evidence.

Chimene had been following Boaz's direction so far.
She looked at his lists, listened to his and Matthew's advice,
uttered the occasional gentle protest the two would expect

her to make out of pity and love. Before leaving Anwara, she and Alim had recorded speeches about the aid Earth was prepared to offer and the goodwill the Mukhtar had shown them. Boaz was now helping her with her next speech, one that would carefully point out the benefits of friendship with Earth and the suspicion of Habbers both worlds had in common.

Boaz thought he had won. She did not let him see that she was preparing to move against him, that his lists of those he distrusted were also showing Chimene her potential allies. She no longer heard the Spirit in his voice, only the sound of a man who would surrender to Earth in return for power here. Lately, at night, she dreamed that the Spirit mocked her: *What have you done? Why have you put chains on My world?*

"We must speak to you," Eva said then, "before it's too late. I can't keep silent any longer, especially after what Josefa's told me today. Maybe you'll finally listen to me. Ever since our meeting with Kaseko, I've wanted to speak. I couldn't believe that you'd give in so easily, that Boaz—"

"What about Boaz?" Chimene, suddenly wary, turned around and leaned against the wall.

The blond woman gestured at Josefa. "Tell her."

"A young man on the patrol came to me," Josefa murmured, "one of those who has often been useful to Boaz. He doesn't shrink from abusing someone under detention or who's being questioned or from extorting a few extra contributions for himself, but he was troubled by some things Boaz has been saying about you lately."

"Such as?"

"That the Spirit has abandoned you." The golden-skinned woman pulled nervously at a strand of her long black hair. "That you no longer love your people and are incapable of guiding us. He's saying that it's time for a new Guide, that you have wandered from the right way."

Chimene folded her arms. "My brothers and sisters will not believe that."

"It doesn't matter whether they do or not," Josefa responded. "Boaz says this only to this man and a few others like him, people who have close ties to Boaz. He tells them how he sorrows over you, how he fears all the fellowship will lose their faith if they ever see what he knows. This man says Boaz means to put you out of the way and raise another in your place. You know what that means. Another can become our Guide only after your death."

"He's clever," Eva said. "I'm sure he can find a way to arrange it with the help of a few like that man, maybe with an accident or even an attack on you that can be blamed on our enemies. Those doing Boaz's bidding will believe they acted in the interests of Ishtar. The rest of the fellowship will mourn for you and perhaps be roused to strike at any of our opponents who might be held responsible for your death."

"He'd probably make Lakshmi the Guide," Josefa said. "The girl adores him—he'd have no trouble manipulating her. Why, he could even bring your child into the world—that would be a nice touch after your death, and everyone knows you planned to have one. Maybe he anticipated that all along, maybe that's why he persuaded you to make arrangements to store your ova. If Lakshmi ever outlives her usefulness or becomes obstinate, he could install his own daughter as the Guide." She took a breath. "If you don't believe me, I can take you to this man, and you can hear this from his own lips. Whether he's moved by love for his Guide or hope of an eventual reward from you, I can't say, but he took a risk in coming to me, since I might have betrayed him to Boaz. I had to convince him that my first loyalty was to you before he told me what he knew."

"And are you loyal to me?" Chimene glanced from Josefa to Eva. "How can I be sure of that? How do I know this isn't some plot to turn me against a man who's been so close to me?"

"The only way you can find out," Eva said, "is to go to Boaz with this story. If that were all it is, he'd silence that young man and that would be the end of the matter. If it isn't, he'd have to move against you immediately, and us as well. You have to trust us and protect yourself. We've put our lives in your hands by telling you this. I know you don't want to believe this—Boaz was to be the father of your child."

"But I do believe you. I've sensed what might be going on in Boaz's mind for a while now. I will take steps." Chimene gazed past the two women at the monument, where a man was now scrubbing at the pillar under the patrol's supervision. "Boaz will repent. He and Matthew will be brought back to the right path." She felt a wave of pity for the two men. The Spirit was with her; she could not hate them even now. She would help them past this obstacle to truth, this lust for power, this eagerness to betray her and her world. They had loved her once, and they would love her again. Ishtar would forgive them if they turned away from error.

"What can you do?" Eva asked.

"The Mukhtar is counting on us to keep his plans secret," Chimene said, "to reveal them only to those who will help us carry them out. By the time his Guardians are on the Platform, it'll be too late for anyone here to make an effective response. He needs time—time for us to weaken the will of our people so that he can impose his rule with a minimum of resistance. We're not going to give him that time. You two will have to help me."

"How?" Josefa said.

"Boaz has a list of people he doesn't trust. They're going to learn about Mukhtar Kaseko's intentions. They're going to hear that Boaz and Administrator Alim betrayed us. The pilots are going to hear it, too—they'll spread the word among more of the fellowship. By the time Boaz realizes that the word is out, he'll have both his enemies and many of our sisters and brothers against him. You'll help me spread this information. Eva, you were always coming to me with stories the discontented had told you— now you can tell them that their Guide has not forgotten them."

"But even if we're believed," Eva said, "what can we do? You might bring about Boaz's downfall and unite us all, only to have us suffer the Mukhtar's wrath. You heard what he said—he wouldn't shrink from a violent confrontation."

"Then why didn't he simply take the Platform before we knew his intentions?" Chimene shook her head. "He wanted us to make it easier for him. He talks of his power, but much of Earth and even most of his fellow Mukhtars might turn against him if they think he's leading them into a protracted and costly siege. He can't win unless his victory costs him little. Our pilots could seize the Platform and make certain his Guardians never land. We can resist the way the Islanders did during Pavel Gvishiani's time, wait them out until they see that we'll never give in."

"And if you're wrong?" Eva said. "An orbiting Guard-

ian ship could disable the Platform and the Islands with
beam weapons, and we have no defenses. Our settlements
would be entirely cut off then, with no way for us to survive indefinitely. The Mukhtar wouldn't even have to
strike at us down here. Can we take that chance?"

"What else would you advise?" Chimene asked.

"Spread the word, disgrace Boaz, blame everything
on him and Alim. The Islanders will be just as unhappy
about this betrayal as anyone here—many of them recall
what it was like when Guardians were stationed there.
They'll be behind you. Then you inform the Mukhtar immediately that you're willing to come to another agreement with him. Let him install his Project Council and
Administrators—you might be able to convince him by
then that there's no need to station Guardians here. Grant
him enough concessions to salve his pride, and he may
grant a few to us. It won't be a satisfactory situation, but
even the most stubborn of our people will see that it's
preferable to the complete capitulation Boaz and Alim
wanted, and they may be grateful to you for at least keeping us from that. That's about the best we can hope for
now."

"But that isn't what I want." Chimene felt very calm.
"The Mukhtar will see our determination. The Spirit will
strike the man down for his arrogance."

"But—"

"And if he decides that he wants a battle, isn't there
glory in dying to preserve our way? Can we give our world
to a man who mocks us and scorns Ishtar? Better to die
speaking the truth and reaching for our freedom. If we
don't have it in this world, we'll claim it in the next, when
no barriers separate us from the Spirit."

Eva, she thought distantly, seemed so pale; Josefa's
hands were trembling as she lifted them to her face. How
sad that after all this time as her companions, the two
women could still lose sight of the truth.

The three patrol members were coming toward them
now. "We'll speak of this again," Chimene said.

A steady tapping on her window woke Risa. She
slipped from her bed, careful not to disturb Sef, and lifted
the curtain. A shadowy form beckoned to her, then moved
in the direction of her door.

Risa smoothed down her shift, pulled on a pair of pants, and hurried toward the common room, wondering who could be calling at this hour. It's about Dyami, she thought. Every caller, every message waiting for her on the screen was an occasion to both hope for and fear news about her son.

For months now, her messages to Dyami had brought no reply; no one else she knew had heard from him either. There had been too many opportunities to dwell on what Evar IngersLens had told her—that the patrol in Turing, according to Dyami, was beating and otherwise abusing the people there. The pilot had not been back to Turing since then, but he had heard other stories from pilots who had traveled there later. One man in the bay had whispered to another pilot about a man nearly dying of a beating, and there were tales of other brutalities. Evar said that many of the pilots now believed them; the haunted, ravaged faces of Turing's people seemed to confirm them. "It isn't the right way," Evar had muttered. "Trying to convince people of the truth is one thing, but this is another." He had begged her to speak to her daughter, certain that the Guide would put a stop to it if she knew. She had not bothered to tell him that Chimene no longer answered her messages.

Dyami was trapped in Turing, probably hoping desperately that someone outside would come to his aid, and there was nothing she could do. Now that Chimene and Administrator Alim had apparently won a promise of more aid from Earth without, it seemed, any demands on the Cytherians in return, some of those who had been grumbling about the Guide were wondering if they might have been wrong about her.

That was what it came down to, Risa thought. If people were themselves inconvenienced or those close to them were harmed, they might summon the courage to act. If they thought that the Guide wouldn't give them what they wanted, they might stand against her. Otherwise, they would not get terribly worked up about the people in Turing, whom they did not have to see and who had probably brought whatever troubles they had upon themselves. They would not have to wrestle with the broader issues of ethics, freedom, and the ideals some of them had once possessed; those were only words that had little to do with their daily lives. Once they had thought they might determine their own fate; now they were becoming accustomed to their powerlessness.

She opened the door. "You'd better let me in," Eva Danas said.

Risa stumbled back. She's going to tell me my son is dead, she thought wildly; Chimene sent her here because she was too afraid to come herself.

"Please," Eva whispered. "I mustn't be seen here. Boaz thinks I'm visiting a man I know. A few people in the patrol whom I can trust are covering for me. I must speak to you." She pushed past Risa. A blue scarf was draped over her blond head; her hands clutched a screen. The door closed behind her.

"Dyami," Risa murmured.

"No. This isn't about your son." Eva settled herself on one of the cushions. "I wish I could tell you some news of him, but I can't. I've heard a few of the rumors. Boaz claims they're lies."

"Why are you here?" Risa said harshly. "You wouldn't be bringing greetings from my daughter in the middle of the night."

Eva slipped off her scarf; it fluttered to the floor. "I have to trust you," she said. "I don't know if you're involved with those who are trying to work against us, but Boaz is suspicious of you. He's just waiting for the right time to do something about you and anyone else he sees as a threat. That's one reason I thought I could come to you."

Risa tensed. Had Boaz already guessed that she was at the center of those who longed to strike out at Ishtar? Some people had been questioned here and in other settlements, but none of them knew about her role.

"I don't know what you're talking about," Risa responded. "I'm worrying about my son, and I have my doubts about how he's being treated, as any mother would. I haven't made any secret about the fact that I can't share my daughter's faith. Other than that, I tend to my work and my household. If this constitutes offensive behavior in the mind of that creature Boaz, then I plead guilty."

"Very well." Eva set down her screen. "Say what you have to now. You'll trust me if you just listen to what I have to say. If you're not involved with any conspiracy now, you may want to be by the time I've finished."

"There'd hardly be any use in conspiring now, would there? Chimene's been back for nearly two weeks, and a Mukhtar has deigned to meet with her in person. I don't hear so much talk against her now. She must be savoring her triumph. They're even saying that the Mukhtar will visit the Islands after various details of the agreement have been worked out."

"The agreement's already been decided," Eva said, "and it isn't a triumph. We've been betrayed—by Administrator Alim and by Boaz and Matthew, too. They knew what the Mukhtar was going to demand even before we arrived on Anwara, and they knew we'd have no choice but to agree. I don't know. Maybe Matthew and Boaz were working for Earth all along. I think of everything that's happened since Kichi left us, and it all—"

"What do you mean about being betrayed?"

"Mukhtar Kaseko came here to reassert Earth's total control. We're to be a new Nomarchy. The Project Council and the Island Administrators will all be the Mukhtar's people. There will be a Guardian force on the Islands, and probably everywhere else eventually—that's what he intends. Any resistance, and he'd destroy the Platform—I heard him say it. It'll be the end of any hope at freedom. We won't be Cytherians any more—just another people in the grip of Earth."

Risa was stunned, yet she knew this had always been a possibility. There was nothing to stop Earth now that the Habbers, who might have stood in Earth's way, were gone. "But why did he meet with you at all?" she asked. "Why didn't he just carry out his plans? We might have fought, but he has plenty of ways to subdue us."

"Because he prefers an easy victory," Eva said. "He wants Alim and the Guide and the dome Councils and the patrol to do his dirty work for him. He wants them to take care of anybody who'd be likely to lead any resistance to his plans. We aren't to say that's the reason, of course. Boaz and the patrol could manufacture evidence of crimes or offenses of some sort. Almost everyone else would probably accept the agreement afterward."

The woman was probably right about that. Turing would make a convenient prison, although it might strain the resources of the patrol a bit to send enough people there to guard the prisoners. She shivered. Boaz might

have other plans—executions, for example. She had provided a precedent he could cite.

"Why are you telling me this?" Risa asked.

"Chimene sent me," Eva answered. "She doesn't
know I chose to come to you—she left contacts to my
discretion. She's determined not to let the Mukhtar have
his victory, and she knows that Boaz is working against
both her interests and our world's. She needs help—not
just from those who are loyal to her but from those who
have been Ishtar's enemies. We have to work together now
if we're going to save our world." She picked up her screen
and thrust it at Risa. "You'd better look at what I've
brought while I give you more details. I assure you that
you'll find it extremely informative."

Risa set down the screen when she was finished with
her viewing. She had grasped the utility of the lists of
names immediately—Boaz's lists, shared with Chimene,
over whom he still believed he had control. The list of
those he considered trustworthy held few surprises; they
were mostly Councilors here and in other settlements and
permanent members of the patrol, along with a few prominent members of the cult. His list of potential enemies was
a bit more striking. Her name was there, as she expected,
but Istu Marnes, her former colleague on the Oberg Council, was also listed; she had assumed Istu had made his
peace with Ishtar long ago. Lena Kerein was under suspicion, in spite of her childhood friendship with Chimene.
She felt a qualm; Boaz might know more about her possible allies than she did herself.

When more people learned of Boaz's treachery, many
would be willing to take a stand. Those who hated Ishtar
would take action to save their world from Earth's rule;
many believers would rally behind their Guide. The
screen held not only lists but also a plea from Chimene
herself, begging her people to rise up against those who
would surrender Venus to Earth. Against her will, Risa
even felt a bit moved; the recording was one of her daughter's most compelling speeches.

She would have to talk to Yakov; their sympathizers in
other settlements would have to be contacted. There had
to be pilots who would be willing to seize the Platform; the
people loyal to Boaz could be detained and disarmed if

necessary. He was planning to rid himself of those who led his enemies; she would do the same to him first. At that point, Chimene's speech, sent out on public channels, might convince any who were wavering to join the resistance. In the meantime, the speech could be circulated in secret to gather support.

"Chimene had to memorize those lists," Eva murmured. "She says she might have missed a few names, but most of them are there, and the ones who aren't may decide to switch sides when they see how many are against them. Galina helped her record the speech at the infirmary while she was supposedly giving Chimene some medical treatment."

"How can I trust you?" Risa stood up and began to pace. "I don't know if those lists are what you claim. I don't even know if Chimene's speech is faked or not. Even if I tried to circulate it, the Guide could always repudiate it."

"Have it analyzed then. Any expert in holograms and screen images will tell you that it's genuine. Just compare it with records of her past speeches—you'll see. And you're her mother—you'd spot a fake."

"Perhaps not. My child was often a mystery to me."

"Please listen." Eva clasped her hands together. "You have to trust me. Don't you see the chance I took in coming here? You could destroy me with what I've given you."

Risa stopped pacing and sat down once more. "I see why you need my help. You want me, and anyone else who might support you, to add to my daughter's glory. If we succeed, she'll be seen as the savior of our world. All the evil could be blamed on Boaz and others, and Chimene would have even more influence than before."

"Does that matter now, with the Mukhtar ready to tighten his grip?"

"And that's another thing. Are you so certain he'll back down if we show him that defeating us would be too costly? You said yourself that he spoke of destroying us if need be. Earth may have backed off long ago, in my mother's time, but the Habbers helped to bring that about. Earth couldn't afford a confrontation with them. We can't use that kind of threat against this Mukhtar. Your people saw to that, fools that you were."

"I thought you'd say that." Eva closed her eyes for a few moments. "May Ishtar forgive me. The Guide is convinced that Kaseko will shrink from the battle, but at the same time she doesn't fear one if it comes. She mentioned the sacrifices the Spirit demands of Her followers. I can't believe that she means it, and yet I saw the same look in her eyes as I saw in the Mukhtar's when he said he was willing to see our people die."

"I won't be responsible for leading our people to that."

Eva bowed her head. "I am prepared to make certain sacrifices. I didn't discuss this with Chimene—she'd only see it as a betrayal, but the Habbers may be our only hope now. We have to appeal to them and pray that they'll forgive us. Whatever my feelings about them, I never believed many of the stories I heard about them. Shuttles have reached the nearest Hab before."

"There might be pilots willing to take the chance," Risa said, "but why should the Habbers listen to their pleas? Why would they do anything for people who asked them to leave and who undoubtedly wouldn't welcome them back?"

Eva looked up; her blue eyes seemed old and weary. "They might listen to me. I would be willing to go and beg them for help, may the Spirit forgive me. I see what's coming otherwise—not the perfect world the Spirit wants but a place that would be either Earth's prison or a graveyard. Maybe they'd listen to one who's so close to the Guide and understand that I wouldn't shame myself that way unless we were desperate. I can tell them of our fears over the fate of the people in Turing. Surely they'd feel some concern over those who were their friends."

Risa's hands were trembling; she pressed them against her thighs. What would happen to her son and his companions when the patrol in Turing learned what was happening outside? She shuddered; she could not think of that. She could only hope that these plans succeeded in time to help Dyami. The Habbers might insist that the people in Turing be freed in return for their help, and Chimene could always blame their ill-treatment on Boaz and the patrol. It was Dyami's only chance now.

"We have to act quickly," Eva said. "There's little time. Boaz is going to have to move against his opponents soon—and against Chimene."

Risa gestured at the screen. "You may leave those

records with me. I'll see that they get to people who'll help
us."

"When you need to speak to me again, contact Devon
Holman. He can be trusted, and even Boaz doesn't suspect
him of any disloyalty. He would do anything to protect
Chimene."

Eva stood up. "You'd better not leave by the front
door," Risa said as she guided the taller woman toward the
corridor. She felt as though she were carrying a heavy
burden, one she could not let slip; it was the same feeling
she had endured when she had been on the Council.

Devon Holman, a young, bearded man wearing the
sash and a patrol member's wand, brought Risa to Lena
Kerein's house three days later. She kept expecting a trap;
only desperation could have led her to trust Eva Danas.
She kept her head down, clinging to Devon's arm as he led
her through the dark, keeping away from the nearby path.
Lena's door would open, and Boaz Huerta would be waiting for her.

Yet when the door opened, she saw only Lena and her
bondmate Carlos sitting with Eva and Yakov Serba. "Speak
softly," Lena said as she guided Risa to a cushion. "My
parents can be trusted, but they're sleeping, and I don't
want the children to hear."

The door to the kitchen opened; Evar IngersLens entered the room, carrying a tray of cups and a teapot. He set
the tray down, then settled himself. "I've given recordings
of the Guide's speech to all the pilots I can trust," he said
without preliminaries. "Some of them have gotten it to the
other settlements, and it's made its way to friends on the
Platform. You'll have most of the pilots with you when they
learn what the Mukhtar intends. We don't care for the idea
of having Guardians aboard our ships again."

Risa gazed at her former lover in surprise. "I knew you
had some pity for my son's plight," she said. "I didn't know
you were with us."

"He has been for a while," Yakov said.

"Not because I've lost my faith, you understand." Evar
ran a hand through his graying brown hair. "I only want to
work against those who have misled and deceived the
Guide. She'll return us to the right way then." He cleared
his throat. "My copilot and I will leave the Platform with

Eva. When we're out of orbit, our allies on the Platform will take over. There may be a little fighting then, but they know who's likely to resist."

She reached for the pilot's hand. "I underestimated you, Evar," she murmured. "I thought your faith had blinded you to so many things."

"I'm not happy about this." His throat moved as he swallowed. "I don't like running to Habbers. I don't know what I'm afraid of more—that the Habbers might not listen and that I wouldn't have any way to get back home or that we won't make it to the Hab in the first place. I can alert the Habbers through our comm once we're on our way, but it'll take a shuttle a week to reach them now, and we have to hope the vessel can make the trip. If they refuse to answer and don't put us under their protection, there will be time enough for Anwara to send a ship after us and disable us. The Mukhtar would probably be happy to let us die out there."

"You mustn't think of that," Risa said. "The Habbers will help—we have to believe that." If they didn't— She pushed the thought away forcefully.

"My arrangements have been made," Eva said. "Matthew was quite pleased that I agreed to make this trip." Matthew, it seemed, had his doubts about some of the people working on the Bats, who were complaining that Ishtar asked for too much of their credit in contributions. Eva had volunteered to go to both polar satellites in an effort to bolster the workers' morale; it had been the excuse she needed to get aboard a shuttle. "We leave in thirty-five hours." She glanced at Yakov. "The rest is going to be up to you."

"I've gotten the lists to my contacts in the other settlements," Yakov said, "and when they hear that the Platform is secure, they'll detain as many councilors and permanent patrol members as possible. Some of the volunteer members will help in disarming them. The Islanders will be able to view Chimene's plea on their screens by then, since we'll be putting it through public channels, but they'll have to fend for themselves. I suspect a lot of them will wait to see what Earth or the Habbers might do before they jump to one side or the other. Some of the pilots will secure our bays. If—when we manage to restore order in the settlements, Administrator Alim will be told that we have no intention of bowing to Earth."

"I guess it's settled then," Risa said softly.

Yakov tugged at his short gray beard. "If Boaz Huerta doesn't find out before we can act. If our allies in the other settlements move on time. I'm hoping there'll be a minimum of violence, but we won't be able to avoid some, and if the Habbers decide to keep out of it—" He sighed. "A lot of people could turn against us again if we accomplish nothing except leaving ourselves at Mukhtar Kaseko's mercy. We'd find out exactly who's with us by then, if not before. Earth might be ready to stand by and let us destroy ourselves."

"Let's go over everything again precisely," Risa said. She would be sending messages to Irina in ibn-Qurrah and Patrick in Kepler later. A battle, possible bloodshed, Cytherian against Cytherian—everything she had hoped to avoid would now become part of her world's history. No wonder Malik, with his burden of knowledge, had held no faith in Venus and had decided to escape this history. It was, after all, only another variation on what lay coiled in a human nature that refused to change. But then she thought of the son she hoped to save—and still might lose if the patrol in Turing, sensing defeat, turned its wrath upon the helpless captives. If she lost Dyami, any victory would be only defeat.

Thirty-two

Dyami's world had been shrinking steadily. Once it was only the size of Turing itself. Events outside these two domes—the lives of people who did their work, visited with friends, lived in households of loved ones, and shared life's simpler joys—were so distant that they hardly seemed real. Such lives were part of a dream world he might have conjured up when he was younger, a world he could never recapture.

The world had then narrowed to become the places where he worked—the refinery, the greenhouse, the kitchen—and the tiny room where he slept. The forest where he had once wandered was now only another place where he labored and where the casual blows of the guards interrupted any reverie that might enlarge the world inside himself.

After that, the core of his world had become a room in the house where Maxim Paz stayed from time to time. He had deceived himself by believing that his tormentor might feel some regret about what he had done, if only because it had taken Dyami days to recover and Jonah had not been pleased at losing his labor. But Maxim had summoned him again, sending two other guards to bring him to the house three weeks later.

Dyami was barely inside the door before he was disabled by the young man's blows, then bound. The horror had begun again, worse this time without any drug to dull his mind and more painful when he struggled. Maxim had been more careful, beating him only enough to subdue him and leave him with a residue of pain while keeping

574

him able to work. The promise Dyami had made to himself, that he would kill Maxim if the guard ever touched him again, had been an empty threat.

He had to think of his friends, who would surely suffer even more if he struck out at the man he hated; Maxim had made that quite clear. He had to make Maxim think that he had lost the capacity to resist, if the prisoners were to have any chance at overpowering their captors.

Maxim hurt him however he could even when Dyami accepted the assaults passively. That was the whole point of the exercise, to make him loathe what he was and become unable to love any others of his kind. But Maxim did not hurt him quite as much when he did not resist and pretended to more agony than he felt. Dyami had lost the last shreds of his pride when he groaned in order to mimic a pain his numbed and beaten body could hardly feel.

Now his world was bounded by his bruised body, the intermittent dizziness and twinges of pain in his skull, the aches of his muscles and bones, the throbbing of his genitals, the inflamed, raw feeling of his insides. Maxim had taught him to hate that body, which had become the instrument of the young man's torture. He had been living in constant dread of the next assault while simultaneously hoping for it, because Maxim would be a little kinder when it was over and leave him alone for a few days afterward.

He had no escape. He was no longer able to entertain the mathematical flights of fancy that had once diverted him or to see an image his mind held shaped by his hands. He could not dwell on memories of the always gentle Balin without remembering how Maxim's brutal assaults parodied their loving acts.

Now he would finally have the chance to strike back. He was awake even before Suleiman reached over to touch his arm. He had been able to sleep soundly until this moment; he felt no righteous rage, no anticipation of revenge. His torment would be over one way or another, and he did not care if it ended with his victory of his death. Just as well, he thought, that he did not care, that his fear of what might happen to him was gone.

Dyami sat up, then rose from his mat and went to the door. Faces peered at him from the room entrances along the hall. He began to pound at the door. "Open up!" he shouted.

"What's going on?" a voice answered from outside.

"Open this door! I can't take it anymore! I have to get out!"

The door slid open; a guard was raising his wand. Dyami knocked him aside, then chopped him on the side of his neck before wresting the wand from him. Another guard came at him; Dyami fired and saw him fall. He aimed toward the dormitory's other door, hitting the guard standing there. People spilled from the doorway behind him; two beams shot through the darkness before the other seven guards were overpowered by a group of prisoners.

"We're all right so far," a man muttered. "They didn't sound the alarm." Dyami took a breath; he had feared that one of the patrol might alert others through a wrist-comm or with a shout.

His eyes were adjusting to the dim dome light; in about two hours the disk above would begin to brighten. Someone called out; the weak cry broke off as a wand struck a guard's head. Two prisoners were opening the other door. The patrol had disconnected the devices allowing the doors to be opened from the inside but had not troubled to install locks; anyone could open the doors from outside. Two women raced from the other door, then turned to run in the direction of the lake; he glimpsed Amina's pale hair before the darkness swallowed her.

Jonah, without knowing it, had provided them with the remaining tools that had made their plans fall into place. The overgrown forest near the lake had to be thinned out and cleared, and Jonah had not wanted to take the prisoners from their other tasks. Two crawlers, with large jaws usually used to clear and crunch up rock, had been brought inside and driven to the woods. That was Jonah's solution; the crawlers, with two guards running them, could cut through the trees and clear away much of the underbrush. That this would also scar the land had not concerned the guard; any damage could be repaired later, when more prisoners arrived. Dyami had seen immediately that the crawlers could also be used as weapons. Amina and Luinne would board the unguarded crawlers, cross the creek farther down, and wait on the other side. The crawlers would provide cover for the prisoners when they advanced on the patrol's dormitory and houses.

Sigurd came outside, followed by Suleiman and a few others. Dyami surrendered his wand to his roommate; three others were quickly handed to other men. Suleiman nodded, then hastened away with five companions. Their job was to get to the tunnel that led into the south dome, stun and disarm the two patrol members who would be guarding it, and make for the airship bay, which would have to be secured. The woods behind the ceramics plant would conceal them for part of the distance; the few guards who stayed on nighttime duty in the south dome would be inside the refinery or the external operations center. The six pilots stationed in Turing would be sleeping in their residence near the bay; Dyami hoped that some of the guards on duty would also be asleep. He had heard a few of the guards complain about Jonah's insistence that they stay awake, since the systems were operating smoothly and alarms would alert them to any problems. But Suleiman and the others had weapons they could use in any case.

"Let's get them inside," Sigurd muttered. The man Dyami had shot was already being dragged through the other dormitory door. A few people would remain outside, to alert the rest if any other guards were seen approaching; they hunkered down in the grass, and one of the women fastened a wrist-comm to her arm. Their captors had grown a bit more careless in recent weeks, convinced that the people they had brutalized were almost completely under their control.

That had been the hard part, Dyami thought; cowering in front of the guards, keeping anger and determination hidden, sacrificing whatever pride they had left, and persuading a few fearful people that they had to fight now, before any more patrol members and prisoners arrived. The other guards were being dragged toward his door. Dyami went inside and waited in the hall with the people standing there. Two men remained outside near the door, to open it when those inside were ready to come out again.

Two of the female guards were unconscious; the guard Dyami had struck looked dazed. The Peeper was with the group. Their wrist-comms were quickly stripped from their arms before they were bound with their sashes; torn clothing became bonds for their legs. The guards had been lax lately; they had been lounging outside, leaving only two of their number to keep an eye on the doors.

"Gag them," Sigurd ordered, "and make sure those knots will hold."

"Killing them would make more sense," Dyami heard himself say. "It'd be fewer we'd have to worry about."

"No killing," Sigurd replied, "unless it can't be helped." He stared at Dyami for a moment, then looked away; they had engaged in this argument before. "Now we have to see about getting more weapons."

This was going to be more difficult. Five guards were on patrol on the other side of the creek; at least two would be on watch outside the patrol's houses and dormitories. If any of them saw the men who were heading for the tunnel, the rest of the guards were certain to be alerted. Dyami pushed that worry aside.

Sigurd handed a wrist-comm to Willis Soran. The slight young man had a talent for mimicking the Peeper, a skill that would now be put to use.

"Steven Ginnes calling," Willis said into the comm, using the Peeper's slightly nasal tones. "Respond."

"This is Lila," a woman's voice replied. "What is it?"

"Some of the penitents are acting up." Willis had captured the guard's speech perfectly; Dyami hoped it would fool the woman. "A man was banging on the door earlier, making a fuss. It's quiet now, but we're going to go in and take a look around. I think you'd better bring the others over here for a bit. I'm not expecting much trouble from this lot, but I'd rather have you nearby, in case we need some support."

"Should I wake up some others?" Lila asked.

"That's not necessary. Just bring the ones patrolling with you. I'm not really expecting anything to happen, but we should be covered."

"You'd think they would have learned by now," the woman said. "We'll have to make a few examples—we can turn them over to the ones who enjoy chastising the recalcitrant. We'll be there in a few minutes. Out."

Sigurd motioned to Dyami. "You proved you were a good shot before. Get out there and take a wand. Remember—wait as long as you can before you shoot. We can't give them a chance to summon help."

Dyami tapped on the door; it opened. He hurried

toward the group outside, then knelt. "I heard," the woman with the wrist-comm said. "They're coming."

"Sigurd says I'm to have a wand."

The woman gave him hers. Dyami squinted into the darkness; now he could see five guards moving toward the opposite bank. The dim light would keep the guards from recognizing them until they were closer; it would be better not to fire at them until they were across the small bridge. He'd been lucky so far; a wand was easier to use than he had expected. He wondered if Suleiman and his group would make it to the bay. If they were seen, and those on duty in that dome guessed at their intentions, the guards might seize the bay themselves and hold it until reinforcements could reach them from outside. A lot of things could go wrong. He considered the possibility dispassionately. His heart beat faster; he felt oddly elated.

Two of the guards were crossing the bridge; a third began to follow. As the fourth moved toward the bridge, the woman behind her halted. "Steven?" she called out. No one answered. The two in front left the bridge and began to move up the small rise toward the waiting prisoners. "Steven?" Dyami tensed as the two came closer. The third guard moved toward the rise; the fourth was on the bridge.

"Something's wrong!" the female guard on the bank suddenly shouted. "Get back!"

"Fire," Dyami said. Beams cut through the dark; the three guards nearest them fell. The woman on the bridge spun around and was caught by another beam. The other female guard was fleeing now; Dyami saw her raise her arm as she ran. He could not hear what she was saying into her wrist-comm but knew she would be calling for help. He aimed, fired, and missed; the woman was quickly out of sight.

"Shit," one man muttered. "We'll have all of them out here now."

"Get their weapons," Dyami said. People were already leaving the dormitory behind him; Sigurd hastened to his side as the fallen guards were dragged up the rise. "One got away," he murmured to Sigurd. "We'll have to fight them here, and we've only got ten wands. I hope none of them guesses we've sent anyone into the other dome, but they may alert the people there anyway."

"We still have a chance," Sigurd said, "if we can hold them until Luinne and Amina get here." He looked around. "All of you, get whatever weapons you can—rocks and sticks and anything else you can find. We've got to make a stand here."

"Why not make for the forest?" Orban Szekely asked. "We'd be hidden there when it's light, and—"

"They'd hunt us down," Dyami said. "They could surround the woods and starve us out. We have to stick together. If any of you start backing down now, we're lost."

"We're lost anyway," another man said.

"Not yet," Sigurd said. "You're forgetting the crawlers. Start looking for possible weapons. Some of you—get those other guards into the dorm."

Dyami followed one group down to the bank; he had a wand, but a few rocks might come in handy. This was the end of their carefully contrived plan—his plan, he thought bitterly, the plan that Sigurd had helped him to contrive. There would be no advance on the patrol from the north and east behind the crawlers, no chance to fire on any of the patrol as they fled from their residences, no chance to acquire more wands, and force the guards to surrender. Jonah was probably already alerting the people on duty in the south dome. He bent over in dismay, searching for rocks.

They did not have to wait long before hearing the approach of the patrol. Two carts moved along the opposite side of the creek, shielding the people behind them. The carts rolled to a stop above the bridge. Dyami flattened himself against the ground, keeping his wand ready; other prisoners lay in the grass or were sheltered behind a few shrubs and the trees near the dormitory. The dome light was already beginning to brighten; before long it would be light enough for the prisoners to be easy targets. Dyami clenched his teeth; where were Luinne and Amina? They might be having problems managing the crawlers; they might never get here at all. Even if they did, the sight of the massed guards might make them lose heart.

"Penitents!" That was Jonah's voice. Dyami could not see him; the patrol members were staying behind the carts. "You had better give up now. You will suffer much less than if you continue to resist. We have more weapons than you, and you cannot escape."

No one replied.

"I know you sent someone into the other dome. I've already alerted my people there, and yours will not succeed in reaching the bay. I must assume that is why they were sent there. We found the bodies of the guards they killed." Dyami swallowed; so Suleiman had decided to take no chances with them. "There will be no mercy for murderers, but there might be some for you if you give up now. You cannot win. I have already sent two of my people for the crawlers—I think you know what that means. We can dig a great many graves with them."

"How can we trust you?" Sigurd shouted. "You won't show us any mercy if we do surrender."

"The Spirit will forgive," Jonah answered, "if you repent of your deeds. That is your choice—to be brought to repentance now or to die forever condemned. You had better consider your choice carefully."

"We have," Sigurd said. "Even death is better than the life we've had in this place."

"Ah, Administrator," Jonah said mockingly. "That is you speaking, isn't it? Then death is what you will have, and it won't be an easy death. Now!"

People were suddenly screaming to Dyami's left. He rolled and stumbled to his feet as a few prisoners fell under beams. Several guards were already on this side of the creek; Jonah had outflanked them, sending guards to sneak up on them from this side. Dyami fired into the crowd, bringing down two sashed figures, then dropped to the grass as another beam shot past him. Guards were rushing down the bank from the carts; he fired at one as the man climbed up from the creek. Other prisoners with wands were firing; he saw one fall.

Then, above the shouting, he heard another sound— the soft, low hum of a motor. A crawler, looking like a tank with jaws, was bearing down on Jonah's people, with another vehicle just behind it. Beams stabbed toward the cabins of the crawlers and were deflected; other guards began to flee along the opposite bank. The two crawlers kept moving; guards shrieked as they fell under the treads. He looked away quickly as one man disappeared into a crawler's jaws.

Rocks flew through the air toward the guards storming the rise. People rushed past Dyami; an arm struck his, making him lose his grip on his wand. He slapped the ground, trying to find it, and was abruptly dragged to his feet.

It was now light enough for him to make out the cruel, handsome features of Maxim Paz. Dyami realized the other man was also unarmed just as Maxim's fist darted toward his face. He ducked and punched the guard in the belly, then pulled a large rock from his pocket and struck him on the side of the head. Maxim crumpled to the ground. Dyami fell to his knees, feeling the other man's skull give way as he continued to pound at him. A light suddenly blinded him; his body jerked convulsively as everything went black.

Dyami opened his eyes. The dome was light; someone was wailing. His head throbbed painfully; he managed to sit up. A few bodies lay on this side of the creek; above the opposite bank, he saw more bodies, their limbs and arms twisted. A few were so crushed that they hardly seemed human.

A beam must have stunned him. He leaned over and retched, then stared at the body next to him. Maxim's head and face were a raw mass of blood, torn flesh, and shattered bone. A sharp-edged rock near the body was covered with blood and matted blond hair.

A shadow fell across the body. Dyami groaned, then looked up at Willis Soran. "What—" he started to say.

"We won," Willis said. "We lost a few people. They lost more—we counted about thirty so far, and a few others probably won't recover. Those crawlers really did a job on them. We have the rest over by their dormitory—they're being watched."

"What about the bay?"

"Suleiman got there. He and the others made it as far as the plant when he saw some guards running out of the refinery toward the bay. He said it looked as if they'd just panicked. He brought them down. They're dead, too—he didn't say how. The pilots gave up after that, and the ones in external operations." Willis stared at Maxim's body, then averted his eyes.

A woman was still wailing. A few people stepped

around the bodies. Dyami looked for the wailer, then found her. Fatima Snow, one of Sigurd's former aides, was sitting next to one body; she lifted her head, wailed again, then covered her face with her loose pale hair.

Willis helped Dyami up. They walked toward Fatima. Tasida hurried to the woman's side, carrying her physician's bag. Dyami looked down at the body. Sigurd's eyes were closed, his pale face composed; he might have been sleeping.

Tasida knelt, scanned the body quickly, then thrust the portable med-scanner into her bag. "It seems his heart gave out," she whispered. "It must have been the wands—I think I saw at least three beams hit him. He wasn't strong enough to take it."

Fatima's shoulders shook; Tasida put her arm around the other woman. "Are you recovering?" Willis asked Dyami, who nodded. "Tasida'll take care of the injured. We've got to get the bodies into those carts."

He looked around numbly at some of those who had paid for their freedom. Helmut Renas-Korbs was lying near the bridge, his head lolling at a peculiar angle. The body of a guard had fallen across his legs. Willis tugged at his arm; Dyami allowed himself to be led away from Sigurd's side.

On their first day of freedom, they buried their dead comrades. The bodies of the guards had been conveyed to the refinery and fed to the recycler, but the former prisoners decided to bury their dead friends in a grave near the tunnel. One of the crawlers dug the grave and covered the bodies with dirt. Fifteen comrades had died with Sigurd, some from heart failure under the onslaught of multiple beams, others by violence at the hands of the guards.

On the second day, the two dormitories and the houses the patrol had used were searched, and possessions confiscated, before the surviving guards were herded inside one of the dorms. They would be fed and given water once a day, half of them in the morning, outside and under guard, the others just before last light. People would be posted by the dormitory at all times, and the patrol would remain inside except when eating their meals.

This was Dyami's suggestion; he wanted as little effort as possible expended in watching the guards. He had also

decided that the pilots would be kept with the patrol. The
pilots had protested; he remained deaf to their pleas. They
whined that they were not guilty of any violence toward
the prisoners; he replied that they had allowed it to continue or had pretended that it did not exist.

He did not know why his comrades were turning to
him, why they waited for his suggestions or looked to him
for some leadership. Perhaps it was because Fatima and
the other former Linkers who had come there with Sigurd
seemed stunned and dazed by his death. Maybe the others
were expecting him to negotiate some sort of agreement
with his sister. Perhaps it was only because they sensed
that his mind was unaffected by any of the feelings of rage,
grief, triumphant joy, and horror at the cost of their victory, emotions that seemed to sweep over them while leaving bewilderment and shock in their wake. He felt almost
as if he had died during the battle and that his body and
the intelligence enclosed inside his skull had not yet realized he was dead.

He offered more directives on the third day of their
freedom. The refinery and the ceramics plant would cease
operations for now. Shifts of people would watch the bay
and see that no ships were allowed to land there. Others
would monitor external operations at all times and see that
their life support was maintained. They would all take
turns in the greenhouse, in the kitchen, and in guarding
the patrol. During what little free time they had, they
could view any messages from the outside that the guards
had not erased, as it seemed many had been.

No one was to contact anyone outside. This was a
temporary prohibition until they could think of what to
say, but it had brought a chorus of protests. Their families
would want to know they were safe; others would have to
be told their loved ones were gone. Dyami had calmly
pointed out what none of them had considered—that their
families could also be used as hostages against them, once
recent events in Turing became known. Soon, of course,
they would have to contact someone, but he wanted to
learn if he would be pleading a cause that would win wide-
spread sympathy or if the settlers had come to believe any
lies Ishtar might have spread about the people in Turing.

Oddly enough, he had not noticed that any calls or
messages were coming in for the patrol. Jonah had appar-

ently not alerted anyone outside before moving against his
rebellious prisoners, perhaps in an effort to protect his
position; he would have had a reprimand at best for not
being able to keep control. He had not retreated and asked
for help from outside. Jonah had paid with his life for that
decision.

A call or message would come in eventually, however,
and it would have to be answered. If they needed to buy
time, one of their captives might be compelled to respond;
Dyami would have to study any message before making a
decision.

He had viewed a few of the messages waiting for him,
gazing at the images abstractedly on a confiscated pocket
screen in the room where he now lived. He had chosen a
room in the other dormitory next to the one where the
patrol and pilots were being held. Suleiman had suggested
that they share one of the houses, but Dyami had refused.
He could not enter a house without thinking of Maxim Paz;
he could not ponder Suleiman's tentative advances without remembering what his tormentor had done to him.

The messages he viewed evoked no love or longing for
the people who had sent them. There was Risa, murmuring of events in Oberg while hinting darkly of conspiracies
and plots. Here was Sef, shielding his fear and concern
with heartiness and false cheer. Irina told him of her
friends in ibn-Qurrah who were curious or worried about
events in Turing; Patrick asked why Dyami had not responded to his last message. Teo, who had made his com-
promises but still mimicked his old recklessness, related
the latest jokes about the Guide and hinted at his recent
sexual exploits. They were only images, imitating people
he had once known. All of the messages were old; it
seemed that the guards had erased more recent ones.

His world had shrunk still more. Now it was no more
than a node of consciousness embedded in a mind that
could no longer feel.

Dyami looked around at the others who had remained
in the dining hall. Some were watching him; others stared
at the large screen they had placed near one wall. They
had brought the screen there three days earlier, but it had
remained blank since then.

A message had come in two days ago; another had

been sent that morning. The people who had seemed so anxious to contact the outside before were now afraid of what the messages might mean.

"Well?" Dyami said. "It's been ten days since anyone outside's heard anything from Turing. We'd better see what's on their minds. Are you all ready?" Those not in the hall would be watching on other screens at their posts.

"Go ahead," Fatima Snow replied, sounding more forceful than she had in a while. "It'll be better than imagining the worst."

Dyami went to the screen, sat down by the console, and called up the first message. An image of Matthew Innes appeared; several people caught their breath.

"Jonah?" Matthew said. "Haven't heard anything from you." The blond man's face was covered with stubble; his thick blond hair looked uncombed. "I couldn't get through to you before, but I assume you've looked at the public channels and know what's going on. We've got mobs against us, thanks to that speech of Chimene's. Most of the Council and our friends on the patrol are under detention, and because of that cursed Eva, we've got the Habbers to worry about now. Two of their ships are on the way here, and they've apparently sent a message to Mukhtar Kaseko. A source on Island Two tells me that they've threatened to disable Anwara if one of their ships isn't allowed to dock there. We may still have a little time—just a little."

Someone screamed behind Matthew. A man holding a wand leaned over Matthew, whispered to him, then disappeared.

"A few of us managed to hide in one house," Matthew went on, "and then we made it to this school. The teachers were keeping the youngest children here until things quieted down. They're our way out, and you've got one, too, if you're ready to use it. Just listen. We've told them that unless we're allowed to get to the Platform and onto a shuttle for Anwara, the children are finished. It's our only chance. I'll risk the justice of the Mukhtar before I give myself up to those people outside."

The blond man panted for breath. "You've got hostages, too, ones the Habbers might still care about. You'd better get a message out to Anwara about what will happen to them if you aren't allowed to follow me. It isn't much of a chance, but it's all you've got. You can't come back here. The pilots are holding most of the bays. There's still some fighting going on in Lyata and Galileo, but I think we're losing there. I don't know where Boaz is—probably being held. Get a message ready and put it out on a public channel. If you don't get a response in a couple of days, show what you're willing to do. Maybe you can begin with that brother of Chimene's—that'd pay her back. Let me know—" His image faded.

"What's going on?" Fatima asked.

Dyami called up the next message. Matthew reappeared, looking even more haggard than before. "Why haven't I heard anything from you? They're going to let us out. They'll take us to the bay, and we'll keep a few kids with us. Listen, don't think you can wait this out—we've even got patrol volunteers against us. Get your message out, and make an example if you have to—we just did, with a teacher here. I—"

Dyami heard shouts, and then the screen suddenly went blank. People were crowding around him. "We'd better bring in a public channel," Fatima said.

Dyami's fingers danced over the console. "—imagined they could give our world to Earth," a familiar voice was saying. He looked up at the face of his sister. "But we shall never bow to the Mukhtars. Those who betrayed us will be called to account."

He bowed his head, bewildered, as he listened to Chimene's forceful, demanding voice.

Thirty-three

Risa sat with Noella outside the house, holding the other woman as she wept on Risa's shoulder. The crowd had stormed the west dome's school before the patrol volunteers stationed outside could stop them. The attack had succeeded; all of the children had been saved, and their parents had been given the satisfaction of seeing Matthew Innes's mutilated body thrown outside the door. But the assault was too late for Theron, whose death at the hands of those holding the school had precipitated the crowd's vengeance. Risa shuddered again with the shock she had felt when Theron's body was dumped outside, and the fear that had swept over her when the crowd suddenly surged forward.

The Council members, except for Boaz, had been detained without incident; patrol volunteers had managed to subdue most of Boaz's allies. Risa had told herself then that they might be able to win without violence, since those who weren't joining the struggle seemed content to wait it out behind the walls of their homes. But a few of Boaz's allies, here and in other settlements, had decided not to give in so easily. Pilots had died in reckless attacks on the bays; households had been threatened by people trying to hide from the patrols who were searching for them. Passive, frightened people had become avenging mobs. They had not been fighting for justice then, or for freedom from Earth, or against those who were allied with the ones who had wanted to impose Earth's rule. They had only been creatures avenging themselves on those who dared to threaten their neighbors or their children.

She did not know how many had died; she had news of only a few. Josefa Huong was dead, after she and a few others had successfully defended the Guide's house against three of Boaz's loyalists. Gupta Benares was gone, trampled by a crowd as he hastened to the side of an injured woman. Theron, trying to protect his pupils, was gone.

Now the orgy of violence was past, and she did not yet know what the dead had purchased with their lives. She had been in the Administrative Center, monitoring several channels on the screens, when a message came from an Administrator on Island Two. Alim ibn-Sharif, according to this woman, was indisposed, and in his place, she had advised the Mukhtar's delegation on Anwara to meet with the Habbers when their ships arrived. The Mukhtar had apparently agreed, swayed by the knowledge that one of the Habber ships would remain in an orbit near Anwara's, ready to disable the satellite.

The Habbers wanted to help resolve the crisis. Risa did not know if Mukhtar Kaseko would listen or if he would decide to fight after all. She did not know if the Habbers were acting out of sympathy for the Cytherians or only because they might view any victory of Earth's as a defeat for themselves. She did not know how fervent her people's wish for autonomy would remain if Venus became a battleground for Earth and the Habitats.

Even if the Habbers succeeded in interceding for the people of Venus, what then? The Cytherians' freedom would mean little without the aid the Project still needed from outside to help the settlements survive. Would Earth continue to aid Venus in return for nothing except the possibility of closer ties and friendship in the future? Would the Habbers want more influence in return for their help?

She feared what still lay ahead of them—recriminations, blame, demands that many be called to account for their deeds.

Noella had stopped crying; she drew away from Risa and wiped her eyes with a sleeve of her shirt. "My children want me to stay with them for a while," she said. "That might be best."

"You have a home here whenever you want to come back," Risa murmured.

"I know. I'll have to see."

The door opened; Nikolai hurried outside. "Risa, you'd better come in. A call came from Turing—Sef's talking to Dyami."

Risa got to her feet. Nikolai went to Noella as she hurried inside. Dyami's face was on the screen—thin and almost as marked by age as his father's. His flared cheekbones were sharper, and his skin was much too pale. Risa halted near the screen and raised a hand to her mouth.

"Sef told me a little of what's been going on," Dyami said. "We had something of a battle of our own, but I'll tell you about that another time. We're safe here—the patrol, what's left of it, is under restraint. Judging by what the screen's been showing us, we may have acted just in time."

"Dyami." She lifted a hand and touched the image.

"We can get along for now. We don't want any airships coming here until we're sure of who's aboard—we're not taking any risks until matters outside are more settled. There are a great many things we want to discuss with the other settlements. My comrades will demand hearings for the people we're holding."

He sounded so cold. Much of her son was still hidden from her, as it had always been. "Theron's dead," she heard herself say. "The rest of us are all right, but he died at the school when—" Her voice caught in her throat.

"I know. Sef told me. I'm sorry." His voice was still steady. "Sigurd Kristens-Vitos is gone, too."

She bowed her head. "I'm afraid I can't talk anymore," Dyami continued. "I'll send a message, when there's more time."

The image flickered out. He might almost have been talking to strangers. Sef reached for her hand; she clung to him for a moment, then let her tears come.

Yakov summoned Risa to the main dome; it seemed that Chimene wanted to speak to both of them. She met him at the Administrative Center, where Andrew Dinel and a few other volunteers were watching over those being held there. Risa smiled sourly at Andrew as she and Yakov passed, thinking of all the business Ishtar had once brought his way. Andrew was not wearing his sash now.

"Your daughter confirmed one rumor for me," Yakov said as they walked. "I heard that Boaz Huerta had been taken to her house three days ago, during the last of the disturbances. He'd been hiding in the house of a friend, but when the friend saw how things were going, she informed Chimene, who had him brought there by a couple of people on the patrol. She says he's there now."

Risa pressed her lips together. Chimene's speech had been useful, but the Guide, except for her recording, had not been much in evidence lately. Hiding in her house, she supposed, anxious to protect all the things she did not own, waiting for the struggle to pass until she could emerge to claim the love of her people. "I wonder if Chimene knows what some are saying about her," Risa muttered.

"I don't know. We've got people seeing her as a heroine, and others who wonder exactly how much she knew about the deeds of some close to her. I've listened to some fairly disturbing stories about events in Turing just today. I don't know how we're going to maneuver between those who admire her and those who think she allowed a great many evils to happen. We'll have to hold hearings, and some of those defending themselves will be quick to point a finger at her. She may have to face a hearing herself, and then—"

"Don't think of that now," Risa responded. "Worry about that after we know the Mukhtar's intentions."

They were silent until they crossed the bridge near Chimene's house. Lang Eberschild and Yusef Deniz were outside with a few of the patrol. "My daughter wishes to see me," she said to Lang as he moved in front of the door. "I trust I'll be allowed to enter."

"I didn't know," the gray-haired man replied.

"Didn't she tell you?"

"She hasn't allowed anyone to enter since Boaz was brought here. Yusef and I have been staying with friends when we're not on watch."

"And you left her in there with that man?" Risa said.

"It was her request." Lang lowered his eyes. "She is our Guide. Two men are inside, to keep Boaz restrained, and Galina and young Lakshmi are with her. Have some pity for your daughter, Risa. When Boaz was brought to her, she didn't curse at him for his betrayal—she wept and spoke of how much she had loved him."

"How moving," Risa said acidly. Lang pressed the door open; she went inside, followed by Yakov.

Chimene lay on a mat in the center of the common

room. She was naked; her head rested on her hands as she stared toward the wall screen. Two young men were reclining on either side of her. The brown-haired one sat up quickly and covered himself with a dark shroud lying near Chimene's feet; the dark-skinned man adjusted the loose open robe that was his only garment.

Chimene looked up and smiled at Risa. She had thought her daughter might at least be viewing some transmissions or trying to comfort some of her followers with calls, but the screen held only an image of a green planet with small continents and vast oceans—Venus as it would be.

"Greetings, Mother." Chimene sat up and nodded at Yakov. "I'm so pleased you both decided to come here."

Risa narrowed her eyes. "Are these the two who are supposed to be guarding Boaz?"

Chimene rose gracefully to her feet, then smoothed some of her long dark hair over one breast. The two men stared at her, looking hypnotized. "There's no need to guard Boaz now," she said. "He's repented of what he's done. He's returned to the truth, and perfect happiness is his. Ishtar has forgiven him. I have forgiven him, too."

"Where is he?"

Chimene beckoned with one arm. The two young men sank back against the mat as the Guide led Risa and Yakov toward her room.

Galina Kolek sat in one corner, her arms around Lakshmi Tiris; a strange, rasping sound was coming from the child's throat. Boaz lay on the bed; his face was contorted in a grimace, his eyes wide, his teeth clamped together. His body seemed stiff under his clothing, and his chest was still. Risa moved a little closer, then realized the man was dead.

Lakshmi looked up at Chimene and screamed. The girl's face was red and swollen; tears spilled from her eyes. "Be quiet," Galina murmured. "He's with the Spirit now." Lakshmi tore herself away from the woman and threw herself across the bed, clawing at the body.

"I thought you gave her something," Chimene said calmly. "It doesn't seem to be working very well." She turned toward the bed. "Calm yourself, Lakshmi. This isn't the way a possible future Guide should behave."

"Boaz!" the child shrieked. "Boaz!"

"Get that girl out of here," Risa said. Yakov pulled Lakshmi from the bed; she screamed again as he carried her out of the room. Galina gazed up at Risa. She was twirling her reddish hair with one hand; the other rested against her physician's bag. "What have you done?" Risa managed to ask.

"He loved me," Chimene replied. "He repented—I gave him the chance to repent. Galina helped me—she gave him something that paralyzes the central nervous system while keeping him conscious. It works slowly—the limbs and the ability to speak are affected first, and one can stay alive for some time before the heart and the lungs stop working, but she can explain it to you in more detail. It's something physicians use when a patient has to remain immobile temporarily, but of course he had a much larger dose."

Risa sagged against the wall, unable to look away from the body.

"I spoke to him," Chimene continued. "I told him that I couldn't allow our world to fall into Kaseko's hands and that I knew he was conspiring against me. But I also told him I still loved him in spite of that, and I proved it to him by letting him atone for his deeds. The Spirit especially loves those who overcome great obstacles and errors to serve Her. I gave him the chance to confront his death and to be sorry for what he had done. He accepted that at the end—I know he felt great joy at being led back to the right way."

Risa stared at Boaz's twisted, frozen face. He did not look like a man who had found joy in dying.

"I also made him happy when I told him our child would live. Galina helped me there, too. Our daughter's embryo is already housed in one of the artificial wombs in the infirmary's laboratory. You see, I knew that we would preserve our world, regardless of what he had done, in spite of Eva's treachery in fleeing to the Habbers." Chimene moved near the bed and smiled down at the dead man. "I would have wanted to carry my child inside myself, but there will be much to do in serving the Spirit during the days to come, so I will give up that joy to carry out my duty. In nine months, my daughter will be with me, and someday she'll hear of how much love her parents shared at the end of her father's life. It was my last gift to him—telling him of the child he had always wanted with me."

Risa heard voices in the hallway; Yakov entered the room, followed by Lang and a few others. "So much lies ahead," Chimene went on. "I must begin to form a new household, to help me and to prepare for my daughter's birth. Don't you think it's time Dyami returned here? I would be so pleased to have my brother at my side—surely he's ready to accept the Spirit now."

Risa reached for Yakov's arm. Lang gaped at the body on the bed, then went to Galina and pulled her to her feet. Chimene was still smiling when a man went to her clothes rod, pulled off a robe, and draped the garment over her before leading her from the room.

Chimene lay on her bed, her hands folded over her chest. She had felt so weary during the past days, ever since Boaz's body had been taken away. She knew that she should be preparing a speech for the fellowship and consulting with Yakov, who, now that Oberg's Council was under detention, had temporarily taken on a Councilor's duties. But she was often too tired for the effort of a speech, and Yakov had sent her no messages asking for her advice.

A few people she did not know were staying in her house now. They were always at the door, ready to follow her if she wanted to stroll along the creek or sit in the clearing behind the house. They fetched her meals that she barely touched and she supposed that they were also turning away visitors; it was almost as if she were under a kind of detention. Maybe it was just as well. She would have some time to renew her energies before resuming her obligations as the Guide.

She had overheard a few comments among the men and women here now and had found out that Mukhtar Kaseko was holding discussions with a delegation of Habbers on Anwara. She had even heard one of her new housemates assert that things had been better when the Habbers dwelled among them, and the others had not troubled to protest such a remark. Maybe they believed that she herself had sent Eva to the Habitat, that the Guide had decided that it was possible to reach out to such people. She would have to put a stop to that and keep her people from falling into such error.

Her door opened; a woman stepped inside. "You have two visitors," she said, "your mother and your friend, Lena Kerein. May I show them in?"

Chimene forced herself to sit up. "Of course." The door closed. She reached for the blue robe lying on the bed and got up; she was settling herself on a cushion when Risa and Lena entered.

"Greetings," Risa said; Lena smiled a little uncertainly. "I hope you're up to discussing a few matters with me. I was just over at the Administrative Center."

"Please sit down," Chimene said. The two women seated themselves. "I've been feeling the need for rest lately. It's been kind of people not to make too many demands on me, but I'm sure I'll soon feel renewed."

Risa's face was solemn. Her small, stocky body was still youthful; one had to get close to her to see the small lines around her eyes and mouth and the flecks of gray in her dark hair. "It seems the Habbers may actually win some sort of agreement from the Mukhtar. When and if they do, we'll have to hold new elections here for our Councils, since those Councilors and the Island Administrators will also have something to say about any agreement with Earth. The Habbers say only that they are willing to act on our behalf and won't return here unless we request it."

Chimene shrugged. "We won't ask for that," she said.

"I'm not so sure." Risa shifted on her cushion. "Some are saying that, when they were here, they interfered as little as possible and that their presence kept Earth at a distance. But a decision about that can come after the election."

"I don't think I should run, do you?" Chimene asked. "Being on Oberg's Council might interfere with my duties, and I'd be too preoccupied with matters in this settlement to pay proper attention to my brothers and sisters elsewhere. The Councilors could still consult with me when necessary."

Risa glanced at Lena, who lowered her eyes. "We'll have to have some hearings after the election," Risa said. "Many are demanding that, and yet if we hold hearings for everybody who's committed some offense, there'd be no end to it. We'd never heal our wounds, only deepen them. We'd go from Councilors and patrol leaders guilty of extortion and intimidation down to people who turned a blind eye to what was going on around them, and there are many such people. We'd have neighbor against neighbor and divided households and families. So we'll have to limit ourselves to the ones who committed the greatest wrongs and who led others to go along with them—the leaders— and those creatures in Turing, of course."

Chimene nodded. "Perhaps the patrol there over-stepped its bounds, but surely some forgiveness is possible for those who were only trying to bring their charges closer to Ishtar. Perhaps I can visit Turing myself to assure my brother and his friends of my concern and love for them."

Risa let out her breath. "They'd probably kill you if you did." Chimene flinched, shocked at the harshness in her mother's voice. "You don't seem to understand. I guessed you wouldn't, but I hoped you might have some sanity left. Do you think you'll escape a hearing now? Do you think we can hold them for others and not for the Guide herself? Those people were acting for you."

"The fellowship knows that I was deceived and mis-led." Chimene's voice trembled a little; she steadied herself. "They know that it was my love for those closest to me that kept me from seeing what I might otherwise have seen, but surely it's no sin for a Guide to love. I did act against those who tried to betray us when my eyes were opened—surely that counts in my favor."

"Oh, yes." Risa's voice rose a little.

"My sisters and brothers love me. They would never allow me to be dragged before a hearing."

"You're wrong," Risa said violently. "You're always saying that the Guide has nothing to fear from the truth. Your followers will allow a hearing if only because a lot of them persist in believing that you can offer a defense. The rest of us will insist on one because there must be a public accounting."

Lena gripped Risa's shoulder. "Please," the brown-haired woman said.

"I don't know what kind of judgment will be made," her mother continued more calmly, "or what kind of sen-tences we can pass. Some might be detained for many years, and reparations will have to be made, although I don't know how some can be repaid for the pain and suf-fering they endured. The disgrace will be enough punishment for some, and the knowledge that they must live among people who may never forgive their deeds. There's a possibility we may be able to negotiate with Earth to take some of the worst ones off our hands, the ones who don't deserve mercy, the ones who would have made Venus a prison. They can contemplate their deeds in the prisons of that world."

"You can't hold a hearing for me," Chimene whispered. "If the Guide is disgraced—why, it could tear Ishtar apart."

"Maybe your followers will come to their senses when they see just how deluded you are. Maybe they'll demand another Guide in your place, especially when your fellow defendants start pointing their fingers at you and speak of how they were only doing your bidding." Risa sighed. "If you say you knew nothing of many of their deeds, you'll be seen as a fool or a liar. If you admit that you did, you'll have to share their punishment. Either way hardly seems a sound position for you."

Chimene lowered her eyes. Disgrace, detention, possible exile—she could not accept such possibilities. Those who loved her could not allow this to happen. She lifted her head. Risa's face had the same severe expression she had seen years before, when she was a child and her mother a Councilor.

She realized then that she had always known Risa would eventually come to judge her. She had known it ever since that night long ago, when she had watched Risa deliver her judgment against three murderers. The future had cast its shadow into the past, and she had glimpsed a time when her mother would condemn her. What could this mean? What was the Spirit trying to reveal to her now?

"I can't—" She clutched at the neckline of her robe. "What about my child? How can I raise her if I—"

"The embryo can be frozen until your fate is clear. There's no reason it can't be allowed to gestate later. In fact, that's what I'd advise, unless you think you can wring out a little more sympathy for yourself by playing the role of an expectant mother. Of course, any judgment against you could also deprive you of the child's custody, but some devoted follower might be willing to adopt her."

"No." These words were not being said to her.

"Would it really matter?" Risa's lip curled. "You talk about sharing and loving all of Ishtar's children equally."

"If my child was taken from me in a hearing—"

"That's all you care about, isn't it—the disgrace, not the child."

"She's part of your line, too."

"May I be cursed for that," Risa muttered. "She's also the child of the man you killed. Lakshmi Tiris will have a tale to tell at your hearing about recent events in this house, and many will wonder about a woman who could expose a young girl to that. When I was on the Council, I was often struck by how a child's testimony could move people."

Risa slowly got to her feet. "I thought you should know exactly what your situation is so that you have a chance to prepare yourself. I must leave you now. I have a darktime shift later—we must get on with our tasks." She paused. "You might get lucky, Chimene. Maybe a physician will find that some sort of physical problem contributed to your derangement. That would destroy much of your credibility as a Guide but might prevent a harsher judgment."

She left the room; Lena remained behind. "Well," Chimene said softly, "have you come to condemn me, too?"

Lena shook her head. "I'll speak for you at any hearing. I'm sure you would have prevented those cruelties in Turing if you'd known—I have to believe that. Some of those close to you misled you and cut you off from many in the fellowship, and maybe there's a lesson for us in that. You did stand against them finally." Lena took her hand for a moment. "I have to speak for you—you were my friend. You might not be here now if I hadn't helped you out all those times you were sneaking off to see Kichi."

"Should you regret that?" Chimene asked. "Kichi chose me, and she was guided by the Spirit. There has to be a reason for all that's past."

"I don't know." Lena was silent for a moment. "You were so young when you became the Guide, and others were able to lead you away from the truth. Maybe the Spirit's trying to show us that there's more to the right way than we were able to see. Kichi always spoke of being patient, the way we must be to terraform a world, and maybe you lost sight of that, being as young as you were."

"Why, Lena. You used to say you had many doubts about the Spirit."

"I still do. Talk of the Spirit never moved me quite as much as speaking of how we could be brothers and sisters, sharing what we had willingly and working for a common end. We talk of barriers, but how many have we raised ourselves against those around us? I had too many doubts myself to believe that pressuring or forcing people to come to us was right—it seemed to me it might be better to set an example and let them come to us instead of giving them an excuse to hate us. I couldn't even see why we had to fear the Habbers after they'd done so much to help us here. I've tried, but then I think of what they must know and how it could help us make the perfect world we say we want."

"You're steeped in error," Chimene said.

"You can say that? Look at what your mistakes have brought. Maybe it'll be good for the fellowship to see the Guide admitting her mistakes and showing us how easy it is to fall into error while seeing it as truth, how easy it is to destroy in the name of love."

"My hearing would destroy the fellowship. How could my people ever trust me again?"

Lena said, "We claim we value truth. If the truth destroys Ishtar, then it means our truth is a lie or a delusion. But I refuse to believe that it will. We can't let what's essential about Ishtar be destroyed, and the important things aren't the rite, the meetings, or all that business about breaking down barriers—it's our bond as Cytherians, trying to make a world that's better than the one our people came from. If some people come to reject you after a hearing, the rest of us will simply have to go on and try to set a better example that might win them back."

"If I lose the love of my brothers and sisters—" Chimene's shoulders slumped. "There'd be nothing left for me."

They did not speak for a while. Lena's gray eyes glistened; she dabbed at her face with a sleeve of her plain gray shirt. *She isn't seeing me as the Guide at all*, Chimene thought, *only as someone to pity, an old friend who's made mistakes. Many would see her that way after the hearing; that prospect was as painful as having to face the hatred and accusations of others.*

"I should go," Lena said at last. "Maybe I can bring Carlos and the children for a visit soon. That might cheer you a little."

"How is your bondmate?" Chimene asked automatically, not really anxious to know.

"As vigorous as ever. Even now, he says there's no one else he'd rather embrace during the rite." A little of Lena's old, slightly mocking tone had crept back into her voice. "Actually, we're not bondmates now. We never renewed our pledge, even though life is exactly as it was. I guess that's my way of trying to follow the right path, living without things like bonds while having most of the advantages of one." She stood up. "Maybe there should be no fellowship of Ishtar—I mean no organized belief. We could keep what's important without that."

"Farewell, Lena."

"Don't sound so final." She leaned over and patted Chimene on the shoulder. "You shouldn't have let us drift apart these past years. I might have helped you when you needed a friend—a real friend, not somebody who either worshipped you or was trying to deceive you for their own ends." Lena moved toward the door. "How odd it is that I can still care about you after all that's past and all I've heard. Maybe it's because you always needed love so much."

"Farewell," Chimene said as the door closed.

Her mind was very clear now. The solitude of her days had given Chimene time to think. The Spirit was guiding her now, and she saw what was needed to preserve both the fellowship and the love her people bore her.

She stood up, crossed the room, and stared at the clothes hanging from her rod before selecting her favorite red robe, then hung the pendant with the black stone around her neck. As she walked to her desk, she pondered what to say. A short statement would be best, more effective than rambling words or elaborate phrases.

She sat down in front of her small screen, then pressed a button to make her recording. "I speak as your Guide," she said, "as one who has always loved the people of this world. Yet I wandered from the right way. I came to love those who betrayed me and turned from those who truly loved me. I allowed evil to be done in my name and blinded myself to the truth. I have repented of what I have done and atoned for it. The Spirit has forgiven me, but I pray that you will as well."

She paused, then leaned closer to the screen. "I have returned to the true path, but much lies ahead for our world—uncertain times, when the truth may be obscured as we try to heal our wounds. I cannot guide you through these times. That must be done by another, someone who will not be so ready to imagine she hears the voice of the Spirit in the mouths of those who are false. You need, I think, one who shares the doubts and uncertainties of many of you and will understand and sympathize with your own. I have waited for the Spirit to reveal the next Guide to me, and I have seen her. She is a woman named Lena Kerein. She claims her faith is weak, and I have known her to question our most deeply held beliefs, but do not doubt her devotion. She will be a Guide in whom you can see what is best in yourselves."

Chimene took a breath. "Ishtar has always demanded much of its followers and of the Guide. Much as I love you, I am now unable to remain with you. You must build on what I tried to accomplish."

She turned off the screen. Kichi had spoken truly when she said that every obstacle, viewed in a certain way, presented an opportunity. At a time when she might have despaired, Chimene had still been able to see what the Spirit asked of her. Ishtar would be preserved, and Chimene would have the love of her people. She would live on, always beautiful in their memories, leaving behind a child who might one day guide her brothers and sisters herself.

The small dagger Mukhtar Kaseko had given her lay next to her hand. She picked it up and felt only a momentary twinge before she slashed at her throat.

Thirty-four

The meeting was drawing to a close. Benzi glanced at his fellow Habbers. Balin's sharp-boned face betrayed no expression; Robira gazed calmly in Kaseko Wugabe's direction with her wide-set gray eyes. Czeslaw and Aaron were watching Tesia as she paced in front of them.

Kaseko glowered at them all from his chair. The blond Commander's thin lips were tightly pressed together. Others of Kaseko's people were seated behind him on cushions, but the Mukhtar had spoken for all of them, as Tesia had for the Habbers.

Benzi shifted a little on his cushion. The Mukhtar, in spite of his impressive height, bluster, and forceful voice, seemed like a child, a bully who threatened and was quick to take offense. Appearances meant so much to him; during all of their meetings, there had been chairs for him and the Guardian Commander, while the Habber delegation had to sit on cushions, gazing up at him as if they were supplicants. Tesia had tolerated this for the first few meetings; they had not wanted to provoke the man. Then Kaseko had begun to give way, and Tesia had taken to standing to make her points. Now she was pacing, halting every so often to move closer to the Mukhtar and hover over him as she spoke.

Tesia stopped in front of the Mukhtar's chair. "You've been both reasonable and fair," she said. "I think we can begin to prepare a public agreement that will serve both your interests and those of the Cytherians. Some details will have to be worked out later, and the Cytherians may have some questions after they've elected their representatives and the Island Administrators have organized themselves, but I shouldn't imagine they'll affect anything essential."

Kaseko scowled at her; he would probably see any agreement as a humiliation.

"I should think you'd be pleased," Tesia continued. "The agreement will show that your presence here helped to bring about the removal of a group who were oppressing their fellows and endangering the Project's future. Many will think it quite clever of you to have come here and played upon their lust for power by offering to be their ally, knowing that the Cytherians would finally rise up against them when their betrayal was made obvious. And you achieved your ends without the great cost of having to use your own forces to settle the matter. Both Earth and Venus will be grateful to you."

"If anyone believes it," Kaseko muttered.

"We must see that they do," Tesia said.

"Oh, yes, and that they'll also believe that your ships came here at the behest of a few panicky Cytherians who thought I was ready to attack them, and that you threatened me into these meetings only to find that we both had the same end in mind." The Mukhtar pulled his white robe closer around himself. "Some may find that hard to swallow, even if there's some truth in it."

"Not at all. You'll be seen as quite magnanimous, dealing with foolish Habbers who either run away from trouble or overreact by anticipating threats that don't exist. You can make us look quite silly for rushing here when we didn't have to do so."

"You think allowing yourselves to be mocked can erase my own disgrace?"

"There's no shame attached to you," Tesia replied, "in either the proposed agreement or the actual facts. You saw an opportunity to impose your rule on Venus with a minimum of trouble by allying yourself with certain Cytherians who would do much of your work for you. You lost that gamble and realized a battle would gain you nothing and cost much. Now you have an opportunity to win goodwill among Cytherians by portraying yourself as one who had their interests at heart and wanted to free them from oppressors."

"That is hardly going to help me with my colleagues," Kaseko said. "They know I hoped for more."

"But you've accomplished a great deal nevertheless, Mukhtar Kaseko. You've saved the Project, and everything will be as it was."

With, Benzi thought, a few differences. Earth's Project Council would remain on Anwara, but a Liaison chosen by the Island Administrators themselves would be one of its members, with the power to make final decisions. Other members of that Council would be chosen by both Islanders and dome-dwellers. Earth might have some influence, but the Cytherians would make their own decisions.

A Habber ship would remain in orbit around the planet, ostensibly to continue studying the process of terraforming and its effect on the world below—so the agreement would state. That the ship would also be a protector could be left unsaid. Other Habber ships would carry any resources Venus needed, and that Earth had problems providing, to the Cytherian satellite if the Project Council requested them. Earth's Cytherian Institute would continue to provide the Project with specialists, but more of its students would be chosen from among the settlers themselves. The Habbers would also make more of their resources available to Earth, which could only benefit a world that had stripped itself of so many.

Bribes and threats—that was what they had used against the Mukhtar. Threats to disable Anwara and to cut off the flow of small asteroids Habbers hurled toward Earth's Lunar plants, where they could be more easily mined; bribes of more aid in any agreement. They had won some freedom for the Cytherians, Benzi thought, but they had not won much for themselves. Habber vessels would once again ferry a few hopeful settlers to Venus, but the Habbers themselves would be only observers in an orbiting ship or pilots bringing settlers and supplies, with no other role on this world unless the Cytherians themselves asked them to return.

Perhaps they would not. Maybe they would prefer being free of people who seemed so alien and who made them question the fears, emotions, and parts of their nature they preferred to accept and rationalize. They had the right to choose; Habbers had to allow them that choice, but for his people and the Cytherians, it might be a defeat.

Habbers would lose that contact with a young, striving culture and become more insular. Cytherians, dreaming of their future world while trapped behind their domes, might turn on one another again; the cauldron could boil over once more.

Small wonder Earthfolk and Cytherians were bemused by Habbers. They might have been even more puzzled if they glimpsed his people's hope—that Cytherians and Habbers might one day move freely between the two societies, bridging the mental distance that lay between them. Cytherians needed to look beyond their world even during the struggle of creating it; Benzi's people needed to remember what they had once been.

"I've never understood what you people wanted," Kaseko said then.

"I doubt you would even if I explained it to you," Tesia replied.

"Power, of course—but you'd also like them to see you as friends—so noble, so caring. You can't even admit openly to what you really want—you have to pretend you have some higher aim."

"You would see things that way." Tesia pulled at the collar of her pale yellow tunic. The strain of the days of discussions was beginning to show; her face was drawn and white. "I suppose you're wondering what will be waiting for you when you get back to Earth. I wouldn't worry about that too much. You have Guardians to enforce your will if necessary."

"Well, you've ensured your precious Cytherians some freedom." The Mukhtar showed his teeth. "See if they use it to invite you back."

"That must be up to them—which reminds me." Tesia moved closer to his chair; Kaseko glared up at her. "There is the matter of a plague that afflicted the Cytherians some fifteen years ago. I think you should have a statement in your part of the agreement that makes it clear how that came about."

The Commander sucked in her breath; Kaseko leaned forward. "We had nothing to do with that."

"But you did." Tesia, Benzi knew, had saved this for last. "A fever broke out near one of your camps. The Guardians there thought they had it under control, but they were careless, and a few people carrying the virus arrived on Venus. The Mukhtars were terribly concerned when they heard of the outbreak there, but there was little they could do and they quickly saw how the illness might be used to their advantage. They ordered that all evidence of the outbreak on Earth be concealed so that our people, whose vessel had brought the infection there, would be blamed for the plague, in the absence of any other suspects."

"That," Kaseko said, "is a ridiculous story."

"I think not, and I'm sure you can buttress it with some evidence. I certainly find it much easier to believe than the suspicions some of our people have—that you deliberately infected a few emigrants in the hope of rousing the hatred of Venus against us. Surely we have to put that story to rest, especially on Venus, or it's going to be much more difficult for you to be allowed any role here at all." Tesia paused. "I would not like to see your reputation sullied by baseless rumors."

Kaseko did not reply.

"Or you can mull this over, and we can argue about it in future discussions while you worry about how many of your colleagues on Earth may be growing impatient with you. I'm sure you'd like to get back as soon as possible."

"I could detain all of you," he said. "I could make you very sorry you came here."

"You'd lose everything then." Tesia smiled. "That satisfaction would cost you much, Mukhtar Kaseko. You'd be throwing away such a lovely agreement, and you'd have only a disabled satellite and a lot of discontented colleagues on Earth in return. Why, I wouldn't be surprised if you came to us then and begged us for refuge."

"Very well." The Mukhtar sank back against his chair. "We'll see if anyone believes it."

"I'll be looking forward to seeing your draft and the images you propose to transmit with it. Your statement will be most inspiring, I'm sure. In the meantime, I think it's your place to announce that we have come to an agreement, so that the Cytherians can proceed with arranging for their elections and getting back to their normal duties. Many will bless you for it."

Kaseko waved a hand wearily. "As God wills."

The other Habbers rose. Czeslaw offered an arm to Tesia as she walked toward him; Benzi and his companions followed them from the room. He had fled this world, only to return as part of an effort to save it; he wondered what Iris and Chen would have thought of that.

Dyami had not gone to meet the arriving airships. It was his turn, and Suleiman's, to guard their prisoners; he felt a sense of relief. At least he would be spared seeing all those greetings, all those relatives and friends of people in Turing rushing to meet their loved ones, sobbing their tears and telling them that everything would now be put right. Some supplies would be arriving in the ships, components and promising new strains for the greenhouse, tents to house the visitors during their stay. When he was relieved of his post, he would go to the bay and help bring in some of the cargo; it would be an excuse to avoid the sight of all those people pretending that everything could be as it once was.

Sef had sent a message saying he would be coming. Dyami had sent one back, saying that wasn't necessary and that his father's household probably needed Sef there. He hoped Sef had taken the hint.

"My sister may be looking for me," Suleiman said. He was sitting on the other side of the dormitory door, his wand in his hands. The dark-haired young man didn't seem terribly anxious to see her, but Suleiman, unlike Dyami, was capable of mimicking emotions he no longer felt when necessary.

Dyami's friend, along with most of the others, had been viewing messages and keeping himself informed during his free moments; Dyami had been unable to work up much curiosity. Even the news of Chimene's suicide left him unmoved; it was only another story from an unreal outside world.

"It'll be a relief when the hearings are over," Suleiman continued.

"You're looking forward to that?" Dyami asked.

"Talking about what's been done to us? Having to live through all of that again?" Suleiman's thin lips twisted into a bitter smile. "I just want it to be finished and for that damned patrol to get what they deserve. It ought to be death, but the new Councils, when they're elected, would never allow that. Anyway, the story is that Earth may agree to take them off our hands, and when they hear what they've done, maybe they'll decide it isn't worth the bother of keeping them locked up and will dispose of the wretches themselves."

Hearings, Dyami thought, might solve little. Every one of those guards probably had a relative or friend who might plead for mercy. Some would argue that the guards were sorry for what had happened. Tasida had been collecting medical evidence with her scanner—the signs of beatings and torture and other injuries—but the former guards might try to cast doubt on the stories of their accusers.

He thought of what lay ahead—the wounds of his body displayed on a screen for all to see, the story he would have to tell in order to justify his own violent acts. He and his friends would be as much the subject of a hearing as their tormentors.

A cart rolled toward them, its treads flattening the grass. The vehicle halted at the edge of the hollow as people began to climb out; Dyami saw the tall frame and broad shoulders of his father. So Sef had decided to come here after all. He was walking toward Dyami now, with a stocky young woman at his side.

Dyami got to his feet. Sef's pace quickened; he held out his arms. Dyami shrank back a little, then endured his father's embrace passively.

"Son." Sef stepped back and released him. "This is Devora Poulis—my son, Dyami Liang-Talis. Devora's one of the people who volunteered to come here and help you out."

Suleiman had mentioned that earlier; some people had offered to come to Turing to take over the duty of guarding their prisoners until their hearings took place. The woman held out a hand; he watched her warily.

"Your wand," she said at last. "I'll need it. You'd probably like to have some time with your father." Dyami gripped the weapon more tightly, then reluctantly surrendered it to her.

"My friend, Suleiman Khan," he muttered as the other man stood up. A woman was suddenly rushing toward Suleiman; she threw herself at him and covered his face with kisses. Dyami suddenly wanted to get away from the people now fanning out around the hollow as they called out names.

"Come with me," he said to Sef. He led him to the other dormitory. "You can leave your pack in my room." They went down the hallway and stopped at Dyami's door; he pressed it open. "Hope you don't mind staying here. It's small, but there should be enough space for both of us." He took the pack from Sef and set it on the floor.

"Risa wanted to come, too," Sef said, "but there's a lot she has to do now. Yakov finally managed to talk her into running for a place on the new Oberg Council, and there's her work and our household's. House seems kind of empty now—just Kolya, Paul, and Grazie—but when you're home—"

"I don't know if I'll be coming home."

Sef ran a hand through his chestnut hair. "Well, the election will be over in a couple of weeks, and everyone wants to settle the hearings after that—no sense in dragging things out. You'd be able to come home any time you like."

Dyami leaned against the wall. "I'm not sure I want to leave Turing. There's work for us here in the plant and refinery. We can start building our own homes. A lot of us are thinking of staying on."

"After what's happened to you here?" Sef shook his head. "I'd think this would be the last place you'd want to stay."

He could not explain; Sef would not understand.

"Teo sends his greetings," Sef went on. "Some of your old friends and schoolmates are anxious to welcome you back. They say they haven't had any replies to the messages they've sent."

"I wonder how many of them would have lifted a finger," Dyami said, "if they hadn't learned about Boaz's and Alim's intentions. They weren't thinking of us, just of what might happen to them if Boaz won out. If that Mukhtar had granted Chimene what she wanted in the first place, they would have been so overjoyed that they wouldn't have troubled themselves over our fate."

"Dyami—"

"Let's walk. Maybe you'd like to see more of Turing." Dyami went into the hall, where others were leading visitors to their rooms. He pushed past the people without speaking; Sef caught up with him when he was outside.

They walked toward the creek in silence. The cheerful but strained voices of visitors and the more muted, hesitant ones of his friends faded until he could hear only the trickle of the creek. The land along the bank was still marked by the wide, flat lines of the crawlers' tracks.

Dyami glanced at his father's plain brown shirt and pants. "I see you're no longer wearing your sash," he said.

"There's no need. You know why I joined in the first place. I admitted that to Lena, but I think she was aware of it anyway. She says she has no wish to hold any members who joined reluctantly or who want to leave Ishtar, although it's her hope some will find their way back." Sef cleared his throat. "You'd be surprised at how many are now saying they only joined to protect their households."

Dyami did not reply.

"Lena's not happy about being the Guide, but she knew refusing it would only cause a lot of dissension. Carlos told me that she said it must have been Chimene's idea of a joke, but it may be one of your sister's good deeds after all. Lena's a reasonable and kind woman—she doesn't want any power, and she's made it clear that the right way demands tolerance while pursuing Ishtar's goals. She's even set a sort of precedent by asking the fellowship to acclaim her as Guide. She's preparing them for the idea that when her time is past, it should be they who select the next Guide, and she has no intention of moving to your sister's house. She'll continue, as much as possible, to lead the life she's always led. She'll encourage those who want to live outside the barriers that confine others and honor them for that, but she thinks those with more flaws are the ones who need her more. She isn't likely to surround herself with an inner circle."

"So Ishtar will go on," Dyami muttered, wondering why it had to exist at all.

"In a somewhat different fashion. I know how you feel, Dyami, but many in the group did turn against much of what was being done in the Guide's name. Trying to destroy Ishtar now wouldn't solve anything. We have to work together now, not keep fighting each other."

They had to be reasonable, he thought; they had to forgive, dispense justice at their hearings, and then go on to heal their wounds. They had to put this behind them, and if he could not, they would all be quick to chide him for refusing to let go of the past, for being hard and unrelenting, for not being able to become what he once had been.

"Your mother could use a message from you," Sef said. "In a way, she blames herself for what happened to your sister. She and Lena were the last people to see Chimene, and Risa was fairly severe with her. Now she wonders if she might have saved Chimene's life if she had been kinder."

"She shouldn't reproach herself for that," Dyami said tonelessly. "Chimene escaped a hearing, and the rest of us are free of her."

Sef made a sound that might have been a moan. Maybe his father was still remembering the times he had lain in Chimene's arms. They were near the small bridge that led to the dormitory where he had been imprisoned; Dyami gestured at the building on the other side.

"That's where they held us," he said. "We're still talking about what to do with it. Some want to tear it down, while others want to leave it as a kind of reminder. We could put in some screens, with images representing some of the things that were done to us here. Perhaps I could contribute some sculptures I might cast, now that I've had an opportunity to observe what certain kinds of treatment do to the human spirit and body. It should prove an interesting subject."

Sef grimaced, sat down, and covered his eyes with one hand. Dyami said, "I meant it as a joke."

"Did you?"

He seated himself next to his father, careful not to get too close. "Do you think the Habbers will be sending people here?" Dyami asked.

"They will if we request it. I have a feeling that we probably will."

"I suppose they've become bored without our foibles to amuse them. They must have been relieved to have an excuse to send ships to Anwara. I trust they won't be unduly upset about what happened after they abandoned us."

"Dyami." Sef gripped his arm; Dyami longed to shake off his hand. "Risa's lost two daughters. You're the only child she has left, you and—" He paused. "I'd better tell you before someone else does. Most people don't know this, but there are rumors, and Risa told me about it herself. There's an embryo in one of the artificial wombs,

Chimene's daughter. If nothing is done, the child will be born in less than eight months."

Dyami tensed.

"Risa's the closest relative," Sef continued. "She has to make a decision. She could let someone else adopt the child, but it is part of her line. She doesn't know what to do, and she's also concerned about your feelings in the matter. She can't bear the thought of giving up her rights and having her grandchild grow up knowing that Risa didn't take her, that her own grandmother decided to have nothing to do with her, but at the same time she doesn't want to lose you over this. She's guessed how you might feel about having the child with us."

"What would she tell it?" Dyami said. "I can't imagine why she'd want it."

"To make up for what's past. She feels she's failed Chimene, that if things had gone differently—" Sef swallowed. "So that we can put what's past behind us instead of blaming an innocent child for the deeds of her parents."

"Her parents?" But he did not have to ask who the father was; Chimene had designated him when she decided to store her ova. A child of Boaz and Chimene might live. His gorge rose. He would never be free of them.

"Risa's going to have the embryo frozen for now," Sef said, "to have more time to decide. She should know what you think. She can't make this decision if you—"

Dyami pushed his father's hand away, then gazed into Sef's brown eyes. "Why, if it's frozen," he said softly, "perhaps her dilemma will resolve itself. It's hardly unknown for something to go wrong in cryonic storage—the technique does carry a very small risk. The longer she waits, the more likely that is, and then the problem's solved. Quite clever of Risa, if you ask me. The embryo could suffer some damage from prolonged freezing, and that would be that. Or an emergency might come up that requires more of the lab's cryonic facilities—they're hardly unlimited. The embryologists might have to dispose of it and the decision would be out of Risa's hands—she could feel that she tried without blaming herself. One can always hope."

Sef was looking at him strangely. His mouth worked; his eyes glistened a little. He said, "We've lost you, haven't we?"

Dyami got up. "I should head for the greenhouse. Now that I'm free of other duties, I should make myself useful elsewhere."

Sef seemed about to say more. Dyami walked away, leaving his father seated on the bank.

Thirty-five

Benzi lifted his eyes to the airship screen. Oberg's domes were visible below; patches of green under the domes surrounded disks of hazy yellow light. Two pilots seated in the front of the cabin leaned over their control panels as the airship dropped through the still, dark clouds.

I might have been one of those pilots, Benzi thought. He contemplated the life he had escaped. He might have followed his father to the surface, and left Oberg later only to ferry settlers and supplies. He would have built a home or shared one with Chen; he might have had a bondmate and children. He would have played a role in the struggles of these people, and wondered what he would have learned about himself. Would he have stood against injustice, or would he have closed his eyes to events for as long as possible? Would he have come to love this world, or grown bitter about its failures?

He had no way of knowing, and if he had stayed, by now he would have been an old man nearing the end of a century of life. He would be clutching at his small joys and sorrowing over his mistakes during the two or three decades he might have remaining to him.

A Habber could believe that there was time to make up for mistakes, to live past regrets, to experience one's feelings fully before letting them drop away. Cytherians and Earthfolk did not have that luxury; their accomplishments and mistakes affected the lives of people who might have no chance to reap their rewards or right their wrongs during their own lifetimes. Cytherians could not escape the consequences of their deeds by living on until even

614

their memories of them had faded. They could not store their experiences in their cyberminds and pretend that these events were part of someone else's life.

In the end, Habbers could not escape the results of their actions, either, although it was much easier to believe that they could. Such a belief was a trap. That was why Habbers had to reach out to these people, before their trap closed around them and left them unable to make any effort at all. Otherwise, forgetting would be too great a temptation. His people would no longer be the companions of their cyberminds, and might become only their pets.

Benzi had not forgotten the promise he had made to Chen—that he would come here and see what his father had helped to build. He had not thought he would ever really keep the promise, yet he was here.

Mukhtar Kaseko, after playing his role of crafty benefactor, had departed with his people for Earth. Benzi had intended to stay on Anwara only until the hearings were over. They had gone on for nearly two months. The embittered statements of accusers and the unrepentant, self-justifying defenses of many of the accused had sickened him, reminding him of all the things he wanted to escape.

The worst were the hearings held in Turing. The people there had carefully assembled their evidence, knowing that if they did not prove their case, they themselves might be held to account for the violence they had unleashed against their captors. Scanner records of damaged bodies showing the effects of abuse had been displayed. Some former prisoners spoke in toneless voices of their beatings, rapes, deprivations, and torture, while others could barely be understood through their weeping. A man in charge of the Turing patrol had foolishly kept recordings indicating that his people had been given free rein with their prisoners. The turning point in those hearings had come when a few on the patrol, hoping for mercy for themselves, verified many of the worst stories.

Earth had finally agreed to take the accused in Turing and some of the worst offenders in other settlements, promising confinement and sessions with Counselors. Benzi had his doubts about that proposed punishment, and suspected that some of the condemned would disappear once they reached the home world. A few might have been Earth's agents all along, and now the Mukhtars and Guardians had reason to silence them for good.

All the negotiating, the subterfuge, and the stories he had heard left Benzi longing to return to his Habitat. Chen was gone; he did not have to keep an old promise to him. Benzi remained unmoved even after a vast majority of the Cytherians had voted in favor of asking the Habbers to return to Venus. It had taken a brief message from Risa Liangharad, the sister he had never seen, to make him decide to stay, at least for a while.

Risa did not mention the referendum. She wanted Benzi to see his father's house and to hear about Chen's life there from those who had loved him. She wanted to share her memories, which were all she had left of some of the people she had loved.

Was it only curiosity and an old promise that had brought him here? Or was it that Risa had reminded him of bonds he thought he had shed? Somehow, he felt that if he left now, he would be repudiating the efforts of Habbers to reach out to these people. By denying what was left of his own family, he might be rejecting the greater human family of which they were a part, and with whom his people might still find a common destiny.

Benzi and the five Habbers traveling with him to Oberg were greeted outside the bay by Risa and a man named Dalal Singh. Both were members of Oberg's Council, there to welcome them officially. Risa kept her eyes averted from Benzi, apparently content to take refuge in formalities during their first meeting; he could not tell what she was thinking.

When the short speech of welcome was over, the Habbers were led away from the bay toward a cluster of buildings overlooking the small grassy space. A few curious onlookers trailed them, but they did not seem anxious to engage them in conversation. Benzi felt uneasy under their gaze. Some might be people who still had their doubts about them, who had only reluctanly voted to allow them back.

They stopped in front of a small round building. "Habbers used to live here," Dalal Singh said. "We've done what we can to make it ready for you, but if there's anything else you require, please let the Council know. You'll have to excuse me now—we're still trying to resume normal operations, and I have other duties."

"Thank you," Czeslaw replied. "We'll look forward to meeting with the Council soon to discuss how we can best be of service."

Dalal bowed a little, then hurried away. Risa remained behind; she was gazing directly at Benzi now. She had Chen's dark hair and pale brown skin, but her small rounded body was Iris's, as was her broad-boned face. Her hair was beginning to gray a little, and lines were etched around her large, almond-shaped brown eyes.

"May I speak to you?" she said a bit stiffly.

"Of course. Would you like to come inside? We could talk while I store my belongings."

"Maybe you'd rather walk. I can show you a little of Oberg." She seemed uncertain about entering the residence.

"Very well. I'd enjoy that." He handed his bag to Czeslaw and followed her away from the building; she was leading him back toward the main road. He grew conscious of the dome overhead, the gardened landscape that resembled and yet was so different from the hollow at the Habitat's center. Here, he could not look up and see the land curving above, or imagine the openness and vastness of the space beyond the Habitat's corridors.

"I hope," Benzi said, "it isn't awkward for you, having a brother who's a Habber."

"A brother. From the way you look, you might be my son."

"We live long lives on the Habs."

She said, "Some say you never die."

"That isn't entirely true. We can lose ourselves eventually." He did not explain. She might not see giving up many of one's memories, or persisting as a pattern of thought inside cyberminds, as death. "We also have our accidents. Like you, we have to depend on an environment we've built and must maintain."

"I didn't understand what you did for a long time," Risa said. "I might as well admit that. Habbers were only people who brought grief to my father by luring his son away. But I think I can understand you a bit more now. After what's happened here, you must feel that you made the right choice."

"But I've chosen to come here now."

"I wonder how much good it'll do," she said. "We never change, do we, people like us. We came here to make something better and look what we've done. We just go on making the same mistakes—Earth's mistakes, the ones we thought we'd never repeat."

"You shouldn't look at it that way," Benzi said. "There was a time when a man such as Kaseko Wugabe would have been incapable of resolving a conflict peacefully. There are restraints on such people now, one of them being their knowledge of their history and what fighting brought to Earth in the past. Earth can be made to back away from such battles now, to see how much might be lost otherwise. Maybe your people have also learned from what's happened here."

"Until we slip again."

"You might," he said, "but probably not as far."

"Not that it matters to you. It's all so theoretical to your people. You can always run away from it."

"No, we can't," he answered. "That's what we've learned."

They crossed the main road and entered a grove of trees. He saw a low wall and the darkness of the dome above it. "We've been told," she said, "that most of the Islanders who fled to the Hab before will return to carry on their work here."

"Yes."

"Do you know if Malik Haddad will be among them?"

He glanced at his sister. "No, he won't."

"So he's happy among your people then."

Happy? Benzi frowned a little. Adrift was a more accurate description. His friend Te-yu called Malik a lost soul, haunted by the past, uncertain of his future. "He's not unhappy," he said. "I think he may choose to visit Venus someday but maybe not until some of his memories have faded."

"Perhaps you remember the message you sent to Chen from Anwara," she said, "before Malik arrived here. Chen put in a request for his services as a teacher in our dome. That's how he came to live with us. You must find it odd that one message from you could have altered our lives so much."

He felt a twinge; maybe that was another reason he had come back.

They were near a clearing; a pillar lay ahead. Benzi was close to it before he recognized his mother's face on the monument. His eyes fell to the inscription that spoke of Iris's sacrifice.

"I thought you might want to see Iris's memorial," Risa murmured. "Chen's image is over there among the memorial pillars." Benzi stared at his feet as he recoiled inwardly from these monuments to death. "Maybe I was mistaken," she continued. "To Habbers, I suppose any death seems too soon."

He took her arm. "I'd like to hear about my father's life here, and your own. You said in your message that I might come to your house. Maybe I could stay there with you while I'm here, in the place where Chen lived. I won't be in Oberg very long, as I told you in my reply to your message. It seems I'll be more useful on Island Two."

She was silent for a while. Perhaps he was pushing too much, assuming she would welcome him into her household for a time. She turned toward him and smiled a little. "So you'd like to hear about the life you might have shared," she said. "Maybe you should stay in my house. It might set a useful example, having a Habber as a guest. Maybe if your people and mine shared more of our lives, we wouldn't be so quick to distrust you again."

"Perhaps."

"And what will you be doing on Island Two?"

"I'm not entirely sure yet," he said. It was too soon to talk of his own hopes, his dream that his people might eventually look out to the stars and voyage beyond this solar system. If they did, they might need companions on their journey, people forged by this world who were unafraid of that challenge and would welcome it, men and women who would teach their fellow Cytherians to look beyond the clouds and the darkness that hid the heavens from them. "I've spent my recent years learning more physics, and I was once a pilot here. I'm sure some use will be found for me."

"Well." She released his arm. "I never thought I'd actually see you, Benzi. I assumed you'd always be just a name and a few stories Chen told me about you. I'm still not sure how I feel."

"Neither am I."

"I wish you could have seen a sister who wasn't just an aging woman burdened by the sorts of sorrows you probably can't understand." Risa waved at the other memorials. "There's an image of my daughter Eleta over there—she died of the fever when she was only a child, the fever some blamed on your people. My other daughter took her own life, and though some are calling it a noble act, it doesn't erase my pain." She lowered her voice. "And my only surviving child has become a man I hardly know."

Benzi had seen her son Dyami on the screen, during the hearings, a man whose eyes seemed as cold and empty as those Dyami had accused. He had not looked like the sensitive young man Benzi's friend Balin remembered.

"And now I have to decide—" Risa shoved her hands into the pockets of her gray tunic. "But that isn't your concern. You'll have to excuse me, Benzi—I hardly find my brother before I have to load my troubles onto his back. I'll come by your residence before last light, and we can go to my house then. I promise you that you'll find a little more cheer among my housemates. Paul Bettinas can tell you about his mother—she was a Plainswoman, like Iris, and she and Chen had many happy years together." Her voice broke off; she left him and went toward the wall.

He hesitated. He could retreat from Risa's worries, go back to the Habber quarters, compose himself before he went to her house. He could open his Link, commune with his friends and the minds of his Habitat; this woman's life did not require his involvement. He could simply listen to her stories and tell her a little about his own life. She was little more than a stranger with whom he shared a genetic heritage.

Benzi walked toward her; she turned and leaned against the wall. "Maybe you should tell me what you have to decide," he said. "At least I can listen, and I may be able to help."

"I doubt that you can help me with this." She sighed. "Chimene was planning to have a child before—" Risa folded her arms and looked away for a moment. "The embryo's frozen at the moment. It's Chimene's daughter —and Boaz Huerta's. As the nearest relative, I can decide to raise her myself or I can give her up to someone else. If I do nothing, the situation will eventually take care of itself, one way or the other."

"I see." He understood the dilemma. The technology to maintain the embryo was available; as long as it remained viable and healthy, it had to be maintained. Ending its existence was not really a choice as long as the embryo's existence did not conflict with the rights of others. Even so, if Risa waited to make a decision, an emergency might require the use of the cryonic chamber now holding that embryo, and if no ectogenetic chamber was available for it then, the matter would be settled by disposing of the potential child. It was not the kind of problem Habbers, with their greater resources, had to face.

"I don't know what to do," Risa said. "That child is part of my line—I couldn't bear to give her up to someone else and have her learn that her own people didn't want her. But my son has made it fairly clear to my bondmate that he wants nothing to do with her. Dyami would like to see every trace of Chimene vanish from this world, and after what he's endured, I can't really blame him. I think I'd lose him altogether if I brought the child into my house."

"He'd blame the child for what its parents did?"

"Blame her? I don't know, but I doubt he'd want anything to do with her or with me. The girl would have to live with that, too."

"I'm sorry, Risa. I don't know what to tell you."

"Maybe you think I'm feeling guilt, or that raising her would be a means of making up for any way I might have failed Chimene." Risa raised her head. "But it isn't just that. We can't keep dwelling on the past and nurturing all our hatreds, or we won't have learned anything from what's happened. I feel that if I refuse to care for that potential child, it's like saying there's no hope for us, that being reconciled is impossible. Does that make any sense to you at all?"

"Yes, it does." A possible solution to her problem was beginning to form in his mind, but he did not know if he was ready to suggest it. Benzi was beginning to regret his decision to talk to her. These concerns were not his; perhaps coming here had been a mistake. He had thought in an abstract way about helping the Cytherians; he had not intended to be drawn into his sister's life.

Risa wiped at her eyes. "Maybe you should go back to your quarters now. I'll come by later—that is, if you still want to stay with me."

He found himself reaching for her arm. "We'll walk back together," he said.

Dyami knew, before he left the refinery, that Balin would be waiting for him. An airship had arrived a few hours earlier, bringing several Habbers who hoped to see their old friends. Maybe Balin would be visiting with someone else; Dyami might be able to make it back to his tent unobserved. Balin would find him eventually, but by then Dyami might have thought of what to say.

Yet when he came outside, Balin was standing beside the wide main road; a slender woman with long reddish hair was at his side. Balin turned, then hurried toward him. Dyami tensed as the other man clutched at his arms; for a moment, he feared he might be embraced.

Balin released him, but he was still searching Dyami's face with concerned, unhappy eyes. His curly dark hair was a little longer, but otherwise he seemed unchanged. Perhaps he was another one who thought they could all go on as they had before.

Balin drew the woman toward him. "My friend, Tesia," he murmured. "This is Dyami Liang-Talis."

"Yes, I know," she said; perhaps she had seen him on a screen during the hearings. He recognized her name now; she was the Habber Sigurd had loved.

"I'm sorry," he said at last. "I wish Sigurd were here to greet you." He did not know what else to say.

"Perhaps you—" She lowered her head. "I'd like to see where he spent his last days. I loved him very much. I begged him to come with us when we left, but he refused —he said he couldn't abandon his world."

"Come with me." He led them along the road toward the tunnel, without speaking. A cart rolled past them, laden with cargo, but Balin and Tesia seemed content to walk the distance.

"Did he say anything about me at all?" the woman asked as they entered the tunnel. "Did he mention anything to you?"

He had never heard Sigurd speak of her here; the Administrator had not talked of the past at all. He was about to say so, then changed his mind. "Yes, he did," Dyami replied. "He didn't say much, only that he loved you and that your years together were happy. He didn't regret that." Sigurd might have said such words; he had probably thought of her often.

They came to the rise outside the tunnel and ascended. In the hollow where the dining hall still stood, the foundations for a few houses had already been finished. The two dormitories near them would be torn down and some of their materials used for other dwellings, when more houses had been built; the houses the patrol had used had already been taken apart. A few of Dyami's friends caught sight of Balin and waved.

Dyami turned toward the grassy mound that lay to his right. "We buried Sigurd there," he said, "along with other friends who fell. We'll be designing some sort of memorial for them as soon—"

Tesia's hazel eyes widened. "I don't want to see his grave," she whispered. "Take me to the place where he died, where he had his last moments of life."

Balin reached for Tesia's arm. "Are you sure—"

"I want to see it."

"I'll take you," Dyami said. "I'm going in that direction anyway."

They walked toward the creek, past a few partly built houses and several tents. The people there raised their hands in greeting, then averted their eyes from Tesia's pale, griefstricken face.

"Sigurd inspired us," Dyami went on. "It wasn't discussed that much at the hearing, but others here will tell you it's true. When he was sent here—he and the other Linkers—we were almost ready to give up any hope. He convinced us that we had to find a way—that there was a way—of fighting for ourselves, that we couldn't wait for help from outside. We'd been hoping for that, you see, thinking that if we just did our best to survive, things would change. If we'd waited for that, things might have been a lot worse for us. Sigurd was a great man in his way."

He guided the two Habbers across the bridge, then climbed toward the building above. "This is where we were confined." He moved toward the spot on the slope where Sigurd had fallen. "Sigurd was here, as nearly as I can recall. He couldn't have felt much when he was hit. If he'd been stronger when he got here, he could have survived, but the beatings and lack of food made him weaker, and the patrol was being more abusive toward the end. They tended to single out some of us for special treatment." His voice had risen a bit. "But you must have heard all about that during the hearings."

Tesia turned toward the creek. "We had a lot of time together," she said. "I'd tell him he was foolish to love me when he might have had a bondmate. He'd say that he felt he already had a bond with me, even though we couldn't have made a pledge. He wanted so much for your people and ours to—" She closed her eyes for a moment. "Leave me. I must have some time by myself."

"Tesia—" Balin began to say.

"Please."

Balin beckoned to Dyami. They began to move along the bank; the two were several paces away before Dyami looked back. Tesia was sitting now, her legs folded; her hands trembled as she lifted them to her face.

"She needs to be alone now," Balin said as they walked on. "This kind of death is hard for us to accept, even to comprehend, and it's difficult for us to grieve in the company of others. She needs to experience it fully, and when it's past, she'll commune with others through her Link and bring herself into balance. The pain will fade, but the memory will be kept."

"How convenient for you," Dyami muttered, "to be able to handle it that way, wallowing in it and then storing it all away."

"Dyami—"

"Why don't you go back to the dining hall? Your old acquaintances here will be delighted to see you again, and they'll find you a place to stay."

Balin did not reply. Dyami quickened his pace, but the other man remained at his side.

A few more houses were being constructed near the creek, beyond the large greenhouse on the eastern bank. Some of those who had decided to stay in Turing preferred sites where there would be few neighbors—for a while anyway. Stacks of materials lay next to raised walls and tents; the people sitting outside the tents called out greetings but did not invite Dyami and Balin to stay.

They want us to enjoy our reunion, Dyami thought; they probably think we want to be alone. Or perhaps they were only used to the fact that he rarely sought their company now.

His own tent stood on a small grassy hill that overlooked the spot where the creek flowed into the lake. The dome light was just beginning to fade when he caught sight of the hill. Walls, with spaces for windows, were up in what would be the back of the house; the space where his common room would be was only a flat open floor. Large glassy windows, tools, a crate of components, and other supplies were stacked on the slope below.

"The bathroom's finished," Dyami said. Balin had not said a word during their walk; he glanced at Dyami and lifted his brows. "That makes things convenient. No roof yet, but the bathroom can be used. It may take me some time to finish the work, since I prefer to do it alone, but I don't lack for supplies. Everyone outside seems anxious to assure us that we'll get whatever we need if they can provide it."

Balin peered up at the wall as they climbed the hill. "It doesn't look like the usual design," he said.

"It isn't. Some of us are planning a few variations. I'm going to have the kitchen, the bathroom, and any other space in the back, and the common room will have windows on three sides. I want a large common room, with windows and no walls. The outside surface will reflect light so no one will be able to see inside. We can manufacture the windows in the ceramics plant now—they're light and they're sturdy. Allen Sirit did a lot of the work—he can tell you more about them."

"From the size of the space," Balin said, "it looks as though that room will be most of the house."

"I plan to spend much of my time in it, and I find I dislike any feeling of confinement lately. This site means a longer walk to the refinery, but I wanted to build near the lake."

Balin gazed at him speculatively. "And away from other people."

"Yes," Dyami replied.

"By yourself?"

"I feel no need for housemates. If it's necessary, I can always allow a new arrival to stay with me temporarily."

He thrust his hands into his pockets. "You didn't bring a bag."

"Tesia and I put ours on a cart. A friend said he'd see they got to the dining hall while we waited for you." Balin lowered his eyes. "I don't know how long she'll be staying. Everything here just reminds her of Sigurd, and yet she feels that he'd want her to be here."

"Maybe you should go back to her now."

Balin tapped his forehead. "If she wants me, she'll summon me." He suddenly gripped Dyami by the arms. "Dyami—"

"You shouldn't have come back here." Dyami freed himself from the Habber's grip. "I'm not the person you knew. I killed a man, one who was barely more than a boy. I wasn't content with disabling him—I kept hitting him with a rock until I knew he was dead. It's not even that I care so much about that. About the only regret I have is that I waited so long before I did it, that I couldn't stop him from doing the things he did to me."

"I still care about you. Don't you believe that?"

"Then I pity you. You were able to leave before. It shouldn't be hard to go now."

Balin said, "I didn't want to leave. I had no choice."

"And now you're back, as though nothing had happened in the meantime. Can't you see I don't want you here?"

Balin stared at him for a long time, then sat down in front of the tent. Dyami clenched his fists; would he have to compel the other man to go? If he lashed out now, it might be the way it was with Maxim Paz, when he hadn't been able to stop, when the hand holding that bloody rock had kept rising and falling of its own accord.

Balin finally spoke. "I still have that sculpture you cast of me. Have you kept the other one?"

"Suleiman seemed interested in it, so I gave it to him." He did not bother to explain his reasons for wanting to be rid of it. The image of Balin had always been nearby whenever Maxim Paz was tormenting him.

"Have you had time to do any others?"

Dyami gritted his teeth. "I've been working on something for the memorial, but it's just sketches so far."

"I'd like to see them, if you'd show them to me."

"Will you leave me alone after that?" Dyami asked. The Habber did not answer.

He lifted the tent flap, went inside, found his pocket screen, then left the tent. Balin leaned toward him as he sat down and called up his sketches.

"It's to be a pillar," Dyami said, "like other such monuments. We'll have images of the faces of the dead and a plaque with their names, but I want to do something different with the rest of it. The others have pretty much left this task to me, but I haven't shown anyone the sketches yet."

An image appeared; he was looking at the base of the monument he planned. Twisted, distorted human bodies ringed the base, their heads bowed; disembodied hands clutched at their necks or were fists against their backs. Above them stood other human figures, their arms outstretched, as if they were pleading with someone. At the top of the pillar, more nude figures with distended bony limbs held up rods that suggested wands; other broken bodies lay at their feet.

"I haven't yet worked out where the faces will go," Dyami said. "They'll be set in at various places along the pillar, with the panorama around them. Their names can appear about a meter or so from the base. Making the molds and casting the images may prove to be a challenge, since I haven't done anything on this scale before."

He blanked the screen and set it on the ground. The dome was darker now; a reflection of the dome's light was a silver disk floating on the smooth black surface of the lake. "You haven't told me what you think," he said.

"I'm impressed. No, that isn't the right word." Balin's voice sounded faint. "I'm moved, and I'm also grieving that such a monument ever had to stand on your world."

Balin took his hand. Dyami let him hold it. "I'm going to stay," the other man continued. "There will be work enough for me, and you should find it easy to avoid me if that's what you want, but I'll be here if you need me."

"If that's what you're hoping for, I don't even know if I'm still capable of it. You'll have to find another bed-partner. The thought of all that repels me now."

"I wasn't thinking of that." Balin stood up. "Tesia's summoning me. I can wait, Dyami. I won't abandon you again."

"You may be waiting for some time."

"One thing I have is time."

Balin began to descend the hill. "Come back tomorrow," Dyami heard himself say. "I won't be at the refinery, and I want to do more on this house. You could keep me company while I work."

He was sorry as soon as he had spoken. Balin was threatening the refuge he had found inside himself, walled off from others; pain, regret, despair, and possibly disappointment lay beyond those walls. Balin might not be asking for love, but he was requesting trust. Dyami wondered if he could risk trusting anyone again.

"I'll come," Balin replied.

THE CYTHERIANS

The screen above Benzi was dark; there were no images of light and clouds to divert the airship's passengers and allow them to pretend they lived on a sunlit world. The airship's outside lights were beams stabbing into the darkness; the sound filling the cabin was the wail of a fierce distant wind. The only passengers, except for Benzi, were two climatologists bound for Island Nine.

He turned and looked back at the man and the woman. Their eyes were staring at the screen; they were silent as they listened to the wind.

The pilots had allowed him to sit up front with them; he had, after all, been a pilot himself. They were two blond young women with closely cropped hair who, except for their differing heights, might have been sisters. The taller woman reached up to adjust the band around her head; the other was gazing at one of the small screens among the panels before her. The two had seemed amused by his request, and his admission that it was an exercise in nostalgia.

He had told them the story in Island Two's bay, while they were waiting for the cargo to be loaded aboard; apparently the two women had not heard the tale before. "I was an apprentice pilot then," he had told them, "bound for Island Eight. The pilot with me was a woman named Te-yu, and my mother was the only passenger, which was probably just as well, as things turned out. First of all, one of our pumps jammed while we were dropping, and then the helium cells sprang a couple of leaks. We knew we couldn't pull out then, and we'd dropped low enough

631

to be caught by a three-hundred-kilometer-an-hour wind. There we were, with leaks and failing pumps. We couldn't pull out, so we had no choice except to land and hope somebody'd find a way to rescue us. We jettisoned the dirigible and rode down on our chutes."

"Obviously you were saved," the shorter pilot said.

"Not until our sensors had failed and our air was going. Even our suits weren't much protection against the increasing heat inside the cabin. A scooper ship, with my father and a pilot aboard, came from the northern Bat for us, but we had to creep down a rocky mountainside on the cabin's treads to reach it."

"Sounds like quite an apprenticeship," the tall pilot murmured. "I'm surprised you're anxious to get on an airship at all."

"On the contrary," Benzi said. "It reminds me of how fortunate I am to be alive."

"Iris Angharads certainly had an adventurous life. I hadn't heard that story about her before. I must keep up with more of our historical records. But what I don't understand is why you were dropping in the first place if you were headed for Island Eight. Weren't you maintaining altitude?"

"Iris had an interesting approach to her work in climatology," Benzi replied, "a quirk, if you will. Even with drones to gather data, and probes sending back information from the surface, she took any opportunity she could to observe things more directly. She relied, in part, on her intuitions, and she often had the feeling she might be able to sense something herself that all those other sensors couldn't. She was being sent to Island Eight, and as long as we were going, she figured we might as well take a sample of the lower atmosphere on the way. She'd listen to the winds when she was aboard airships, whenever she could talk the pilots into opening the sound sensors so she could hear them for herself."

"A bit risky for you," the pilot said, "descending like that, with no bays where you might land. I always say you can trust maintenance to keep you safe only if you don't take foolish chances."

But Iris, he thought now, had always been one to take chances; she was incapable of simply observing from afar. Benzi had believed that he might, that he could watch her world from a distance, untouched by its storms and up-heavals. Decades ago, sitting in airships much like this one, he had felt only resentment and the urge to escape, to free himself of everything holding him here. Soon, if it was necessary, he might have to accept more bonds with Cytherians that might not so easily be broken.

Risa had promised him a message when he was back on Island Two. He wondered what she would tell him. It did not matter; he was finally prepared to accept the responsibility she might feel forced to give him. He might find the first of the Cytherians who would share his dream of going to the stars.

Dyami was leading Amina away from Oberg's bay when a familiar voice called out to him.

"Dyami!" Teo was running toward him, past a few tents that housed the recent arrivals from Earth. "I wanted to greet you." He pumped Dyami's arms. "I can't talk long —I have to get back to the lab."

Dyami tried to smile. Teo was still the same slender, dark-haired man he had seen on his last visit nearly eight years ago. He noticed one difference; his friend was no longer wearing Ishtar's sash. He thought of the occasional messages he had received from Teo. In the earlier ones, Teo had spoken of how concerned he had always been when he had not known what was happening in Turing and of how he had tried to rouse others to indignation. In later messages, his deeds had grown in the telling until Dyami might almost have thought that Teo was at the center of those working against Ishtar.

Dyami let go of Teo's hands and adjusted his pack. Teo's messages resembled those some of his other school-mates had sent. They had all seen that those close to the Guide were committing excesses; they had not known what was going on in Turing or they surely would have done something about it. They certainly did not want him to think they would have tolerated such abuses of their fellow citizens. But that was all past, and they wanted him to know that they all expected a visit whenever he came back to Oberg.

They did not say what some of them probably thought, what a few newcomers in Turing had said before being silenced by icy stares. Turing's monument was a bit on the dramatic side, wasn't it? Surely some of the stories told during the hearings there were a trifle exaggerated, and anyway, hadn't the former prisoners, by not trying to conceal their indifference to Ishtar, brought some of their trouble on themselves? It had all been a terrible mistake, of course, but they could not think the Guide and most of her followers had much to do with what the patrol in Turing had done.

Dyami pulled Amina forward gently. "My housemate, Amina Astarte. This is my old friend, Teo Lingard."

"You may have glimpsed my image on his screens," Teo said to the blond woman. He raised his brows as he turned toward Dyami again. "You mentioned a new housemate in your last message, but you didn't provide any details. Does this signal a change in your inclinations?"

Amina laughed. "We're only friends. My own inclinations run in an entirely different direction."

Teo's smile widened; he seemed relieved. "In that case, Dyami, I should tell you that I know a couple of interesting men who would very much like to meet you."

Dyami sighed; he had expected that sort of invitation. He thought of a young man who had recently come to live in Turing, who had been quick to seek Dyami out. The man had been disappointed when Dyami shied away from talking of the past, and even more downcast when his advances were politely but firmly refused. Teo's friends were probably like that young man, anxious to feed on the tales of suffering that might provide fuel for their own fantasies. Perhaps the notion of comforting a victim appealed to them, or maybe their fantasies were darker ones; he had seen something of Maxim Paz in the young man's eyes.

Teo's smile had faded. "You needn't worry now," he said. "Some people may still look askance at us, but as long as we're not blatant—well, discretion is preferable to deception, I suppose. Things are better, and maybe that's all we can expect for now."

Dyami tried to think of what to say. "It isn't that," he murmured at last. "I'm content with Balin as a lover. I haven't felt the need for others." This much was true. Balin had been patient, and Dyami had found contentment and love with him again, but there were still times when he needed to retreat, when fear and distrust still inhibited him.

"Ah, yes, the Habber." Teo tilted his head. "Well, you could meet these men anyway—they'd like to talk to you at least. You see—" He looked away. "I know what you're thinking, that all I did was try to protect myself, that I wasn't really thinking of anyone else as long as they left me alone. I have learned something since then, and so have others. You do believe that, don't you?"

"Of course," Dyami replied, not sure he did.

"You must come to visit me, both of you. Amina can hear all about our childish adventures. Will you be staying here long enough to welcome in 634?"

Dyami shook his head. "We're only here for a week. We'll be in ibn-Qurrah with Amina's family for the new year."

"Well, then. I must get back to the lab, and you're probably anxious to get to your parents' house."

"Amina wants to see the monument first."

"Of course."

Dyami clutched Teo's shoulder; the other man brightened a little. "We will visit you," Dyami said.

A cart filled with passengers rolled past as Dyami and Amina left the main road. Dyami glanced at the group; a few of the people wore sashes. He found himself wondering how many of them had stood by, closing their minds to anything that might require them to act, and how many had actively aided Ishtar, convinced that anything the Guide did was right.

In the clearing where the monument stood, a small gardening robot was watering the grass. Amina took his arms as they approached the pillar. "Here it is," Dyami said. "I trust it's what you expected." She looked up at the faces of Iris and Amir without speaking. "My grandfather came here once in a while to polish the monument—he never thought anyone else was tending to it properly. His own memorial's with the other pillars."

They walked toward the other monuments. He was about to point out Chen's image to her when a holo image on the pillar next to it caught his eye. Chimene's large dark eyes stared out from the top of that pillar; the image was alone, far above the other faces clustered near the center and base of the memorial. A trampled wreath of flowers lay in front of the monument; a torn banner was attached to the wreath.

He bent forward and read the banner's lettering:

TO THE MEMORY OF OUR GUIDE,
CHIMENE LIANG-HADDAD,
WHO LOVED US ALL AND WHO LIVES ON

Dyami straightened. "Playing a martyr's role," he said hoarsely, "is becoming something of a family tradition." Amina's hand tightened around his arm. "We'll never be free of her, will we?"

"You shouldn't have seen this now," she said. "Have you decided what you're going to tell your parents?"

"I think I have." He turned away from the pillar. "When the hearings were over, I expected that one of the things we'd have to endure was the pity of others and their efforts to reassure us that everything was fine now. What I didn't expect was that they'd want us to reassure them. They want to forget—they don't want to think that all of us are capable of certain deeds. They prefer to think it was just all caused by a few misguided or malicious people."

"Dyami—"

"And now I'm supposed to forgive and forget."

"No. We're supposed to remember without passing those hatreds on." She pulled at his sleeve. "Your parents will be waiting. Let's not put this off any longer."

Risa and Grazie were leaving the greenhouse as Dyami and Amina walked up the path toward them. The two women quickly set down their baskets and hurried to him; Risa threw her arms around him as Grazie dabbed at her eyes.

"It's been so long," his mother said; her tears were wetting his shirt. He finally managed to free himself before leaning over to kiss her. "And you must be Amina." Risa clasped the blond woman's hands. "This is Grazie Lauro, one of my housemates. I—"

Dyami was afraid his mother might cry again. Amina glanced from Risa to him, then said, "Perhaps Grazie can show me the house while you two talk. You'd probably like a chance to visit alone first."

Dyami shrugged out of his pack and handed it to

Amina; Grazie picked up the baskets. "Kolya's made some of his bread," Grazie said, "and there's fresh fish, and when Andy Dinel heard you'd be visiting, he sent over a bottle of his whiskey. We have a fine dinner planned for you later."

He narrowed his eyes. "Just the household," Risa said; he relaxed a little. "Go ahead, you two. I'll sit with my son out here for a little."

Grazie led Amina into the house; Risa seated herself on the grass. "Well," she whispered.

He sat down next to her. "Well."

She smoothed back his hair, then touched his cheek lightly. "So you have a housemate now. You didn't tell me very much about your arrangement."

"Don't look so hopeful, Risa. Amina's no more interested in me sexually than I am in her, but we're friends, and we've been close. We have certain scars in common." He paused. "Amina's lover Tasida wanted to form a household with some friends, and Amina's still shy of living with that many other people, so I offered her a place in my house. It suits us, and our lovers visit us there."

"That's all right then." She patted his arm. "I'm just happy to know you won't be alone in that house anymore. I worried about you being so alone. And are you going to stay in Turing?"

"For the foreseeable future."

"You know you can always come back here," she said. "This house seems so empty now sometimes, but that will probably change soon. With my work and the Council's business, I'll need help here, but I'm sure I'll find someone among the new settlers."

She was avoiding the issue that had brought him here. "You finally got the child," he said.

"Yes. They took her out of the womb chamber two weeks ago. She seems strong enough and healthy, but of course we expected that."

"You told me in your message," he said.

"You didn't tell me how you felt."

He put his larger hands around her small ones. "Why don't you tell me how you feel about it now?"

She rested her graying head against his arm. "Do you remember what I used to tell you about Chen, how bitter and despairing he was when Iris died? All he wanted to do was to forget—that's what he told me. He didn't want a child that would only remind him of her and of all the ways he might have failed her himself. But bringing me into the world helped him heal, and he was glad he'd made that decision afterward, that he'd decided to stay here instead of trying to escape his grief."

"This is hardly the same sort of situation."

"But Mahala has given me some consolation. Still, I have someone else I must consider, and that's you."

The door to the house opened; Sef walked outside, carrying a small bundle in his arms. It stirred, and Dyami heard a faint cry.

He was about to speak when Risa pulled her hands from his. "Don't say anything yet until I've finished. My brother Benzi has offered to care for Mahala if you can't bear the thought of her living among us. He's a relative, too, and he could make a case for raising her himself. He's willing to stay on Island Two until she reaches maturity, and maybe it would be good for others to see that kind of bond between a Habber and one of our people. I'll give her up if keeping her here is just going to divide us. You wouldn't have to think about her any more." Her mouth twisted. "You might even take a kind of perverse pleasure in seeing Chimene's child raised by one of the people she hated so much. It would be one kind of revenge, and perhaps that's all you want now."

Sef was standing next to him. Dyami got to his feet and peered at the infant as Sef drew the cloth from her face. Her dark eyes gazed up at him; a few strands of fine black hair curled against her nearly bald head. She opened her mouth as if about to wail, then reached out with one tiny hand. He did not know what he had expected to feel; she was only another child after all.

"She usually cries around strangers," Sef said. "She seems to like you."

"I suspect she didn't cry only because I look so much like you."

Risa stood up. "I promised Benzi a message. You can think of what you want me to tell him. He'll come here as soon as he can if that's your decision—I wouldn't want her to bond too closely with us before he takes her."

Dyami said, "I don't know if that's a good idea."

"Better than waiting too much longer," she replied.

"What I meant," Dyami said, "is that it might be hard

for her—being raised by a Habber without being one herself, knowing she might have had a home here, thinking that her own family would see only her mother in her. That would be a burden. She'd grow up as an outsider, in a way, always wondering if anyone really cared about her. It'd make more sense for her to stay here and for Benzi to visit her—they could still establish a bond that way."

"Are you saying—" Risa raised a hand to her mouth. "You wouldn't be angry with me?"

"No. I won't be angry." He swallowed. "She might want to visit Turing eventually. She'd have a place to stay, get to know me in case I come back to Oberg later."

Mahala caught one of his fingers; Dyami let her hold on. Another burden, he thought, another creature who would share the history of this world, who would look out from this dome and try to imagine a world of light and life outside. Yet for the first time since leaving the place that had been his prison, he felt free.

Author's Afterword

In the 1970s, when I first thought of writing a novel about Venus, we already knew that the environment of this world was truly hellish and hostile. No longer could a tale be told of tropical Venusian swamps, deserts, or vast oceans that covered the planet's surface. Our "sister planet" turned out to be a barren world, smothered in an atmosphere composed largely of carbon dioxide, with a surface temperature of 900° Fahrenheit and clouds liberally laced with sulphuric acid. The Soviet Union's *Venera* probes of the mid-1960s, the first designed to reach the planet's surface, were crushed and burned in the inhospitable atmosphere long before they landed. It seemed highly unlikely that human beings would ever set foot on a planet where the heat and a surface pressure nearly one hundred times that of Earth would destroy an unprotected body.

Yet I wanted to put my characters there, and terraforming Venus offered a way to do this. The obstacles to altering the planet did not seem that great when I began outlining my novel. One popular notion was that Venus could be terraformed by seeding the atmosphere with algae that would, through photosynthesis, change the carbon dioxide to oxygen; the planet would cool rapidly, rains would fall, and we would be left with a planet that might sustain life. I could, so I thought, get my fictional terraforming out of the way fairly simply and move on to the story I wanted to tell—one of a family seeking to realize their dreams, and meeting both failure and success—on a new world.

This congenial vision quickly vanished when I began my research. The more I learned about Venus, the greater the obstacles became; to terraform that world would take a project that spanned centuries. The story I thought could be told in one book soon burgeoned beyond that length; the problems in telling it, along with the technical difficulties any planetary engineers would realistically face, seemed insurmountable.

Over the years, some have asked why the full range of techniques often used by other novelists have so rarely been applied to so-called "hard" science fiction. One reason may be that the scope of such ideas, and the technical problems in working them out with attention to realism and scientific detail, can be overwhelming. Questions of character, in this context, can seem either irrelevant or, as some have argued, inappropriate. Large ideas can dwarf the people in a story; their human concerns seem small. One traditional way out of the difficulty is to write an entertaining adventure story, since the ideas will still be interesting for themselves.

Yet the hard science fiction story presents opportunities more writers are grasping. Scientific ideas and technological developments affect the ways in which people view themselves; their cultures and personal concerns influence the ways these developments are used. Hard science fiction should be thoroughly hard—as demanding in its depictions of characters and attention to literary virtues as it is with ideas; each part is diminished without the other. Ideally, such a story, rooted in realistic possibilities and in human character, will have a depth and resonance with our own experience that might be lacking if either were ignored.

I had to view the problems in writing about the terraforming of Venus as artistic opportunities. The difficulties of my Venus Project determined how my characters would behave and the choices they would make. The story, like the Project, had to be epic in scope if the people in it weren't to be lost. The restrictions of realism, which can seem so confining (one scientific impossibility can force the writer to jettison whole scenes), can also open up a story in unexpected ways. One major problem facing me was the motivation for my Venus Project: what reasons would people have for undertaking this centuries-long endeavor, even if I assumed it would become technically feasible? The problems we may soon face on our own planet provided one answer. We are unwittingly changing our own world, and Venus as it is shows us the consequences of a runaway greenhouse effect. Terraforming may become as much an act of desperation as a grand, challenging engineering endeavor, thus linking both intellectual and human concerns. Terraforming another world may eventually give us the tools we need to save our own.

Writing about the generations of one family has allowed me to tell two stories that are complete in themselves, but also unified by both that family's experience and the setting in which they lead their lives. *Venus of Dreams* is largely the story of visionaries dreaming of a world they will not see; *Venus of Shadows* depicts possible social, cultural, and political obstacles that are as great to Venus's settlers as the technological ones. One story remains to be told in the concluding novel—the personal story of one who will see the green and sun-lit world her ancestors have created.

ABOUT THE AUTHOR

Pamela Sargent published her first short story in 1970. Her novels include *Cloned Lives, The Sudden Star, Watchstar, The Golden Space, The Alien Upstairs,* and *Venus of Dreams,* about which the Chicago *Sun-Times* wrote: "Sargent has combined the family saga and social-science science fiction, both on the grand scale, and produced a thoroughly impressive book." Her novel *The Shore of Women* was called "one of the few perfect novels of the '80s" by Orson Scott Card in *The Magazine of Fantasy and Science Fiction* and "a compelling and emotionally involving novel" by *Publishers Weekly.* She has also published two short story collections and edited five anthologies, including *Women of Wonder, Bio-Futures,* and, with Ian Watson, *Afterlives.* Among her novels for young adults are *Earthseed, Eye of the Comet, Homesmind,* and *Alien Child.* She lives in upstate New York, where she is writing the third novel in the *Venus* series, *Child of Venus.*